Laughing Gas

the Best of Maxine

By Marian Henley

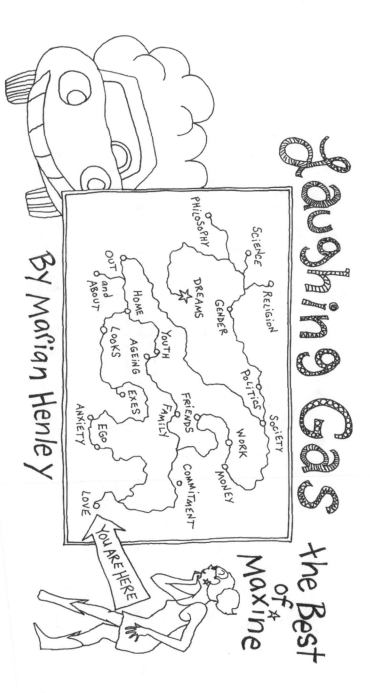

PHILOSOPHY
SCIENCE
RELIGION
OUT
and
ABOUT
DREAMS
GENDER
HOME
YOUTH
POLITICS
LOOKS
AGEING
SOCIETY
EXES
FRIENDS
WORK
FAMILY
ANXIETY
EGO
COMMITMENT
MONEY
LOVE
YOU ARE HERE

Republic of Texas Press

Republic of Texas Press is an imprint of Wordware Publishing, Inc.

Printed in the United States of America

ISBN 1-55622-932-1
10 9 8 7 6 5 4 3 2 1
0207

All inquiries for volume purchases of this book should be addressed to Wordware Publishing, Inc., at 2320 Los Rios Boulevard, Plano, Texas 75074. Telephone inquiries may be made by calling:

(972) 423-0090

This book is dedicated
to my parents,
Mimi and Bill Henley;
to Aunt Chick; and to the memory of
Uncle Neddy, Aunt Connie, and Aunt Nancy.
Hilarity is hereditary.

Contents

Acknowledgements, vii

Introduction, ix

Love, 1

Commitment, 35

Ego and Anxiety, 53

Friends and Family, 75

Youth and Ageing, 93

Exes, 111

v

Looks, 125
Out and About, 147
Home, 161

Work and Money, 171
Society and Politics, 187
Gender, 209
Science and Religion, 233
Philosophy, 245
Dreams, 261

Acknowledgements

Like any artist or writer, I live in two places: inside my head and out in the world. It's like being an amphibian. I swim back and forth. Without the help of the following people, Maxine might have stayed inside my head:

Kay Huckabee, Julie Oliver, and Anne Simon gave me their friendship and a taste for divine foolishness. I returned the favor by turning them into Cece and Simone, Maxine's madcap Soul Sisters.

Lynn Lenau, Temple Wynne, Shannon Wynne, Henry Frost, Lewis Shiner, Bob and JoAnn Baker, and Angus Wynne gave me much-needed encouragement during the early days when Maxine first bopped into being. And Brave Combo kept me on my toes. Dancing, of course.

David Seeley and Bob Walton, formerly of the Dallas Observer, were the first to publish Maxine. I will never forget the first moment I saw her on the October 1, 1981, issue's cover. It was a thrill beyond all thrills. Joe Dishner, formerly of the Austin Chronicle, and Louis Black and Nick Barbaro, now and forever of the Austin Chronicle, were the second to publish Maxine. Ellen Kampinsky was third. The thrill continues.

My work has been enriched immeasurably by creative associations with Melissa Berry, Mara Harris, Sara Hickman, Sarah Jordan, Candice Land, Bill Mathers, Malford Milligan, Ed Newmann, Derek O'Brien, my sisters Connie and Cindy, Octavio Solis, Lisa Taylor, Bart Weiss, Joe Yancey, and dear God who am I forgetting? Oh, Yes! My cats Angel, Penelope, and Ted. They inspire me to clownish heights with their antics and affection, as did the dearly departed Agnes, Agatha, Glad, and Napoleon the noble Beagle.

Rick Wupperman can't be thanked enough, and I am grateful to writers and journalists Sophia Dembling, Rebecca Sherman, Shermakaye Bass, and Raymond Lesser for writing about Maxine and me in a way that revealed to me how much I reveal.

Finally, this book would not have found its publisher without the detective skills and fearless plodding of Ruth Pennebaker. Without Pamela Nelson's wit, it would not have its title.

Many thanks to Ginnie Bivona for believing in this book and signing me on the dotted line. And thanks to Alan and Martha McCuller for making it look good.

Introduction

I like to laugh. Not only does it tone the abdominal muscles, it is also a handy, all-purpose response to life.

Let me tell you a story.

At the end of my sophomore year in high school, I was reading MAD magazine in my dorm room. Exams were over. Birds were singing. At some point, I started laughing. I laughed so hard that I fell off my chair. I could not stop. I rolled from side to side on the floor. A group of friends gathered around. "What's so funny?" one asked. I was laughing too hard to speak. "Marian? "Our housemother appeared in the doorway. Pink curlers bobbed on her head. "Do you need to go to the infirmary?" That did it. I doubled up. Someone had the presence of mind to time me, and I laughed for fifteen minutes and twenty-three seconds. My abdomen ached for days.

"What was so funny?" my two roommates asked me later. "I don't know," I said. We all burst out laughing.

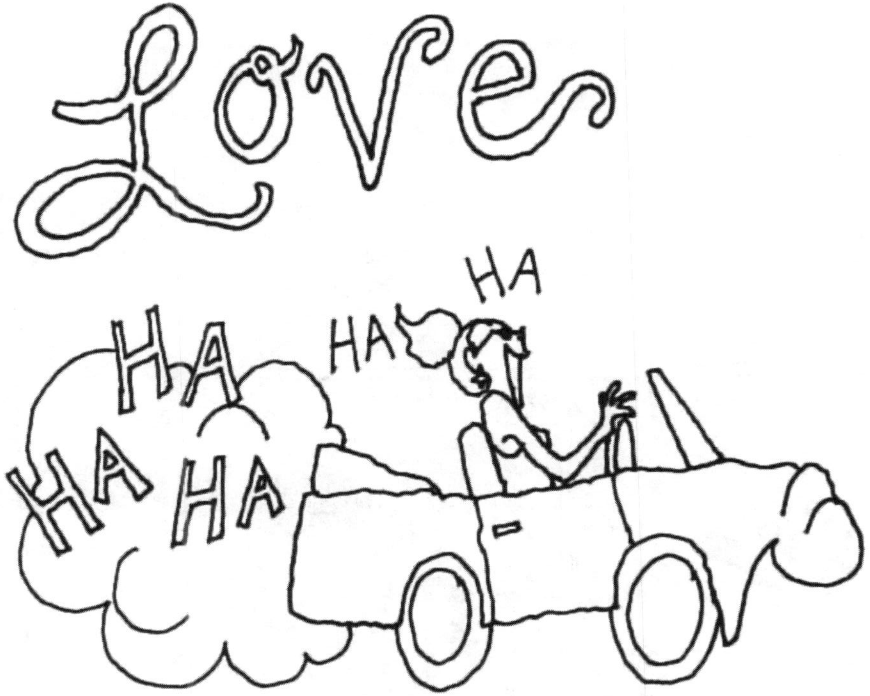
Love
HA
HA HA
HA
HA

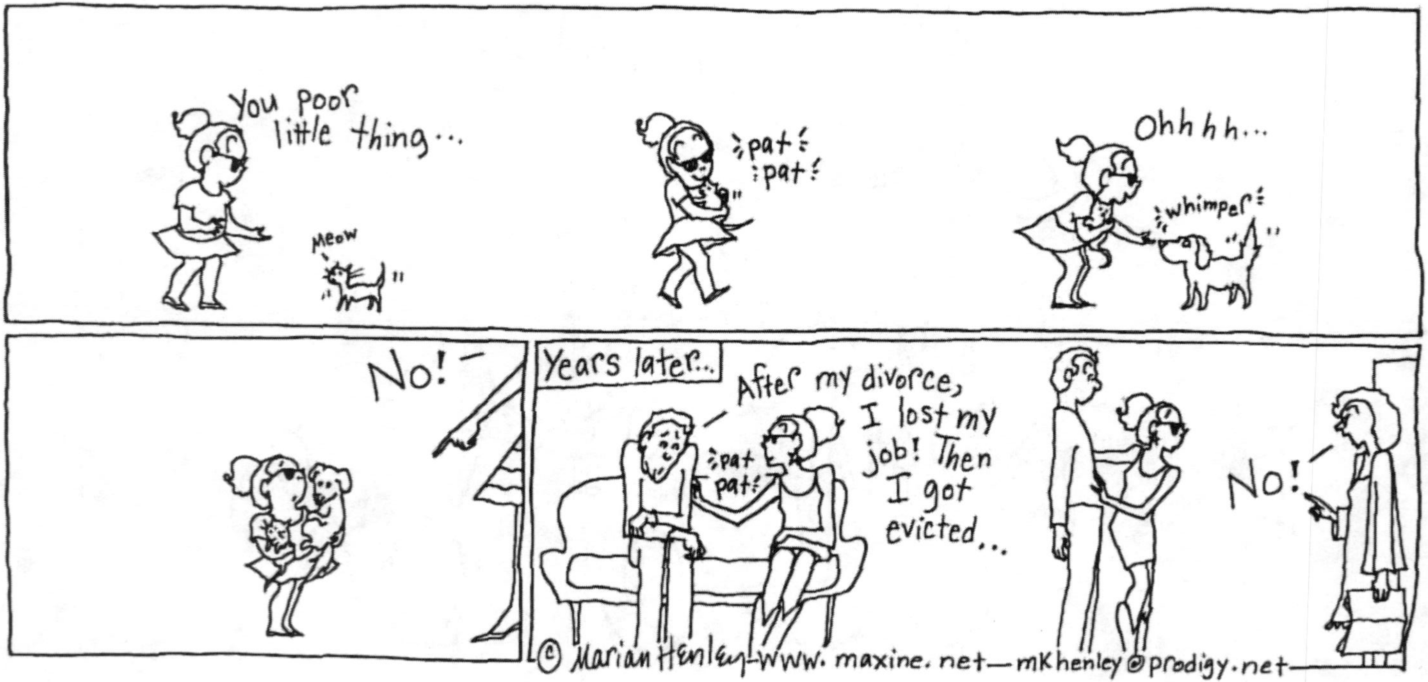
You poor little thing...
Meow
pat pat
Ohhhh...
whimper
No!
Years later...
After my divorce, I lost my job! Then I got evicted...
pat pat
No!
© Marian Henley—www.maxine.net—mkhenley@prodigy.net

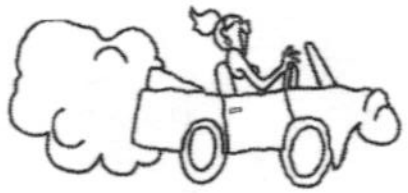

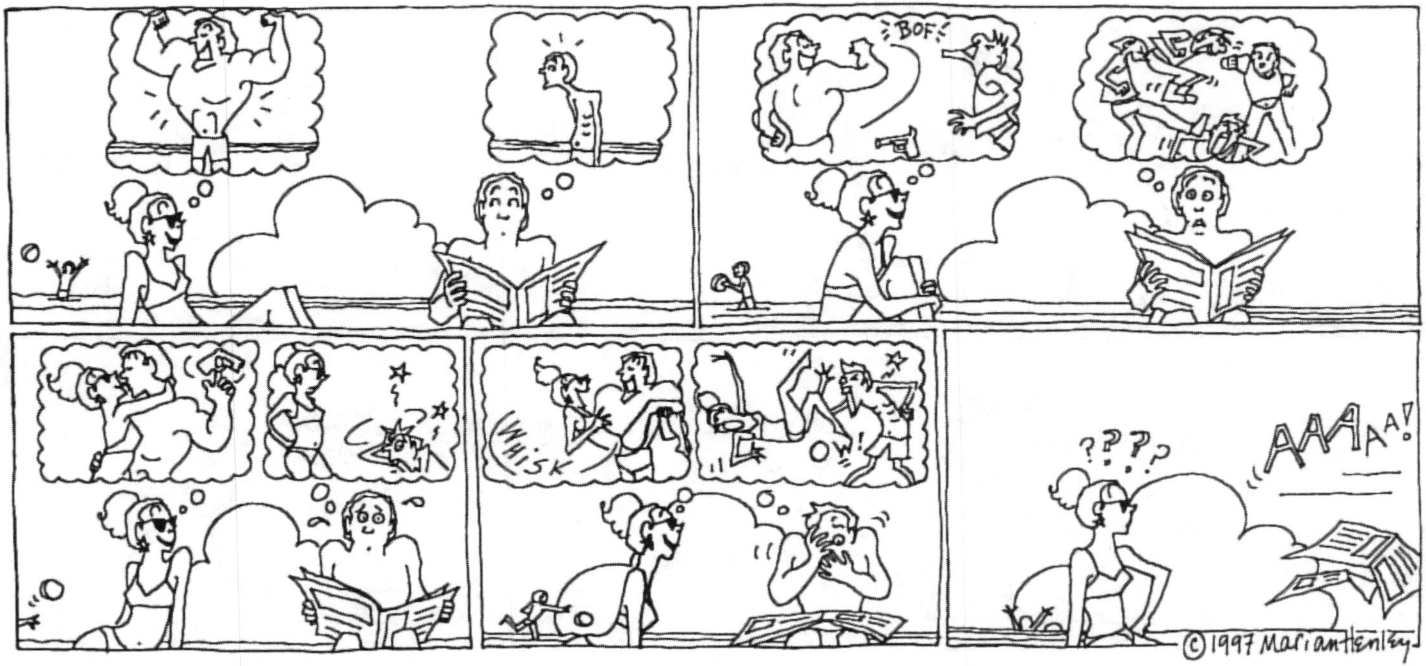
BOF
WHISK
OW!
?????
AAAAA!
©1997 Marian Henley

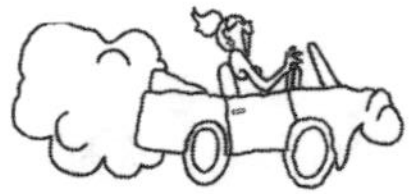

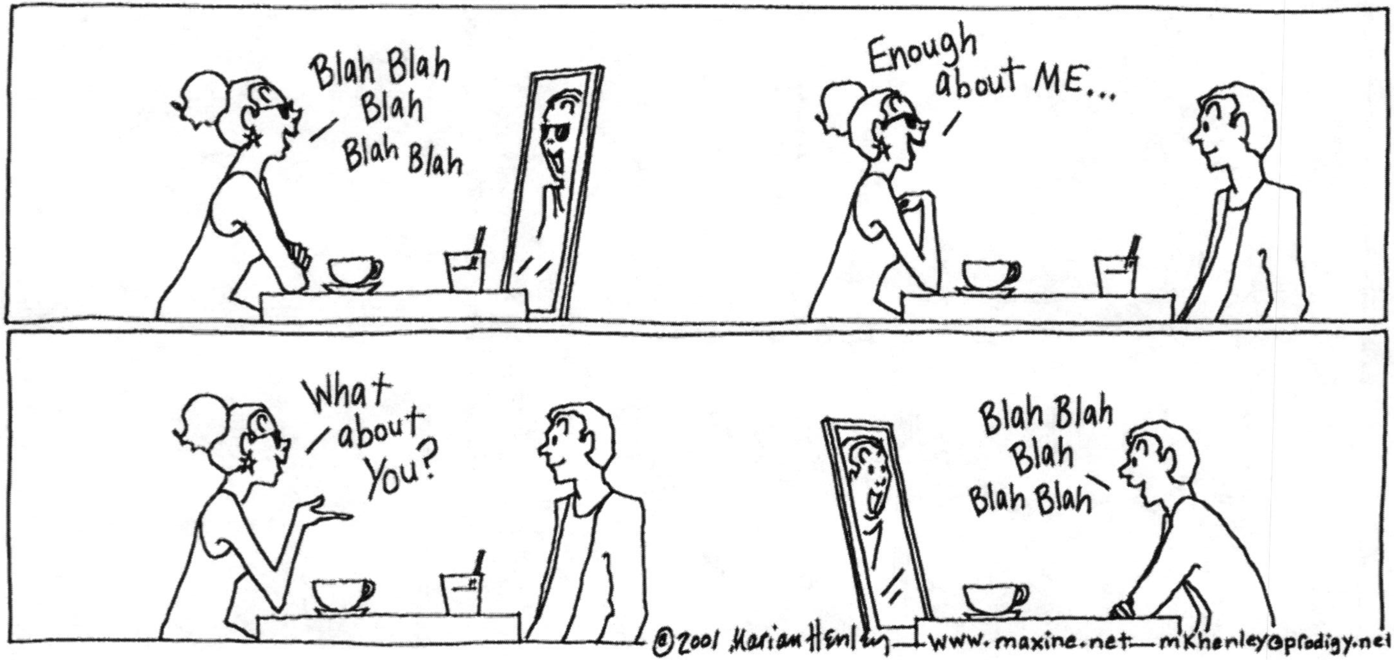
Blah Blah
Blah
Blah Blah
Enough about ME...
What about You?
Blah Blah
Blah
Blah Blah
©2001 Marian Henley — www.maxine.net — mkhenley@prodigy.net

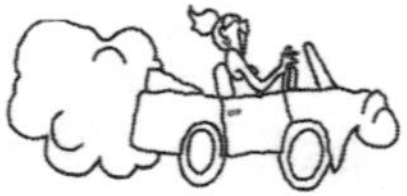

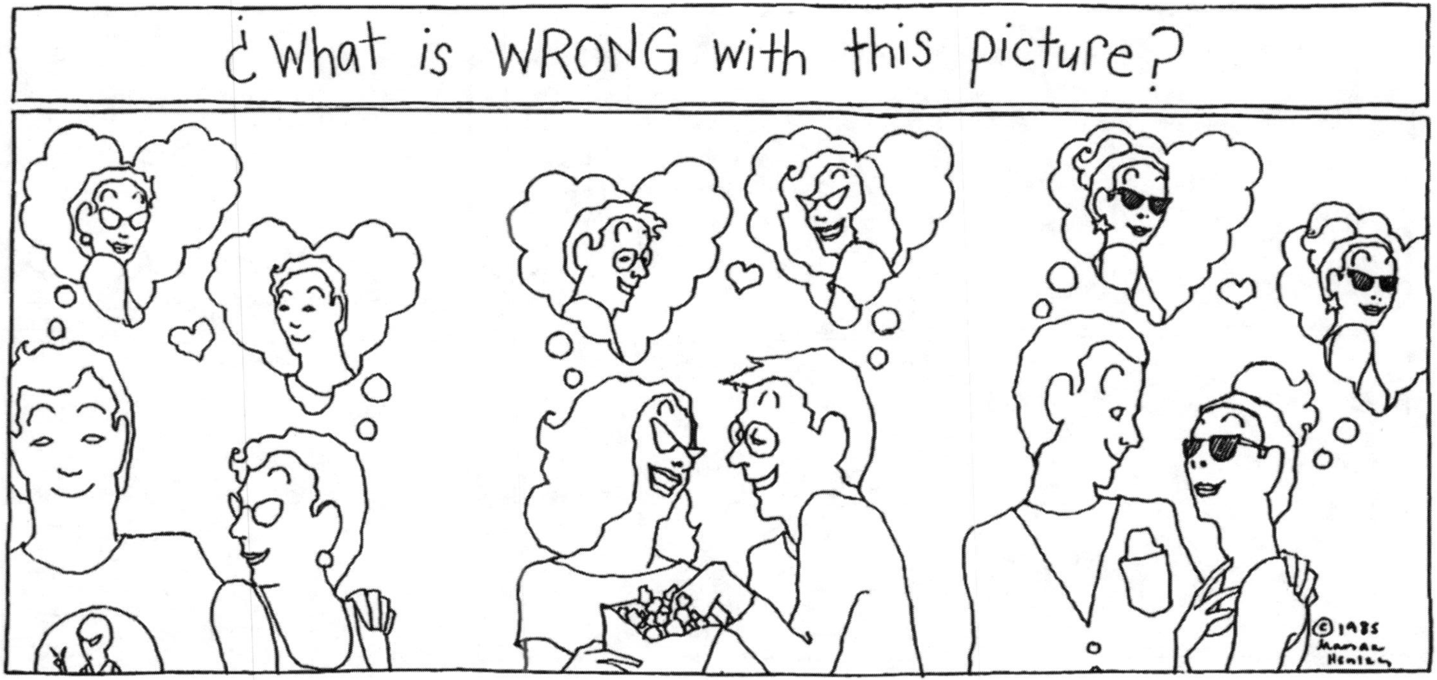
¿What is WRONG with this picture?
©1985 Marian Henley

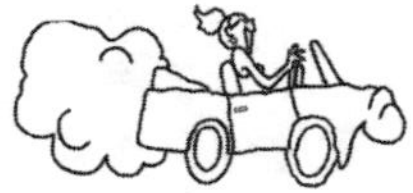

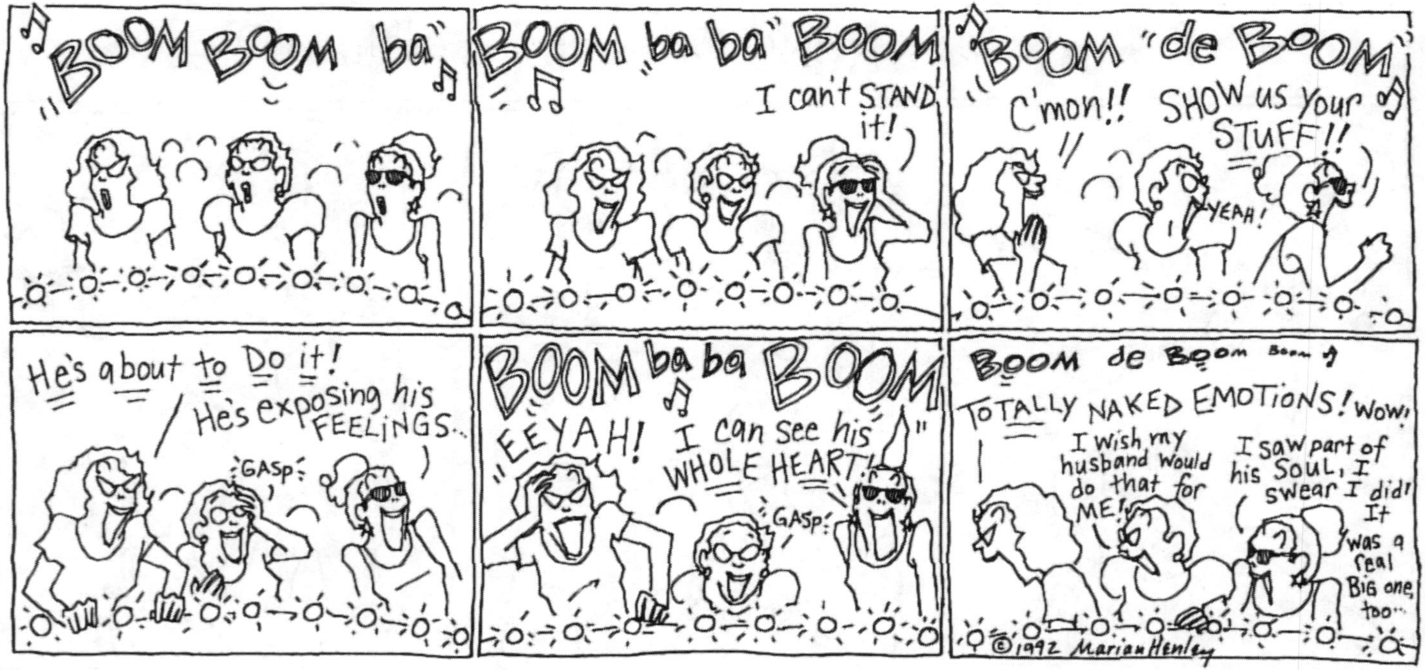
"BOOM BOOM ba"
BOOM "ba ba" BOOM
I can't STAND it!
"BOOM "de BOOM"
C'mon!!
SHOW us your STUFF!!
YEAH!
He's about to Do it!
He's exposing his FEELINGS...
GASp
BOOM ba ba BOOM
EEYAH!
I can see his WHOLE HEART!"
GASp
BOOM de BOOM Boom
TOTALLY NAKED EMOTIONS! WOW!
I wish my husband would do that for ME!
I saw part of his SOUL, I swear I did! It was a real BIG one, too...
©1992 Marian Henley

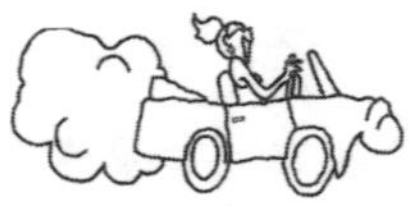

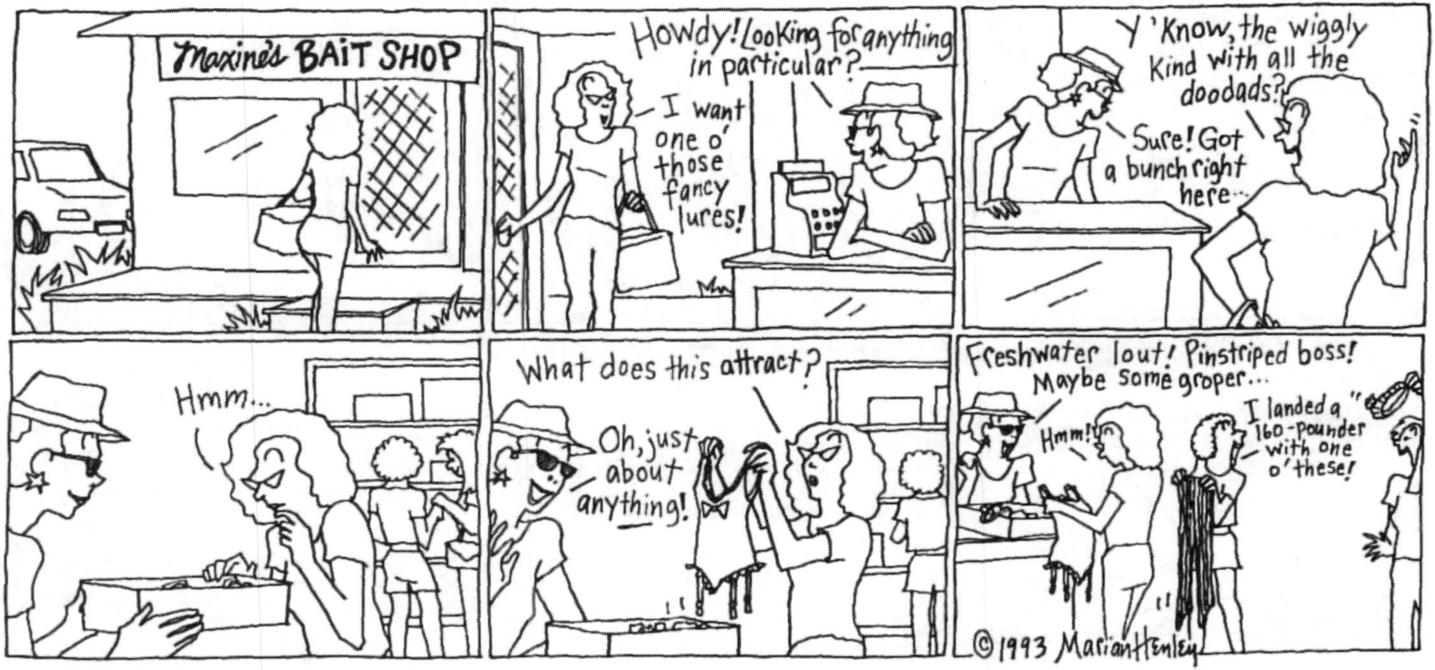
Maxine's BAIT SHOP
Howdy! Looking for anything in particular?
I want one o' those fancy lures!
Y'Know, the wiggly Kind with all the doodads?
Sure! Got a bunch right here...
Hmm...
What does this attract?
Oh, just about anything!
Freshwater lout! Pinstriped boss! Maybe some groper...
Hmm!
I landed a 160-pounder with one o' these!
©1993 MarianHenley

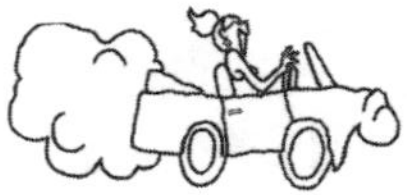

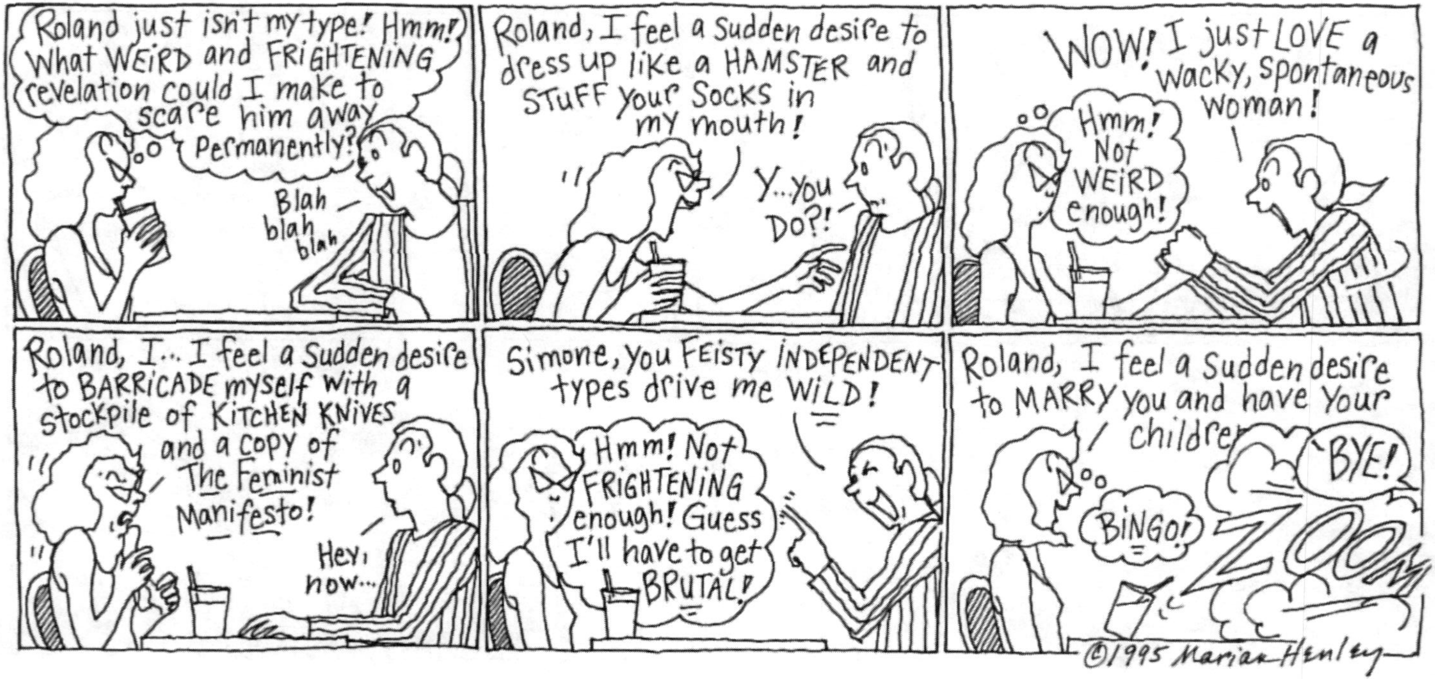
Roland just isn't my type! Hmm! What WEIRD and FRIGHTENING revelation could I make to scare him away permanently?
Blah blah blah
Roland, I feel a sudden desire to dress up like a HAMSTER and STUFF your socks in my mouth!
Y...You DO?!
WOW! I just LOVE a wacky, spontaneous woman!
Hmm! Not WEIRD enough!
Roland, I... I feel a sudden desire to BARRICADE myself with a stockpile of KITCHEN KNIVES and a copy of The Feminist Manifesto!
Hey, now...
Simone, you FEISTY INDEPENDENT types drive me WILD!
Hmm! Not FRIGHTENING enough! Guess I'll have to get BRUTAL!
Roland, I feel a sudden desire to MARRY you and have your childre
BINGO!
BYE!
ZOOM
©1995 Marian Henley

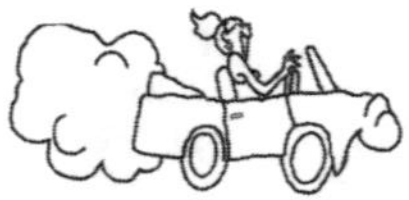

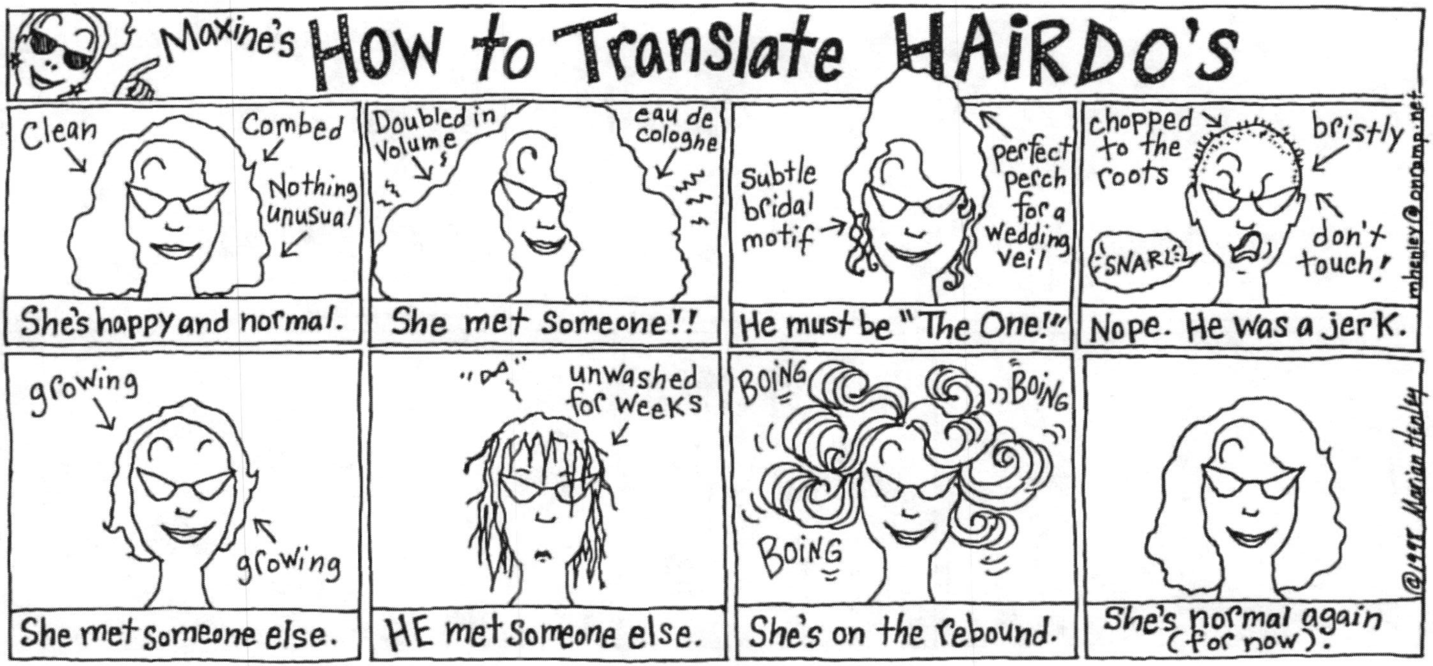
Maxine's How to Translate HAiRDO's
Clean
Combed
Nothing unusual
She's happy and normal.
Doubled in Volume
eau de cologne
She met Someone!!
Subtle bridal motif
perfect perch for a wedding veil
He must be "The One!"
chopped to the roots
bristly
SNARL!
don't touch!
Nope. He was a jerk.
mhenley@onramp.net
growing
growing
She met someone else.
unwashed for weeks
HE met Someone else.
BOING
BOING
BOING
She's on the rebound.
She's normal again (for now).
@1998 Marian Henley

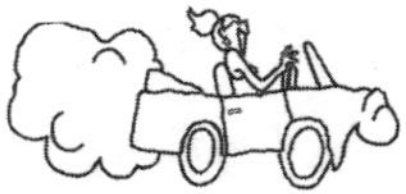

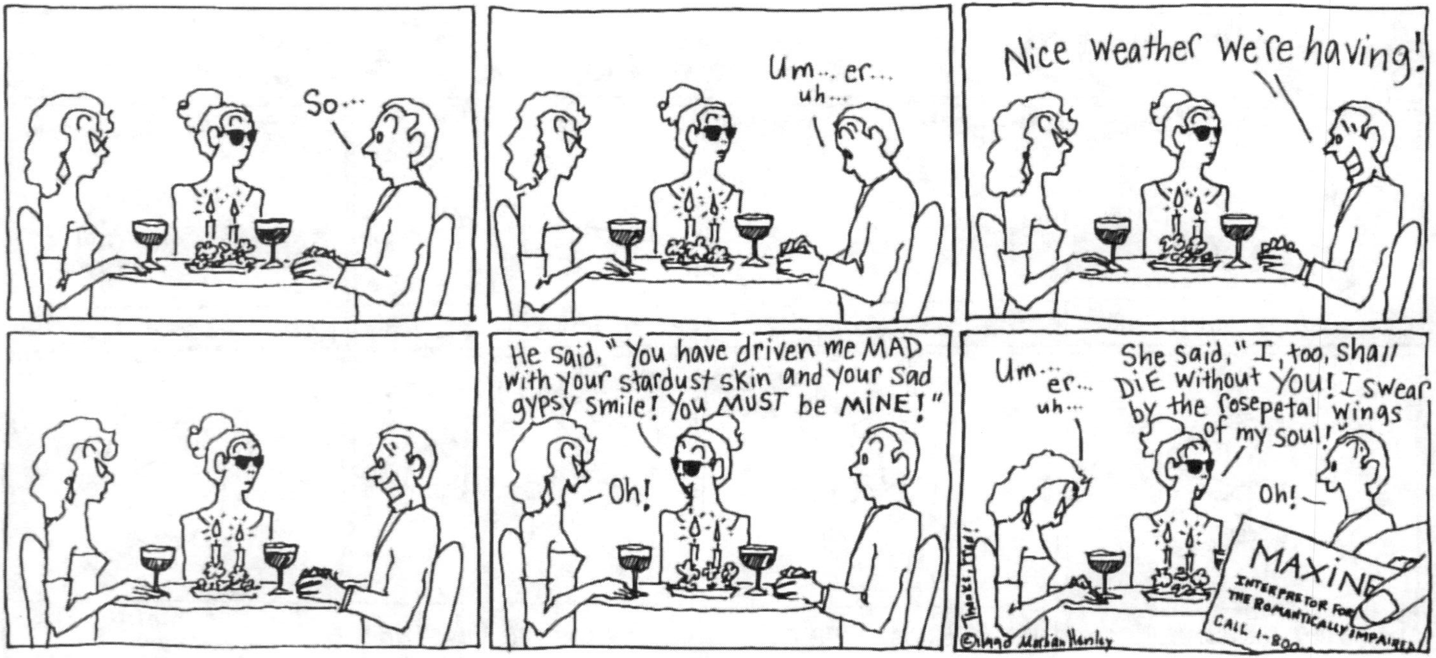
So…
Um… er… uh…
Nice weather we're having!
He said, "You have driven me MAD with your stardust skin and your sad gypsy smile! You MUST be MINE!"
Oh!
Um… er… uh…
She said, "I, too, shall DIE without YOU! I swear by the rosepetal wings of my soul!"
Oh!
MAXINE
INTERPRETOR FOR THE ROMANTICALLY IMPAIRED
CALL 1-800…

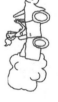

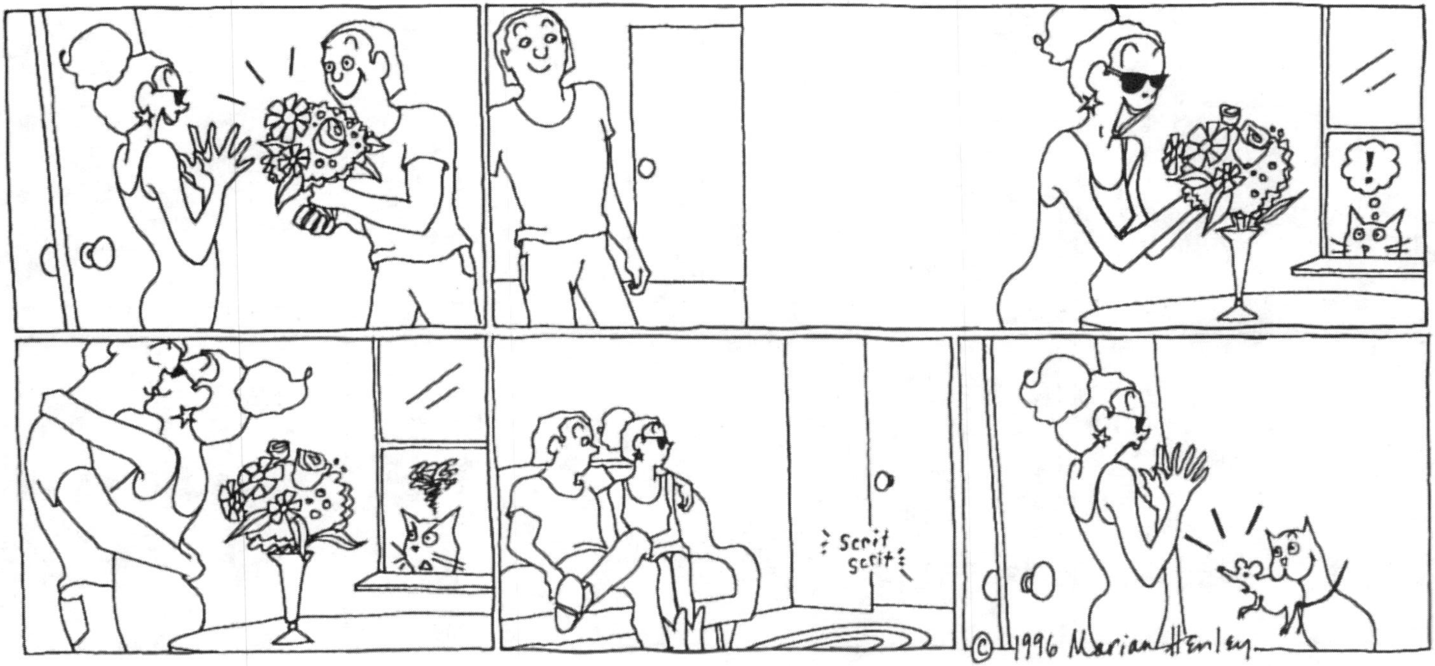
!
scrit
scrit
© 1996 Marian Henley

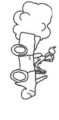

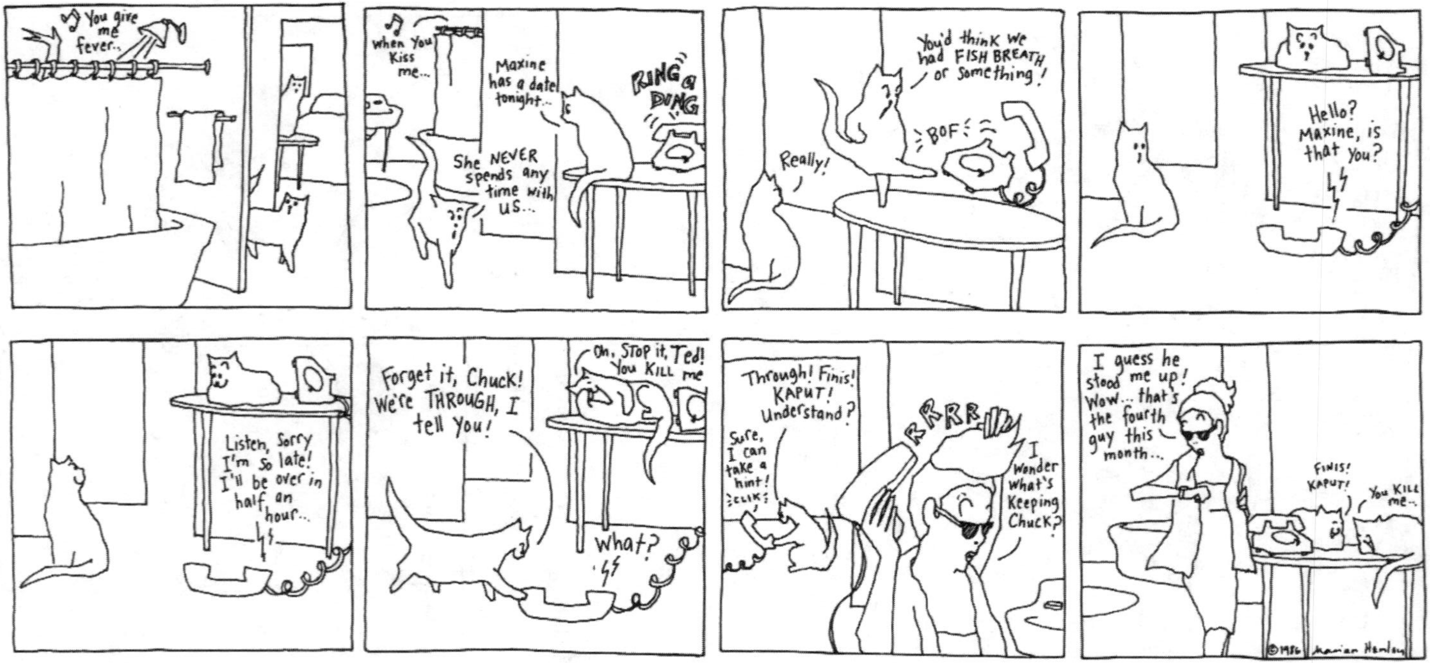
You give me fever..
when You Kiss me...
Maxine has a date tonight...
She NEVER spends any time with US...
RING DING
You'd think we had FISH BREATH or Something!
BOF
Really!
Hello? Maxine, is that you?
Listen, Sorry I'm so late! I'll be over in half an hour...
Forget it, Chuck! We're THROUGH, I tell you!
Oh, STOP it, Ted! You KILL me
What?
Through! Finis! KAPUT! Understand?
Sure, I can take a hint!
CLIK
RRRR
I wonder what's Keeping Chuck?
I guess he stood me up! Wow... that's the fourth guy this month...
FINIS! KAPUT!
You KILL me..
©1986 Marian Henley

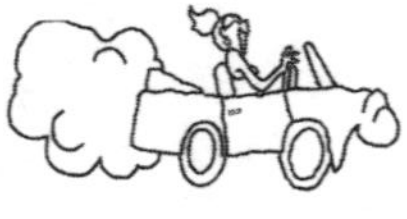

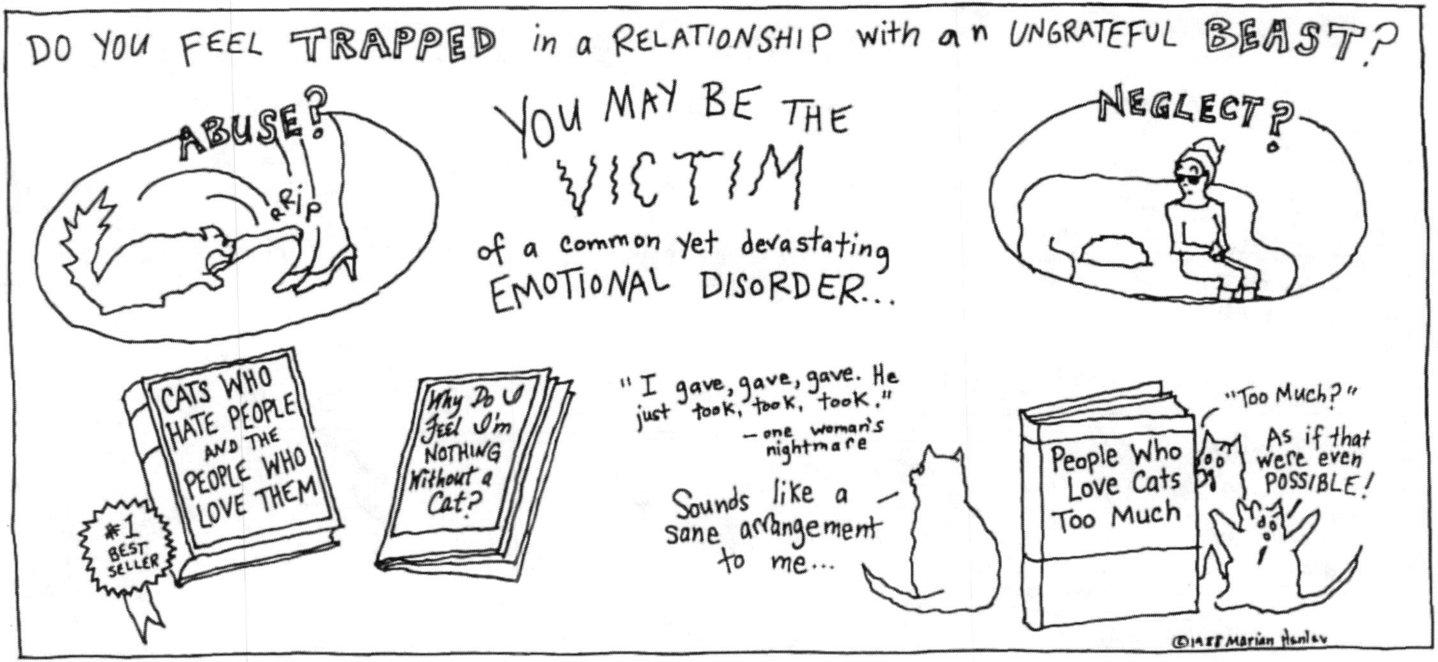
DO YOU FEEL TRAPPED in a RELATIONSHIP with an UNGRATEFUL BEAST?
ABUSE?
RIP
YOU MAY BE THE VICTIM of a common yet devastating EMOTIONAL DISORDER...
NEGLECT?
CATS WHO HATE PEOPLE AND THE PEOPLE WHO LOVE THEM
#1 BEST SELLER
Why Do U Feel I'm NOTHING Without a Cat?
"I gave, gave, gave. He just took, took, took." – one woman's nightmare
Sounds like a sane arrangement to me...
People Who Love Cats Too Much
"Too Much?"
As if that were even POSSIBLE!
©1988 Marian Henley

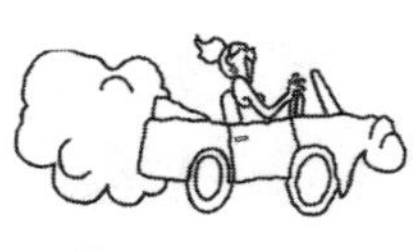

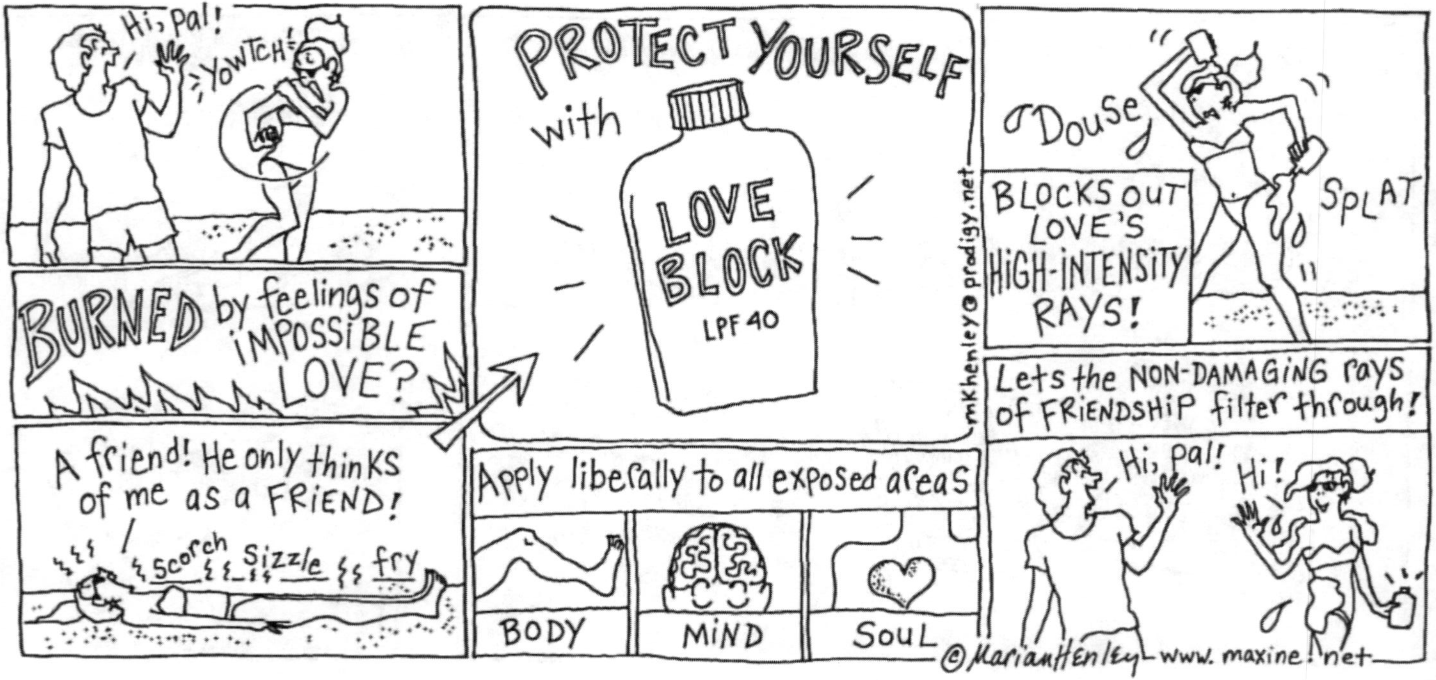
Hi, pal!
YOWTCH!
BURNED by feelings of IMPOSSIBLE LOVE?
A friend! He only thinks of me as a FRIEND!
scorch sizzle fry
PROTECT YOURSELF with
LOVE BLOCK
LPF 40
mkhenley@prodigy.net
Apply liberally to all exposed areas
BODY
MIND
SOUL
Douse
SPLAT
BLOCKS OUT LOVE'S HIGH-INTENSITY RAYS!
Lets the NON-DAMAGING rays of FRIENDSHIP filter through!
Hi, pal!
Hi!
©MarianHenley www.maxine!.net

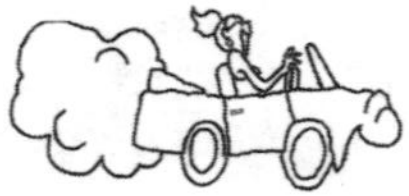

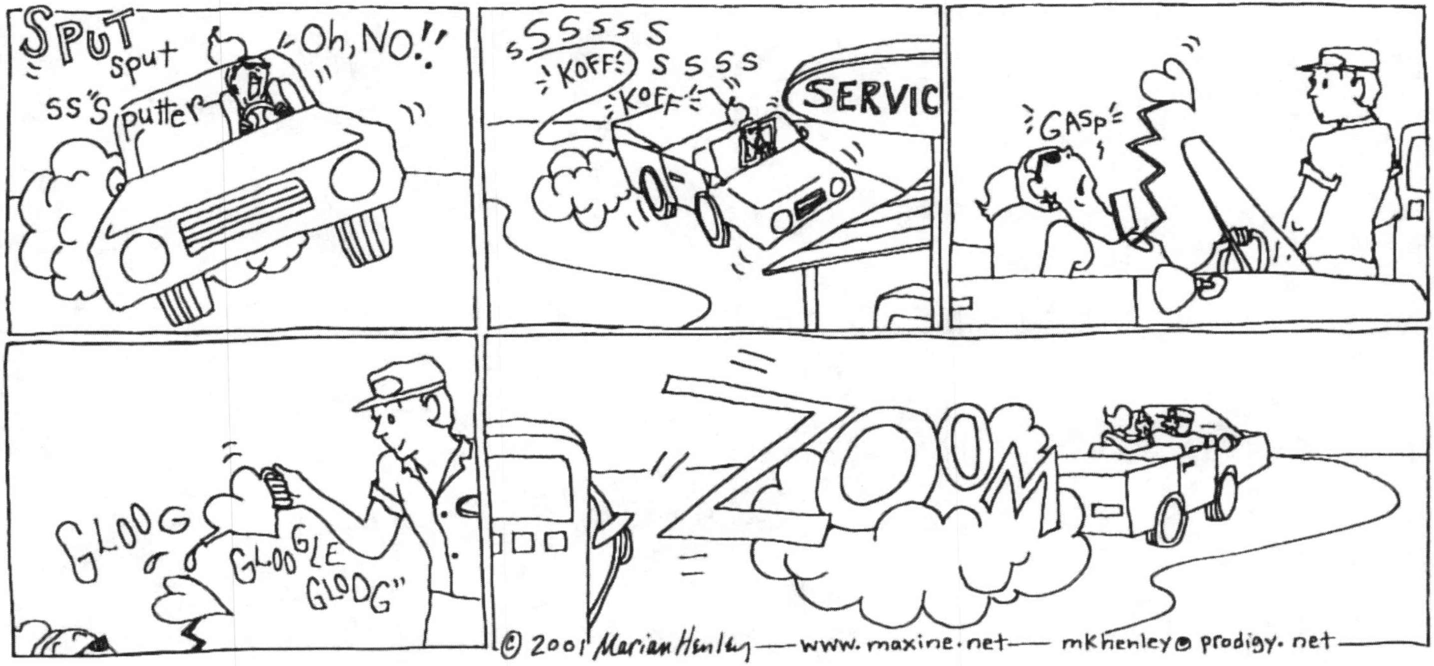
SPUT
sput
SSS putter
"Oh, NO!!"
sSSsss
KOFF
SSSS
KOFF
SERVIC
GASP
GLOOG
GLOOGLE
GLODG"
ZOOM
© 2001 Marian Henley — www.maxine.net — mkhenley@prodigy.net

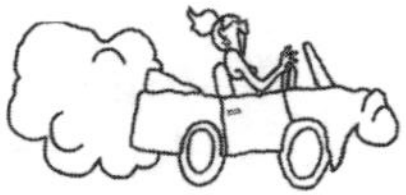

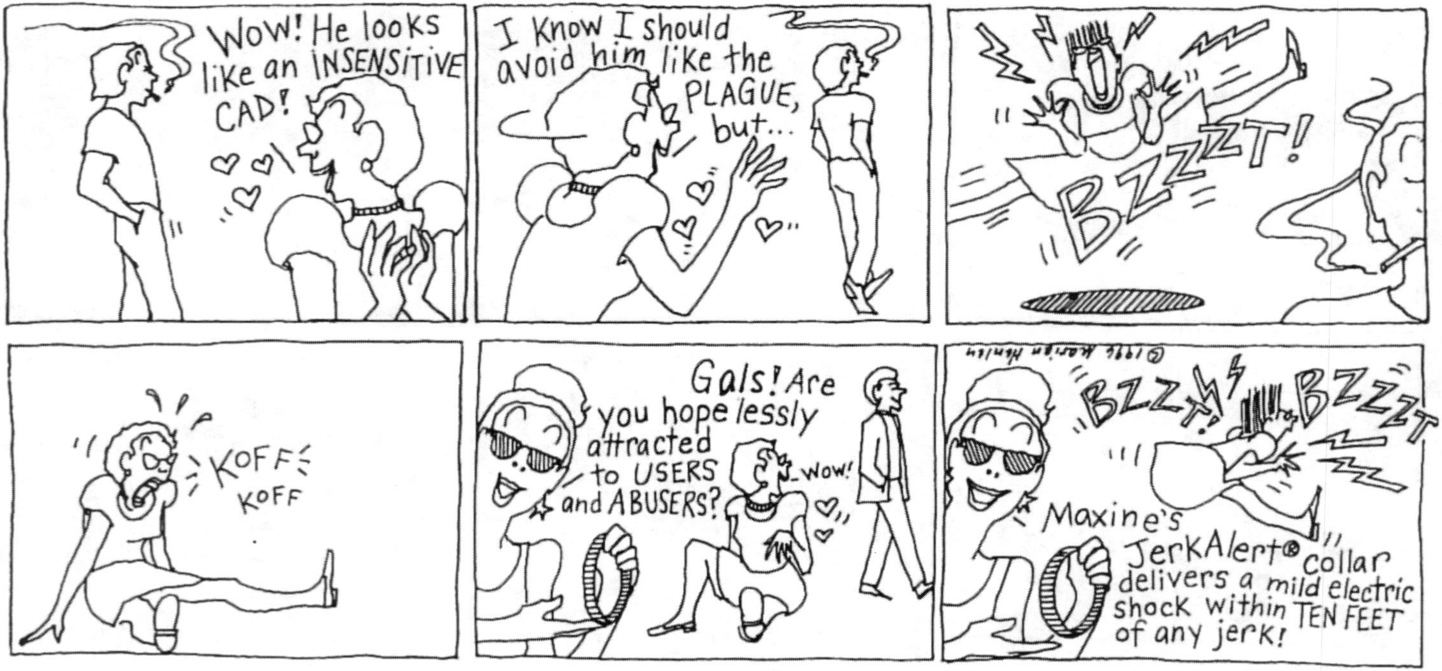
Wow! He looks like an INSENSITIVE CAD!
I Know I should avoid him like the PLAGUE, but...
BZZZZT!
KOFF KOFF
Gals! Are you hopelessly attracted to USERS and ABUSERS?
WOW!
BZZZT! BZZZZT
Maxine's JerkAlert® collar delivers a mild electric shock within TEN FEET of any jerk!

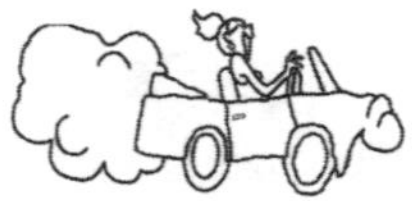

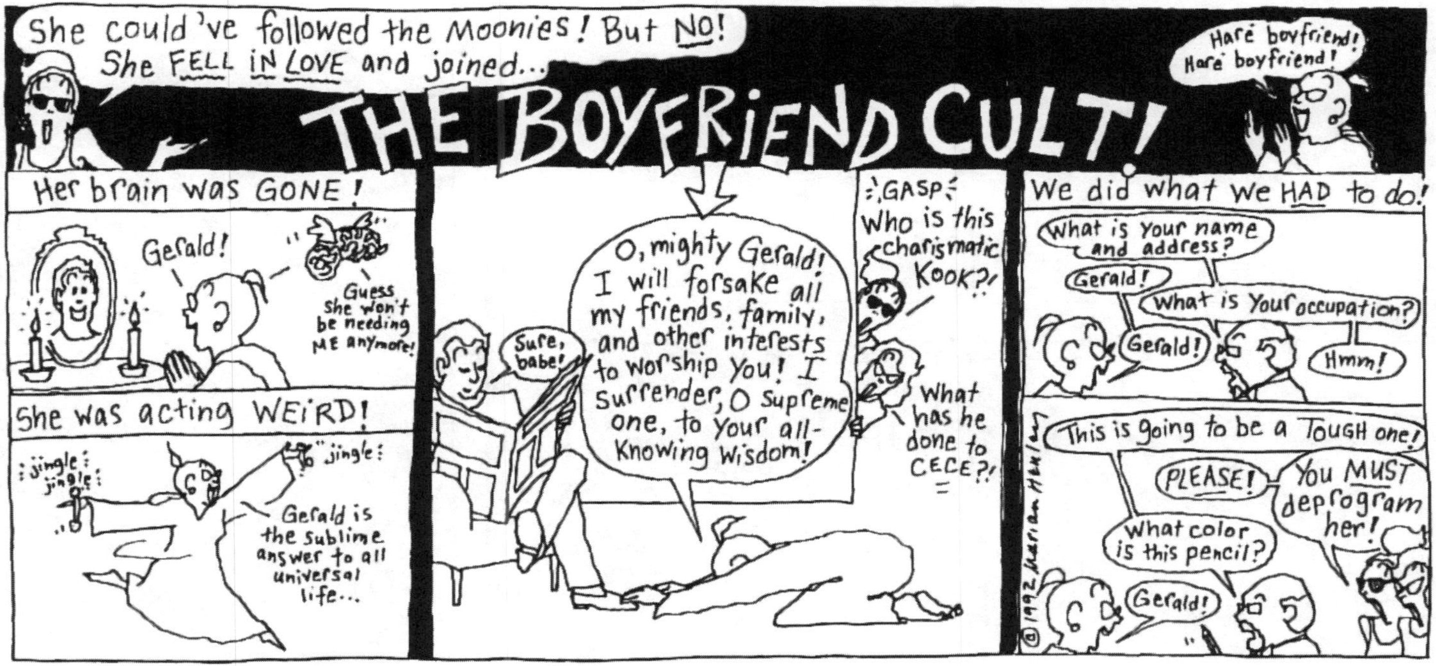
She could've followed the Moonies! But NO! She FELL IN LOVE and joined...
Haré boyfriend! Haré boyfriend!
THE BOYFRIEND CULT!
Her brain was GONE!
Gerald!
Guess she won't be needing ME anymore!
She was acting WEIRD!
jingle jingle
jingle
Gerald is the sublime answer to all universal life...
O, mighty Gerald! I will forsake all my friends, family, and other interests to worship You! I surrender, O supreme one, to your all-knowing wisdom!
Sure, babe!
GASP
Who is this charismatic Kook?!
What has he done to CECE?!
We did what we HAD to do!
What is your name and address?
Gerald!
What is your occupation?
Gerald!
Hmm!
This is going to be a TOUGH one!
PLEASE!
You MUST deprogram her!
What color is this pencil?
Gerald!
© 1992 Marian Henley

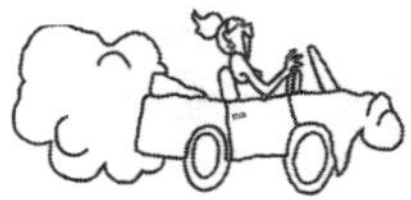

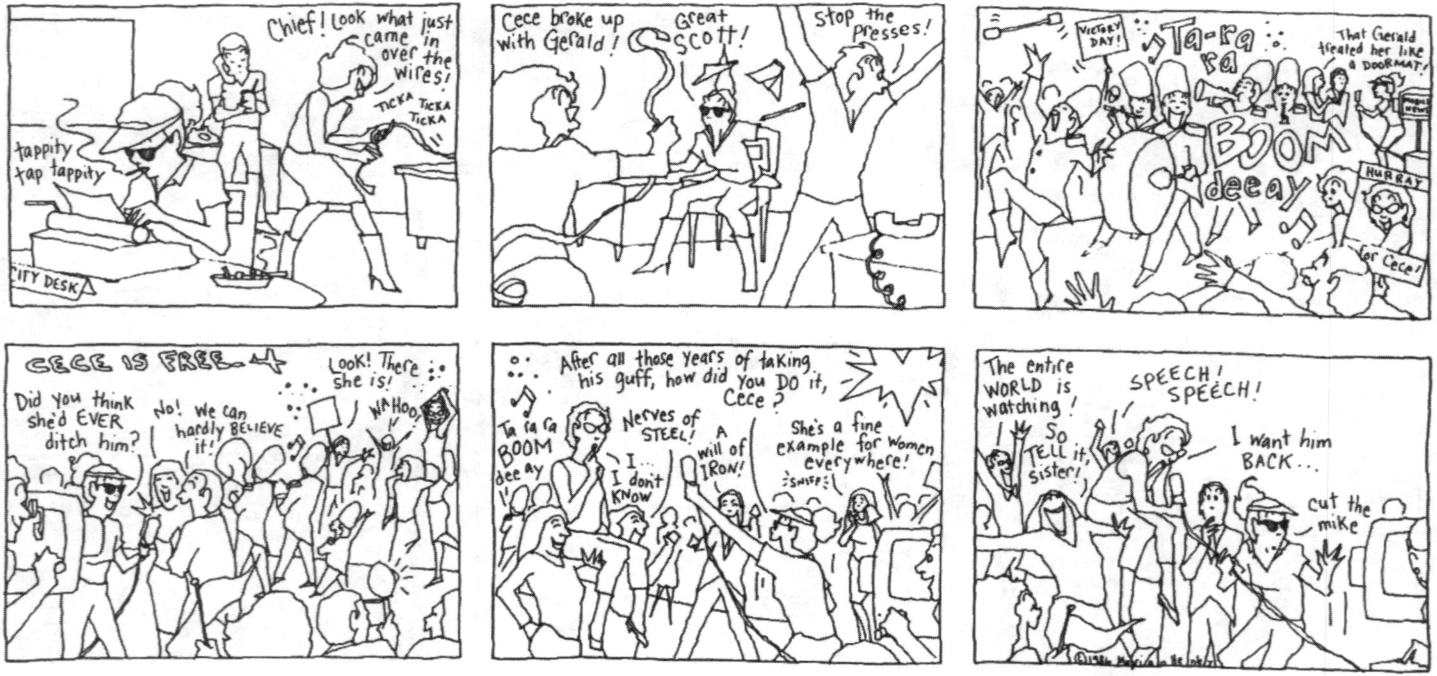
tappity tap tappity
Chief! Look what just came in over the wires!
TICKA TICKA TICKA
CITY DESK
Cece broke up with Gerald!
Great SCOTT!
Stop the presses!
VICTORY DAY!
Ta-ra ra BOOM deeay
That Gerald treated her like a DOORMAT!
HURRAY for Cece!
CECE IS FREE
Did you think she'd EVER ditch him?
No! We can hardly BELIEVE it!
LOOK! There she is!
WAHOO!
After all those years of taking his guff, how did you DO it, Cece?
Ta ra ra BOOM dee ay
Nerves of STEEL!
I... I don't KNOW
A will of IRON!
She's a fine example for women everywhere!
SNIFF
The entire WORLD is watching!
So TELL it, sister!
SPEECH! SPEECH!
I want him BACK...
cut the mike

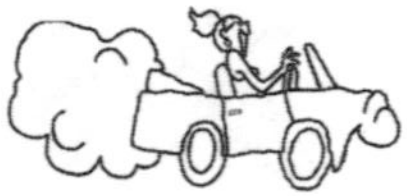

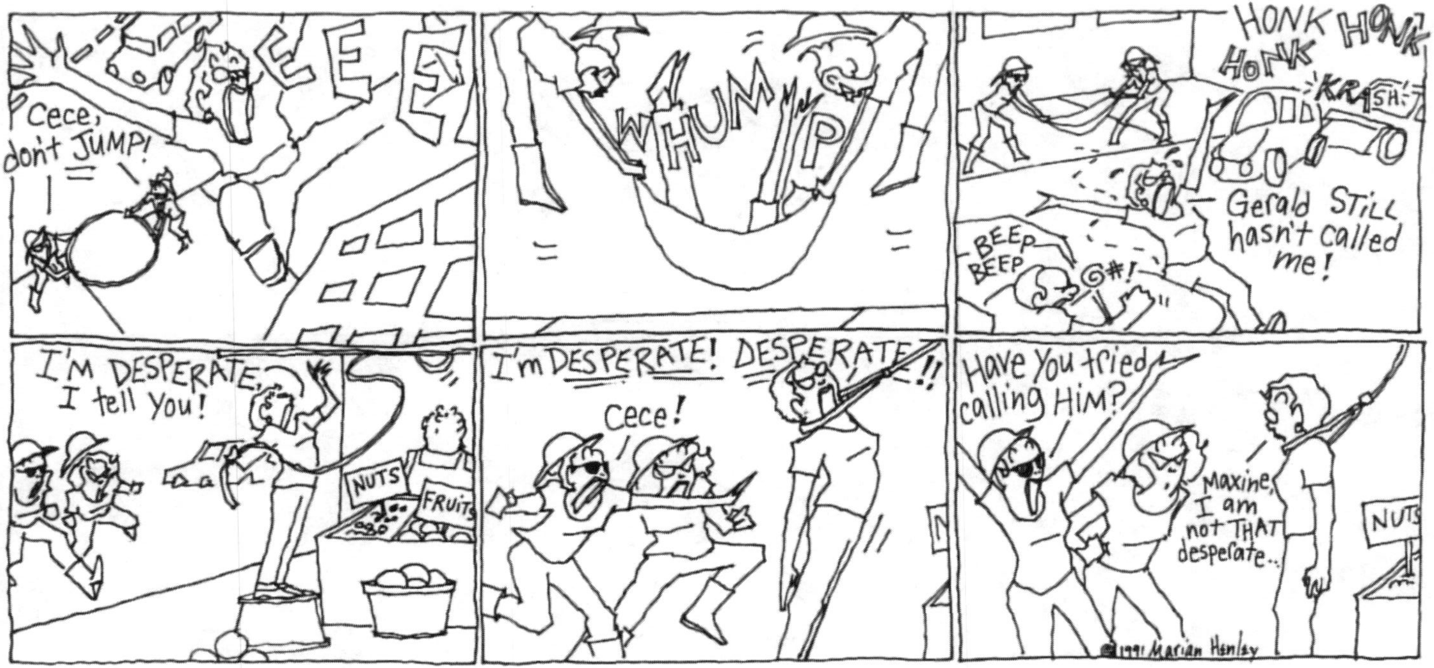
EEE
Cece, don't JUMP!
WHUMP
HONK HONK HONK
KRASH
Gerald STILL hasn't called me!
BEEP BEEP
@#!
I'M DESPERATE, I tell you!
NUTS
FRUITS
I'm DESPERATE! DESPERATE!!
Cece!
Have you tried calling HIM?
Maxine, I am not THAT desperate..
NUTS
©1991 Marian Henley

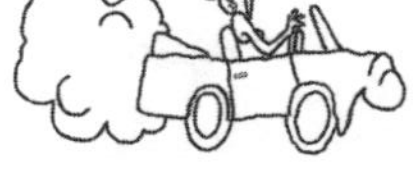

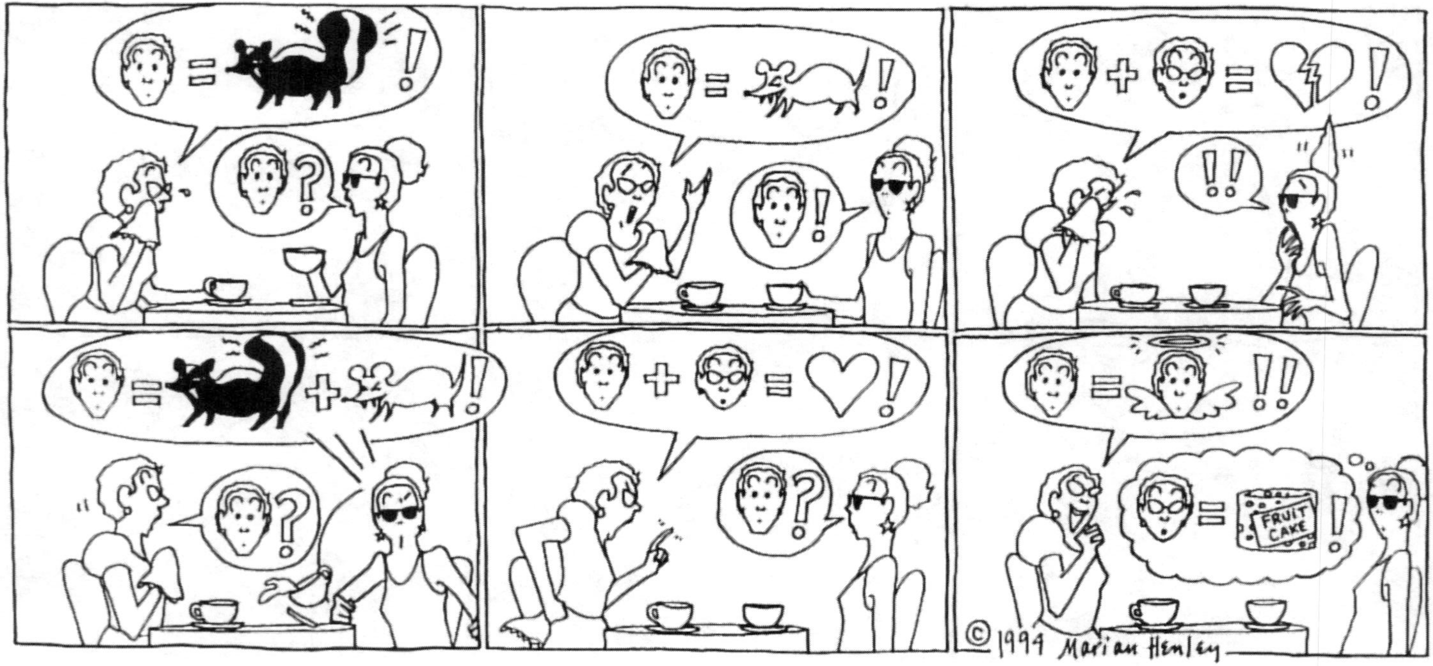
FRUIT CAKE
© 1994 Marian Henley

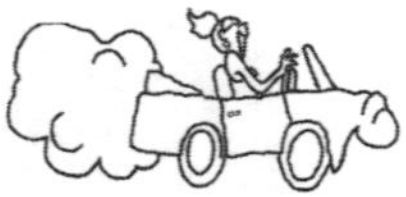

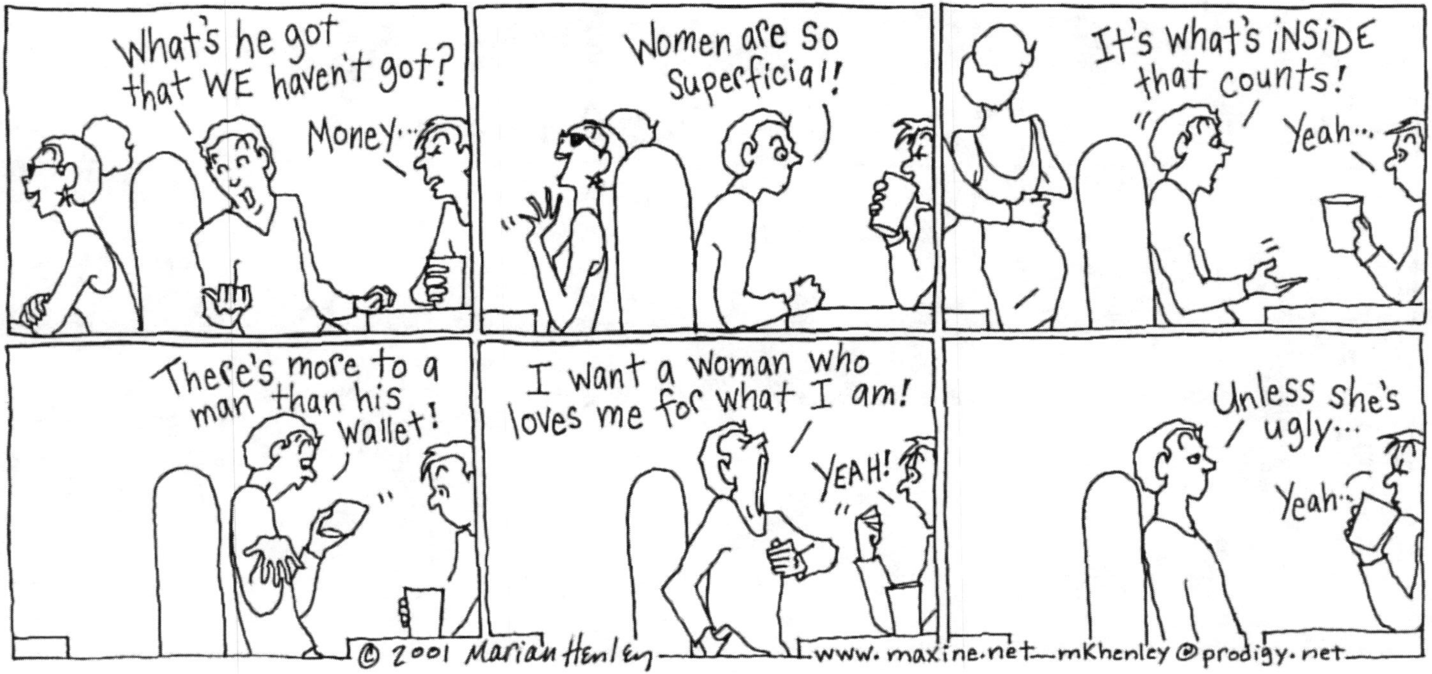
What's he got that WE haven't got?
Money...
Women are so superficial!
It's what's INSIDE that counts!
Yeah...
There's more to a man than his wallet!
I want a woman who loves me for what I am!
YEAH!
Unless she's ugly...
Yeah...
© 2001 Marian Henley www.maxine.net mKhenley@prodigy.net

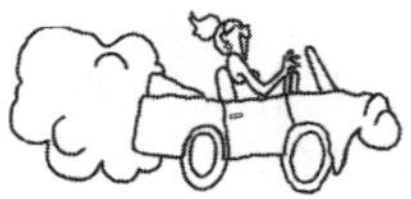

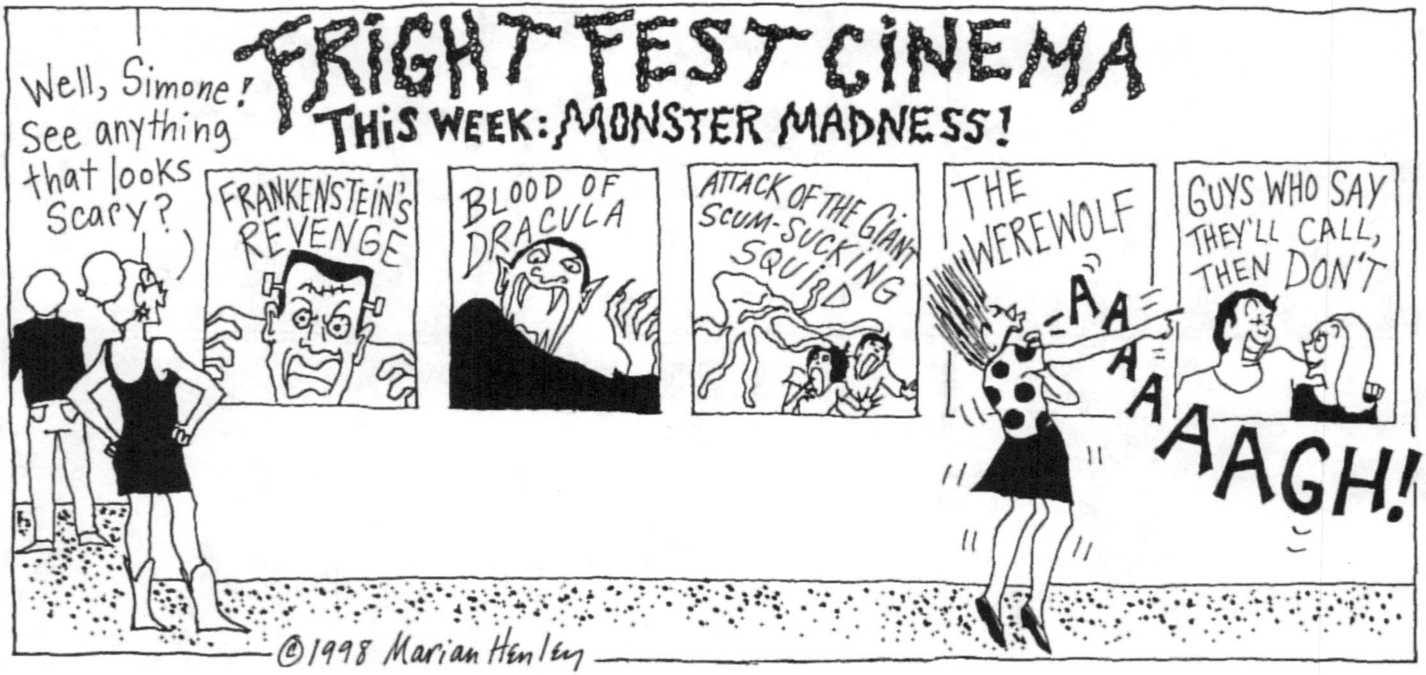
Well, Simone! See anything that looks scary?
FRIGHT FEST CINEMA
THIS WEEK: MONSTER MADNESS!
FRANKENSTEIN'S REVENGE
BLOOD OF DRACULA
ATTACK OF THE GIANT SCUM-SUCKING SQUID
THE WEREWOLF
GUYS WHO SAY THEY'LL CALL, THEN DON'T
AAAAAAGH!
©1998 Marian Henley

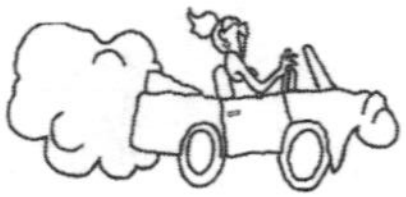

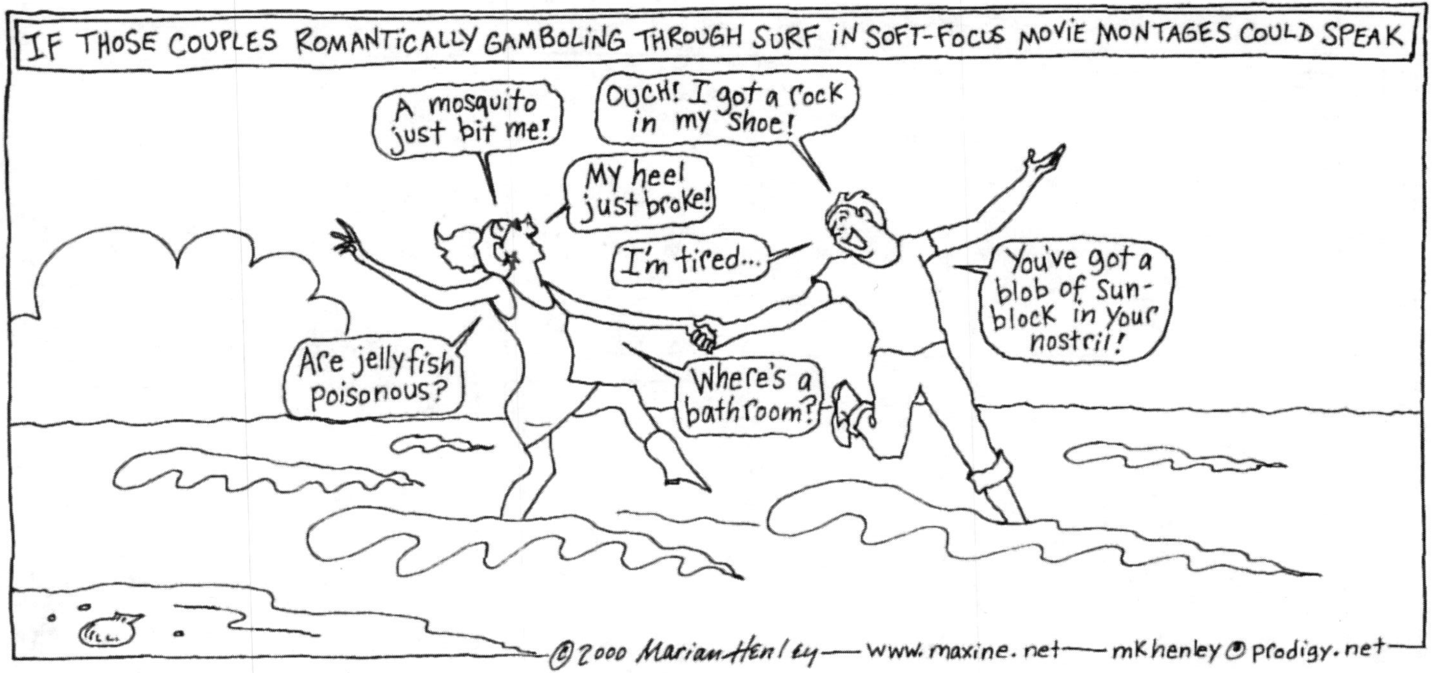
IF THOSE COUPLES ROMANTICALLY GAMBOLING THROUGH SURF IN SOFT-FOCUS MOVIE MONTAGES COULD SPEAK
A mosquito just bit me!
OUCH! I got a rock in my shoe!
My heel just broke!
I'm tired...
You've got a blob of Sun-block in your nostril!
Are jellyfish poisonous?
Where's a bathroom?
©2000 Marian Henley — www.maxine.net — mkhenley@prodigy.net

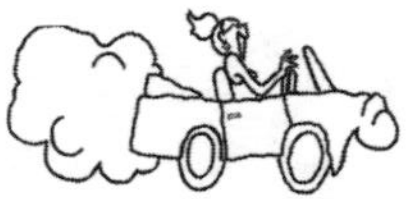

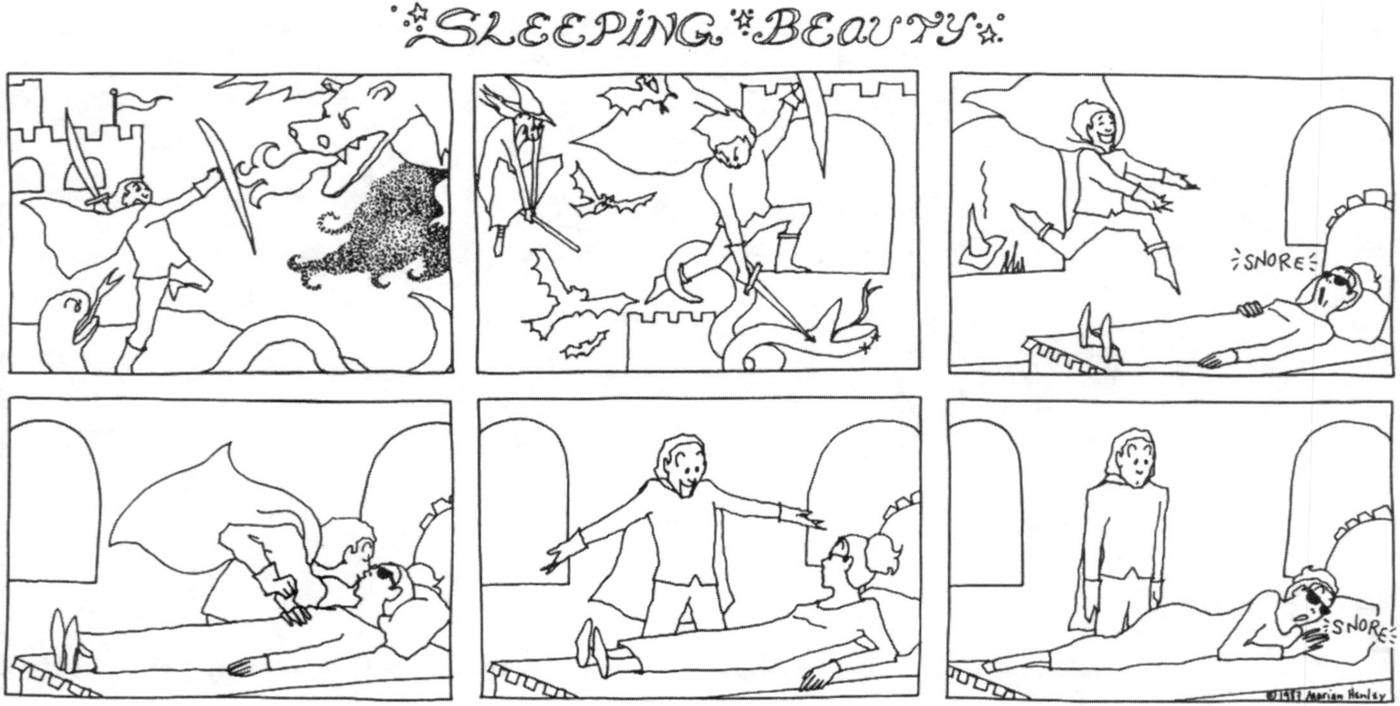
SLEEPING BEAUTY
SNORE
SNORE
Marian Henley

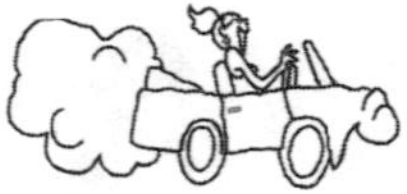

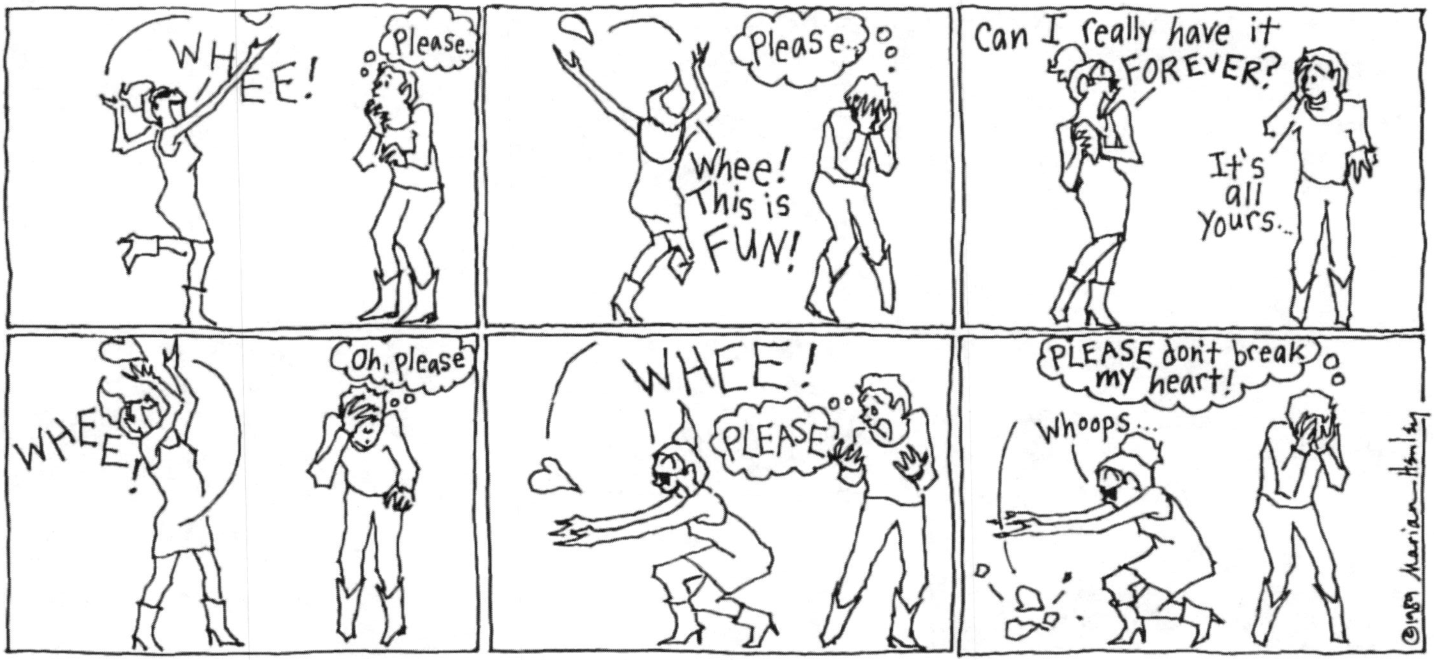
WHEE!
Please..
Please...
Whee! This is FUN!
Can I really have it FOREVER?
It's all Yours...
WHEE!
Oh, please
WHEE!
PLEASE
PLEASE don't break my heart!
Whoops...
©1989 Marian Henley

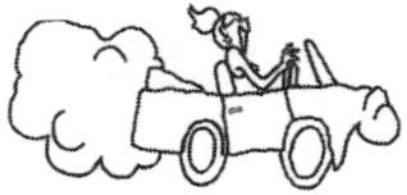

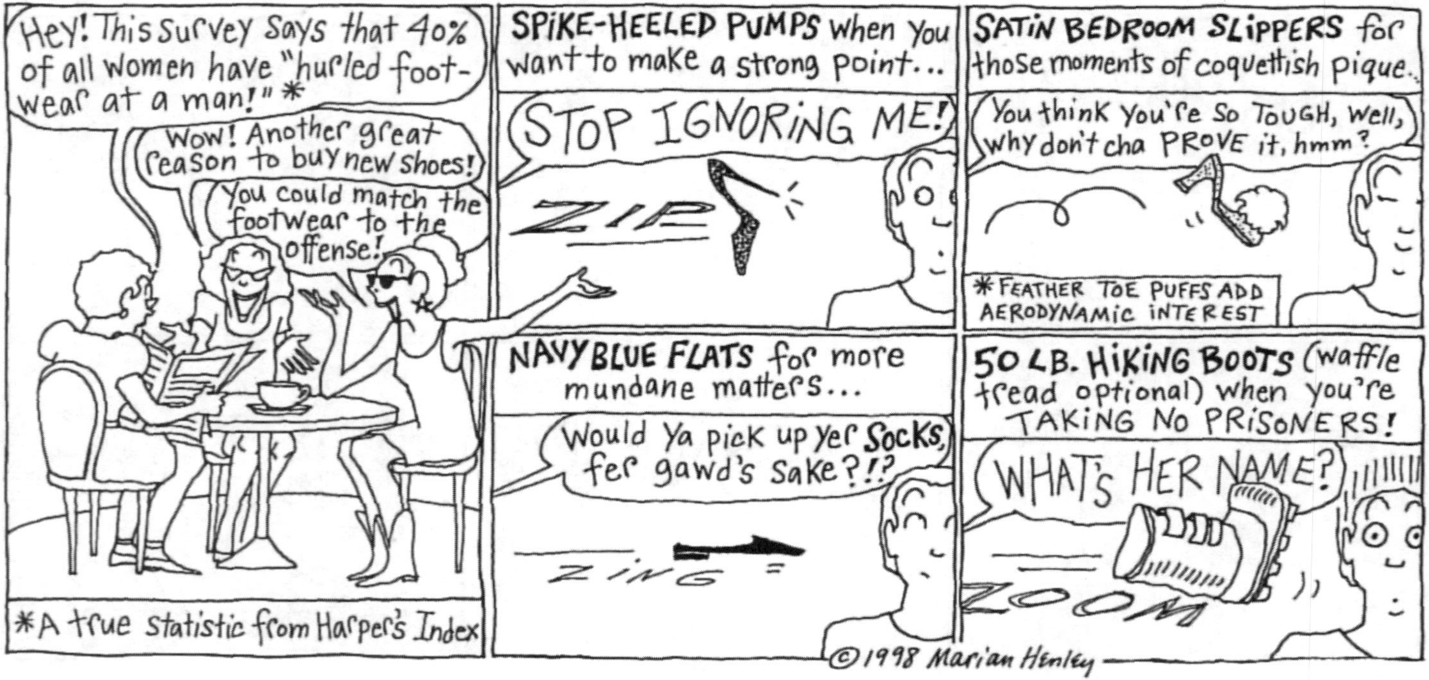
Hey! This Survey Says that 40% of all women have "hurled foot-wear at a man!" *
Wow! Another great reason to buy new shoes!
You could match the footwear to the offense!
*A true statistic from Harper's Index
SPIKE-HEELED PUMPS when you want to make a strong point...
STOP IGNORING ME!
ZIP
NAVY BLUE FLATS for more mundane matters...
Would ya pick up yer SOCKS, fer gawd's sake?!?
ZING
SATIN BEDROOM SLIPPERS for those moments of coquettish pique...
You think you're so TOUGH, well, why don't cha PROVE it, hmm?
* FEATHER TOE PUFFS ADD AERODYNAMIC INTEREST
50 LB. HIKING BOOTS (waffle tread optional) when you're TAKING NO PRISONERS!
WHAT'S HER NAME?
ZOOM
©1998 Marian Henley

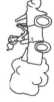

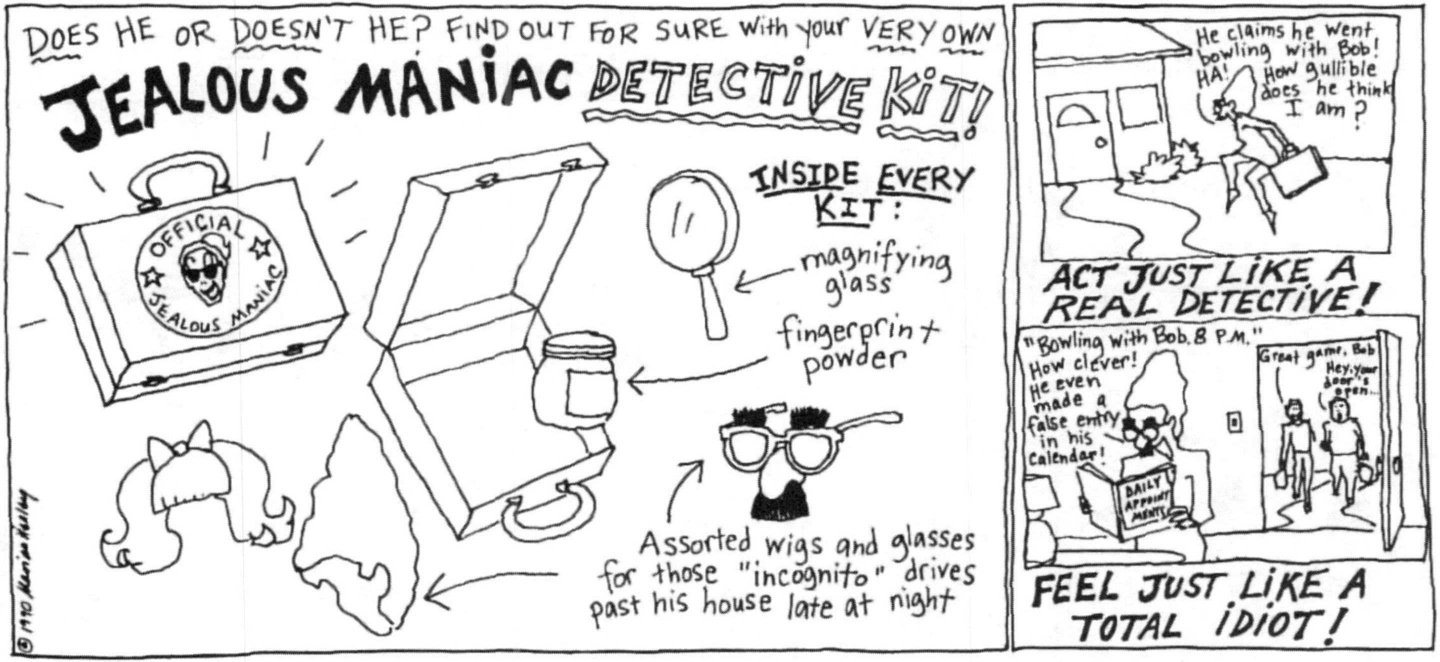
© 1990 Marian Henley
DOES HE OR DOESN'T HE? FIND OUT FOR SURE with your VERY OWN
JEALOUS MANIAC DETECTIVE KIT!
OFFICIAL JEALOUS MANIAC
INSIDE EVERY KIT:
magnifying glass
fingerprint powder
Assorted wigs and glasses for those "incognito" drives past his house late at night
He claims he went bowling with Bob! HA! How gullible does he think I am?
ACT JUST LIKE A REAL DETECTIVE!
"Bowling with Bob. 8 P.M." How clever! He even made a false entry in his calendar!
DAILY APPOINTMENTS
Great game, Bob
Hey, your door's open...
FEEL JUST LIKE A TOTAL IDIOT!

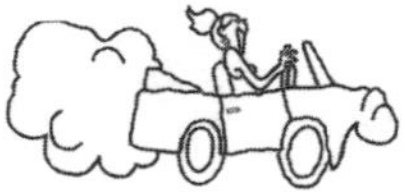

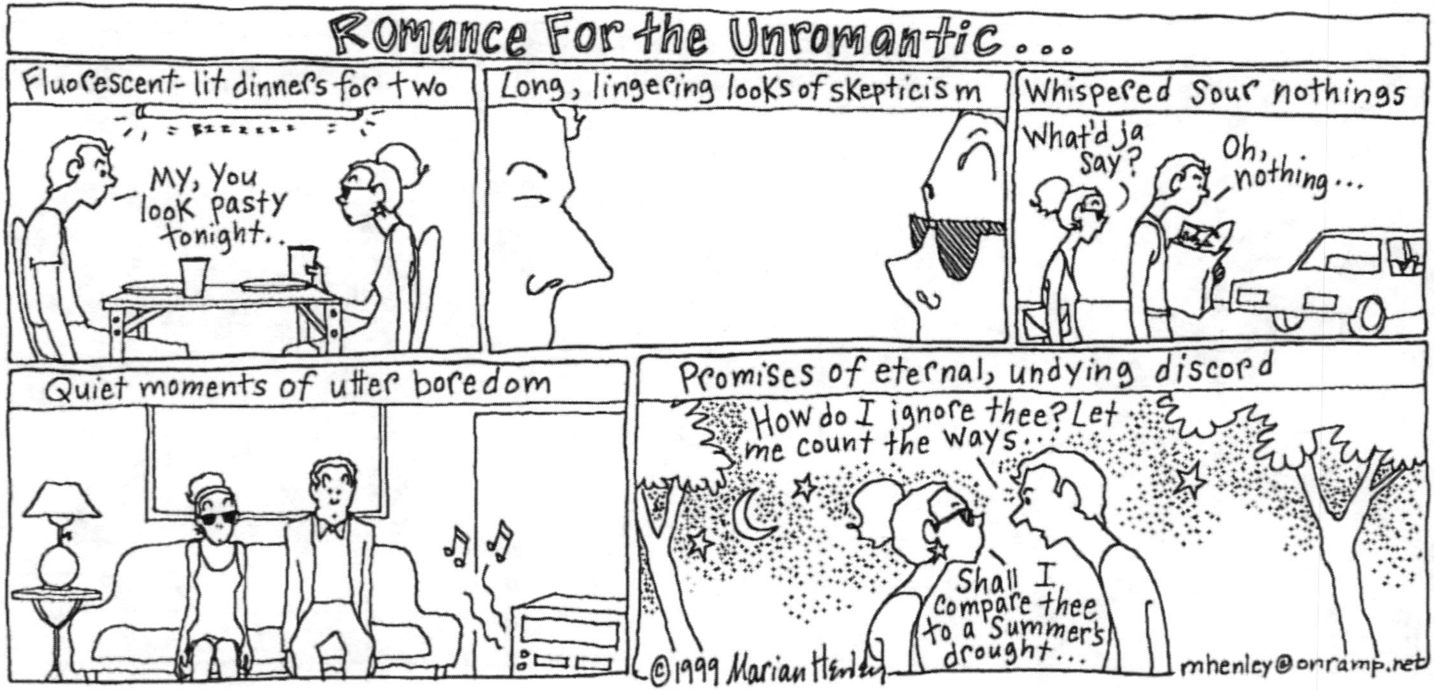
Romance For the Unromantic...
Fluorescent-lit dinners for two
BZZZZZZ
My, You look pasty tonight..
Long, lingering looks of skepticism
Whispered Sour nothings
What'd ja say?
Oh, nothing...
Quiet moments of utter boredom
Promises of eternal, undying discord
How do I ignore thee? Let me count the ways...
Shall I compare thee to a Summer's drought...
©1999 Marian Henley
mhenley@onramp.net

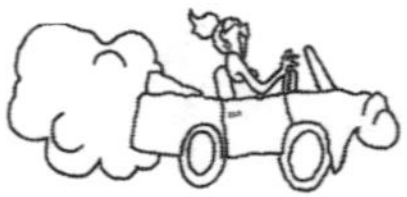

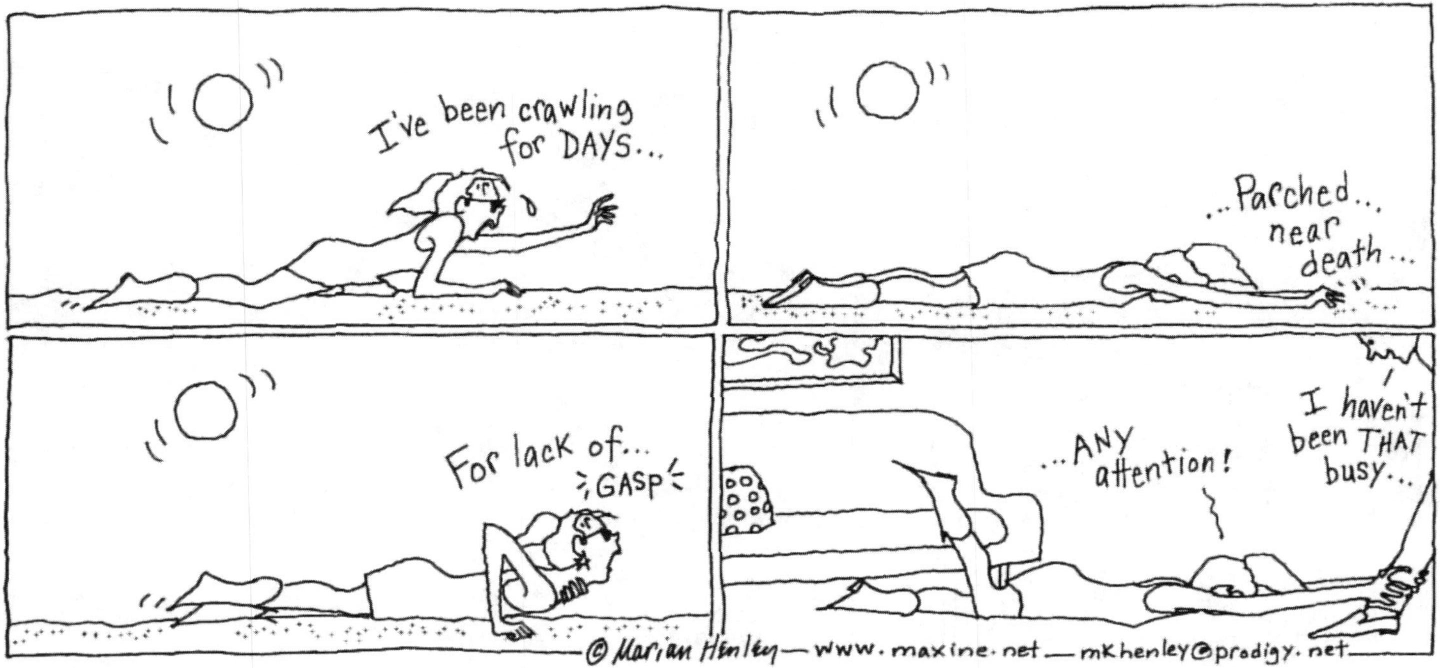
I've been crawling for DAYS...
...Parched... near death...
For lack of...
GASP
...ANY attention!
I haven't been THAT busy...
© Marian Henley—www.maxine.net—mkhenley@prodigy.net

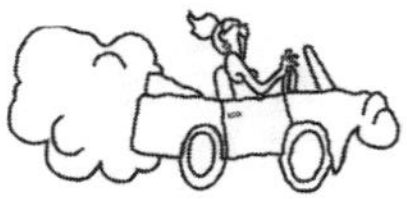

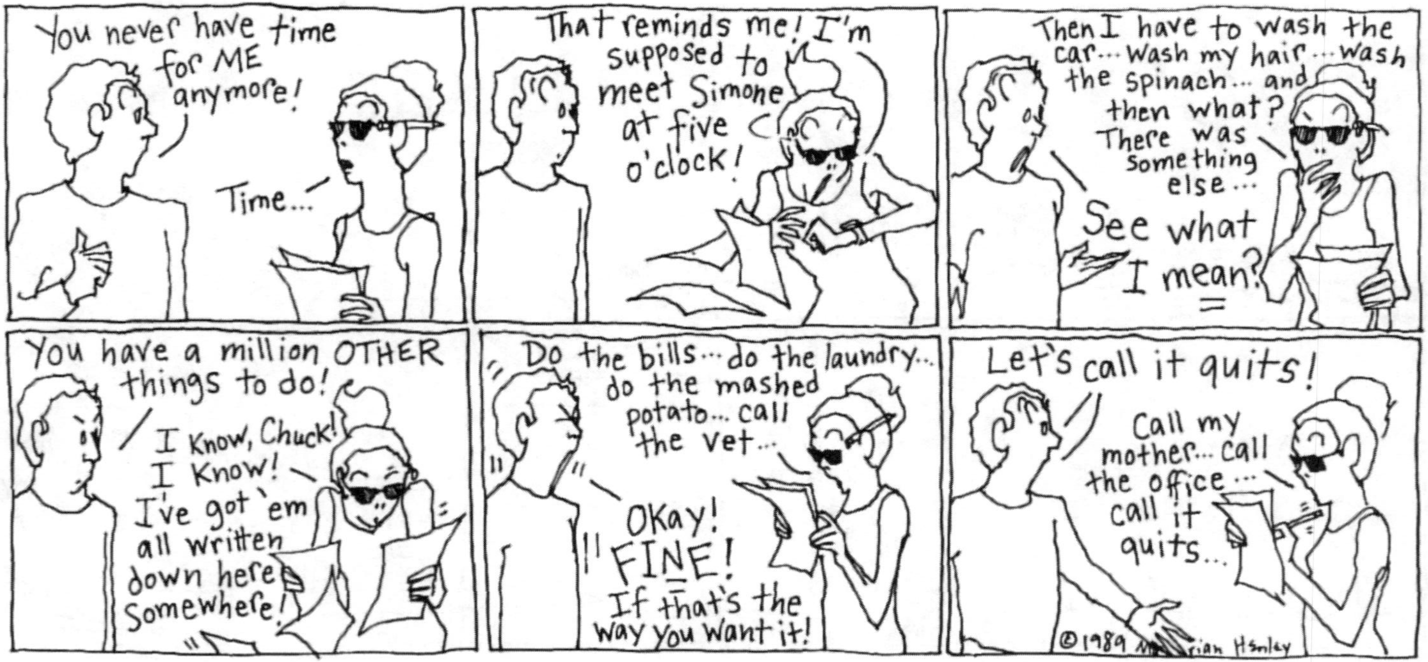
You never have time for ME anymore!
Time...
That reminds me! I'm supposed to meet Simone at five o'clock!
Then I have to wash the car... wash my hair... wash the spinach... and then what? There was something else...
See what I mean?
You have a million OTHER things to do!
I know, Chuck! I know! I've got 'em all written down here somewhere!
Do the bills... do the laundry... do the mashed potato... call the vet...
OKAY! FINE! If that's the way you want it!
Let's call it quits!
Call my mother... call the office... call it quits...
©1989

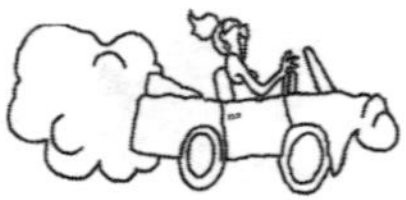

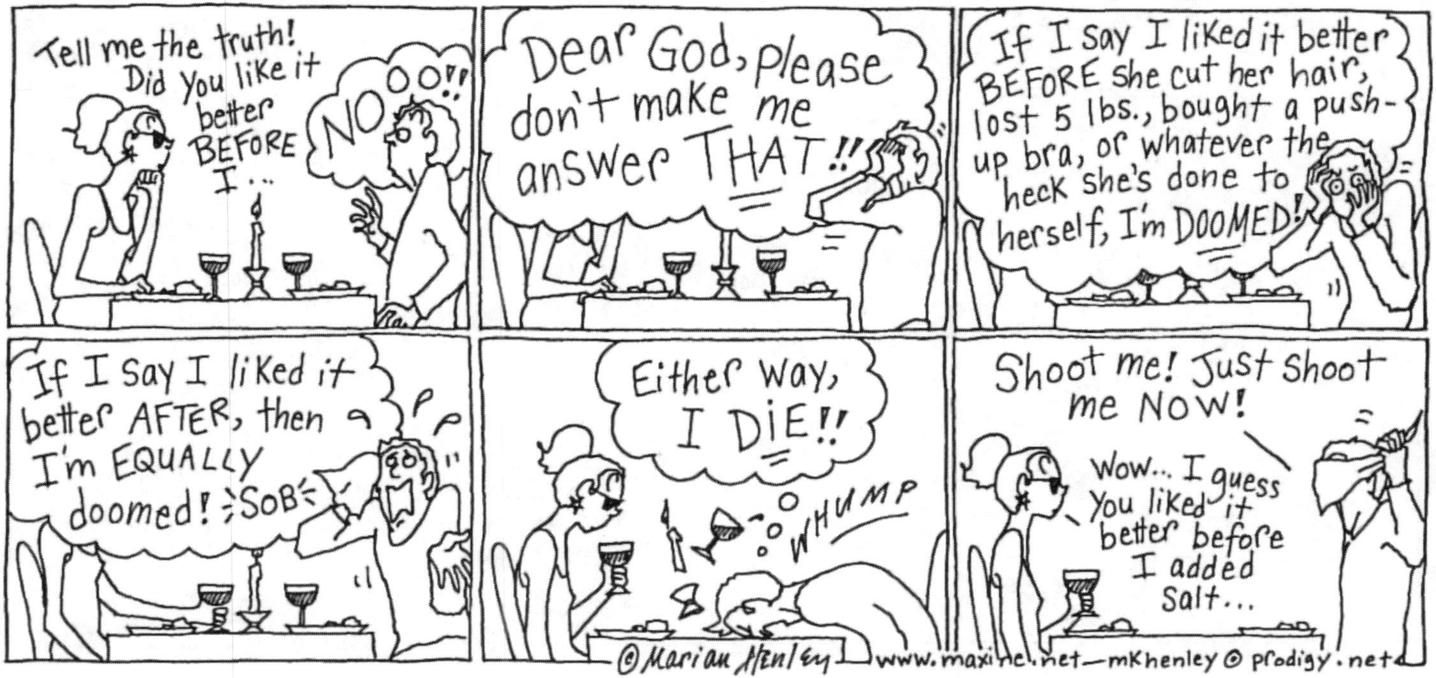
Tell me the truth! Did you like it better BEFORE I...
NOOOO!!
Dear God, please don't make me answer THAT!!
If I say I liked it better BEFORE she cut her hair, lost 5 lbs., bought a push-up bra, or whatever the heck she's done to herself, I'm DOOMED!
If I say I liked it better AFTER, then I'm EQUALLY doomed! ;SOB;
Either way, I DIE!!
WHUMP
Shoot me! Just Shoot me NOW!
Wow... I guess You liked it better before I added Salt...
©Marian Henley www.maxine.net—mKhenley@prodigy.net

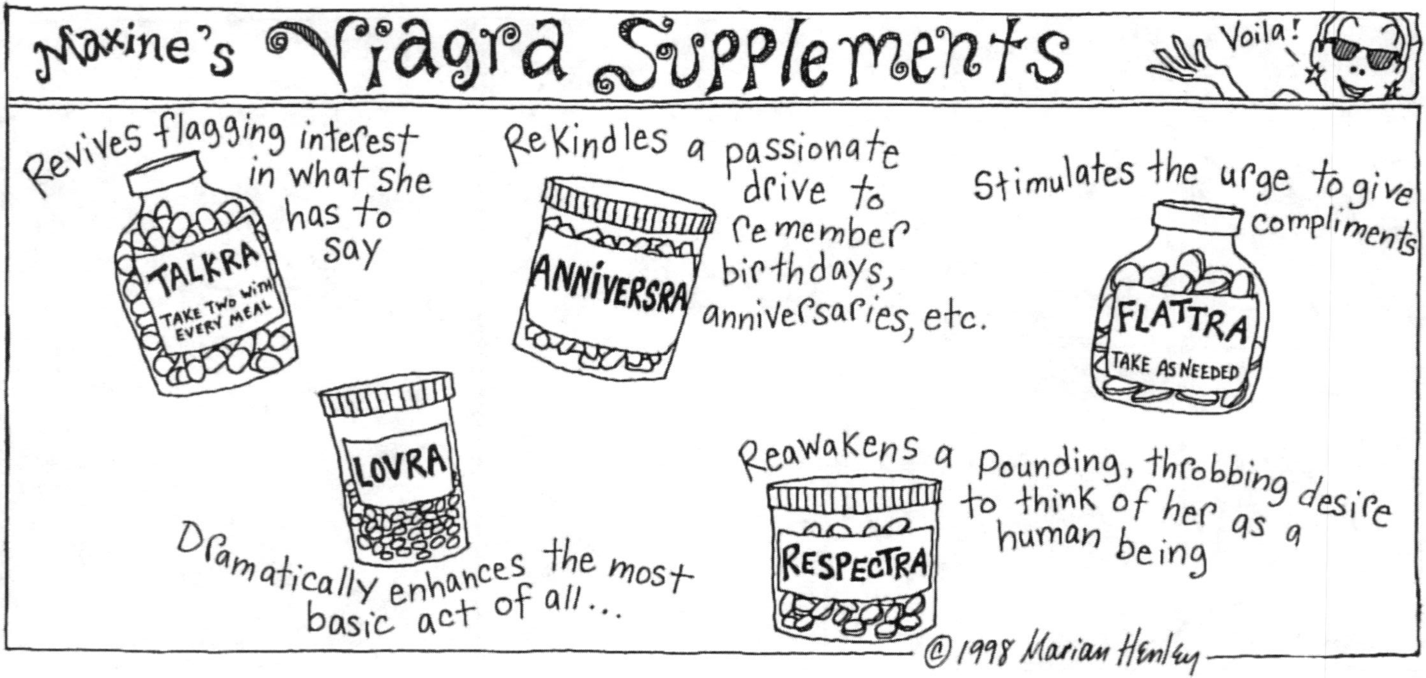
Maxine's Viagra Supplements
Voila!
Revives flagging interest in what she has to say
TALKRA
TAKE TWO WITH EVERY MEAL
Rekindles a passionate drive to remember birthdays, anniversaries, etc.
ANNIVERSRA
Stimulates the urge to give compliments
FLATTRA
TAKE AS NEEDED
LOVRA
Dramatically enhances the most basic act of all...
Reawakens a pounding, throbbing desire to think of her as a human being
RESPECTRA
© 1998 Marian Henley

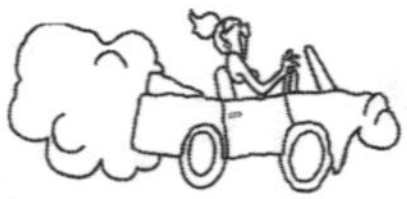

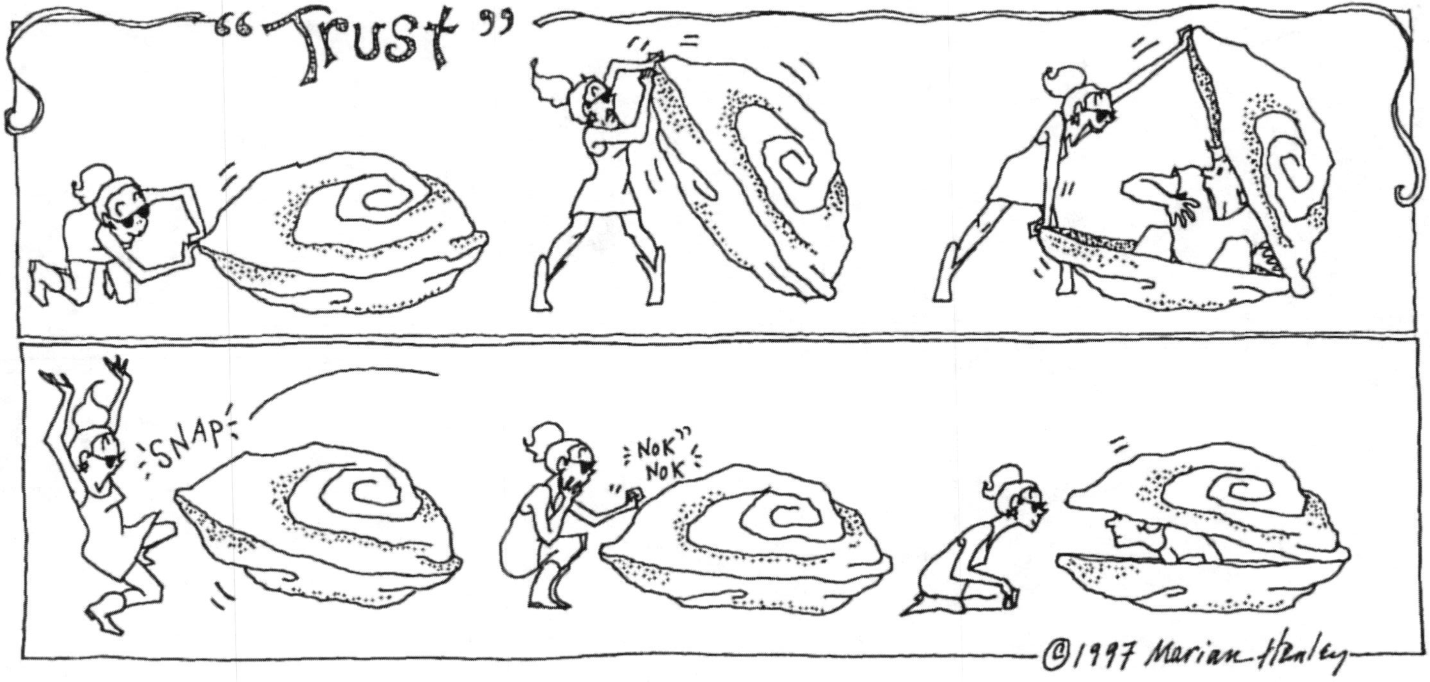
"Trust"
SNAP
NOK NOK
©1997 Marian Henley

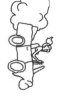

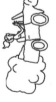

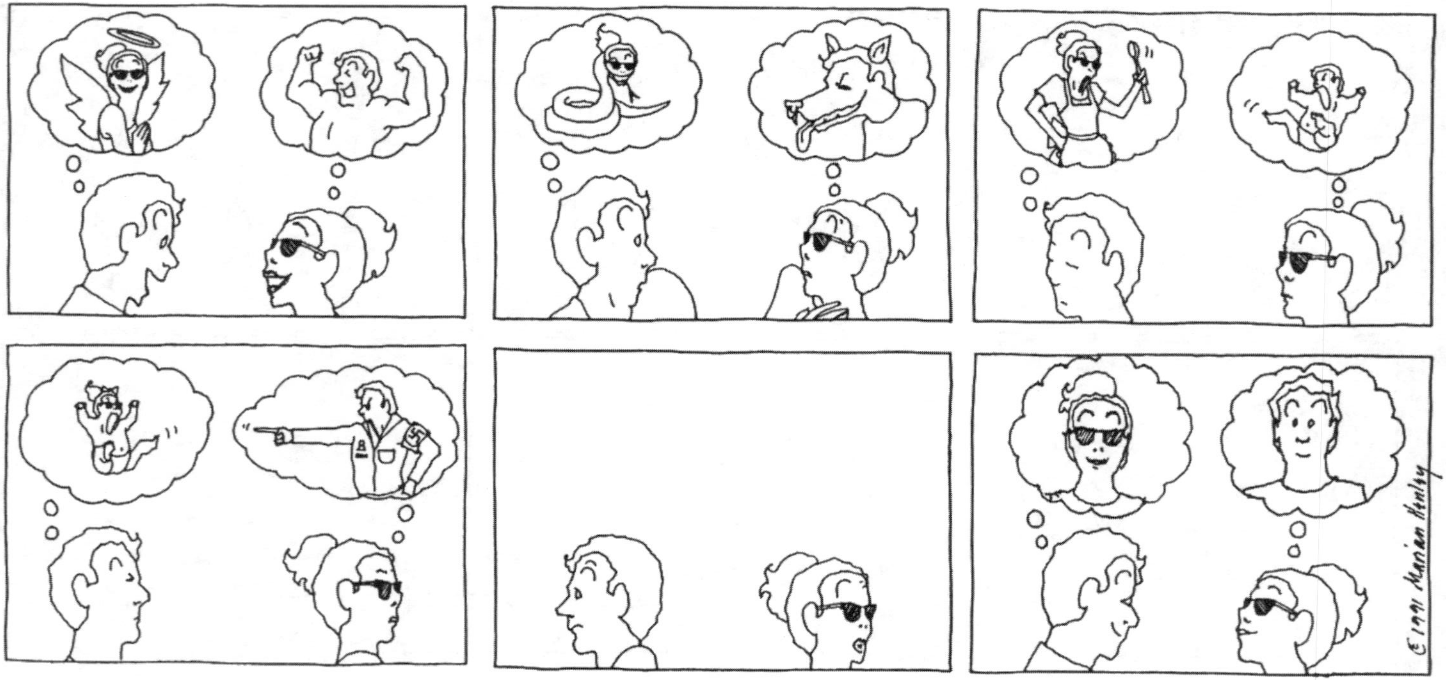
©1991 Marian Henley

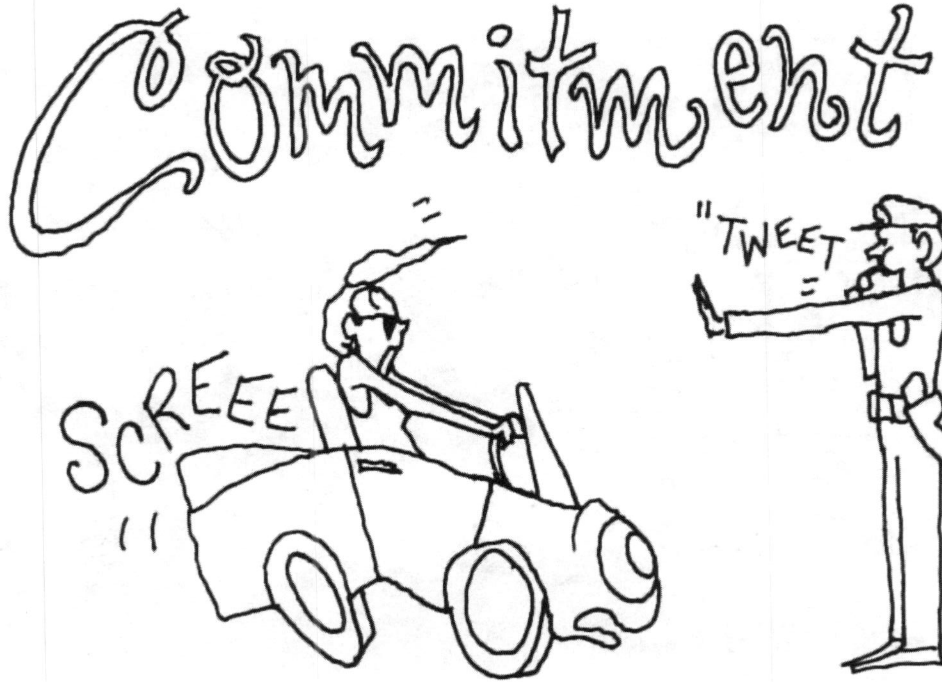
Commitment
SCREEE
"TWEET"

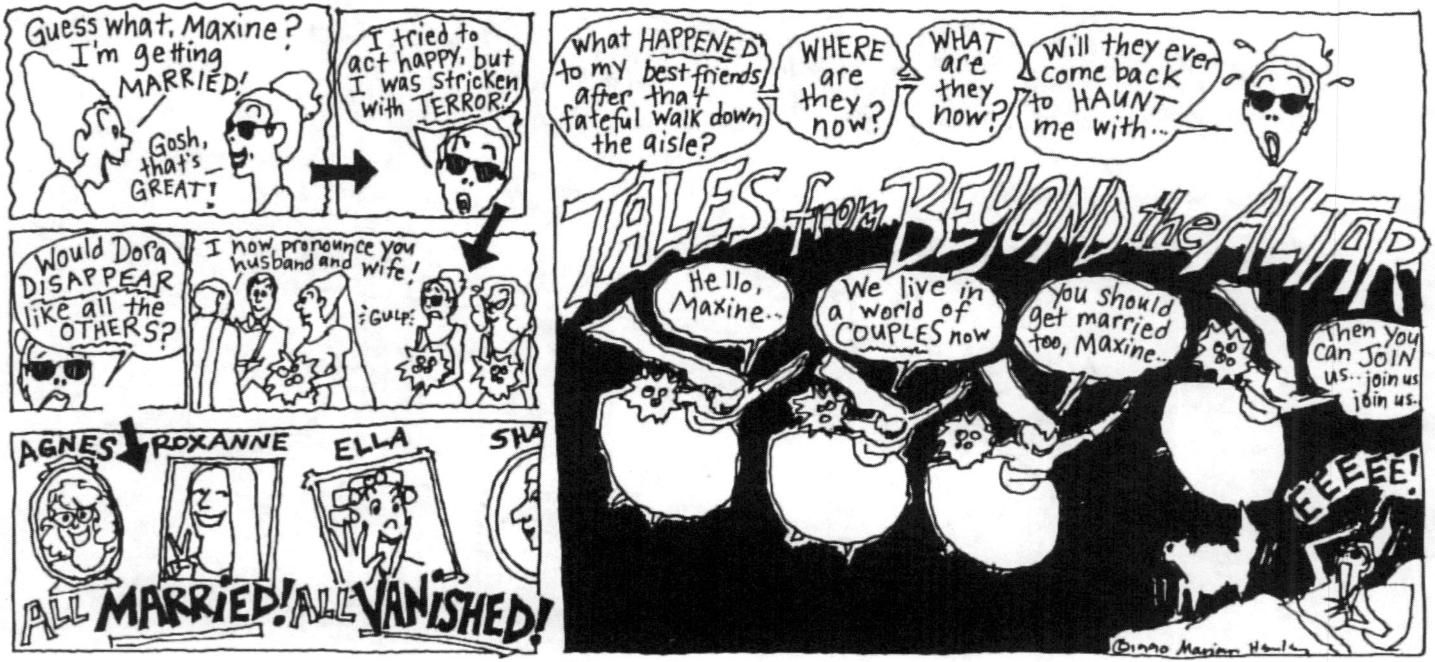
Guess what, Maxine? I'm getting MARRIED!
Gosh, that's GREAT!
I tried to act happy, but I was stricken with TERROR!
Would Dora DISAPPEAR like all the OTHERS?
I now pronounce you husband and wife!
GULP!
AGNES
ROXANNE
ELLA
ALL MARRIED! ALL VANISHED!
What HAPPENED to my best friends after that fateful walk down the aisle?
WHERE are they now?
WHAT are they now?
Will they ever come back to HAUNT me with...
TALES from BEYOND the ALTAR
Hello, Maxine...
We live in a world of COUPLES now
You should get married too, Maxine...
Then you can JOIN us... join us join us...
EEEEE!

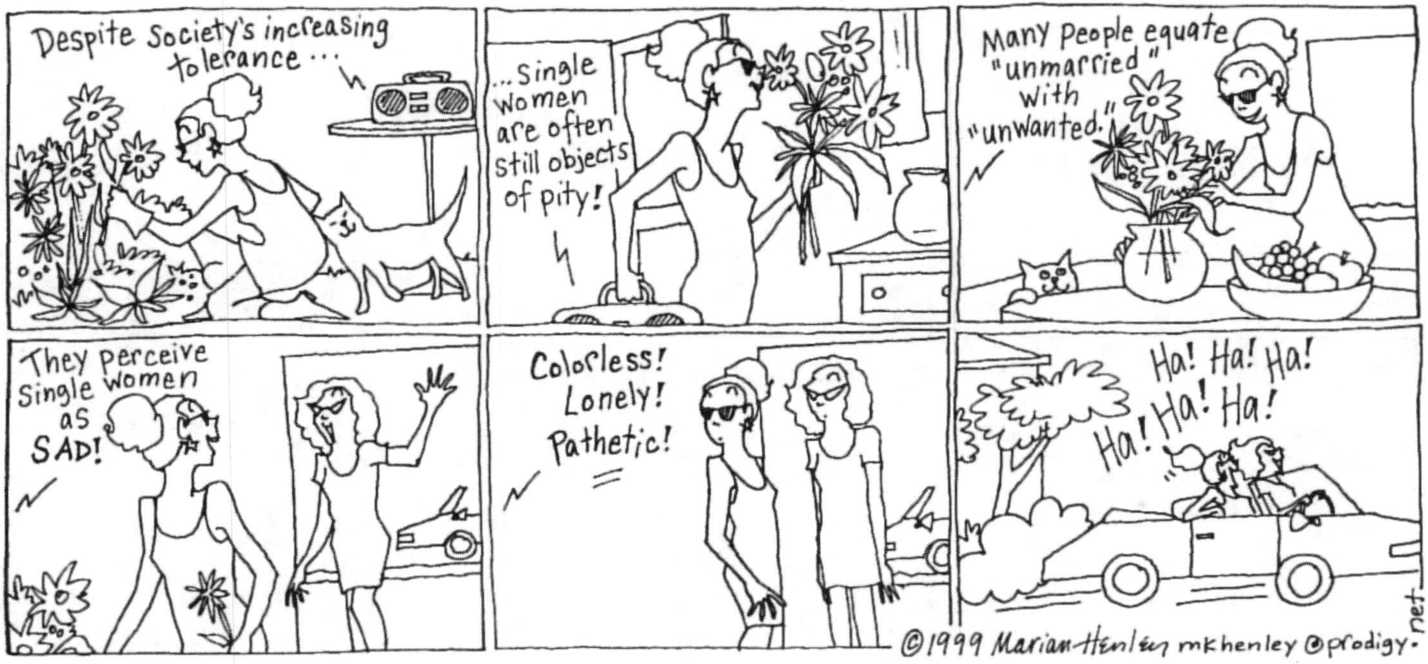
Despite Society's increasing tolerance ...
... Single women are often still objects of pity!
Many People equate "unmarried" with "unwanted."
They perceive single women as SAD!
Colorless! Lonely! Pathetic!
Ha! Ha! Ha! Ha! Ha! Ha!
©1999 Marian Henley mkhenley@prodigy.net

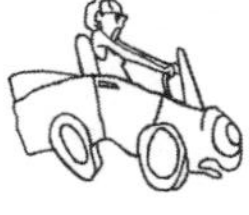

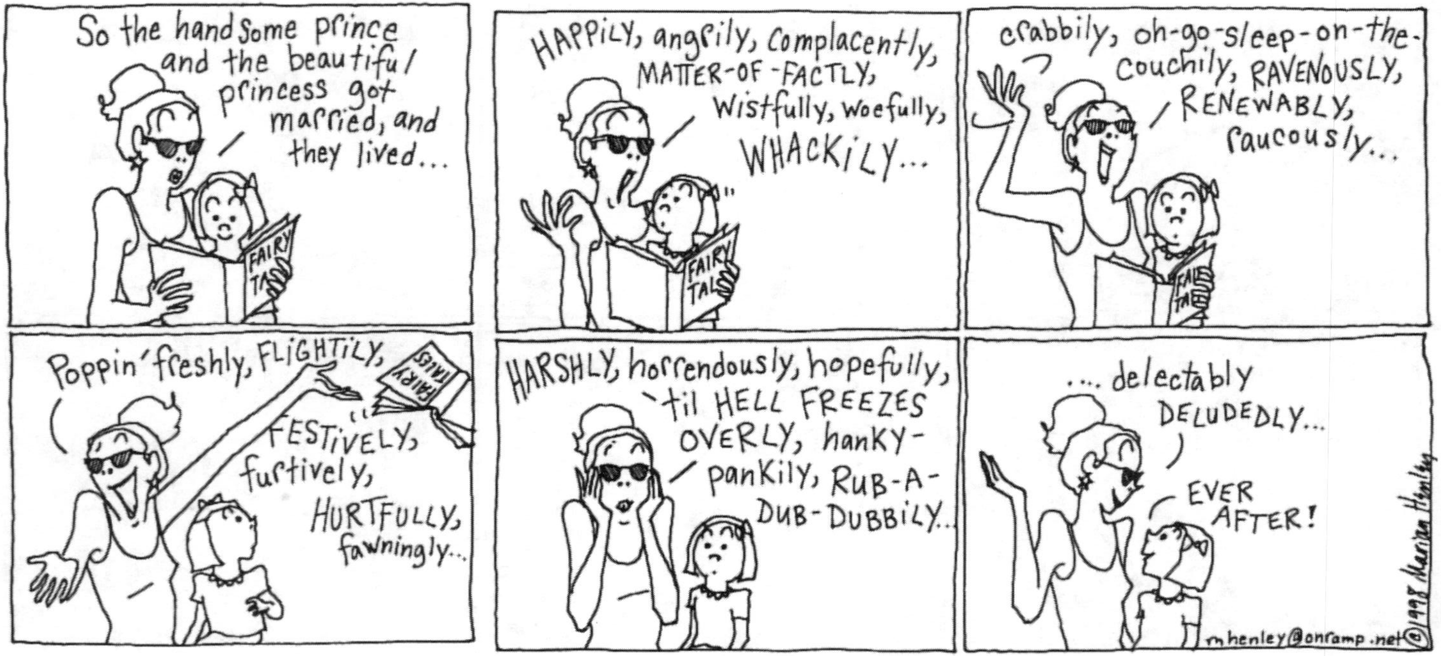
So the handsome prince and the beautiful princess got married, and they lived...
FAIRY TA
HAPPILY, angrily, complacently, MATTER-OF-FACTLY, wistfully, woefully, WHACKILY...
FAIRY TAL
crabbily, oh-go-sleep-on-the-couchily, RAVENOUSLY, RENEWABLY, raucously...
Poppin' freshly, FLIGHTILY, FESTIVELY, furtively, HURTFULLY, fawningly...
FAIRY TALES
HARSHLY, horrendously, hopefully, 'til HELL FREEZES OVERLY, hanky-pankily, RUB-A-DUB-DUBBILY...
.... delectably DELUDEDLY...
EVER AFTER!
©1998 Marian Henley
mhenley@onramp.net

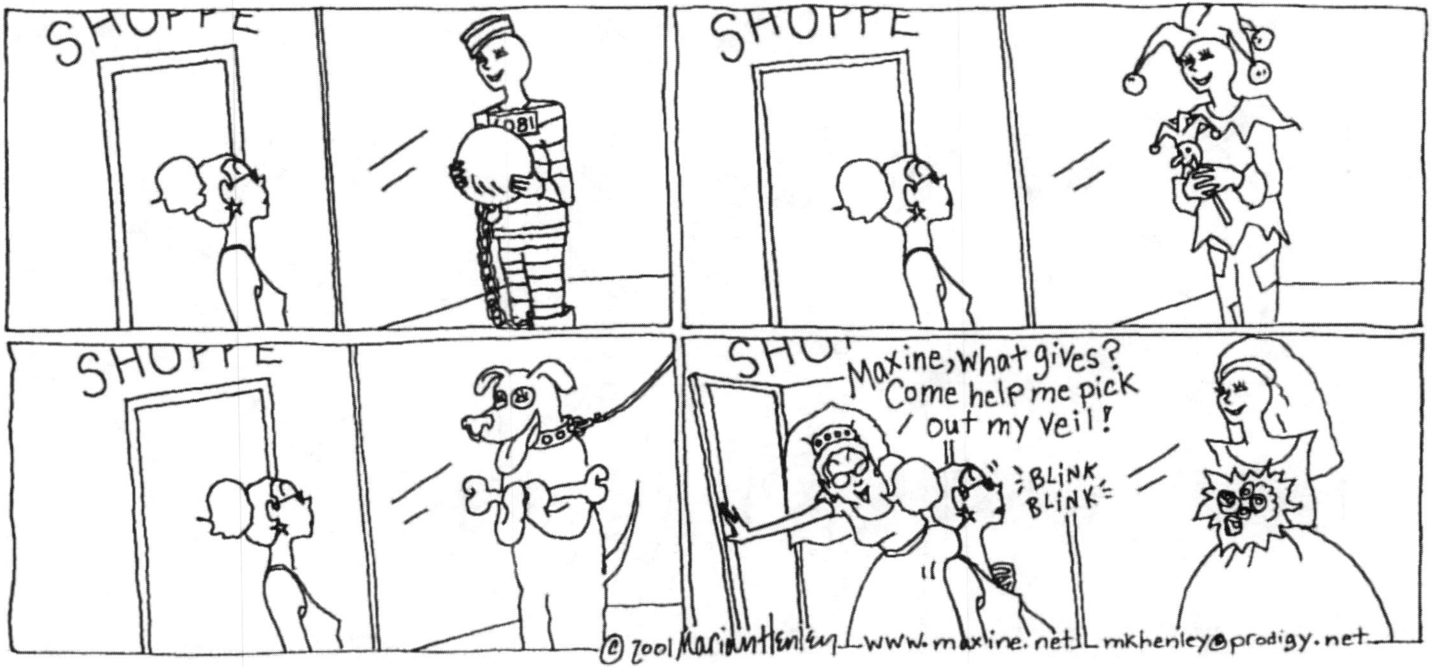
SHOPPE
1081
SHOPPE
SHOPPE
SHO
Maxine, what gives? Come help me pick out my veil!
BLINK BLINK
© 2001 Marian Henley www.maxine.net mkhenley@prodigy.net

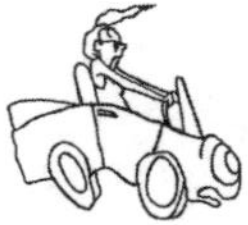

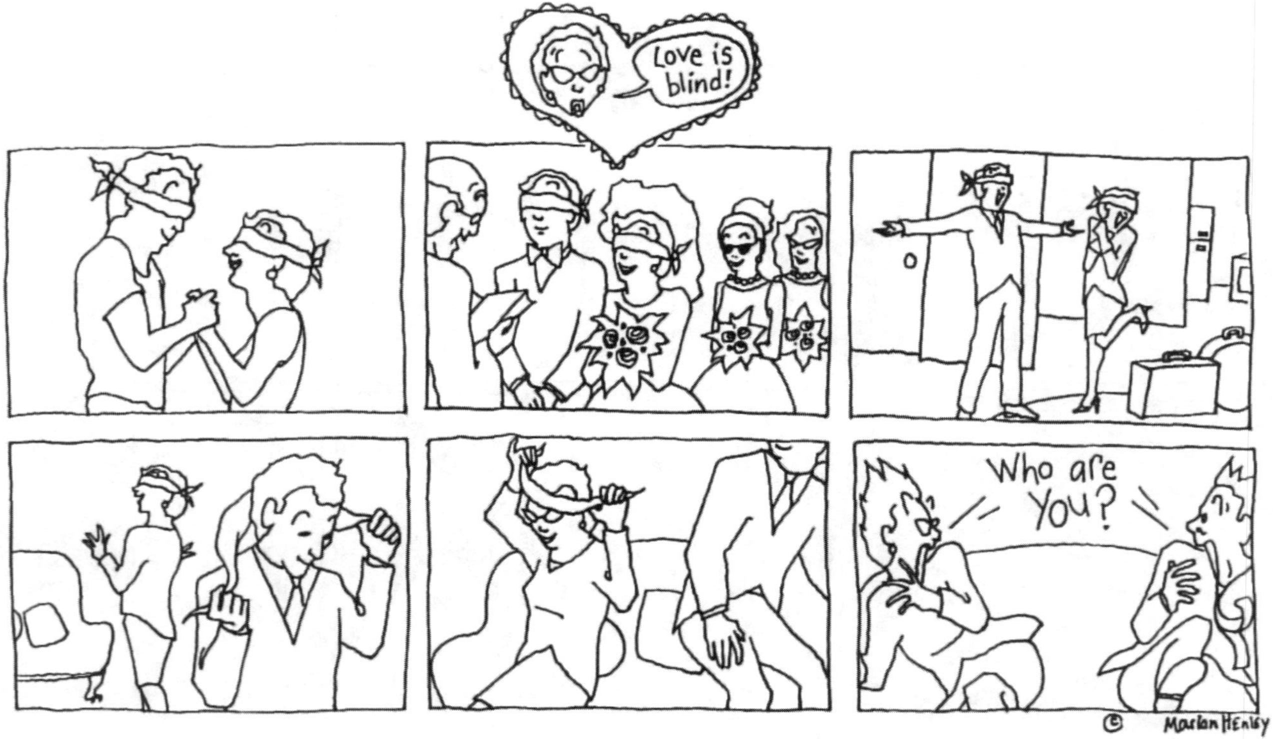
Love is blind!
Who are You?
© Marian Henley

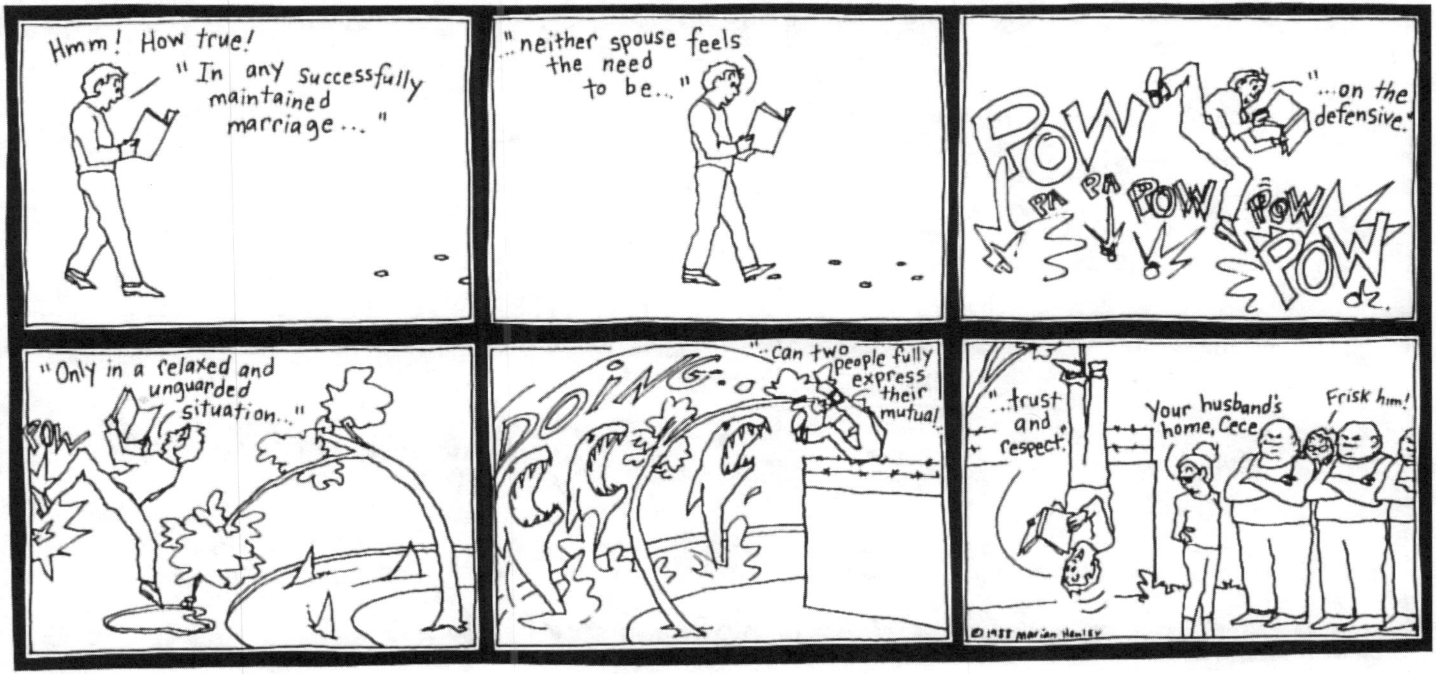
Hmm! How true!
"In any successfully maintained marriage..."
"...neither spouse feels the need to be..."
POW
PA PA
POW
POW
POW
"...on the defensive."
"Only in a relaxed and unguarded situation..."
POW
DOING
"...can two people fully express their mutual..."
"...trust and respect."
Your husband's home, Cece.
Frisk him!
© 1988 Marian Henley

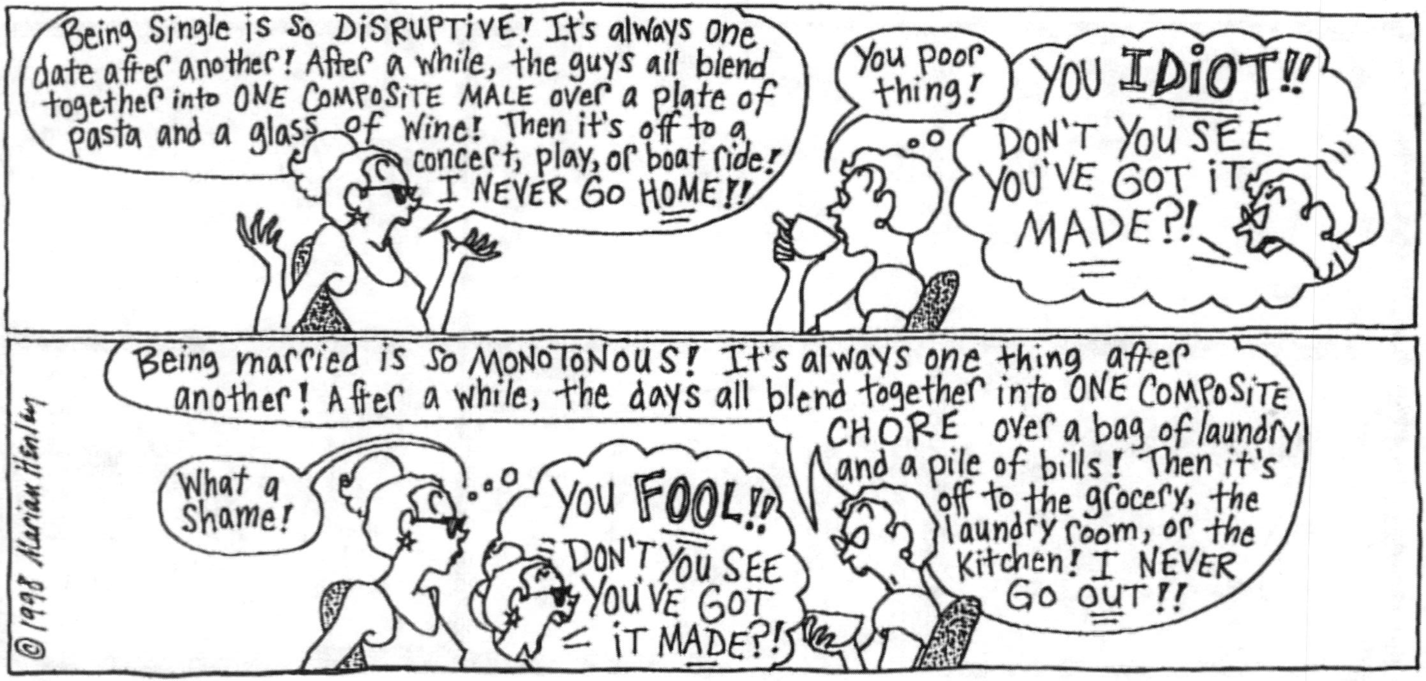
Being Single is so DISRUPTIVE! It's always one date after another! After a while, the guys all blend together into ONE COMPOSITE MALE over a plate of pasta and a glass of wine! Then it's off to a concert, play, or boat ride! I NEVER GO HOME!!
You poor thing!
YOU IDIOT!! DON'T YOU SEE YOU'VE GOT IT MADE?!
Being married is so MONOTONOUS! It's always one thing after another! After a while, the days all blend together into ONE COMPOSITE CHORE over a bag of laundry and a pile of bills! Then it's off to the grocery, the laundry room, or the Kitchen! I NEVER GO OUT!!
What a Shame!
YOU FOOL!! DON'T YOU SEE YOU'VE GOT IT MADE?!
© 1998 Marian Henley

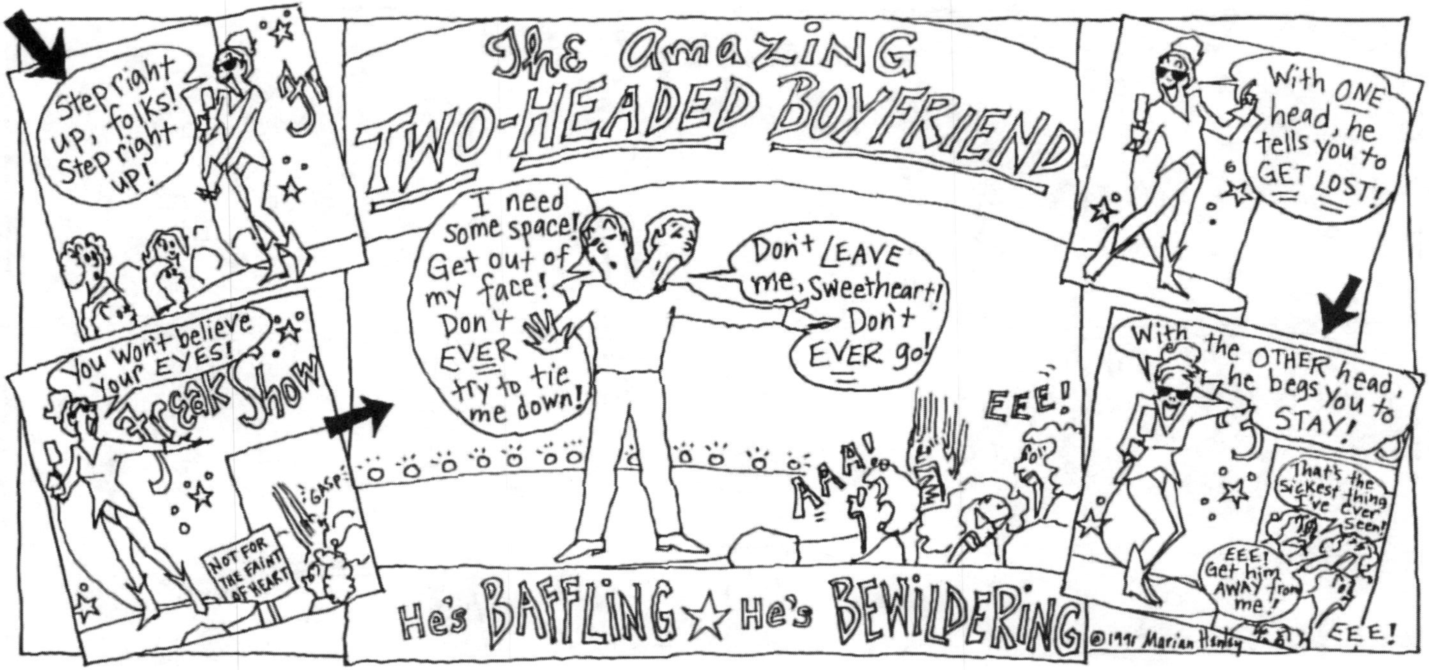
Step right up, folks! Step right up!
You won't believe your EYES!
Freak Show
NOT FOR THE FAINT OF HEART
GASP!
The Amazing TWO-HEADED BOYFRIEND
I need some space! Get out of my face! Don't EVER try to tie me down!
Don't LEAVE me, Sweetheart! Don't EVER go!
AAA!
EEE!
He's BAFFLING ★ He's BEWILDERING
With ONE head, he tells you to GET LOST!
With the OTHER head, he begs you to STAY!
That's the sickest thing I've ever seen!
EEE! Get him AWAY from me!
EEE!
©1991 Marian Henley

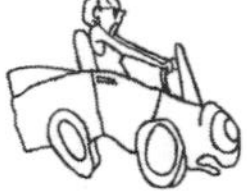

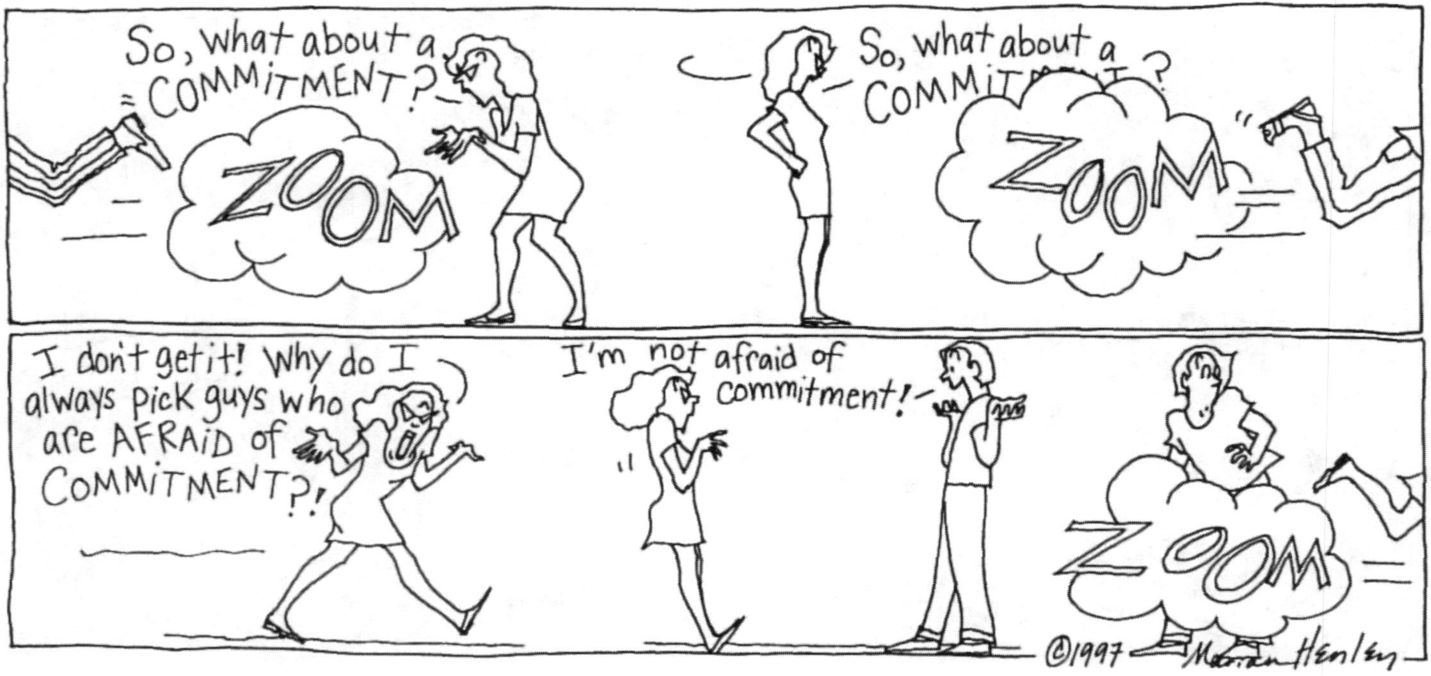
So, what about a COMMITMENT?
ZOOM
So, what about a COMMIT
ZOOM
I don't get it! Why do I always pick guys who are AFRAID of COMMITMENT?!
I'm not afraid of commitment!
ZOOM
©1997 Marian Henley

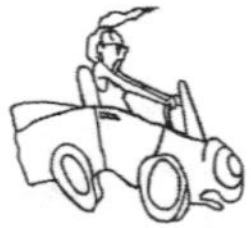

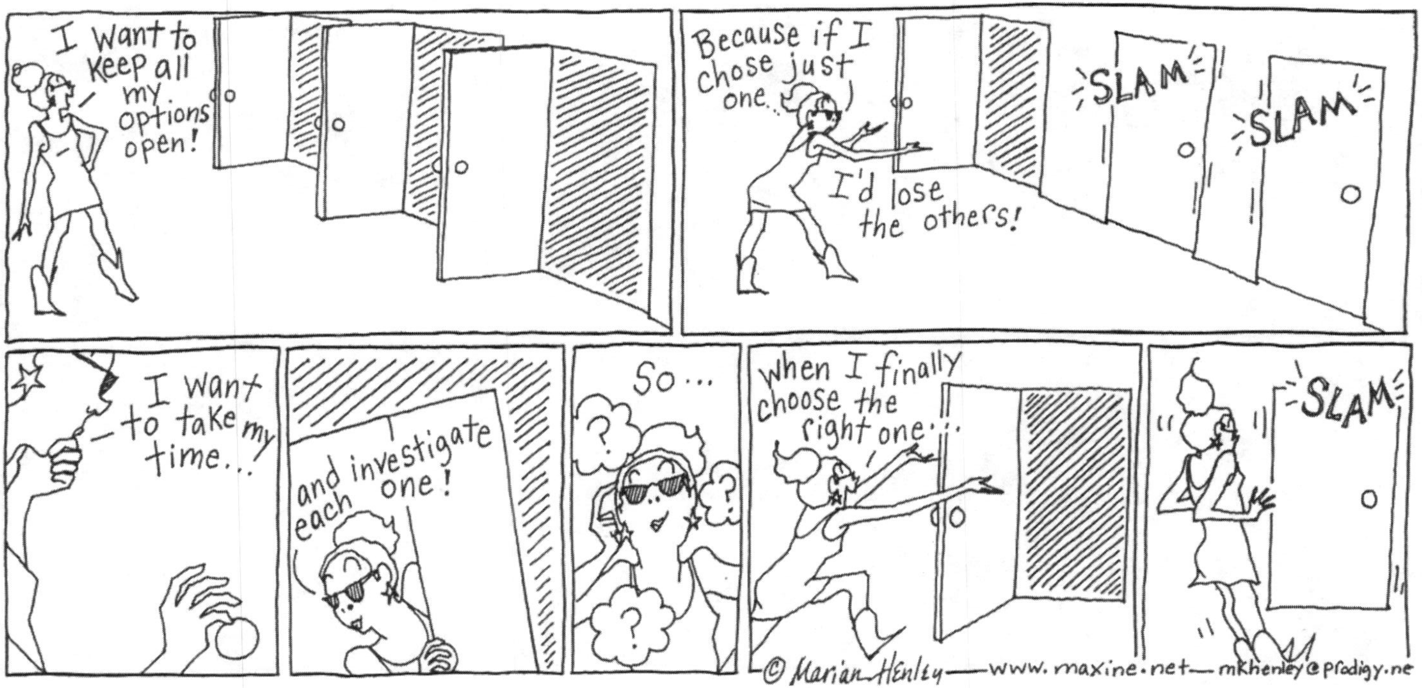
I want to keep all my options open!
Because if I chose just one...
I'd lose the others!
SLAM
SLAM
I want to take my time...
and investigate each one!
So...
when I finally choose the right one...
SLAM
© Marian Henley—www.maxine.net—mkhenley@prodigy.ne

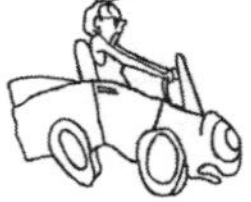

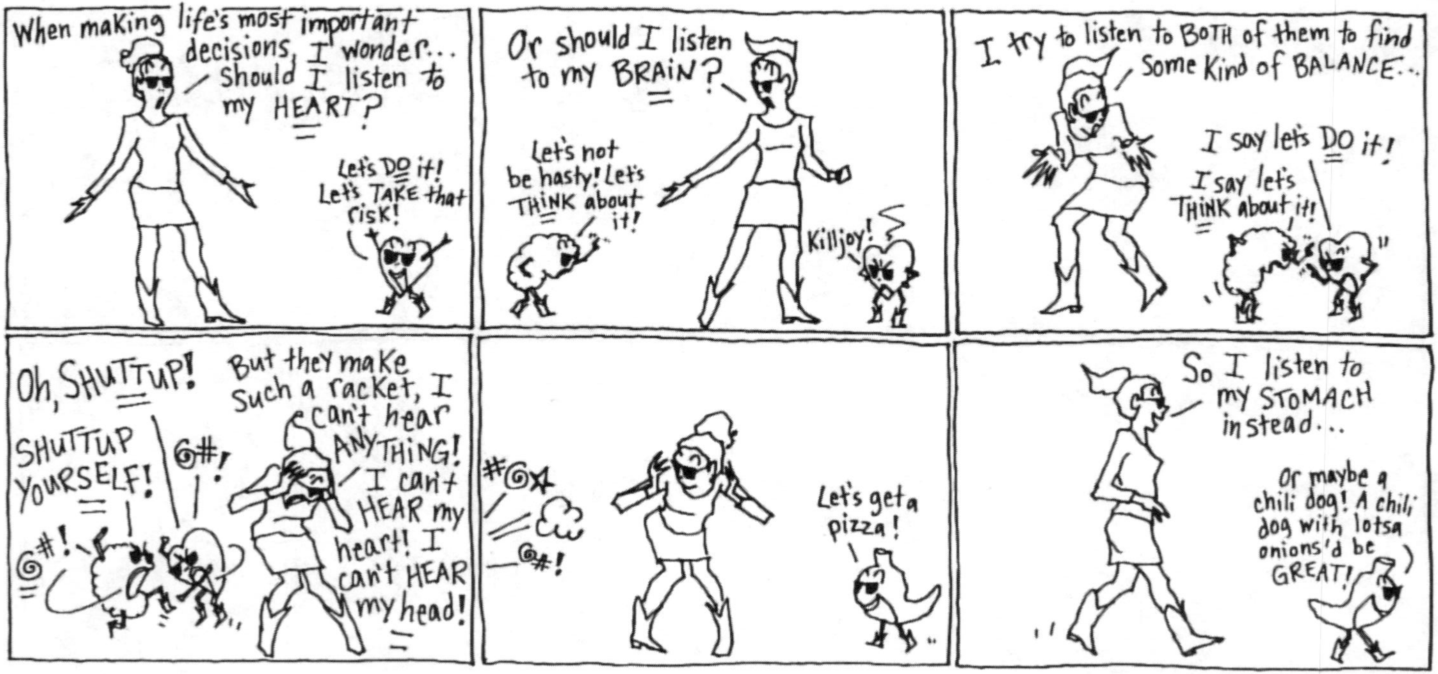
When making life's most important decisions, I wonder... Should I listen to my HEART?
Let's DO it! Let's TAKE that risk!
Or should I listen to my BRAIN?
Let's not be hasty! Let's THINK about it!
Killjoy!
I try to listen to BOTH of them to find Some Kind of BALANCE...
I say let's DO it!
I say let's THINK about it!
Oh, SHUTTUP!
SHUTTUP YOURSELF!
@#!
@#!
But they make such a racket, I can't hear ANYTHING! I can't HEAR my heart! I can't HEAR my head!
#@☆
@#!
Let's get a pizza!
So I listen to my STOMACH instead...
Or maybe a chili dog! A chili dog with lotsa onions'd be GREAT!

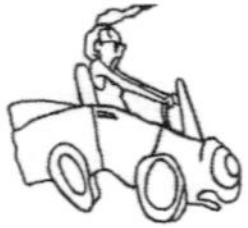

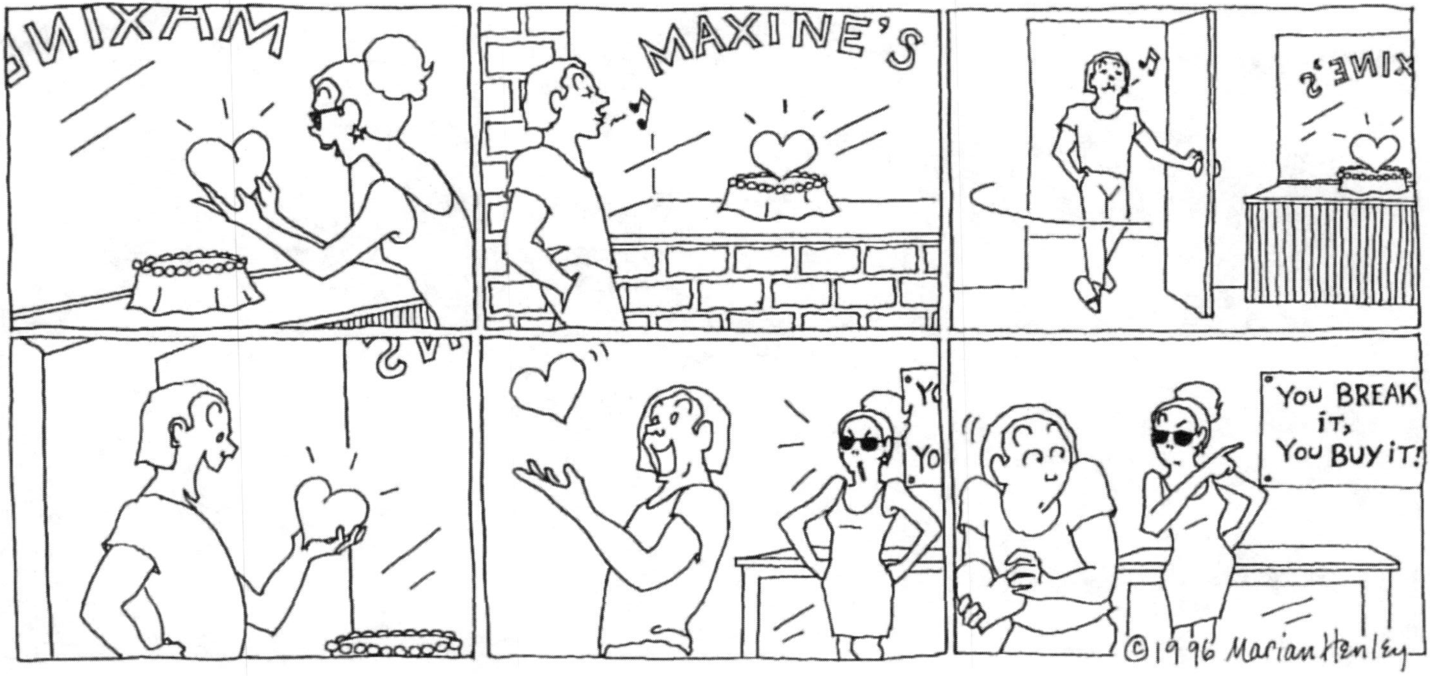
MAXINE'S
You BREAK iT, You BUY iT!
©1996 Marian Henley

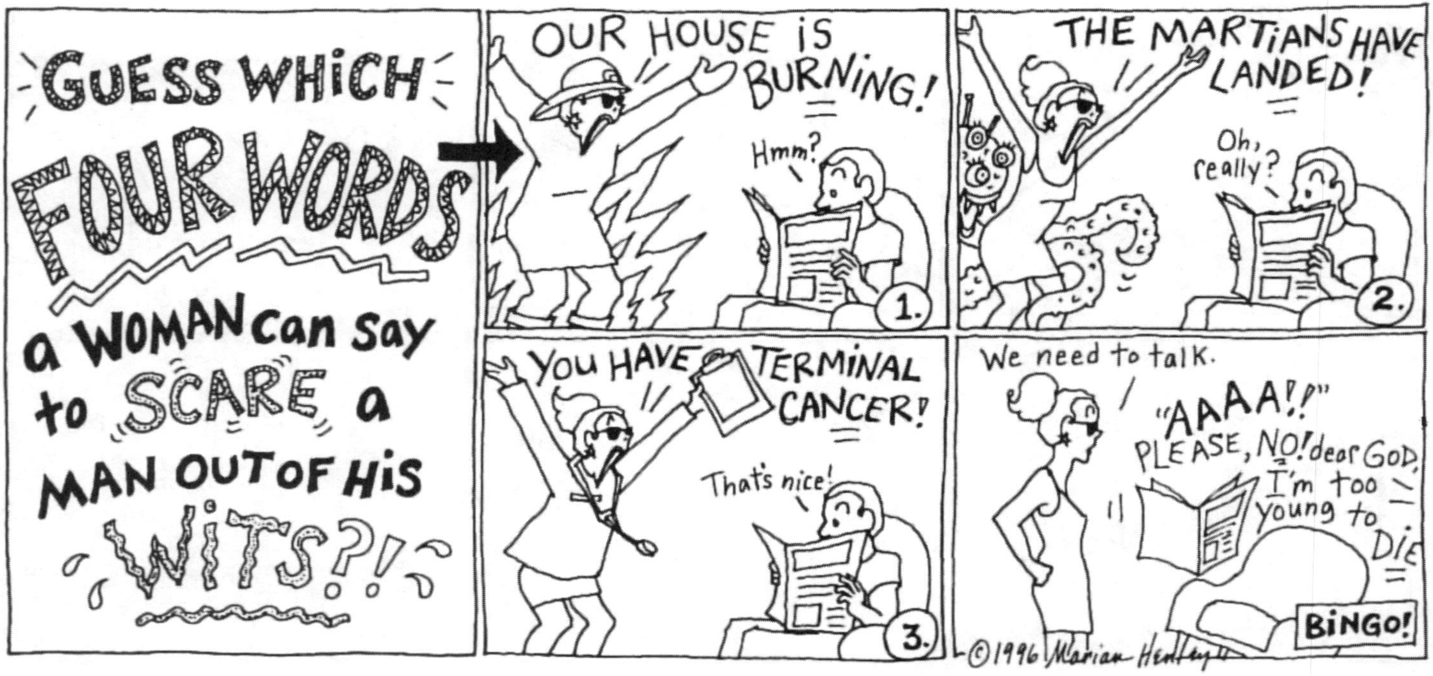
GUESS WHICH FOUR WORDS a WOMAN can say to SCARE a MAN OUT OF HIS WITS?!
OUR HOUSE IS BURNING!
Hmm?
1.
THE MARTIANS HAVE LANDED!
Oh, really?
2.
YOU HAVE TERMINAL CANCER!
That's nice!
3.
We need to talk.
"AAAA!!"
PLEASE, NO! dear GOD, I'm too young to DIE
BINGO!
©1996 Marian Henley

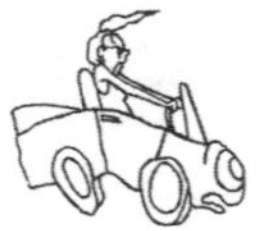

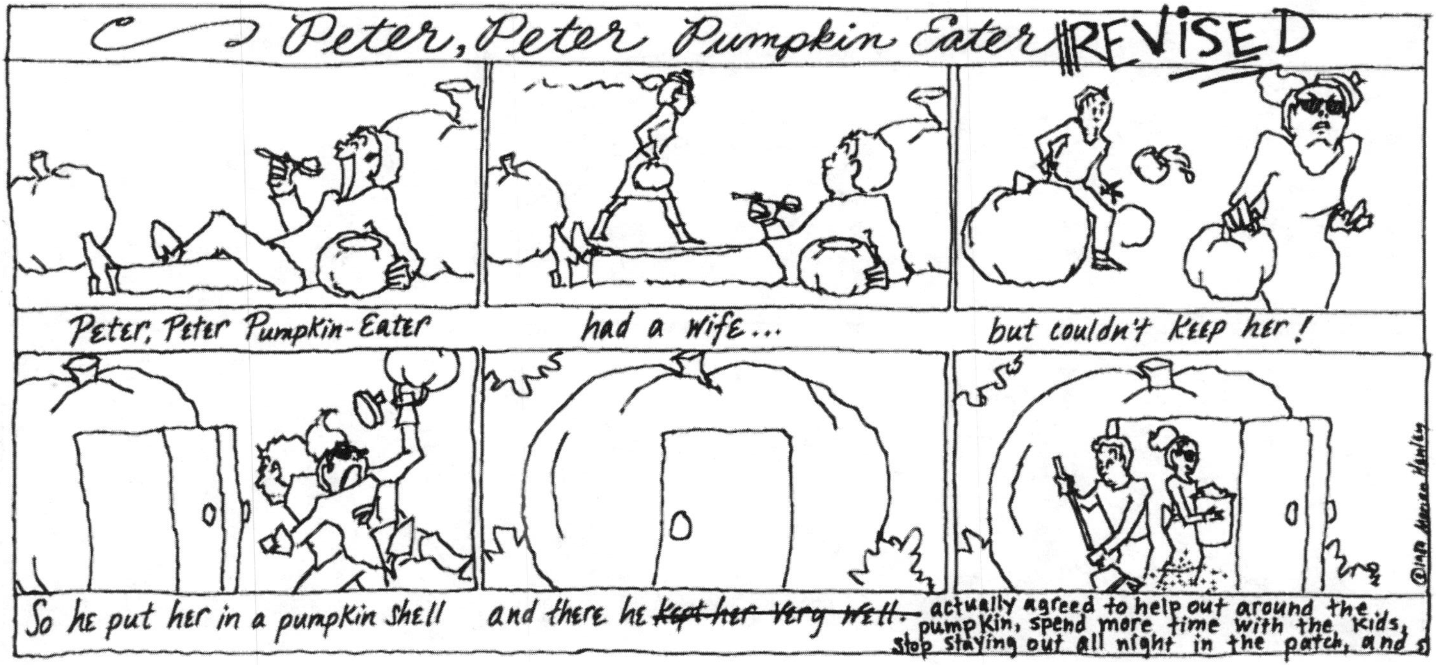
Peter, Peter Pumpkin Eater REVISED
Peter, Peter Pumpkin-Eater
had a wife...
but couldn't keep her!
So he put her in a pumpkin shell
and there he ~~kept her very well.~~ actually agreed to help out around the pumpkin, spend more time with the kids, stop staying out all night in the patch, and s
©1988 Marian Henley

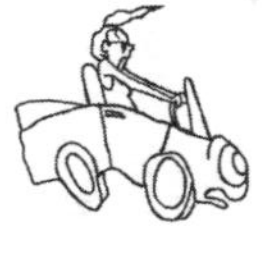

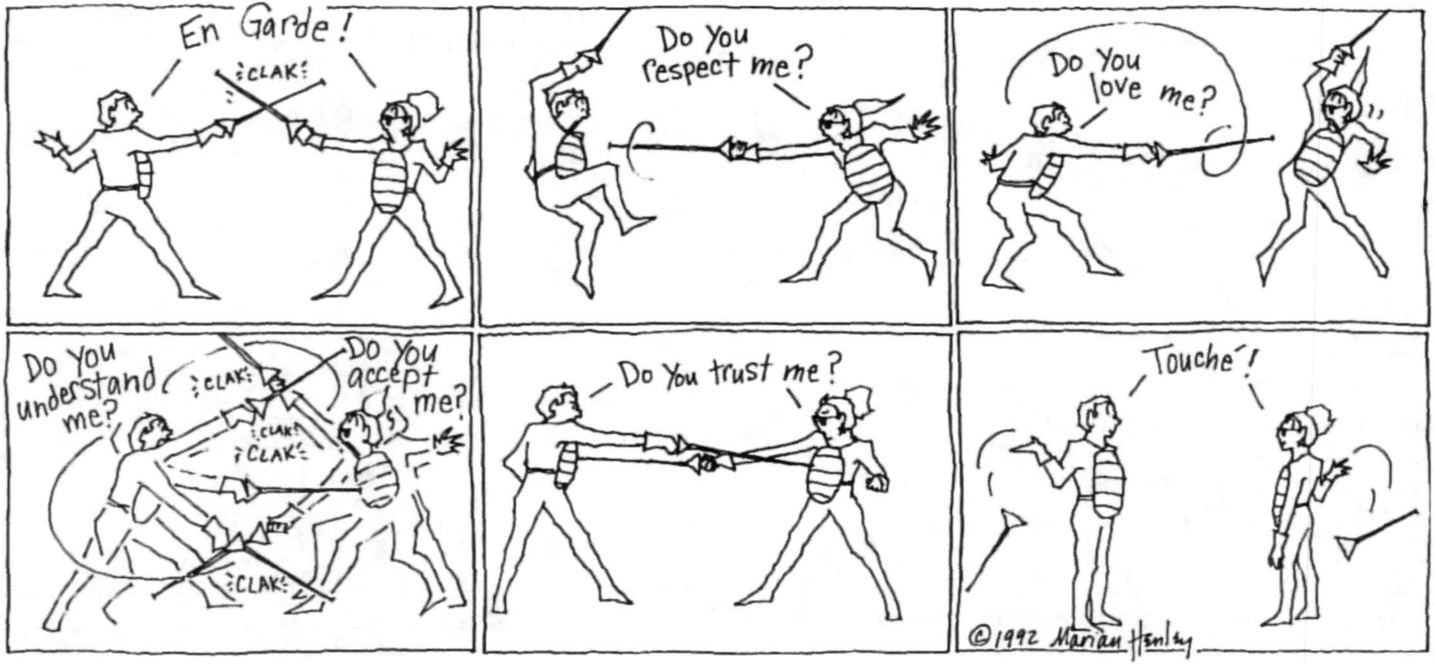
En Garde!
¡CLAK!
Do you respect me?
Do you love me?
Do you understand me?
¡CLAK!
Do you accept me?
¡CLAK!
¡CLAK!
¡CLAK!
Do You trust me?
Touche'!
©1992 Marian Henley

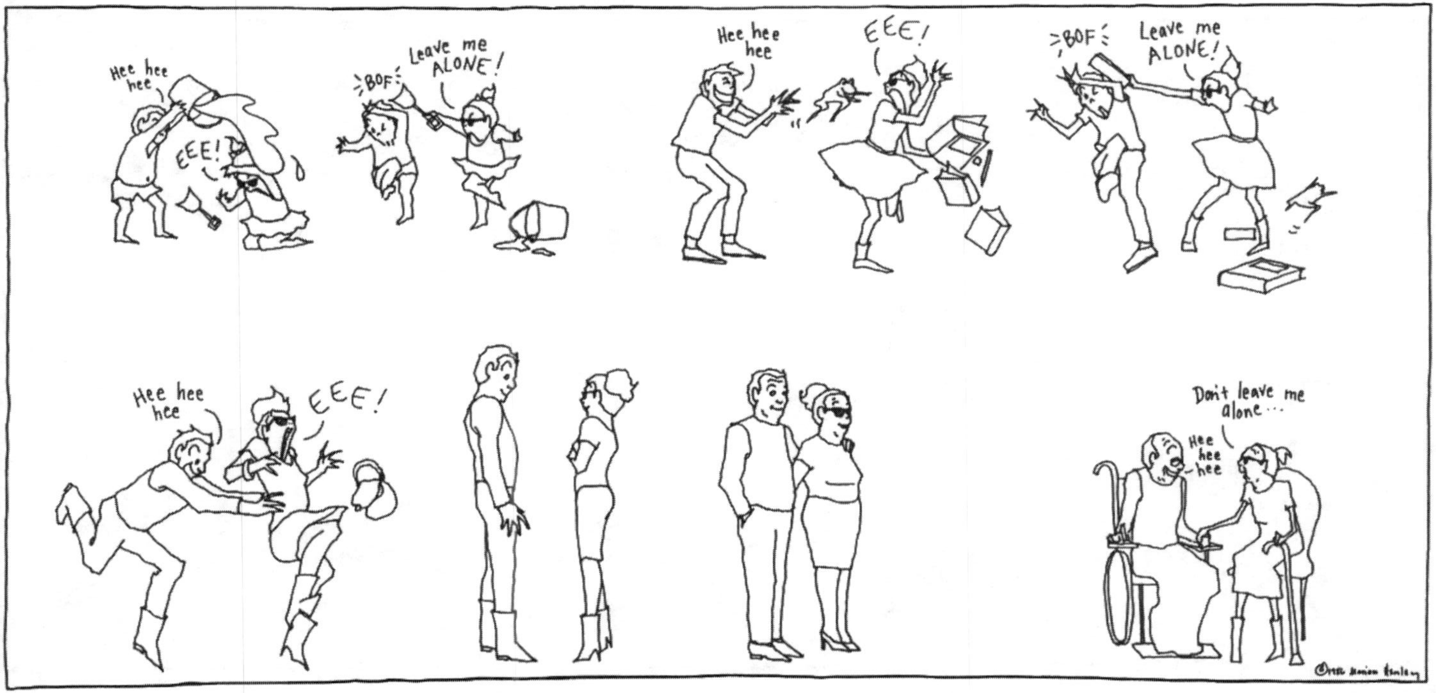
Hee hee hee
EEE!
BOF
Leave me ALONE!
Hee hee hee
EEE!
BOF
Leave me ALONE!
Hee hee hee
EEE!
Don't leave me alone…
Hee hee hee

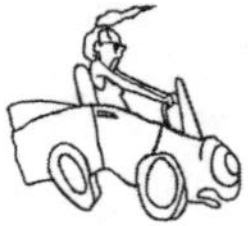

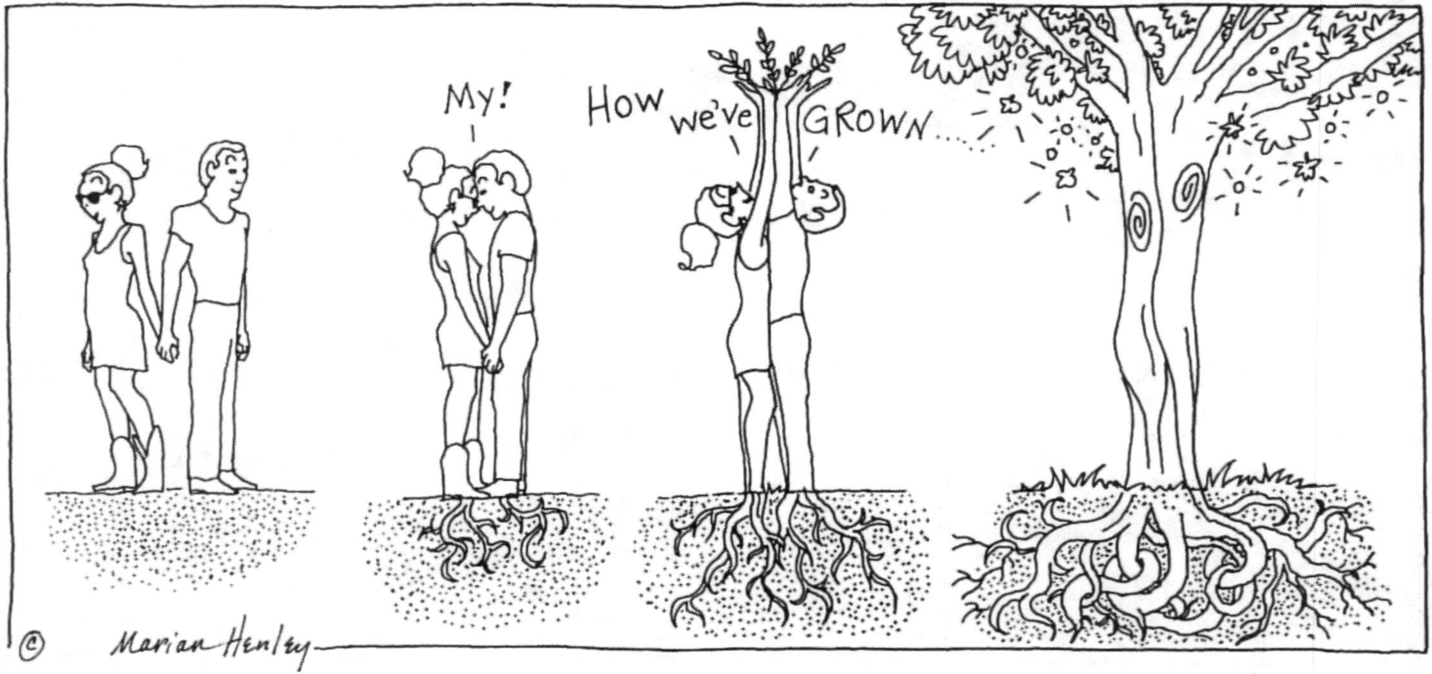
My!
How we've GROWN....
© Marian Henley

Ego and Anxiety

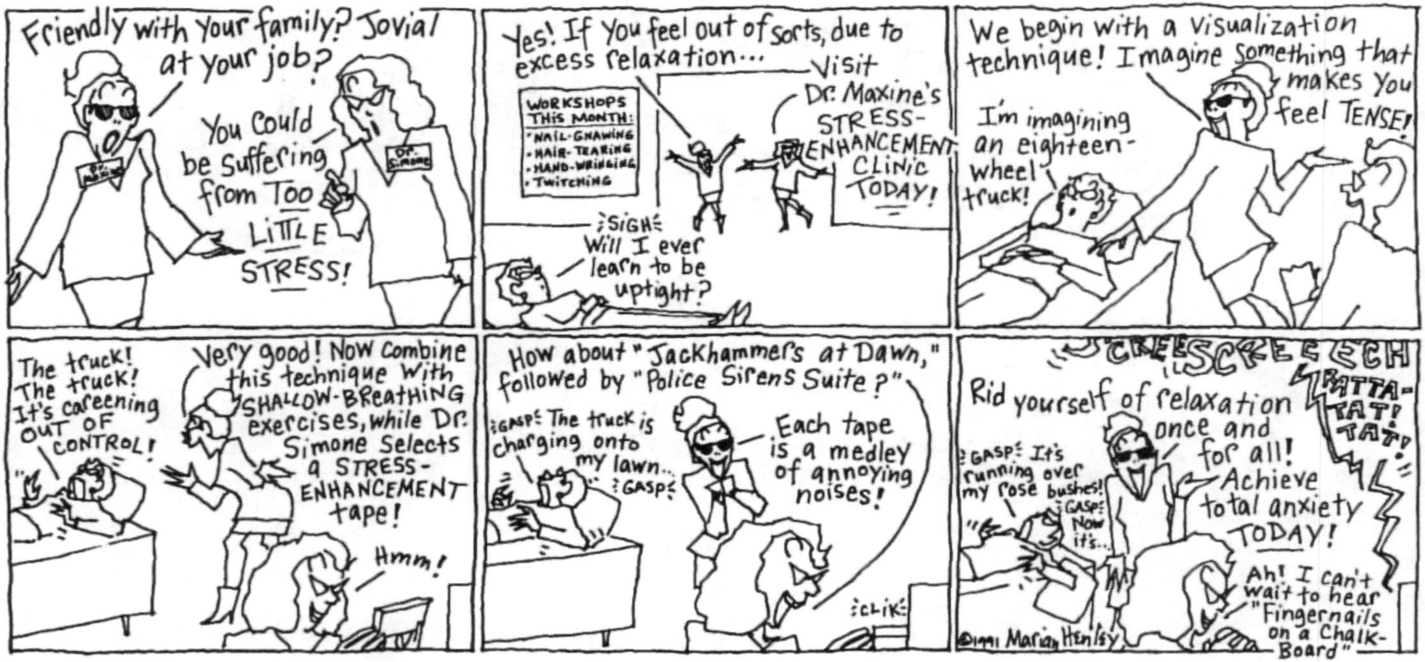
Friendly with your family? Jovial at your job?
You could be suffering from TOO LITTLE STRESS!
Yes! If you feel out of sorts, due to excess relaxation...
WORKSHOPS THIS MONTH:
• NAIL-GNAWING
• HAIR-TEARING
• HAND-WRINGING
• TWITCHING
Visit Dr. Maxine's STRESS-ENHANCEMENT CLINIC TODAY!
¡SIGH!
Will I ever learn to be uptight?
We begin with a visualization technique! Imagine something that makes you feel TENSE!
I'm imagining an eighteen-wheel truck!
The truck! The truck! It's careening OUT OF CONTROL!
Very good! Now combine this technique with SHALLOW-BREATHING exercises, while Dr. Simone selects a STRESS-ENHANCEMENT tape!
Hmm!
How about "Jackhammers at Dawn," followed by "Police Sirens Suite?"
¡GASP! The truck is charging onto my lawn...
¡GASP!
Each tape is a medley of annoying noises!
¡CLIK!
SCREEECH
RATTA-TAT! TAT!
Rid yourself of relaxation once and for all! Achieve total anxiety TODAY!
¡GASP! It's running over my rose bushes!
¡GASP! Now it's...
Ah! I can't wait to hear "Fingernails on a Chalk-Board"
©1991 Marian Henley

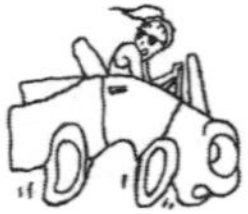

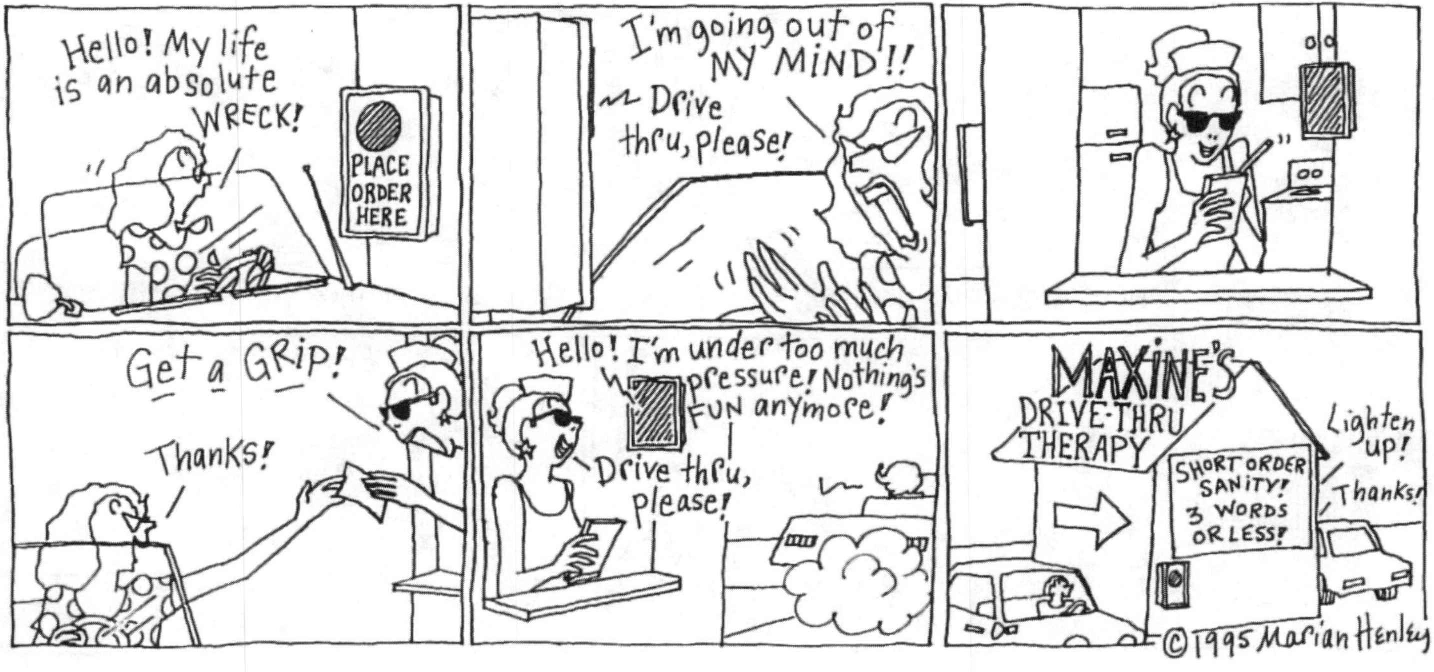
Hello! My life is an absolute WRECK!
PLACE ORDER HERE
Drive thru, please!
I'm going out of MY MIND!!
Get a GRIP!
Thanks!
Hello! I'm under too much pressure! Nothing's FUN anymore!
Drive thru, please!
MAXINE'S DRIVE-THRU THERAPY
SHORT ORDER SANITY! 3 WORDS OR LESS!
Lighten up!
Thanks!
©1995 Marian Henley

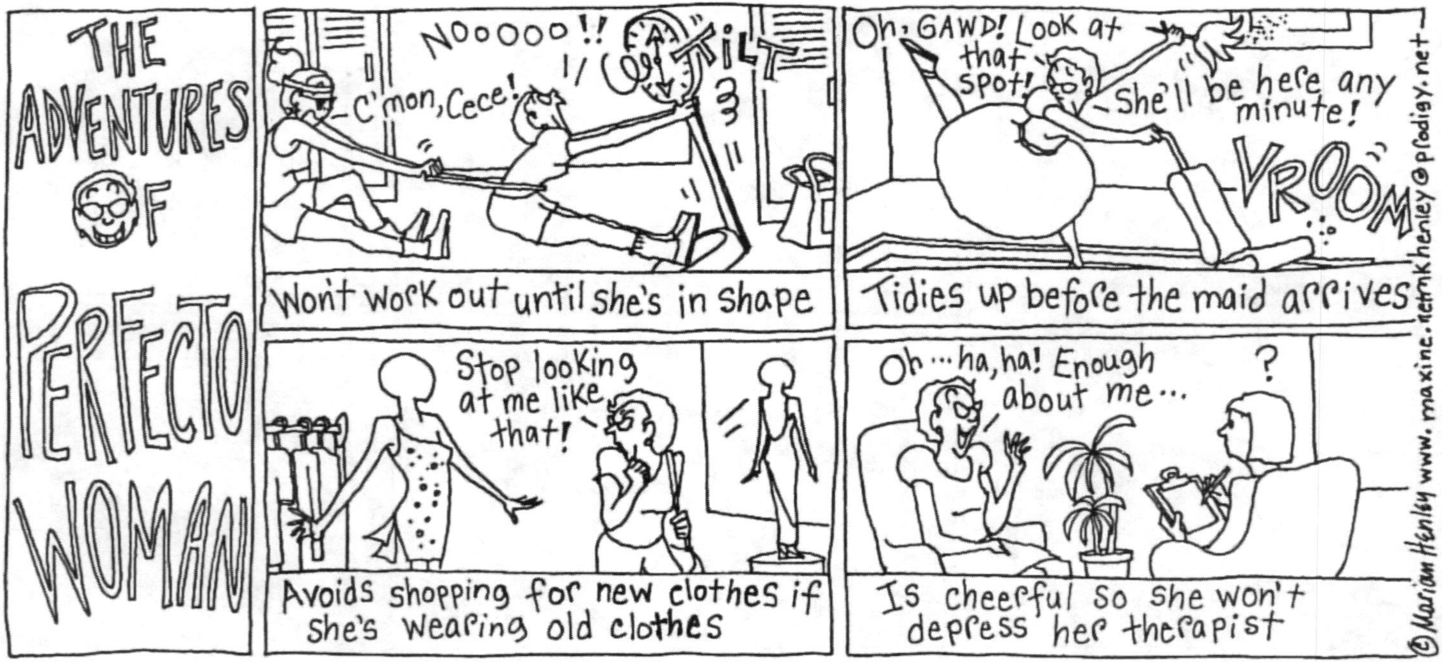
THE ADVENTURES OF PERFECTO WOMAN
NOooooo!!
C'mon, Cece!
TILT
Won't work out until she's in shape
Oh, GAWD! Look at that spot!
She'll be here any minute!
VROOM
Tidies up before the maid arrives
Stop looking at me like that!
Avoids shopping for new clothes if she's wearing old clothes
Oh...ha, ha! Enough about me...
?
Is cheerful so she won't depress her therapist
© Marian Henley www.maxine.net mkhenley@prodigy.net

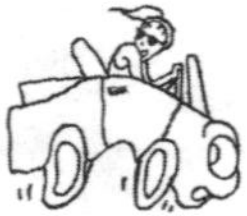

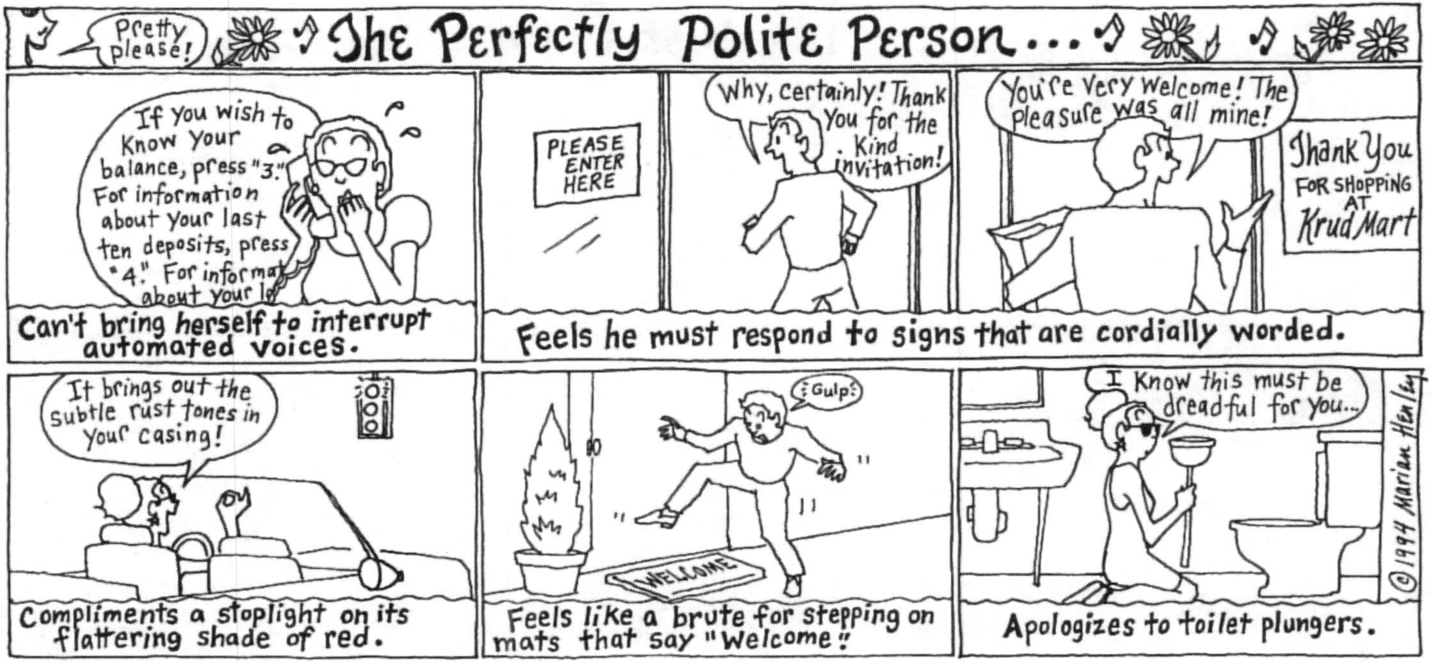
Pretty please!
The Perfectly Polite Person...
If you wish to know your balance, press "3." For information about your last ten deposits, press "4." For informat about your l
Can't bring herself to interrupt automated voices.
PLEASE ENTER HERE
Why, certainly! Thank you for the kind invitation!
You're very welcome! The pleasure was all mine!
Thank You FOR SHOPPING AT Krud Mart
Feels he must respond to signs that are cordially worded.
It brings out the subtle rust tones in your casing!
Compliments a stoplight on its flattering shade of red.
Gulp
WELCOME
Feels like a brute for stepping on mats that say "Welcome!"
I know this must be dreadful for you...
©1994 Marian Henley
Apologizes to toilet plungers.

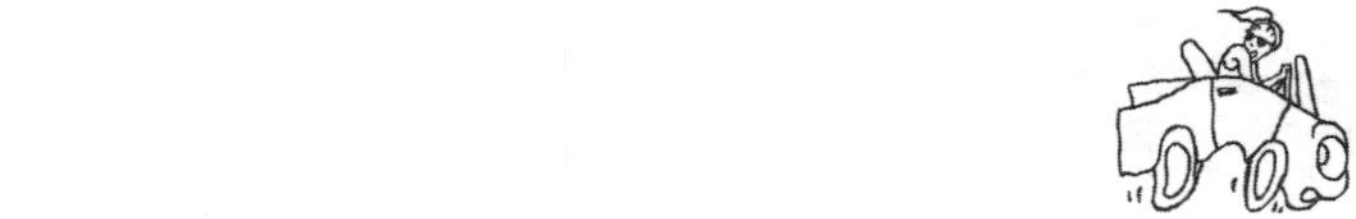

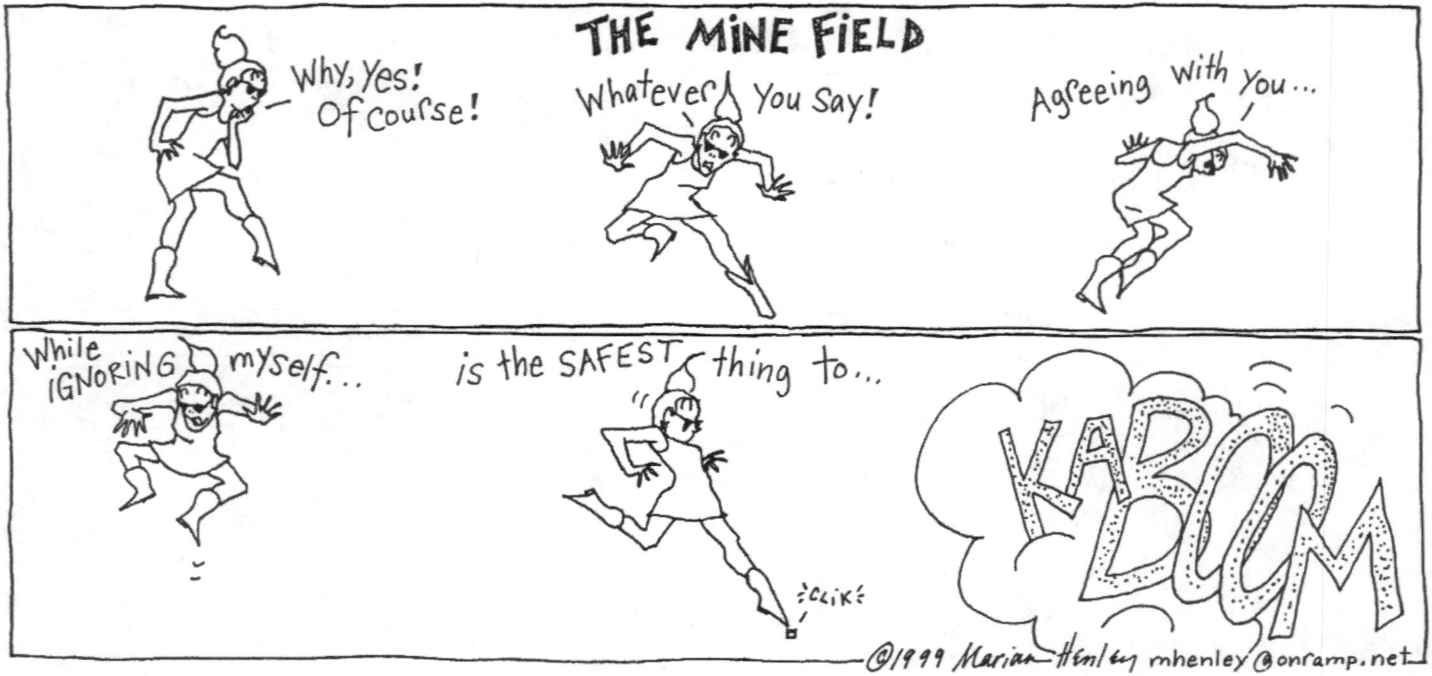
THE MINE FIELD
Why, Yes! Of course!
Whatever You Say!
Agreeing with You...
While IGNORING myself...
is the SAFEST thing to...
CLIK
KABOOM
©1999 Marian Henley mhenley@onramp.net

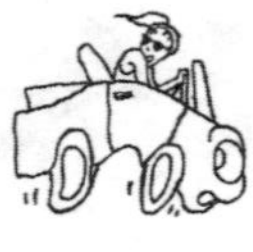

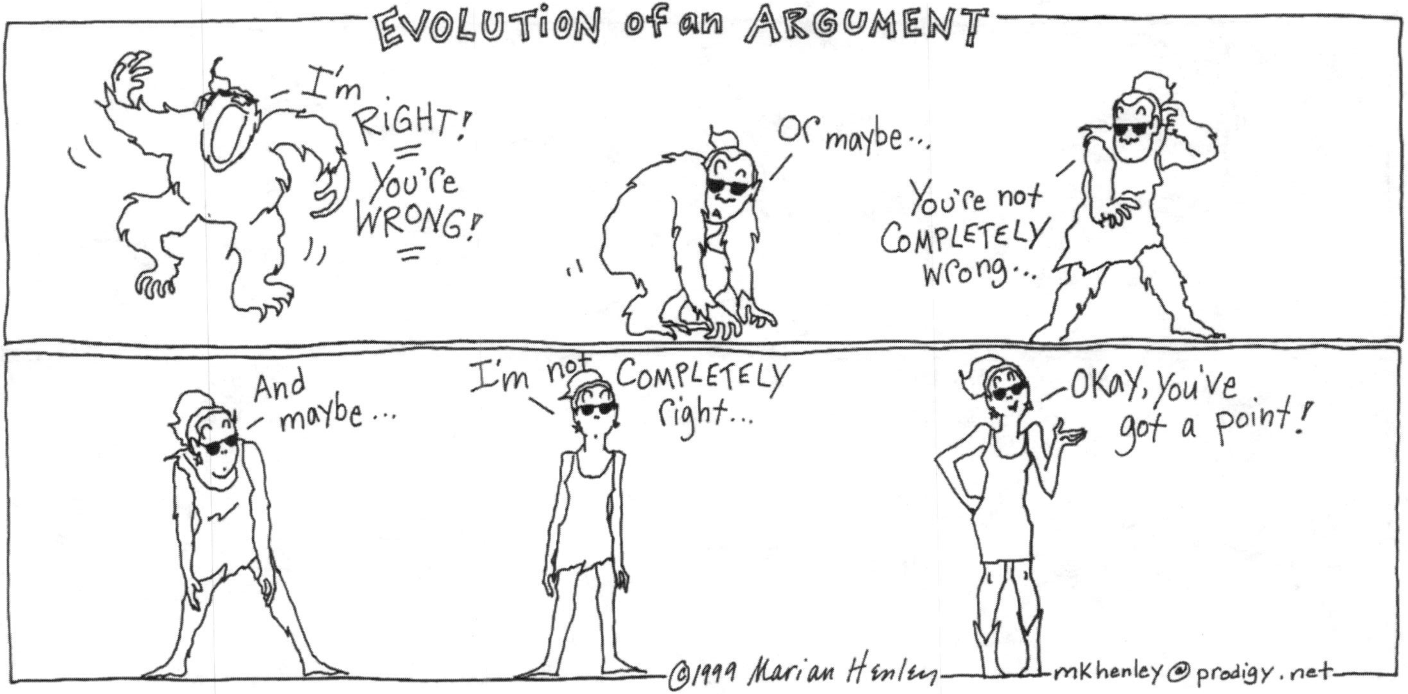
EVOLUTION of an ARGUMENT
I'm RIGHT! You're WRONG!
Or maybe...
You're not COMPLETELY wrong...
And maybe...
I'm not COMPLETELY right...
OKAY, You've got a point!
©1999 Marian Henley
mkhenley@prodigy.net

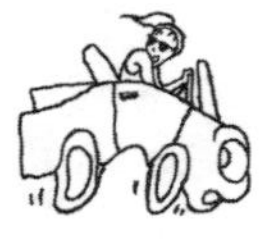

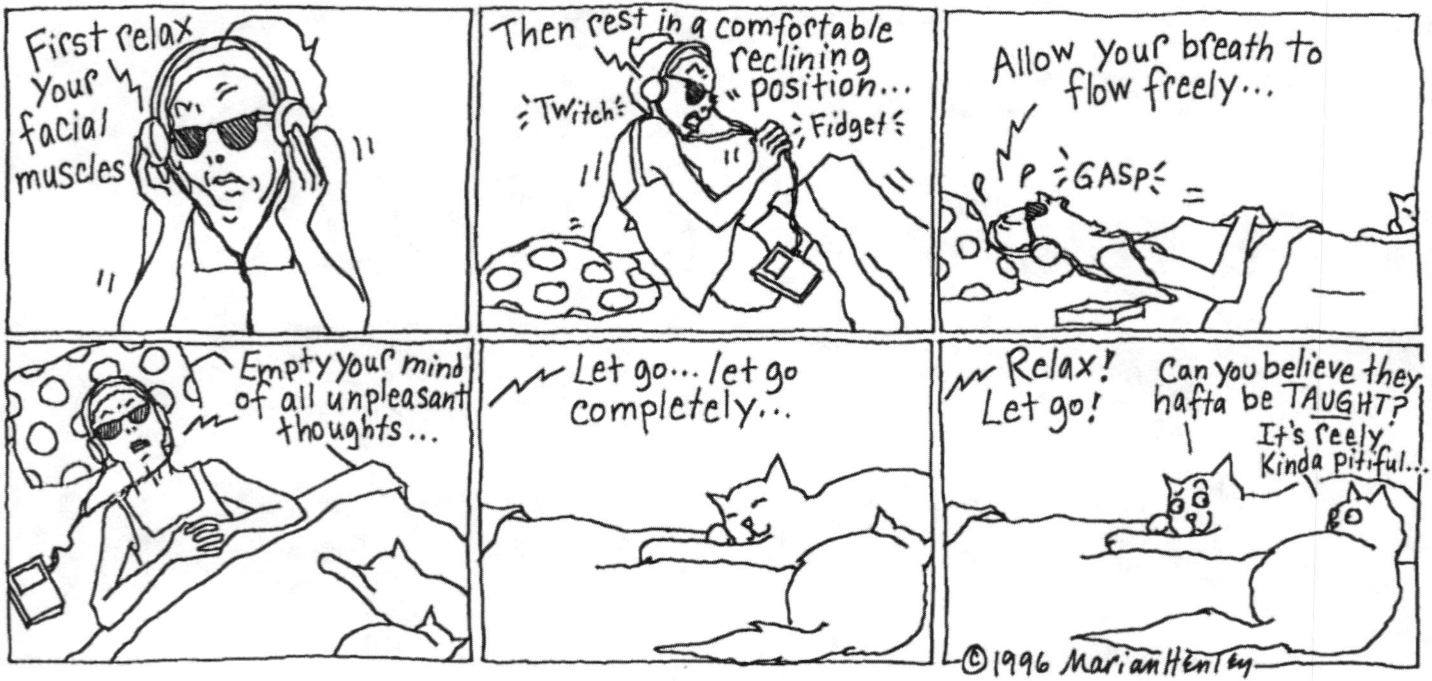
First relax your facial muscles
Then rest in a comfortable reclining position...
Twitch
Fidget
Allow your breath to flow freely...
P P
GASP
Empty your mind of all unpleasant thoughts...
Let go... let go completely...
Relax! Let go!
Can you believe they hafta be TAUGHT?
It's reely kinda pitiful...
©1996 Marian Henley

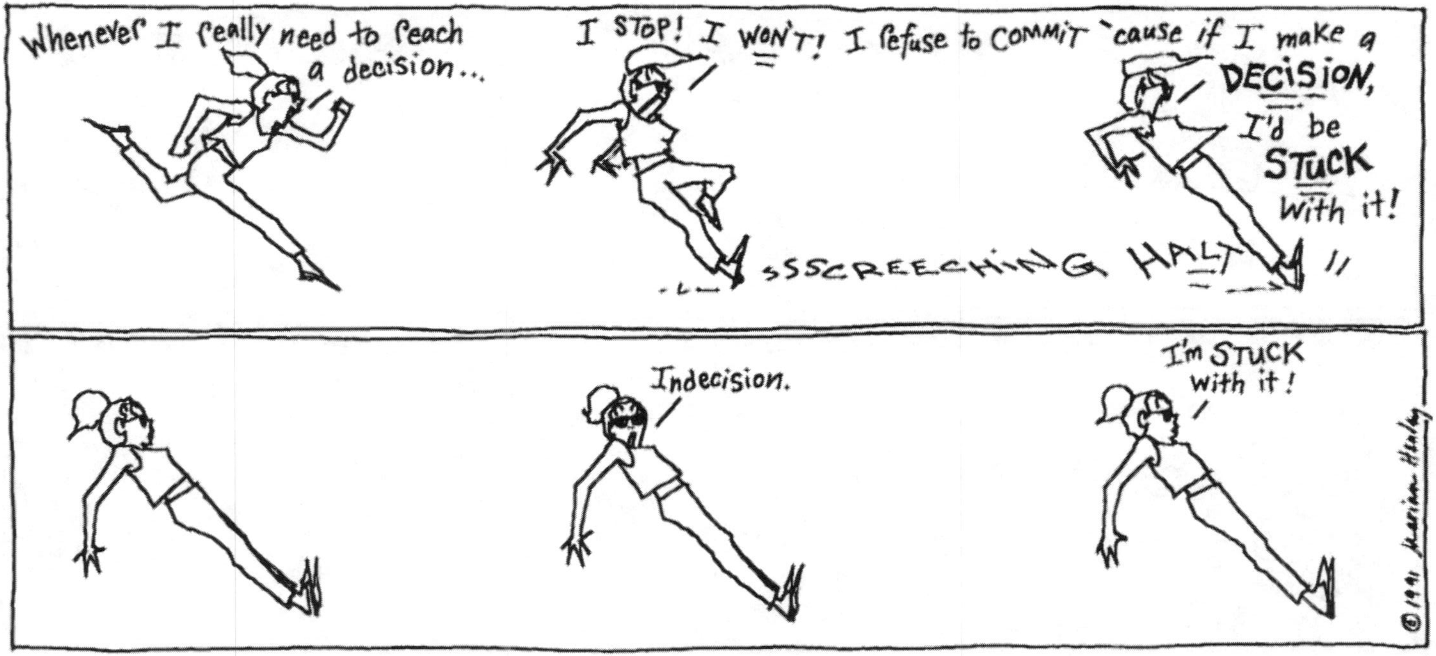
Whenever I really need to reach a decision...
I STOP! I WON'T! I refuse to COMMIT 'cause if I make a DECISION, I'd be STUCK with it!
"SSSCREECHING HALT"
Indecision.
I'm STUCK with it!
©1991 Marian Healy

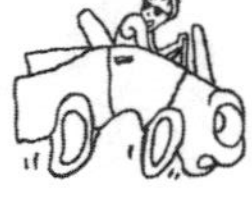

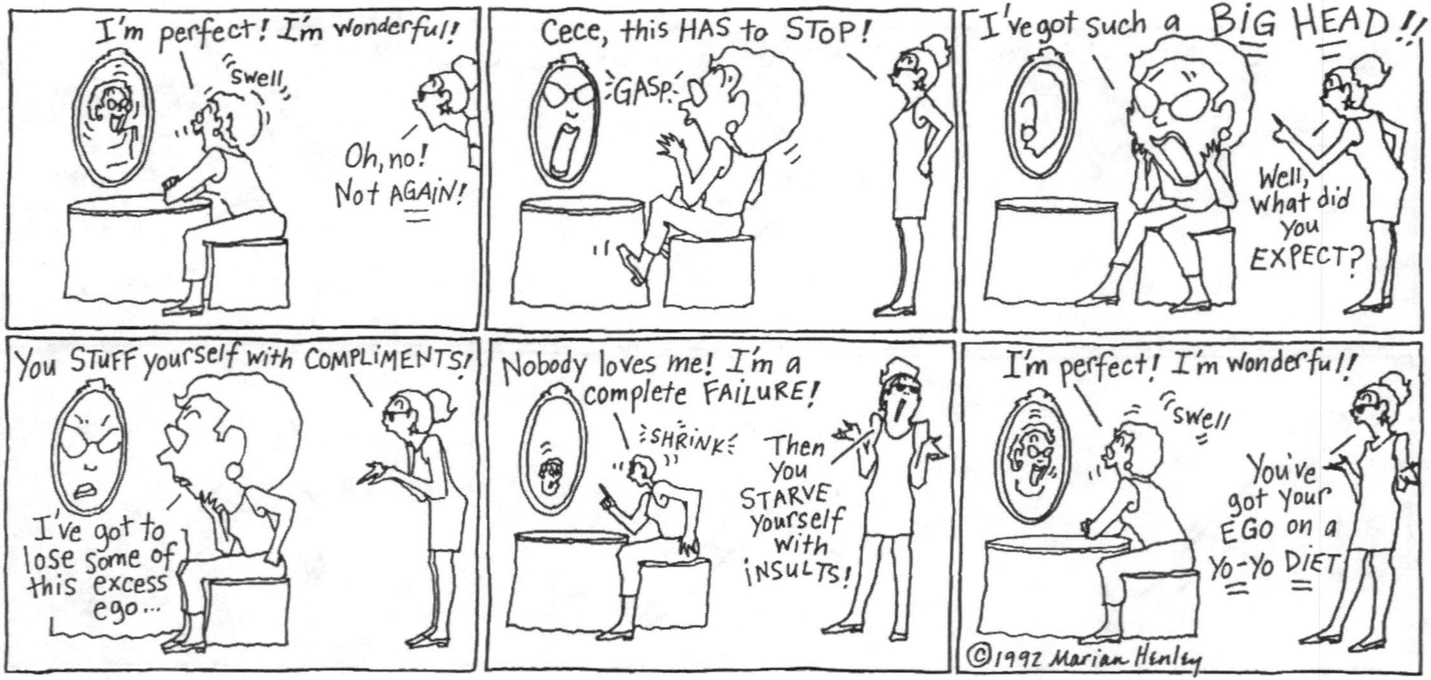
I'm perfect! I'm wonderful!
SWELL
Oh, no! Not AGAIN!
Cece, this HAS to STOP!
GASP
I've got such a BIG HEAD!!
Well, what did you EXPECT?
You STUFF yourself with COMPLIMENTS!
I've got to lose some of this excess ego...
Nobody loves me! I'm a complete FAILURE!
SHRINK
Then you STARVE yourself with INSULTS!
I'm perfect! I'm wonderful!
SWELL
You've got your EGO on a YO-YO DIET
©1992 Marian Henley

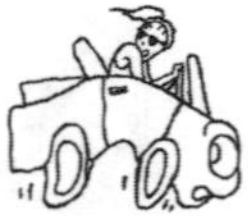

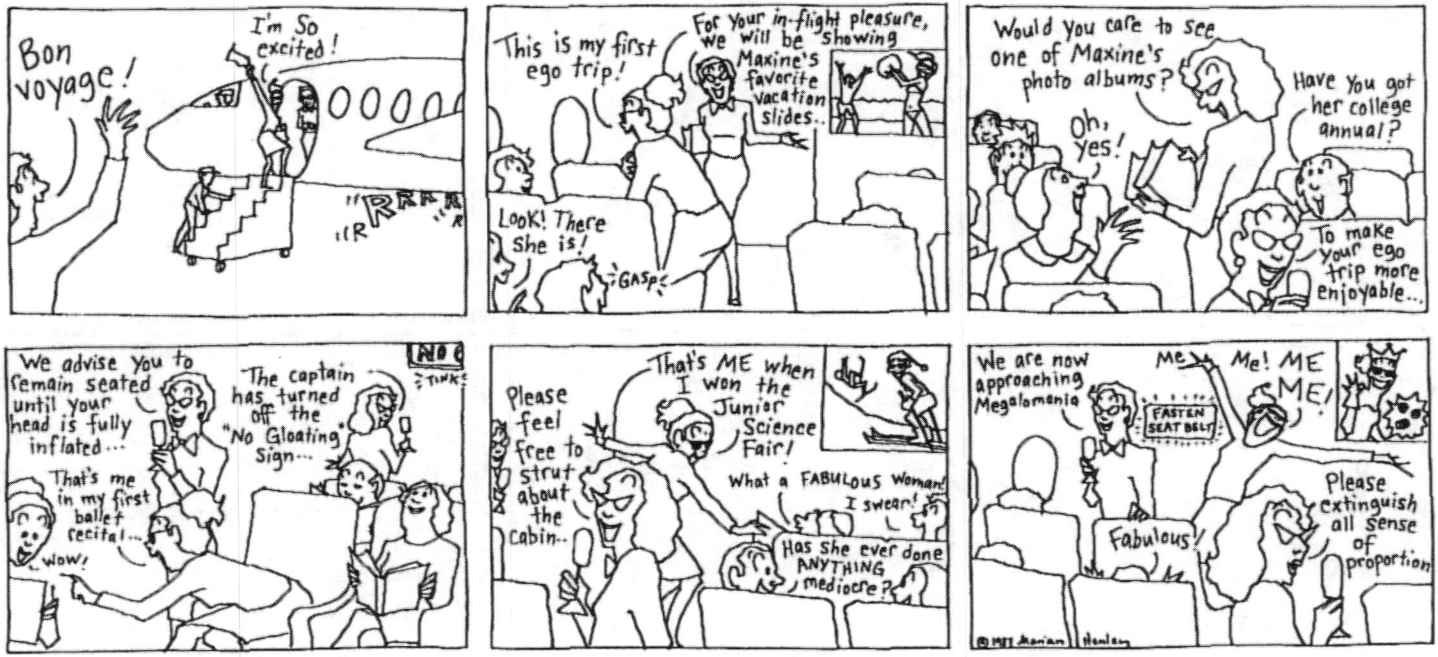
Bon voyage!
I'm So excited!
"RRRR "R "R
This is my first ego trip!
For your in-flight pleasure, we will be showing Maxine's favorite vacation slides..
Look! There she is!
GASP
Would you care to see one of Maxine's photo albums?
Oh, yes!
Have you got her college annual?
To make your ego trip more enjoyable...
We advise you to remain seated until your head is fully inflated...
The captain has turned off the "No Gloating" Sign...
That's me in my first ballet recital...
WOW!
TINK
That's ME when I won the Junior Science Fair!
Please feel free to strut about the cabin..
What a FABULOUS Woman!
I swear!
Has she ever done ANYTHING mediocre?
We are now approaching Megalomania
FASTEN SEAT BELT
ME Me! ME ME!
Please extinguish all sense of proportion
Fabulous!

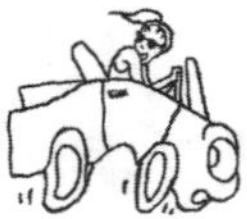

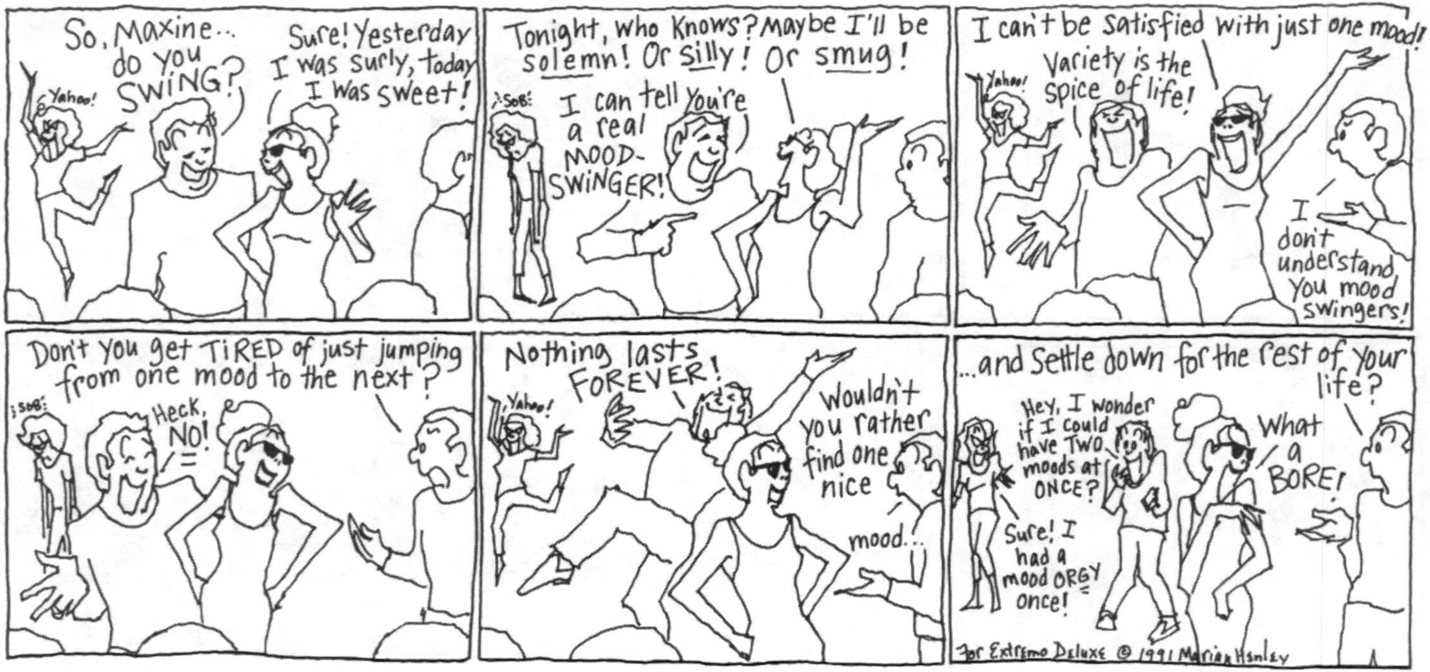
So, Maxine... do you SWING?
Yahoo!
Sure! Yesterday I was surly, today I was sweet!
Tonight, who Knows? Maybe I'll be solemn! Or silly! Or smug!
;SOB;
I can tell you're a real MOOD-SWINGER!
I can't be satisfied with just one mood!
Yahoo!
Variety is the spice of life!
I don't understand you mood swingers!
Don't you get TIRED of just jumping from one mood to the next?
;SOB;
Heck, NO!
Nothing lasts FOREVER!
Yahoo!
Wouldn't you rather find one nice mood...
...and settle down for the rest of your life?
Hey, I wonder if I could have TWO moods at ONCE?
Sure! I had a mood ORGY once!
What a BORE!
For Extremo Deluxe © 1991 Marian Henley

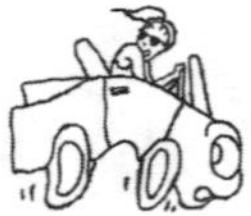

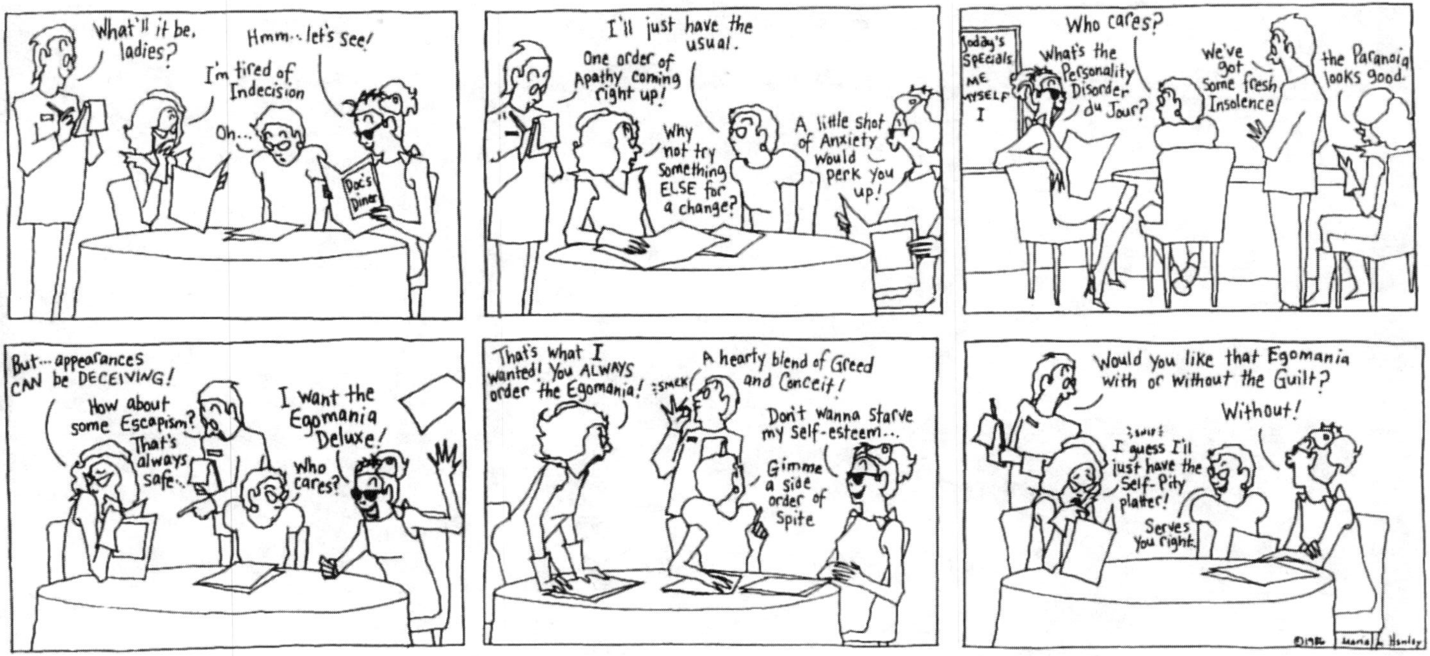
What'll it be, ladies?
Hmm... let's see!
I'm tired of Indecision
Oh...
Doc's Diner
I'll just have the usual.
One order of Apathy coming right up!
Why not try Something ELSE for a change?
A little shot of Anxiety would perk you up!
Today's Specials
ME
MYSELF
I
Who cares?
What's the Personality Disorder du Jour?
We've got Some fresh Insolence
the Paranoia looks good.
But... appearances CAN be DECEIVING!
How about some Escapism? That's always safe...
I want the Egomania Deluxe!
Who cares?
That's what I wanted! You ALWAYS order the Egomania!
A hearty blend of Greed and Conceit!
Don't wanna starve my Self-esteem...
Gimme a side order of Spite
Would you like that Egomania with or without the Guilt?
Without!
I guess I'll just have the Self-Pity platter!
Serves you right.

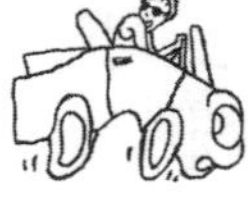

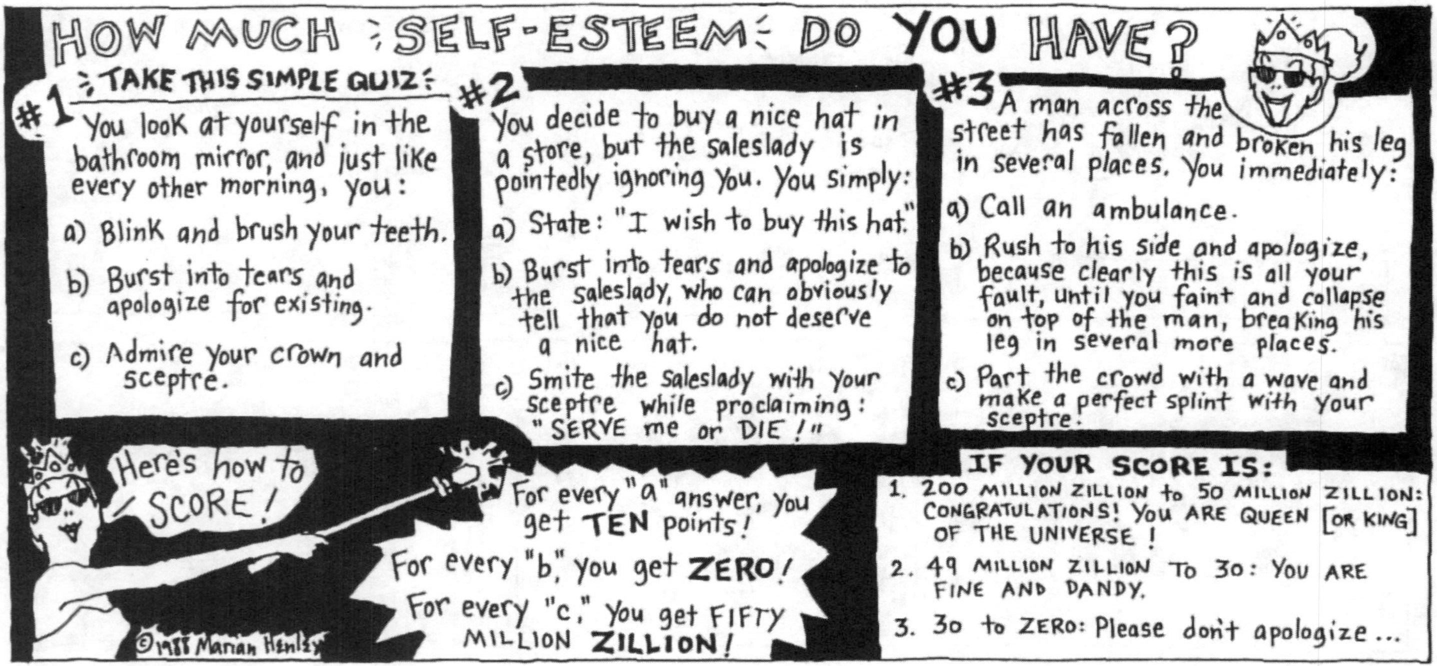
HOW MUCH SELF-ESTEEM DO YOU HAVE?
TAKE THIS SIMPLE QUIZ
#1 You look at yourself in the bathroom mirror, and just like every other morning, you:
a) Blink and brush your teeth.
b) Burst into tears and apologize for existing.
c) Admire your crown and sceptre.
#2 You decide to buy a nice hat in a store, but the saleslady is pointedly ignoring you. You simply:
a) State: "I wish to buy this hat."
b) Burst into tears and apologize to the saleslady, who can obviously tell that you do not deserve a nice hat.
c) Smite the saleslady with your sceptre while proclaiming: "SERVE me or DIE!"
#3 A man across the street has fallen and broken his leg in several places. You immediately:
a) Call an ambulance.
b) Rush to his side and apologize, because clearly this is all your fault, until you faint and collapse on top of the man, breaking his leg in several more places.
c) Part the crowd with a wave and make a perfect splint with your sceptre.
Here's how to SCORE!
For every "a" answer, you get TEN points!
For every "b," you get ZERO!
For every "c," you get FIFTY MILLION ZILLION!
IF YOUR SCORE IS:
1. 200 MILLION ZILLION to 50 MILLION ZILLION: CONGRATULATIONS! YOU ARE QUEEN [OR KING] OF THE UNIVERSE!
2. 49 MILLION ZILLION TO 30: YOU ARE FINE AND DANDY.
3. 30 to ZERO: Please don't apologize...
©1988 Marian Henley

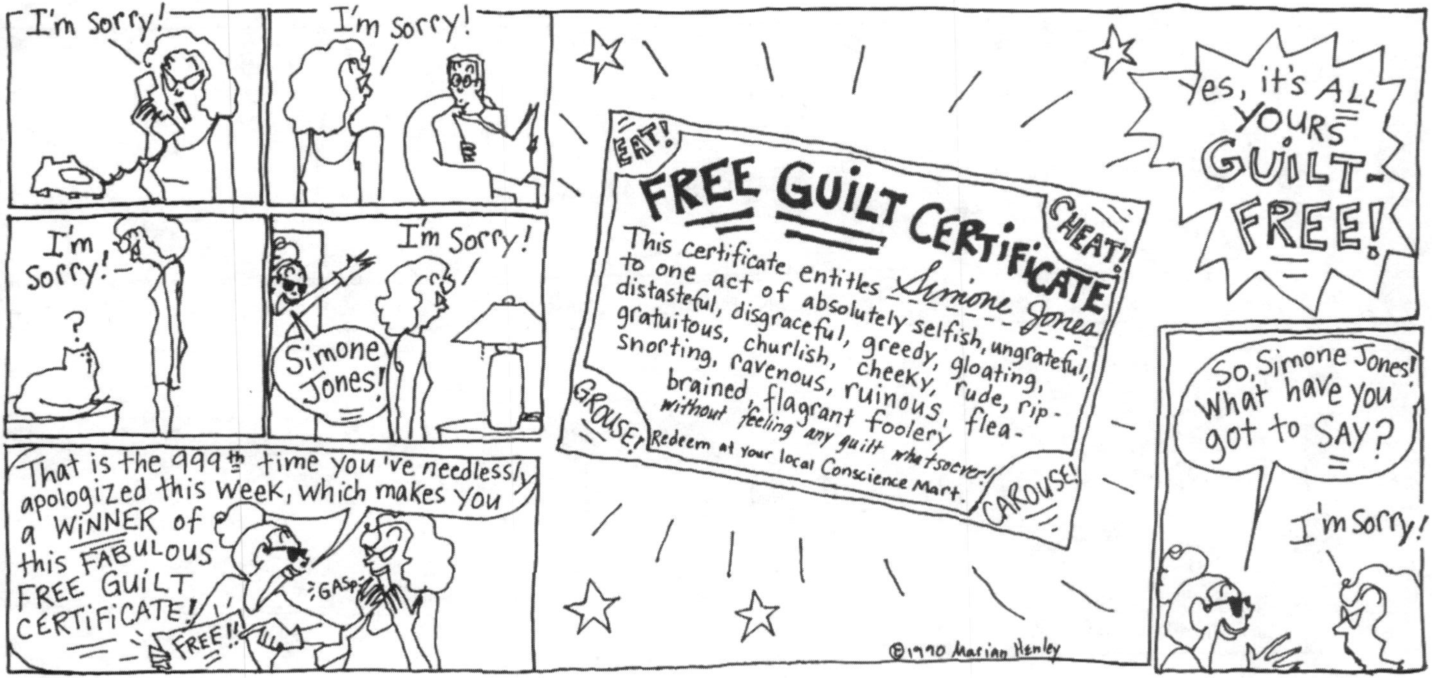
I'm sorry!
I'm sorry!
I'm sorry!
?
I'm sorry!
Simone Jones!
That is the 999th time you've needlessly apologized this week, which makes you a WINNER of this FABULOUS FREE GUILT CERTIFICATE!
FREE!!
GASP
FREE GUILT CERTIFICATE
This certificate entitles Simone Jones to one act of absolutely selfish, ungrateful, distasteful, disgraceful, greedy, gloating, gratuitous, churlish, cheeky, rude, rip-snorting, ravenous, ruinous, flea-brained, flagrant foolery without feeling any guilt whatsoever!
Redeem at your local Conscience Mart.
EAT!
CHEAT!
GROUSE!
CAROUSE!
©1990 Marian Henley
Yes, it's ALL YOURS GUILT-FREE!
So, Simone Jones! What have you got to SAY?
I'm sorry!

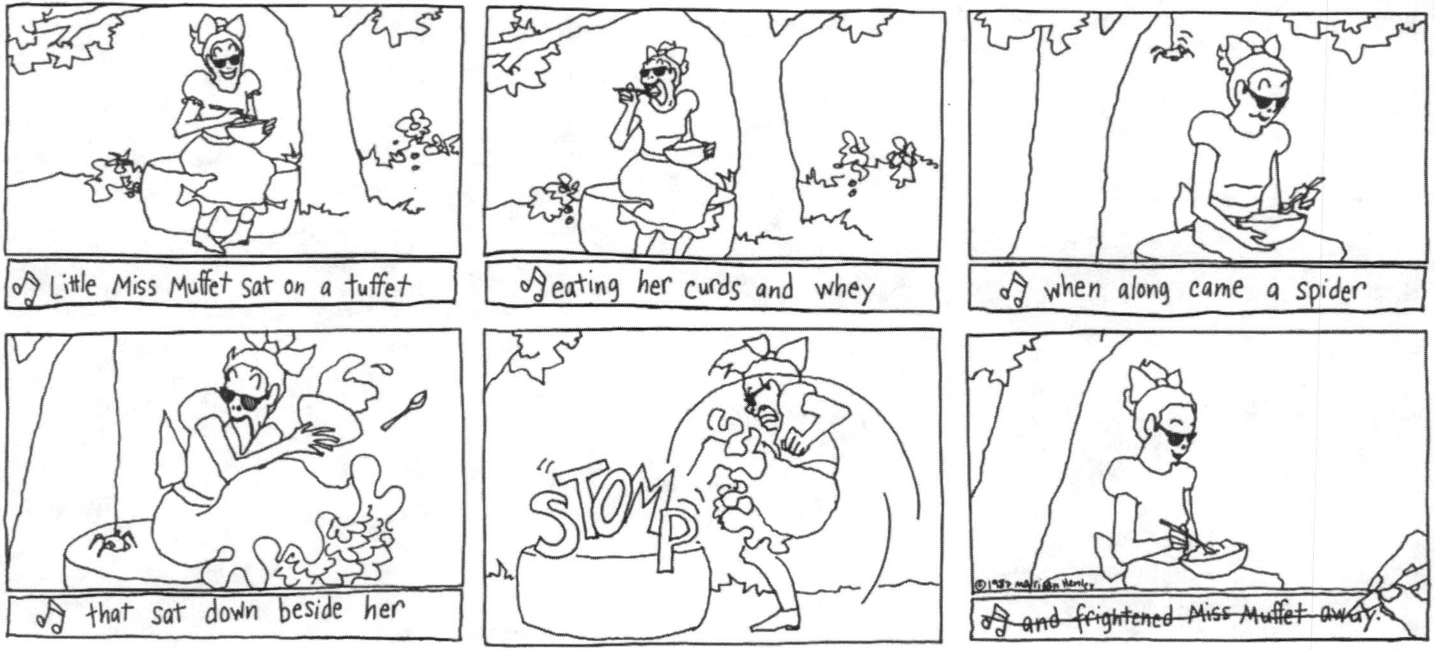
Little Miss Muffet sat on a tuffet
eating her curds and whey
when along came a spider
that sat down beside her
STOMP
and frightened Miss Muffet away.

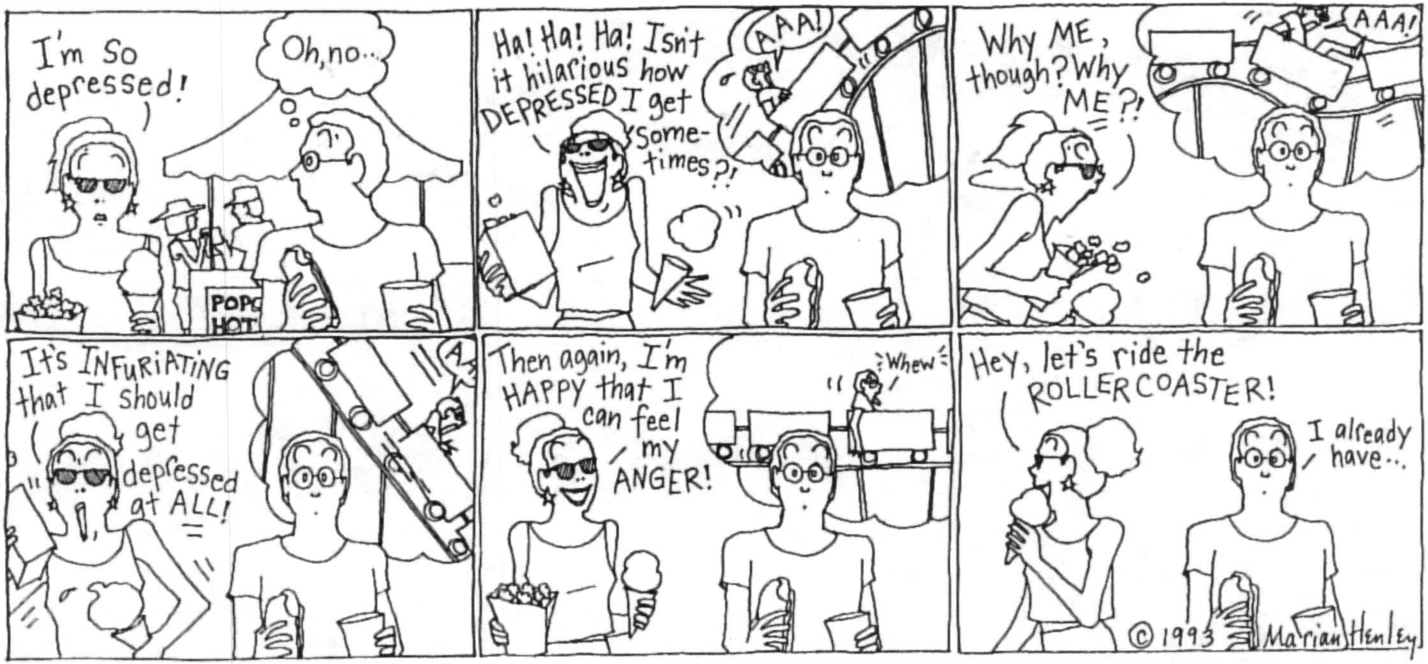
I'm so depressed!
Oh, no...
POPC
HOT
Ha! Ha! Ha! Isn't it hilarious how DEPRESSED I get sometimes?!
AAA!
Why ME, though? Why ME?!
AAA!
It's INFURIATING that I should get depressed at ALL!
A
Then again, I'm HAPPY that I can feel my ANGER!
Whew
Hey, let's ride the ROLLERCOASTER!
I already have...
© 1993 Marian Henley

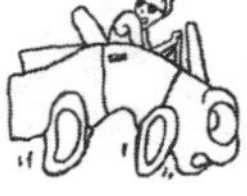

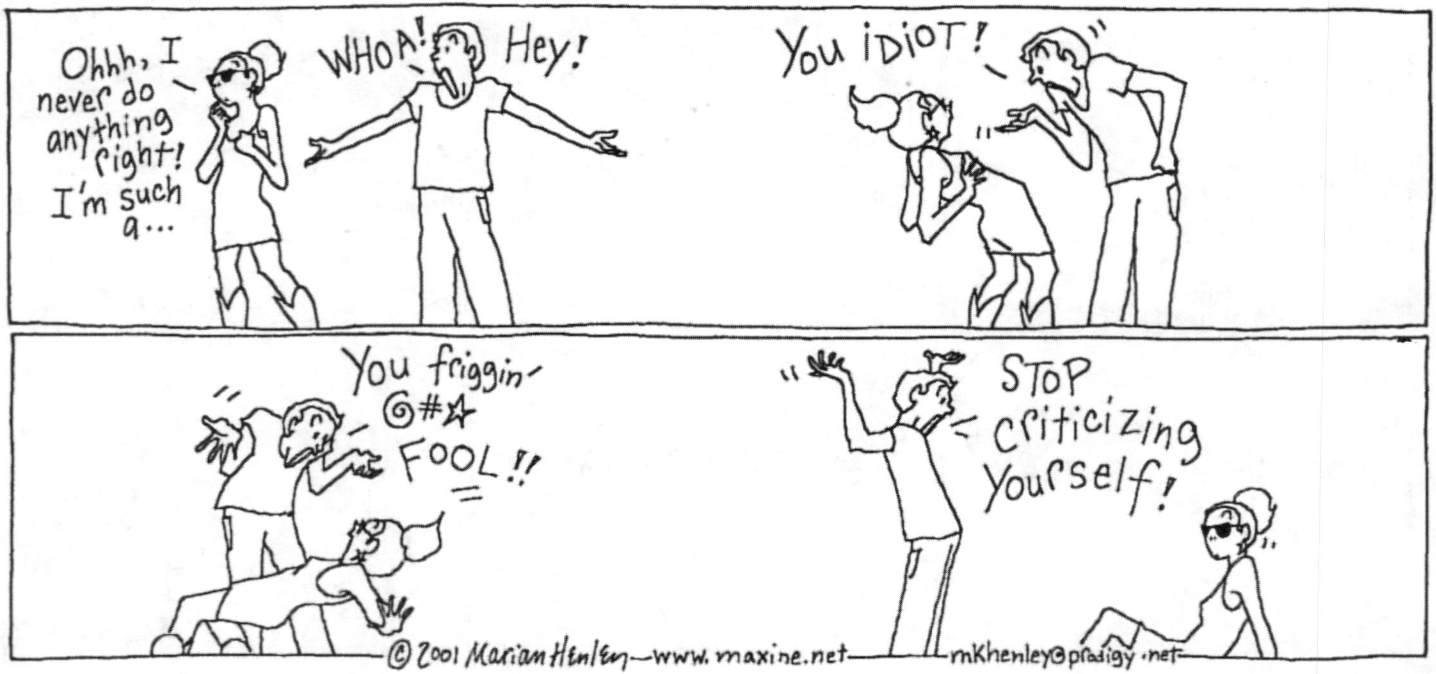
Ohhh, I never do anything right! I'm such a...
WHOA! Hey!
You IDIOT!
You friggin' @#☆ FOOL!!
STOP criticizing yourself!
© 2001 Marian Henley—www.maxine.net—mkhenley@prodigy.net

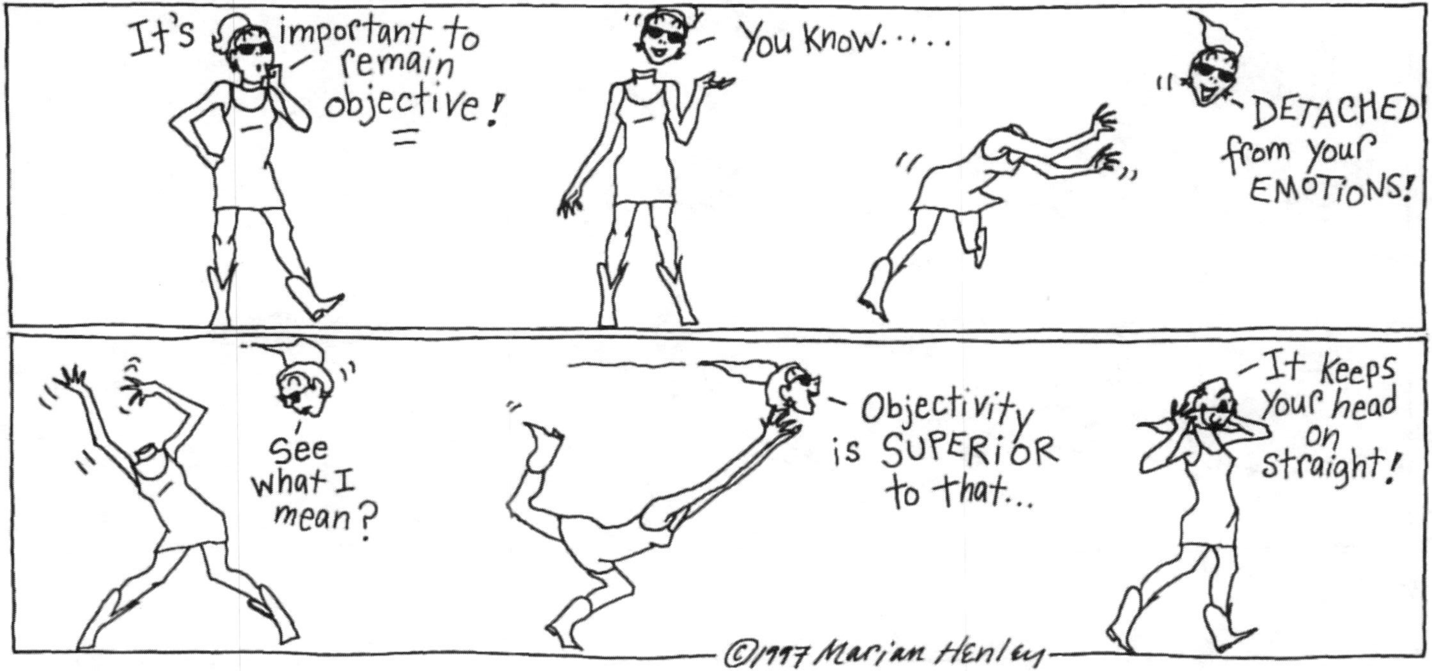
It's important to remain objective!
You know.....
DETACHED from your EMOTIONS!
See what I mean?
Objectivity is SUPERIOR to that...
It keeps your head on straight!
©1997 Marian Henley

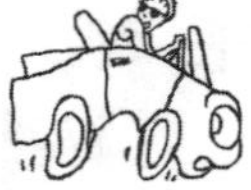

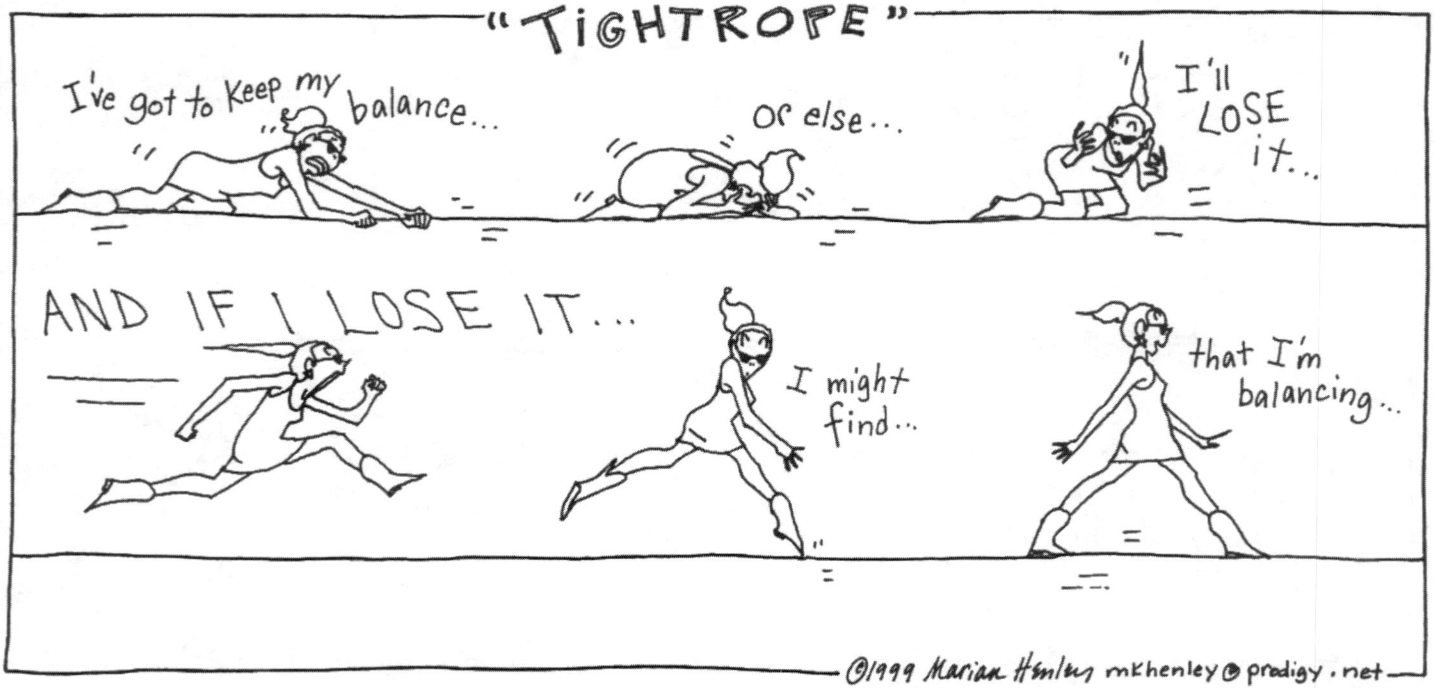
"TIGHTROPE"
I've got to keep my balance...
or else...
I'll LOSE it...
AND IF I LOSE IT...
I might find...
that I'm balancing...
©1999 Marian Henley mkhenley@prodigy.net

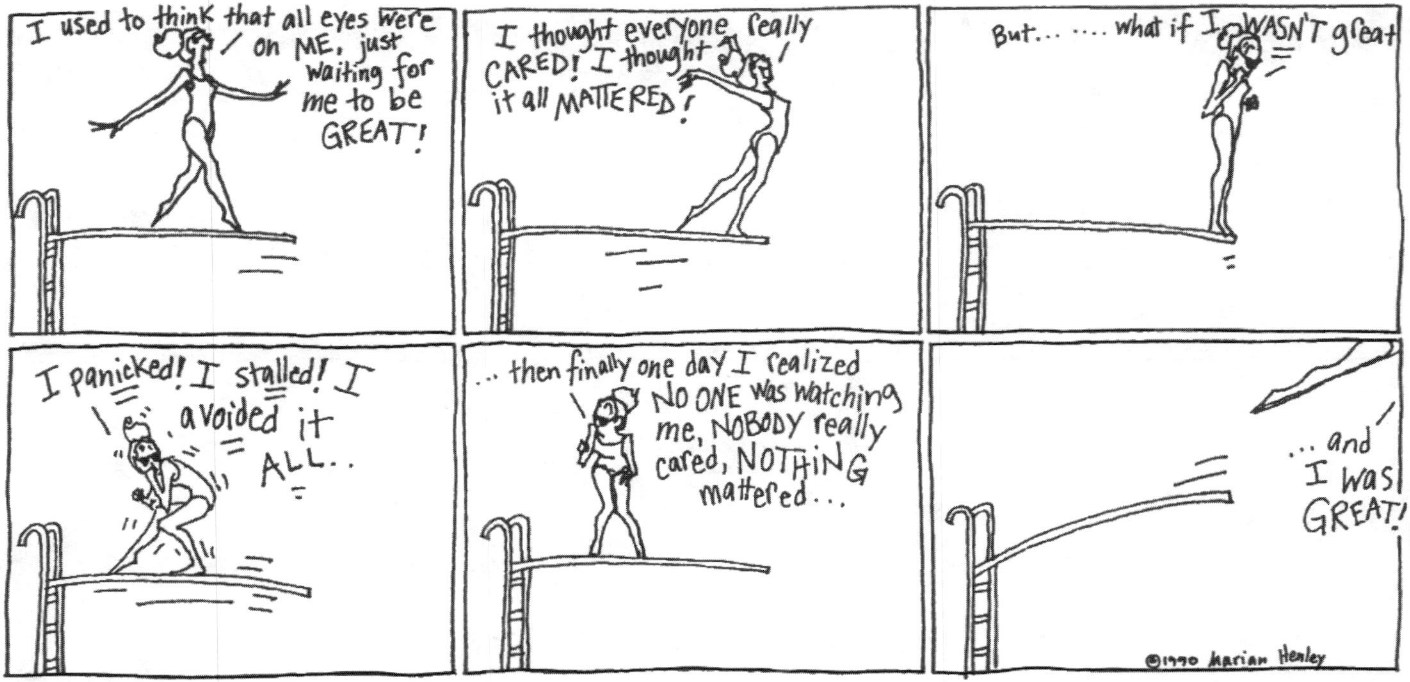
I used to think that all eyes were on ME, just waiting for me to be GREAT!
I thought everyone really CARED! I thought it all MATTERED!
But... ....what if I WASN'T great
I panicked! I stalled! I avoided it ALL..
...then finally one day I realized NO ONE was watching me, NOBODY really cared, NOTHING mattered...
...and I was GREAT!
©1990 Marian Henley

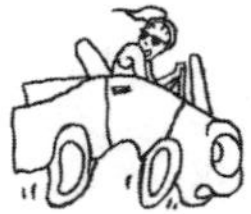

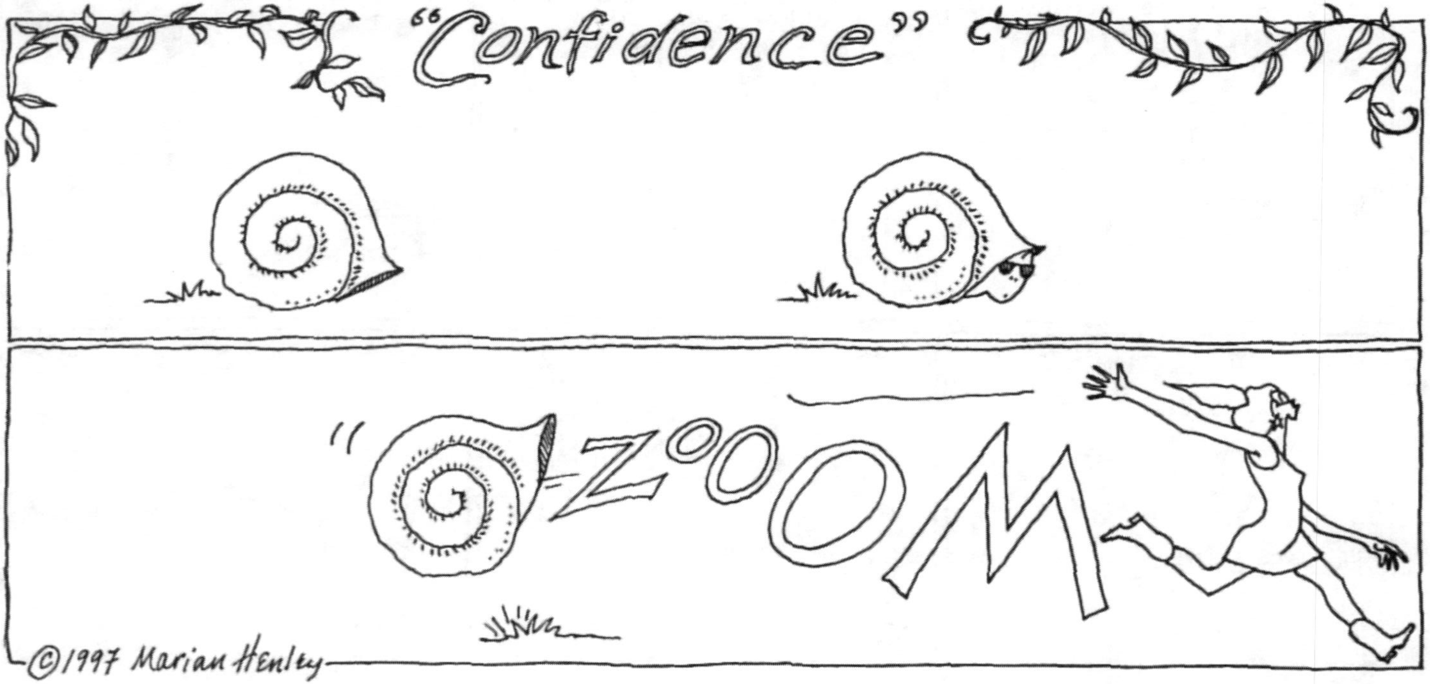
"Confidence"
ZoooM
©1997 Marian Henley

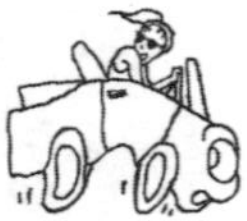

Friends and Family

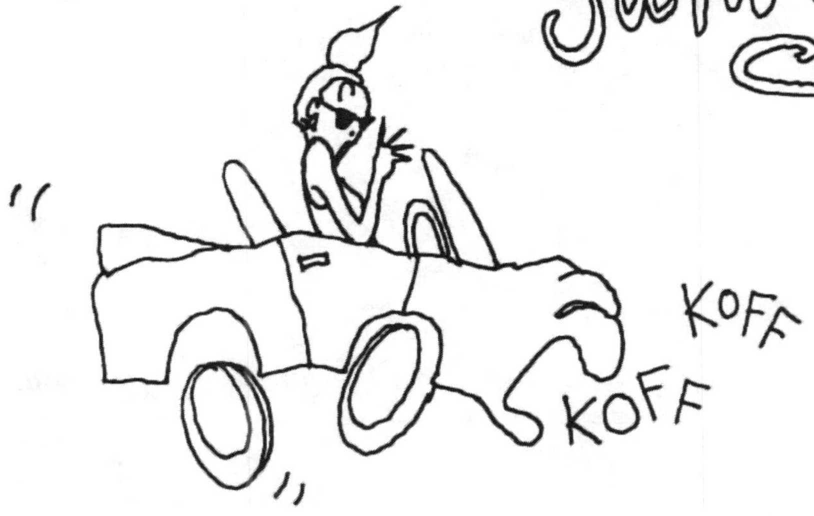
KOFF
KOFF

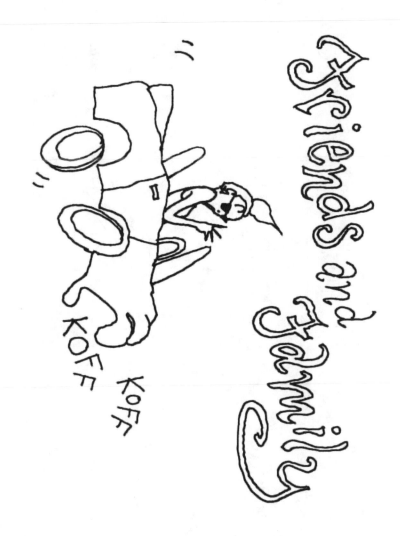

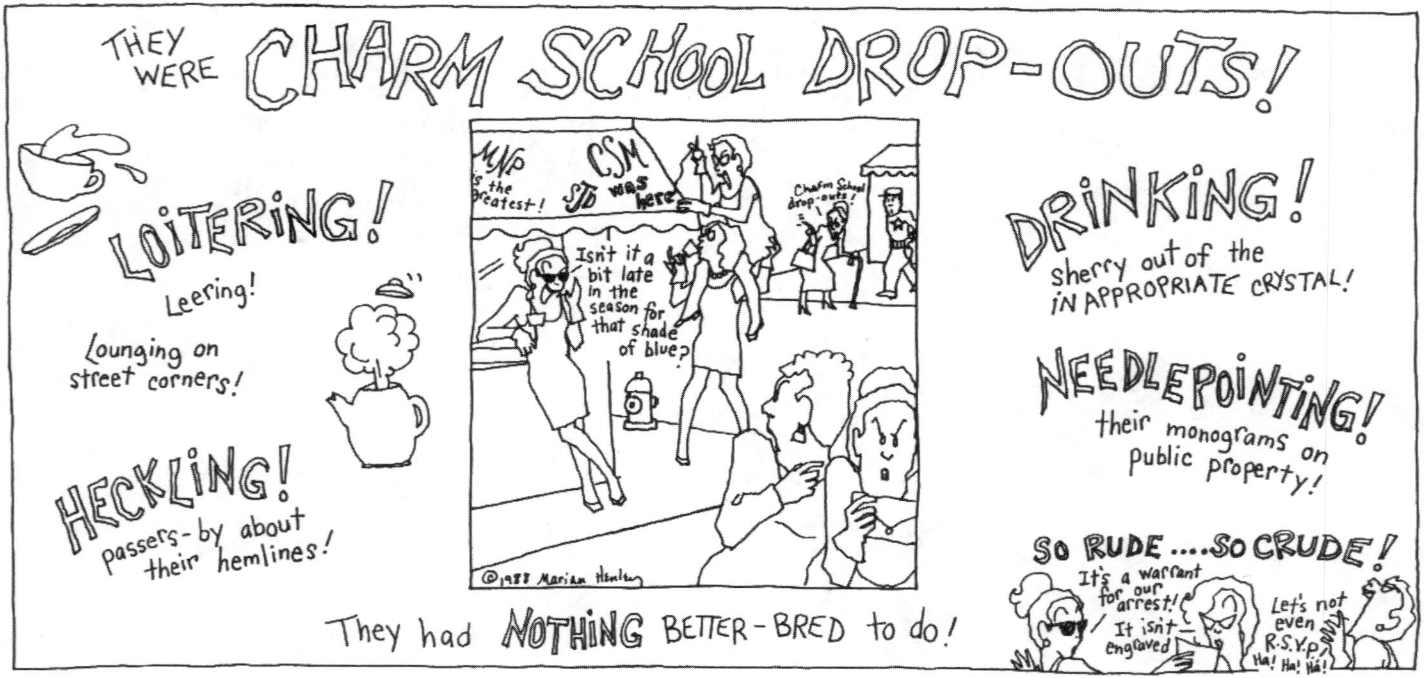
THEY WERE CHARM SCHOOL DROP-OUTS!
LOITERING!
Leering!
Lounging on street corners!
HECKLING!
passers-by about their hemlines!
MNP is the greatest!
CSM
STB was here
Isn't it a bit late in the season for that shade of blue?
Charm School drop-outs!
©1988 Marian Henley
DRINKING!
sherry out of the INAPPROPRIATE CRYSTAL!
NEEDLEPOINTING!
their monograms on public property!
SO RUDE ....SO CRUDE!
It's a warrant for our arrest!
It isn't engraved
Let's not even R.S.V.P.!
Ha! Ha! Ha!
They had NOTHING BETTER-BRED to do!

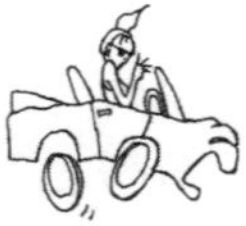

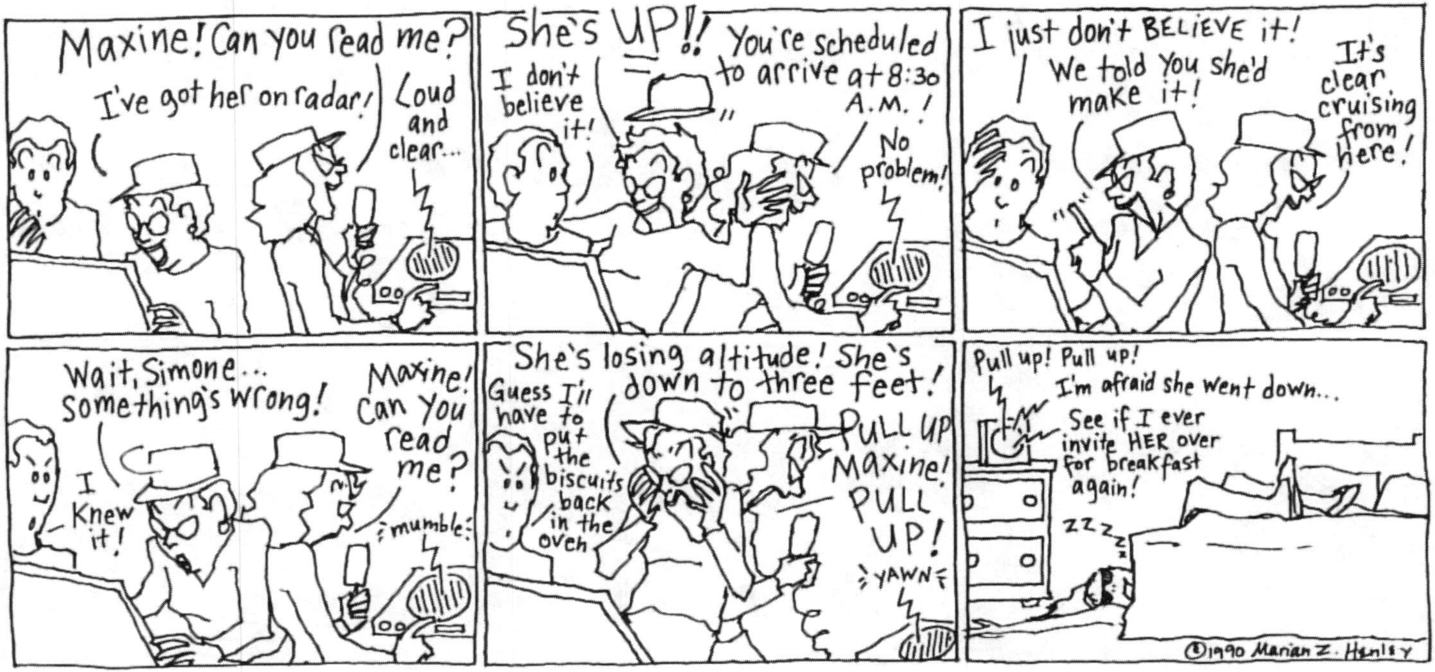
Maxine! Can you read me?
I've got her on radar!
Loud and clear...
She's UP!!
I don't believe it!
You're scheduled to arrive at 8:30 A.M.!
No problem!
I just don't BELIEVE it!
We told you she'd make it!
It's clear cruising from here!
Wait, Simone... something's wrong!
I knew it!
Maxine! Can you read me?
mumble
She's losing altitude! She's down to three feet!
Guess I'll have to put the biscuits back in the oven
PULL UP Maxine! PULL UP!
YAWN
Pull up! Pull up!
I'm afraid she went down...
See if I ever invite HER over for breakfast again!
ZZZ
©1990 Marian Z. Henley

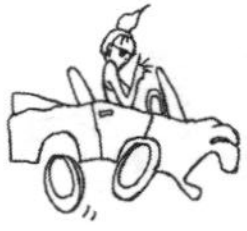

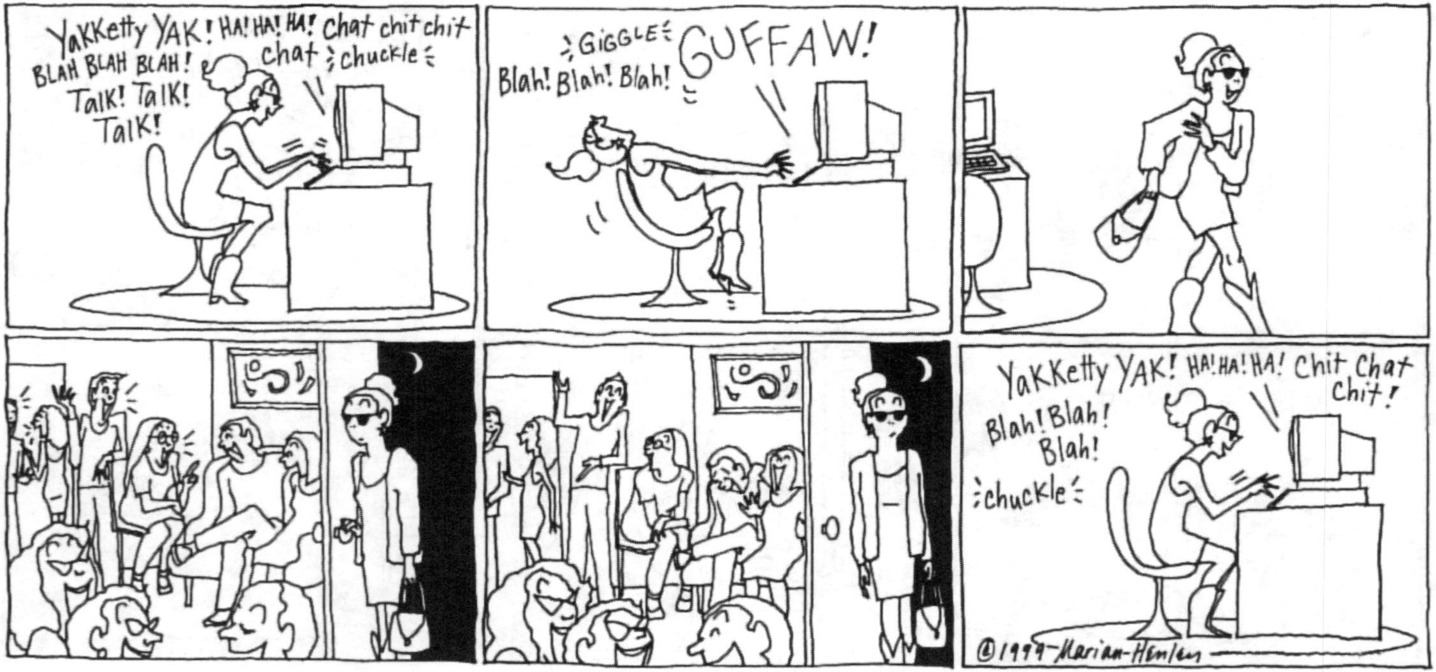
YaKKetty YAK! HA! HA! HA! Chat chit chit chat
chuckle
BLAH BLAH BLAH! Talk! Talk! Talk!
GIGGLE
Blah! Blah! Blah!
GUFFAW!
YaKKetty YAK! HA! HA! HA! Chit Chat Chit!
Blah! Blah! Blah!
chuckle
© 1999 Marian Henley

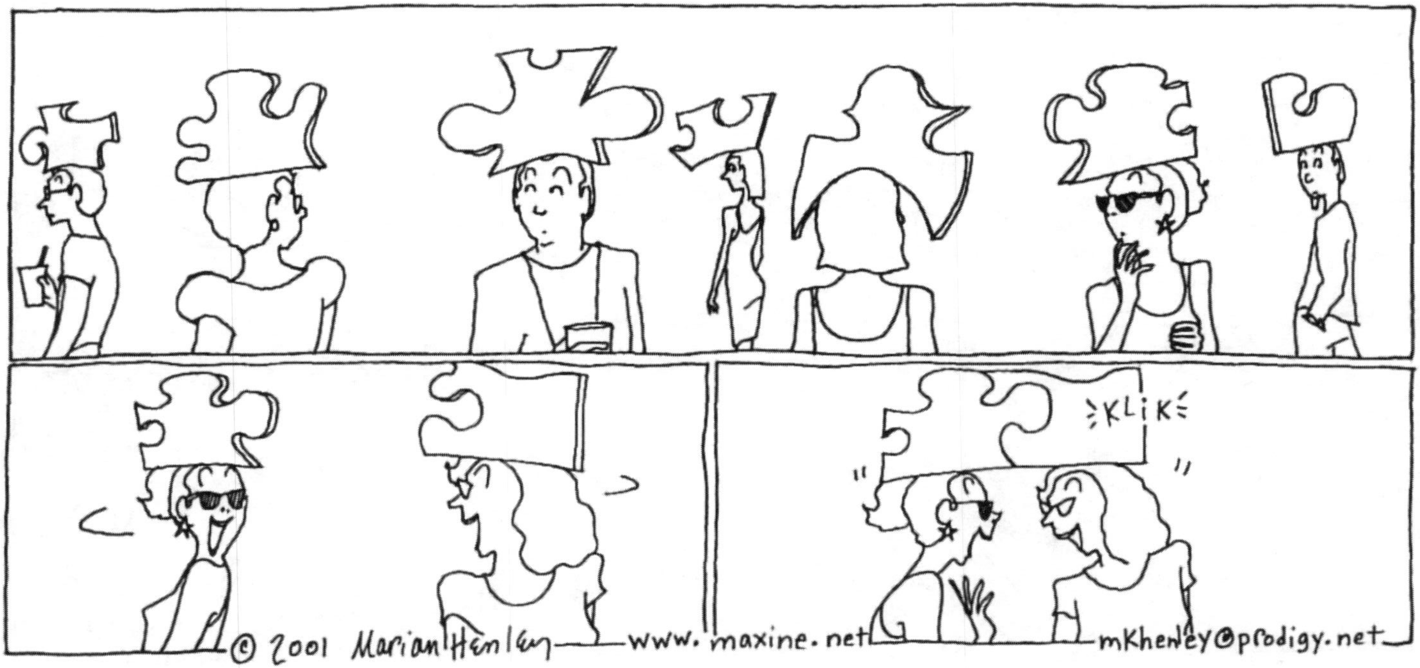
KLiK
© 2001 Marian Henley — www.maxine.net — mKhenley@prodigy.net

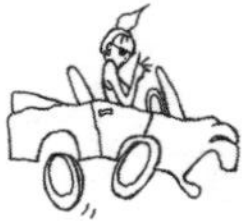

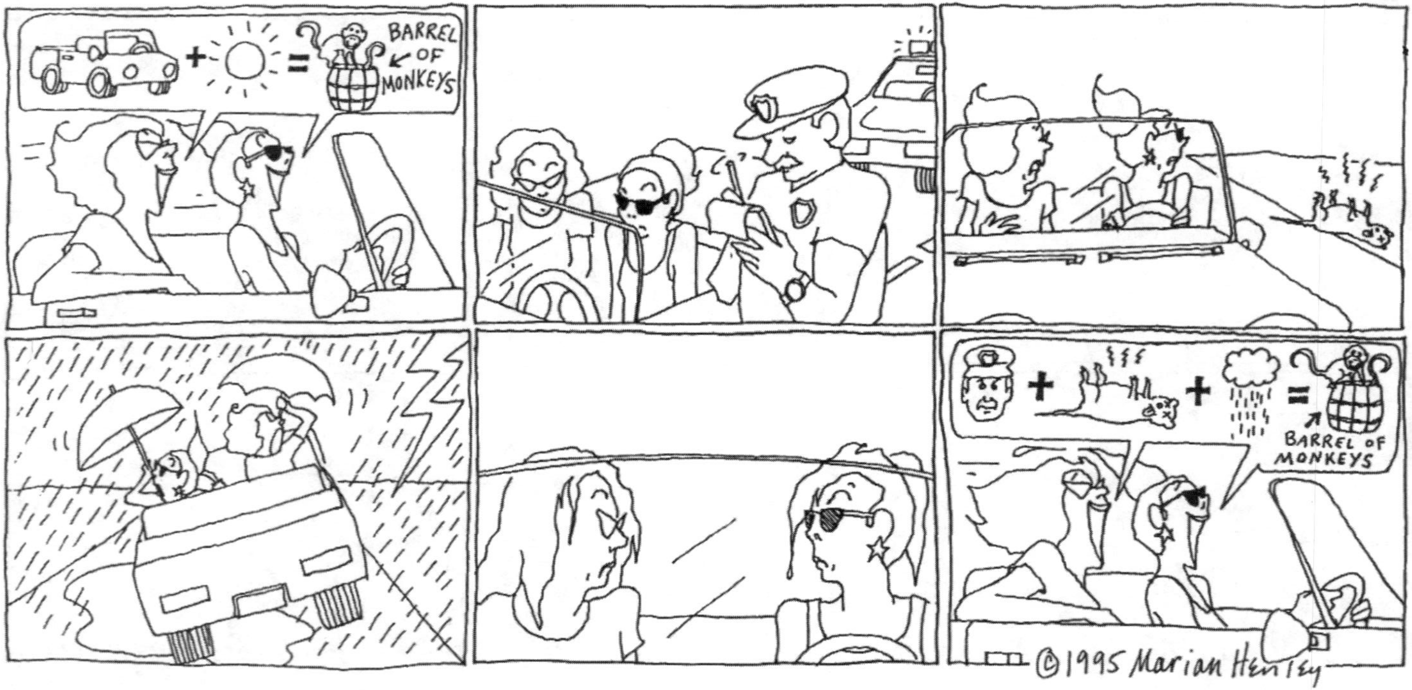
BARREL OF MONKEYS
BARREL OF MONKEYS
©1995 Marian Henley

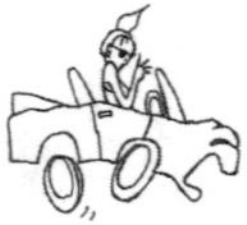

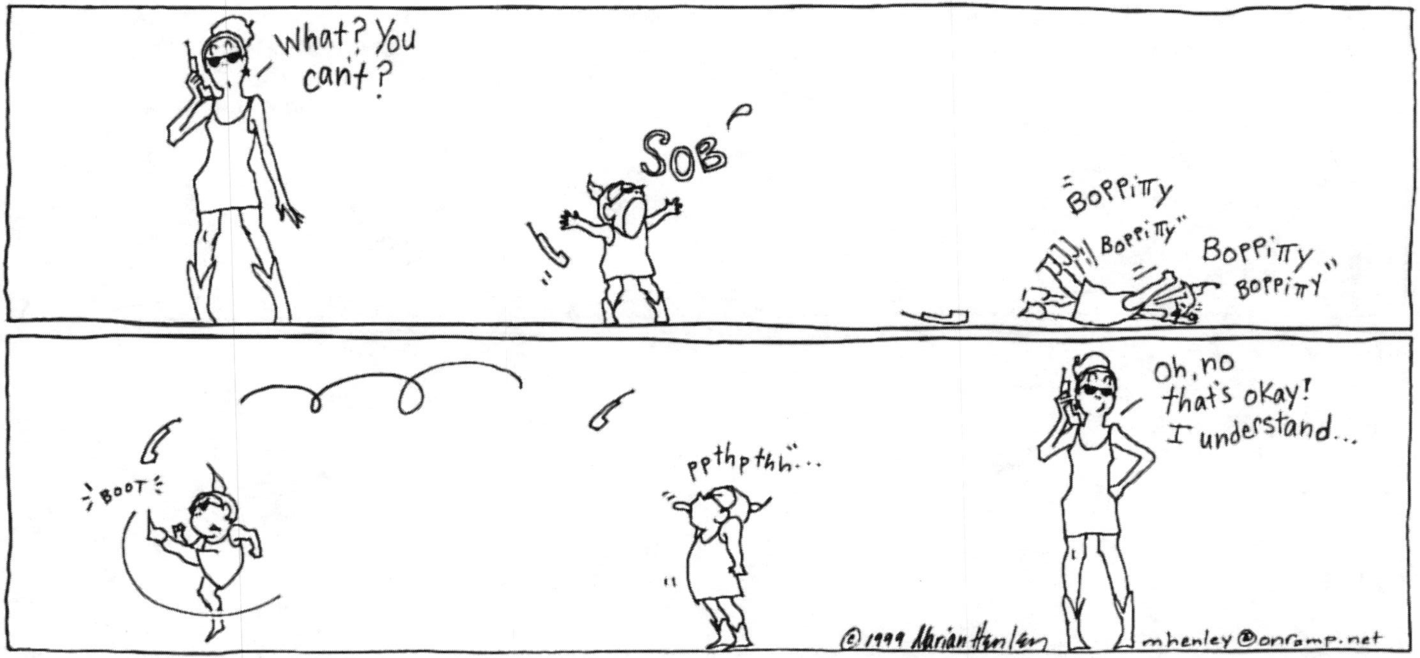
What? You can't?
SOB
BOPPITTY
BOPPITTY
BOPPITTY
BOPPITTY
BOOT
ppthpthh...
Oh, no that's okay! I understand...
© 1999 Marian Henley
mhenley@onramp.net

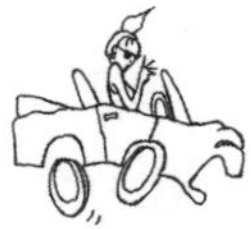

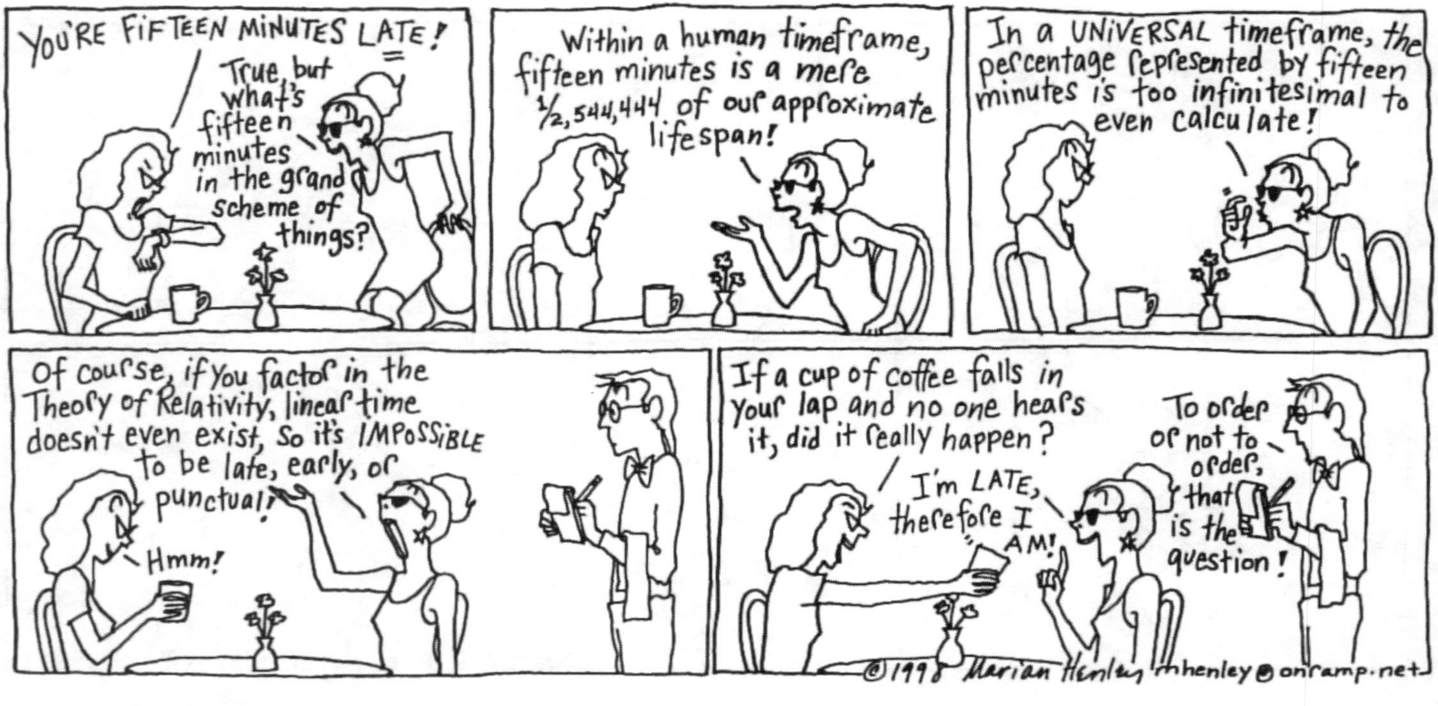
YOU'RE FIFTEEN MINUTES LATE!
True, but what's fifteen minutes in the grand scheme of things?
Within a human timeframe, fifteen minutes is a mere 1/2,544,444 of our approximate lifespan!
In a UNIVERSAL timeframe, the percentage represented by fifteen minutes is too infinitesimal to even calculate!
Of course, if you factor in the Theory of Relativity, linear time doesn't even exist, so it's IMPOSSIBLE to be late, early, or punctual!
Hmm!
If a cup of coffee falls in your lap and no one hears it, did it really happen?
I'm LATE, therefore I AM!
To order or not to order, that is the question!
©1998 Marian Henley mhenley@onramp.net

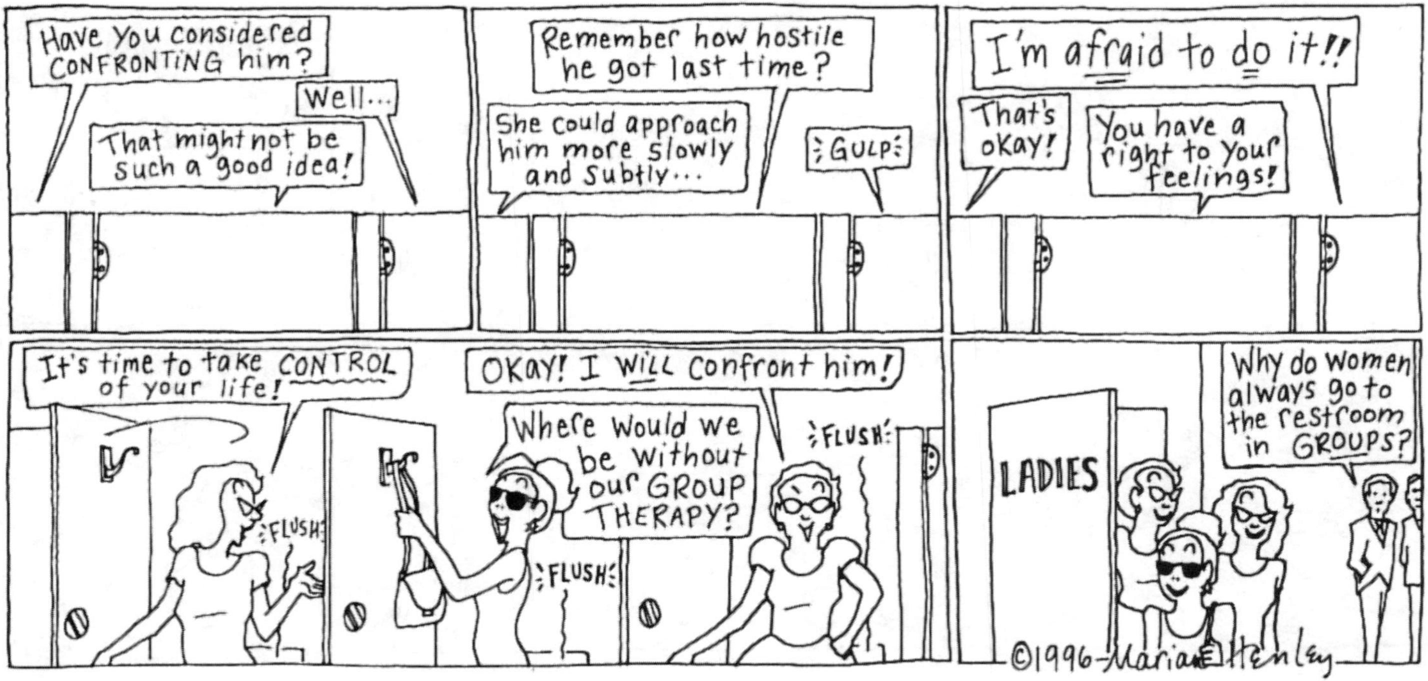
Have you considered CONFRONTING him?
Well...
That might not be such a good idea!
Remember how hostile he got last time?
She could approach him more slowly and subtly...
GULP
I'm afraid to do it!!
That's okay!
You have a right to your feelings!
It's time to take CONTROL of your life!
FLUSH
OKAY! I WILL confront him!
Where would we be without our GROUP THERAPY?
FLUSH
FLUSH
LADIES
Why do women always go to the restroom in GROUPS?
©1996-Marian Henley

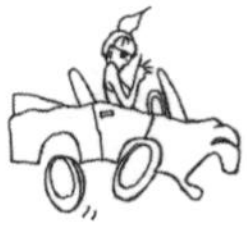

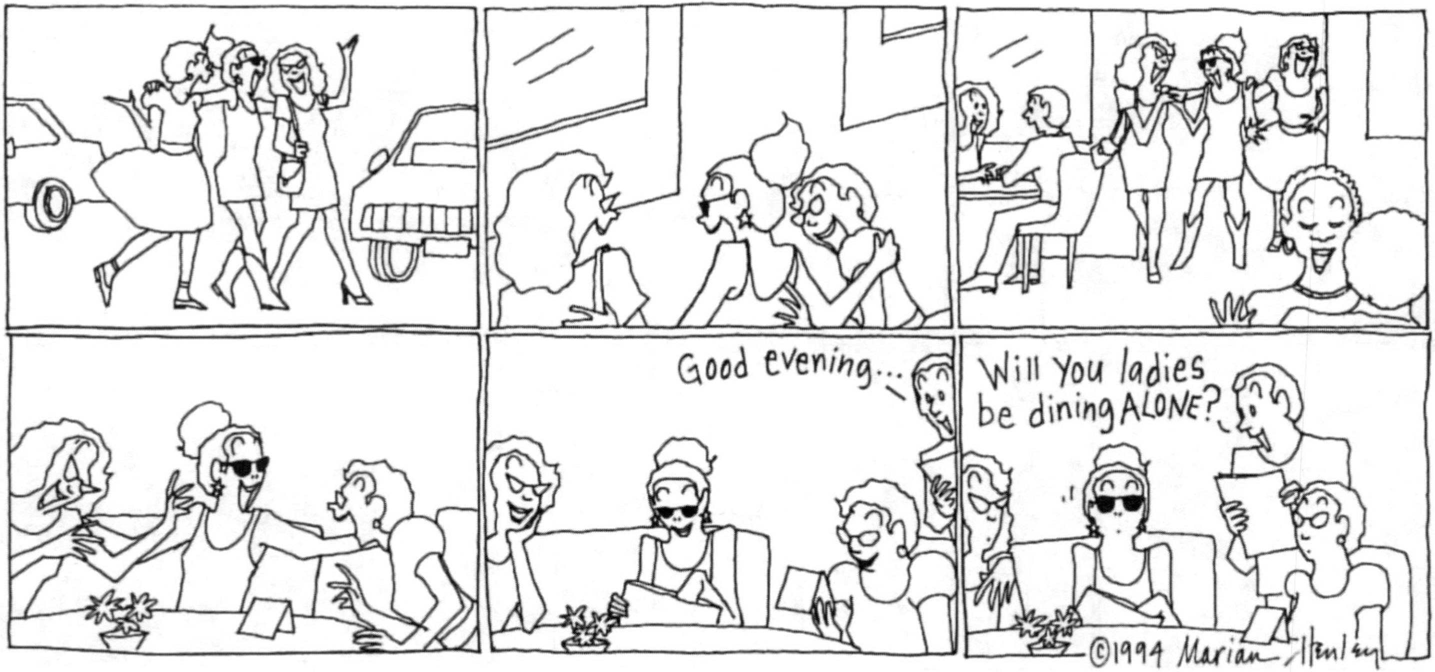
Good evening...
Will You ladies be dining ALONE?
©1994 Marian Henley

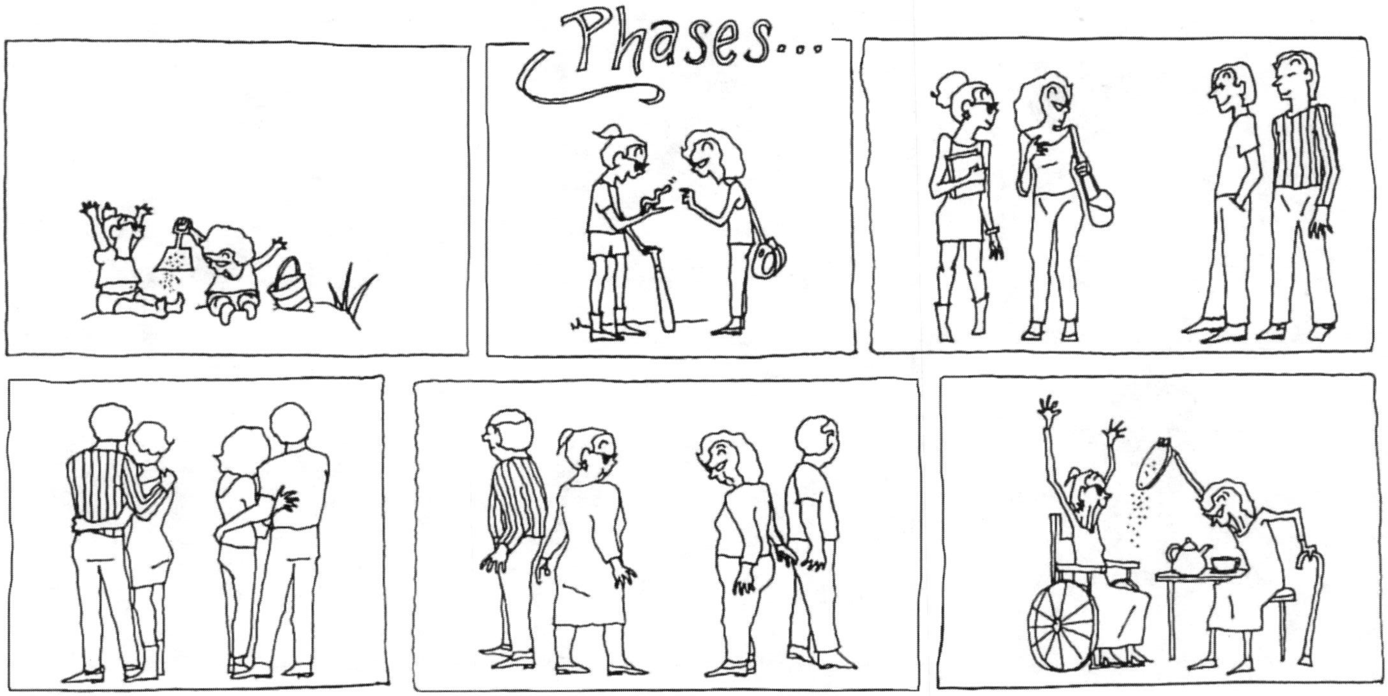
Phases...

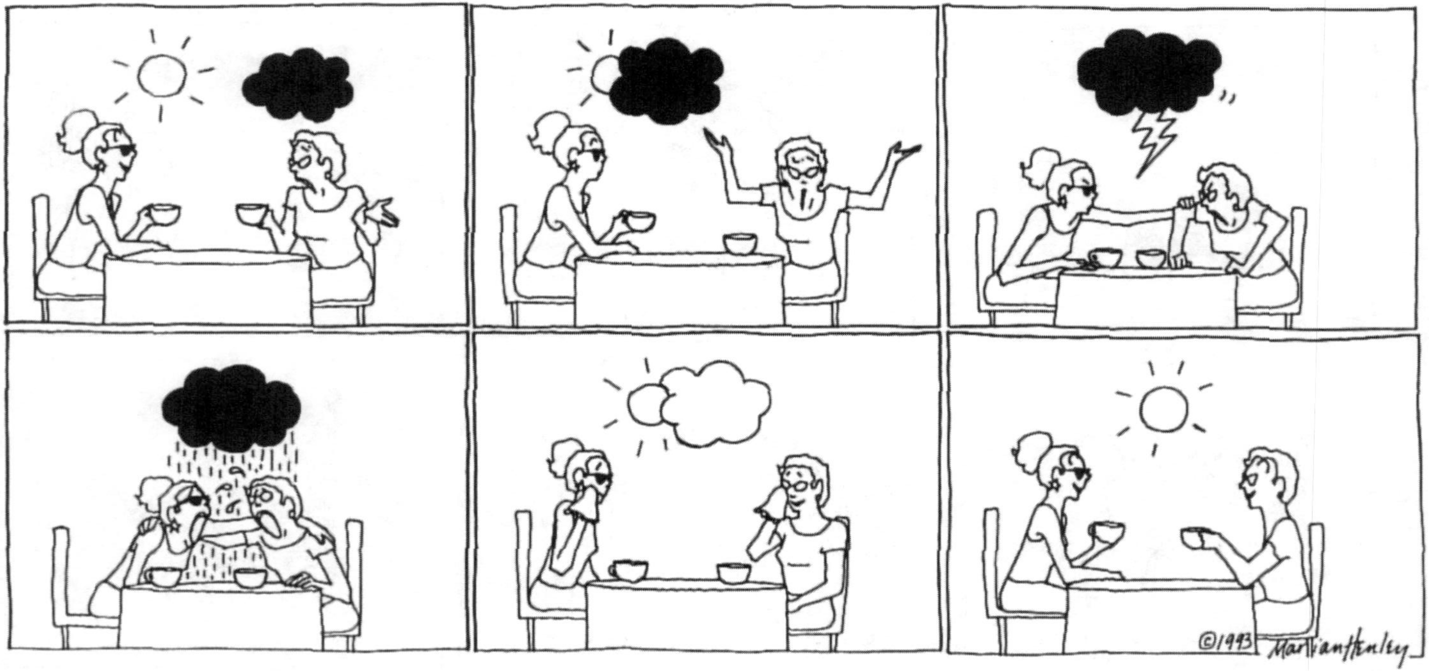
©1993 MarlianHenley

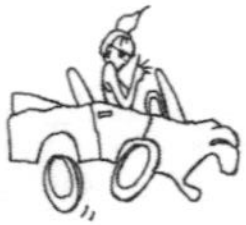

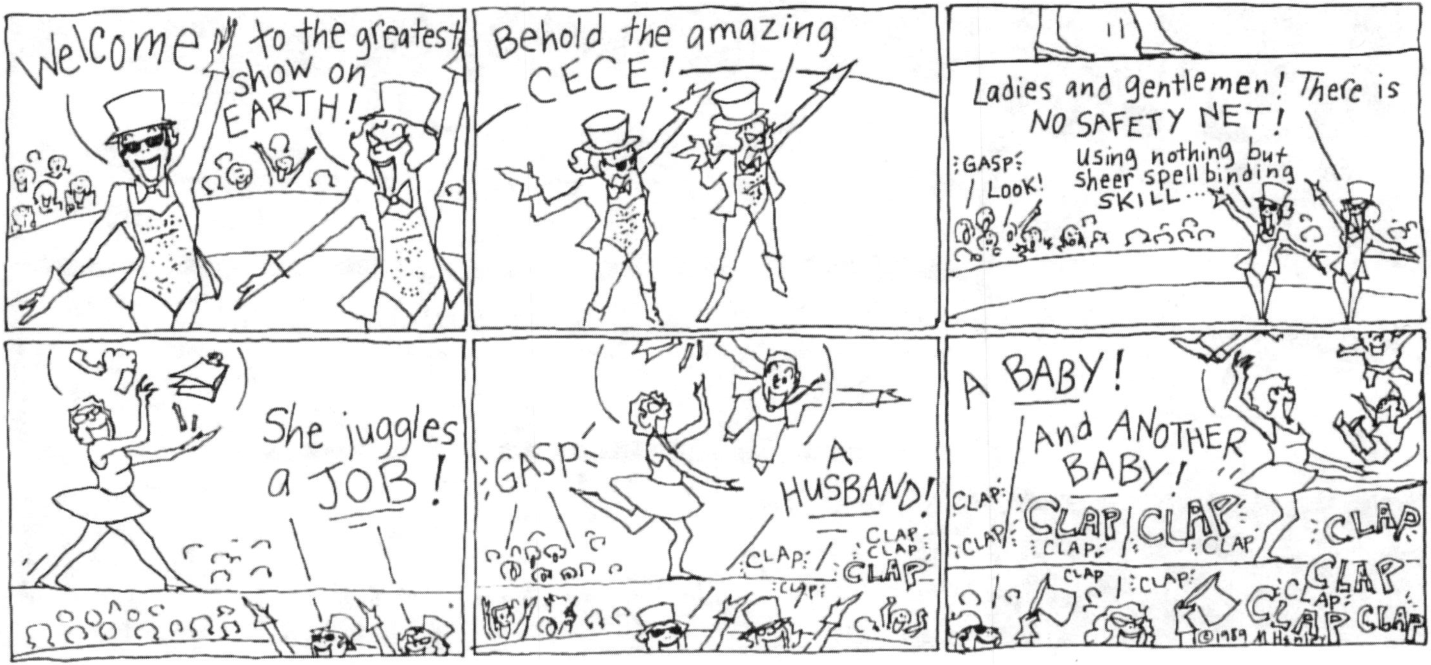
Welcome to the greatest show on EARTH!
Behold the amazing CECE!
Ladies and gentlemen! There is NO SAFETY NET!
GASP
LOOK!
Using nothing but sheer spellbinding SKILL...
She juggles a JOB!
GASP
A HUSBAND!
CLAP
CLAP CLAP CLAP
A BABY!
And ANOTHER BABY!
CLAP CLAP CLAP CLAP CLAP CLAP CLAP CLAP CLAP
©1989 M Hanley

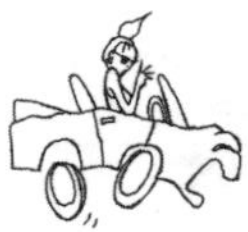

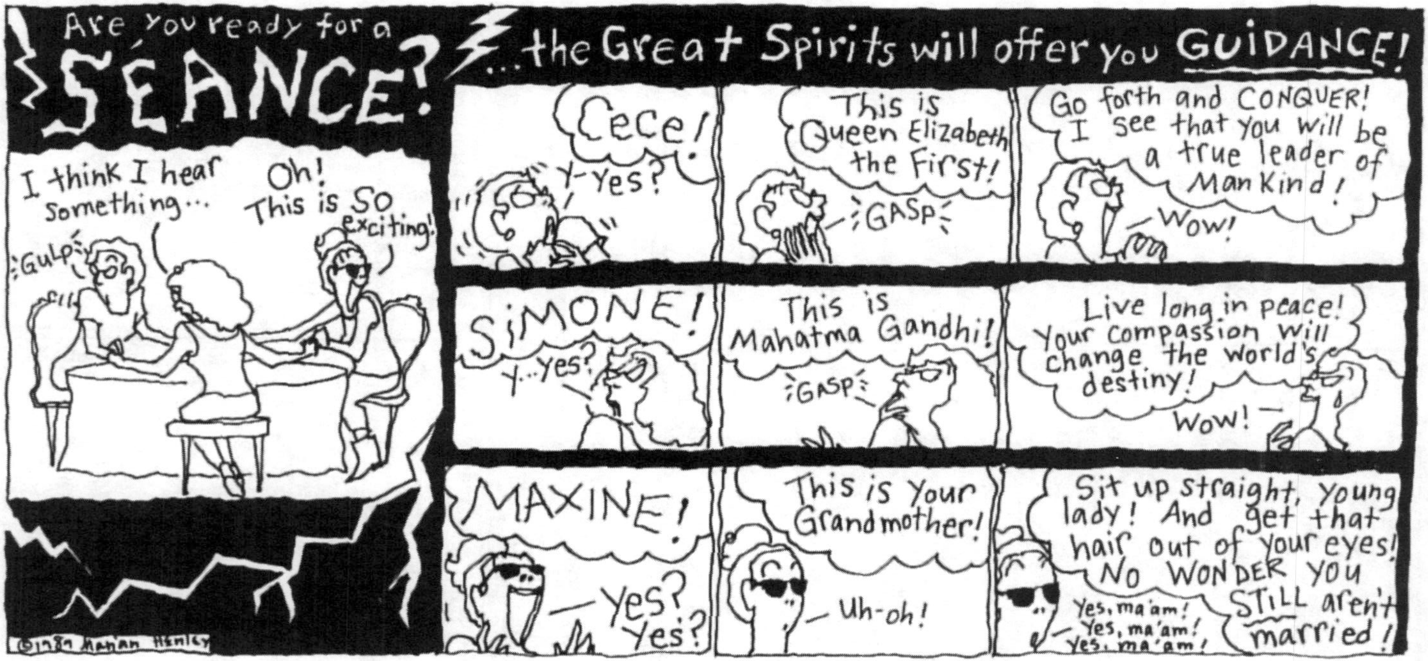
Are you ready for a SÉANCE?
I think I hear something...
Gulp
Oh! This is SO exciting!
...the Great Spirits will offer you GUIDANCE!
Cece!
Y-Yes?
This is Queen Elizabeth the First!
GASP
Go forth and CONQUER! I see that you will be a true leader of ManKind!
Wow!
SiMONE!
Y...Yes?
This is Mahatma Gandhi!
GASP
Live long in peace! Your compassion will change the world's destiny!
Wow!
MAXINE!
Yes? Yes?
This is Your Grandmother!
Uh-oh!
Sit up straight, young lady! And get that hair out of your eyes! NO WONDER YOU STILL aren't married!
Yes, ma'am! Yes, ma'am! Yes, ma'am!

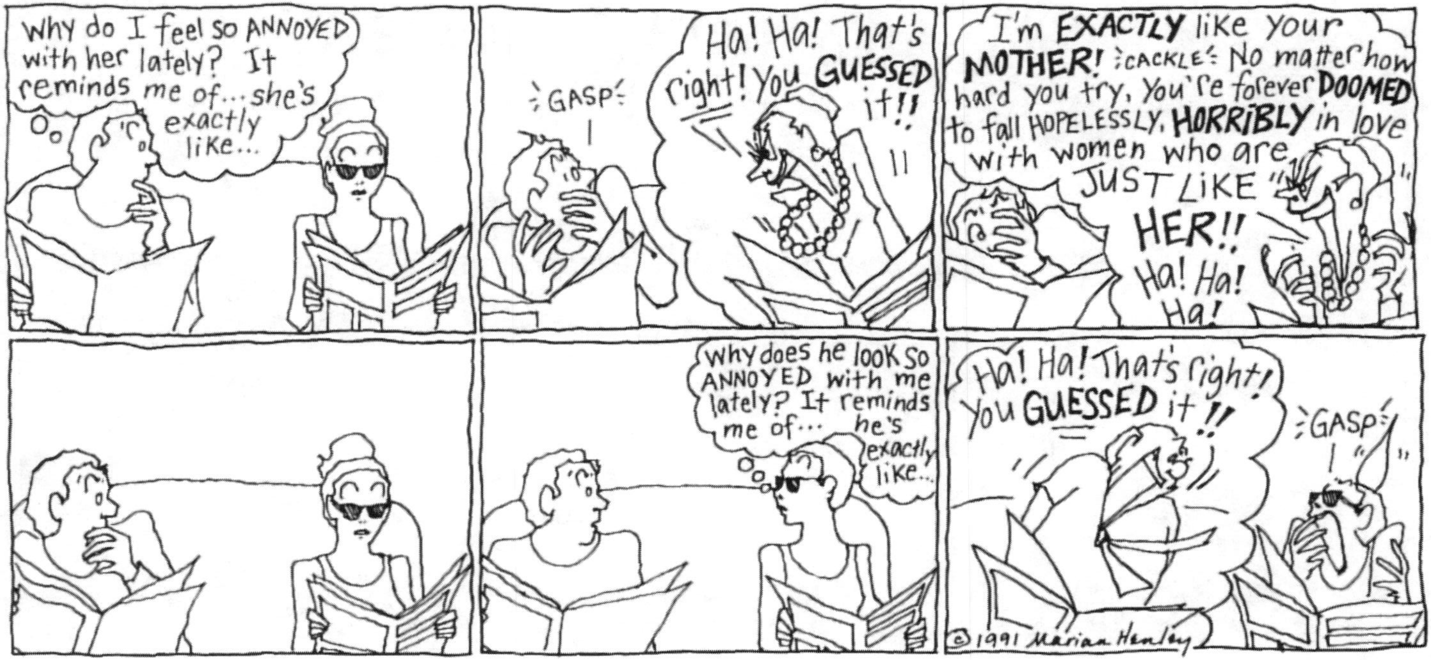
Why do I feel so ANNOYED with her lately? It reminds me of... she's exactly like...
GASP
Ha! Ha! That's right! You GUESSED it!!
I'm EXACTLY like your MOTHER! CACKLE No matter how hard you try, You're forever DOOMED to fall HOPELESSLY, HORRIBLY in love with women who are JUST LIKE HER!! Ha! Ha! Ha!
Why does he look so ANNOYED with me lately? It reminds me of... he's exactly like...
Ha! Ha! That's right! You GUESSED it!!
GASP
© 1991 Marian Henley

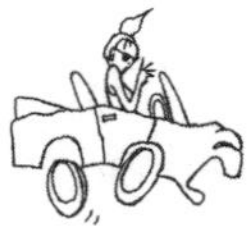

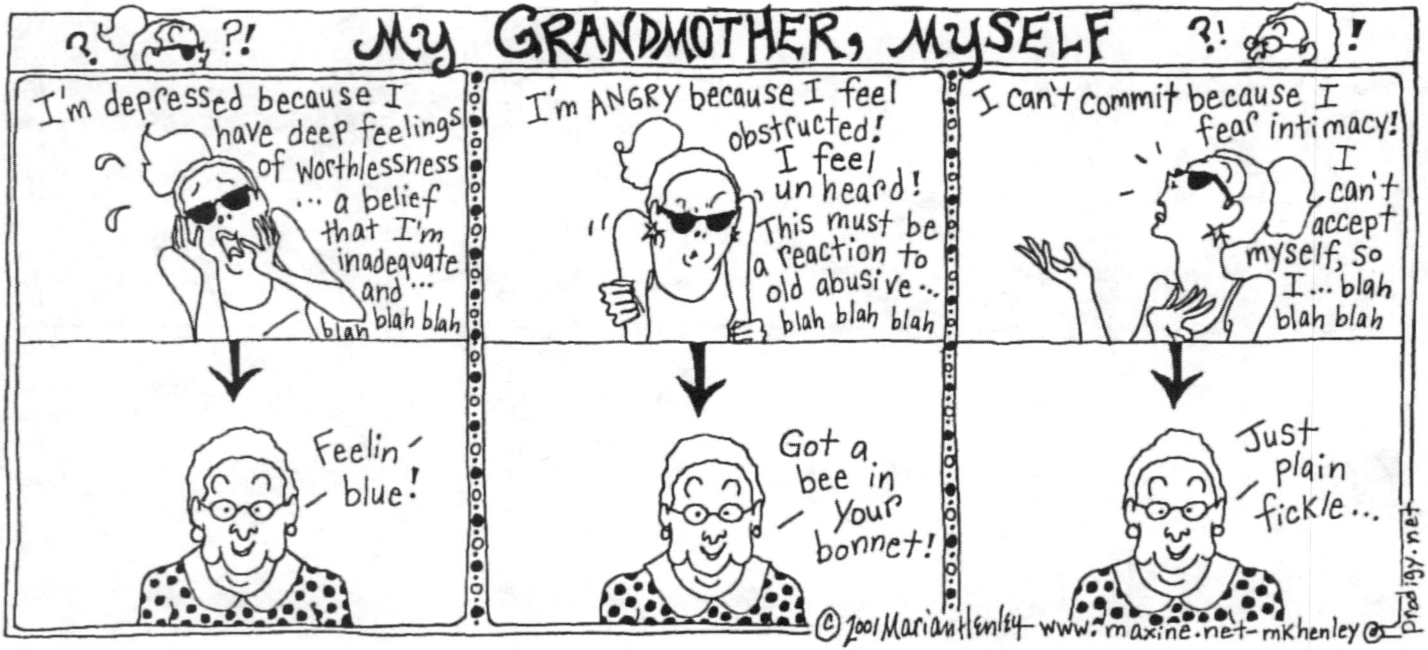
MY GRANDMOTHER, MYSELF
?. ?!
?! !
I'm depressed because I have deep feelings of worthlessness ... a belief that I'm inadequate and ... blah blah blah
Feelin' blue!
I'm ANGRY because I feel obstructed! I feel unheard! This must be a reaction to old abusive ... blah blah blah
Got a bee in your bonnet!
I can't commit because I fear intimacy! I can't accept myself, so I ... blah blah blah
Just plain fickle ...
© 2001 MarianHenley www.maxine.net-mkhenley@prodigy.net

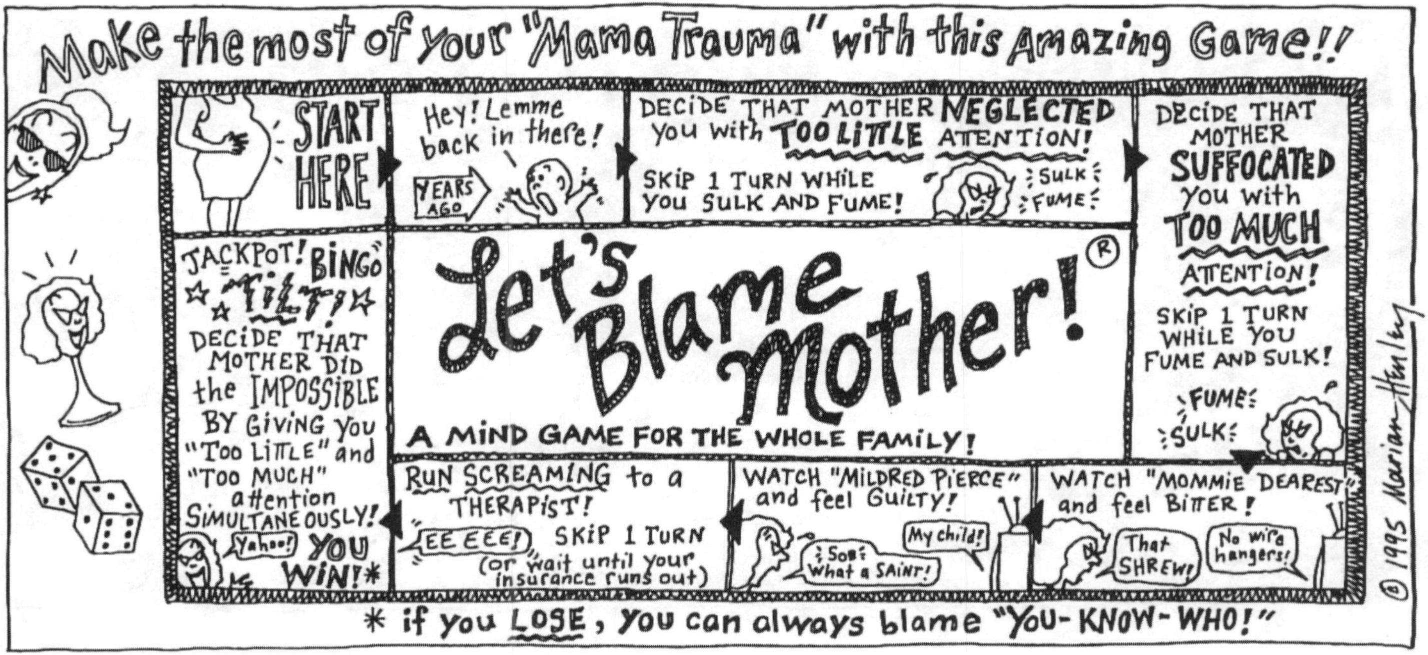
Make the most of your "Mama Trauma" with this Amazing Game!!
START HERE
Hey! Lemme back in there!
YEARS AGO
DECIDE THAT MOTHER NEGLECTED you with TOO LITTLE ATTENTION!
SKIP 1 TURN WHILE YOU SULK AND FUME!
SULK
FUME
DECIDE THAT MOTHER SUFFOCATED you with TOO MUCH ATTENTION!
SKIP 1 TURN WHILE YOU FUME AND SULK!
FUME
SULK
Let's Blame Mother!®
A MIND GAME FOR THE WHOLE FAMILY!
WATCH "MOMMIE DEAREST" and feel BITTER!
That SHREW!
No wire hangers!
WATCH "MILDRED PIERCE" and feel GUILTY!
My child!
Sob! What a SAINT!
RUN SCREAMING to a THERAPIST!
EE EEE!
SKIP 1 TURN
(or wait until your insurance runs out)
JACKPOT! BINGO TILT!
DECIDE THAT MOTHER DID the IMPOSSIBLE BY GIVING YOU "TOO LITTLE" and "TOO MUCH" attention SIMULTANEOUSLY!
Yahoo!
YOU WIN!*
* if you LOSE, you can always blame "YOU-KNOW-WHO!"
© 1995 Marian Henley

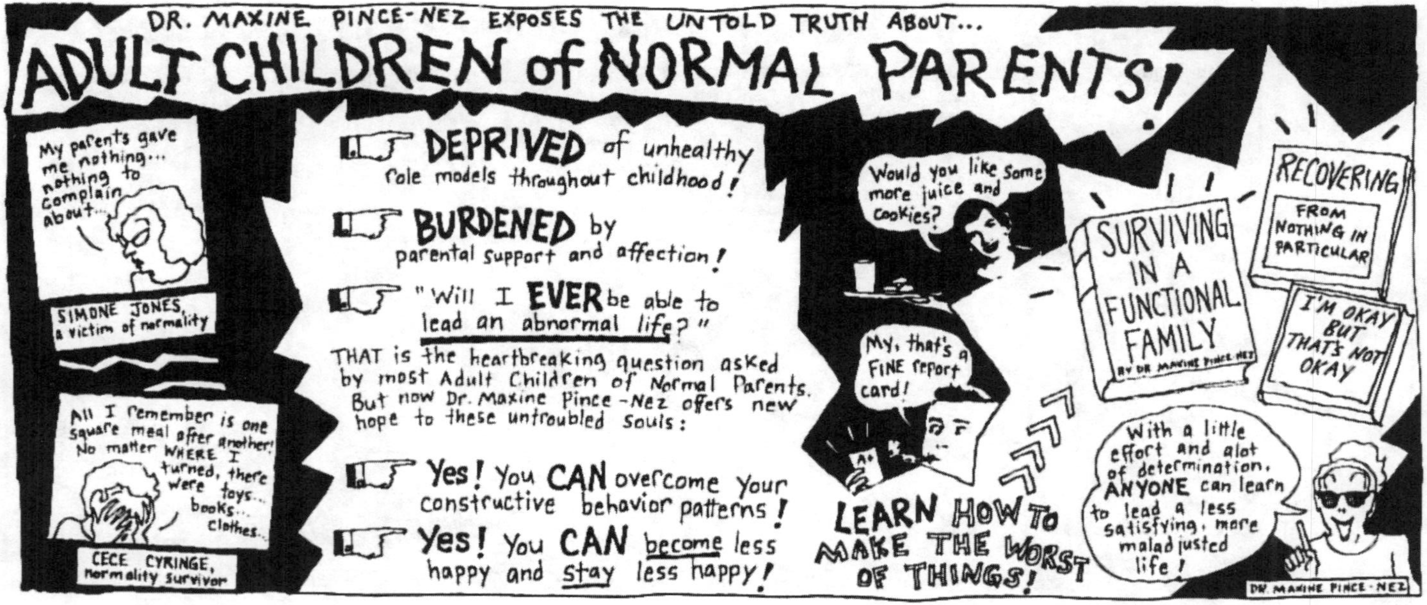
DR. MAXINE PINCE-NEZ EXPOSES THE UNTOLD TRUTH ABOUT...
ADULT CHILDREN of NORMAL PARENTS!
My parents gave me nothing... nothing to complain about...
SIMONE JONES, a victim of normality
All I remember is one square meal after another! No matter WHERE I turned, there were toys... books... clothes...
CECE CYRINGE, normality survivor
DEPRIVED of unhealthy role models throughout childhood!
BURDENED by parental support and affection!
"Will I EVER be able to lead an abnormal life?"
THAT is the heartbreaking question asked by most Adult Children of Normal Parents. But now Dr. Maxine Pince-Nez offers new hope to these untroubled souls:
Yes! You CAN overcome your constructive behavior patterns!
Yes! You CAN become less happy and stay less happy!
Would you like some more juice and cookies?
My, that's a FINE report card!
LEARN HOW TO MAKE THE WORST OF THINGS!
SURVIVING IN A FUNCTIONAL FAMILY
BY DR. MAXINE PINCE-NEZ
RECOVERING FROM NOTHING IN PARTICULAR
I'M OKAY BUT THAT'S NOT OKAY
With a little effort and alot of determination, ANYONE can learn to lead a less satisfying, more maladjusted life!
DR. MAXINE PINCE-NEZ

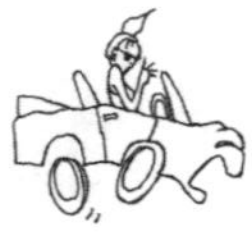

Youth and Ageing

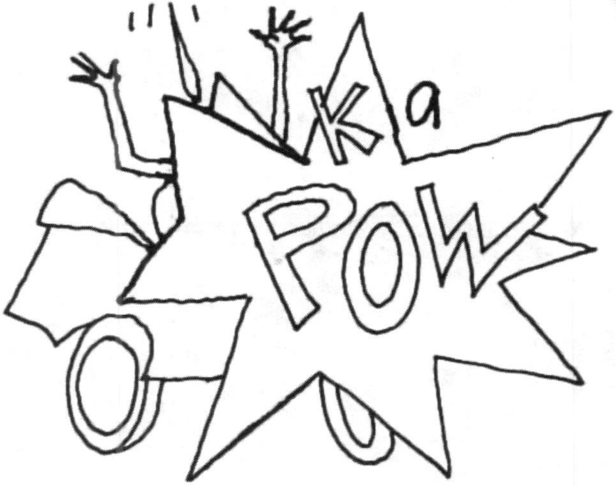
Ka
POW

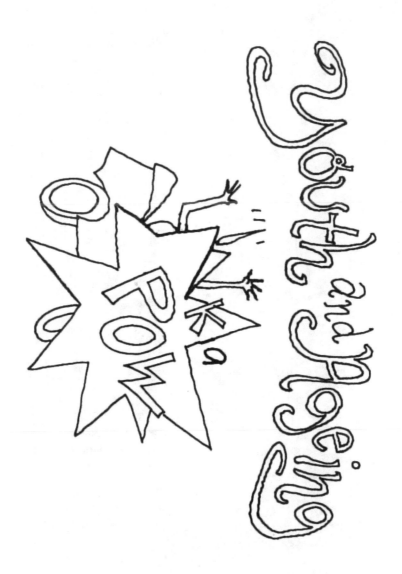

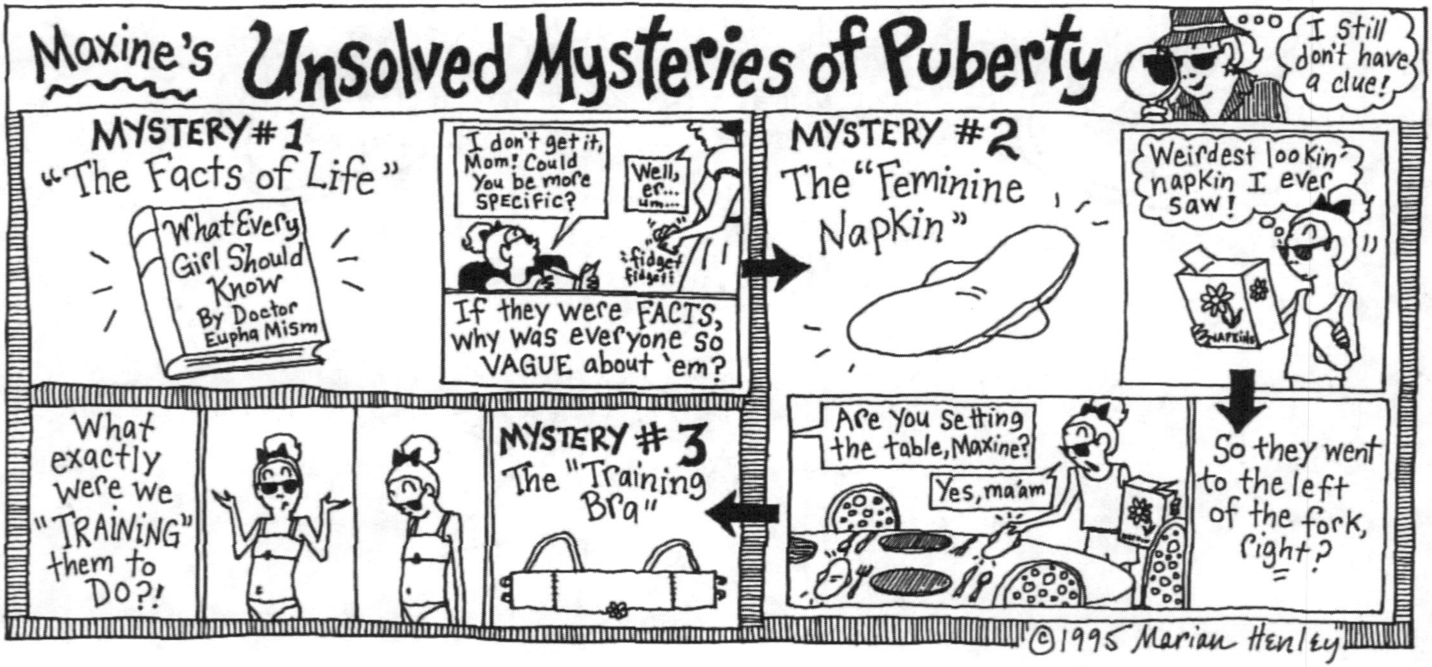
Maxine's Unsolved Mysteries of Puberty
I still don't have a clue!
MYSTERY #1
"The Facts of Life"
What Every Girl Should Know
By Doctor Eupha Mism
I don't get it, Mom! Could you be more SPECIFIC?
Well, er... um...
fidget fidget
If they were FACTS, why was everyone so VAGUE about 'em?
MYSTERY #2
The "Feminine Napkin"
Weirdest lookin' napkin I ever saw!
Are you setting the table, Maxine?
Yes, ma'am
So they went to the left of the fork, right?
MYSTERY #3
The "Training Bra"
What exactly were we "TRAINING" them to DO?!
©1995 Marian Henley

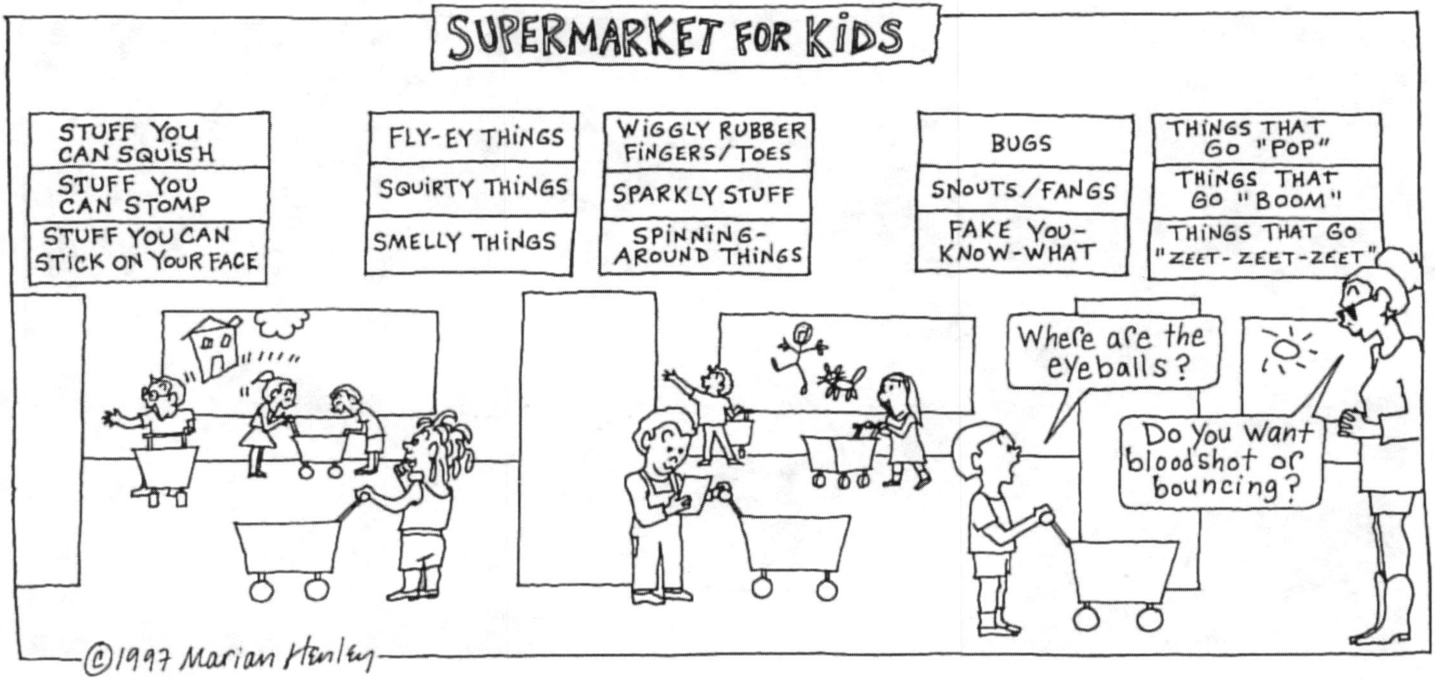
SUPERMARKET FOR KIDS
STUFF YOU CAN SQUISH
STUFF YOU CAN STOMP
STUFF YOU CAN STICK ON YOUR FACE
FLY-EY THINGS
SQUIRTY THINGS
SMELLY THINGS
WIGGLY RUBBER FINGERS/TOES
SPARKLY STUFF
SPINNING-AROUND THINGS
BUGS
SNOUTS/FANGS
FAKE YOU-KNOW-WHAT
THINGS THAT GO "POP"
THINGS THAT GO "BOOM"
THINGS THAT GO "ZEET-ZEET-ZEET"
Where are the eyeballs?
Do you want bloodshot or bouncing?
©1997 Marian Henley

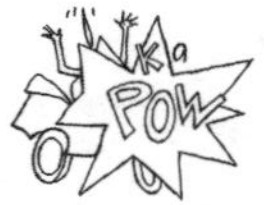

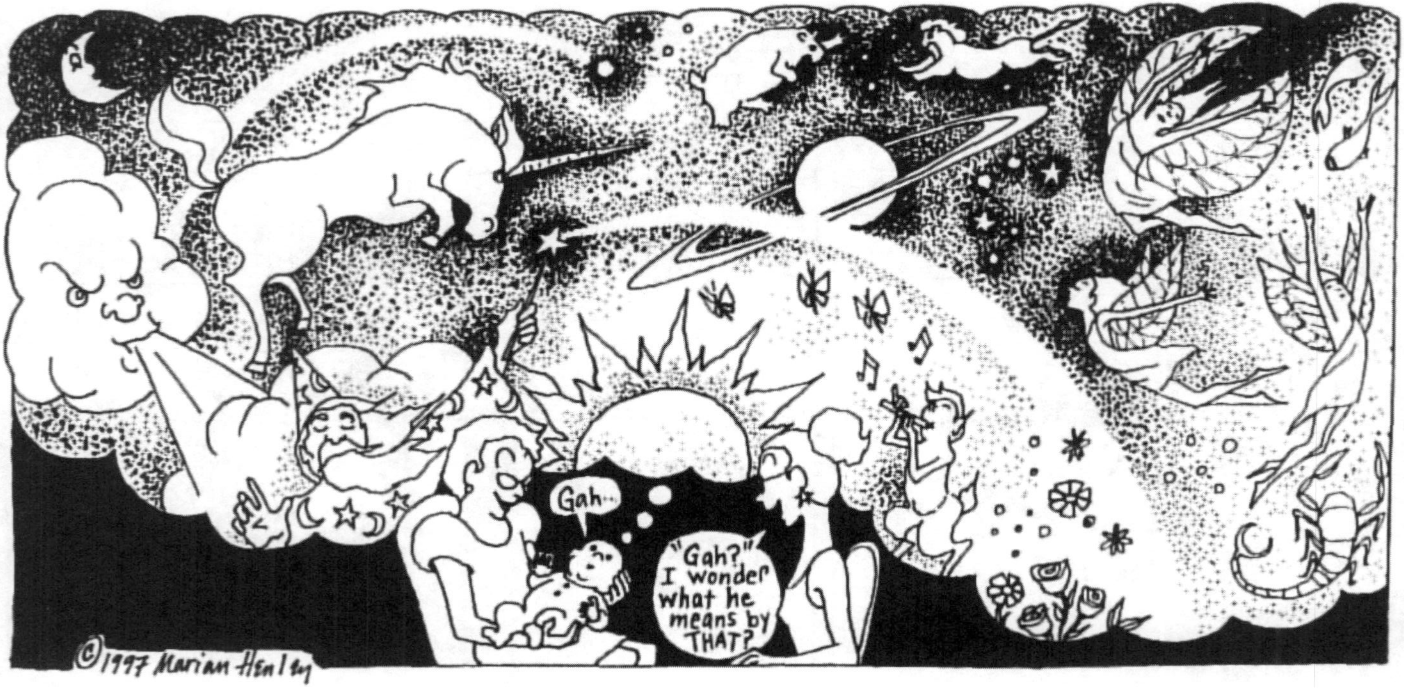
Gah...
"Gah?" I wonder what he means by THAT?
©1997 Marian Henley

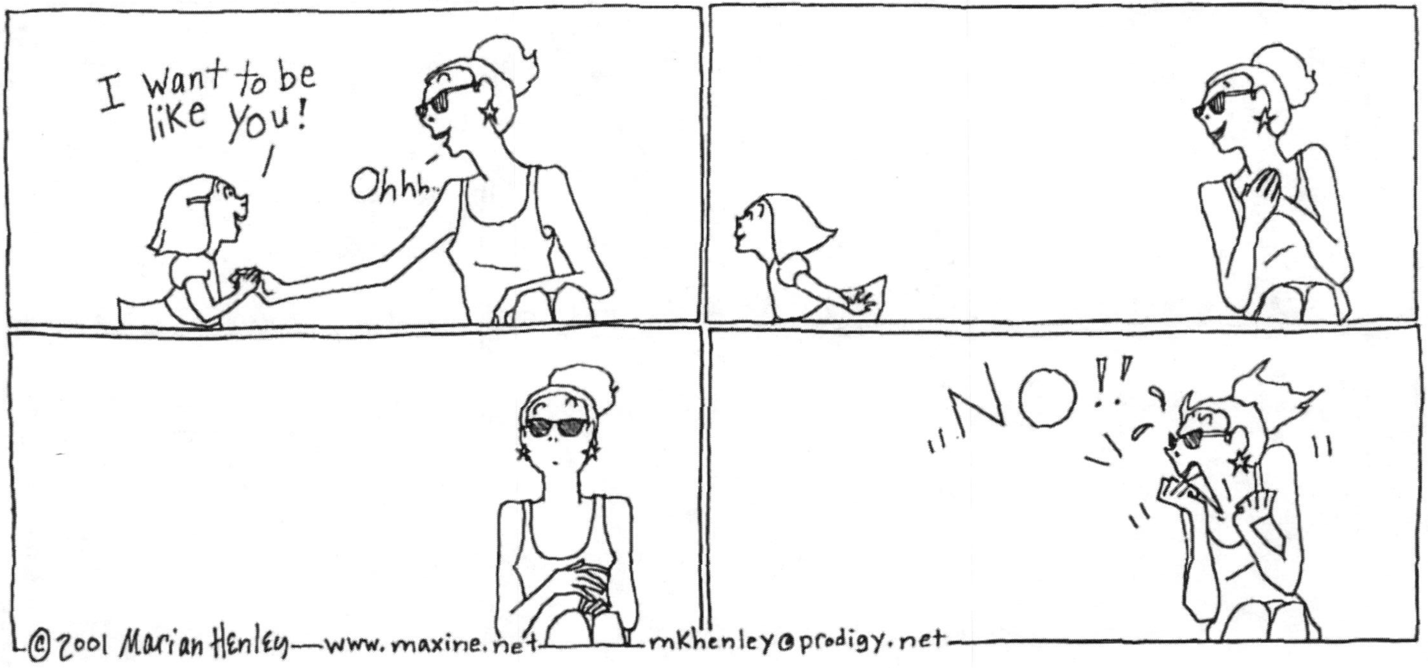
I want to be like you!
Ohhh...
"NO!!"
©2001 Marian Henley—www.maxine.net—mkhenley@prodigy.net

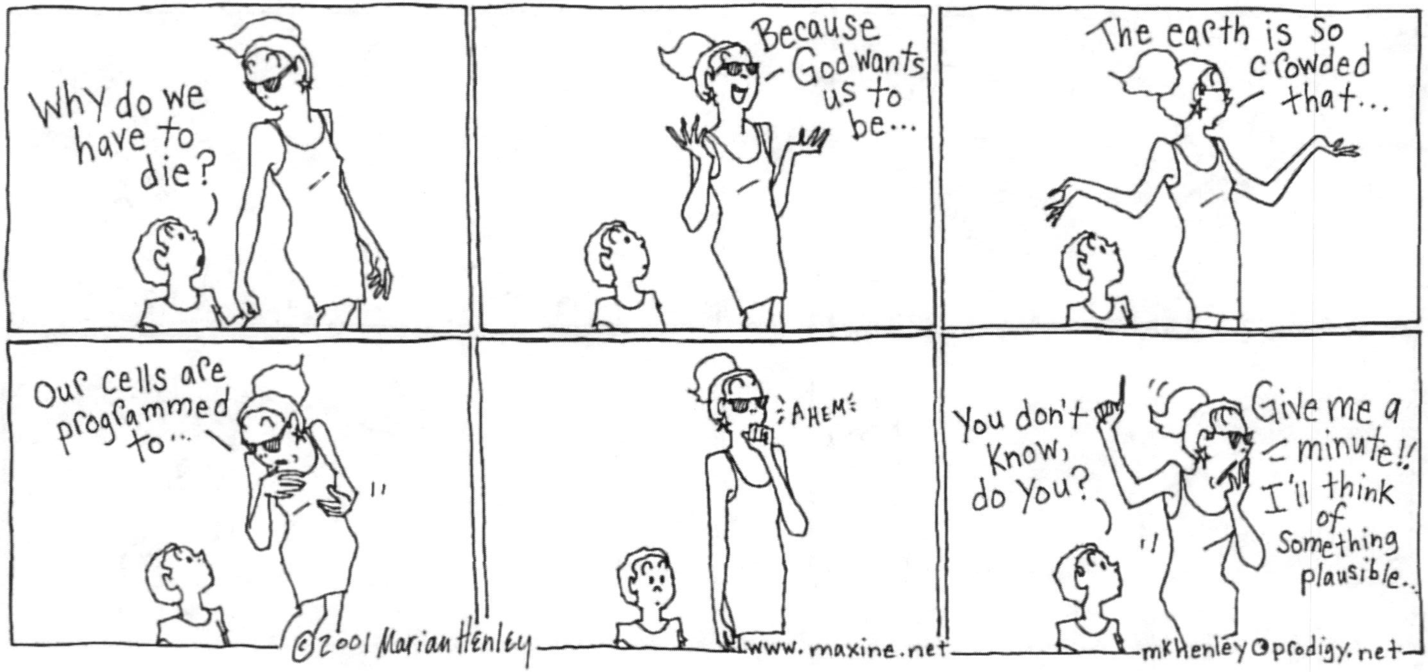
Why do we have to die?
Because God wants us to be...
The earth is so crowded that...
Our cells are programmed to...
AHEM
You don't know, do you?
Give me a minute!! I'll think of something plausible...
©2001 Marian Henley
www.maxine.net
mkhenley@prodigy.net

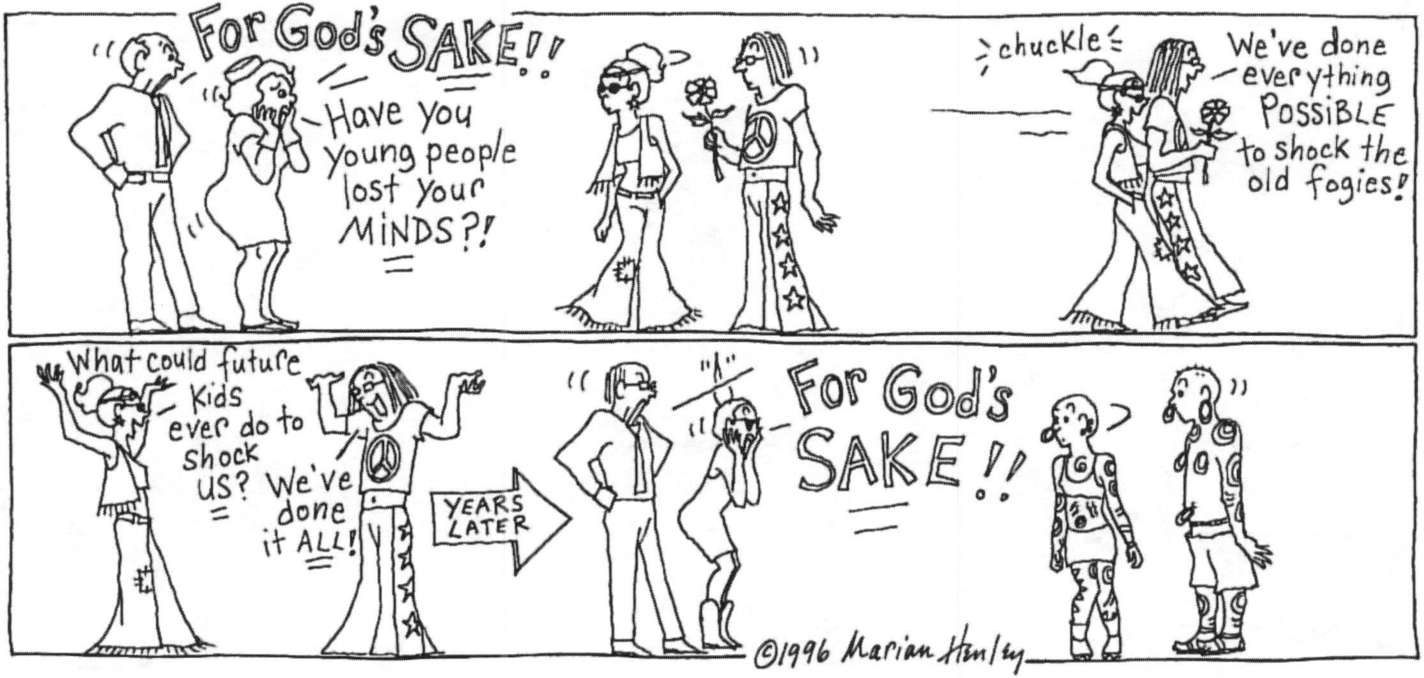
FOR GOD'S SAKE!!
Have you young people lost your MINDS?!
chuckle
We've done everything POSSIBLE to shock the old fogies!
What could future kids ever do to shock US?
We've done it ALL!
YEARS LATER
FOR GOD'S SAKE!!
©1996 Marian Henley

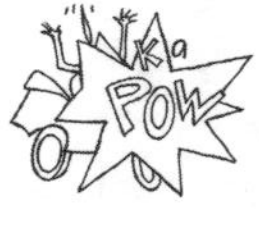

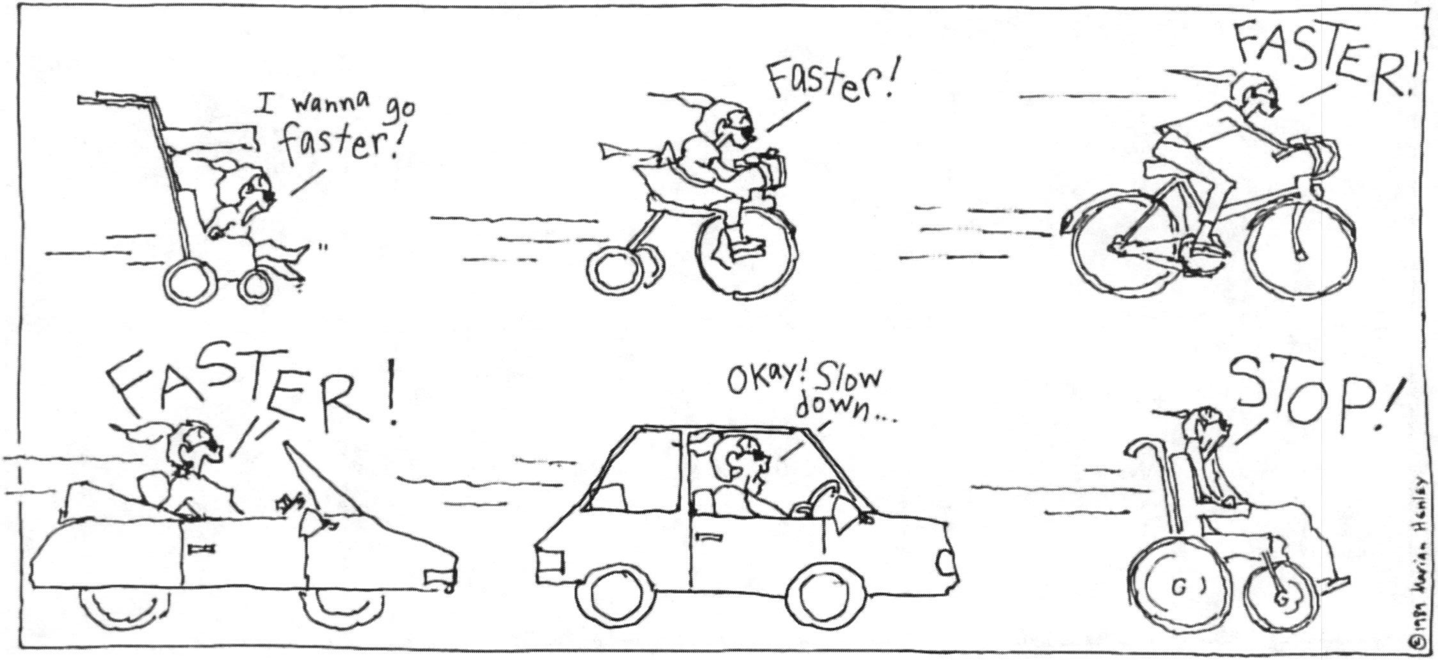
I wanna go faster!
Faster!
FASTER!
FASTER!
OKAY! Slow down...
STOP!
© 1989 Marian Henley

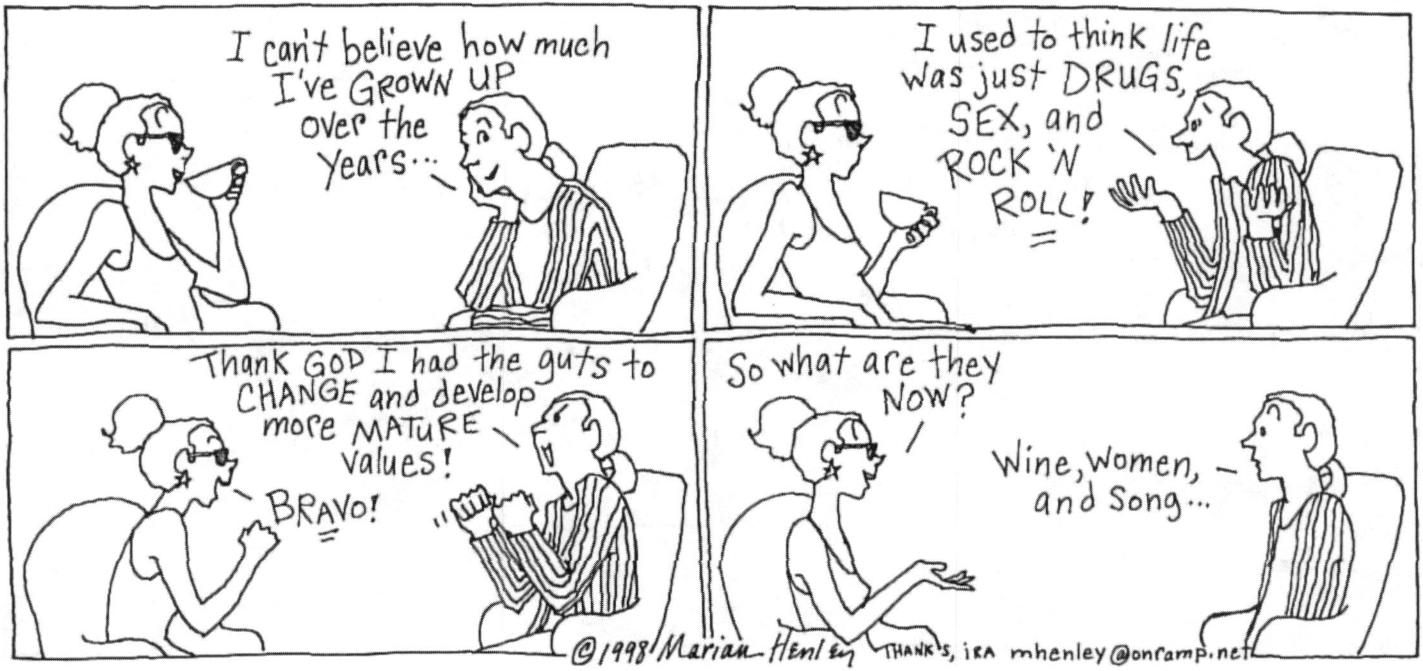
I can't believe how much I've GROWN UP over the years...
I used to think life was just DRUGS, SEX, and ROCK 'N ROLL!
Thank GOD I had the guts to CHANGE and develop more MATURE values!
BRAVO!
So what are they NOW?
Wine, women, and Song...
©1998 Marian Henley
THANK'S, IRA mhenley@onramp.net

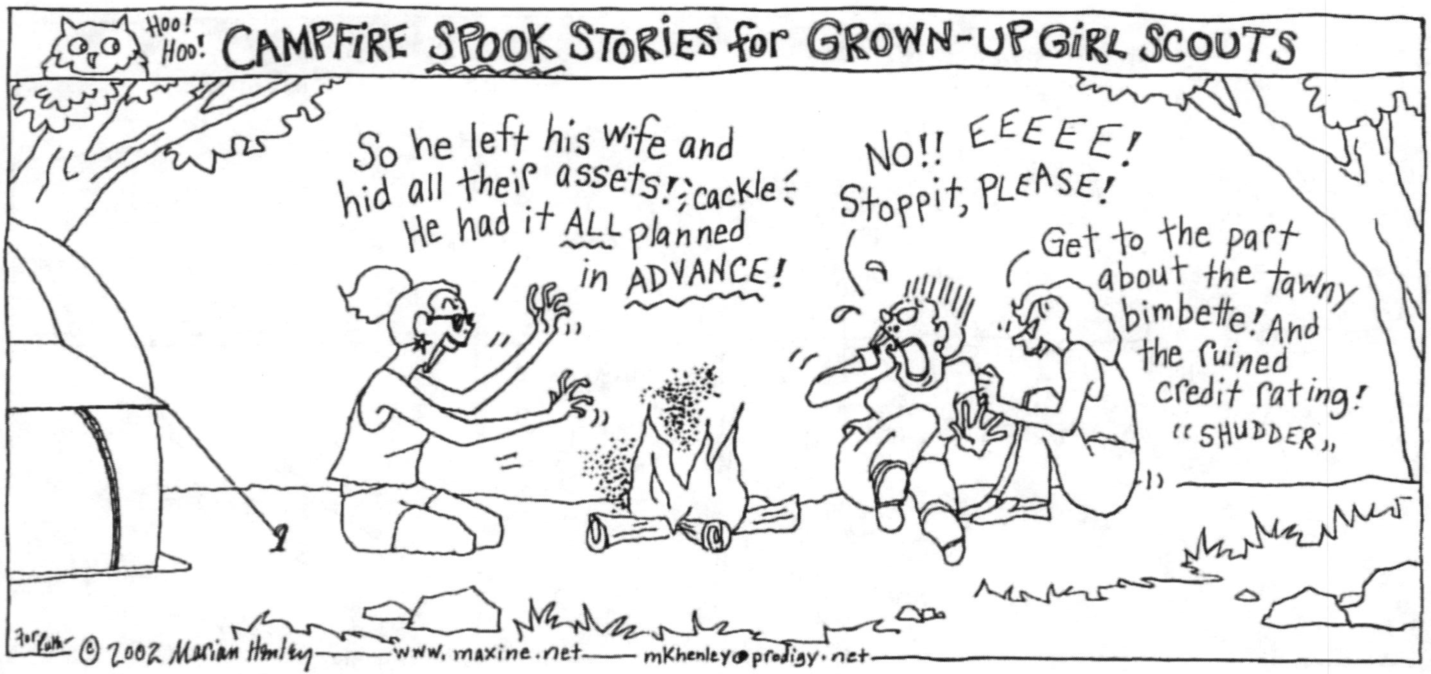
HOO! HOO!
CAMPFIRE SPOOK STORIES for GROWN-UP GIRL SCOUTS
So he left his wife and hid all their assets! ;cackle; He had it ALL planned in ADVANCE!
No!! EEEEE! Stoppit, PLEASE!
Get to the part about the tawny bimbette! And the ruined credit rating! "SHUDDER"
© 2002 Marian Henley —— www.maxine.net —— mkhenley@prodigy.net

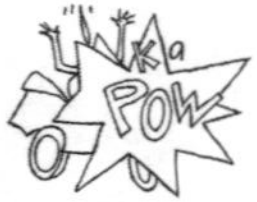

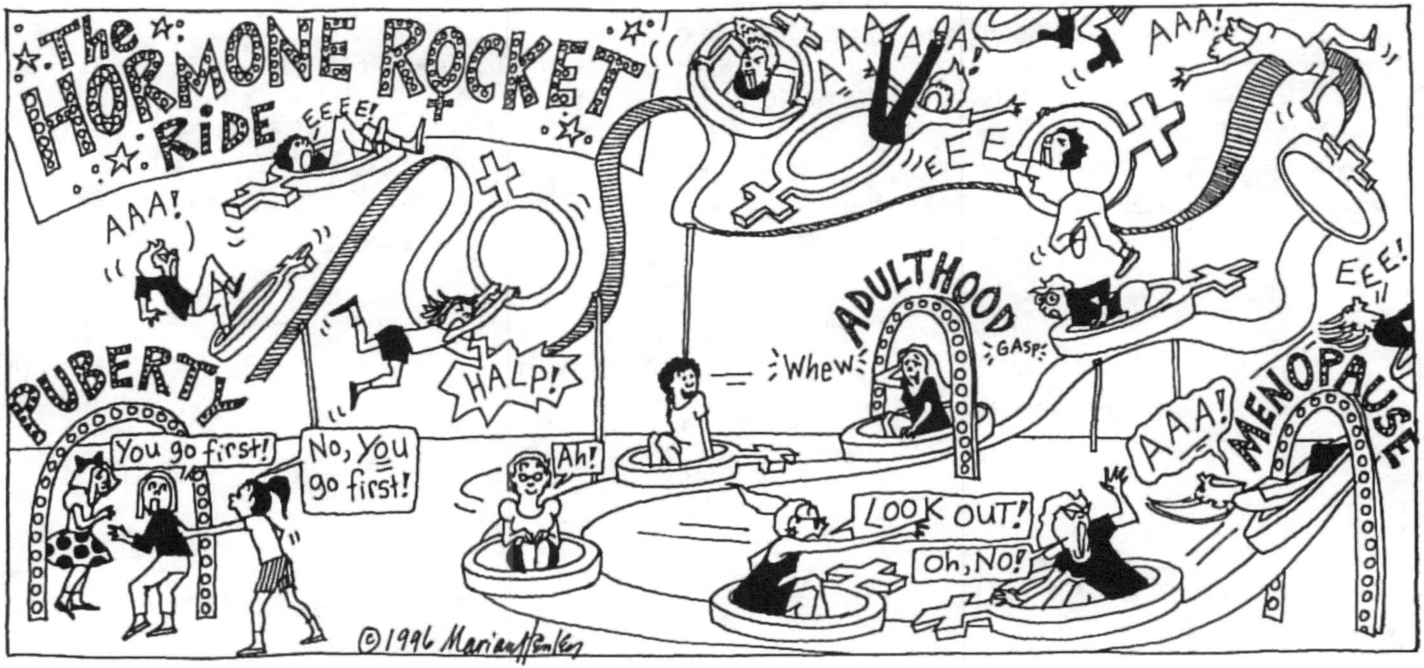
The HORMONE ROCKET RiDE
EEEE!
AAA!
PUBERTY
HALP!
You go first!
No, You go first!
Ah!
Whew
ADULTHOOD
GASP
AAAAAA!
EEE
AAA!
EEE!
MENOPAUSE
AAA!
LOOK OUT!
Oh, NO!
©1996 Marian Henley

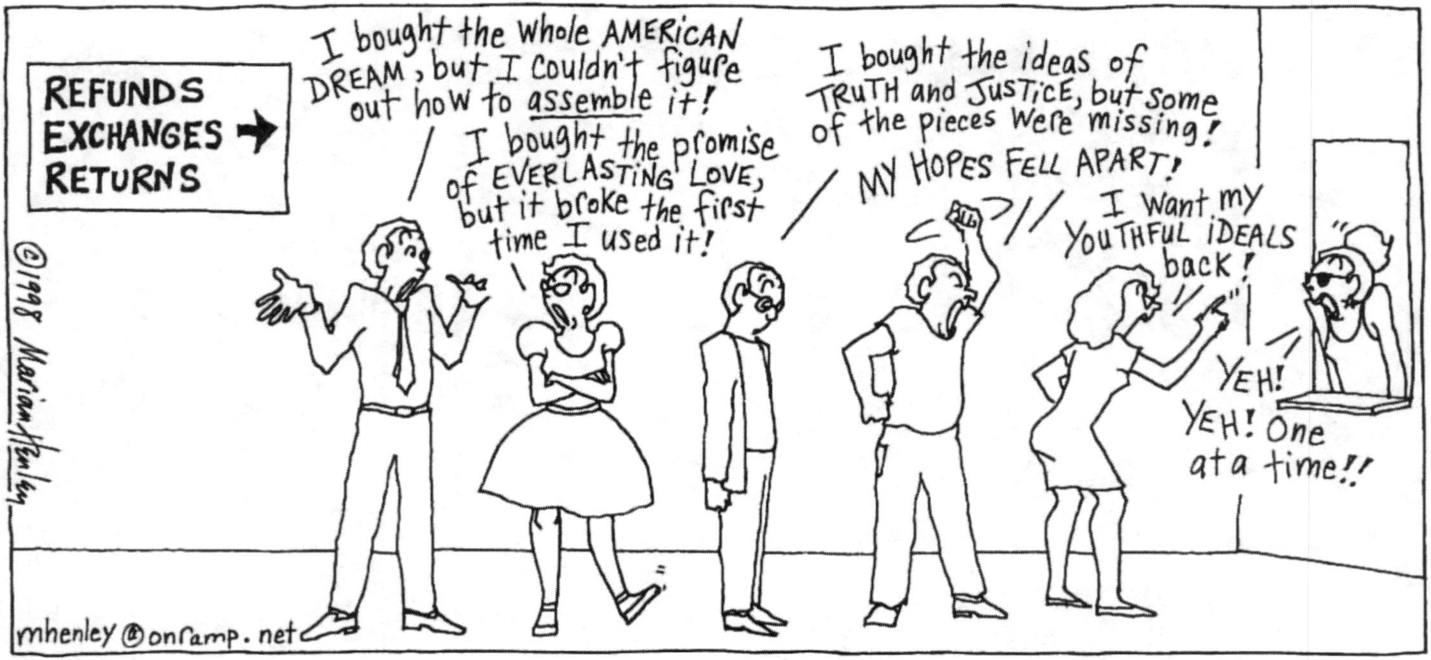
REFUNDS
EXCHANGES
RETURNS
I bought the whole AMERICAN DREAM, but I couldn't figure out how to assemble it!
I bought the promise of EVERLASTING LOVE, but it broke the first time I used it!
I bought the ideas of TRUTH and JUSTICE, but some of the pieces were missing!
MY HOPES FELL APART!
I want my YOUTHFUL IDEALS back!
YEH!
YEH!
One at a time!!
©1998 Marian Henley
mhenley@onramp.net

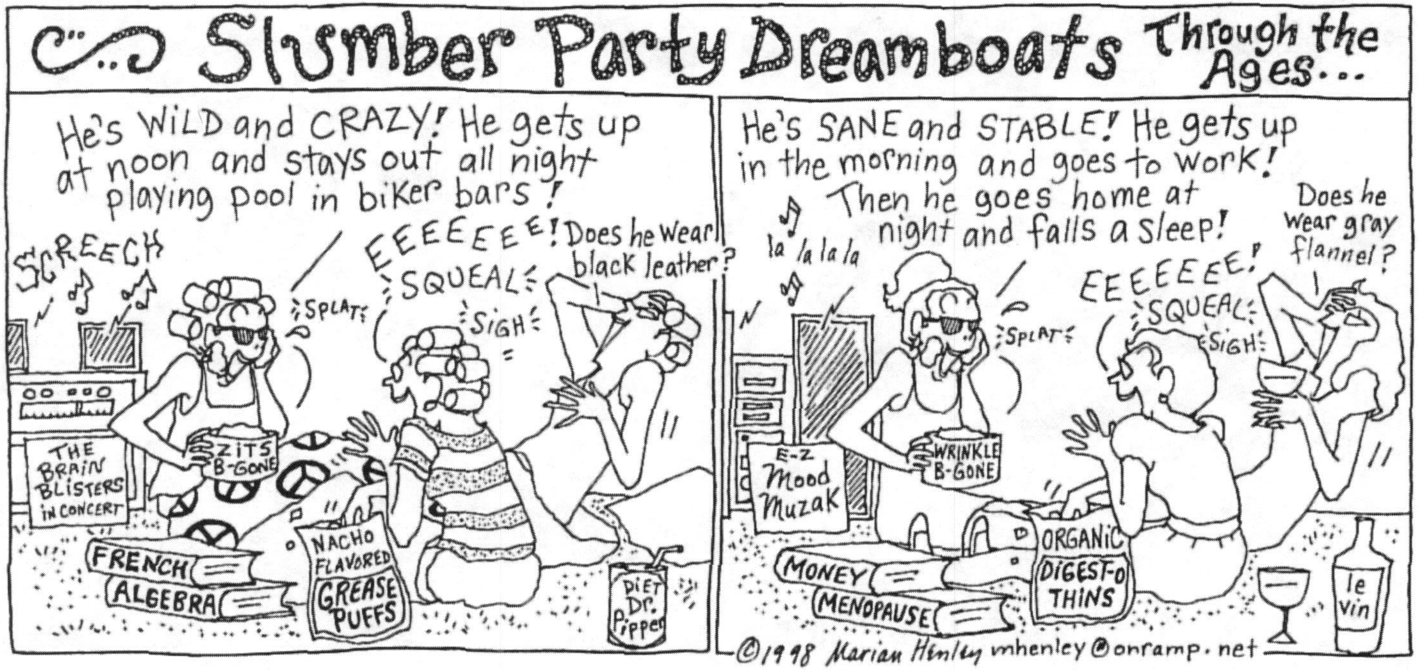
Slumber Party Dreamboats Through the Ages...
He's WILD and CRAZY! He gets up at noon and stays out all night playing pool in biker bars!
SCREECH
SPLAT
EEEEEEE!
SQUEAL
SIGH
Does he wear black leather?
THE BRAIN BLISTERS IN CONCERT
ZITS B-GONE
FRENCH
ALGEBRA
NACHO FLAVORED GREASE PUFFS
DIET Dr. Pipper
He's SANE and STABLE! He gets up in the morning and goes to work! Then he goes home at night and falls asleep!
la la la la
SPLAT
EEEEEEE!
SQUEAL
SIGH
Does he wear gray flannel?
E-Z Mood Muzak
WRINKLE B-GONE
MONEY
MENOPAUSE
ORGANIC DIGEST-O THINS
le vin
©1998 Marian Henley mhenley@onramp.net

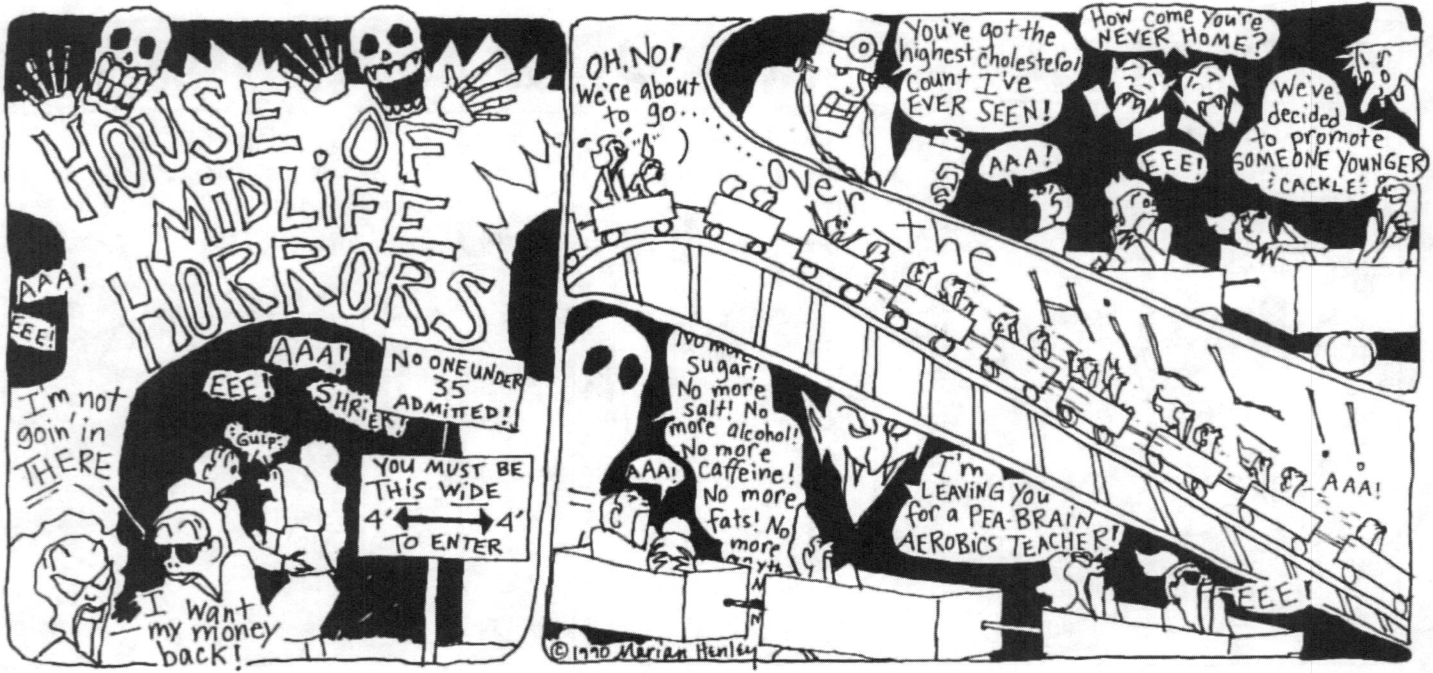
HOUSE OF MIDLIFE HORRORS
AAA!
EEE!
I'm not goin' in THERE
AAA!
EEE!
SHRIEK!
GULP:
NO ONE UNDER 35 ADMITTED!
YOU MUST BE THIS WIDE 4' 4' TO ENTER
I want my money back!
OH, NO! We're about to go....
over the Hill!!
You've got the highest cholesterol count I've EVER SEEN!
AAA!
How come you're NEVER HOME?
EEE!
We've decided to promote SOMEONE YOUNGER ¡CACKLE!
No more Sugar! No more salt! No more alcohol! No more caffeine! No more fats! No more
AAA!
I'm LEAVING You for a PEA-BRAIN AEROBICS TEACHER!
AAA!
EEE!
©1990 Marian Henley

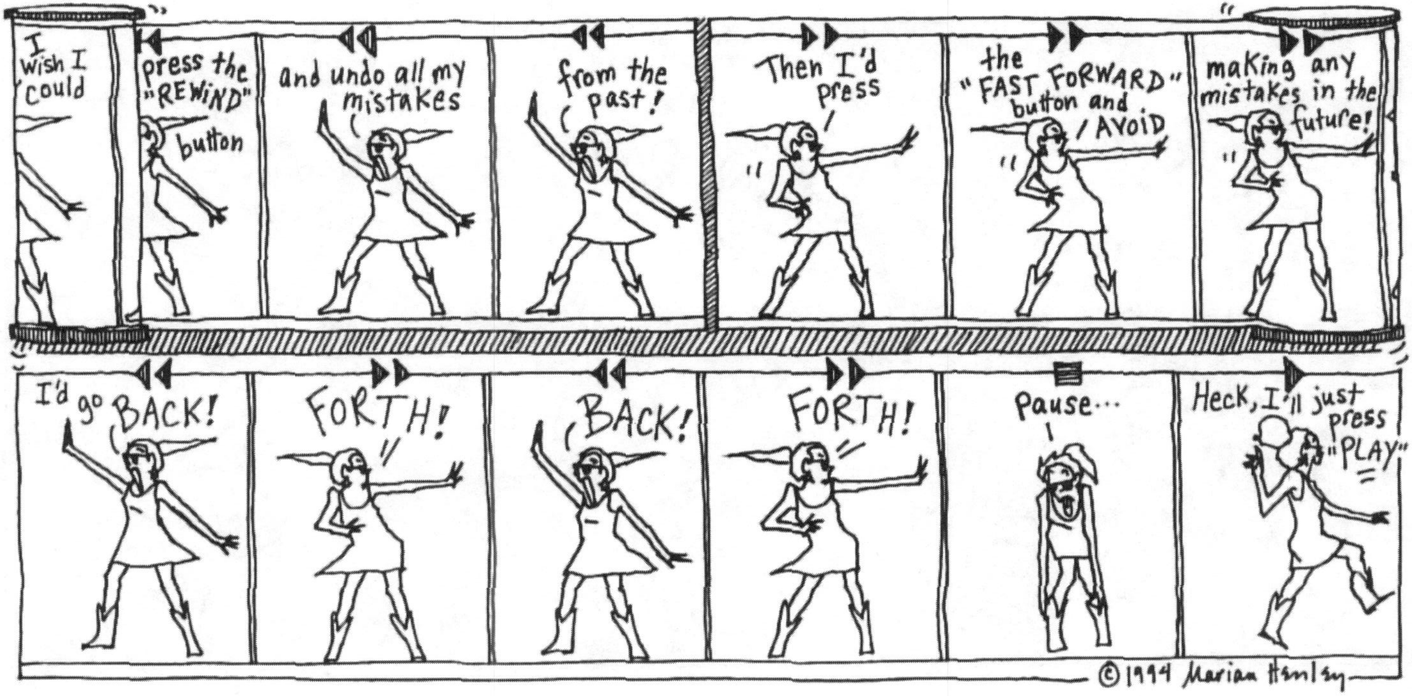
I wish I could
press the "REWIND" button
and undo all my mistakes
from the past!
Then I'd press
the "FAST FORWARD" button and AVOID
making any mistakes in the future!
I'd go BACK!
FORTH!
BACK!
FORTH!
Pause...
Heck, I'll just press "PLAY"
©1994 Marian Henley

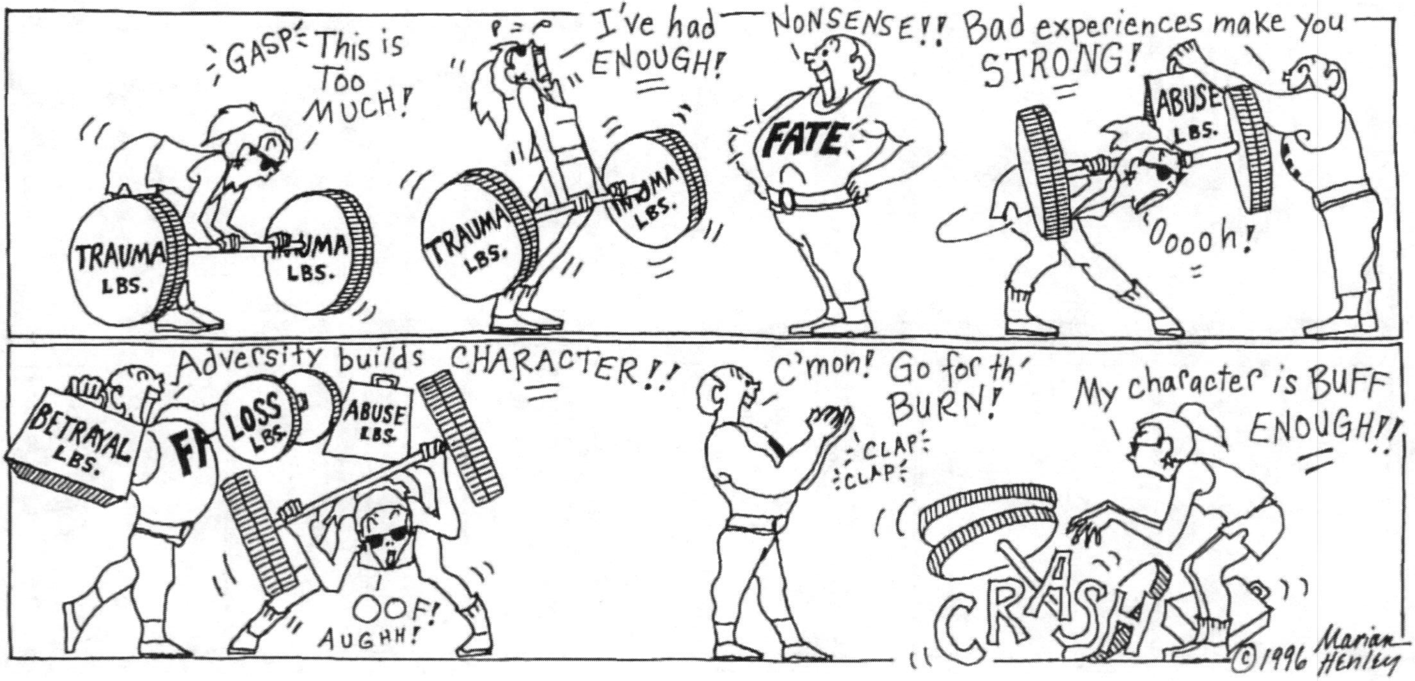
GASP! This is Too MUCH!
TRAUMA LBS.
TRAUMA LBS.
I've had ENOUGH!
NONSENSE!! Bad experiences make you STRONG!
FATE
ABUSE LBS.
Ooooh!
Adversity builds CHARACTER!!
BETRAYAL LBS.
LOSS LBS.
ABUSE LBS.
OOF! AUGHH!
C'mon! Go for th' BURN!
CLAP CLAP
My character is BUFF ENOUGH!!
CRASH
©1996 Marian Henley

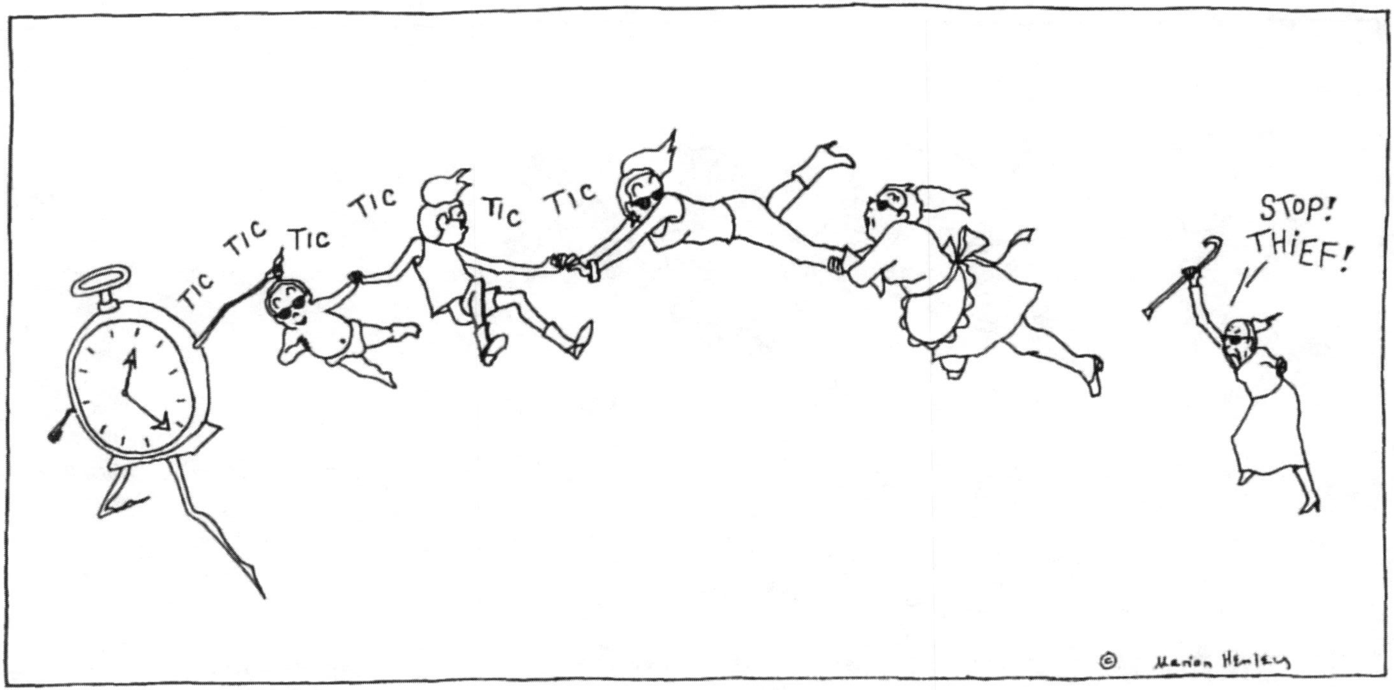
TIC TIC TIC TIC TIC TIC
STOP! THIEF!
© Marion Henley

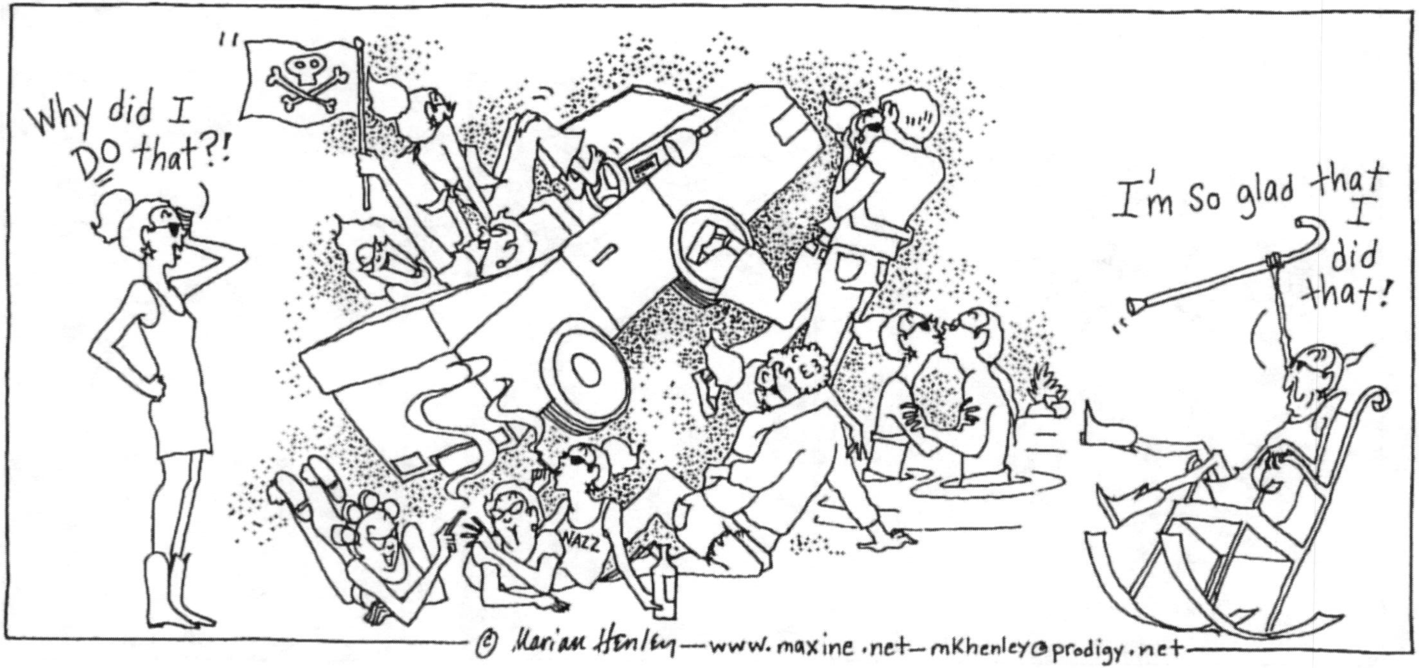
Why did I DO that?!
I'm so glad that I did that!
NAZZ
© Marian Henley—www.maxine.net—mkhenley@prodigy.net

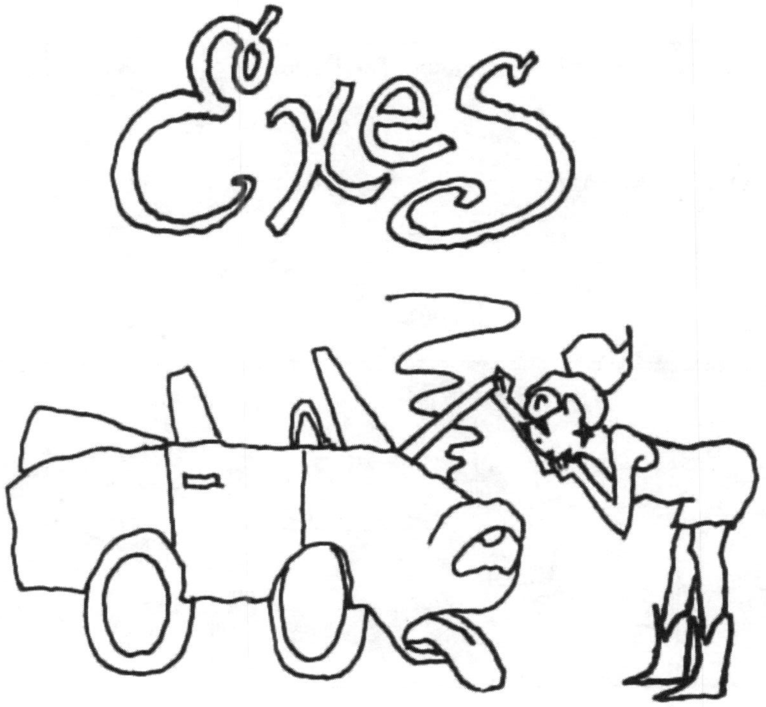
Exes

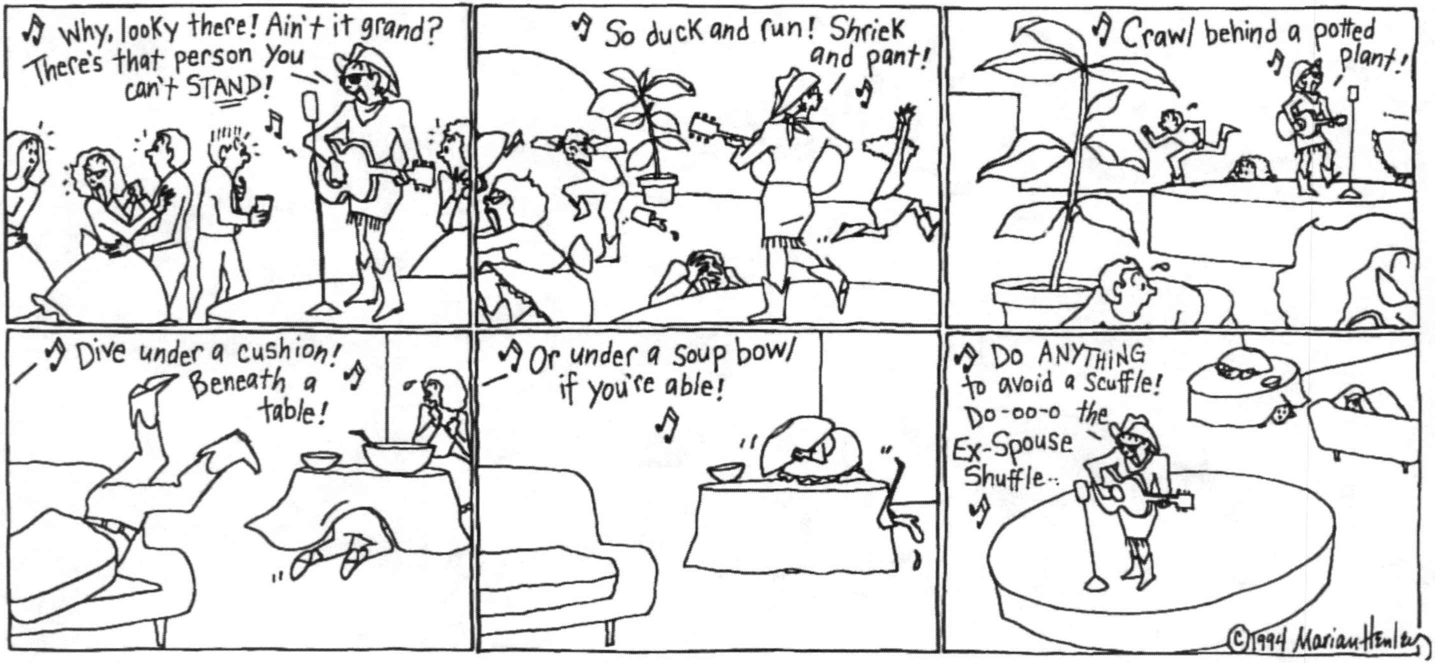
Why, looky there! Ain't it grand? There's that person you can't STAND!
So duck and run! Shriek and pant!
Crawl behind a potted plant!
Dive under a cushion! Beneath a table!
Or under a soup bowl if you're able!
Do ANYTHING to avoid a Scuffle! Do-oo-o the Ex-Spouse Shuffle...
©1994 Marian Henley

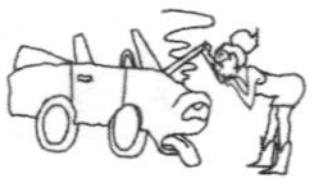

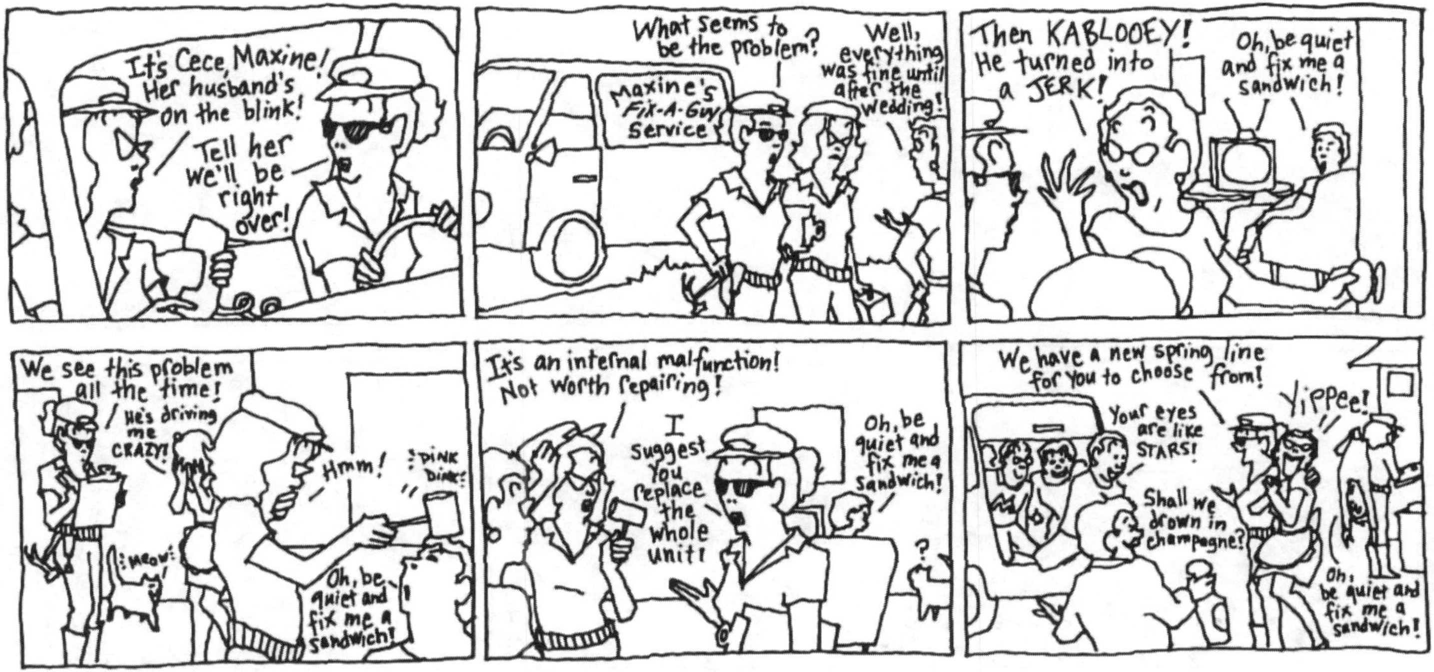
It's Cece, Maxine! Her husband's on the blink!
Tell her we'll be right over!
What seems to be the problem?
Maxine's Fix-A-Guy Service
Well, everything was fine until after the wedding!
Then KABLOOEY! He turned into a JERK!
Oh, be quiet and fix me a sandwich!
We see this problem all the time!
He's driving me CRAZY!
Hmm!
DINK DINK!
MEOW!
Oh, be quiet and fix me a sandwich!
It's an internal malfunction! Not worth repairing!
I suggest you replace the whole unit!
Oh, be quiet and fix me a sandwich!
?
We have a new spring line for you to choose from!
Your eyes are like STARS!
Shall we drown in champagne?
Yippee!
Oh, be quiet and fix me a sandwich!

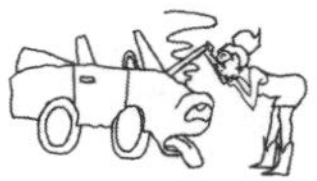

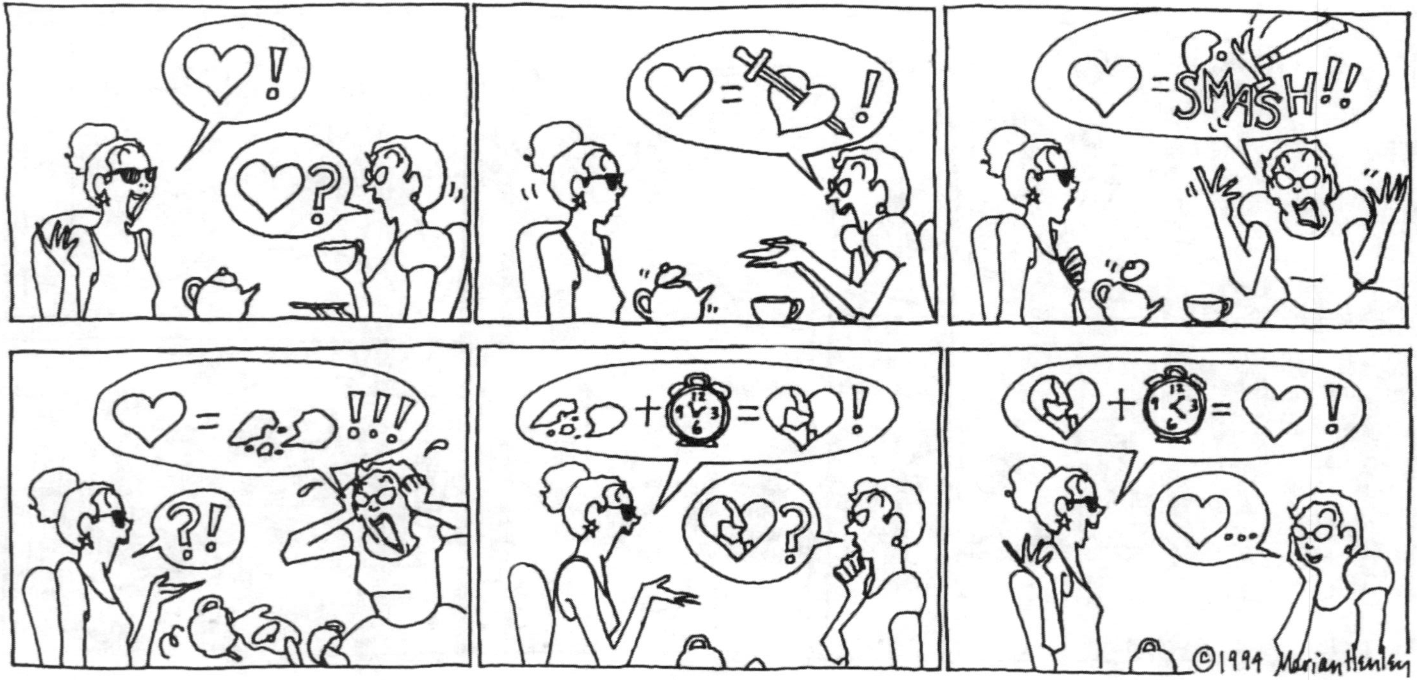
!
?
= !
= SMASH!!
= !!!
?!
+ = !
?
+ = !
...
©1994 Marian Henley

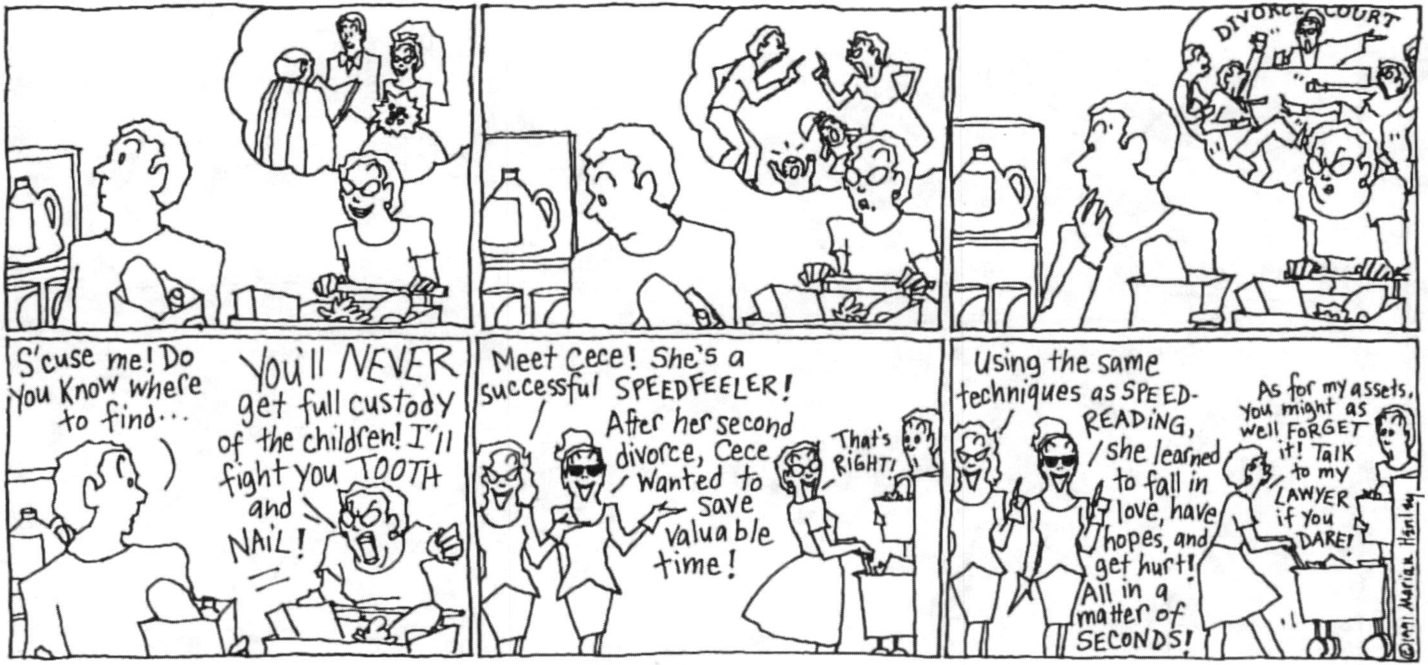
DIVORCE COURT
S'cuse me! Do You Know where to find...
You'll NEVER get full custody of the children! I'll fight you TOOTH and NAIL!
Meet Cece! She's a successful SPEEDFEELER!
After her second divorce, Cece wanted to save valuable time!
That's RIGHT!
Using the same techniques as SPEED-READING, she learned to fall in love, have hopes, and get hurt! All in a matter of SECONDS!
As for my assets, You might as well FORGET it! TALK to my LAWYER if You DARE!
©1991 Marian Hanley

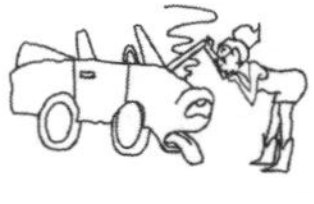

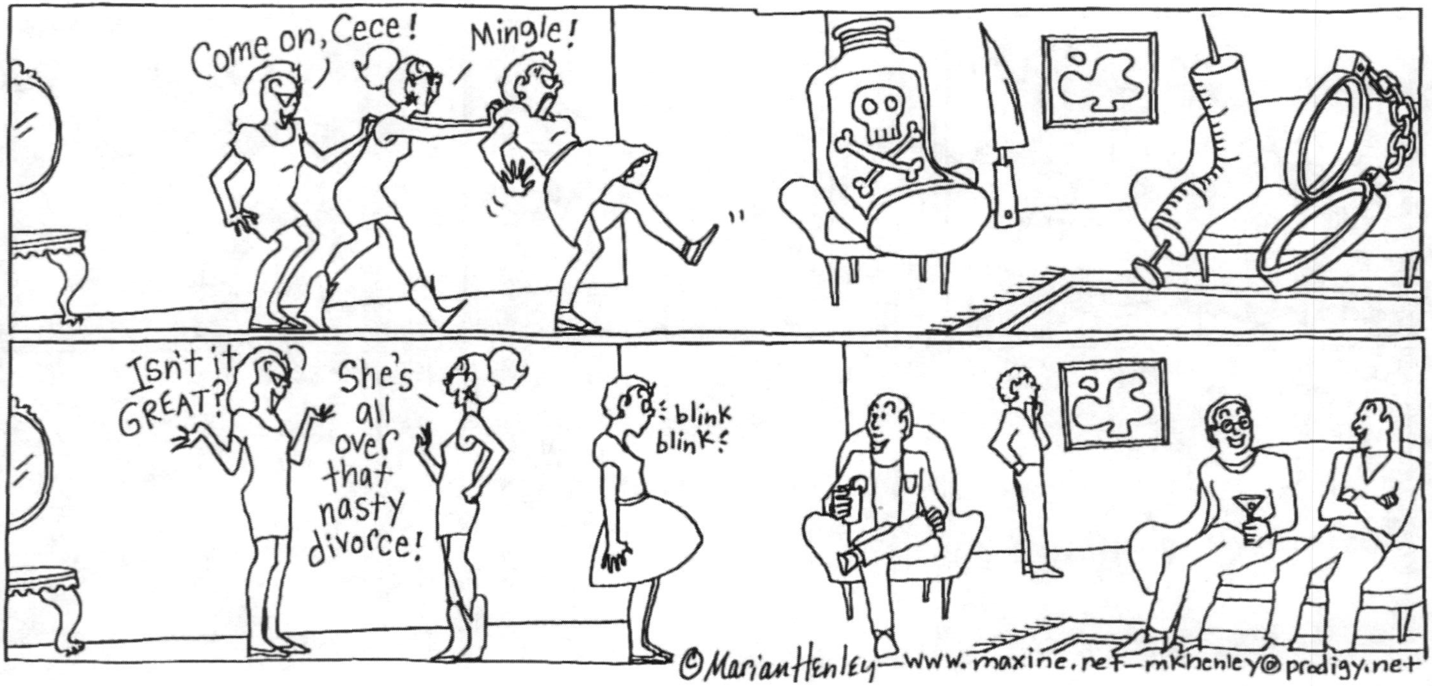
Come on, Cece!
Mingle!
Isn't it GREAT?
She's all over that nasty divorce!
blink blink!
©MarianHenley—www.maxine.net—mkhenley@prodigy.net

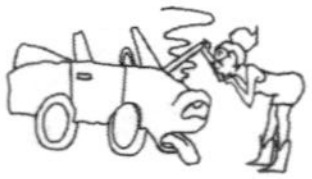

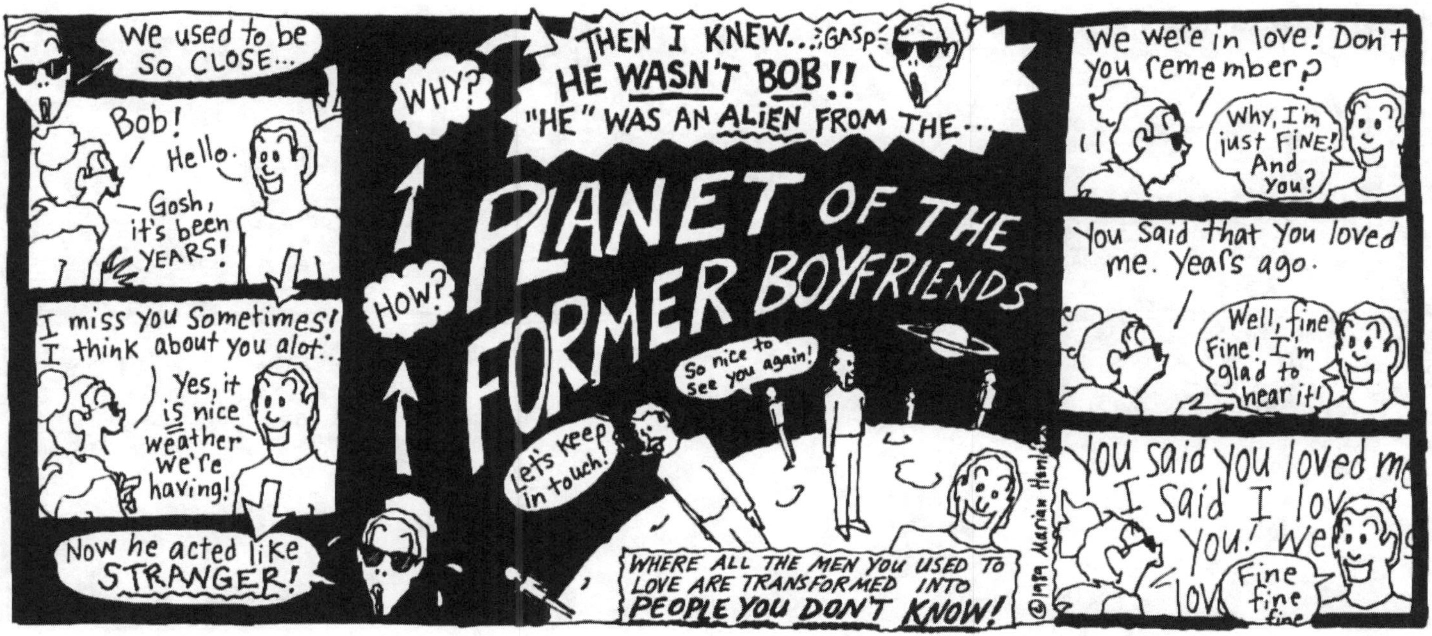
We used to be so CLOSE...
Bob!
Hello.
Gosh, it's been YEARS!
I miss you Sometimes! I think about you alot...
Yes, it is nice weather we're having!
Now he acted like STRANGER!
WHY?
HOW?
THEN I KNEW... :GASP:
HE WASN'T BOB!!
"HE" WAS AN ALIEN FROM THE...
PLANET OF THE FORMER BOYFRIENDS
So nice to see you again!
Let's keep in touch!
WHERE ALL THE MEN YOU USED TO LOVE ARE TRANSFORMED INTO PEOPLE YOU DON'T KNOW!
©1989 Marian Henley
We were in love! Don't you remember?
Why, I'm just FINE! And you?
You said that you loved me. Years ago.
Well, fine Fine! I'm glad to hear it!
You said you loved m
I said I lov
you! We
lov
Fine fine

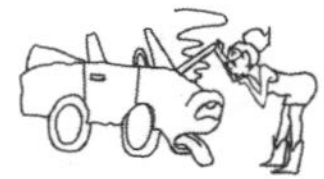

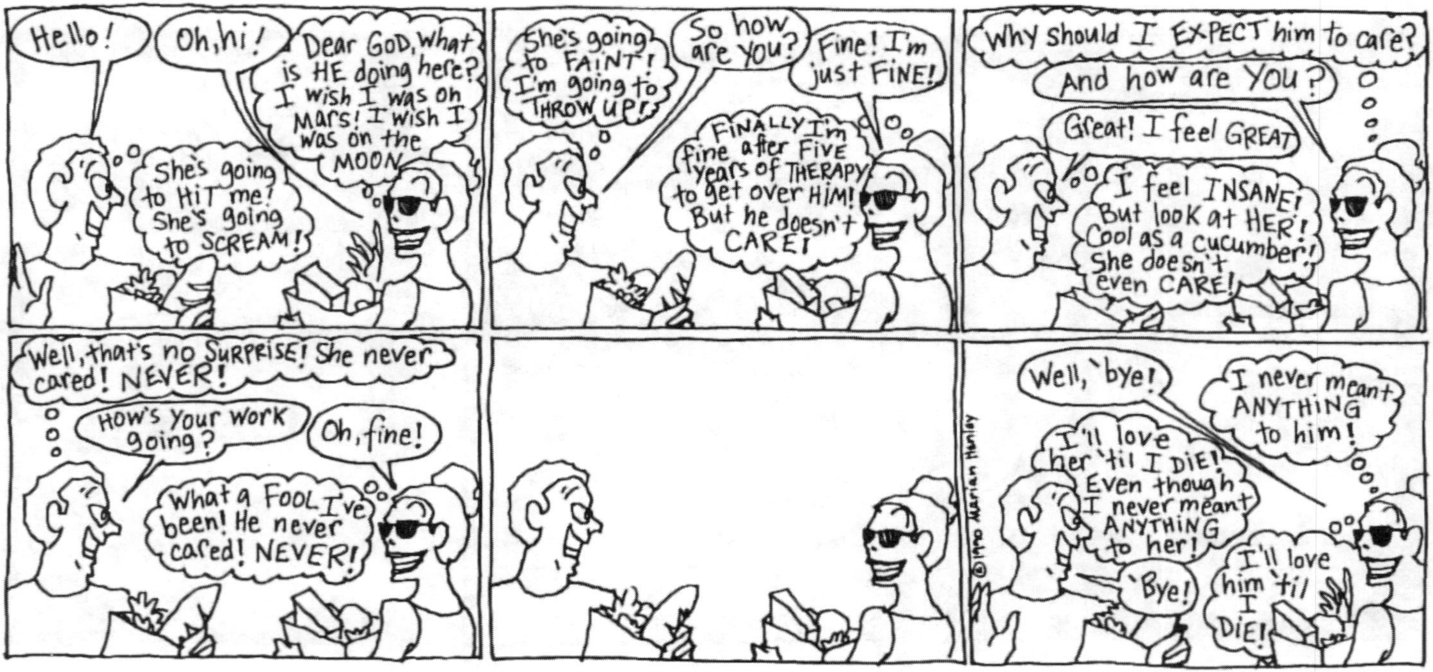
Hello!
Oh, hi!
Dear GOD, what is HE doing here? I wish I was on Mars! I wish I was on the MOON
She's going to HIT me! She's going to SCREAM!
She's going to FAINT! I'm going to THROW UP!
So how are YOU?
Fine! I'm just FINE!
FINALLY I'm fine after FIVE years of THERAPY to get over HIM! But he doesn't CARE!
Why should I EXPECT him to care?
And how are YOU?
Great! I feel GREAT
I feel INSANE! But look at HER! Cool as a cucumber! She doesn't even CARE!
Well, that's no SURPRISE! She never cared! NEVER!
HOW'S your work going?
Oh, fine!
What a FOOL I've been! He never cared! NEVER!
© 1990 Marian Henley
Well, 'bye!
I never meant ANYTHING to him!
I'll love her 'til I DIE! Even though I never meant ANYTHING to her!
'Bye!
I'll love him 'til I DIE!

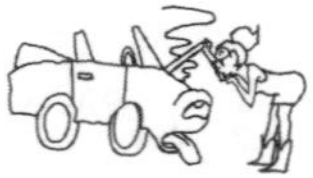

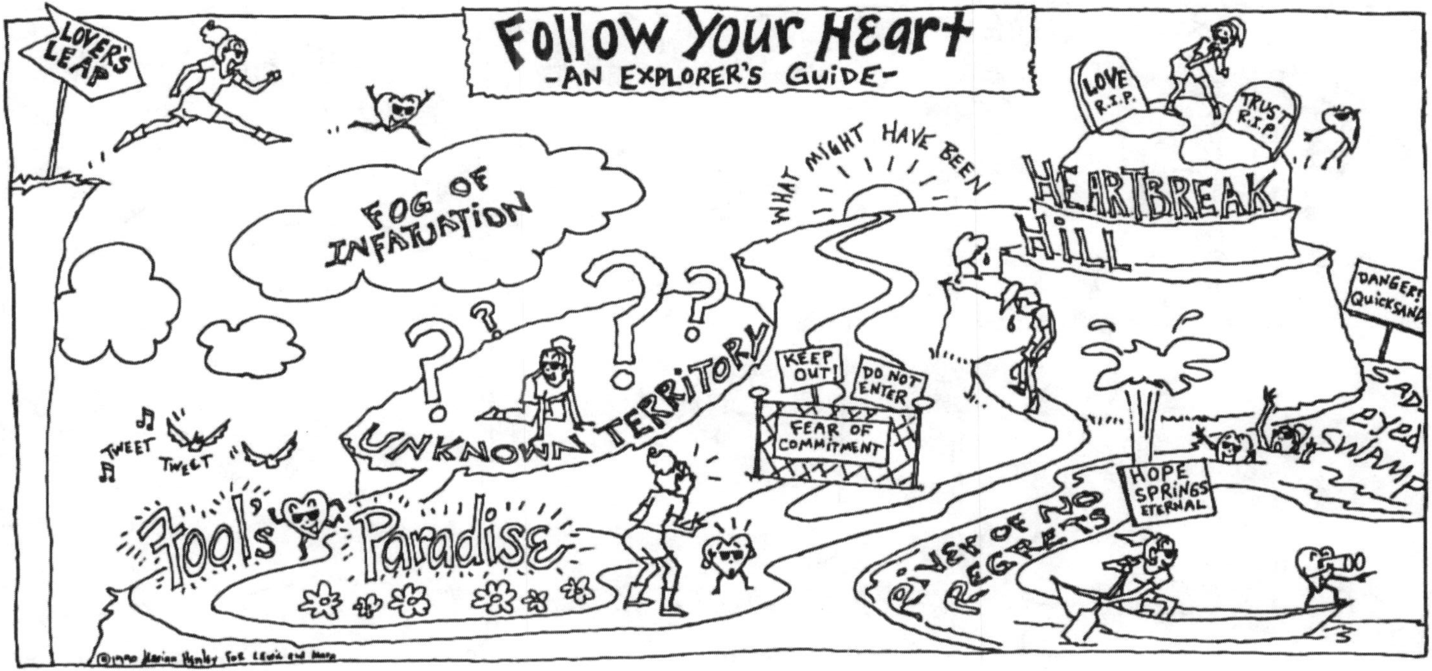
Follow Your Heart
-AN EXPLORER'S GUIDE-
LOVER'S LEAP
FOG OF INFATUATION
UNKNOWN TERRITORY
WHAT MIGHT HAVE BEEN
LOVE R.I.P.
TRUST R.I.P.
HEARTBREAK HILL
DANGER! QUICKSAND
KEEP OUT!
DO NOT ENTER
FEAR OF COMMITMENT
TWEET TWEET
Fool's Paradise
RIVER OF NO REGRETS
HOPE SPRINGS ETERNAL
SAD-EYED SWAMP

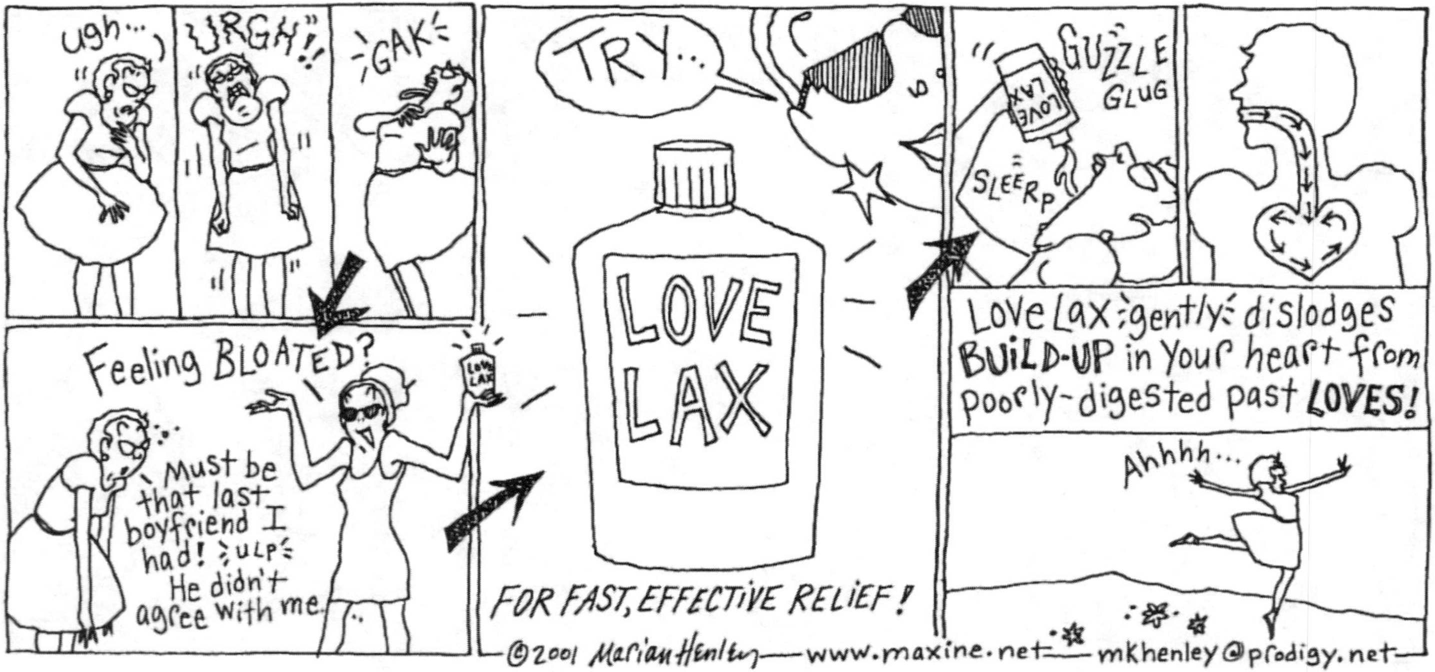
ugh...
URGH!!
GAK
Feeling BLOATED?
Must be that last boyfriend I had! ULP He didn't agree with me.
LOVE LAX
TRY...
LOVE LAX
FOR FAST, EFFECTIVE RELIEF!
LOVE LAX
GUZZLE
GLUG
SLEERP
Love Lax gently dislodges BUILD-UP in your heart from poorly-digested past LOVES!
Ahhhh...
©2001 Marian Henley — www.maxine.net — mkhenley@prodigy.net

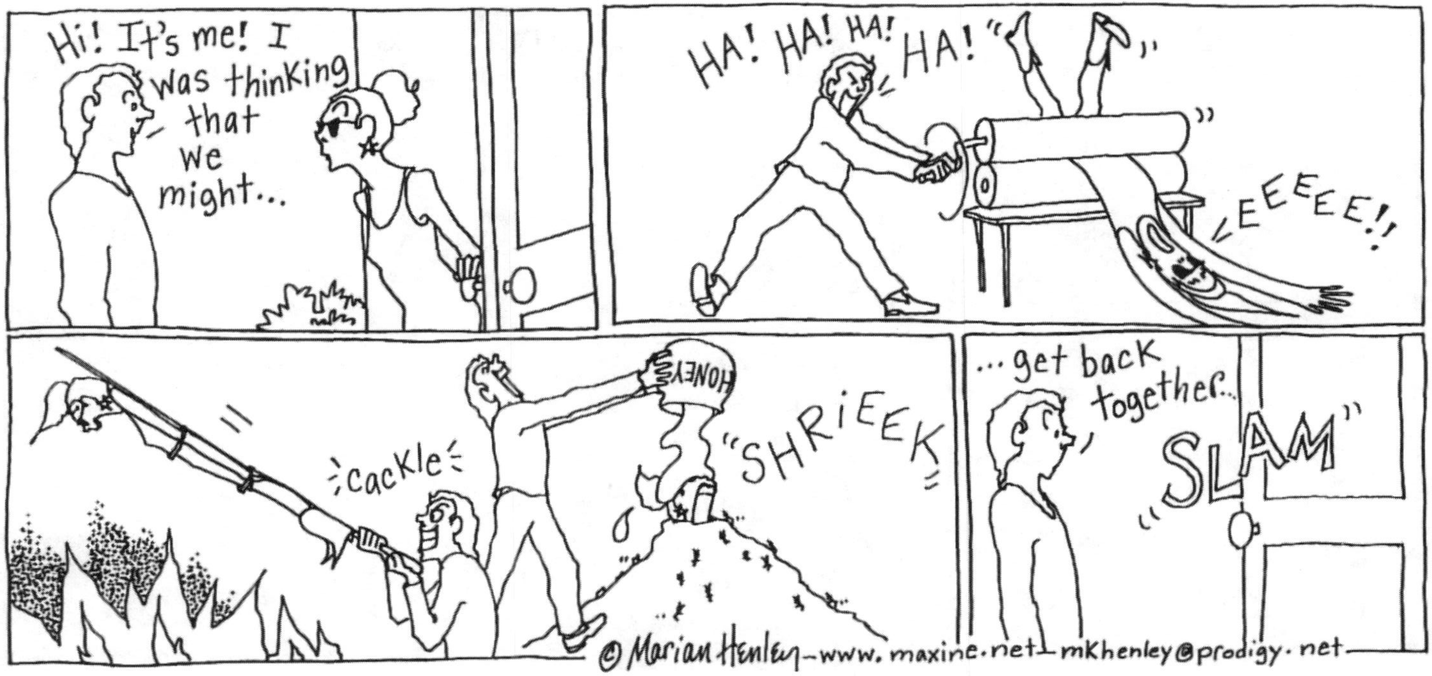
Hi! It's me! I was thinking that we might...
"HA! HA! HA! HA!"
"EEEEEE!!"
cackle
HONEY
"SHRIEEK"
...get back together...
"SLAM"
© Marian Henley—www.maxine.net—mkhenley@prodigy.net

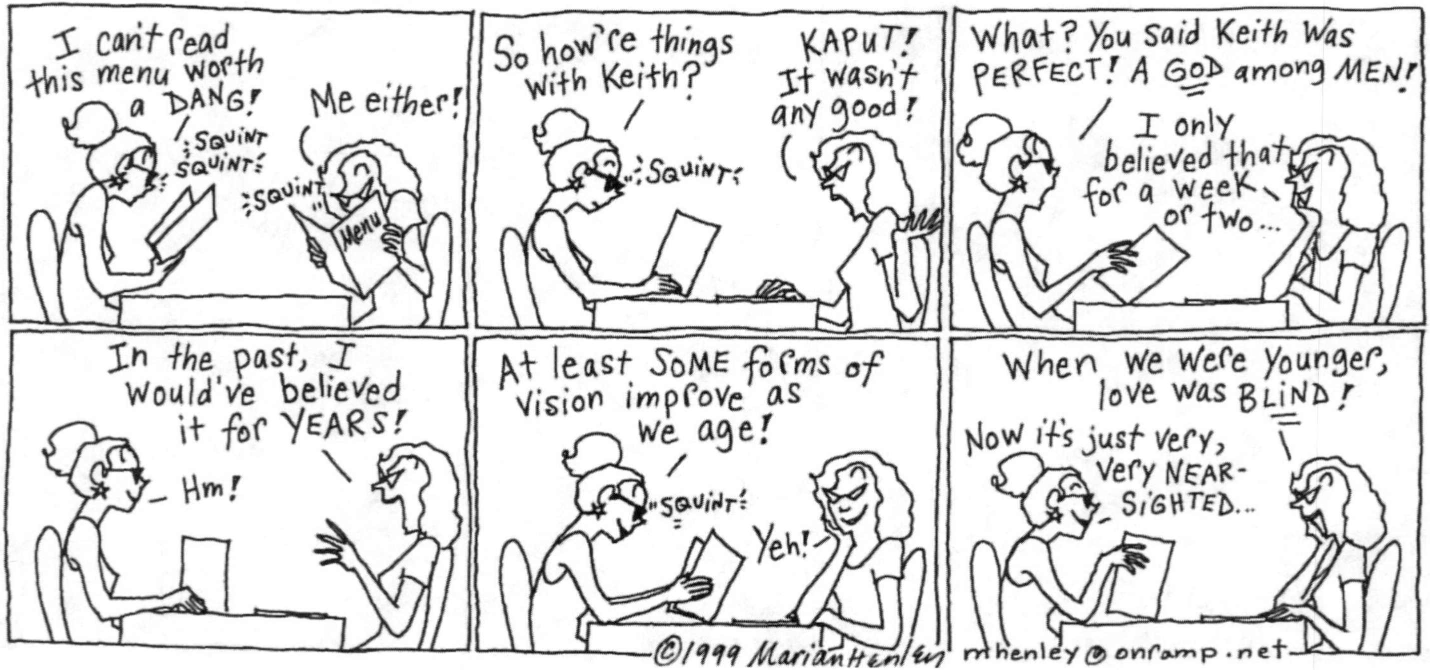
I can't read this menu worth a DANG!
:SQUINT SQUINT:
Me either!
:SQUINT:
Menu
So how're things with Keith?
:SQUINT:
KAPUT! It wasn't any good!
What? You said Keith was PERFECT! A GOD among MEN!
I only believed that for a week or two...
In the past, I would've believed it for YEARS!
Hm!
At least SOME forms of vision improve as we age!
:SQUINT:
Yeh!
When we were younger, love was BLIND!
Now it's just very, very NEAR-SIGHTED...
©1999 Marian Henley mhenley@onramp.net

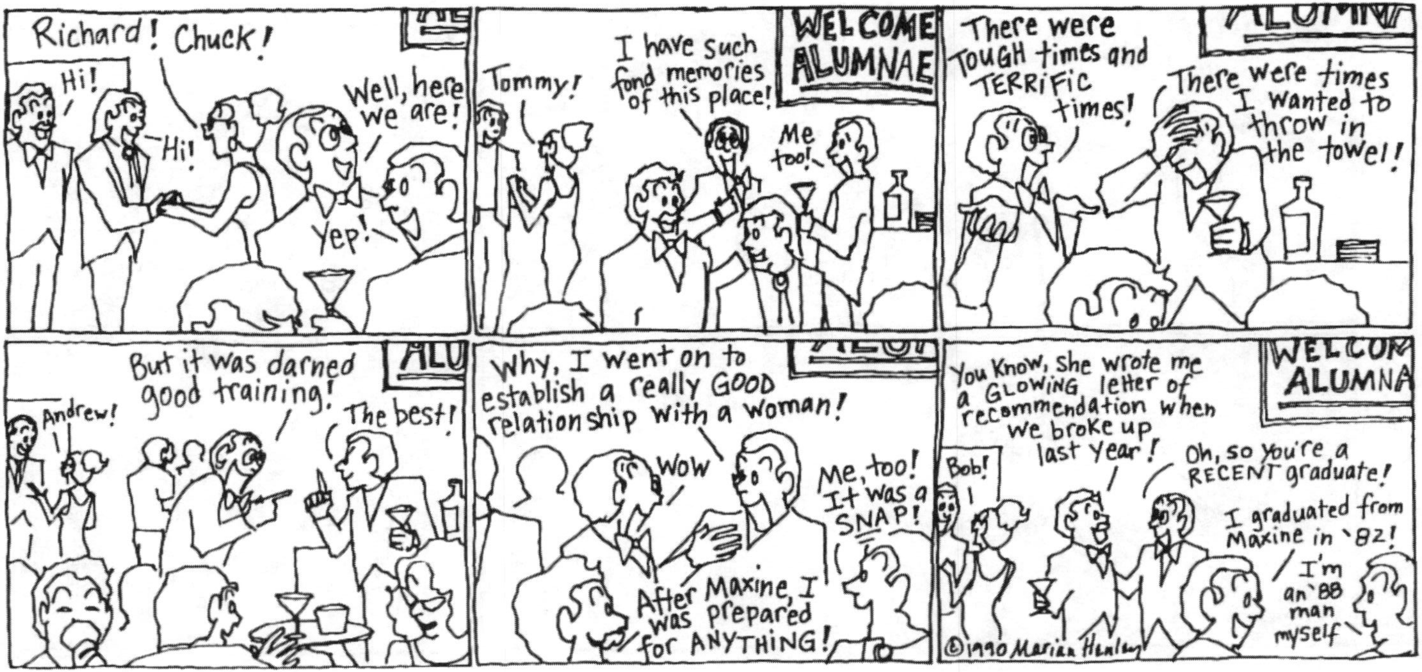
Richard!
Chuck!
Hi!
Hi!
Well, here we are!
Yep!
WELCOME ALUMNAE
Tommy!
I have such fond memories of this place!
Me too!
There were TOUGH times and TERRIFIC times!
There were times I wanted to throw in the towel!
But it was darned good training!
Andrew!
The best!
Why, I went on to establish a really GOOD relationship with a woman!
Wow
Me, too! It was a SNAP!
After Maxine, I was prepared for ANYTHING!
WELCOM ALUMNA
You know, she wrote me a GLOWING letter of recommendation when we broke up last year!
Bob!
Oh, so you're a RECENT graduate!
I graduated from Maxine in '82!
I'm an '88 man myself
©1990 Marian Henley

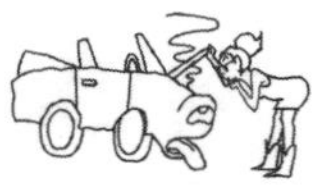

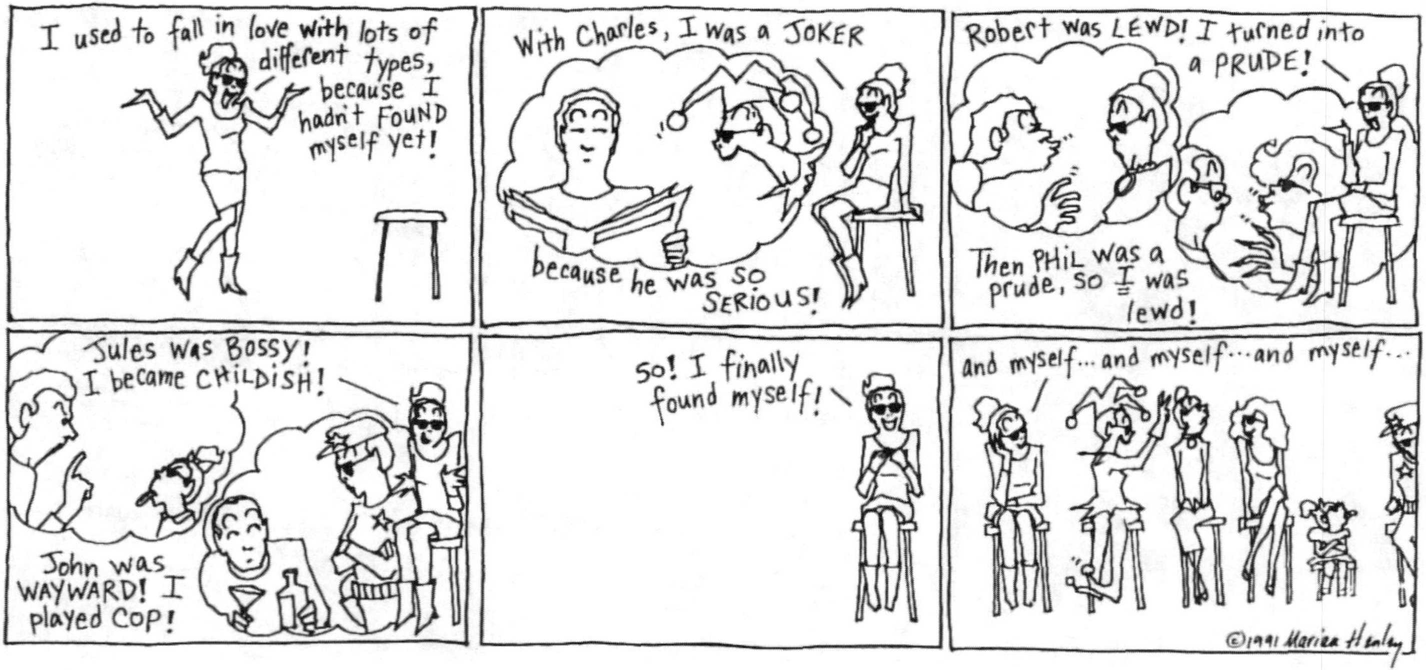
I used to fall in love with lots of different types, because I hadn't FOUND myself yet!
With Charles, I was a JOKER
because he was SO SERIOUS!
Robert was LEWD! I turned into a PRUDE!
Then PHIL was a prude, so I was lewd!
Jules was BOSSY! I became CHILDISH!
John was WAYWARD! I played COP!
So! I finally found myself!
and myself... and myself... and myself...
©1991 Marian Henley

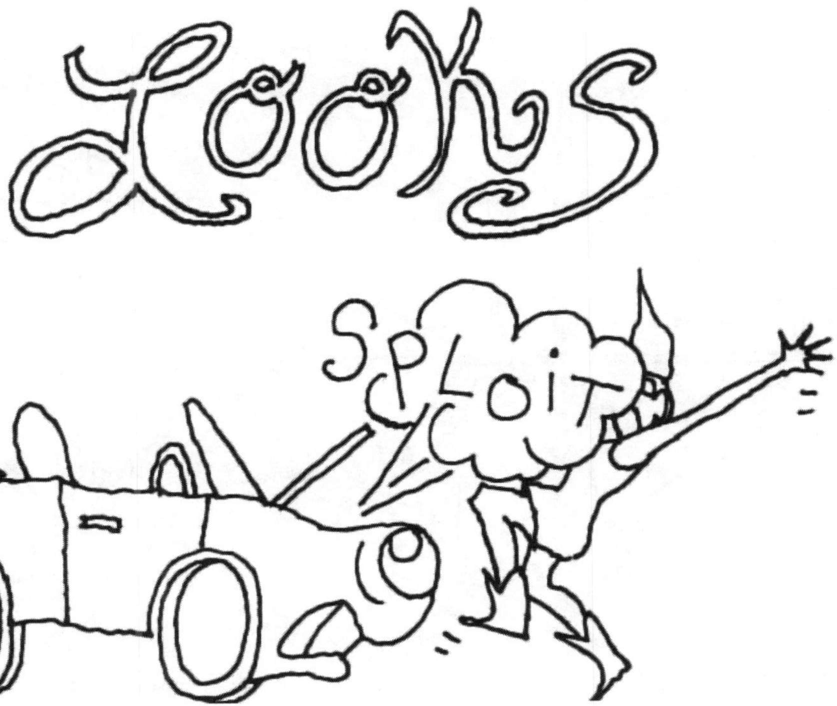
Looks
SPLOIT

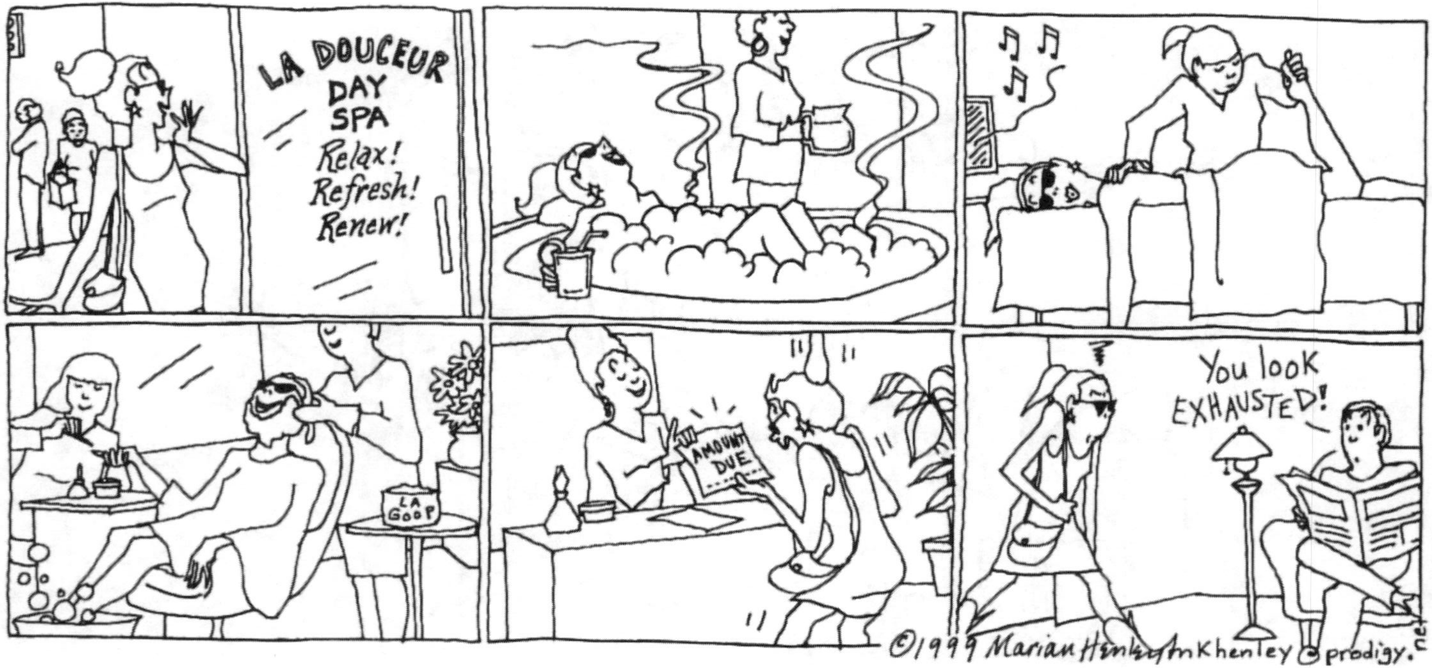
LA DOUCEUR
DAY
SPA
Relax!
Refresh!
Renew!
LA GOOP
AMOUNT DUE
You look EXHAUSTED!
©1999 Marian Henley mkhenley@prodigy.net

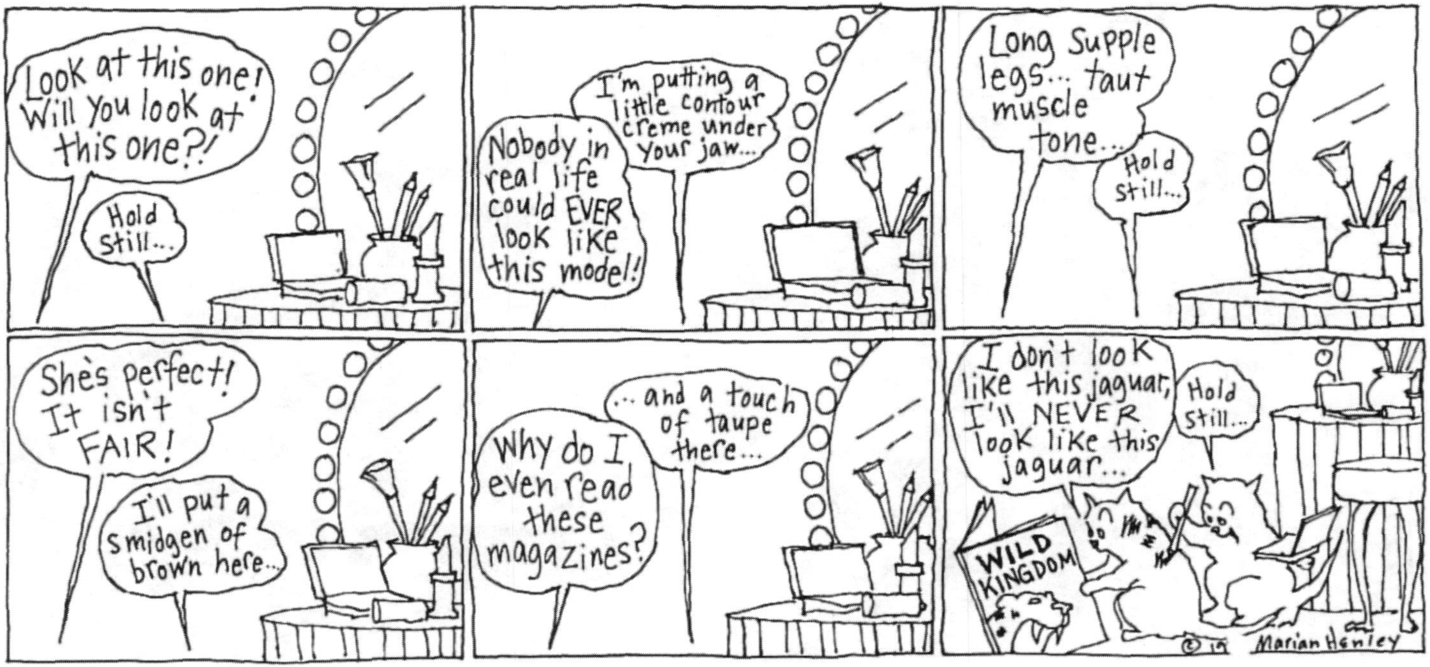
Look at this one! Will you look at this one?!
Hold still...
Nobody in real life could EVER look like this model!!
I'm putting a little contour creme under your jaw...
Long supple legs... taut muscle tone...
Hold still...
She's perfect! It isn't FAIR!
I'll put a smidgen of brown here...
Why do I even read these magazines?
... and a touch of taupe there...
I don't look like this jaguar, I'll NEVER look like this jaguar...
Hold still...
WILD KINGDOM
© 19 Marian Henley

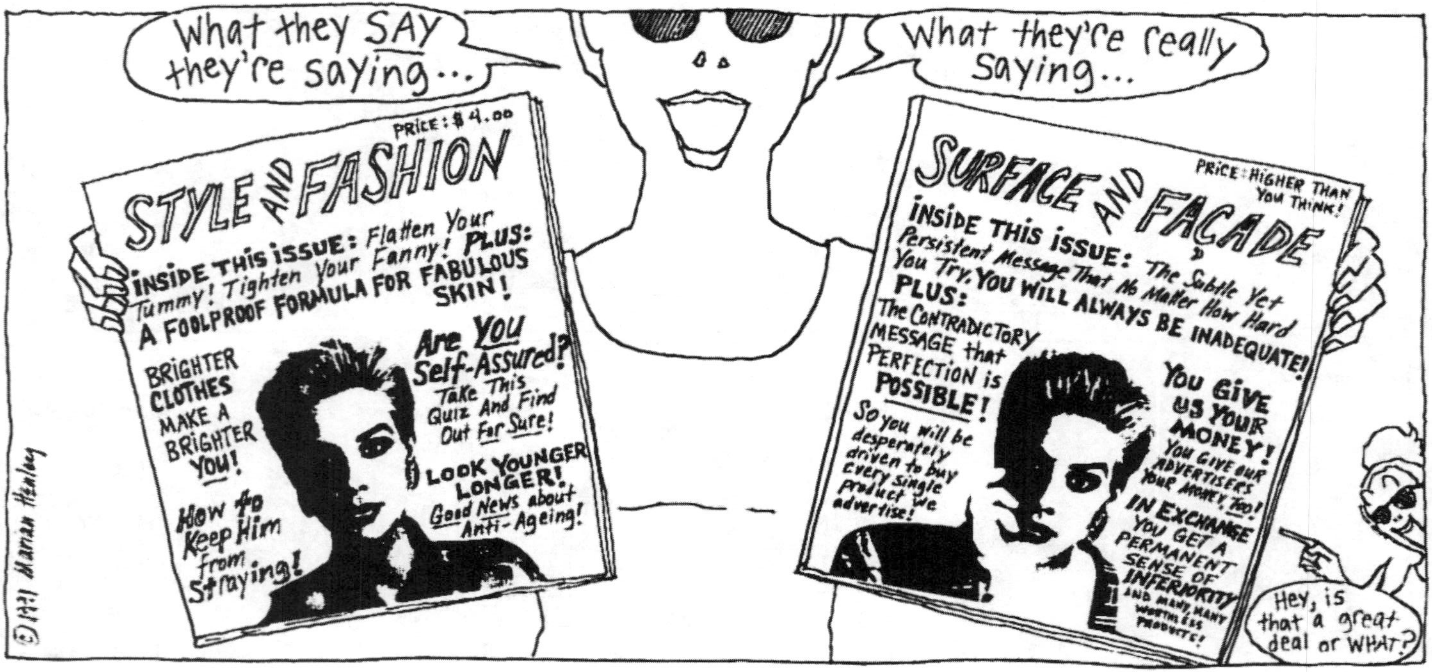
What they SAY they're saying...
PRICE: $4.00
STYLE AND FASHION
INSIDE THIS ISSUE: Flatten Your Tummy! Tighten Your Fanny! PLUS: A FOOLPROOF FORMULA FOR FABULOUS SKIN!
BRIGHTER CLOTHES MAKE A BRIGHTER YOU!
Are YOU Self-Assured? Take This Quiz And Find Out For Sure!
LOOK YOUNGER LONGER! Good News about Anti-Ageing!
How to Keep Him from Straying!
© 1991 Marian Henley
What they're really saying...
SURFACE AND FACADE
PRICE: HIGHER THAN YOU THINK!
INSIDE THIS ISSUE: The Subtle Yet Persistent Message That No Matter How Hard You Try, YOU WILL ALWAYS BE INADEQUATE!
PLUS: The CONTRADICTORY MESSAGE that PERFECTION is POSSIBLE!
So you will be desperately driven to buy every single product we advertise!
YOU GIVE US YOUR MONEY! You give our advertisers your money, too!
IN EXCHANGE YOU GET A PERMANENT SENSE OF INFERIORITY AND MANY, MANY WORTHLESS PRODUCTS!
Hey, is that a great deal or WHAT?

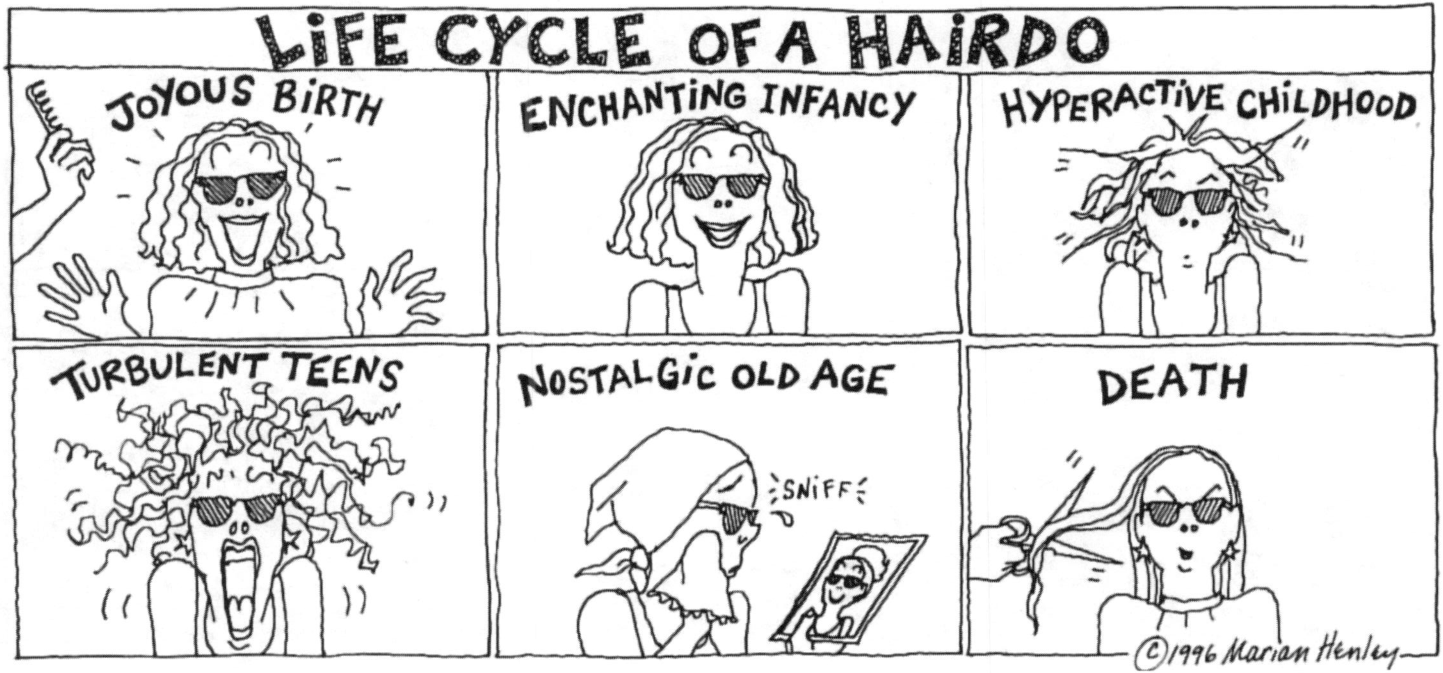
LIFE CYCLE OF A HAIRDO
JOYOUS BIRTH
ENCHANTING INFANCY
HYPERACTIVE CHILDHOOD
TURBULENT TEENS
NOSTALGIC OLD AGE
SNIFF
DEATH
©1996 Marian Henley

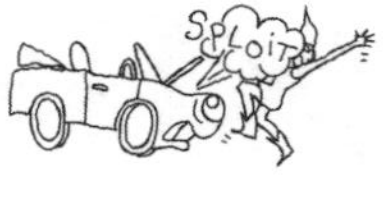
SPLOIT

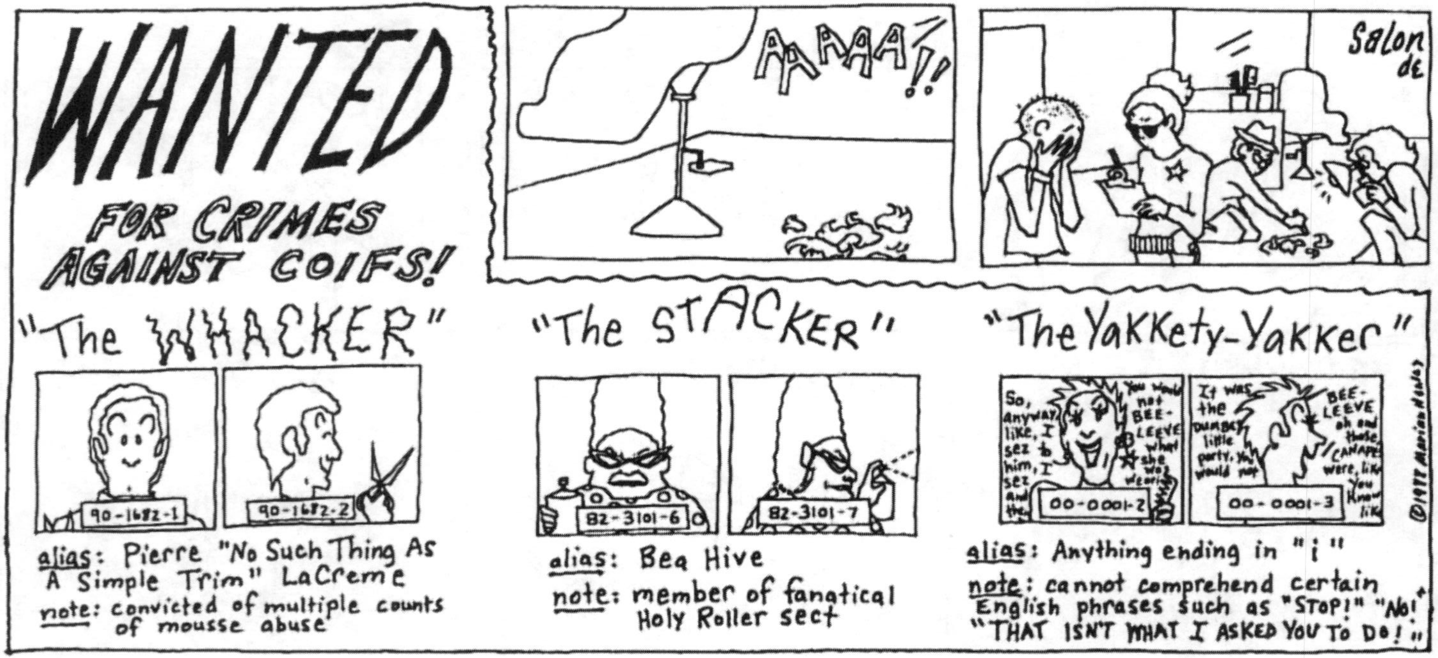
WANTED
FOR CRIMES AGAINST COIFS!
AAAA!!
Salon de
"The WHACKER"
90-1682-1
90-1682-2
alias: Pierre "No Such Thing As A Simple Trim" LaCreme
note: convicted of multiple counts of mousse abuse
"The STACKER"
82-3101-6
82-3101-7
alias: Bea Hive
note: member of fanatical Holy Roller sect
"The Yakkety-Yakker"
So, anyway, like, I sez to him, I sez and the
You would not BEE-LEEVE what she was wearing
00-0001-2
It was the dumbest little party, you would not
BEE-LEEVE oh and those CANAPES were, like, you know, like
00-0001-3
alias: Anything ending in "i"
note: cannot comprehend certain English phrases such as "STOP!" "NO!" "THAT ISN'T WHAT I ASKED YOU TO DO!"
©1977 Marian Henley

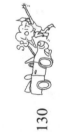

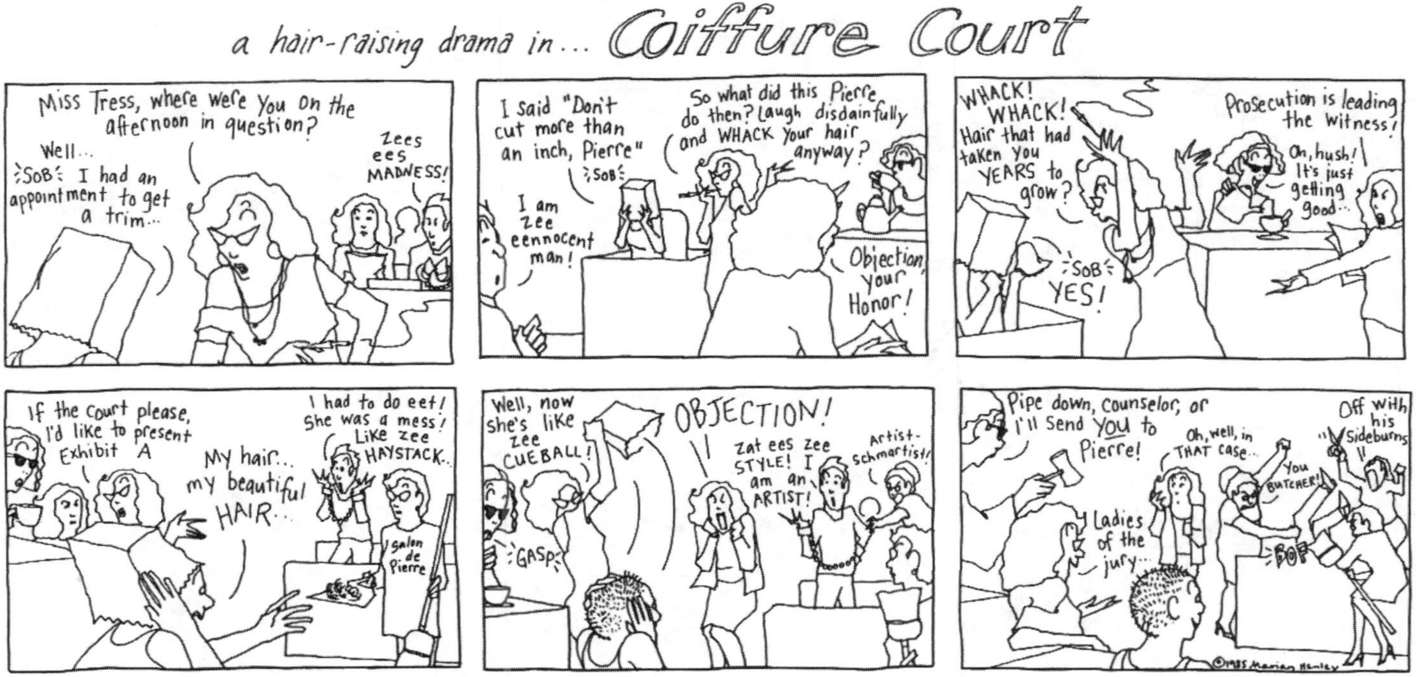
a hair-raising drama in... Coiffure Court
Miss Tress, where were you on the afternoon in question?
Well... :SOB: I had an appointment to get a trim...
Zees ees MADNESS!
I said "Don't cut more than an inch, Pierre" :SOB:
I am zee eennocent man!
So what did this Pierre do then? Laugh disdainfully and WHACK your hair anyway?
Objection, your Honor!
WHACK! WHACK! Hair that had taken you YEARS to grow?
:SOB: YES!
Prosecution is leading the witness!
Oh, hush! It's just getting good...
If the court please, I'd like to present Exhibit A
My hair... my beautiful HAIR...
I had to do eet! She was a mess! Like zee HAYSTACK..
Salon de Pierre
Well, now she's like zee CUEBALL!
:GASP:
OBJECTION!
Zat ees zee STYLE! I am an ARTIST!
Artist-Schmartist!
Pipe down, counselor, or I'll send YOU to Pierre!
Ladies of the jury...
Oh, well, in THAT case...
You BUTCHER!
POP
"Off with his Sideburns"
©1985 Marian Henley

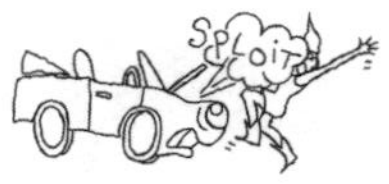
SPLOIT

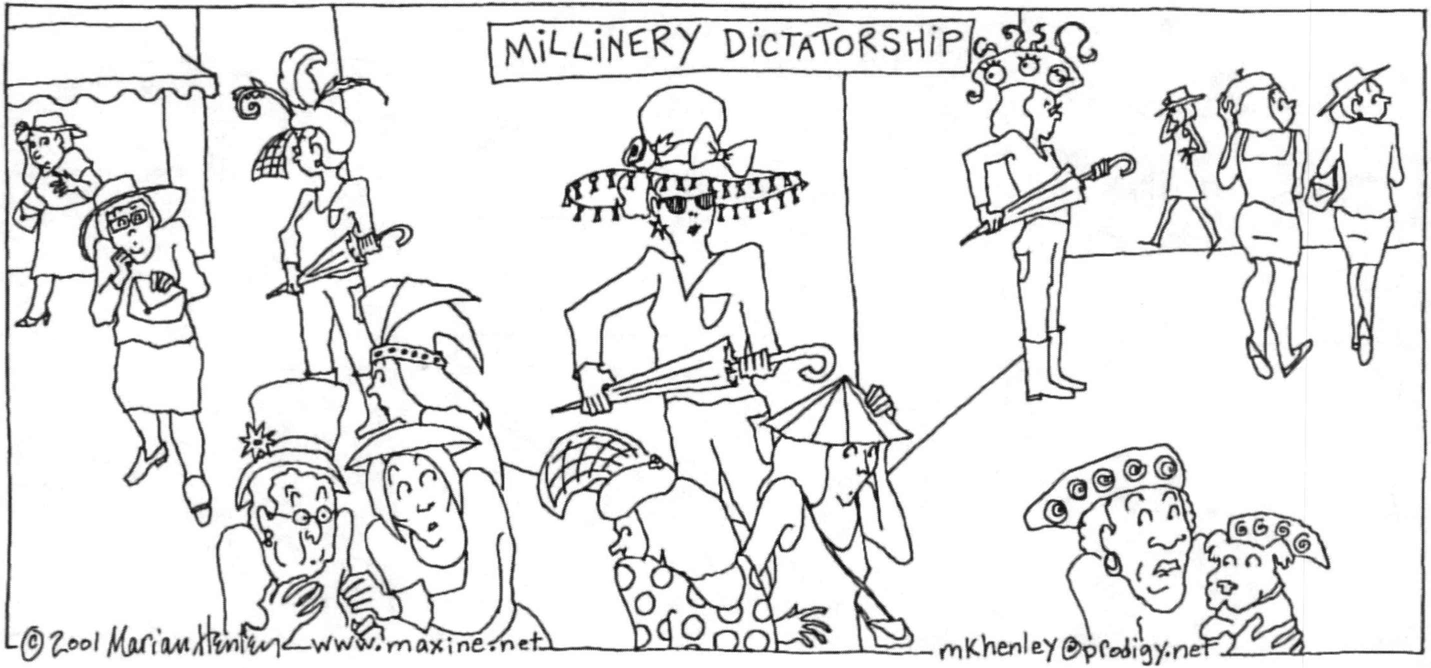
MiLLiNERY DiCTATORSHiP
© 2001 Marian Henley www.maxine.net
mkhenley@prodigy.net

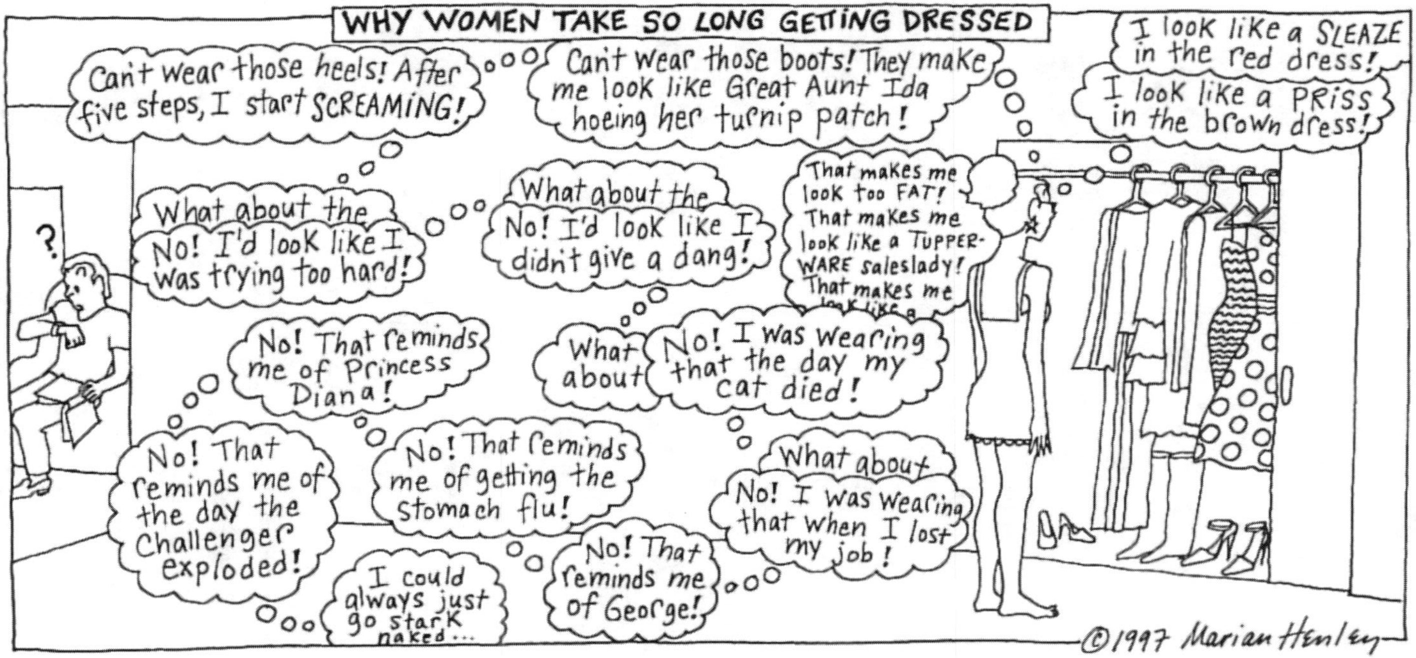
WHY WOMEN TAKE SO LONG GETTING DRESSED
I look like a SLEAZE in the red dress!
I look like a PRISS in the brown dress!
Can't wear those boots! They make me look like Great Aunt Ida hoeing her turnip patch!
Can't wear those heels! After five steps, I start SCREAMING!
That makes me look too FAT! That makes me look like a TUPPERWARE saleslady! That makes me
What about the
No! I'd look like I didn't give a dang!
What about the
No! I'd look like I was trying too hard!
?
What about
No! I was wearing that the day my cat died!
No! That reminds me of Princess Diana!
What about
No! I was wearing that when I lost my job!
No! That reminds me of getting the stomach flu!
No! That reminds me of the day the Challenger exploded!
No! That reminds me of George!
I could always just go stark naked...
©1997 Marian Henley

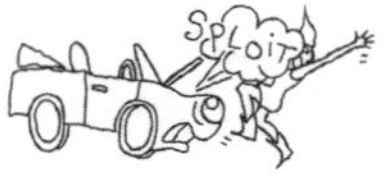
SPLOIT

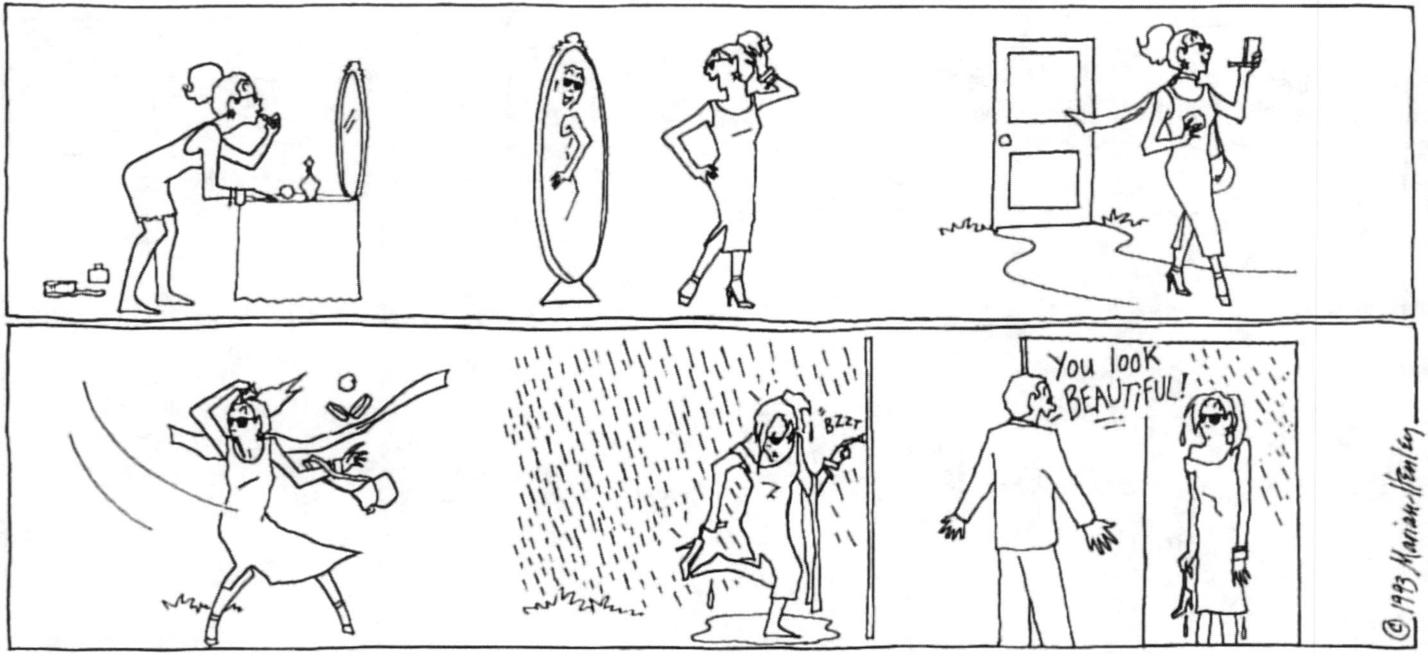
BZZT
You look BEAUTIFUL!
© 1993 Marian Henley

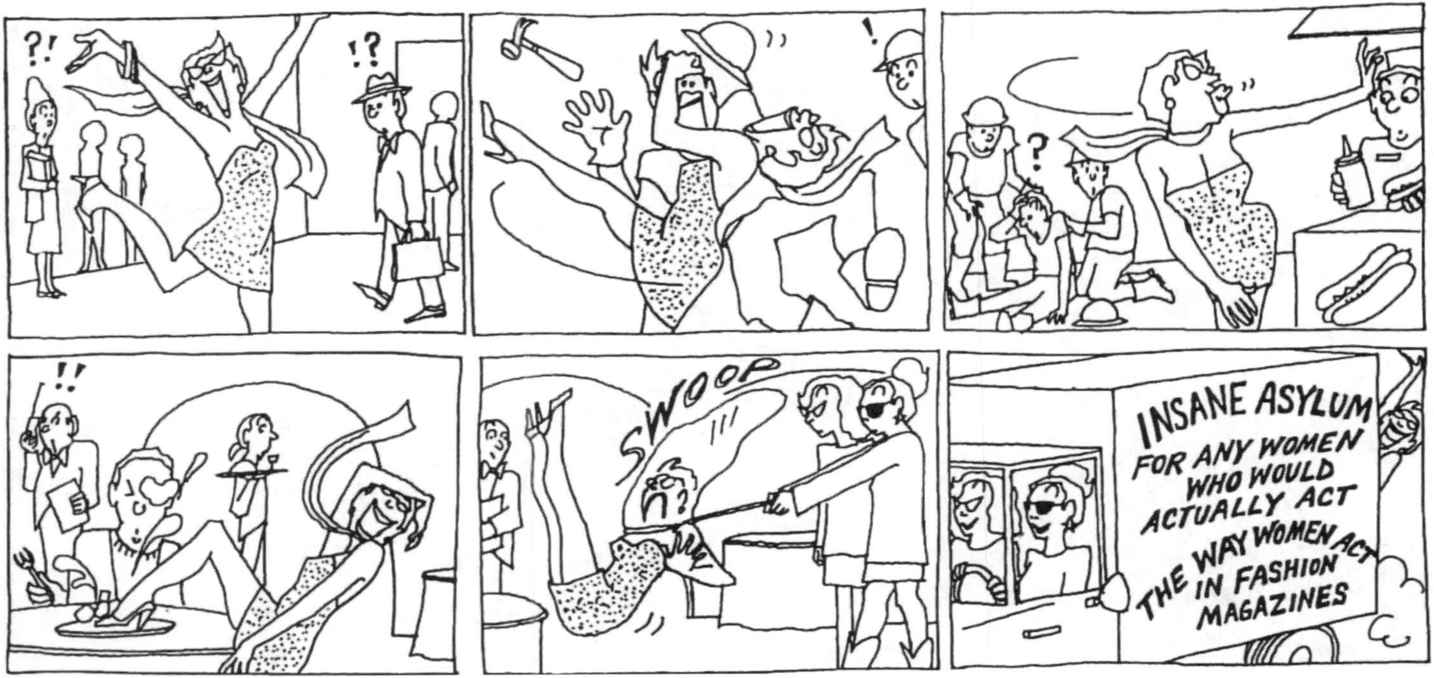
?!
!?
!
?
!!
SWOOP
?
INSANE ASYLUM
FOR ANY WOMEN
WHO WOULD
ACTUALLY ACT
THE WAY WOMEN ACT
IN FASHION
MAGAZINES

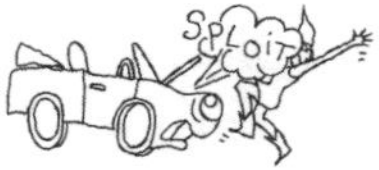
SPLOIT

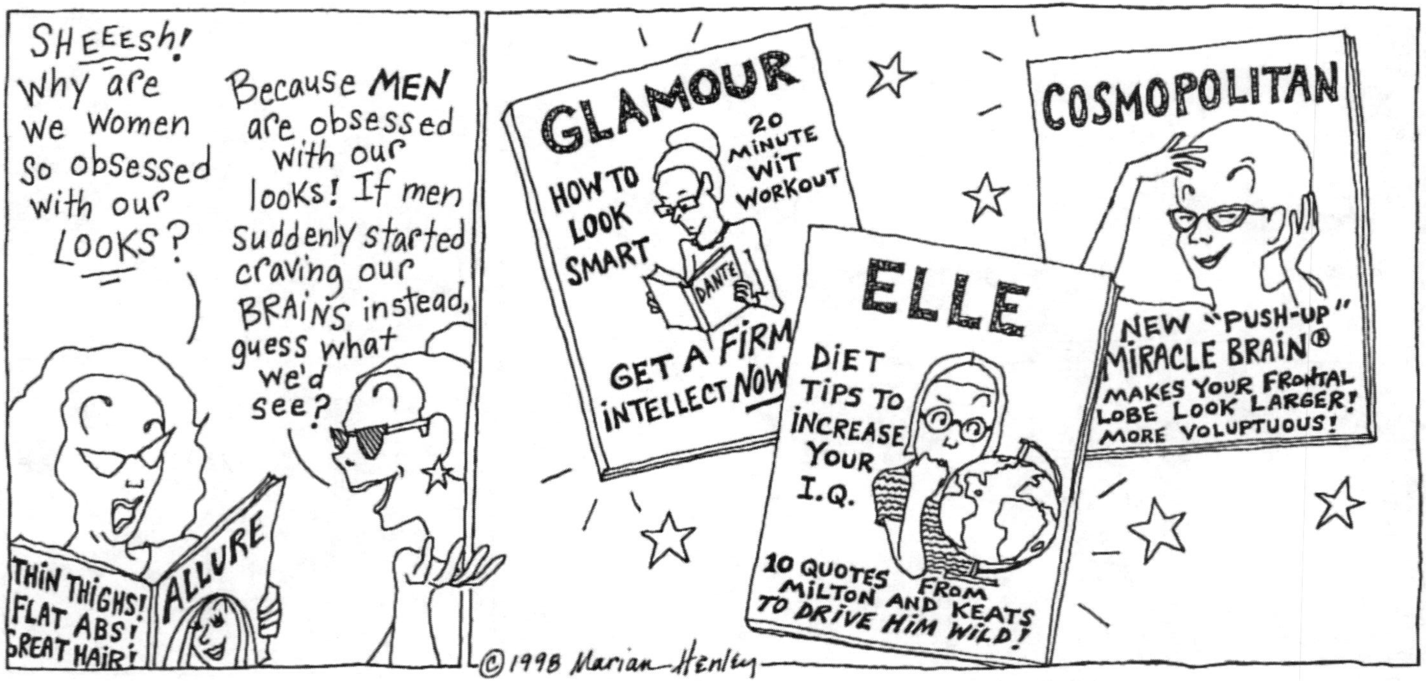
SHEEESH! Why are we women so obsessed with our LOOKS?
Because MEN are obsessed with our looks! If men suddenly started craving our BRAINS instead, guess what we'd see?
THIN THIGHS! FLAT ABS! GREAT HAIR!
ALLURE
GLAMOUR
HOW TO LOOK SMART
20 MINUTE WIT WORKOUT
DANTE
GET A FIRM INTELLECT NOW
ELLE
DIET TIPS TO INCREASE YOUR I.Q.
10 QUOTES FROM MILTON AND KEATS TO DRIVE HIM WILD!
COSMOPOLITAN
NEW "PUSH-UP" MIRACLE BRAIN®
MAKES YOUR FRONTAL LOBE LOOK LARGER! MORE VOLUPTUOUS!
©1998 Marian Henley

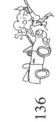

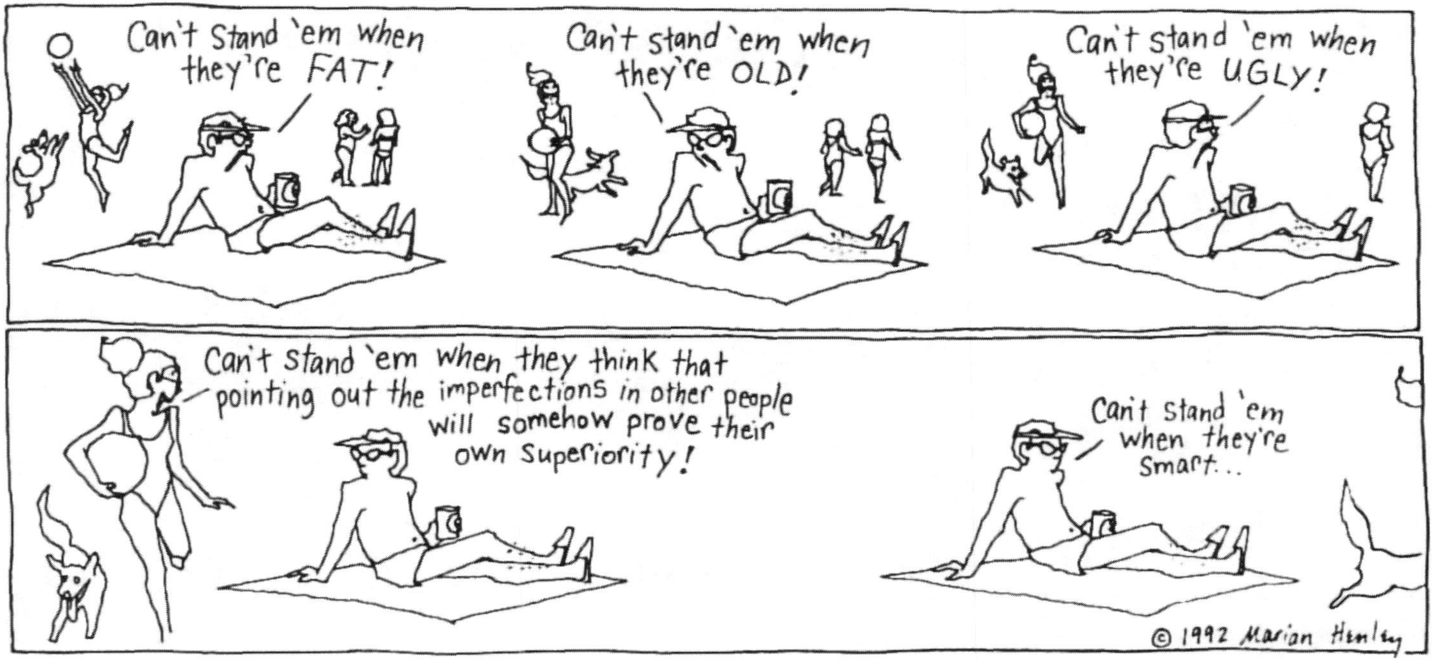
Can't Stand 'em when they're FAT!
Can't stand 'em when they're OLD!
Can't stand 'em when they're UGLY!
Can't stand 'em when they think that pointing out the imperfections in other people will somehow prove their own Superiority!
Can't stand 'em when they're smart...
© 1992 Marian Henley

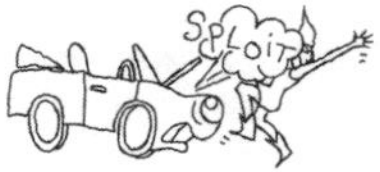
SPLOIT

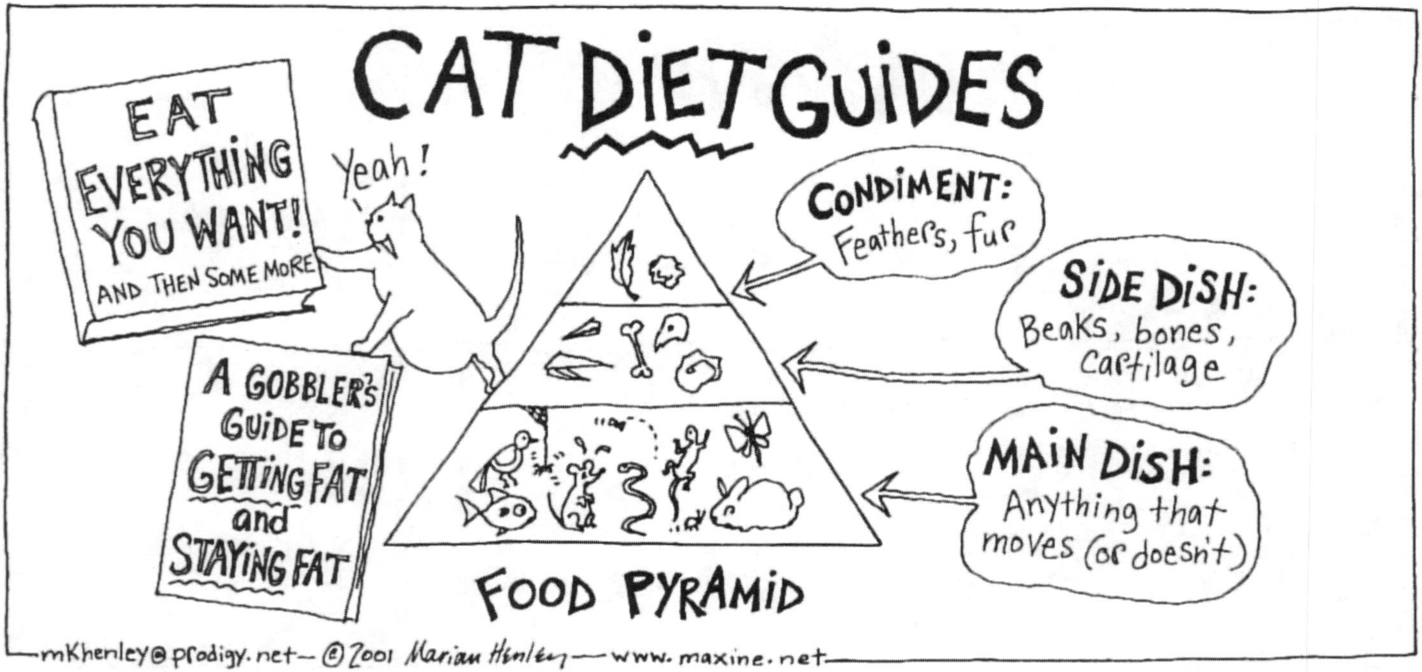
CAT DIET GUIDES
EAT EVERYTHING YOU WANT! AND THEN SOME MORE
Yeah!
A GOBBLER'S GUIDE TO GETTING FAT and STAYING FAT
CONDIMENT: Feathers, fur
SIDE DISH: Beaks, bones, cartilage
MAIN DISH: Anything that moves (or doesn't)
FOOD PYRAMID
mKhenley@prodigy.net — ©2001 Marian Henley — www.maxine.net

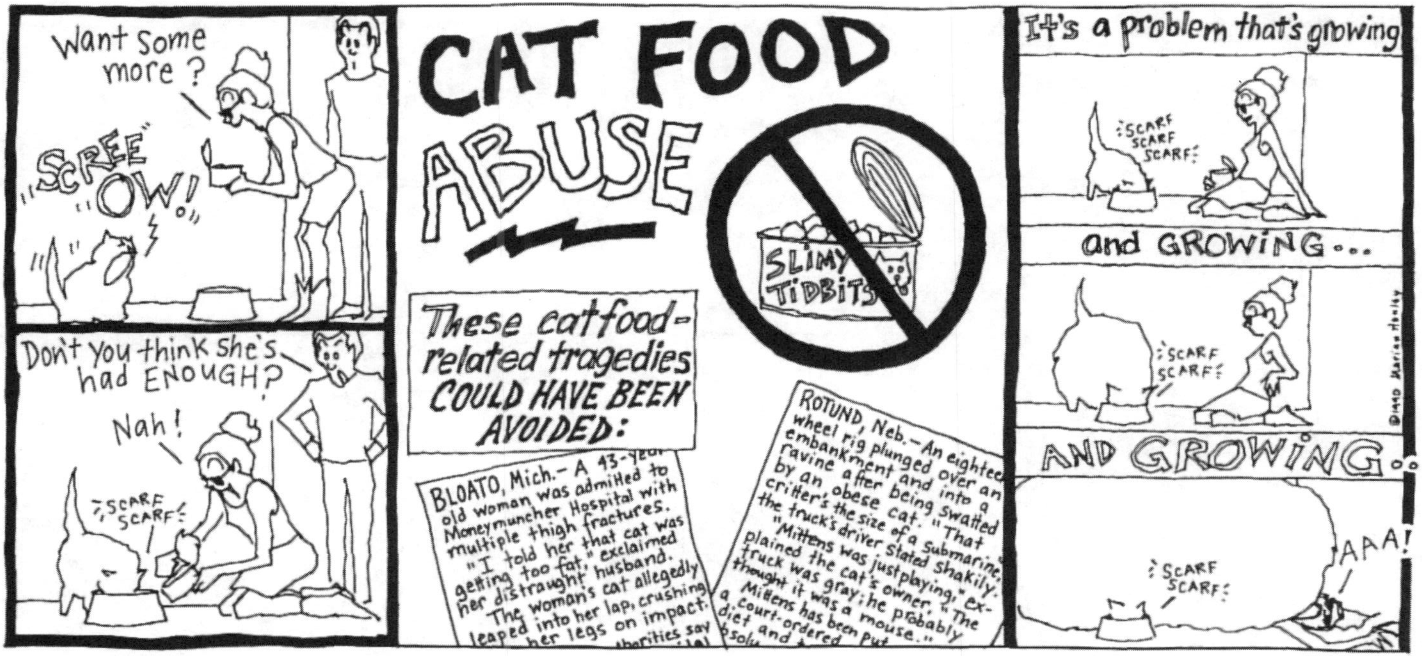
Want some more?
"SCREE" "OW!"
Don't you think she's had ENOUGH?
Nah!
SCARF SCARF
CAT FOOD ABUSE
SLIMY TIDBITS
These catfood-related tragedies COULD HAVE BEEN AVOIDED:
BLOATO, Mich.— A 43-year old woman was admitted to Moneymuncher Hospital with multiple thigh fractures.
"I told her that cat was getting too fat," exclaimed her distraught husband.
The woman's cat allegedly leaped into her lap, crushing her legs on impact.
ROTUND, Neb.—An eighteen wheel rig plunged over an embankment and into a ravine after being swatted by an obese cat. "That critter's the size of a submarine," the truck's driver stated shakily.
"Mittens was just playing," explained the cat's owner. "The truck was gray; he probably thought it was a mouse.."
Mittens has been put on a court-ordered diet and
It's a problem that's growing
SCARF SCARF SCARF
and GROWING...
SCARF SCARF
AND GROWING..
SCARF SCARF
AAA!
©1990 Marian Henley

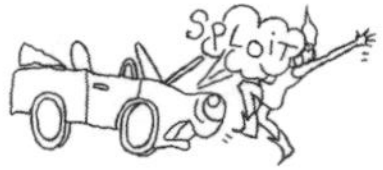
SPLOIT

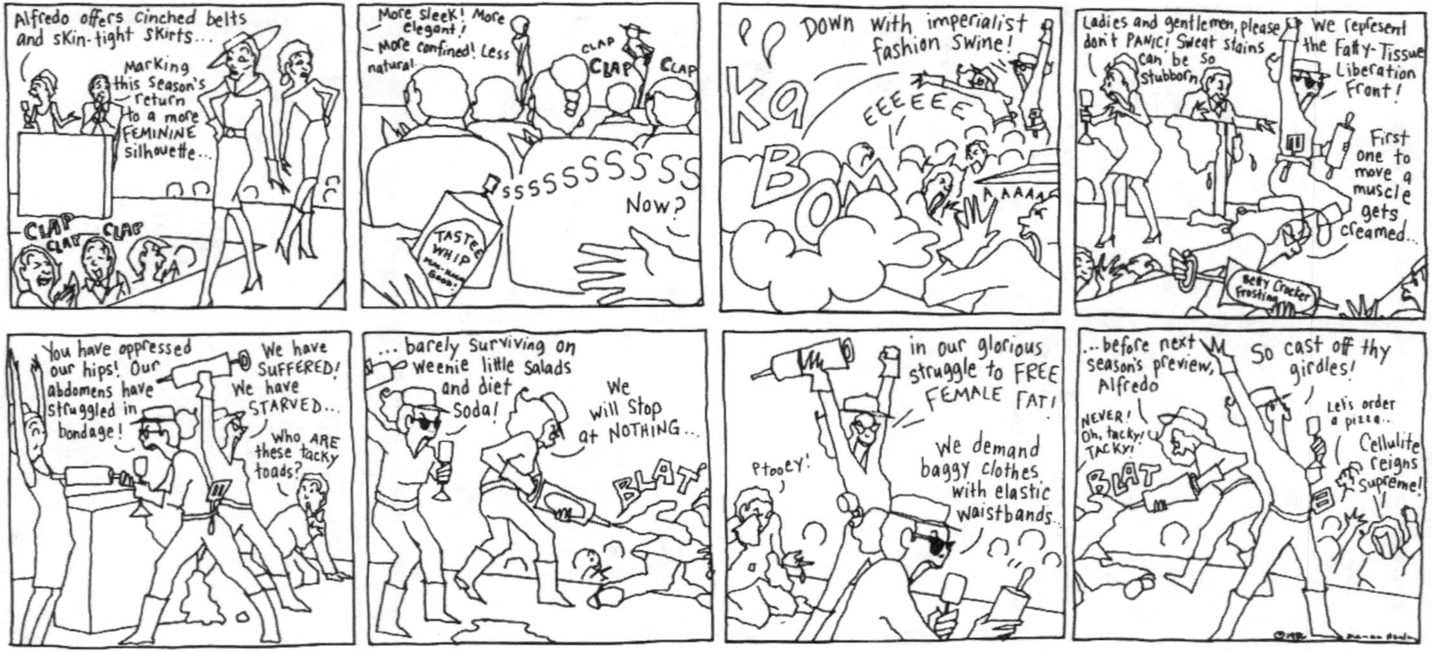
Alfredo offers cinched belts and skin-tight skirts...
Marking this season's return to a more FEMININE silhouette...
CLAP CLAP CLAP
More sleek! More elegant!
More confined! Less natural...
CLAP CLAP CLAP
TASTEE WHIP
sssssSSSSSS
Now?
Down with imperialist fashion swine!
KA
BOOM
EEEEEE
AAAAA
Ladies and gentlemen, please don't PANIC! Sweat stains can be so stubborn.
We represent the Fatty-Tissue Liberation Front!
First one to move a muscle gets creamed...
Betty Crocker Frosting
You have oppressed our hips! Our abdomens have struggled in bondage!
We have SUFFERED! We have STARVED...
Who ARE these tacky toads?
... barely surviving on weenie little salads and diet soda!
We will stop at NOTHING...
BLAT
in our glorious struggle to FREE FEMALE FAT!
Ptooey!
We demand baggy clothes with elastic waistbands...
...before next season's preview, Alfredo
So cast off thy girdles!
NEVER! Oh, tacky! TACKY!
BLAT
Let's order a pizza...
Cellulite reigns supreme!

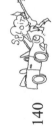

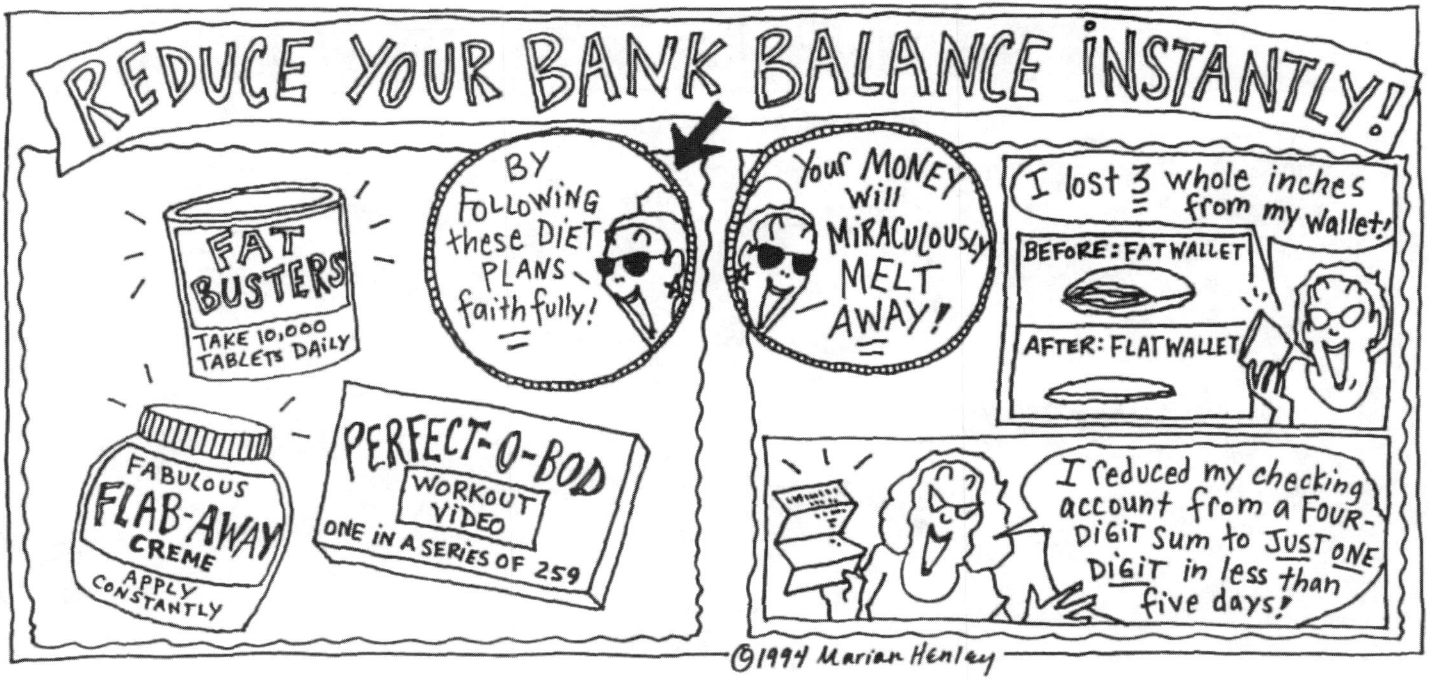
REDUCE YOUR BANK BALANCE INSTANTLY!
FAT BUSTERS
TAKE 10,000 TABLETS DAILY
FABULOUS FLAB-AWAY CREME
APPLY CONSTANTLY
PERFECT-O-BOD
WORKOUT VIDEO
ONE IN A SERIES OF 259
BY FOLLOWING these DIET PLANS faithfully!
Your MONEY will MIRACULOUSLY MELT AWAY!
I lost 3 whole inches from my wallet!
BEFORE: FAT WALLET
AFTER: FLAT WALLET
I reduced my checking account from a FOUR-DIGIT sum to JUST ONE DIGIT in less than five days!
©1994 Marian Henley

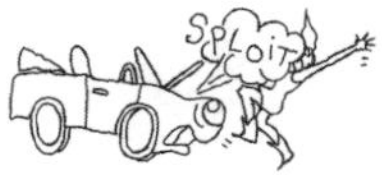
SPLOIT

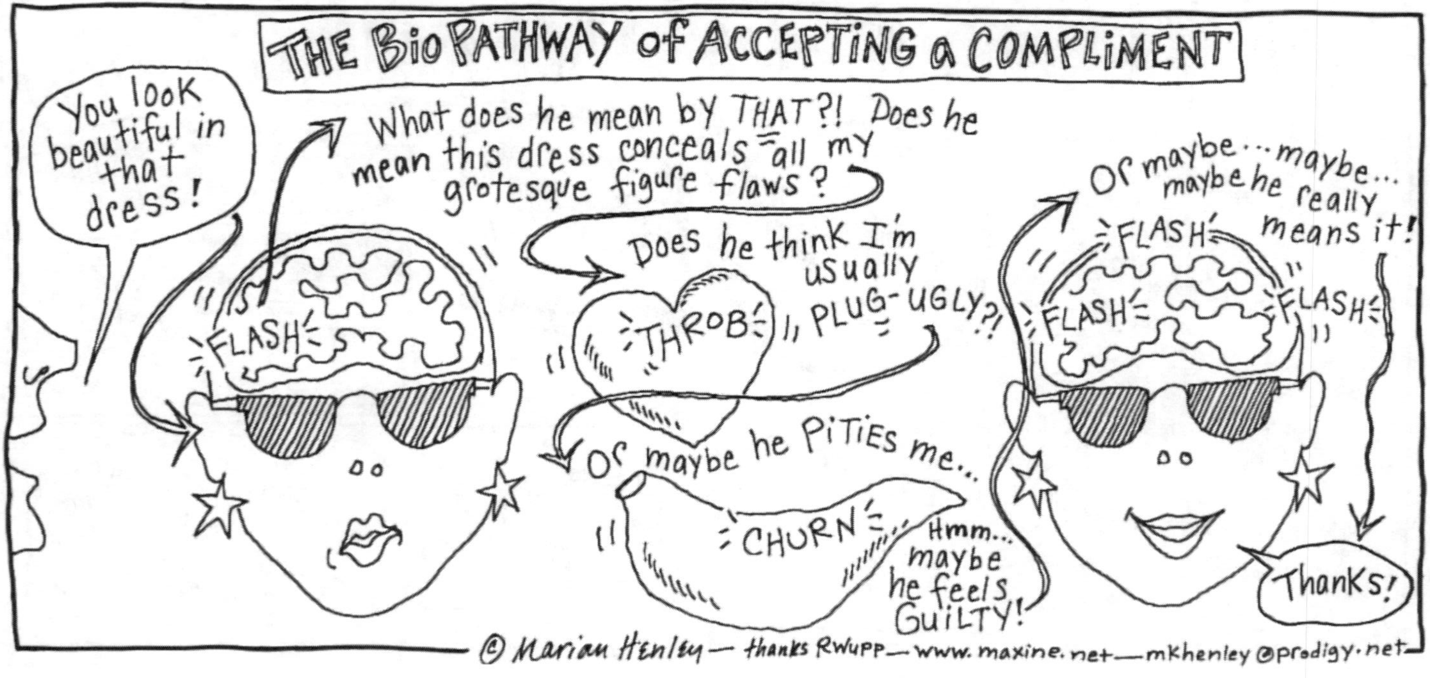
THE BIO PATHWAY of ACCEPTING a COMPLIMENT
You look beautiful in that dress!
FLASH
What does he mean by THAT?! Does he mean this dress conceals all my grotesque figure flaws?
Does he think I'm usually PLUG-UGLY?!
THROB
Or maybe he PITIES me...
CHURN
Hmm... maybe he feels GUILTY!
FLASH
FLASH
FLASH
Or maybe... maybe... maybe he really means it!
Thanks!
© Marian Henley — thanks RWupp — www.maxine.net — mkhenley@prodigy.net

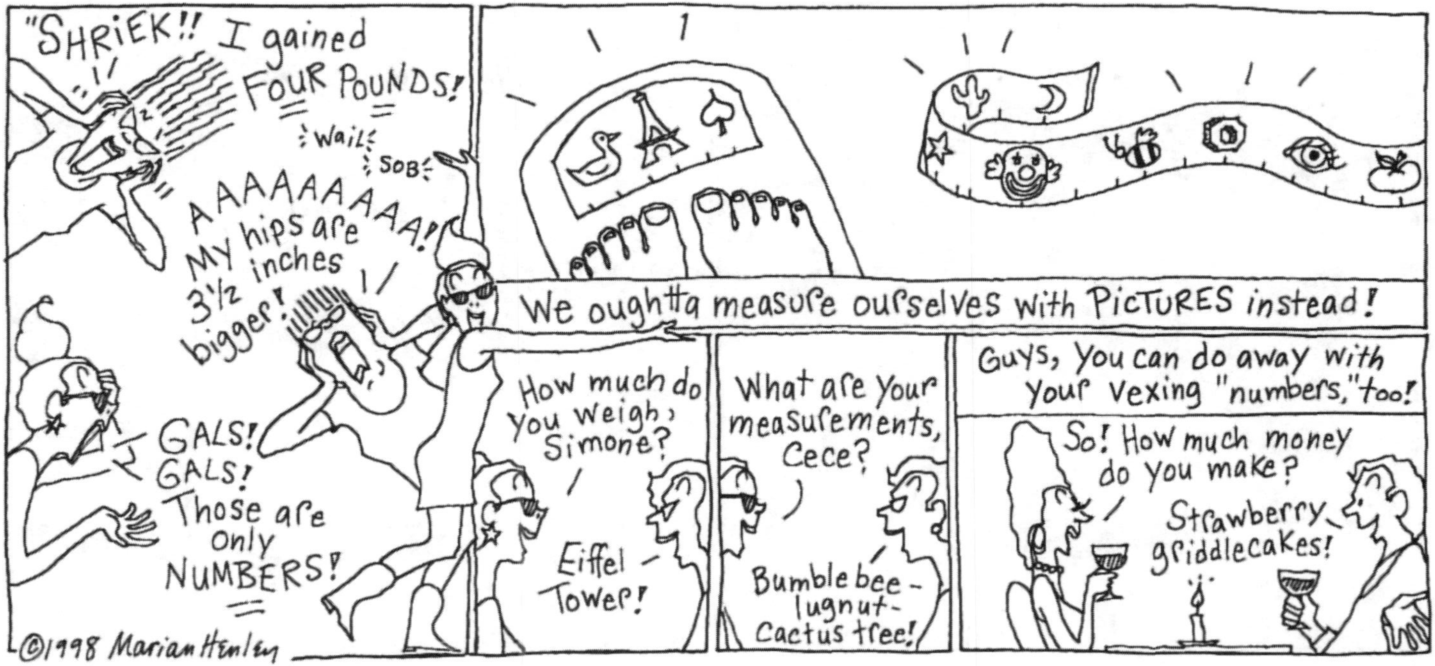
"SHRIEK!! I gained FOUR POUNDS!
WAIL
SOB
AAAAAAAAAA!
My hips are 3½ inches bigger!
GALS! GALS! Those are only NUMBERS!
We oughtta measure ourselves with PICTURES instead!
How much do you weigh, Simone?
Eiffel Tower!
What are your measurements, Cece?
Bumblebee-lugnut-cactus tree!
Guys, you can do away with your vexing "numbers," too!
So! How much money do you make?
Strawberry griddlecakes!
©1998 Marian Henley

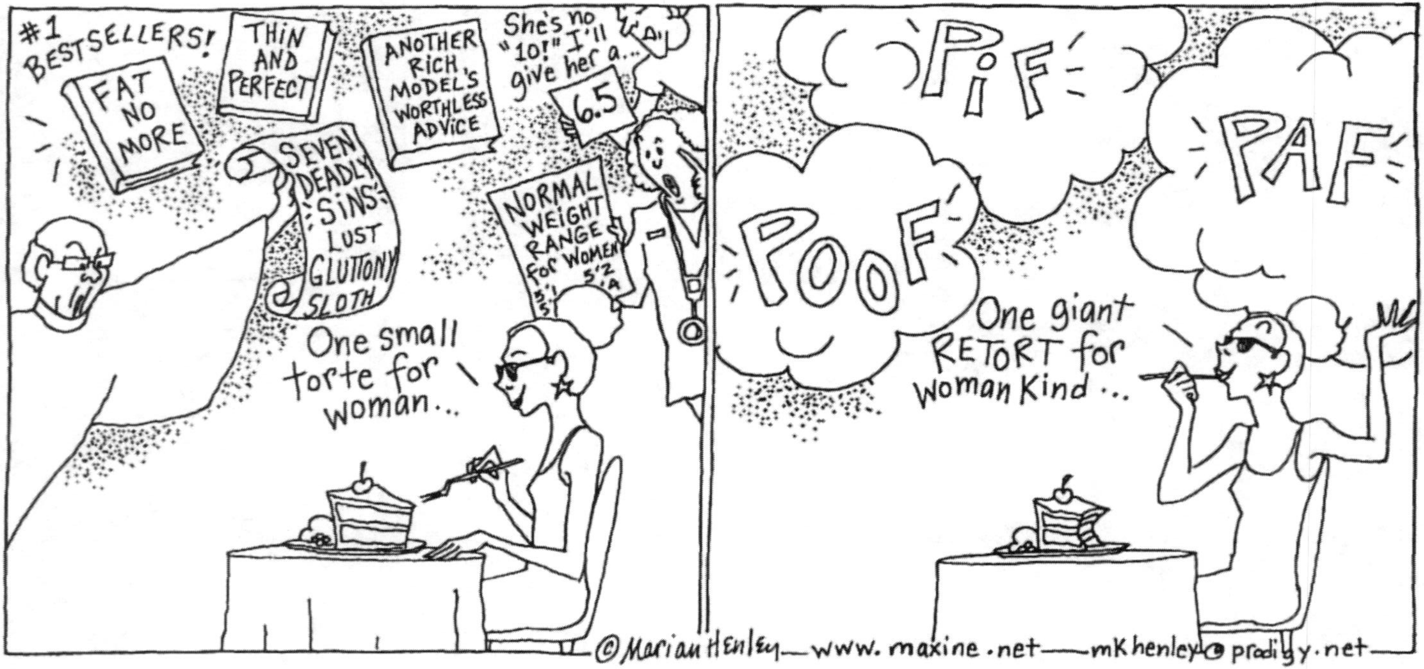
#1 BESTSELLERS!
FAT NO MORE
THIN AND PERFECT
ANOTHER RICH MODEL'S WORTHLESS ADVICE
SEVEN DEADLY SINS: LUST GLUTTONY SLOTH
She's no "10!" I'll give her a...
6.5
NORMAL WEIGHT RANGE FOR WOMEN
One small torte for woman...
PiF
PAF
POOF
One giant RETORT for woman kind...
©Marian Henley—www.maxine.net—mkhenley@prodigy.net

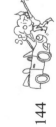

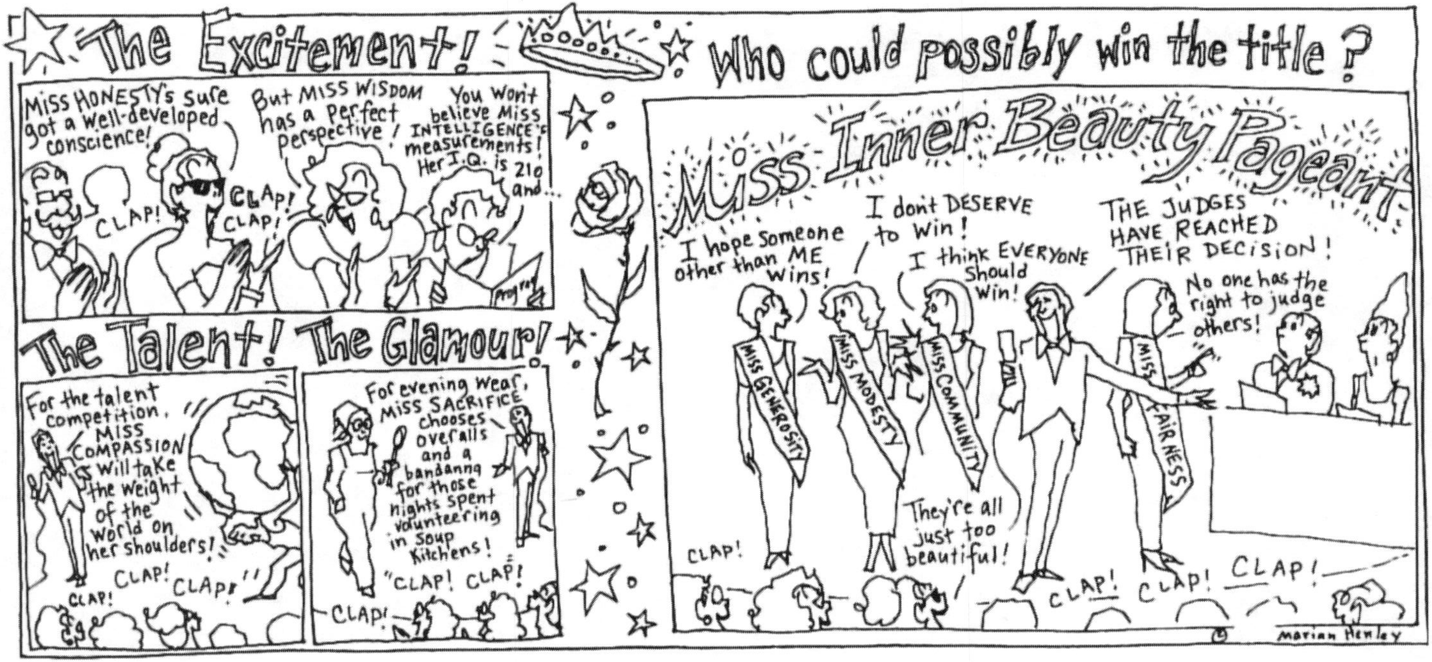
The Excitement!
Who could possibly win the title?
MISS HONESTY's sure got a well-developed conscience!
CLAP!
CLAP! CLAP!
But MISS WISDOM has a perfect perspective!
You won't believe MISS INTELLIGENCE's measurements! Her I.Q. is 210 and...
The Talent! The Glamour!
For the talent competition, MISS COMPASSION will take the weight of the world on her shoulders!
CLAP! CLAP! CLAP!
For evening wear, MISS SACRIFICE chooses overalls and a bandanna for those nights spent volunteering in soup kitchens!
"CLAP! CLAP!
CLAP!
Miss Inner Beauty Pageant
I hope someone other than ME wins!
I don't DESERVE to win!
I think EVERYONE should win!
THE JUDGES HAVE REACHED THEIR DECISION!
No one has the right to judge others!
MISS GENEROSITY
MISS MODESTY
MISS COMMUNITY
MISS FAIRNESS
They're all just too beautiful!
CLAP!
CLAP! CLAP! CLAP!
Marian Henley

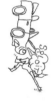

Out and About

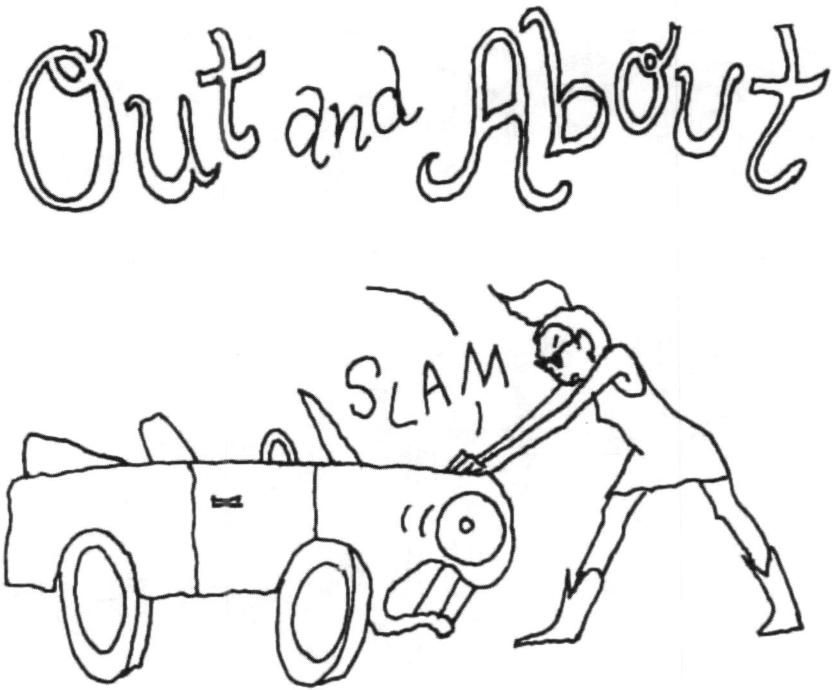
SLAM

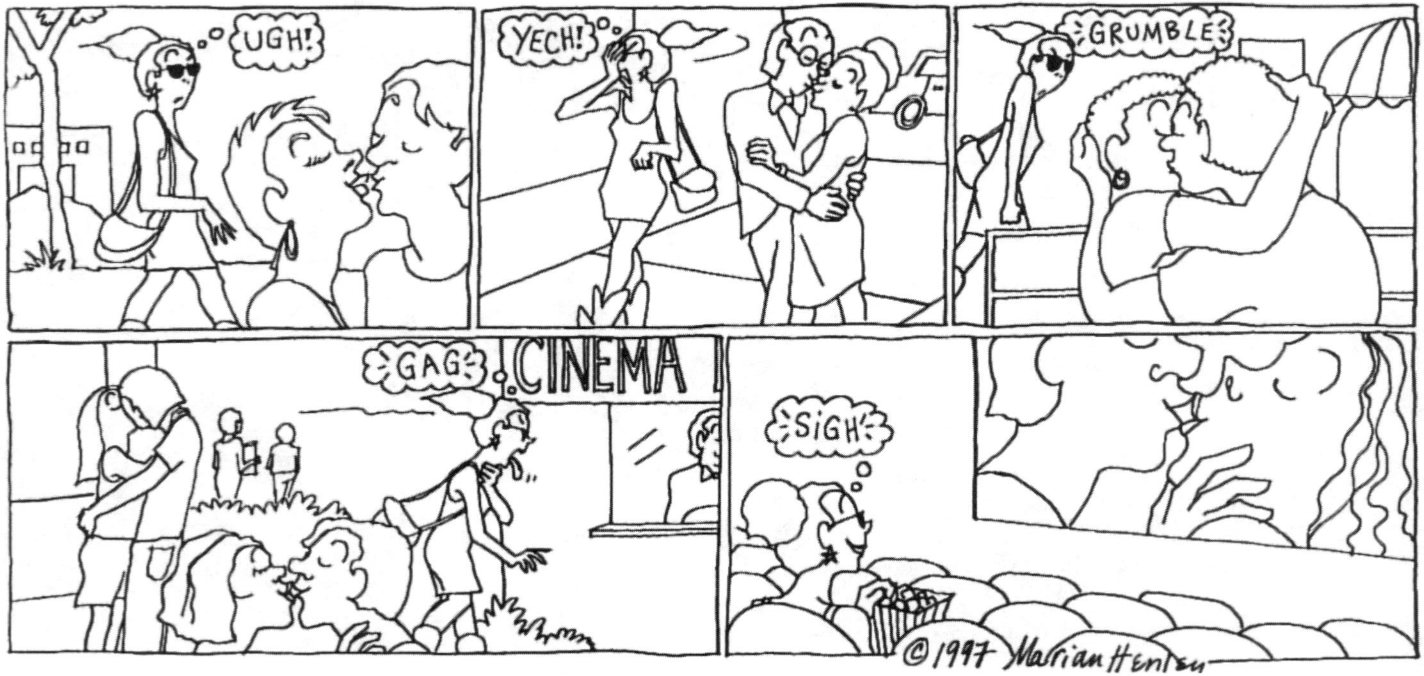
UGH!
YECH!
GRUMBLE
GAG
CINEMA
SIGH
©1997 Marian Henley

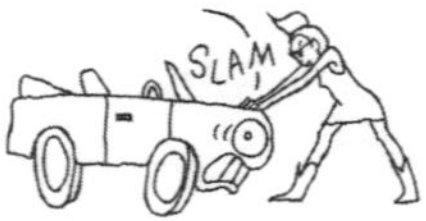
SLAM

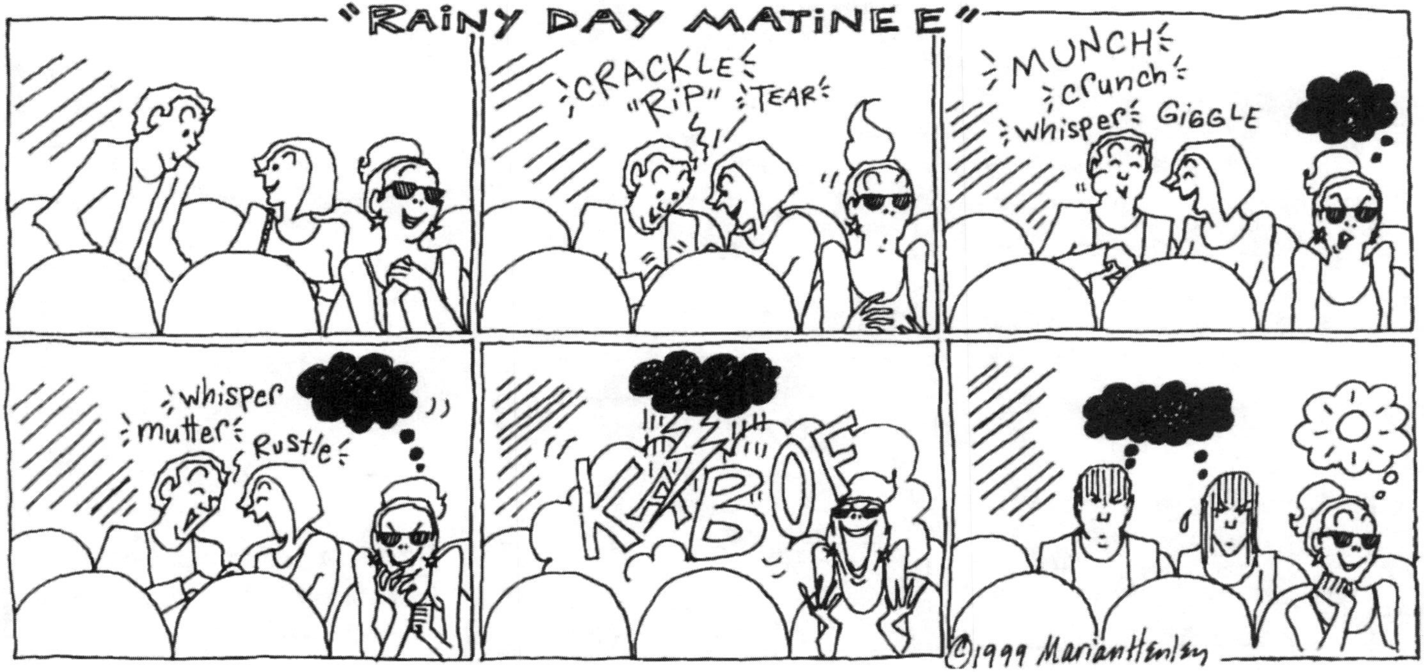
"RAINY DAY MATINEE"
CRACKLE
"RIP"
TEAR
MUNCH
crunch
whisper
GIGGLE
whisper
mutter
Rustle
KABOE
©1999 MarianHenley

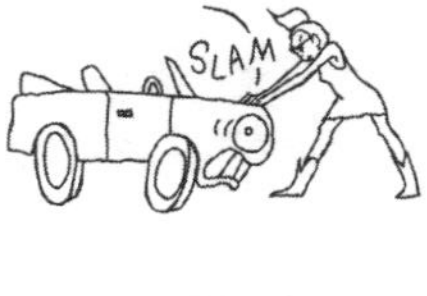
SLAM

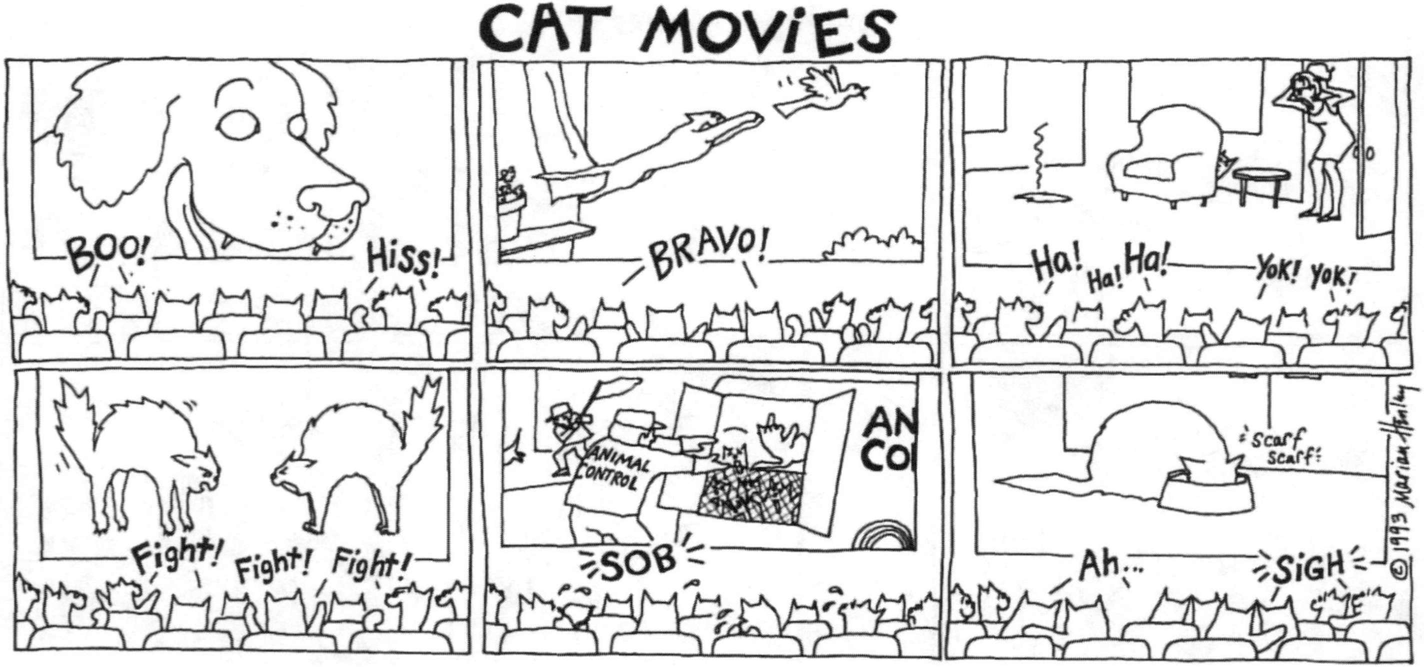
CAT MOViES
BOO!
HiSS!
BRAVO!
Ha! Ha! Ha!
YOK! YOK!
Fight! Fight! Fight!
ANIMAL CONTROL
AN CO
SOB
Scarf scarf
Ah...
SiGH
© 1993 Marian Henley

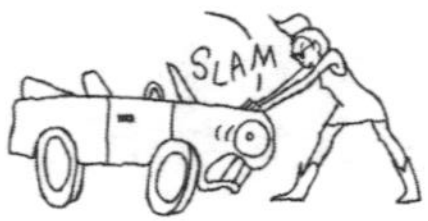
SLAM

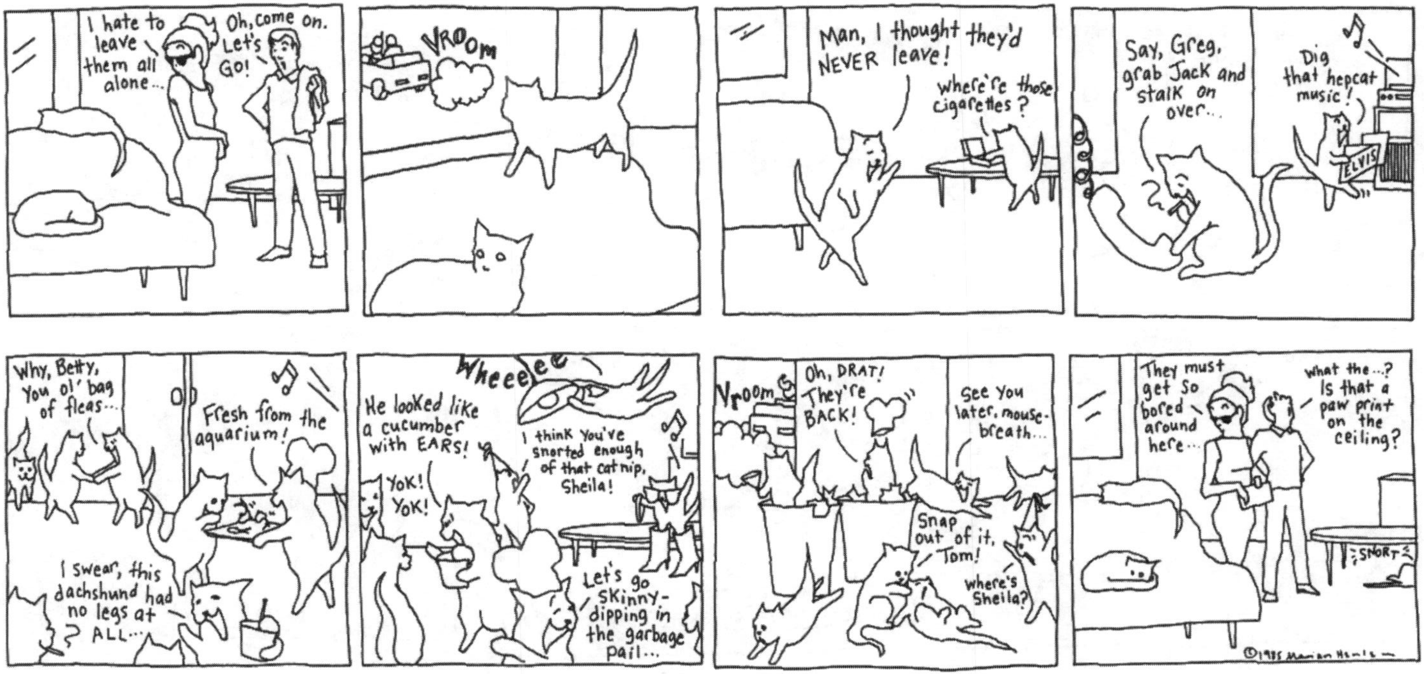
I hate to leave them all alone...
Oh, come on. Let's GO!
VROOM
Man, I thought they'd NEVER leave!
Where're those cigarettes?
Say, Greg, grab Jack and stalk on over...
Dig that hepcat music!
ELVIS
Why, Betty, You ol' bag of fleas...
Fresh from the aquarium!
I swear, this dachshund had no legs at ALL...
Wheeeeee
He looked like a cucumber with EARS!
YOK! YOK!
I think You've snorted enough of that catnip, Sheila!
Let's go SKinny-dipping in the garbage pail...
Vroom
Oh, DRAT! They're BACK!
See You later, mouse-breath...
Snap out of it, Tom!
Where's Sheila?
They must get so bored around here...
What the...? Is that a paw print on the ceiling?
SNORT
©1985 Marian Henley

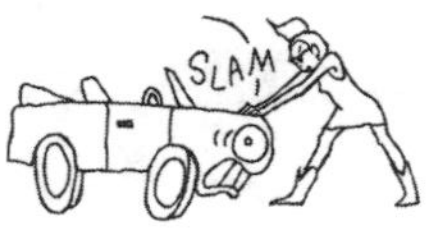
SLAM

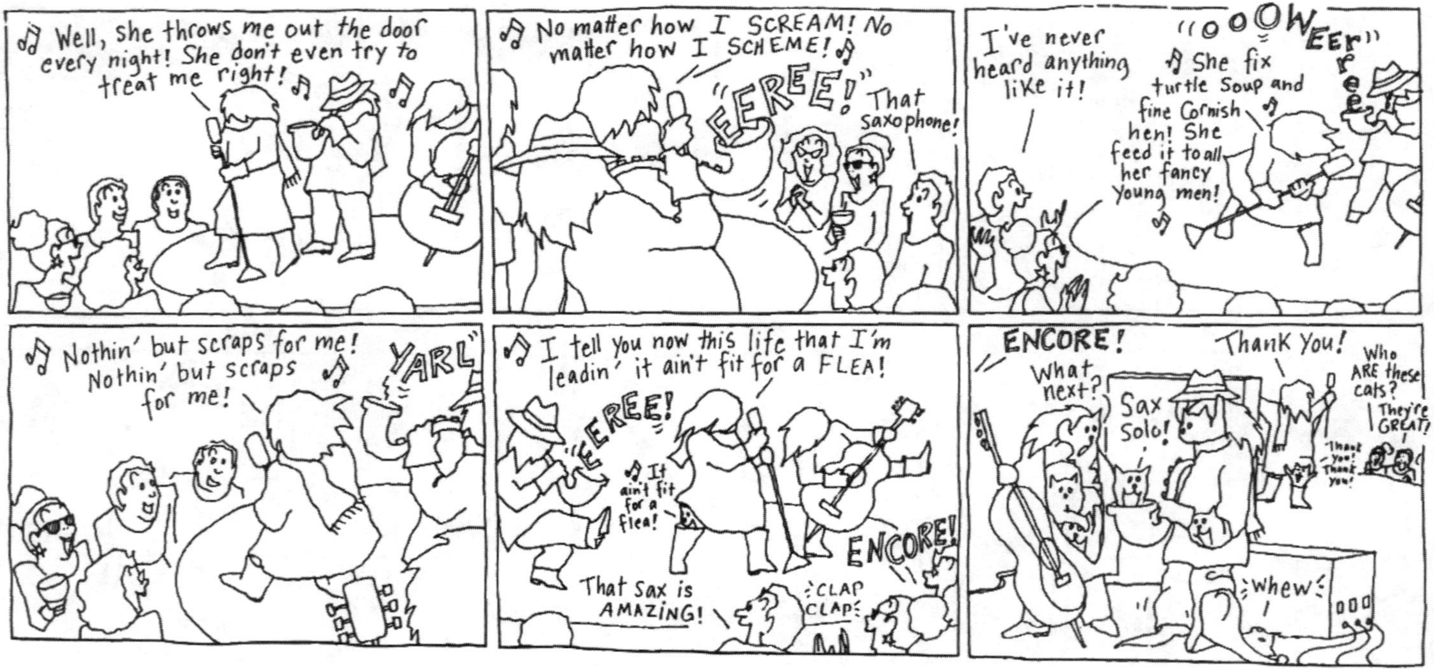
Well, she throws me out the door every night! She don't even try to treat me right!
No matter how I SCREAM! No matter how I SCHEME!
"EEREE!"
That saxophone!
I've never heard anything like it!
"OOOOWEEreee"
She fix turtle Soup and fine Cornish hen! She feed it to all her fancy young men!
Nothin' but scraps for me! Nothin' but scraps for me!
"YARL"
I tell you now this life that I'm leadin' it ain't fit for a FLEA!
"EEREE!"
It ain't fit for a flea!
That Sax is AMAZING!
CLAP CLAP
ENCORE!
ENCORE!
What next?
Sax Solo!
Thank You!
Who ARE these cats?
They're GREAT!
Whew!

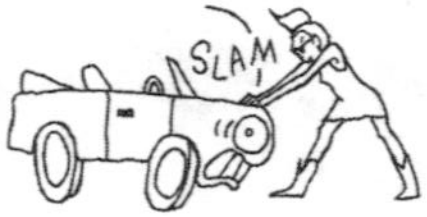
SLAM

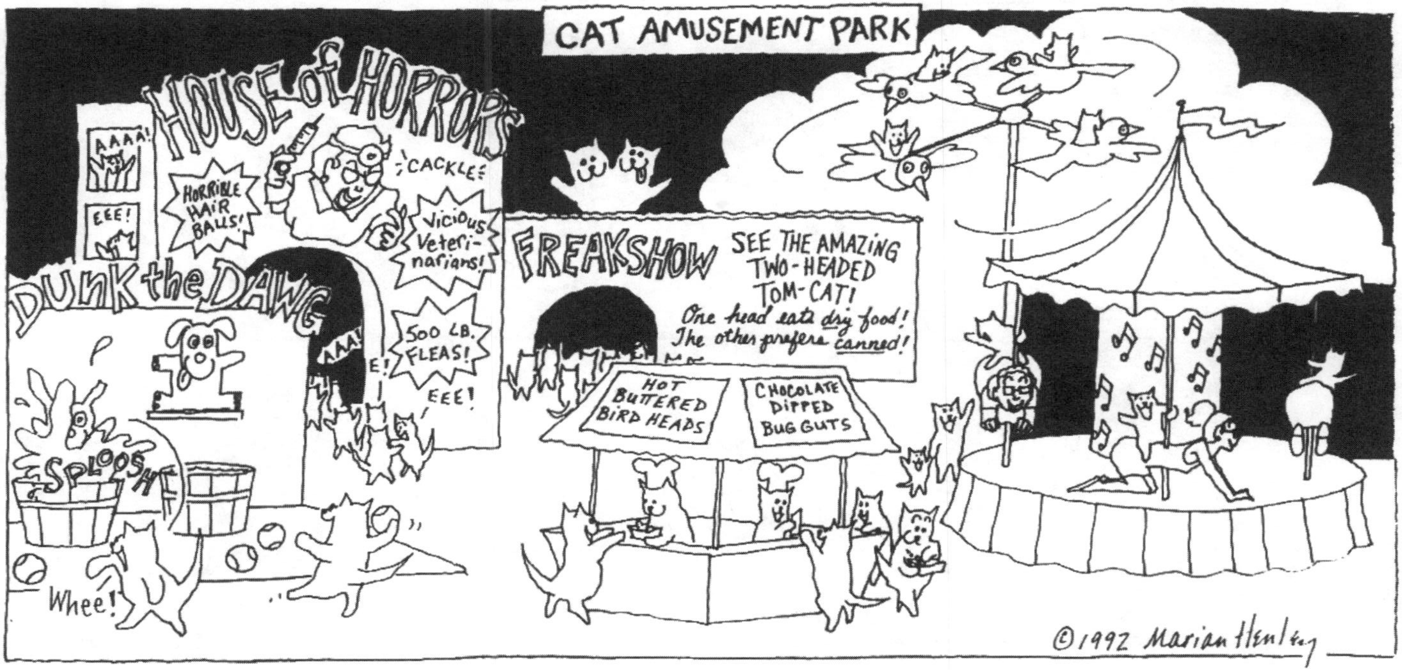
CAT AMUSEMENT PARK
HOUSE of HORRORS
AAAA!
EEE!
HORRIBLE HAIR BALLS!
CACKLE
Vicious Veterinarians!
500 LB. FLEAS!
AAA!
E!
EEE!
DUNK the DAWG
SPLOOSH
Whee!
FREAKSHOW
SEE THE AMAZING TWO-HEADED TOM-CAT!
One head eats dry food! The other prefers canned!
HOT BUTTERED BIRD HEADS
CHOCOLATE DIPPED BUG GUTS
©1992 Marian Henley

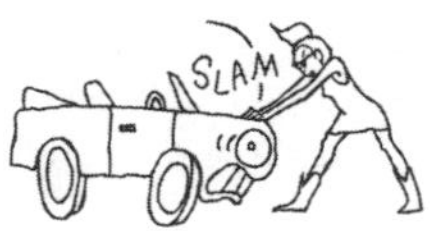
SLAM

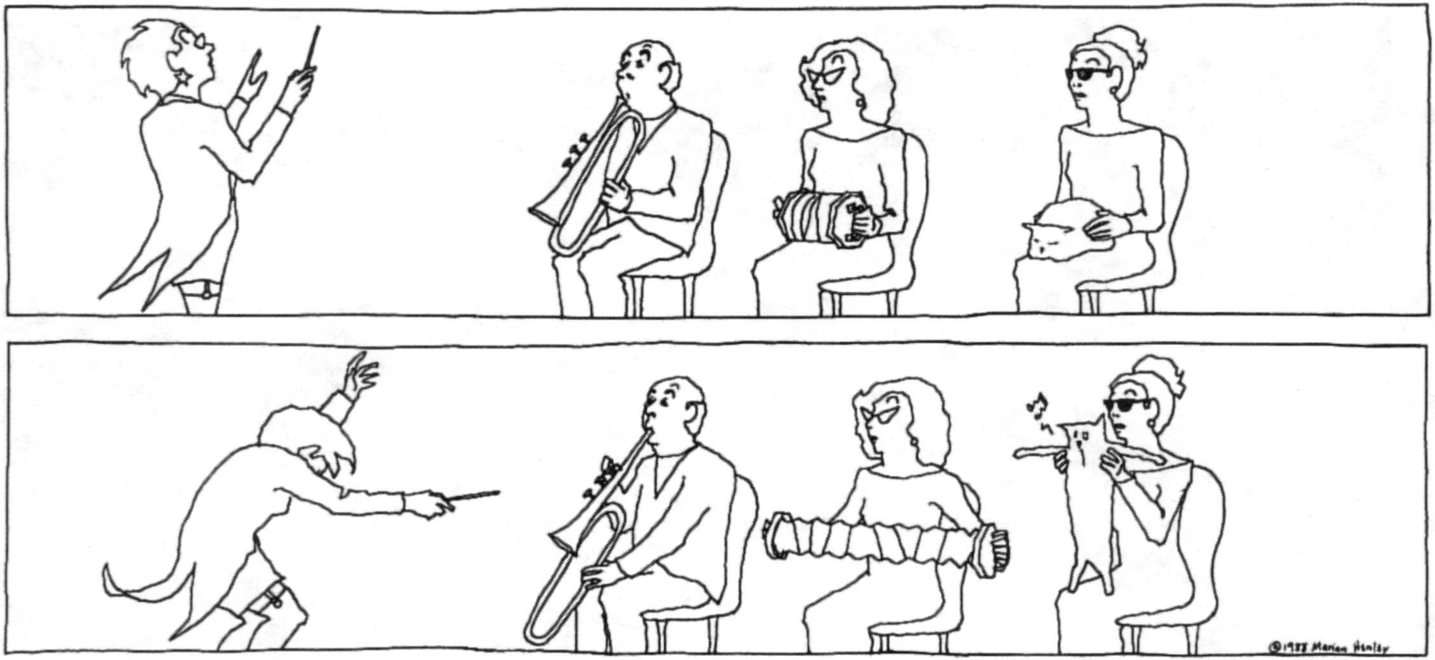
©1988 Marian Henley

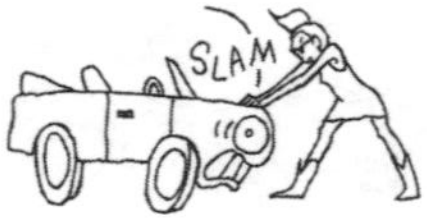
SLAM!

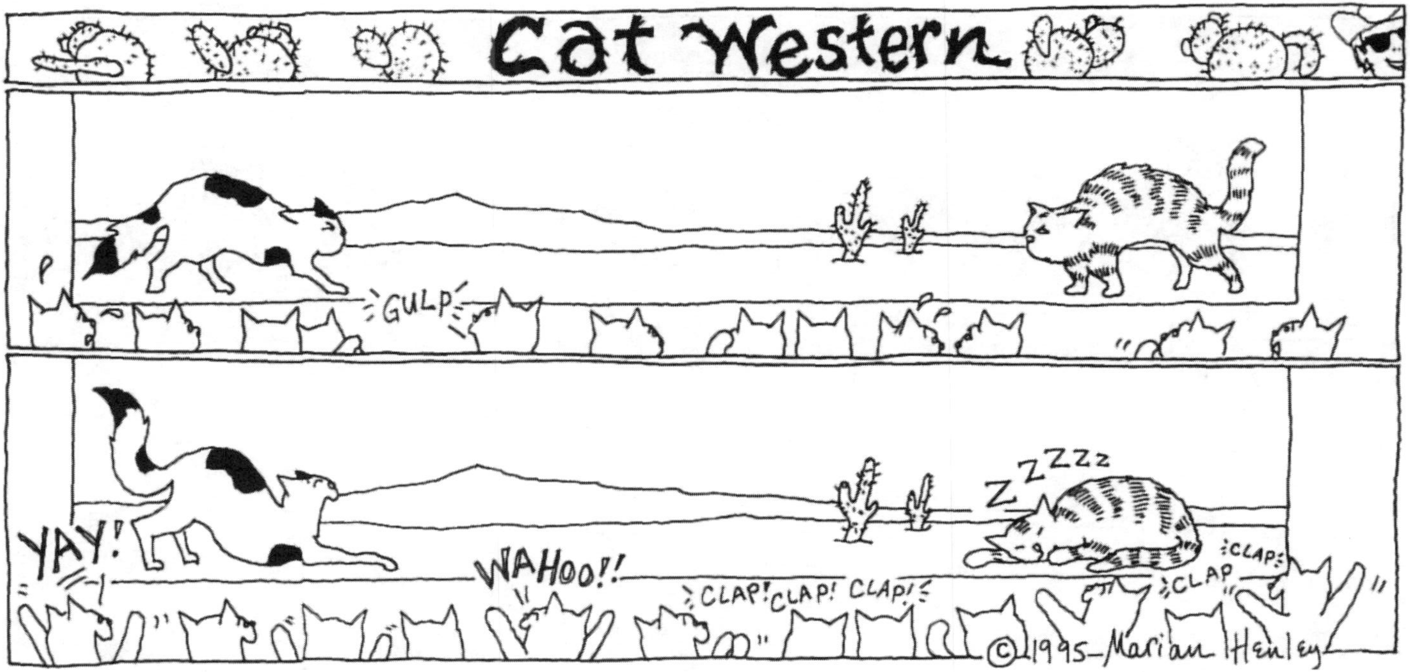
Cat Western
GULP
YAY!
WAHOO!!
CLAP! CLAP! CLAP!
CLAP
CLAP
Z Z Z Z z
© 1995–Marian Henley

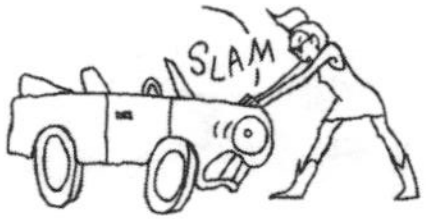
SLAM

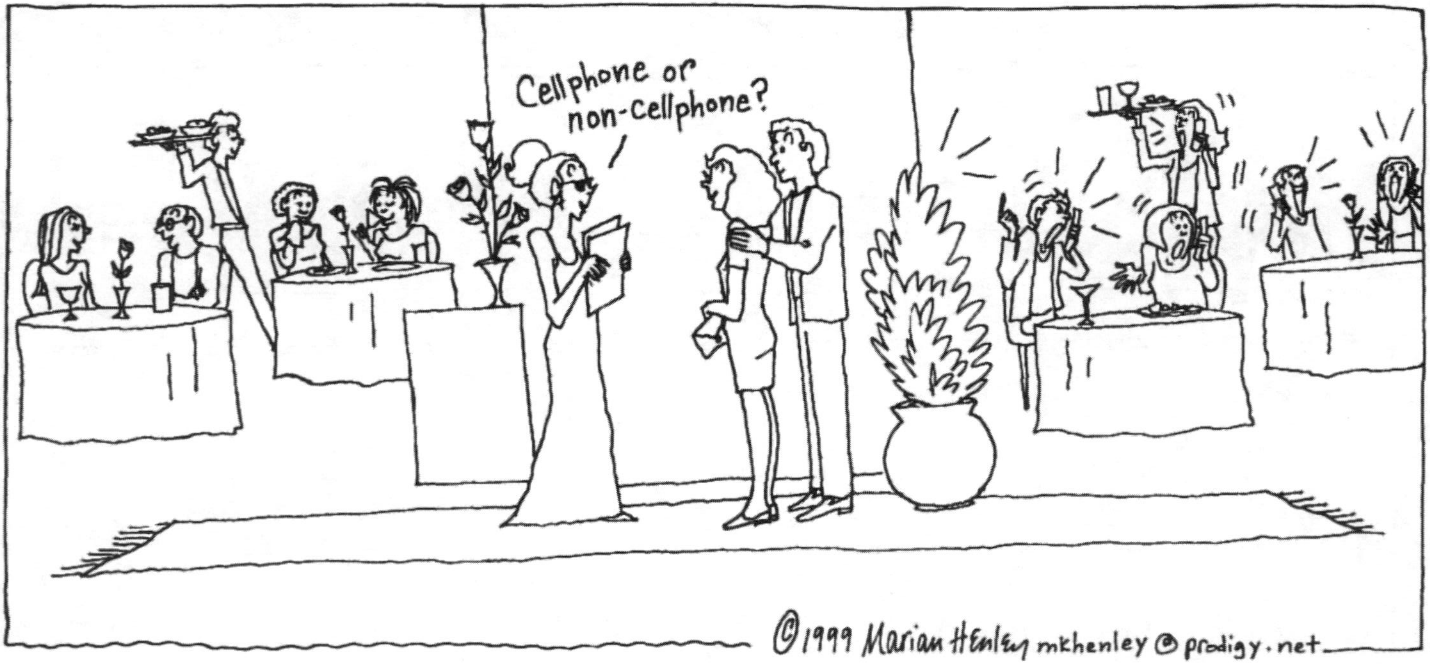
Cellphone or non-cellphone?
©1999 Marian Henley mkhenley@prodigy.net

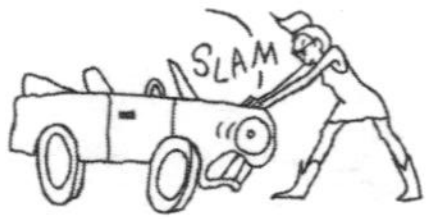
SLAM

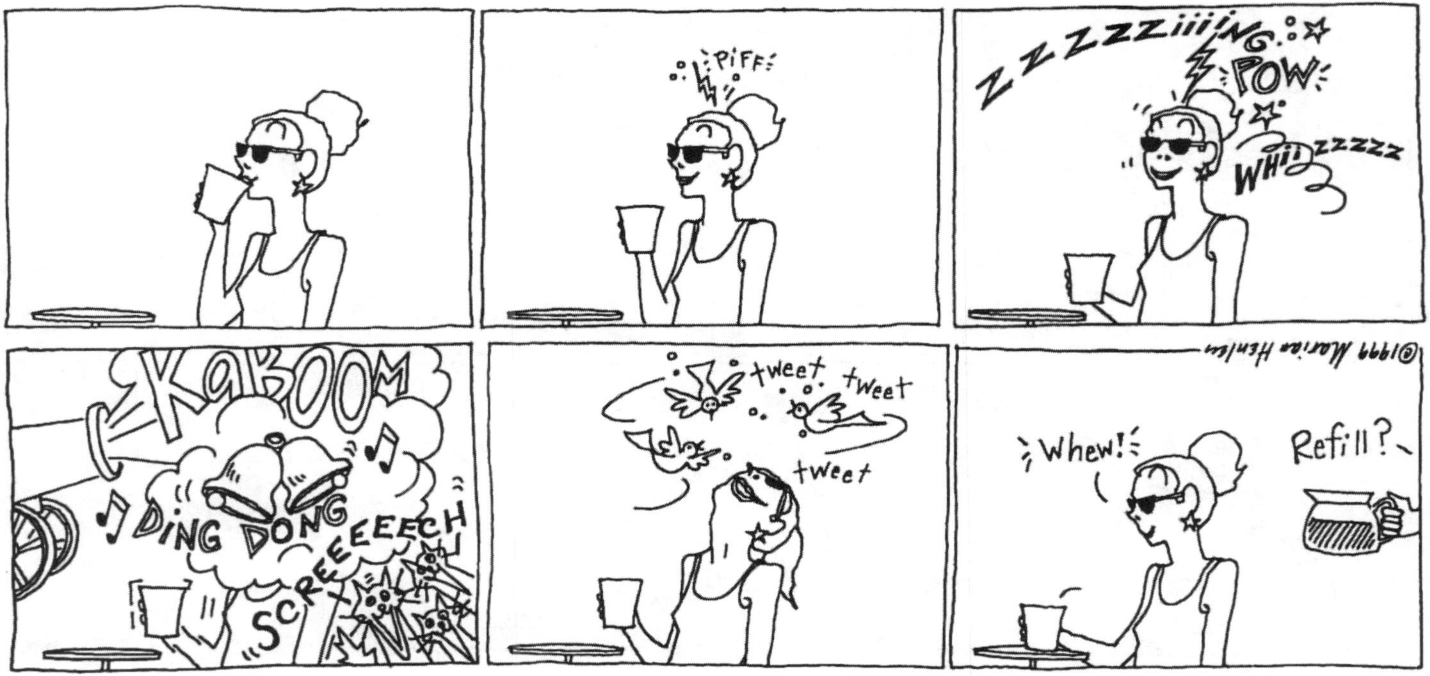
PIFF
ZZZZZZiiiiiNG
POW
WHIIZZZZZ
KABOOM
DING DONG
SCREEEEEECH
tweet
tweet
tweet
Whew!
Refill?
©1999 Marian Henley

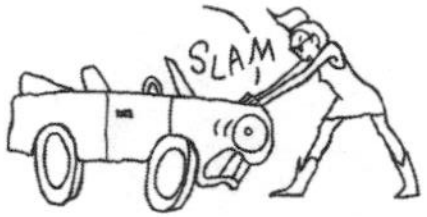
SLAM

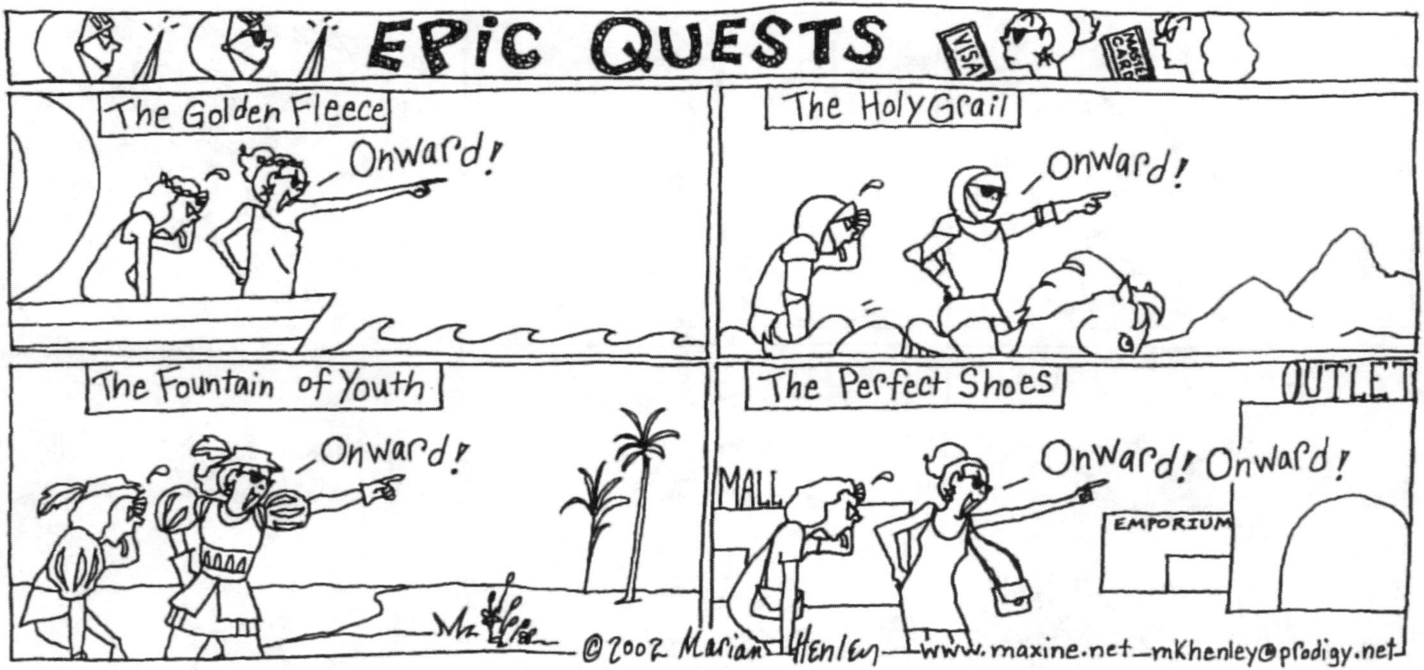
EPIC QUESTS
VISA
MASTERCARD
The Golden Fleece
Onward!
The Holy Grail
Onward!
The Fountain of Youth
Onward!
The Perfect Shoes
MALL
Onward! Onward!
EMPORIUM
OUTLET
©2002 Marian Henley www.maxine.net mKhenley@prodigy.net

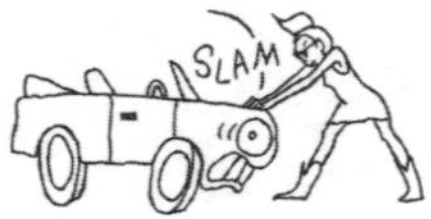
SLAM

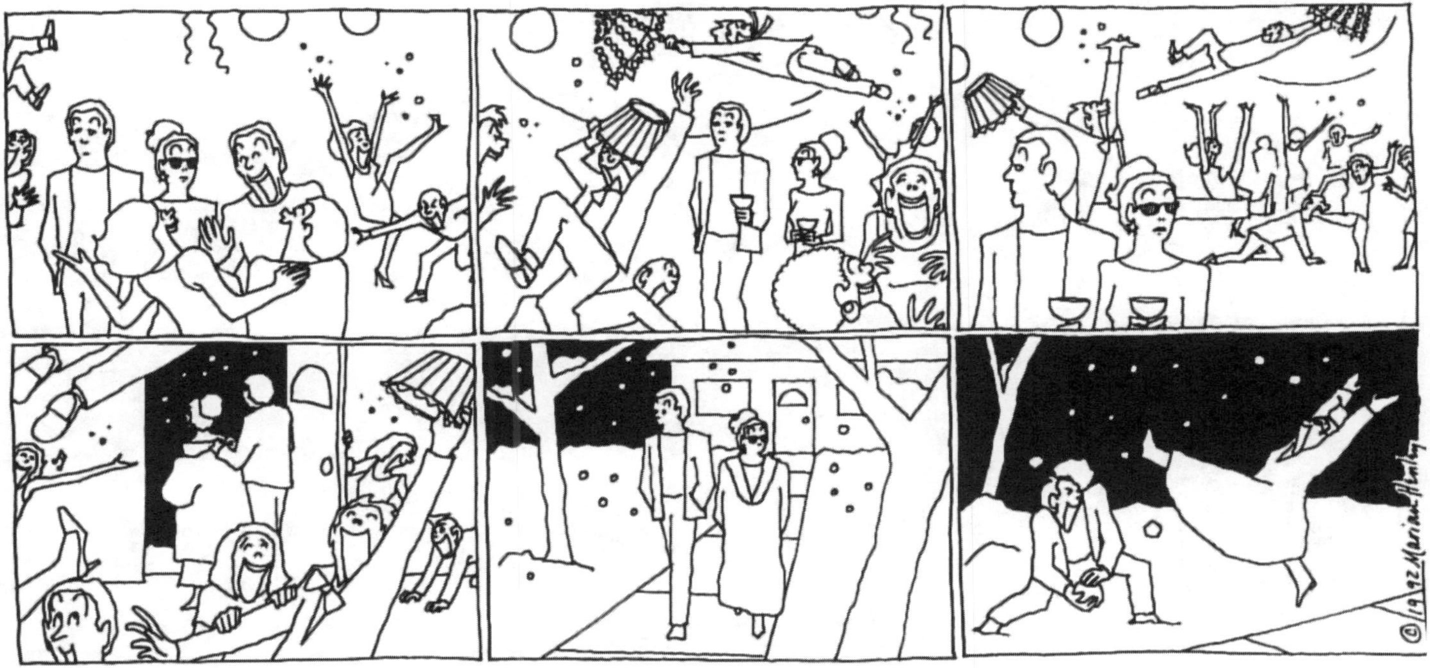
© 1992 Marian Henley

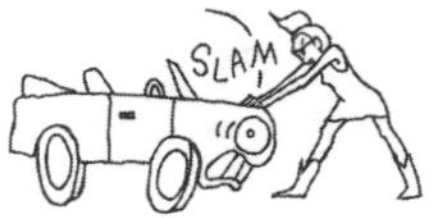
SLAM

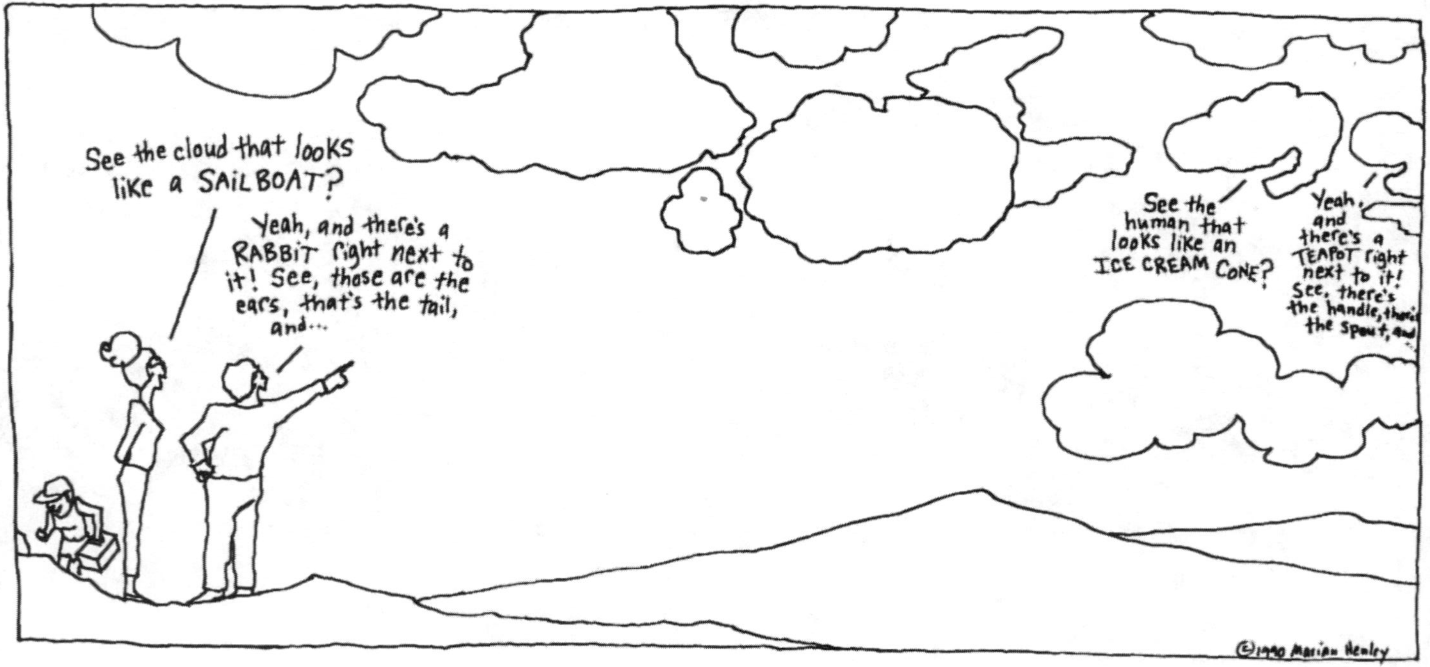
See the cloud that looks like a SAILBOAT?
Yeah, and there's a RABBIT right next to it! See, those are the ears, that's the tail, and...
See the human that looks like an ICE CREAM CONE?
Yeah, and there's a TEAPOT right next to it! See, there's the handle, there's the spout, and
©1990 Marian Henley

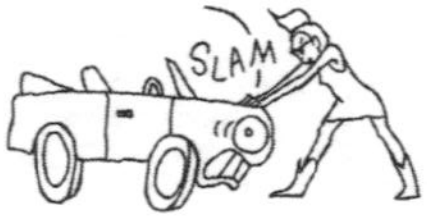
SLAM

Home

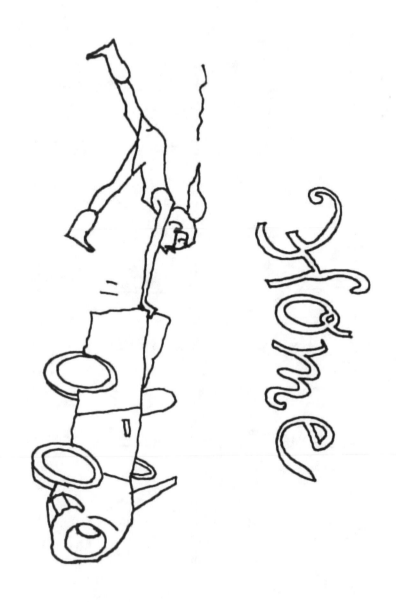

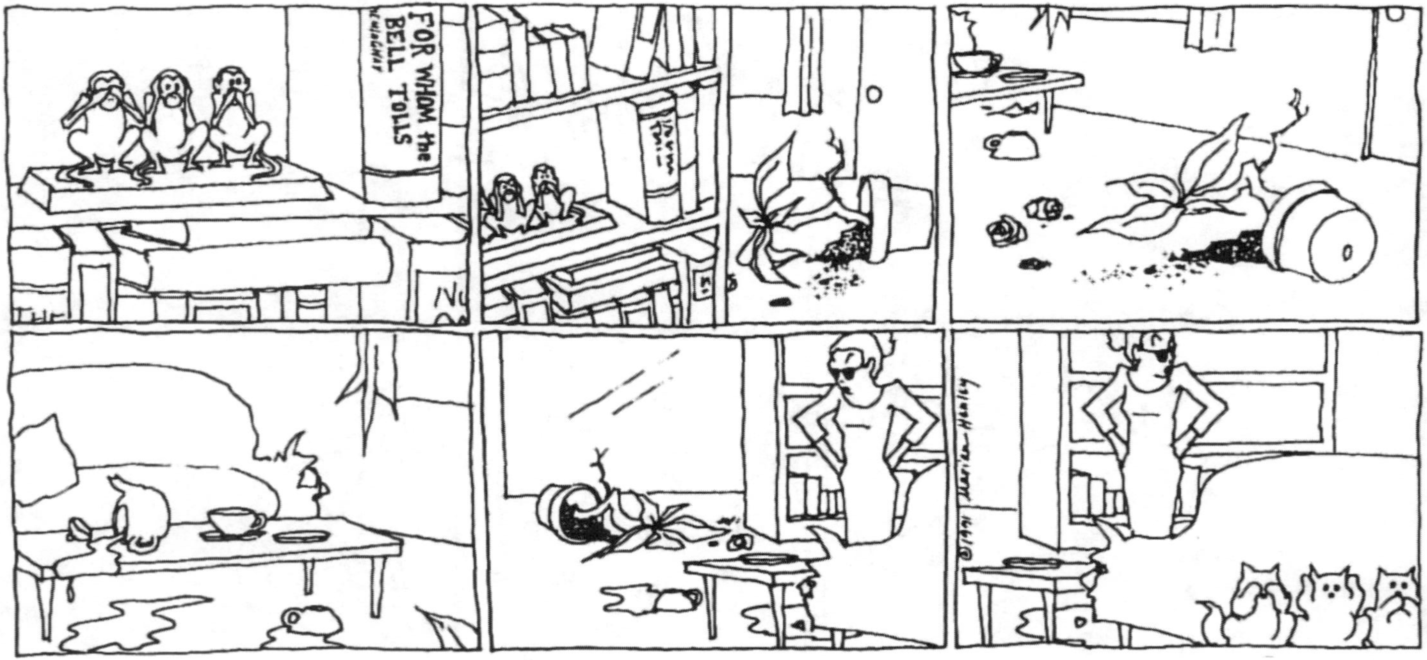
FOR WHOM the BELL TOLLS

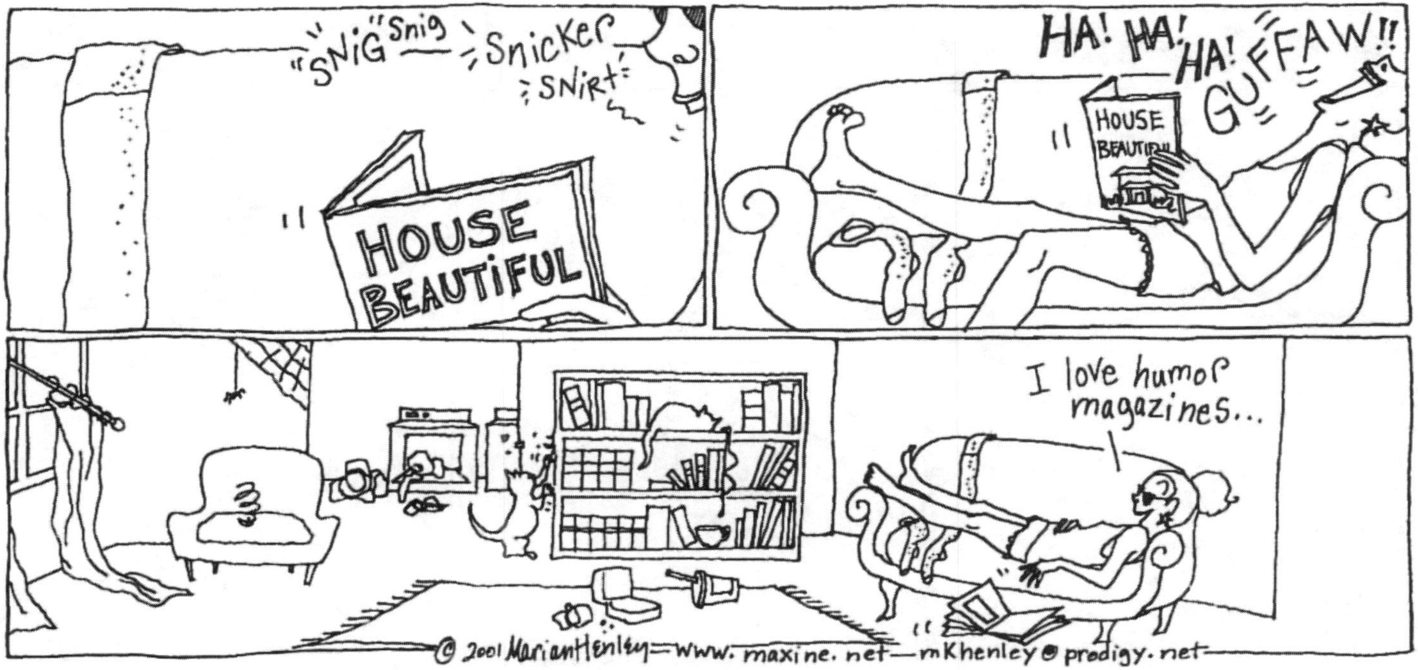
"SNIG "Snig — Snicker
SNIRT
HOUSE BEAUTIFUL
HA! HA! HA! GUFFAW!!
HOUSE BEAUTIFUL
I love humor magazines...
© 2001 MarianHenley—www.maxine.net—mKhenley@prodigy.net

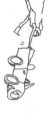

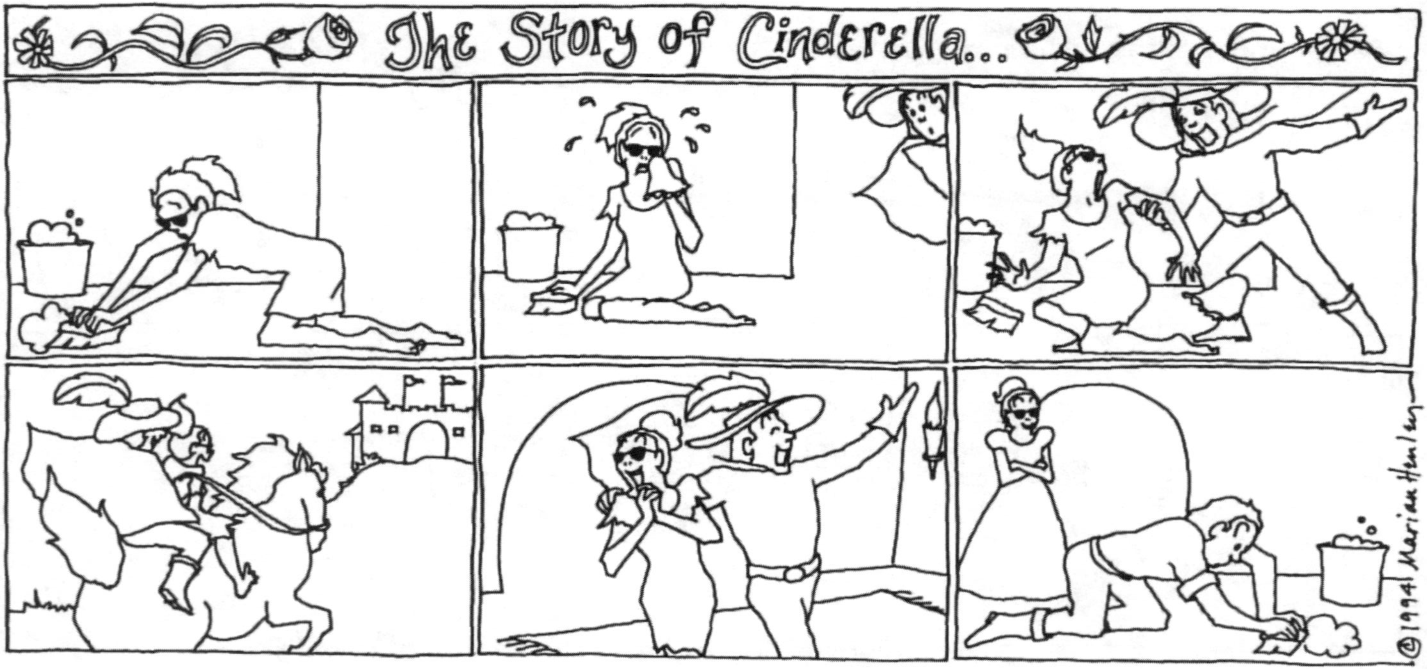
The Story of Cinderella...
©1994 Marian Henley

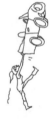

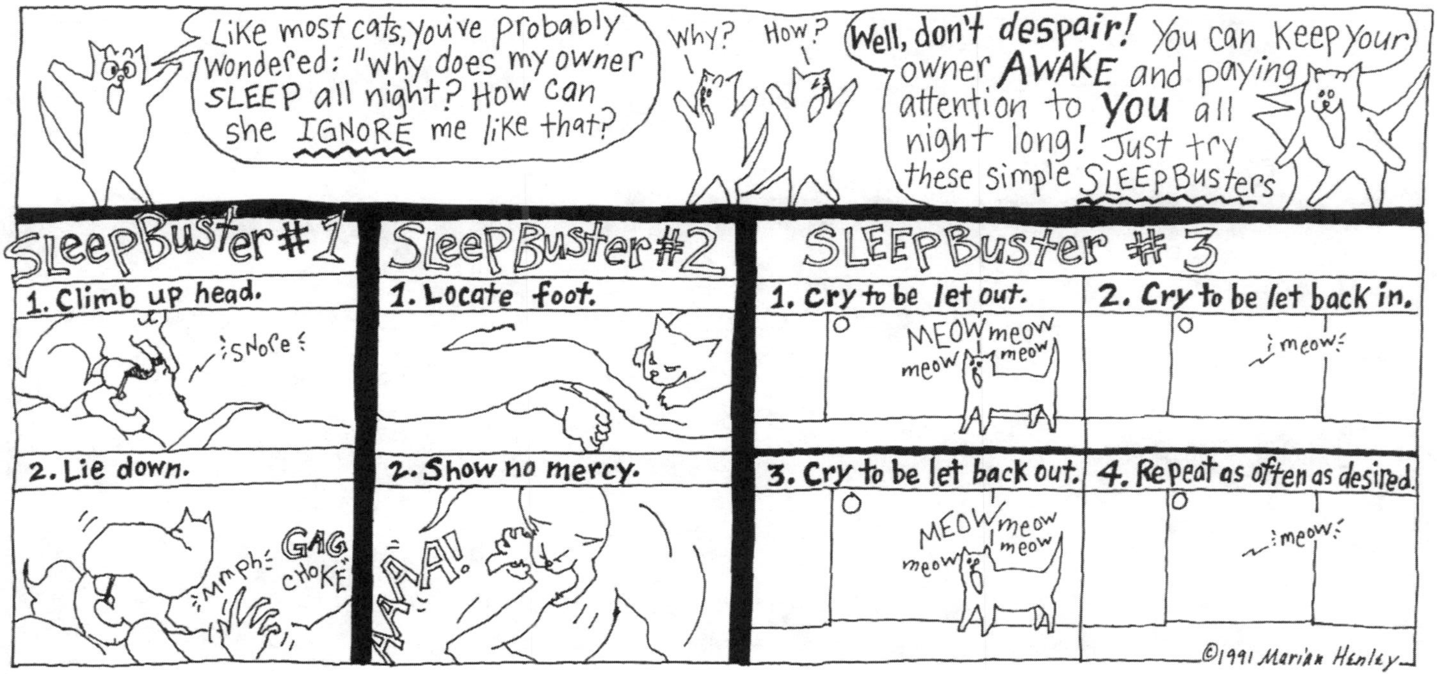
Like most cats, you've probably wondered: "Why does my owner SLEEP all night? How can she IGNORE me like that?
Why?
How?
Well, don't despair! You can keep your owner AWAKE and paying attention to YOU all night long! Just try these simple SLEEPBusters
SleepBuster #1
1. Climb up head.
snore
2. Lie down.
mmph
GAG
CHOKE
SleepBuster #2
1. Locate foot.
2. Show no mercy.
AAAA!
SLEEPBuster #3
1. Cry to be let out.
MEOW meow
meow
meow
2. Cry to be let back in.
meow
3. Cry to be let back out.
MEOW meow
meow
meow
4. Repeat as often as desired.
meow
©1991 Marian Henley

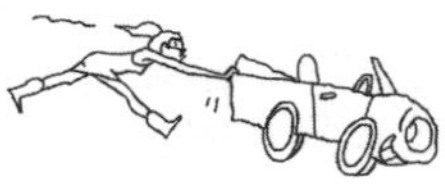

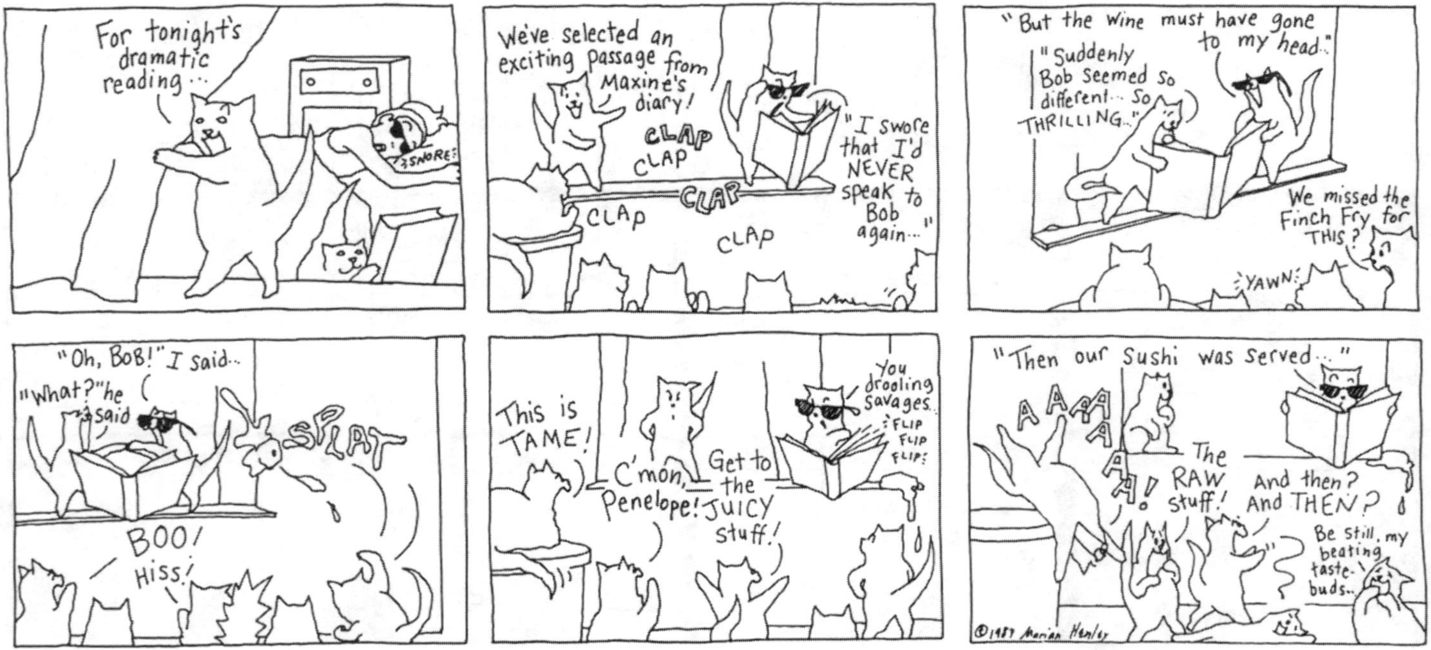
For tonight's dramatic reading...
SNORE
We've selected an exciting passage from Maxine's diary!
CLAP
CLAP
CLAP
CLAP
CLAP
"I swore that I'd NEVER speak to Bob again..."
"But the wine must have gone to my head."
"Suddenly Bob seemed so different... So THRILLING..."
We missed the Finch Fry for THIS?
YAWN
"Oh, BOB!" I said...
"What?" he said
SPLAT
BOO!
HISS!
This is TAME!
C'mon, Penelope!
Get to the JUICY stuff!
You drooling savages...
FLIP
FLIP
FLIP
"Then our Sushi was served..."
AAAAAA!
The RAW stuff!
And then? And THEN?
Be still, my beating taste-buds...
©1987 Marian Henley

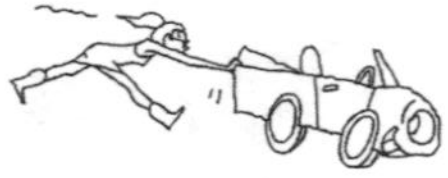

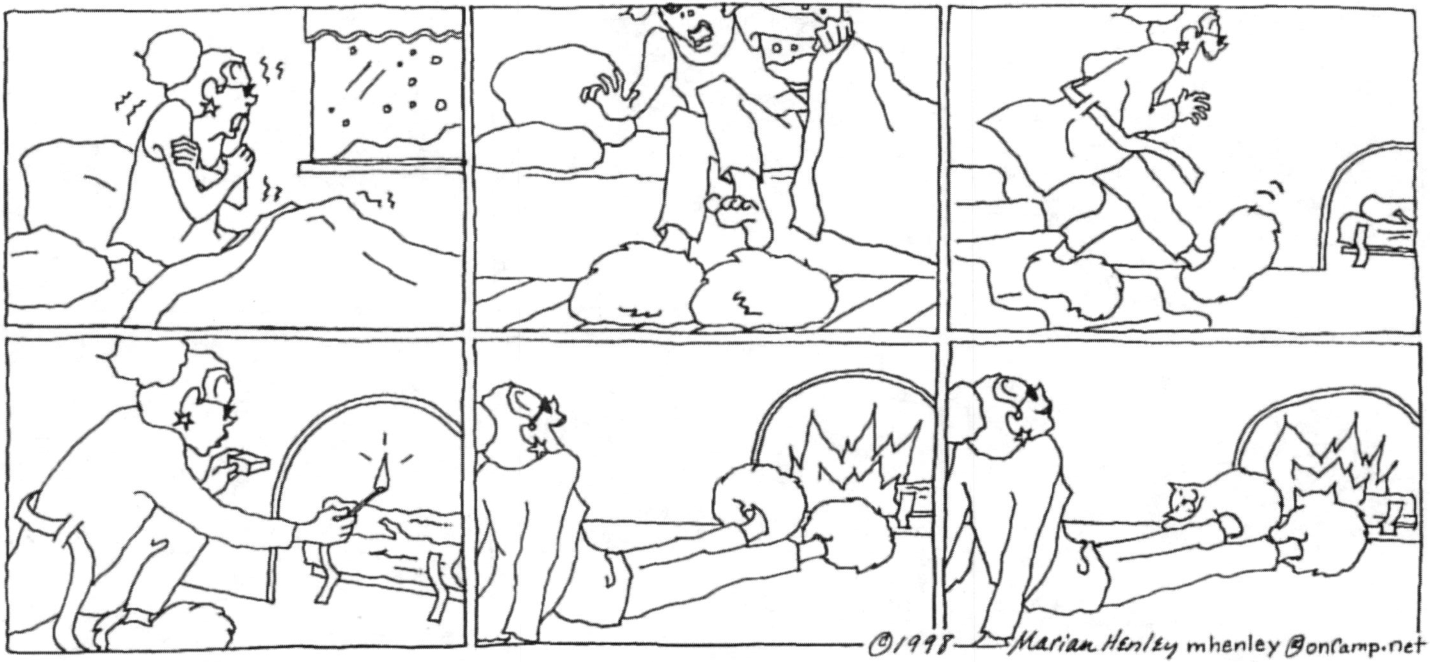
©1998 Marian Henley mhenley@onramp.net

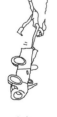

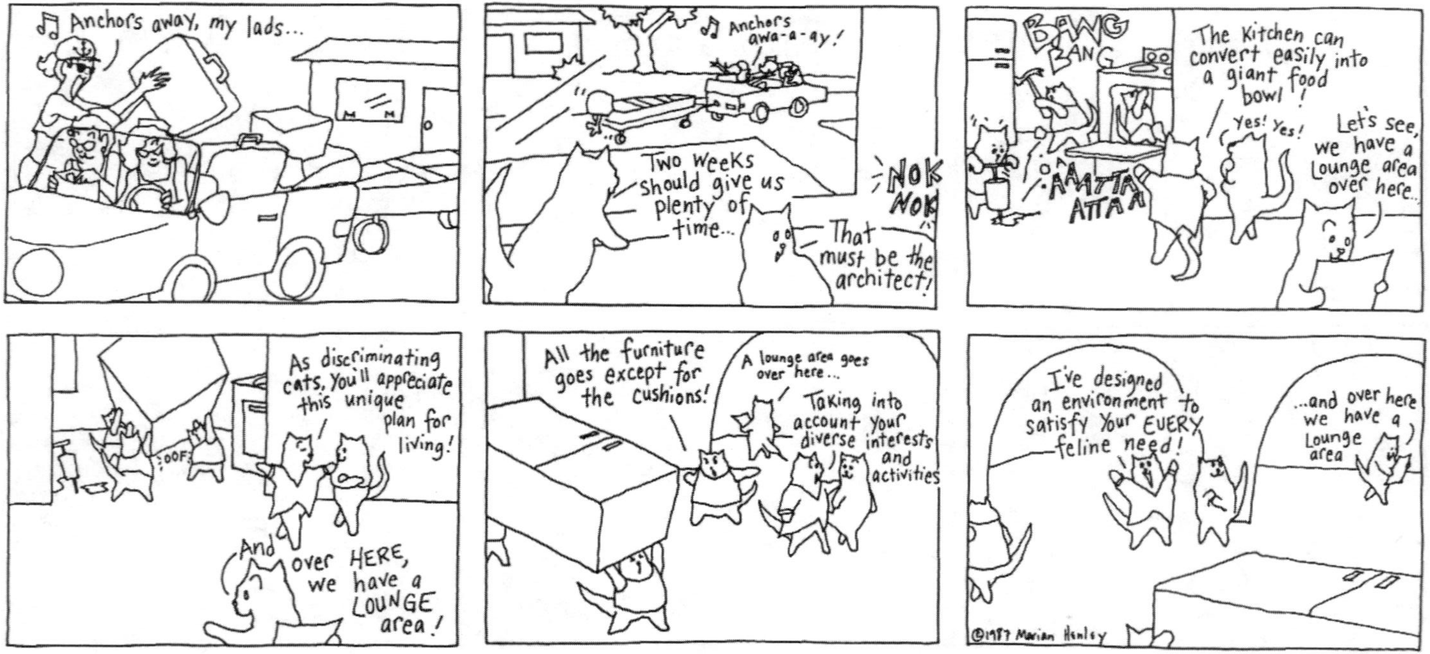
Anchors away, my lads...
Anchors awa-a-ay!
Two weeks should give us plenty of time...
NOK NOK
That must be the architect!
BAWG BANG
AAATTA ATTA
The kitchen can convert easily into a giant food bowl!
Yes! Yes!
Let's see, we have a lounge area over here...
OOF
As discriminating cats, you'll appreciate this unique plan for living!
And over HERE, we have a LOUNGE area!
All the furniture goes except for the cushions!
A lounge area goes over here...
Taking into account your diverse interests and activities
I've designed an environment to satisfy your EVERY feline need!
...and over here we have a lounge area
©1987 Marian Henley

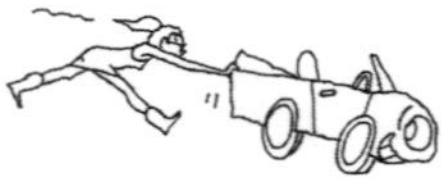

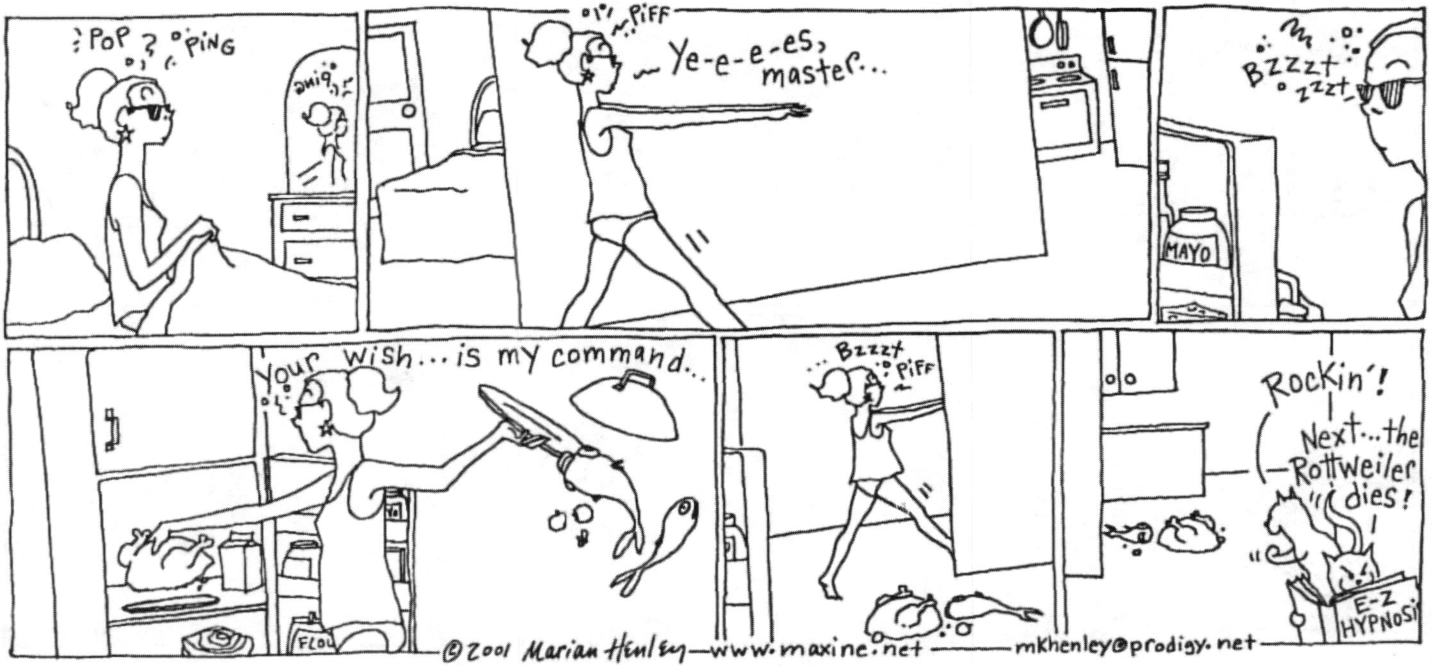
POP
PING
Ye-e-e-es, master...
PIFF
BZZZT
ZZZT
MAYO
Your wish... is my command...
Bzzzt
PIFF
Rockin'!
Next...the Rottweiler dies!
E-Z HYPNOSI
©2001 Marian Henley—www.maxine.net——mkhenley@prodigy.net

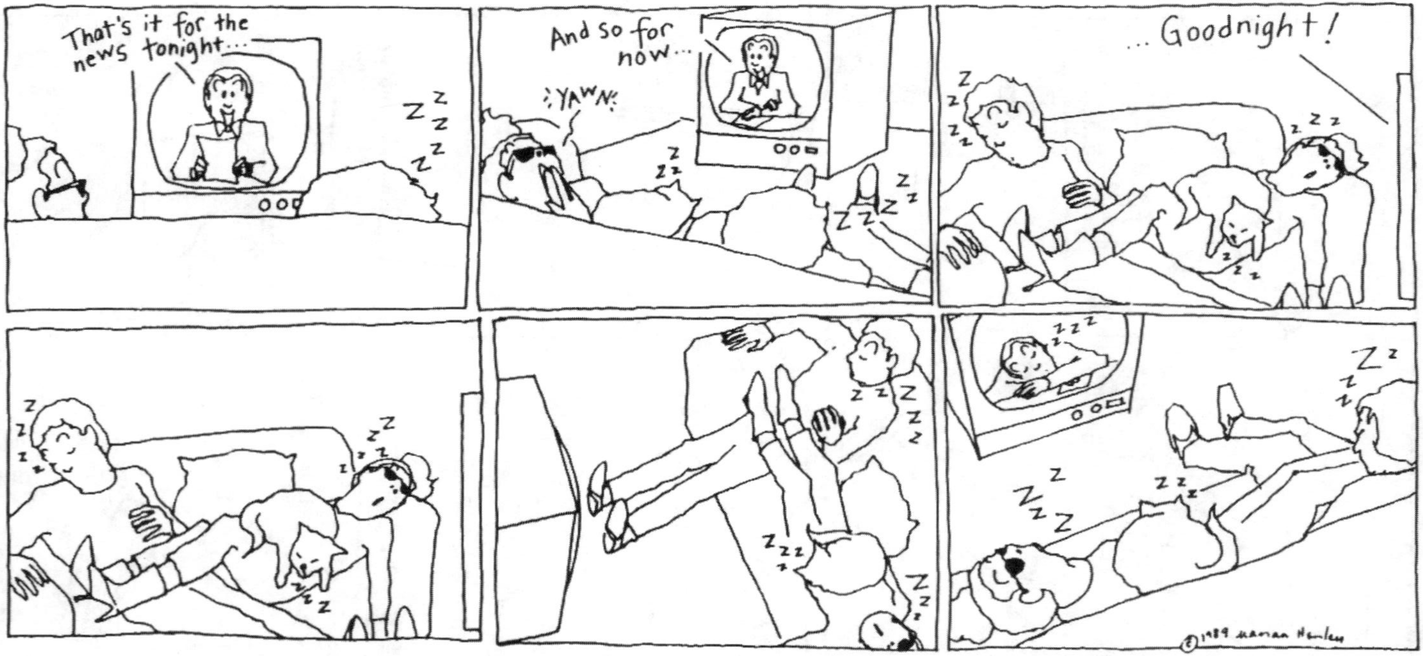
That's it for the news tonight...
And so for now...
YAWN
... Goodnight!
©1989 Marian Henley

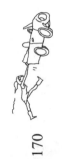

Work and Money

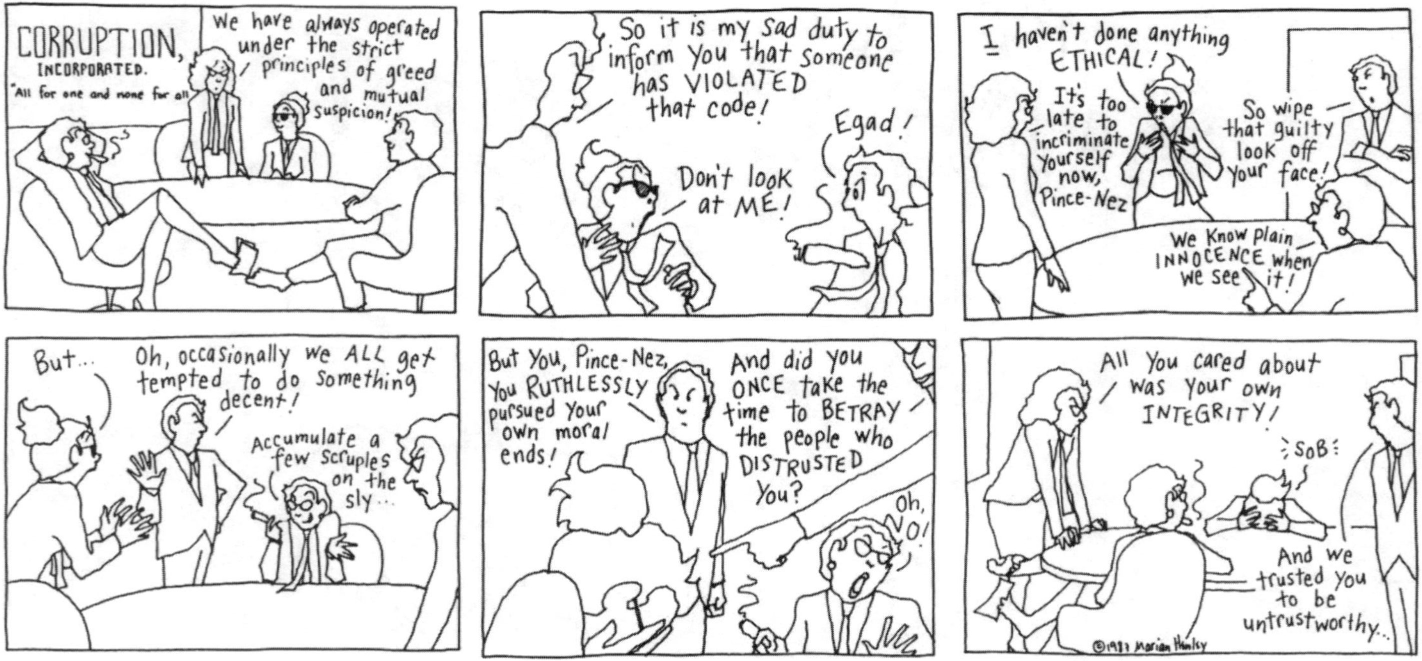
CORRUPTION, INCORPORATED.
"All for one and none for all"
We have always operated under the strict principles of greed and mutual suspicion!
So it is my sad duty to inform you that someone has VIOLATED that code!
Don't look at ME!
Egad!
I haven't done anything ETHICAL!
It's too late to incriminate yourself now, Pince-Nez
So wipe that guilty look off your face!
We know plain INNOCENCE when we see it!
But...
Oh, occasionally we ALL get tempted to do something decent!
Accumulate a few scruples on the sly...
But you, Pince-Nez, you RUTHLESSLY pursued your own moral ends!
And did you ONCE take the time to BETRAY the people who DISTRUSTED you?
Oh, NO!
All you cared about was your own INTEGRITY!
SOB
And we trusted you to be untrustworthy...
©1987 Marian Henley

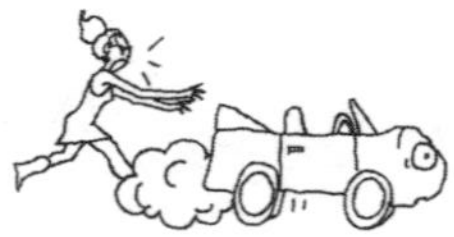

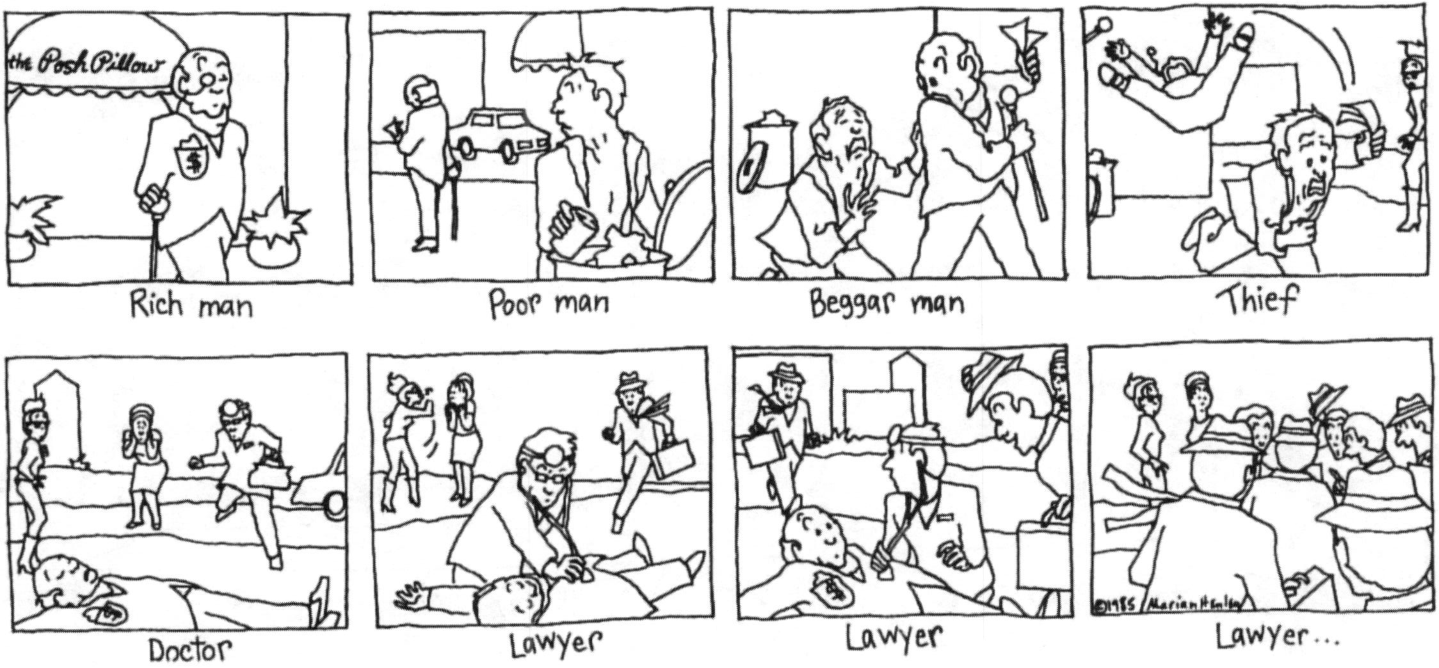
the Posh Pillow
Rich man
Poor man
Beggar man
Thief
Doctor
Lawyer
Lawyer
©1985 Marian Henley
Lawyer...

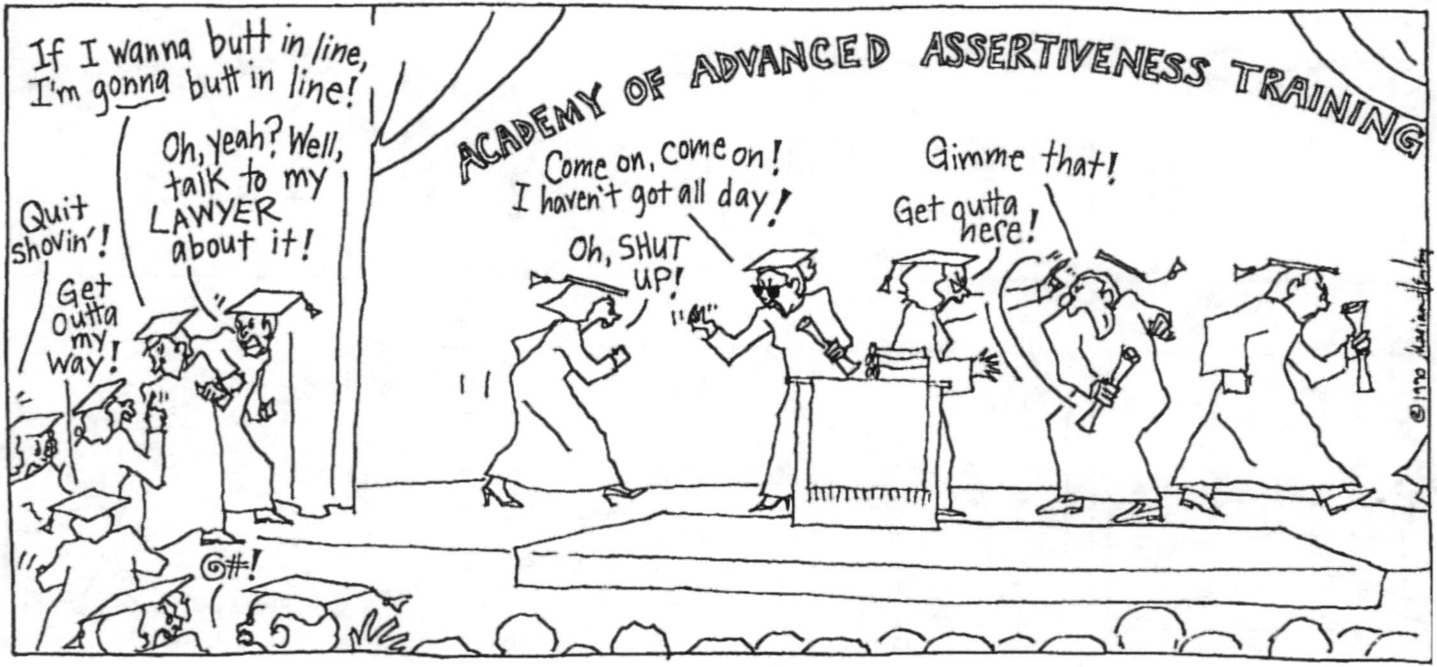
If I wanna butt in line, I'm gonna butt in line!
Oh, yeah? Well, talk to my LAWYER about it!
Quit shovin'!
Get outta my way!
G#!
ACADEMY OF ADVANCED ASSERTIVENESS TRAINING
Come on, come on! I haven't got all day!
Oh, SHUT UP!
Gimme that!
Get outta here!

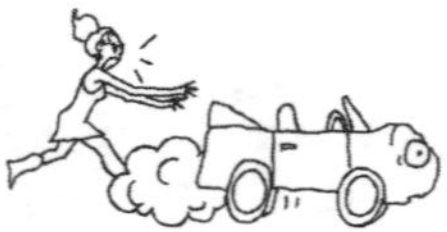

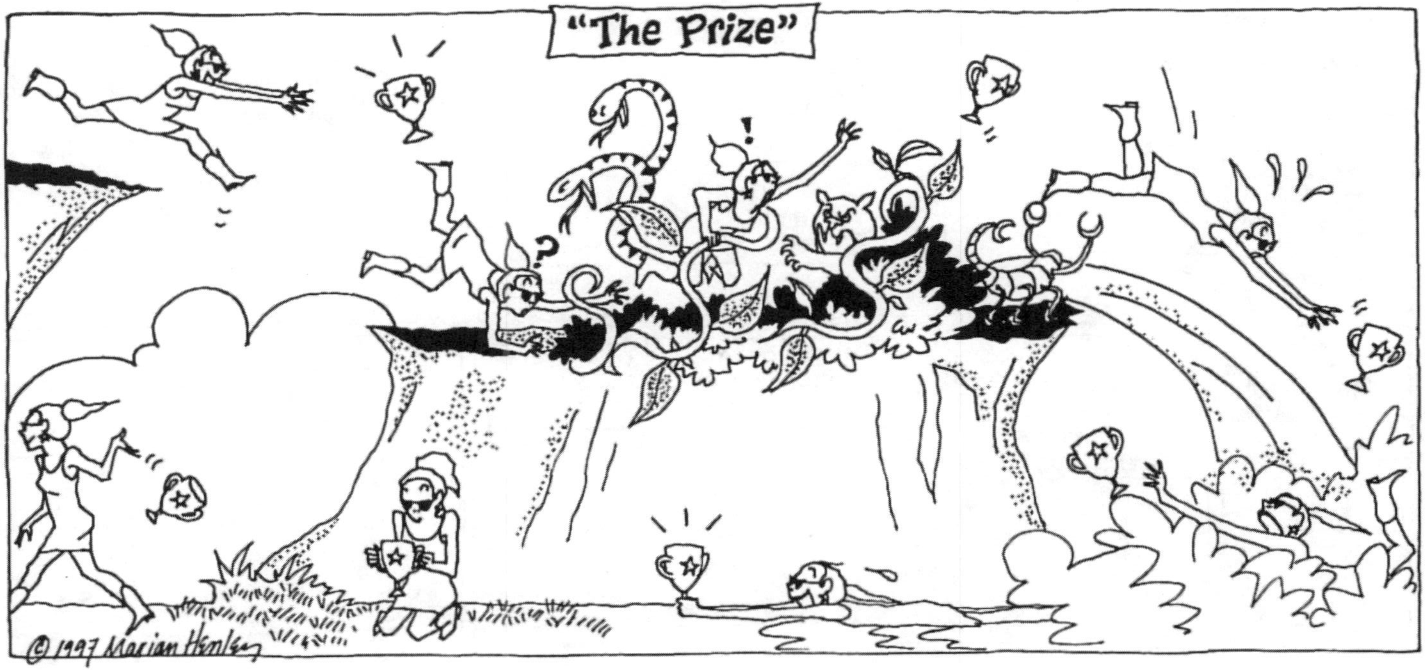
"The Prize"
?
!
© 1997 Marian Henley

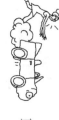

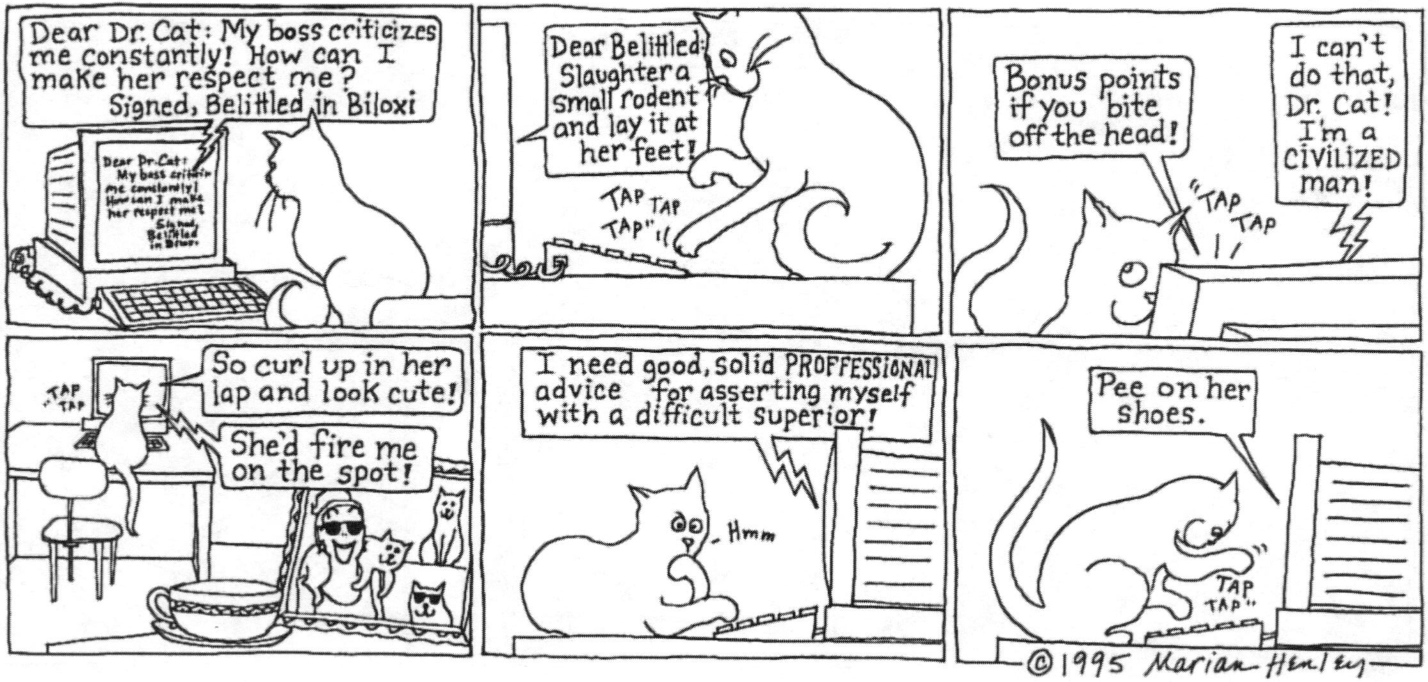
Dear Dr. Cat: My boss criticizes me constantly! How can I make her respect me? Signed, Belittled in Biloxi
Dear Belittled: Slaughter a small rodent and lay it at her feet!
TAP TAP TAP"
Bonus points if you bite off the head!
"TAP TAP
I can't do that, Dr. Cat! I'm a CIVILIZED man!
TAP TAP
So curl up in her lap and look cute!
She'd fire me on the spot!
I need good, solid PROFFESSIONAL advice for asserting myself with a difficult superior!
Hmm
Pee on her shoes.
TAP TAP"
©1995 Marian Henley

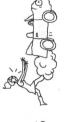

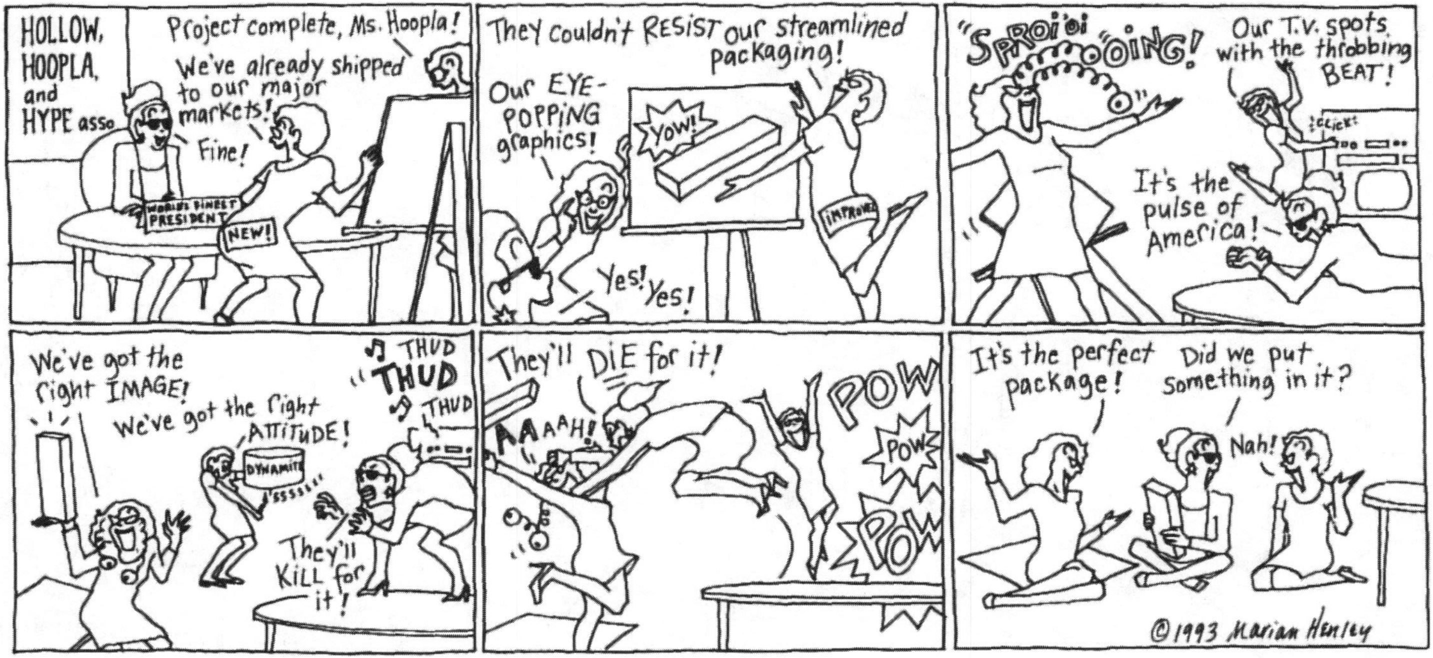
HOLLOW, HOOPLA, and HYPE asso
Project complete, Ms. Hoopla!
We've already shipped to our major markets!
Fine!
WORLD'S FINEST PRESIDENT
NEW!
They couldn't RESIST our streamlined packaging!
Our EYE-POPPING graphics!
YOW!
IMPROVED
Yes! Yes!
"SPROiOiOiOOING!"
Our T.V. spots with the throbbing BEAT!
CLICK!
It's the pulse of America!
We've got the right IMAGE!
We've got the right ATTITUDE!
DYNAMITE
SSSSSS
THUD THUD THUD
They'll KILL for it!
They'll DIE for it!
AAAAH!
POW POW POW
It's the perfect package!
Did we put something in it?
Nah!
©1993 Marian Henley

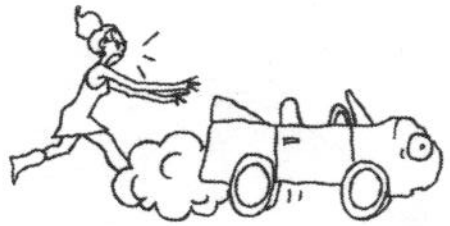

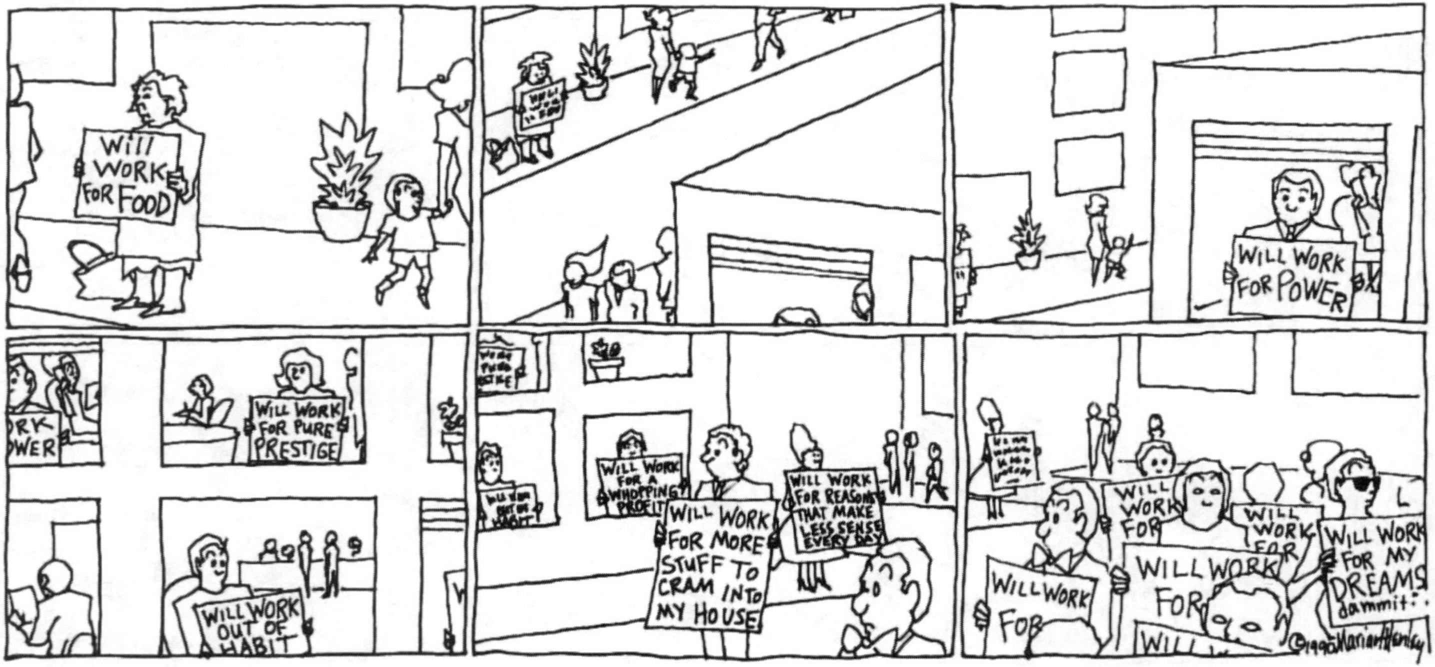
WILL WORK FOR FOOD
WILL WORK FOR POWER
WILL WORK FOR PURE PRESTIGE
WILL WORK OUT OF HABIT
WILL WORK FOR A WHOPPING PROFIT
WILL WORK FOR MORE STUFF TO CRAM INTO MY HOUSE
WILL WORK FOR REASONS THAT MAKE LESS SENSE EVERY DAY
WILL WORK FOR
WILL WORK FOR
WILL WORK FOR
WILL WORK FOR
WILL WORK FOR MY DREAMS dammit!!
©1990 Marian Henley

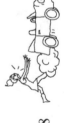

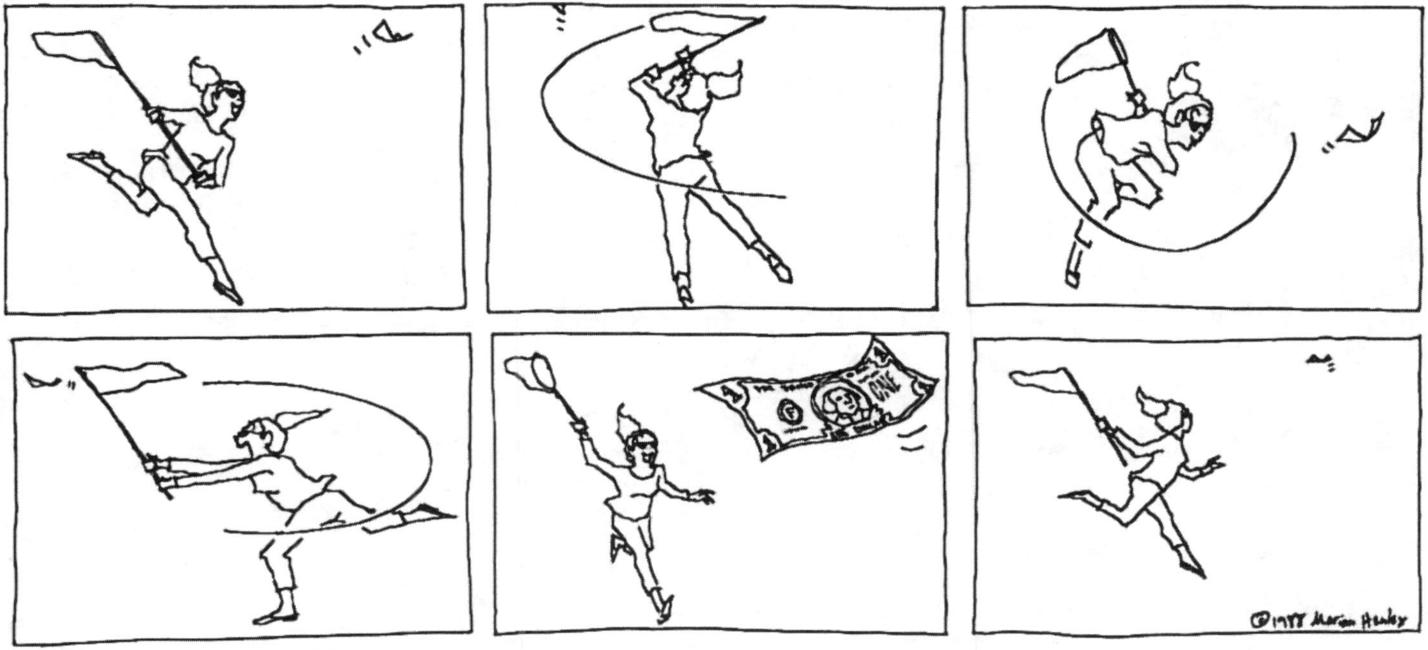
ONE

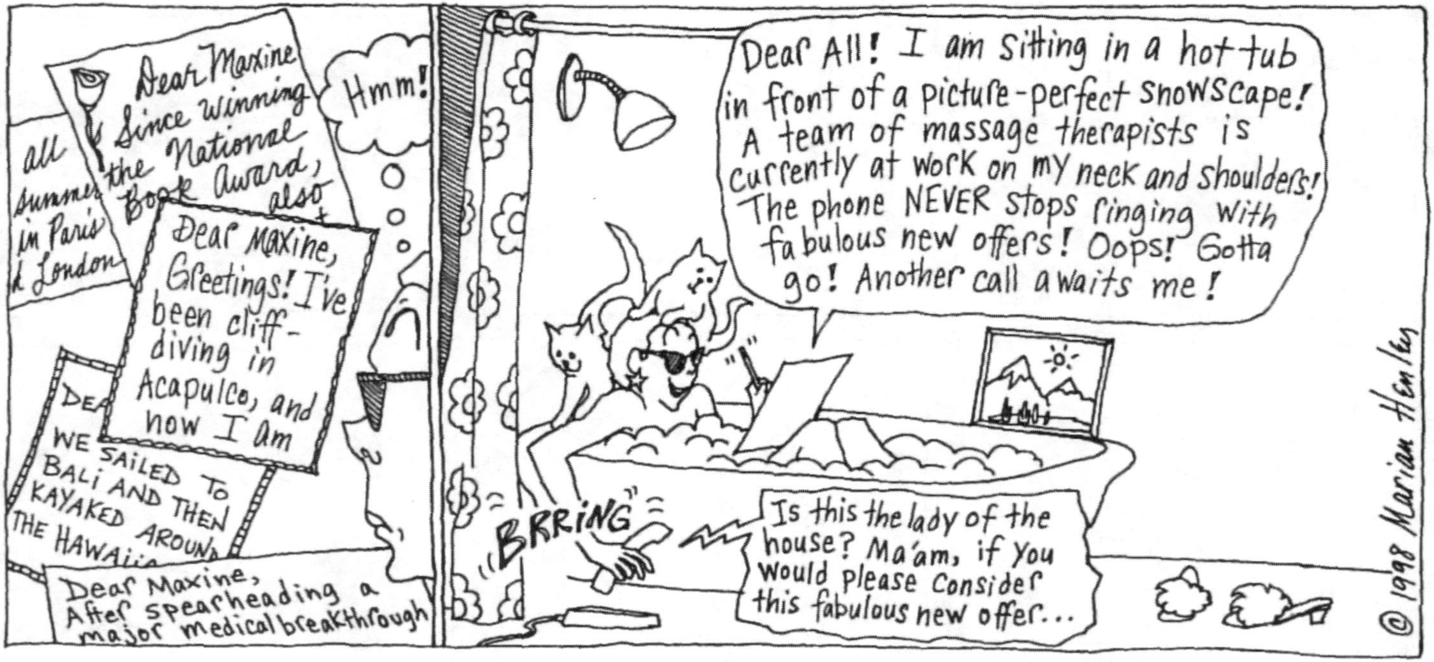
all summer in Paris London
Dear Maxine Since winning the National Book Award, also
Dear Maxine, Greetings! I've been cliff-diving in Acapulco, and now I am
WE SAILED TO BALI AND THEN KAYAKED AROUND THE HAWAII
Dear Maxine, After spearheading a major medical breakthrough
Hmm!
Dear All! I am sitting in a hot tub in front of a picture-perfect snowscape! A team of massage therapists is currently at work on my neck and shoulders! The phone NEVER stops ringing with fabulous new offers! Oops! Gotta go! Another call awaits me!
BRRING
Is this the lady of the house? Ma'am, if you would please consider this fabulous new offer...
© 1998 Marian Henley

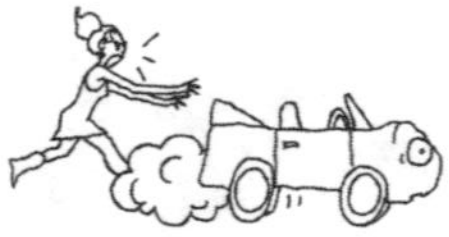

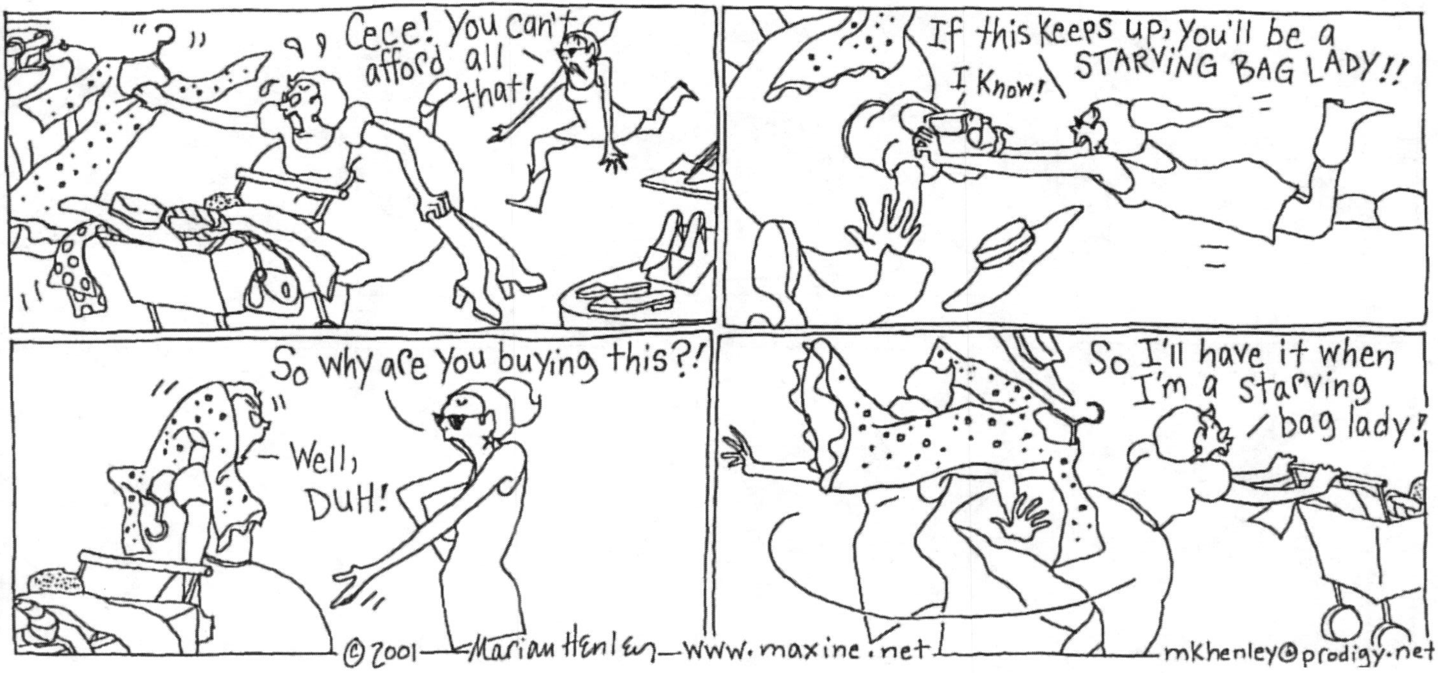
"?"
Cece! You can't afford all that!
If this keeps up, you'll be a STARVING BAG LADY!!
I Know!
So why are you buying this?!
Well, DUH!
So I'll have it when I'm a starving bag lady!
© 2001—Marian Henley—www.maxine.net—mkhenley@prodigy.net

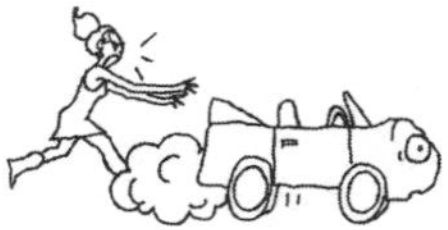

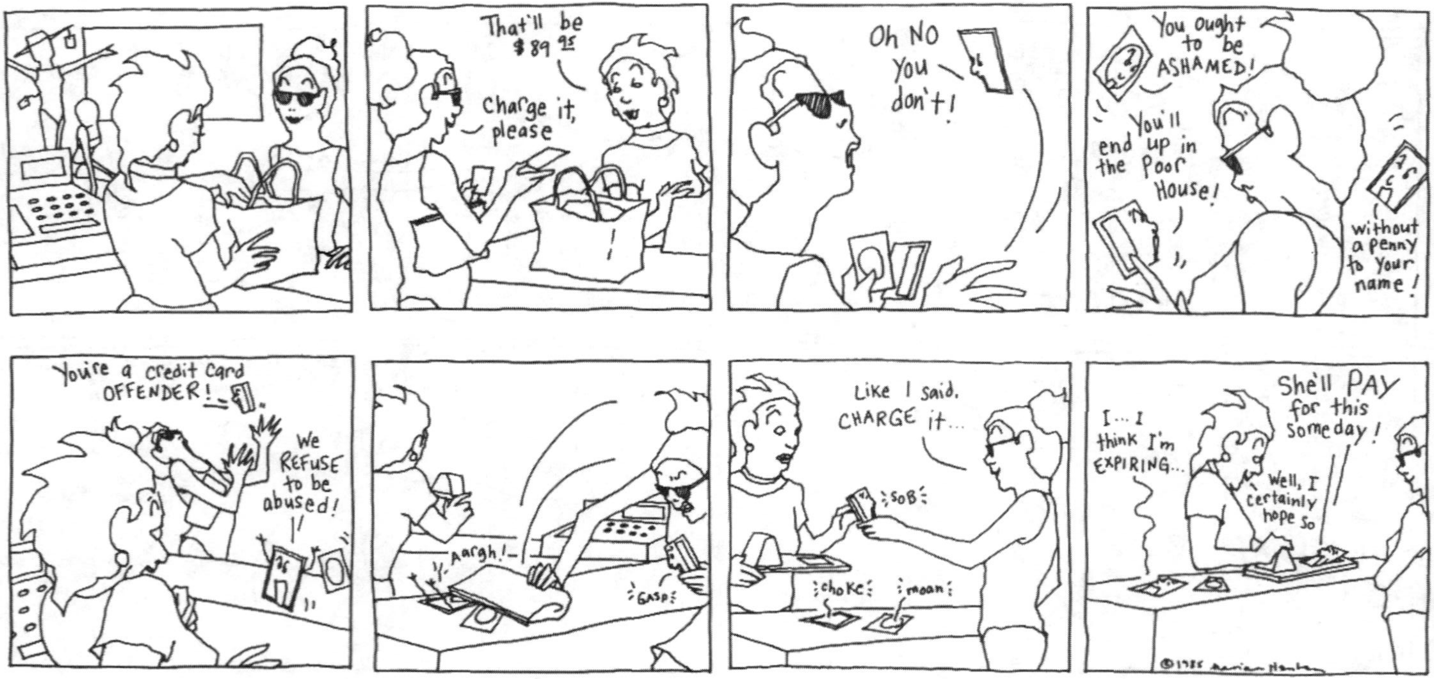
That'll be $89 95
Charge it, please
Oh NO You don't!
You ought to be ASHAMED!
You'll end up in the Poor House!
without a penny to your name!
You're a credit card OFFENDER!
We REFUSE to be abused!
Aargh!
GASP
Like I said. CHARGE it...
SOB
choke
moan
I... I think I'm EXPIRING...
She'll PAY for this someday!
Well, I certainly hope so
©1985

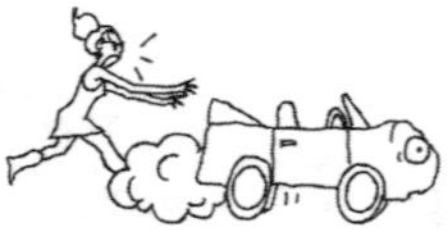

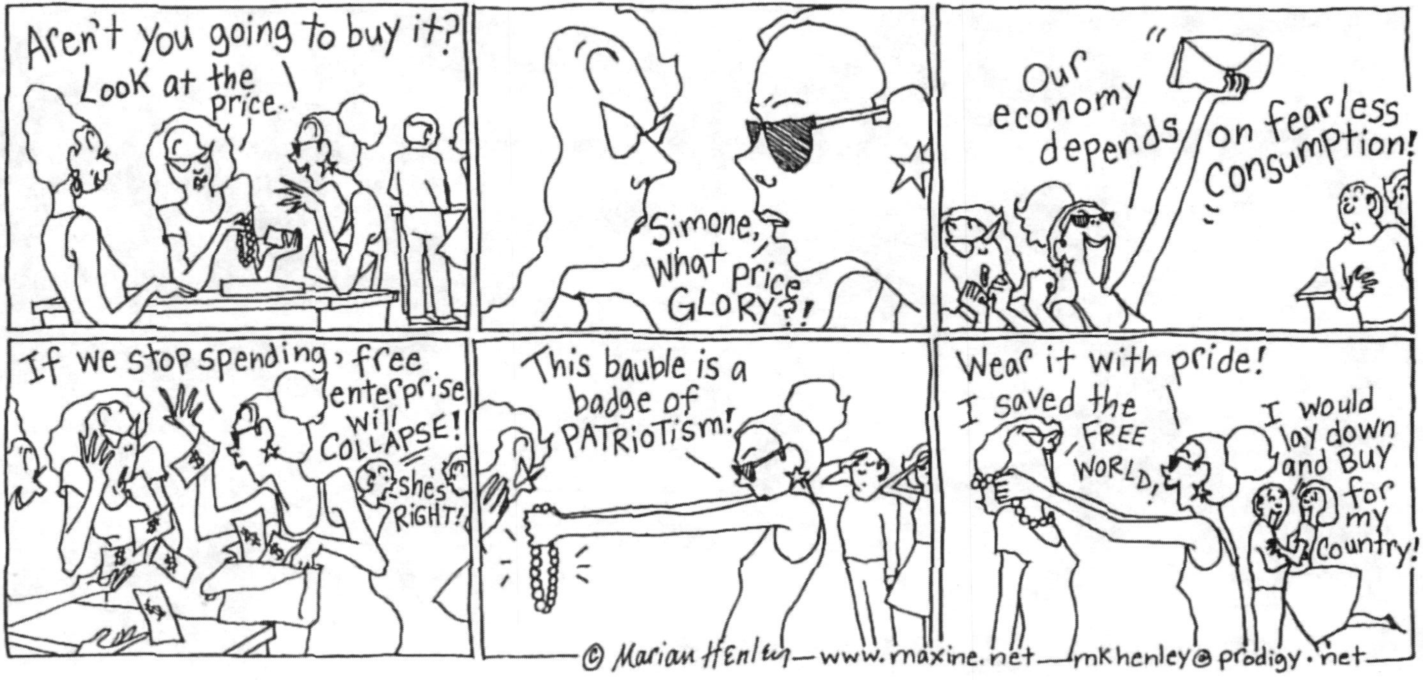
Aren't you going to buy it?
Look at the price..
Simone, what price GLORY?!
Our economy depends on fearless Consumption!
If we stop spending, free enterprise will COLLAPSE!
she's RIGHT!
This bauble is a badge of PATRIOTISM!
Wear it with pride!
I saved the FREE WORLD!
I would lay down and BUY for my Country!
© Marian Henley—www.maxine.net—mkhenley@prodigy.net

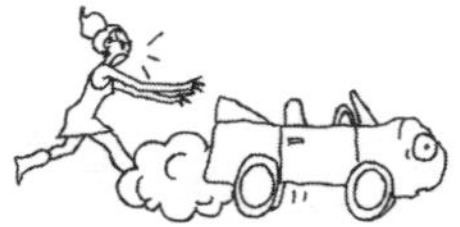

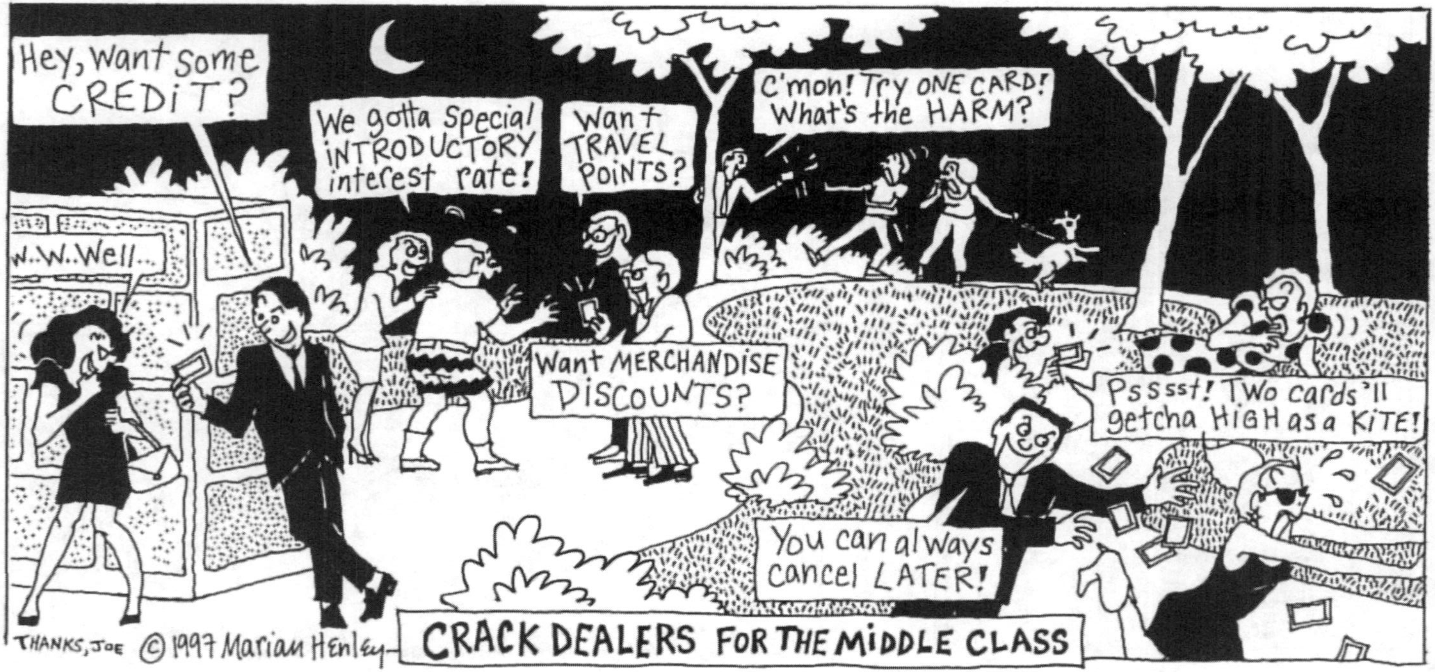
Hey, want some CREDiT?
W..W..Well...
We gotta special INTRODUCTORY interest rate!
Want TRAVEL POINTS?
C'mon! Try ONE CARD! What's the HARM?
Want MERCHANDISE DISCOUNTS?
Psssst! Two cards'll getcha HIGH as a KiTE!
You can always cancel LATER!
CRACK DEALERS FOR THE MiDDLE CLASS
THANKS, JOE © 1997 Marian Henley

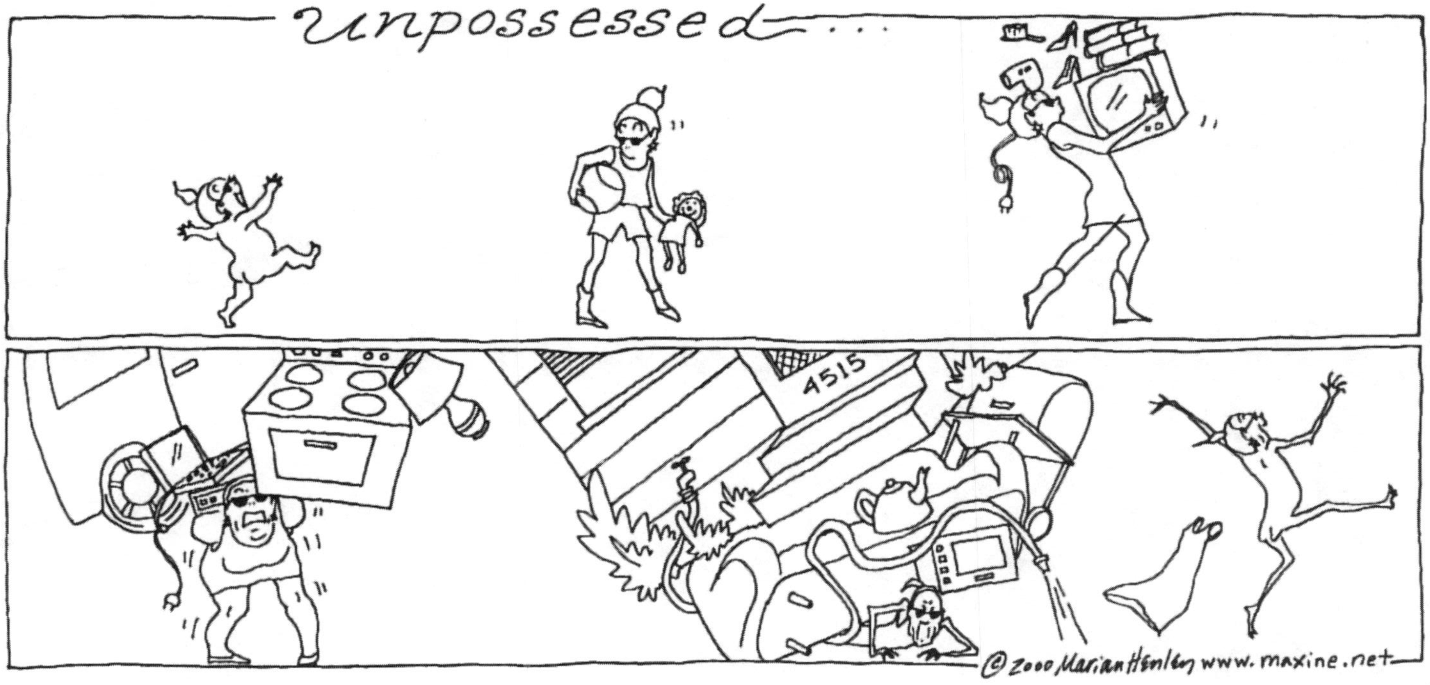
unpossessed...
4515
© 2000 Marian Henley www.maxine.net

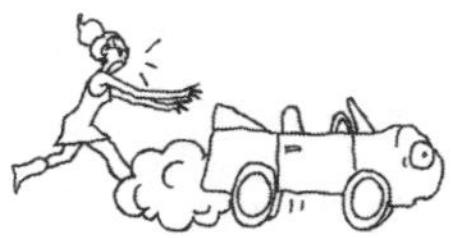

Society and Politics

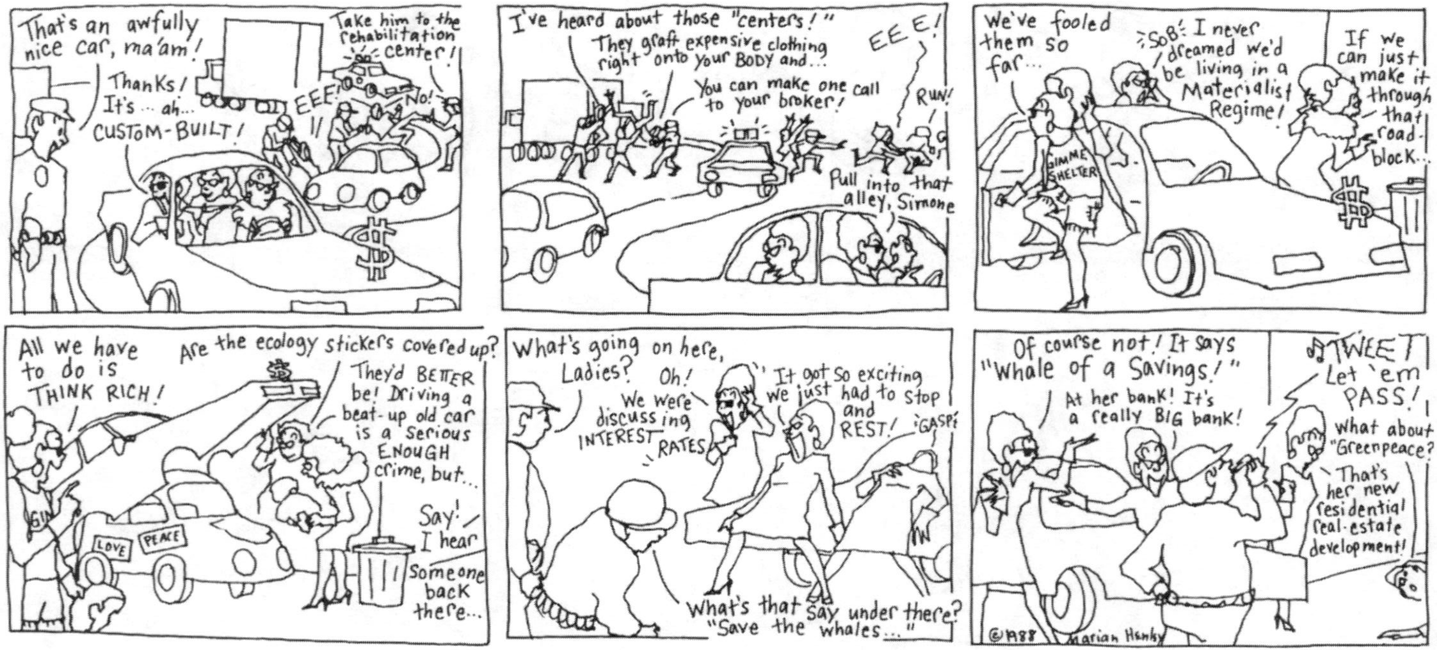
That's an awfully nice car, ma'am!
Thanks! It's ... ah... CUSTOM-BUILT!
Take him to the rehabilitation center!
EEE!
No!
I've heard about those "centers!"
They graft expensive clothing right onto your BODY and...
You can make one call to your broker!
EEE!
RUN!
Pull into that alley, Simone
We've fooled them so far...
SOB! I never dreamed we'd be living in a Materialist Regime!
GIMME SHELTER
If we can just make it through that road-block...
All we have to do is THINK RICH!
Are the ecology stickers covered up?
They'd BETTER be! Driving a beat-up old car is a serious ENOUGH crime, but...
Say! I hear Someone back there...
LOVE
PEACE
What's going on here, Ladies?
Oh! We were discussing INTEREST RATES
It got so exciting we just had to stop and REST!
GASP!
What's that say under there? "Save the whales..."
Of course not! It says "Whale of a Savings!"
At her bank! It's a really BIG bank!
TWEET! Let 'em PASS!
What about "Greenpeace?"
That's her new residential real-estate development!
©1988 Marian Henley

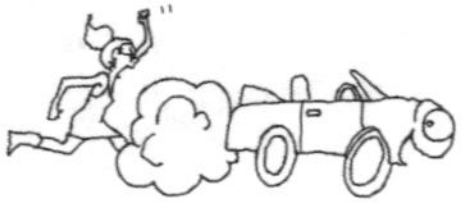

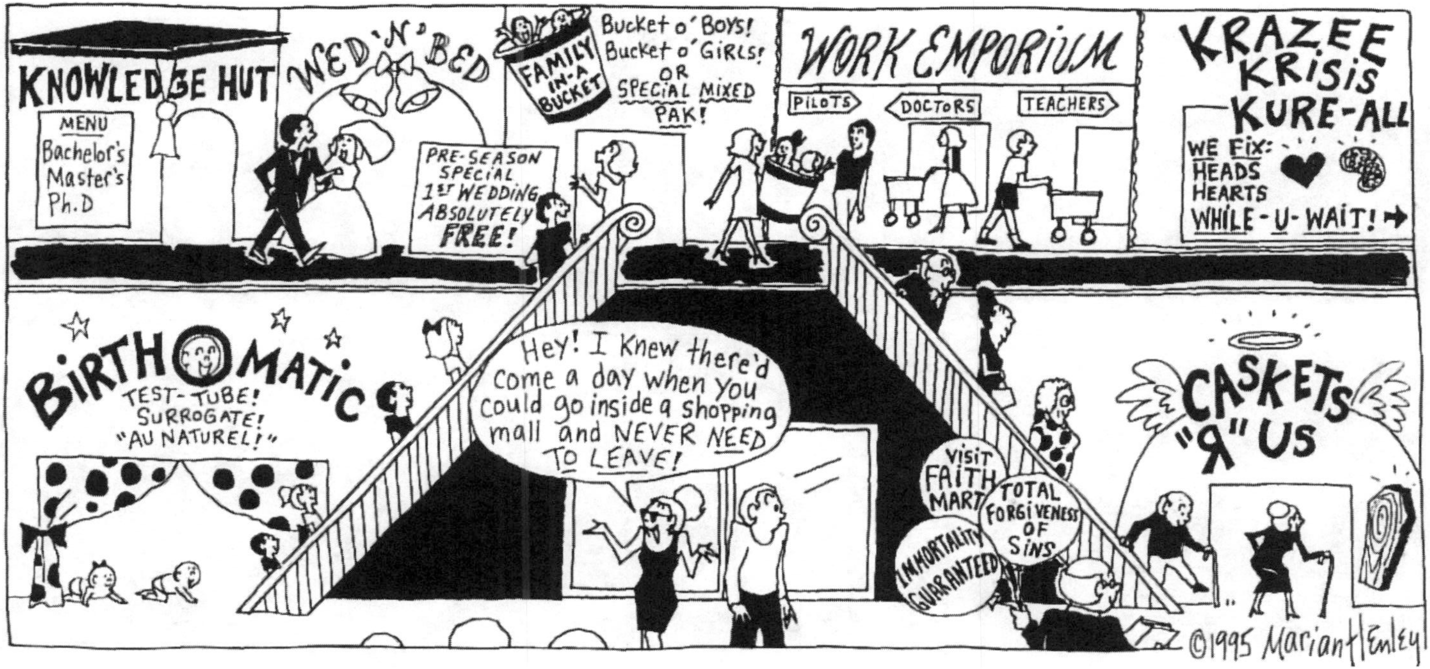
KNOWLEDGE HUT
MENU
Bachelor's
Master's
Ph.D
WED 'N' BED
PRE-SEASON SPECIAL
1ST WEDDING ABSOLUTELY FREE!
FAMILY IN-A BUCKET
Bucket o' Boys!
Bucket o' Girls!
OR
SPECIAL MIXED PAK!
WORK EMPORIUM
PILOTS
DOCTORS
TEACHERS
KRAZEE KRISIS KURE-ALL
WE FIX:
HEADS
HEARTS
WHILE-U-WAIT! →
BIRTHOMATIC
TEST-TUBE!
SURROGATE!
"AU NATUREL!"
Hey! I Knew there'd come a day when you could go inside a shopping mall and NEVER NEED TO LEAVE!
VISIT FAITH MART
IMMORTALITY GUARANTEED
TOTAL FORGIVENESS OF SINS
CASKETS "R" US
©1995 Marian Henley

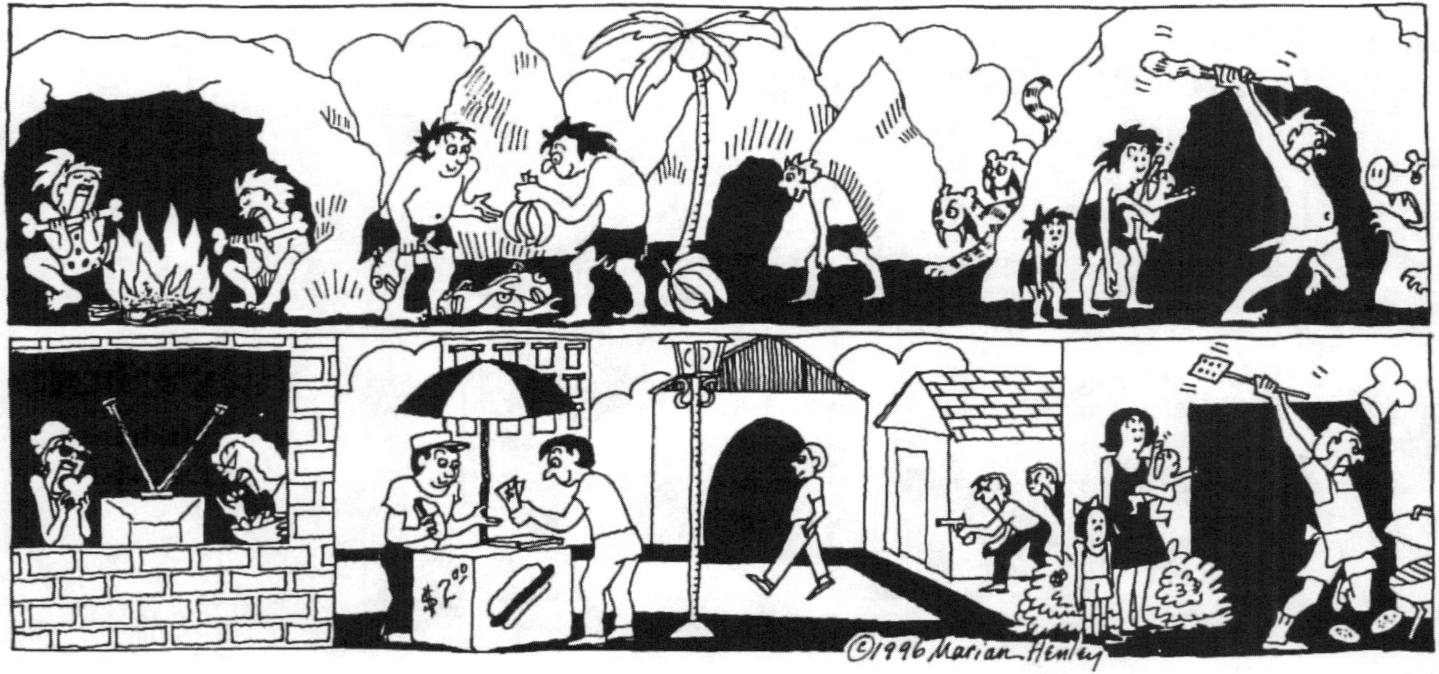
$2.00
©1996 Marian Henley

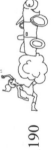

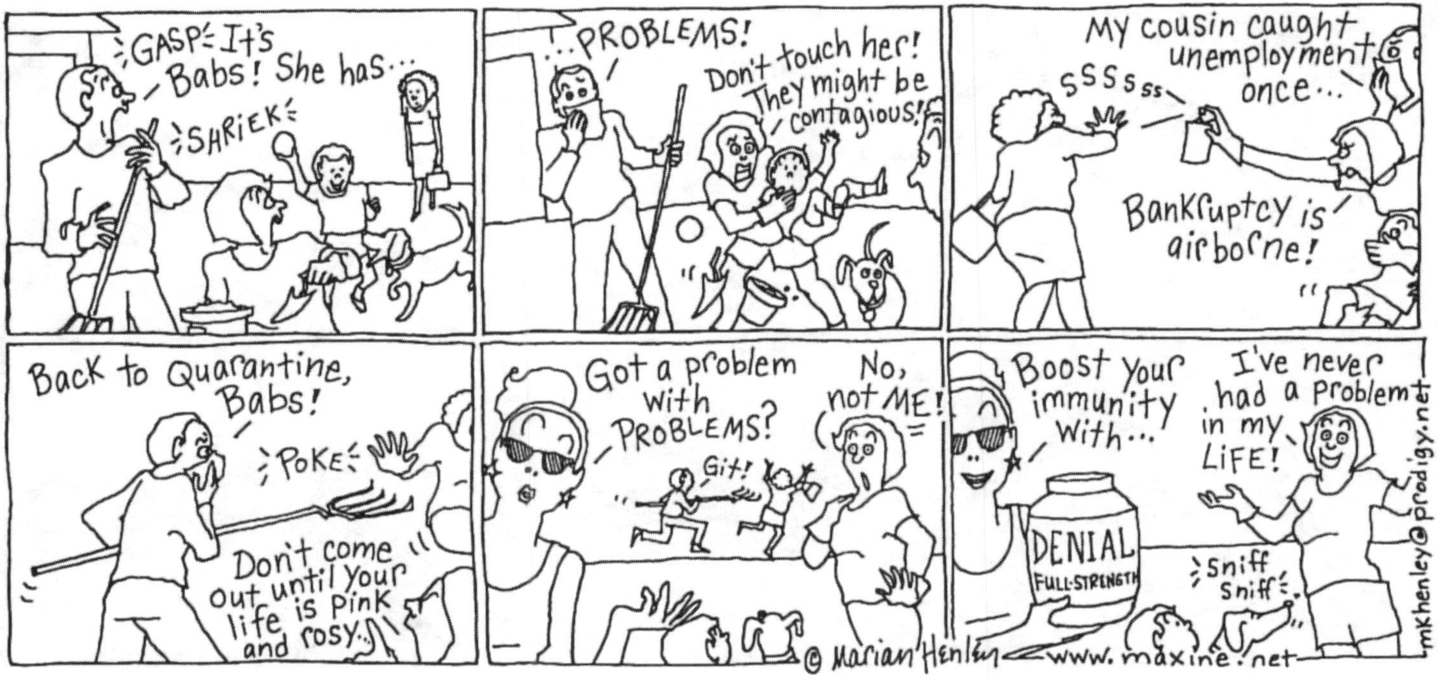
GASP! It's Babs! She has...
SHRIEK!
...PROBLEMS!
Don't touch her! They might be contagious!
My cousin caught unemployment once...
SSSsss
Bankruptcy is airborne!
Back to Quarantine, Babs!
POKE!
Don't come out until your life is pink and rosy...
Got a problem with PROBLEMS?
Git!
No, not ME!
Boost your immunity with...
DENIAL
FULL-STRENGTH
I've never had a problem in my LIFE!
Sniff Sniff
© Marian Henley
www.maxine.net
mkhenley@prodigy.net

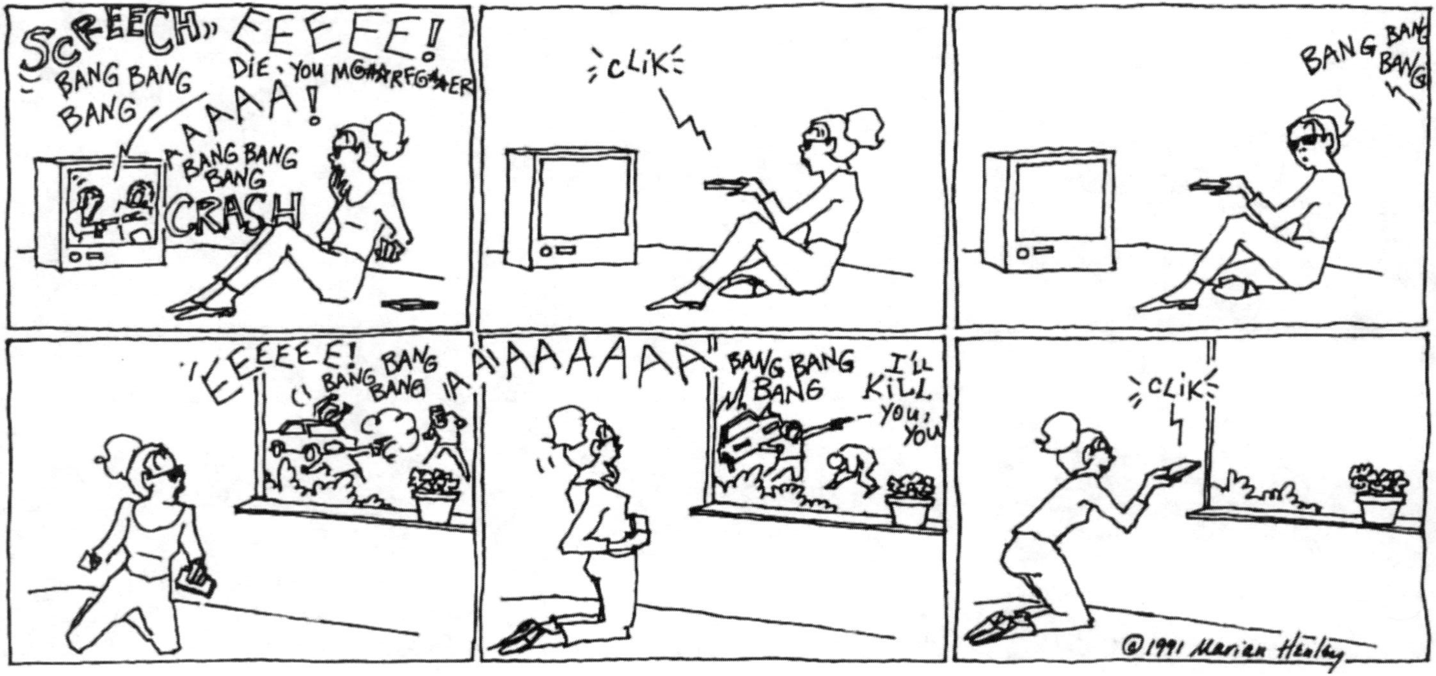
SCREECH
EEEEE!
BANG BANG BANG
DIE, YOU
AAAAA!
BANG BANG BANG
CRASH
CLIK
BANG BANG BANG
EEEEEE!
BANG BANG BANG
AAAAAAA
BANG BANG BANG
I'LL KILL YOU, YOU
CLIK
©1991 Marian Henley

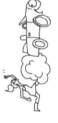

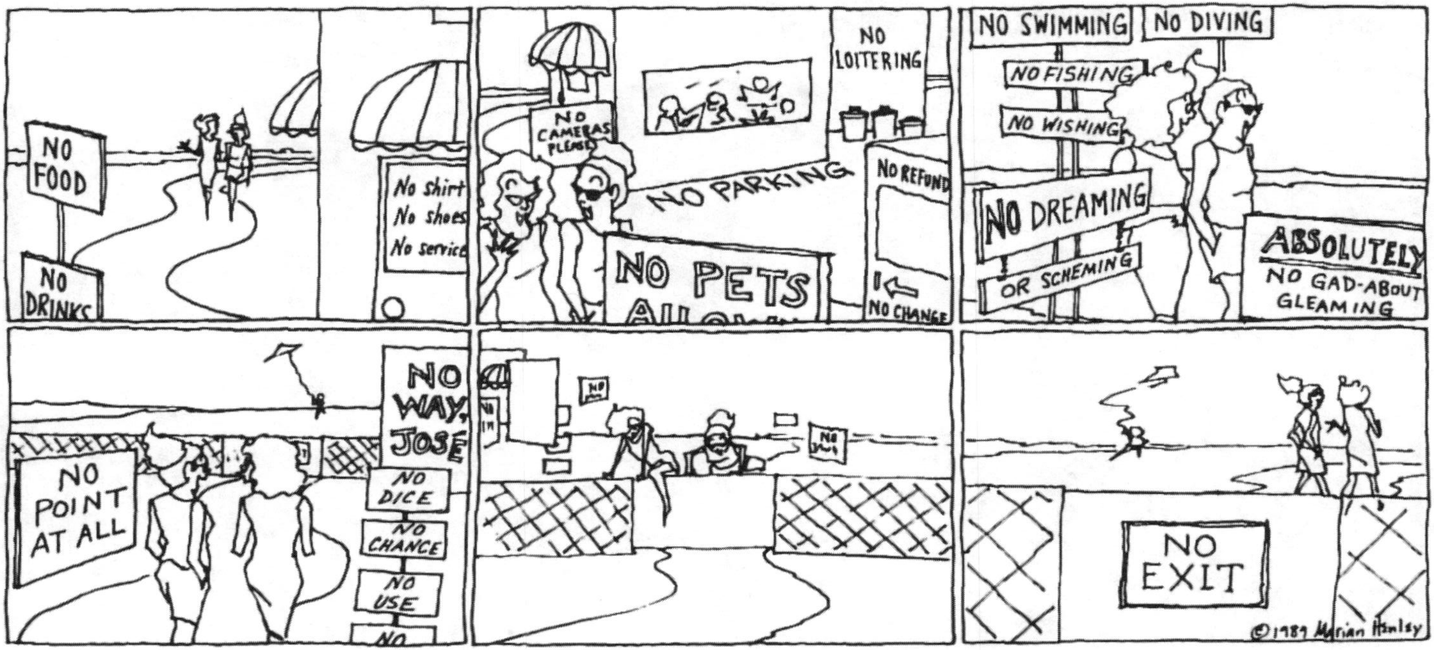
NO FOOD
NO DRINKS
No shirt
No shoes
No service
NO CAMERAS PLEASE
NO PARKING
NO LOITERING
NO REFUND
NO CHANGE
NO PETS
NO SWIMMING
NO DIVING
NO FISHING
NO WISHING
NO DREAMING
OR SCHEMING
ABSOLUTELY
NO GAD-ABOUT GLEAMING
NO POINT AT ALL
NO WAY, JOSÉ
NO DICE
NO CHANCE
NO USE
NO EXIT
©1989 Marian Henley

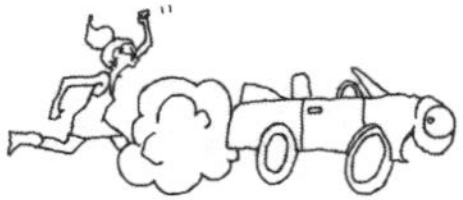

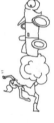

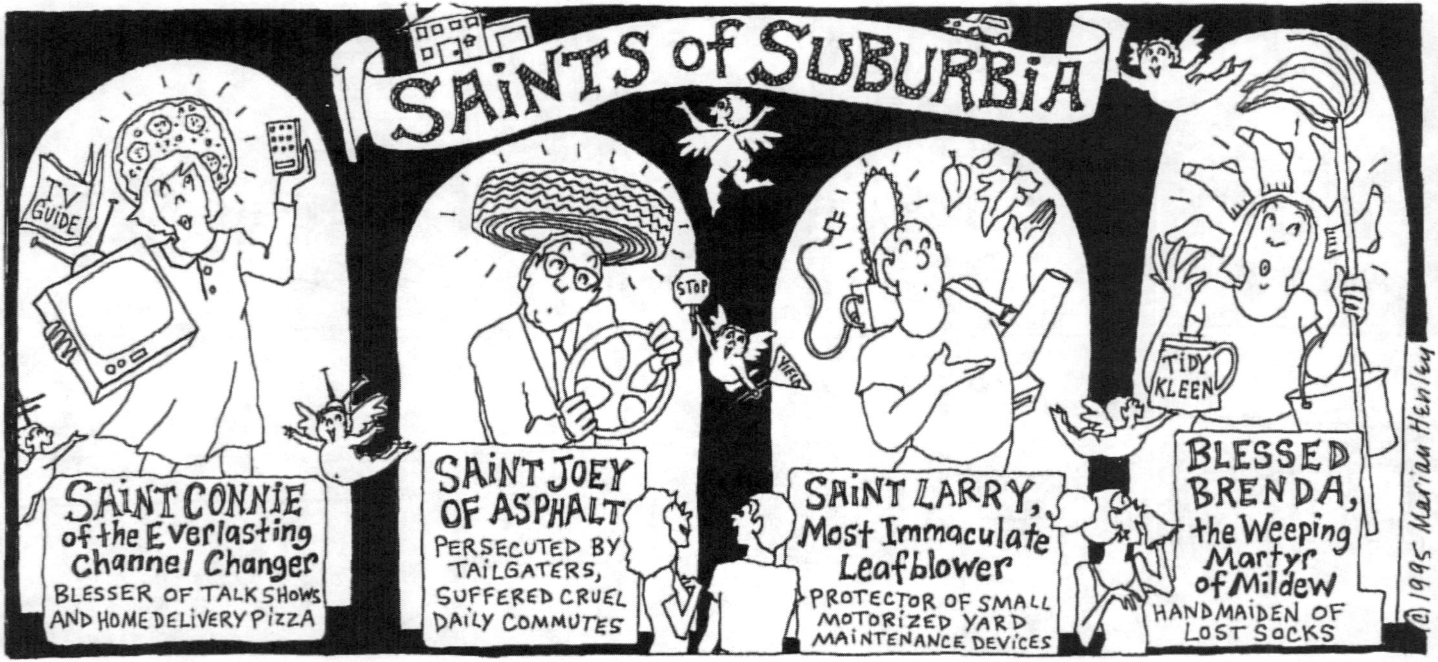
SAINTS of SUBURBIA
TV GUIDE
SAINT CONNIE of the Everlasting Channel Changer
BLESSER OF TALK SHOWS AND HOME DELIVERY PIZZA
STOP
SAINT JOEY OF ASPHALT
PERSECUTED BY TAILGATERS, SUFFERED CRUEL DAILY COMMUTES
SAINT LARRY, Most Immaculate Leafblower
PROTECTOR OF SMALL MOTORIZED YARD MAINTENANCE DEVICES
TIDY KLEEN
BLESSED BRENDA, the Weeping Martyr of Mildew
HANDMAIDEN OF LOST SOCKS
© 1995 Marian Henley

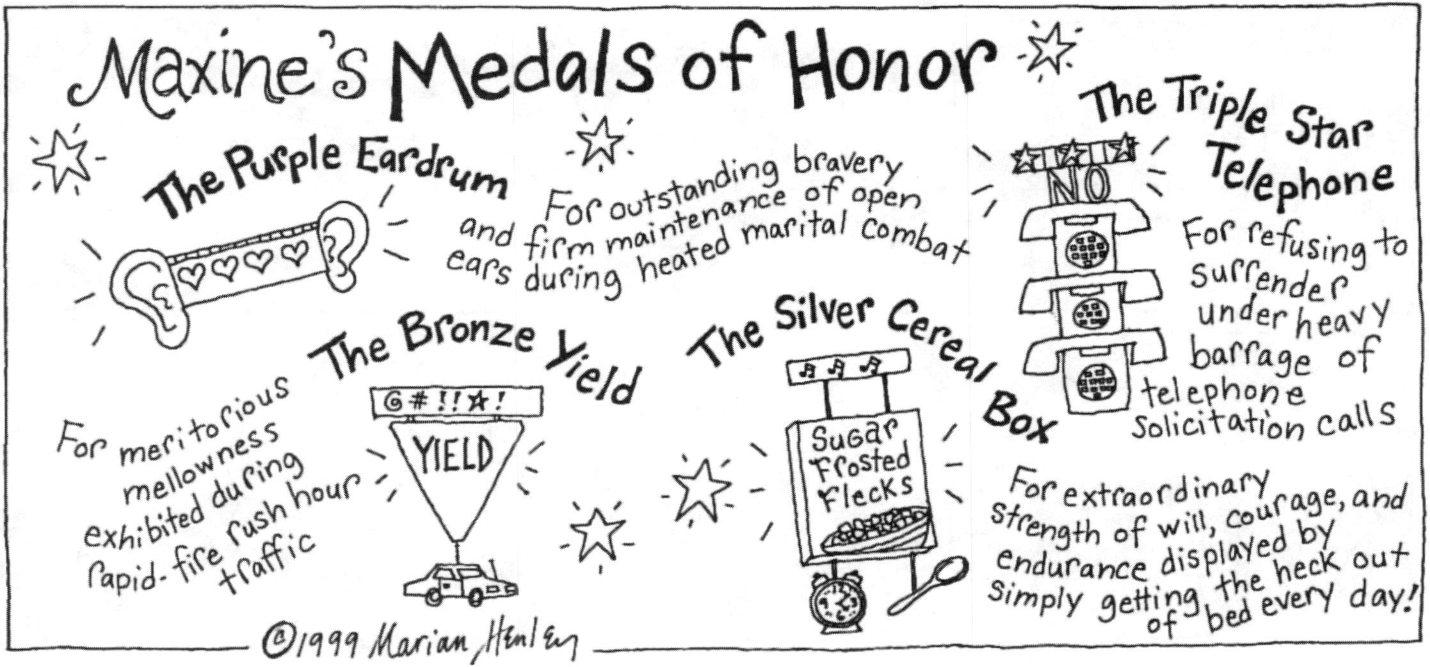
Maxine's Medals of Honor
The Purple Eardrum
For outstanding bravery and firm maintenance of open ears during heated marital combat
The Triple Star Telephone
NO
For refusing to surrender under heavy barrage of telephone solicitation calls
The Bronze Yield
@#!!☆!
YIELD
For meritorious mellowness exhibited during rapid-fire rush hour traffic
The Silver Cereal Box
Sugar Frosted Flecks
For extraordinary strength of will, courage, and endurance displayed by simply getting the heck out of bed every day!
©1999 Marian Henley

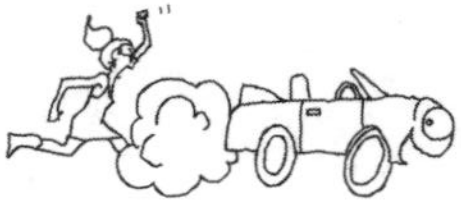

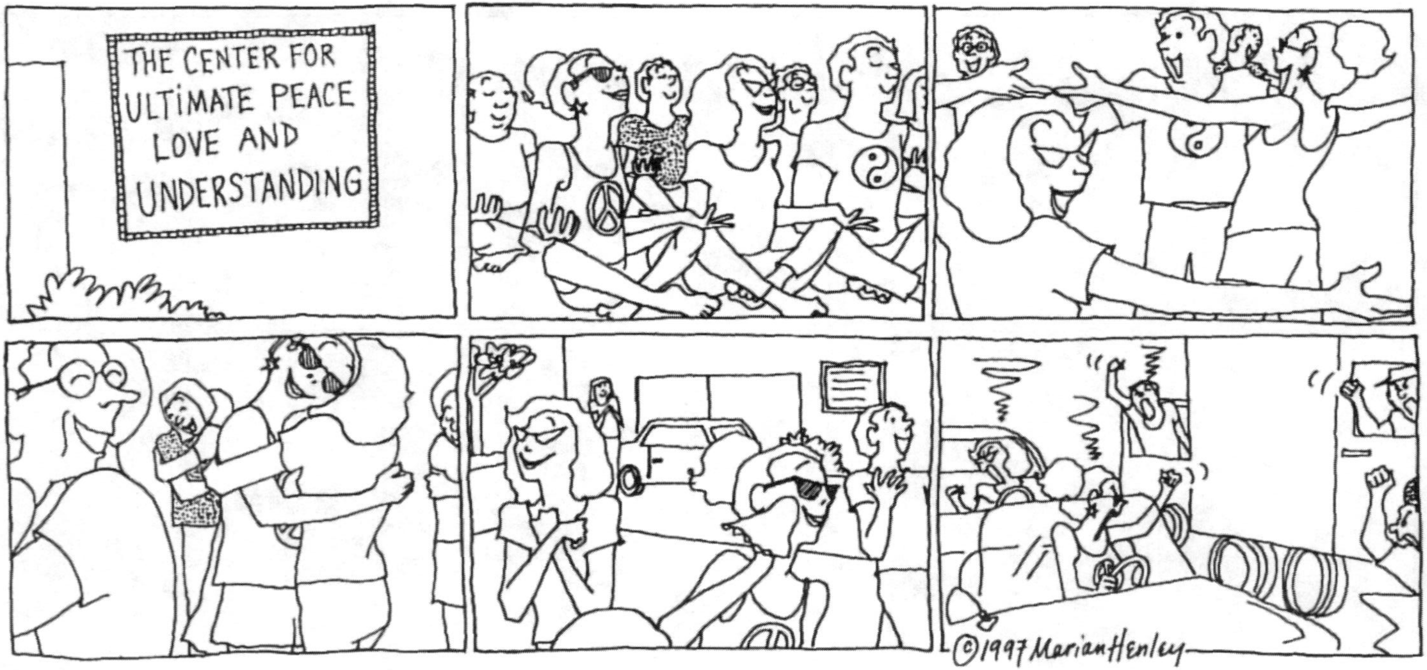
THE CENTER FOR ULTIMATE PEACE LOVE AND UNDERSTANDING
©1997 MarianHenley

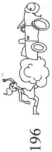

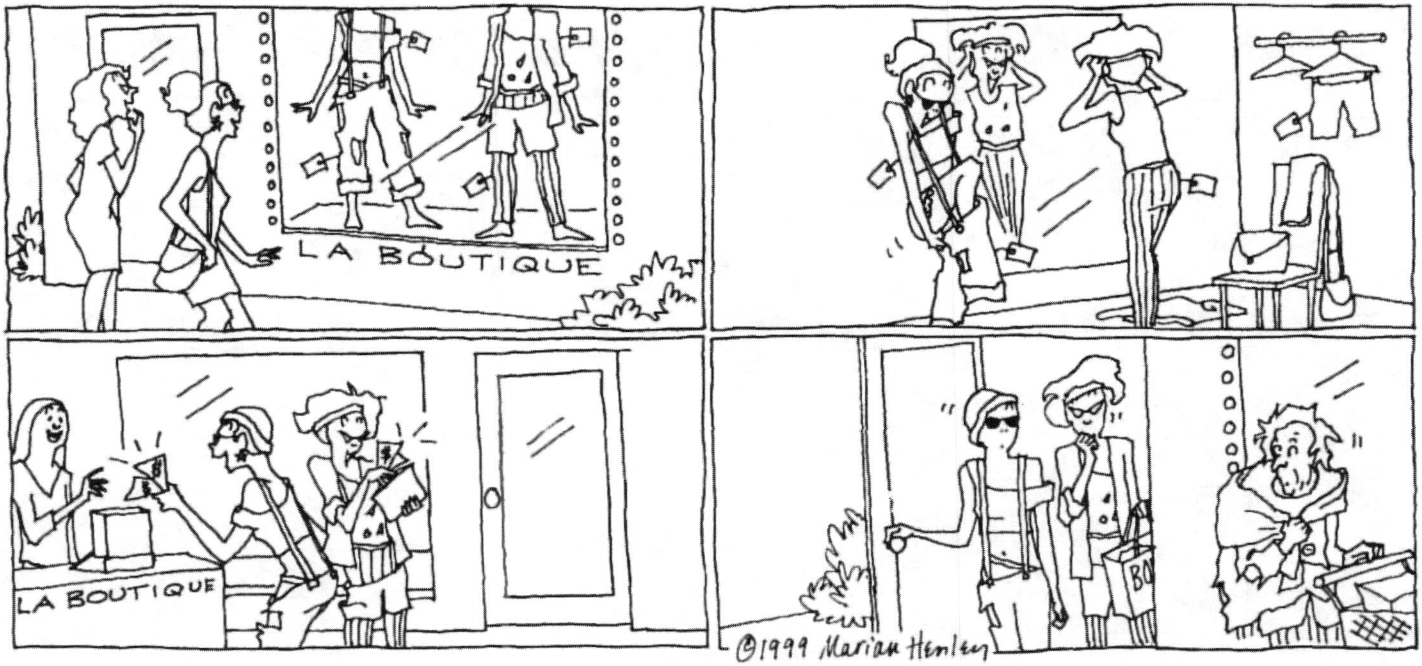
LA BOUTIQUE
LA BOUTIQUE
BO
©1999 Marian Henley

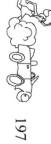

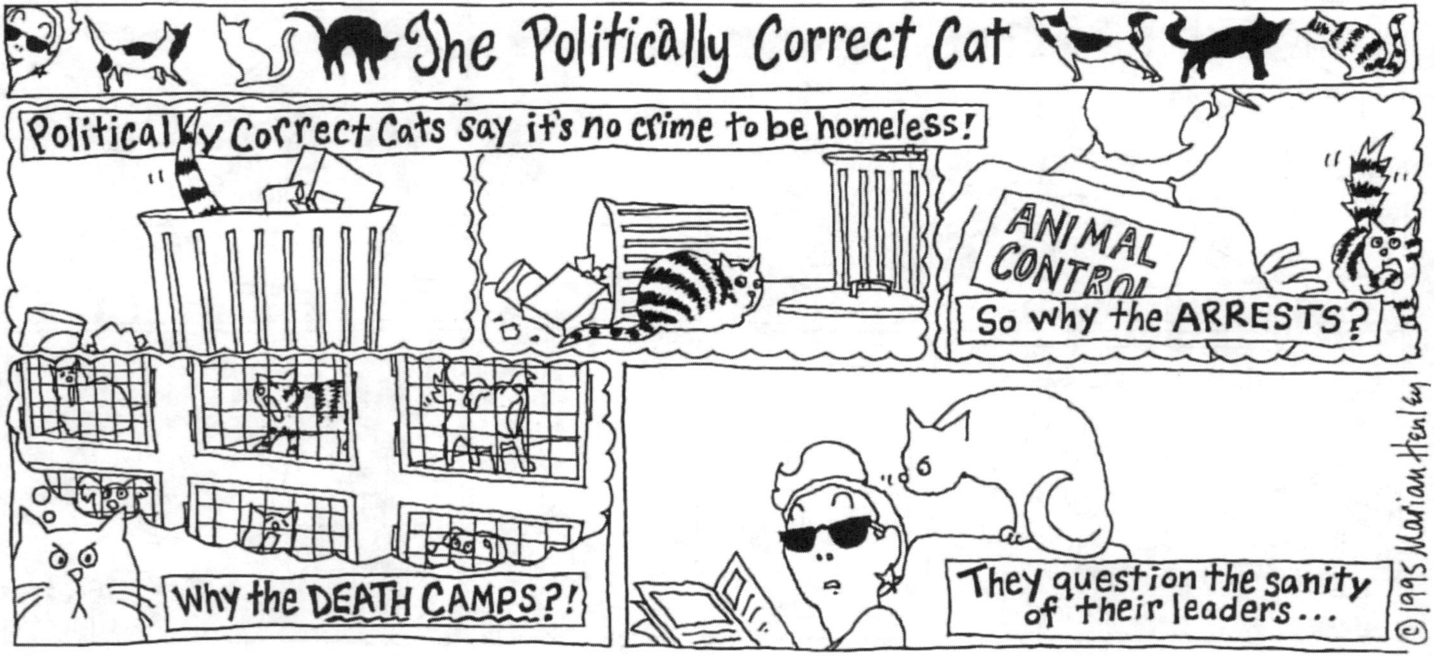
The Politically Correct Cat
Politically Correct Cats say it's no crime to be homeless!
ANIMAL CONTROL
So why the ARRESTS?
Why the DEATH CAMPS?!
They question the sanity of their leaders...
© 1995 Marian Henley

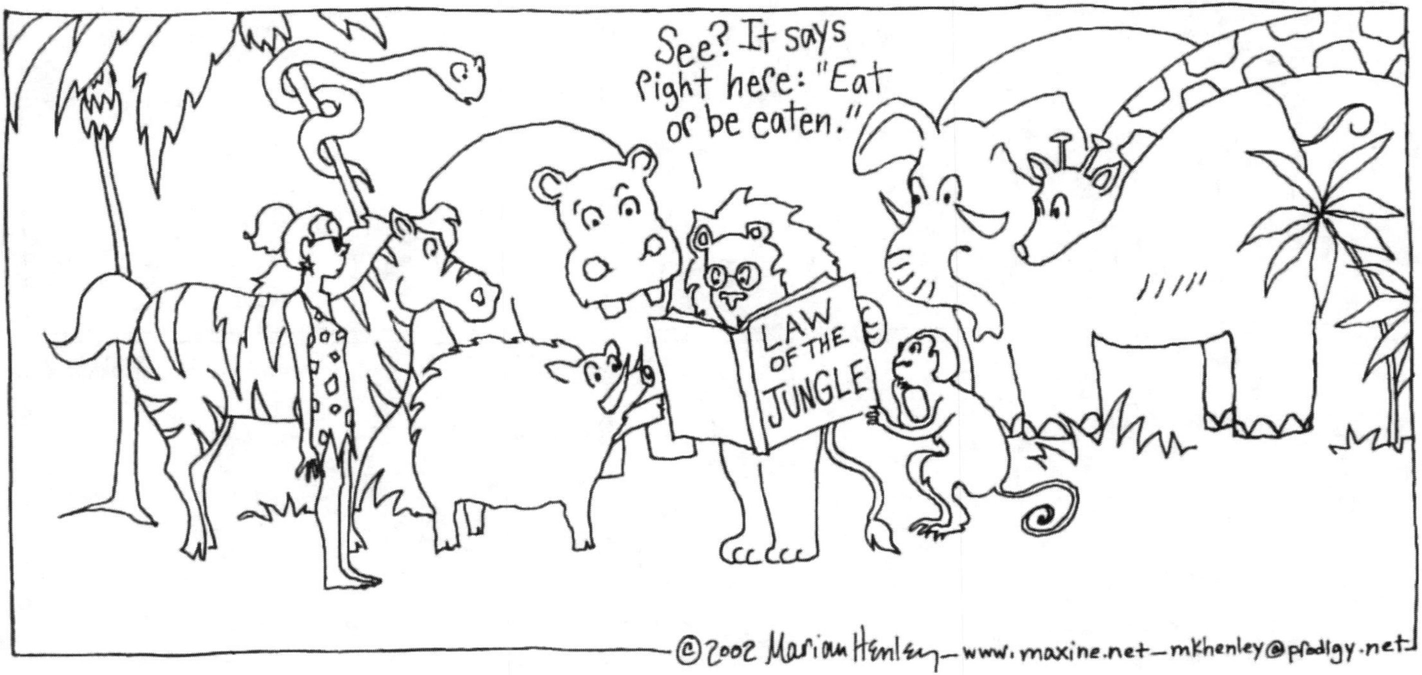
See? It says right here: "Eat or be eaten."
LAW OF THE JUNGLE
©2002 Marian Henley—www.maxine.net—mkhenley@prodigy.net

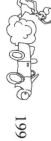

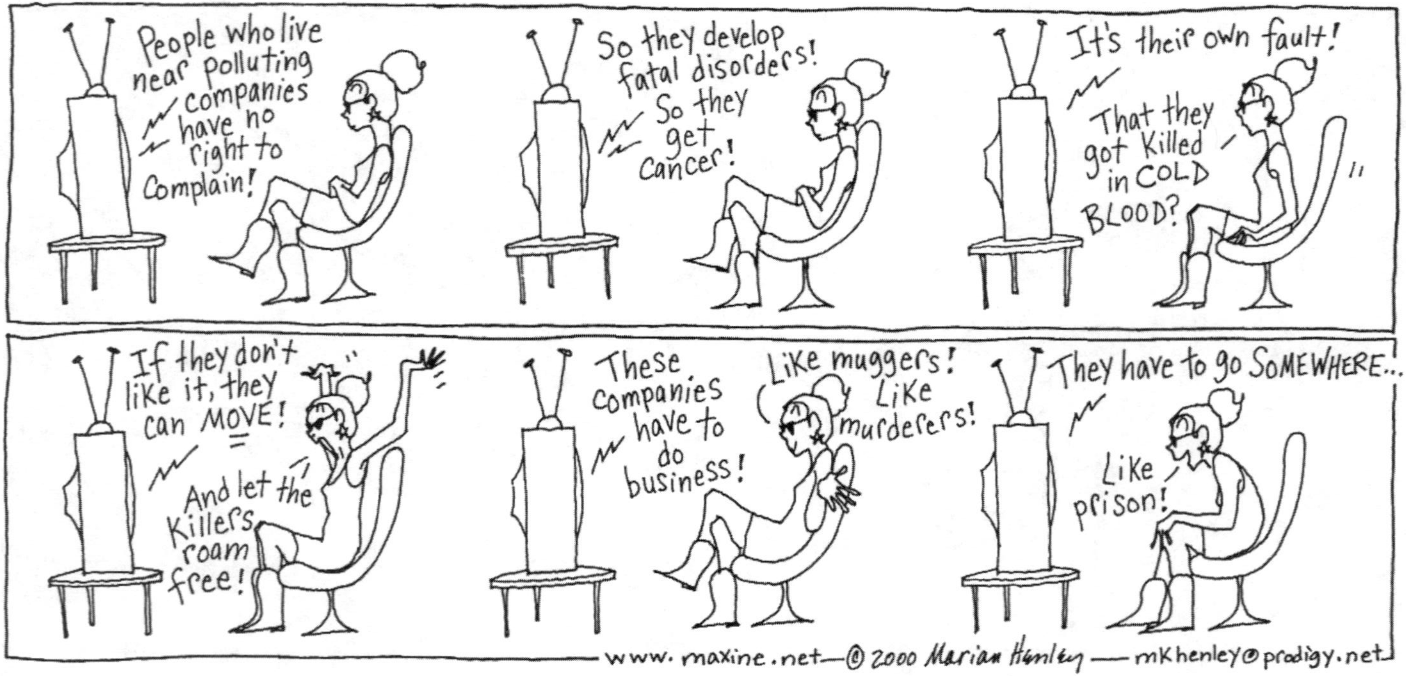
People who live near polluting companies have no right to complain!
So they develop fatal disorders!
So they get cancer!
It's their own fault!
That they got killed in COLD BLOOD?
If they don't like it, they can MOVE!
And let the killers roam free!
These companies have to do business!
Like muggers! Like murderers!
They have to go SOMEWHERE...
Like prison!
www.maxine.net—© 2000 Marian Henley—mkhenley@prodigy.net

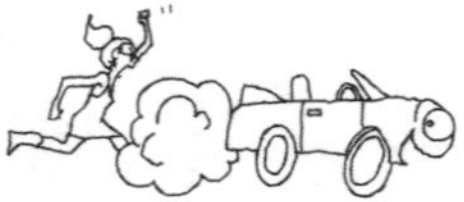

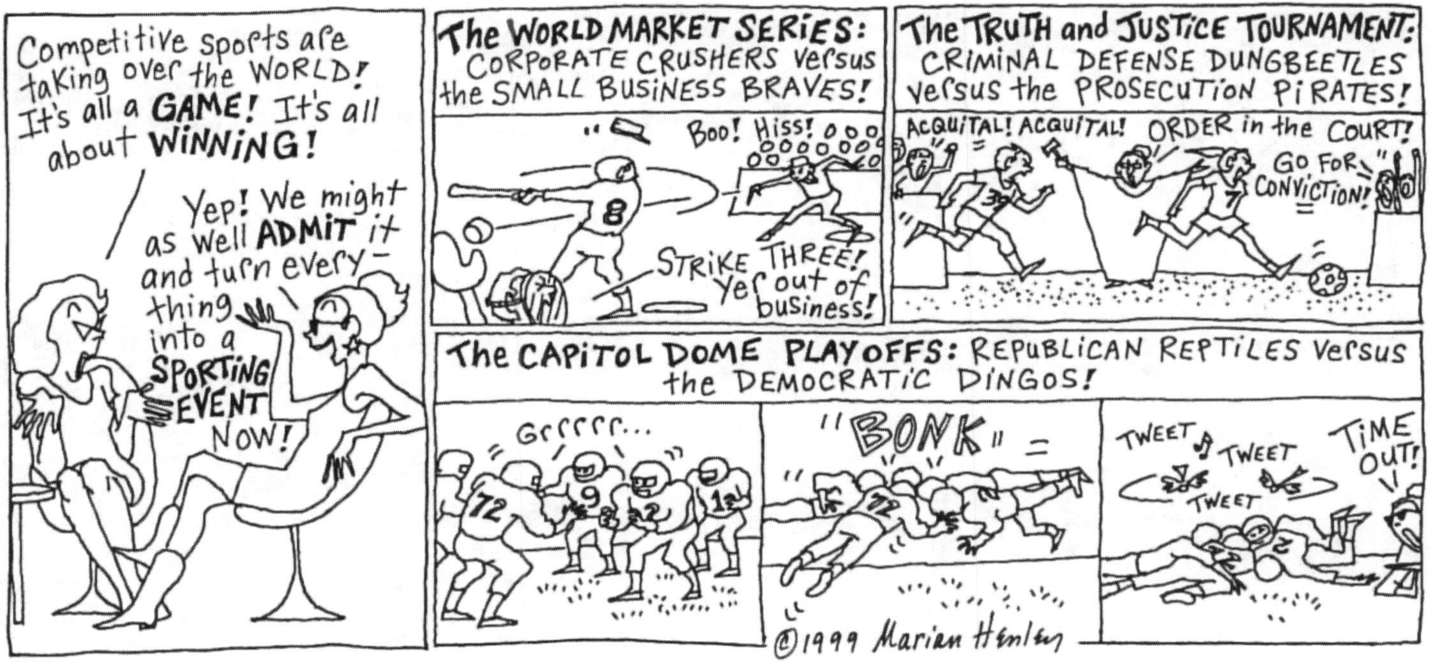
Competitive sports are taking over the WORLD! It's all a GAME! It's all about WINNING!
Yep! We might as well ADMIT it and turn every-thing into a SPORTING EVENT NOW!
The WORLD MARKET SERIES: CORPORATE CRUSHERS versus the SMALL BUSINESS BRAVES!
Boo! Hiss!
STRIKE THREE! Yer out of business!
The TRUTH and JUSTICE TOURNAMENT: CRIMINAL DEFENSE DUNGBEETLES versus the PROSECUTION PIRATES!
ACQUITAL! ACQUITAL!
ORDER in the COURT!
GO FOR CONVICTION!
The CAPITOL DOME PLAYOFFS: REPUBLICAN REPTILES versus the DEMOCRATIC DINGOS!
Grrrrr...
BONK
TWEET TWEET TWEET
TIME OUT!
©1999 Marian Henley

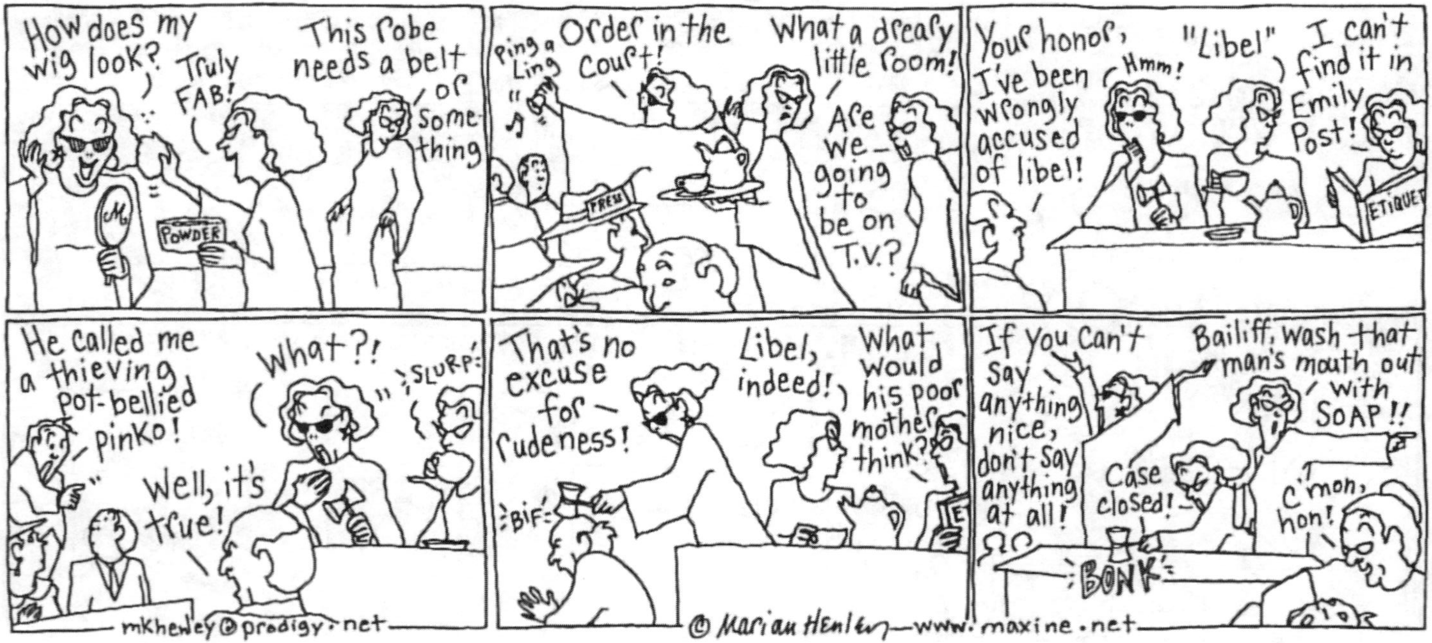
How does my wig look?
Truly FAB!
This robe needs a belt or something
Ping a Ling
Order in the court!
What a dreary little room!
Are we going to be on T.V.?
PRESS
Your honor, I've been wrongly accused of libel!
Hmm!
"Libel" I can't find it in Emily Post!
ETIQUET
He called me a thieving pot-bellied pinko!
What?!
SLURP!
Well, it's true!
POWDER
That's no excuse for rudeness!
BIF!
Libel, indeed!
What would his poor mother think?
If you can't say anything nice, don't say anything at all!
Bailiff, wash that man's mouth out with SOAP!!
Case closed!
BONK!
C'mon, hon!
mkhewley@prodigy.net
© Marian Henley www.maxine.net

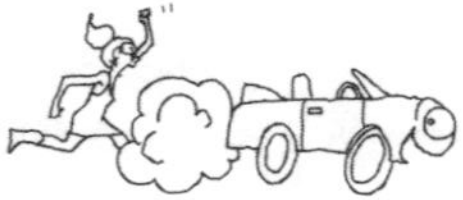

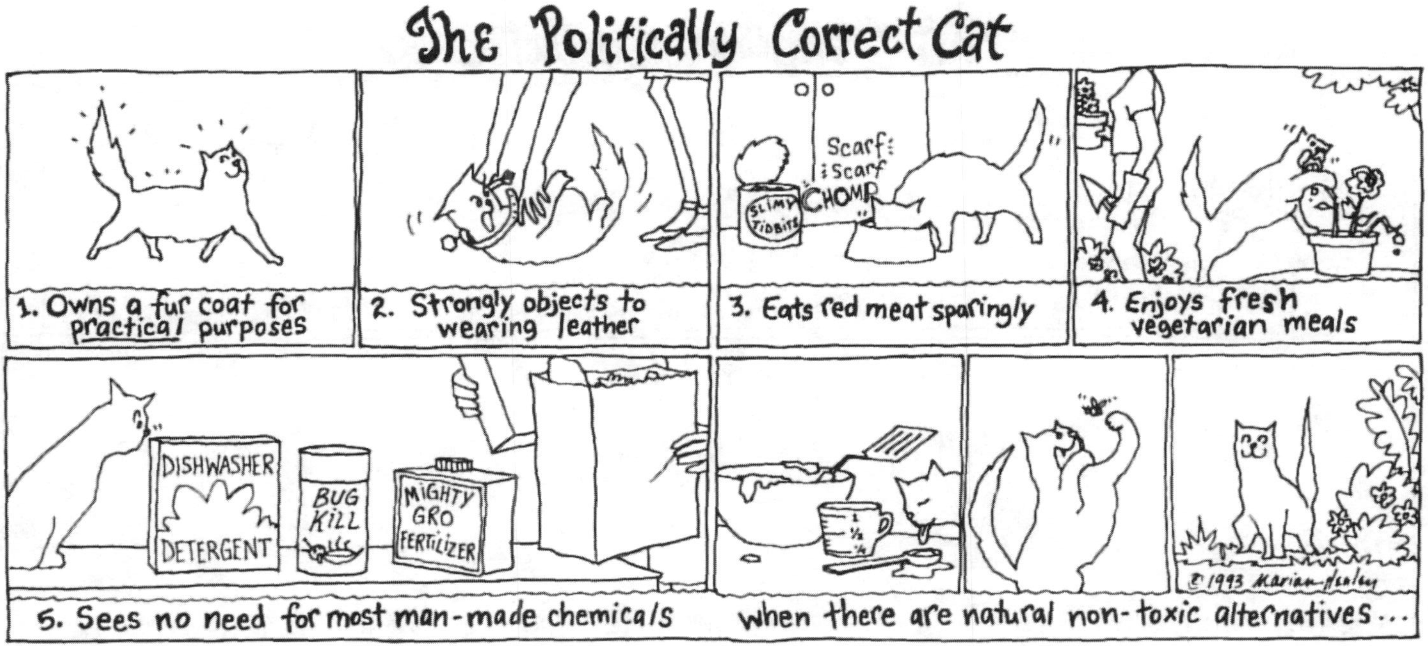
The Politically Correct Cat
1. Owns a fur coat for practical purposes
2. Strongly objects to wearing leather
SLIMY TIDBITS
Scarf: Scarf
CHOMP
3. Eats red meat sparingly
4. Enjoys fresh vegetarian meals
DISHWASHER DETERGENT
BUG KILL
MIGHTY GRO FERTILIZER
5. Sees no need for most man-made chemicals
when there are natural non-toxic alternatives...
© 1993 Marian Henley

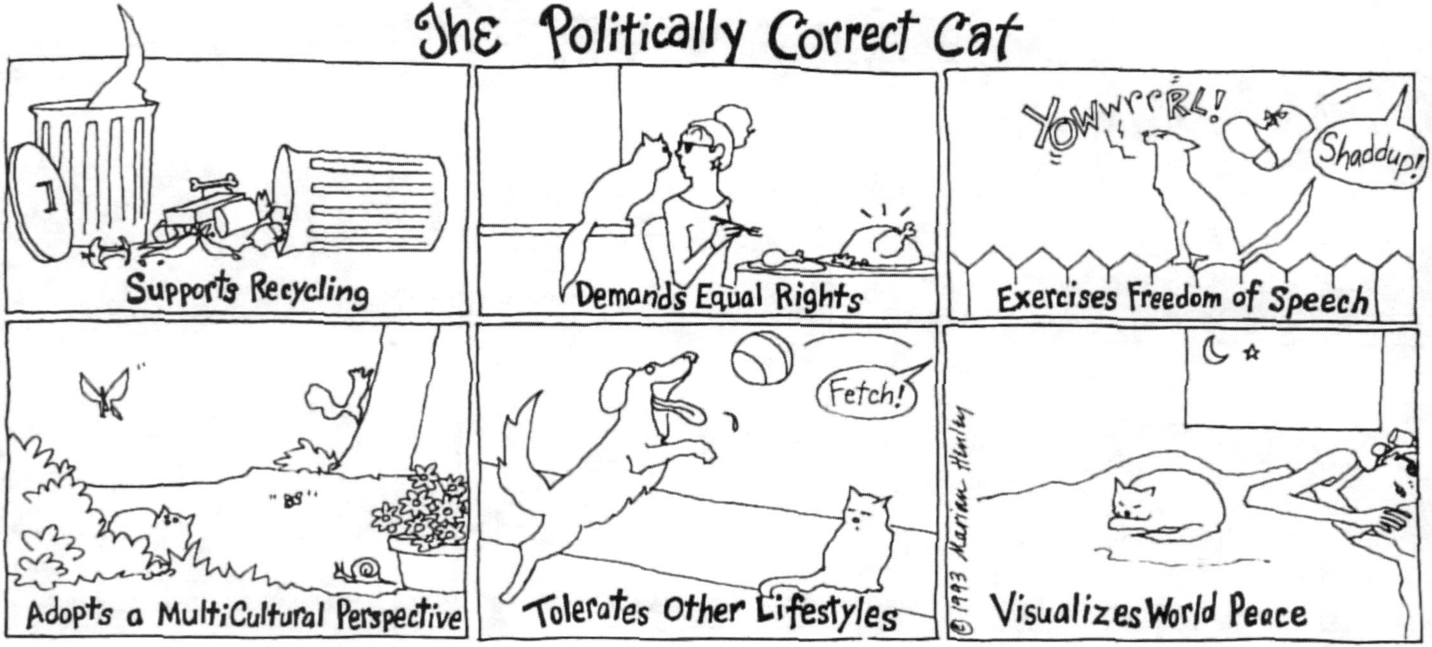
The Politically Correct Cat
Supports Recycling
Demands Equal Rights
YOWWrrrRL!
Shaddup!
Exercises Freedom of Speech
"BS"
Adopts a MultiCultural Perspective
Fetch!
Tolerates Other Lifestyles
© 1993 Marian Henley
Visualizes World Peace

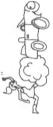

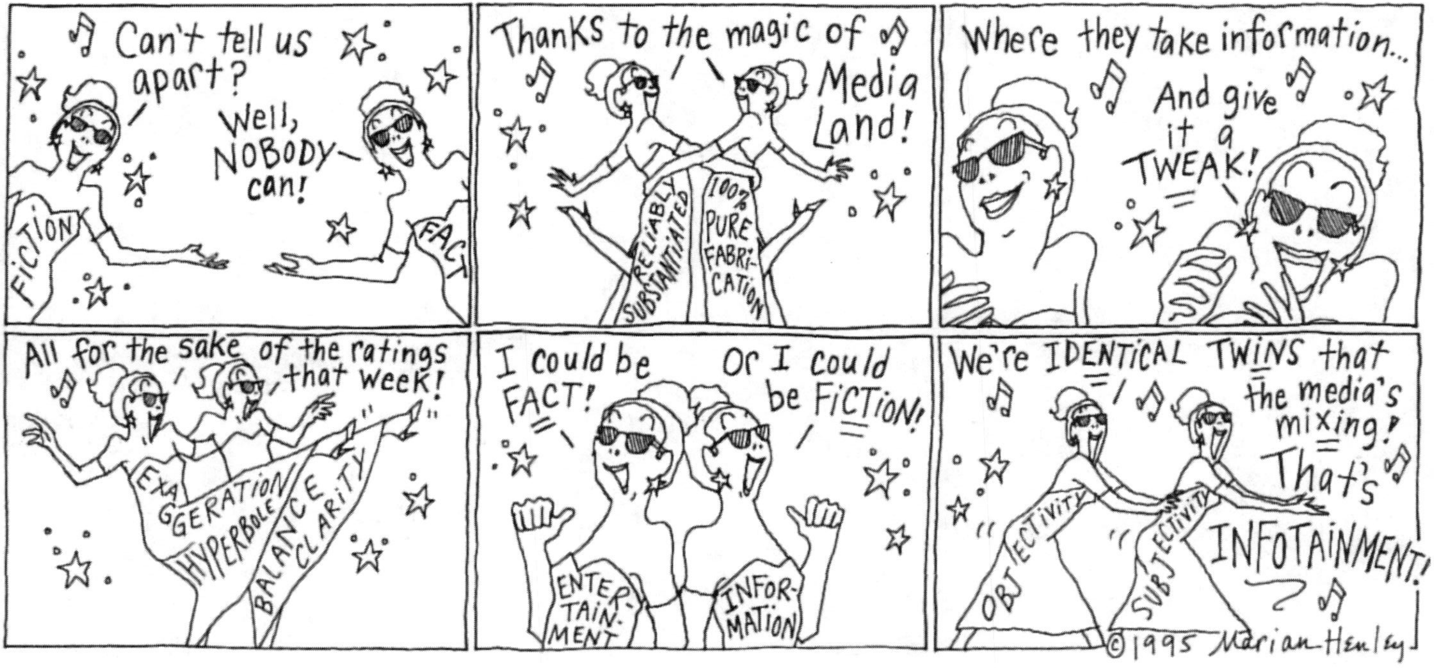
Can't tell us apart?
Well, NOBODY— can!
FICTION
FACT
Thanks to the magic of Media Land!
RELIABLY SUBSTANTIATED
100% PURE FABRICATION
Where they take information...
And give it a TWEAK!
All for the sake of the ratings that week!
EXAGGERATION
HYPERBOLE
BALANCE
CLARITY
I could be FACT!
Or I could be FICTION!
ENTERTAINMENT
INFORMATION
We're IDENTICAL TWINS that the media's mixing!
That's INFOTAINMENT!
OBJECTIVITY
SUBJECTIVITY
©1995 Marian Henley

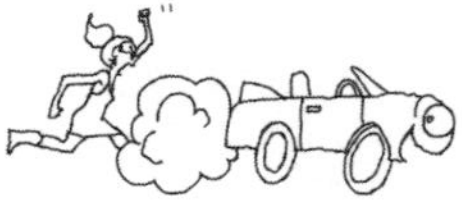

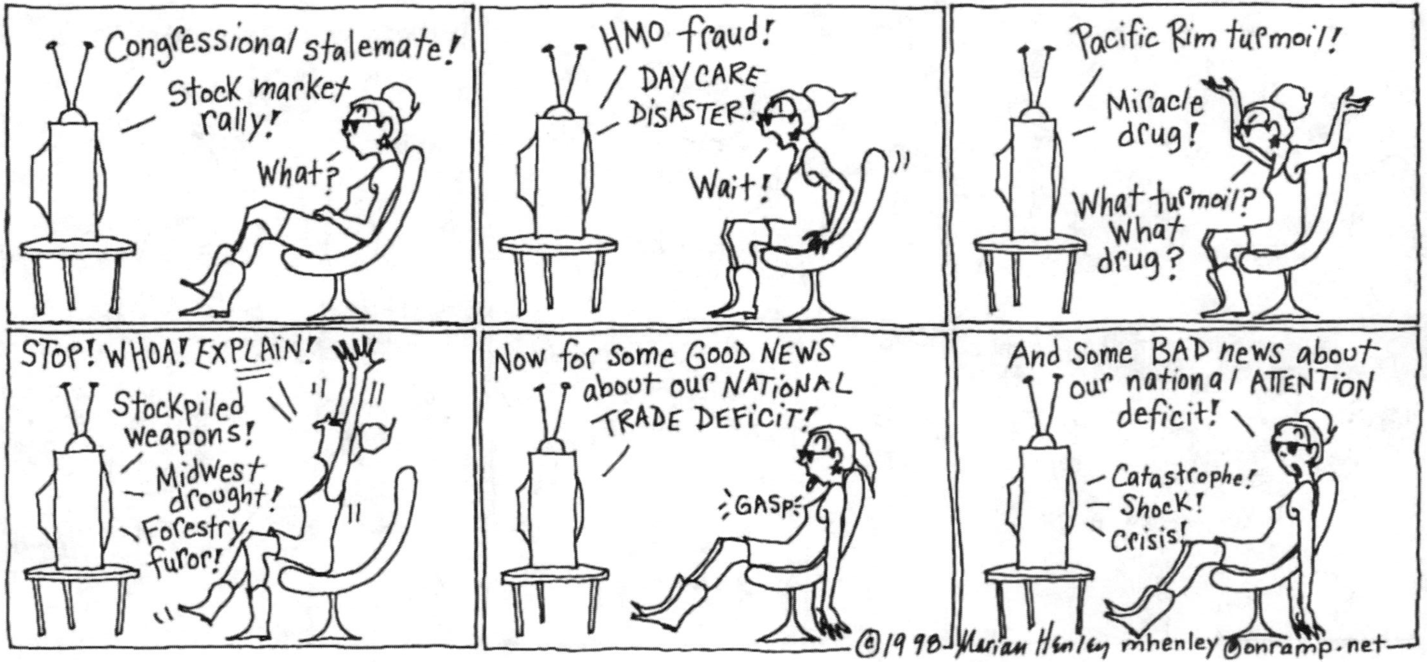
Congressional stalemate!
Stock market rally!
What?
HMO fraud!
DAY CARE DISASTER!
Wait!
Pacific Rim turmoil!
Miracle drug!
What turmoil? What drug?
STOP! WHOA! EXPLAIN!
Stockpiled weapons!
Midwest drought!
Forestry furor!
Now for some GOOD NEWS about our NATIONAL TRADE DEFICIT!
GASP
And some BAD news about our national ATTENTION deficit!
Catastrophe!
Shock!
Crisis!
©1998 Marian Henley mhenley@onramp.net

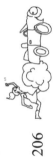

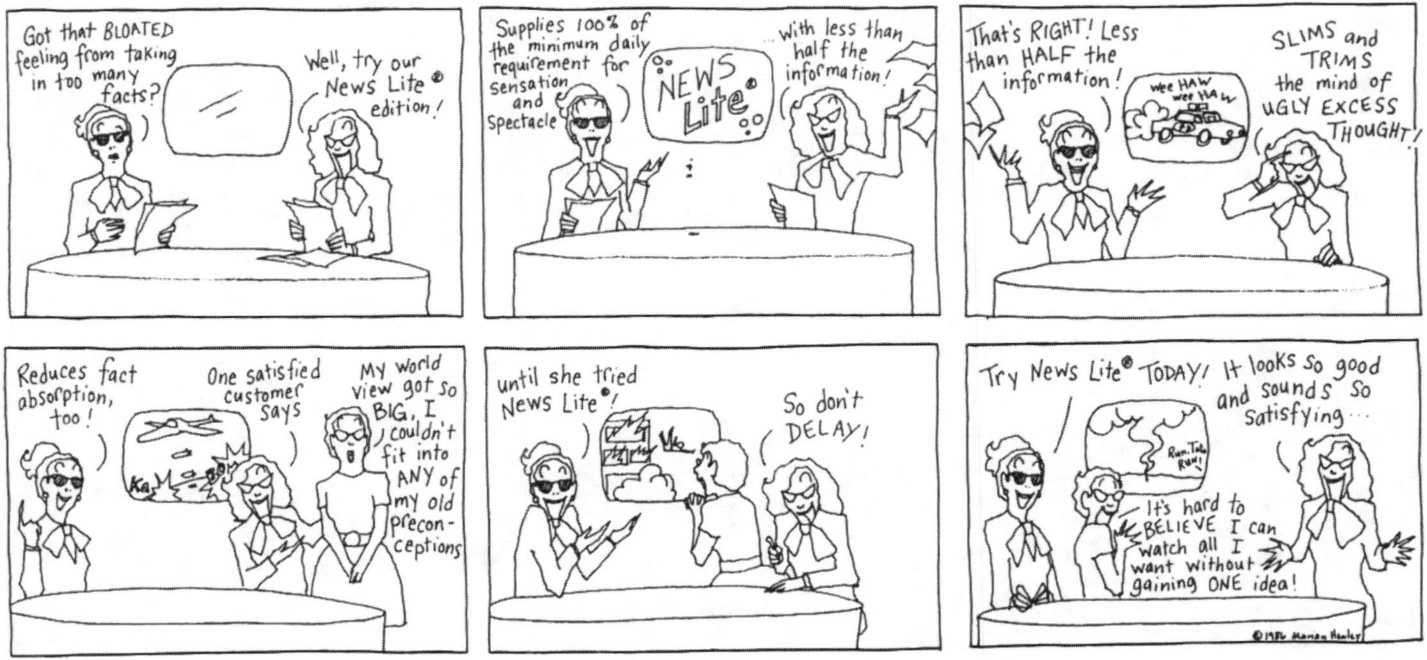
Got that BLOATED feeling from taking in too many facts?
Well, try our News Lite® edition!
Supplies 100% of the minimum daily requirement for sensation and spectacle
NEWS Lite®
...with less than half the information!
That's RIGHT! Less than HALF the information!
WEE HAW WEE HAW
SLIMS and TRIMS the mind of UGLY EXCESS THOUGHT!
Reduces fact absorption, too!
One satisfied customer says
My world view got so BIG, I couldn't fit into ANY of my old precon-ceptions
until she tried News Lite®!
So don't DELAY!
Try News Lite® TODAY! It looks so good and sounds so satisfying...
Run, Toto, RUN!
It's hard to BELIEVE I can watch all I want without gaining ONE idea!

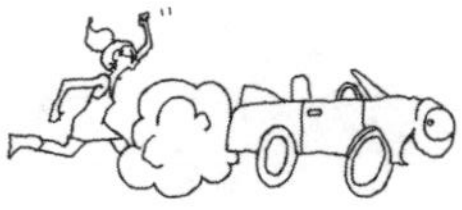

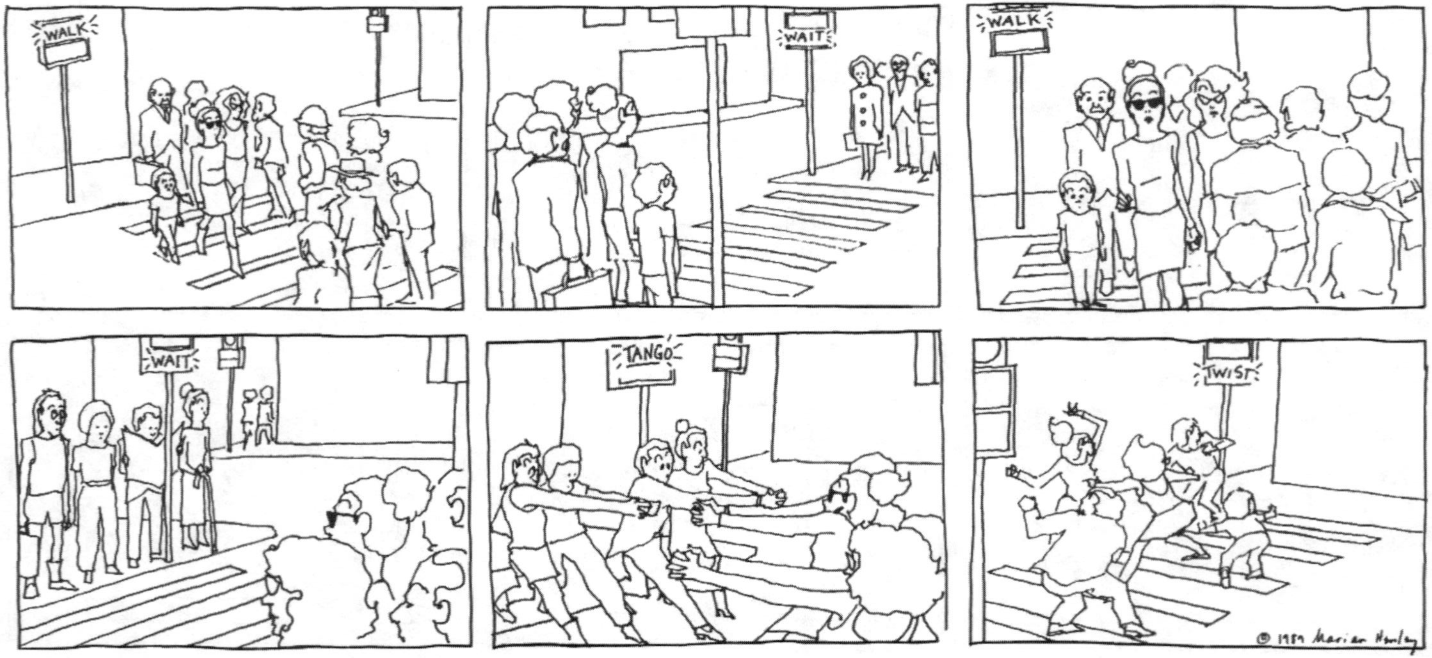
WALK
WAIT
WALK
WAIT
TANGO
TWIST

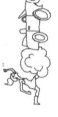

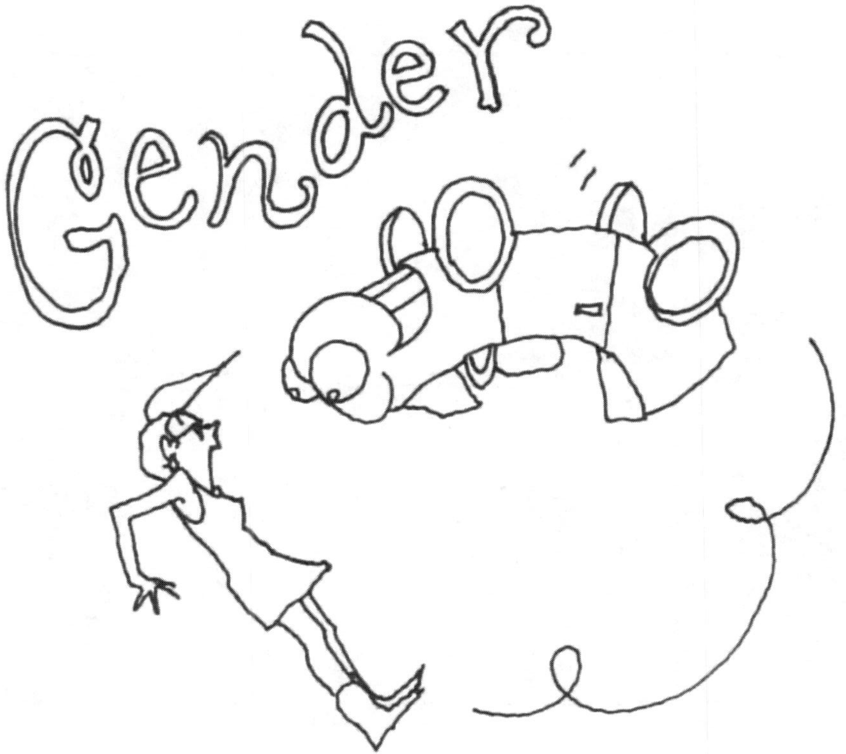
Gender

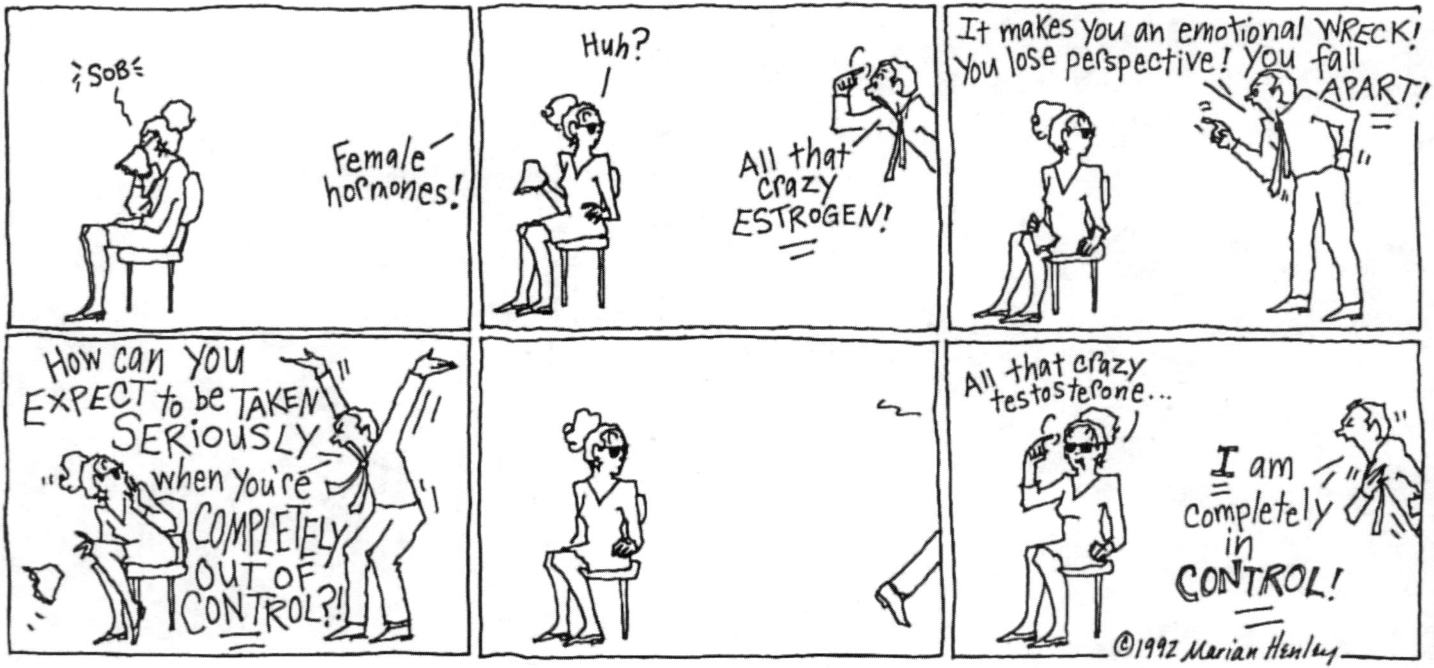
¡SOB!
Female hormones!
Huh?
All that crazy ESTROGEN!
It makes you an emotional WRECK! You lose perspective! You fall APART!
How can you EXPECT to be TAKEN SERIOUSLY when you're COMPLETELY OUT OF CONTROL?!
All that crazy testosterone...
I am completely in CONTROL!
©1992 Marian Henley

Did MODERN WOMAN Evolve from a DOOR MAT?

Oh, it's alright! Go ahead and walk all over me!
I don't mind! I really don't!
I really...
I...
I...
I really...
I really DO mind!
So watch your step!

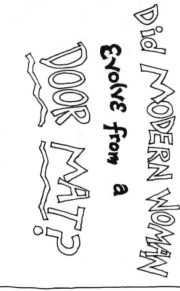

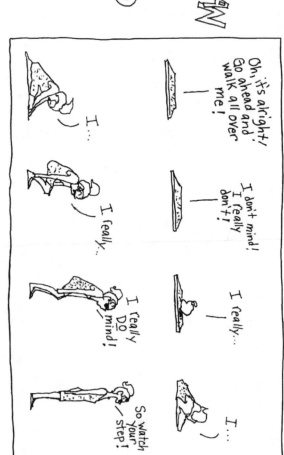

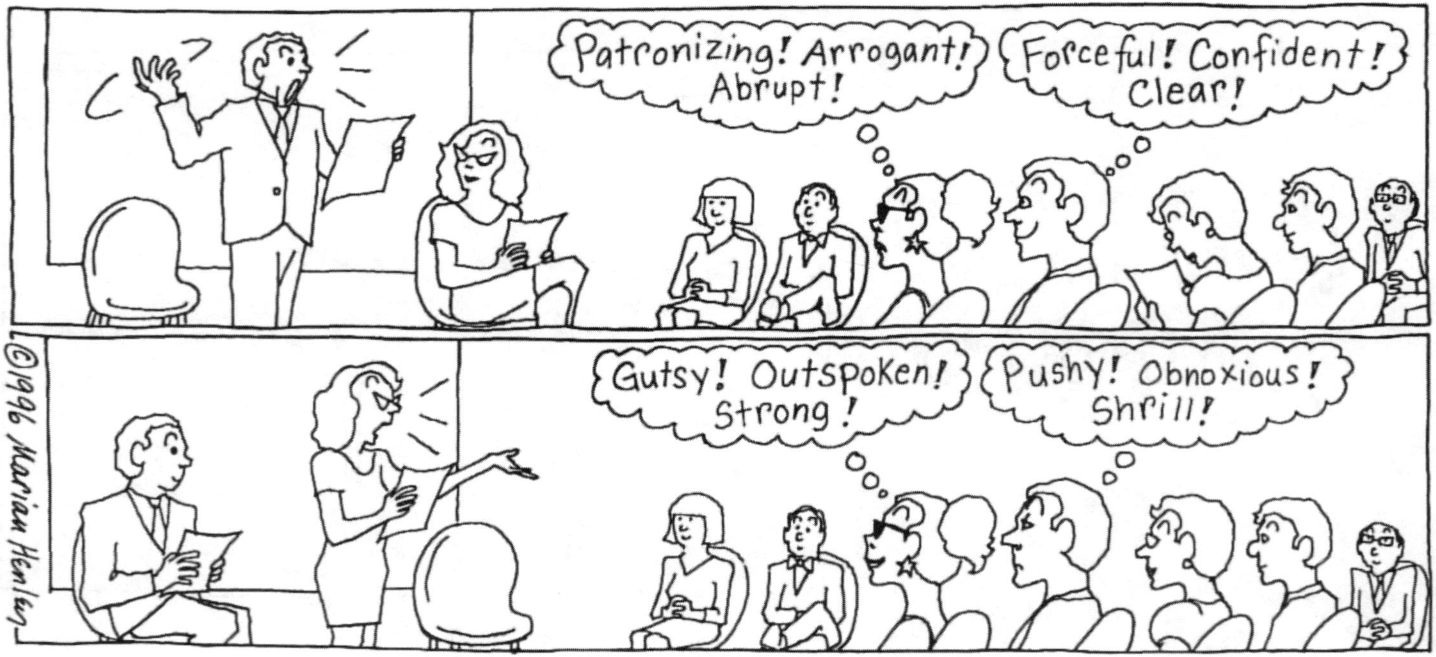
Patronizing! Arrogant! Abrupt!
Forceful! Confident! Clear!
Gutsy! Outspoken! Strong!
Pushy! Obnoxious! Shrill!
©1996 Marian Henley

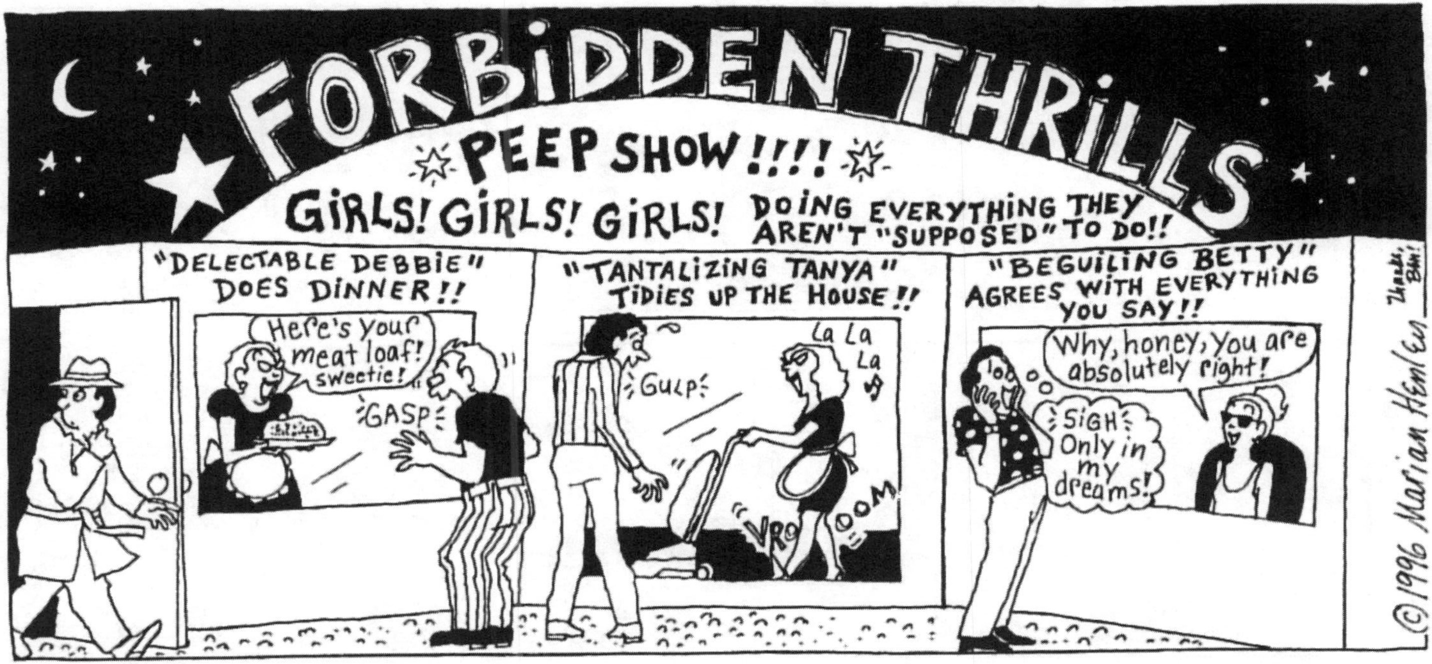
FORBIDDEN THRILLS
PEEP SHOW!!!!
GIRLS! GIRLS! GIRLS! DOING EVERYTHING THEY AREN'T "SUPPOSED" TO DO!!
"DELECTABLE DEBBIE" DOES DINNER!!
Here's your meat loaf! sweetie!
GASP
"TANTALIZING TANYA" TIDIES UP THE HOUSE!!
GULP
La La La
VROOOOM
"BEGUILING BETTY" AGREES WITH EVERYTHING YOU SAY!!
Why, honey, you are absolutely right!
SIGH Only in my dreams!
©1996 Marian Henley
Thanks, Ben!

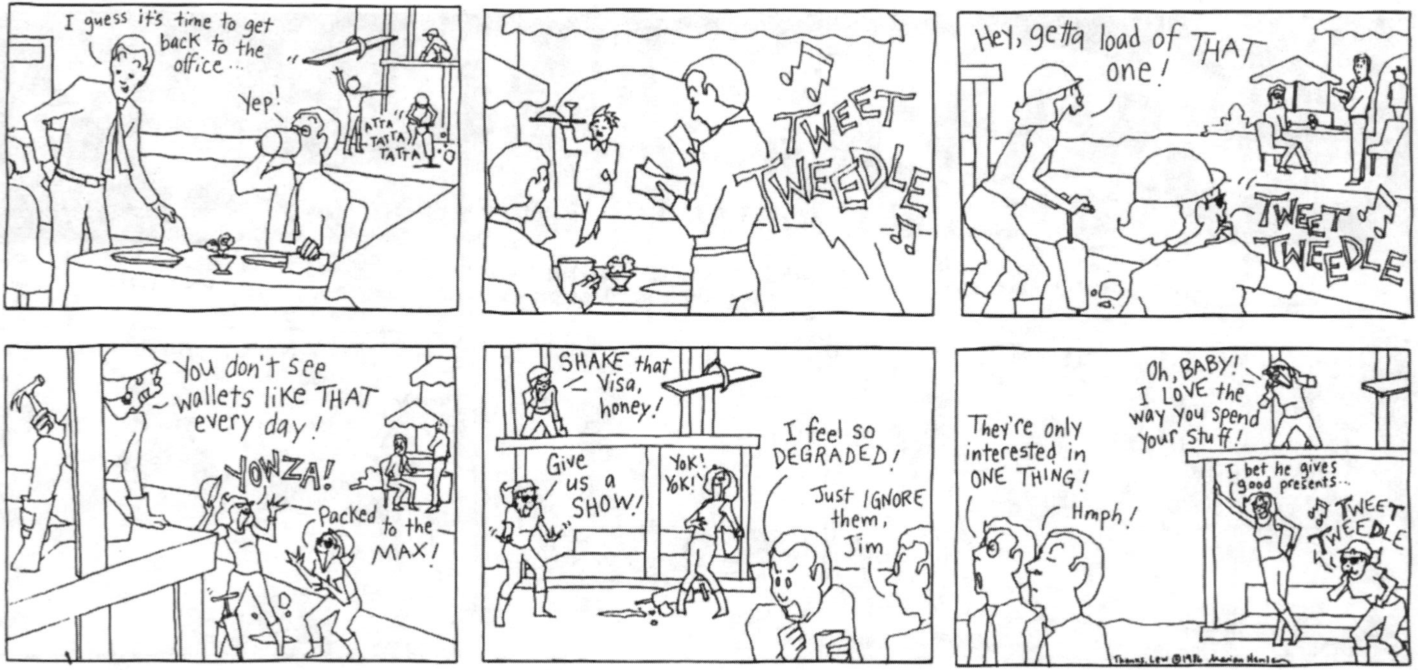
I guess it's time to get back to the office...
Yep!
ATTA TATTA TATTA
TWEET TWEEDLE
Hey, getta load of THAT one!
TWEET TWEEDLE
You don't see wallets like THAT every day!
YOWZA!
Packed to the MAX!
SHAKE that Visa, honey!
Give us a SHOW!
YOK! YOK!
I feel so DEGRADED!
Just IGNORE them, Jim
They're only interested in ONE THING!
Hmph!
Oh, BABY! I LOVE the way you spend your stuff!
I bet he gives good presents...
TWEET TWEEDLE

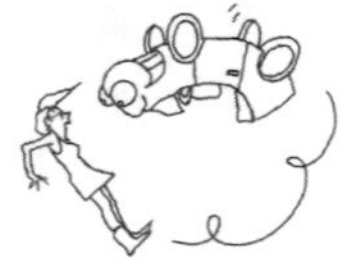

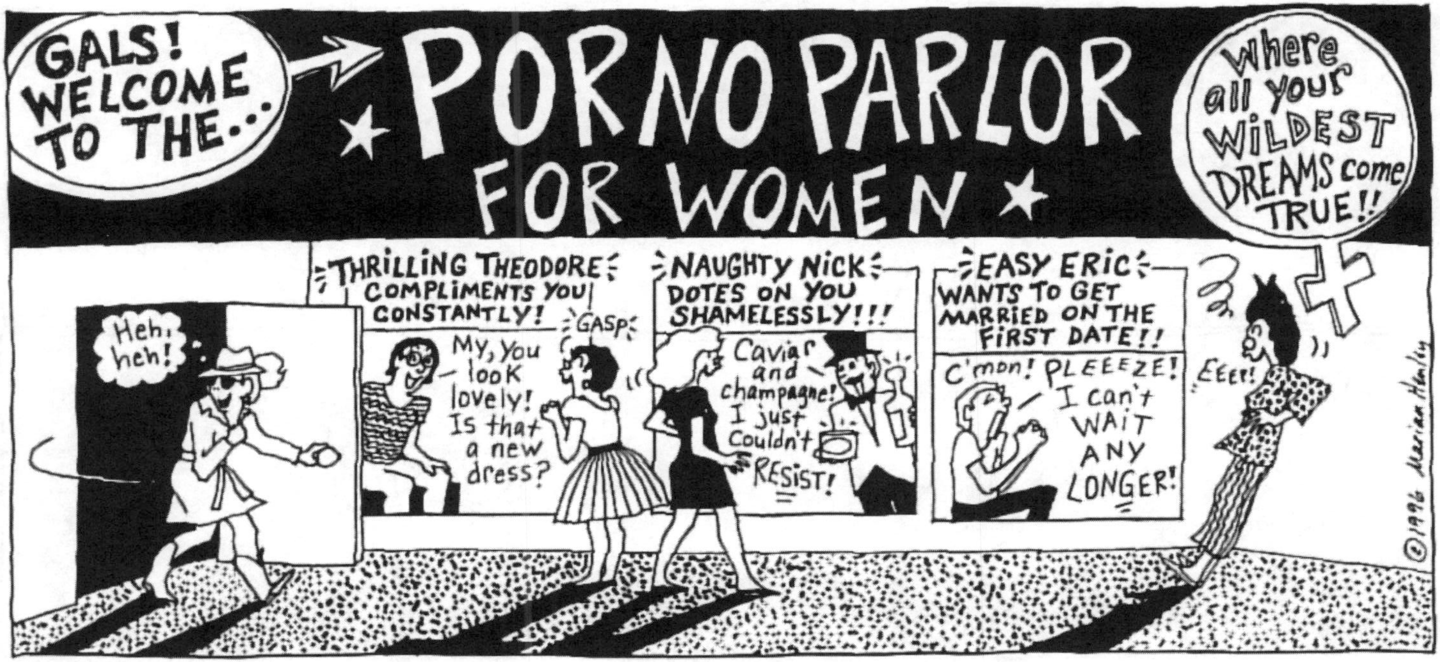
GALS! WELCOME TO THE...
PORNO PARLOR FOR WOMEN
Where all your WILDEST DREAMS come TRUE!!
Heh, heh!
THRILLING THEODORE COMPLIMENTS YOU CONSTANTLY!
My, You look lovely! Is that a new dress?
GASP
NAUGHTY NICK DOTES ON YOU SHAMELESSLY!!!
Caviar and champagne! I just Couldn't RESIST!
EASY ERIC WANTS TO GET MARRIED ON THE FIRST DATE!!
C'mon! PLEEEZE! I can't WAIT ANY LONGER!
EEEE!
©1996 Marian Henley

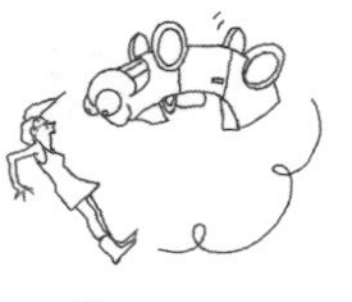

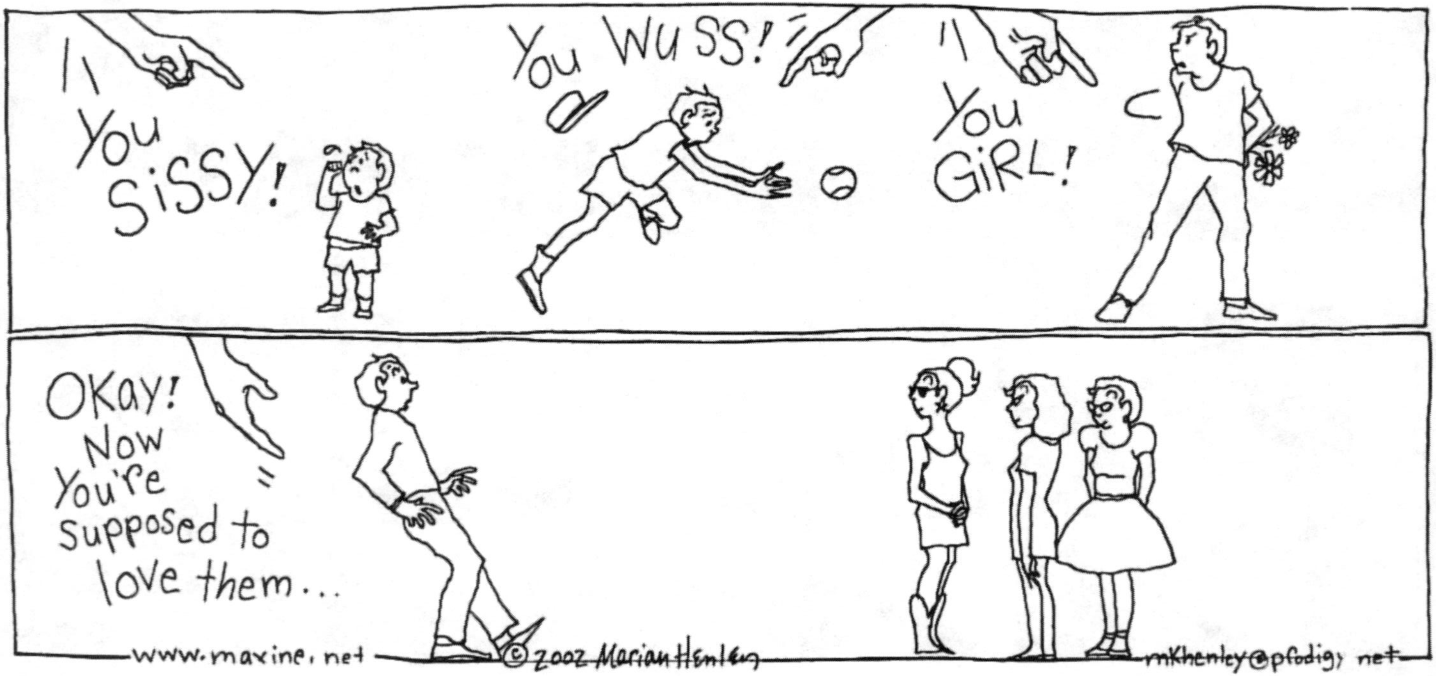
"You SiSSY!"
"You WUSS!"
"You GiRL!"
"OKay! Now You're supposed to love them..."
www.maxine.net
© 2002 Marian Henley
mkhenley@prodigy.net

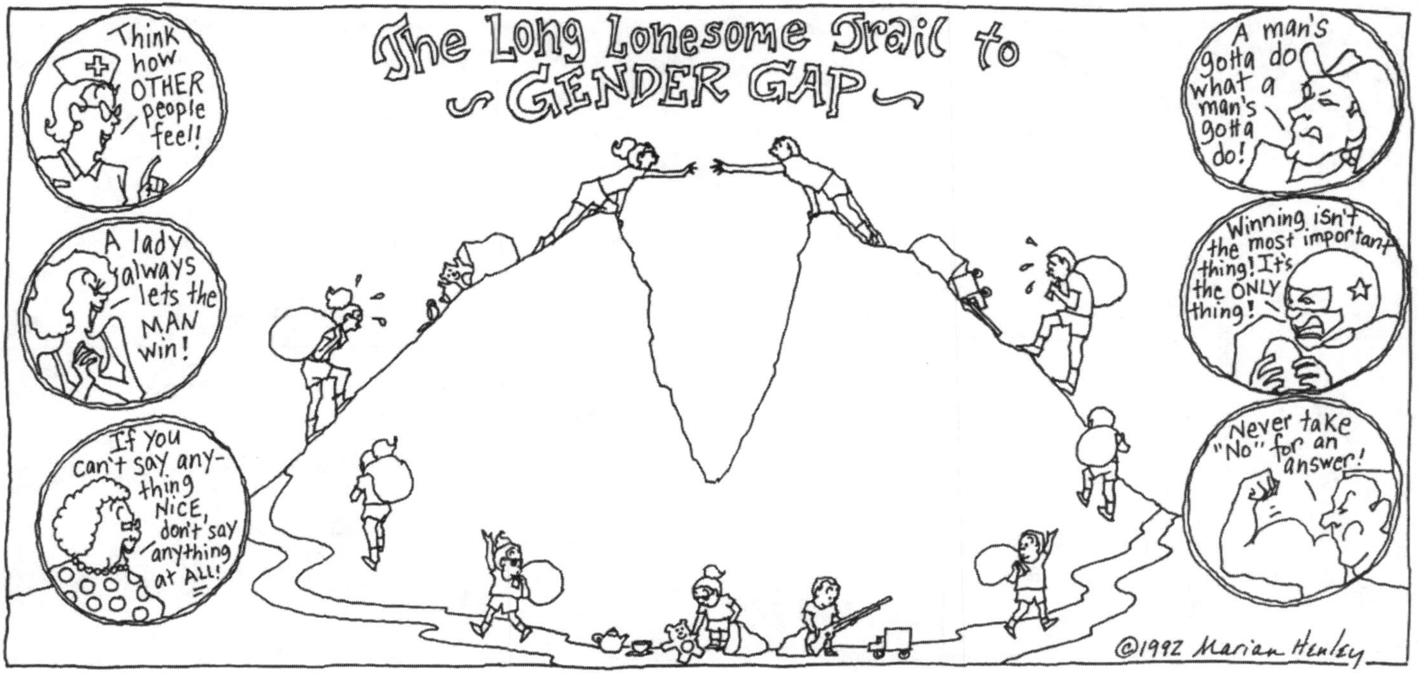
The Long Lonesome Trail to ~GENDER GAP~
Think how OTHER people feel!!
A lady always lets the MAN win!
If you can't say anything NICE, don't say anything at ALL!
A man's gotta do what a man's gotta do!
Winning isn't the most important thing! It's the ONLY thing!
Never take "No" for an answer!
©1992 Marian Henley

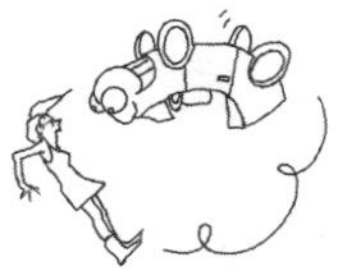

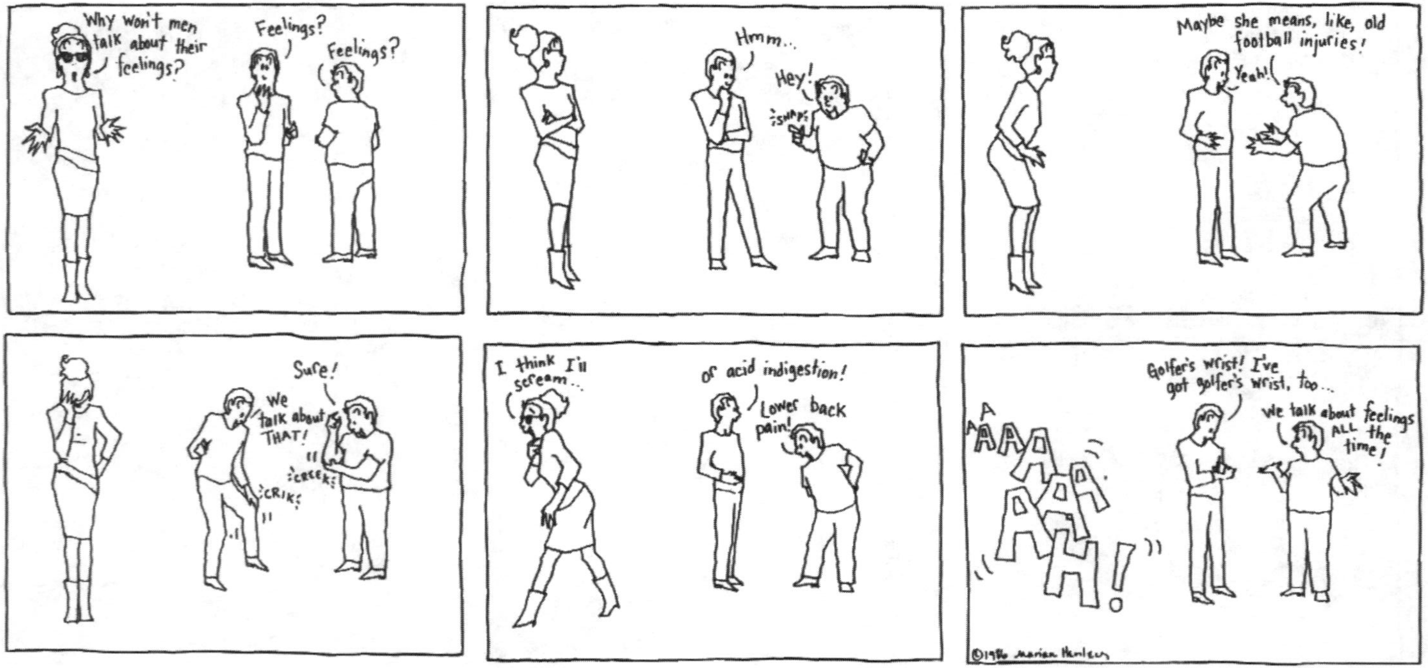
Why won't men talk about their feelings?
Feelings?
Feelings?
Hmm...
Hey!
SNAP!
Maybe she means, like, old football injuries!
Yeah!
Sure!
We talk about THAT!
CREEK!
CRIK!
I think I'll scream...
or acid indigestion!
Lower back pain!
Golfer's wrist! I've got golfer's wrist, too...
We talk about feelings ALL the time!
AAAAAAAAH!
©1986 Marian Henley

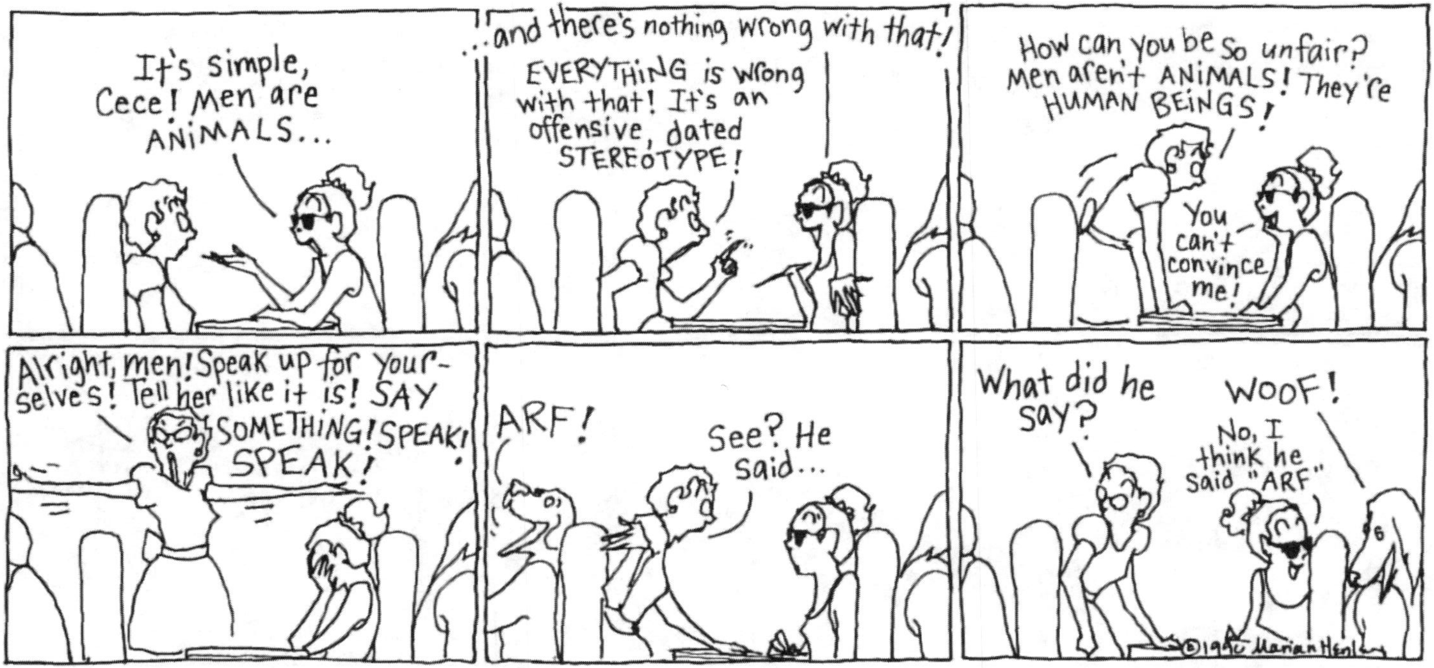
It's simple, Cece! Men are ANIMALS...
...and there's nothing wrong with that!
EVERYTHING is wrong with that! It's an offensive, dated STEREOTYPE!
How can you be so unfair? Men aren't ANIMALS! They're HUMAN BEINGS!
You can't convince me!
Alright, men! Speak up for your-selves! Tell her like it is! SAY SOMETHING! SPEAK! SPEAK!
ARF!
See? He said...
What did he say?
WOOF!
No, I think he said "ARF"

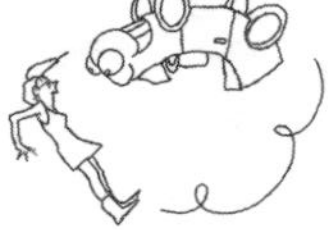

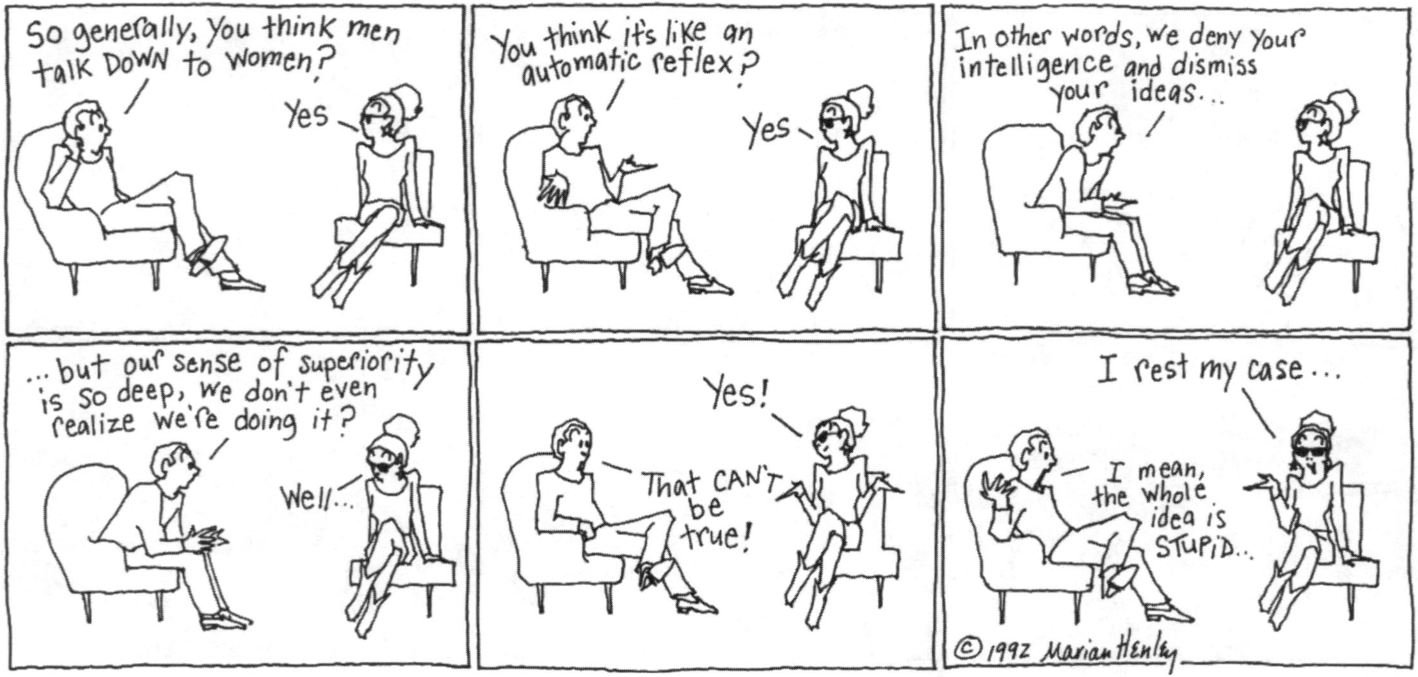
So generally, you think men talk DOWN to women?
Yes
You think it's like an automatic reflex?
Yes
In other words, we deny your intelligence and dismiss your ideas...
...but our sense of superiority is so deep, we don't even realize we're doing it?
Well...
That CAN'T be true!
Yes!
I mean, the whole idea is STUPID...
I rest my case...
© 1992 Marian Henley

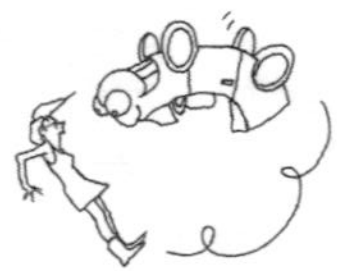

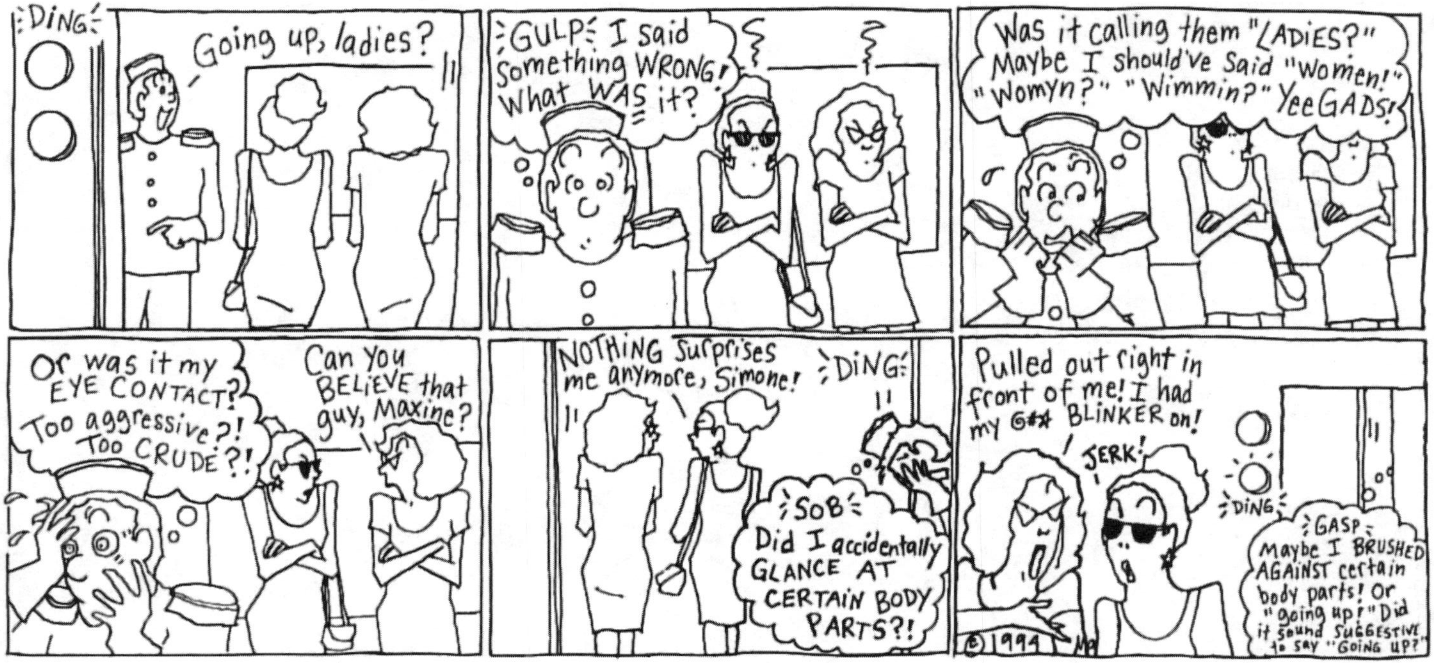
DING
Going up, ladies?
GULP I said something WRONG! What WAS it?
Was it calling them "LADIES?" Maybe I should've said "women!" "Womyn?" "Wimmin?" YeeGADS!
Or was it my EYE CONTACT? Too aggressive?! Too CRUDE?!
Can you BELIEVE that guy, Maxine?
NOTHING surprises me anymore, Simone!
DING
SOB Did I accidentally GLANCE AT CERTAIN BODY PARTS?!
Pulled out right in front of me! I had my G#* BLINKER on!
JERK!
DING
GASP Maybe I BRUSHED AGAINST certain body parts! Or "going up?" Did it sound SUGGESTIVE to say "GOING UP?"
© 1994

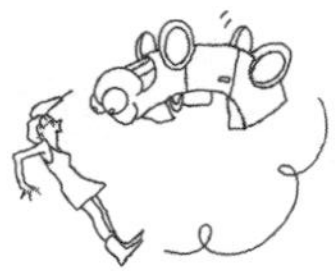

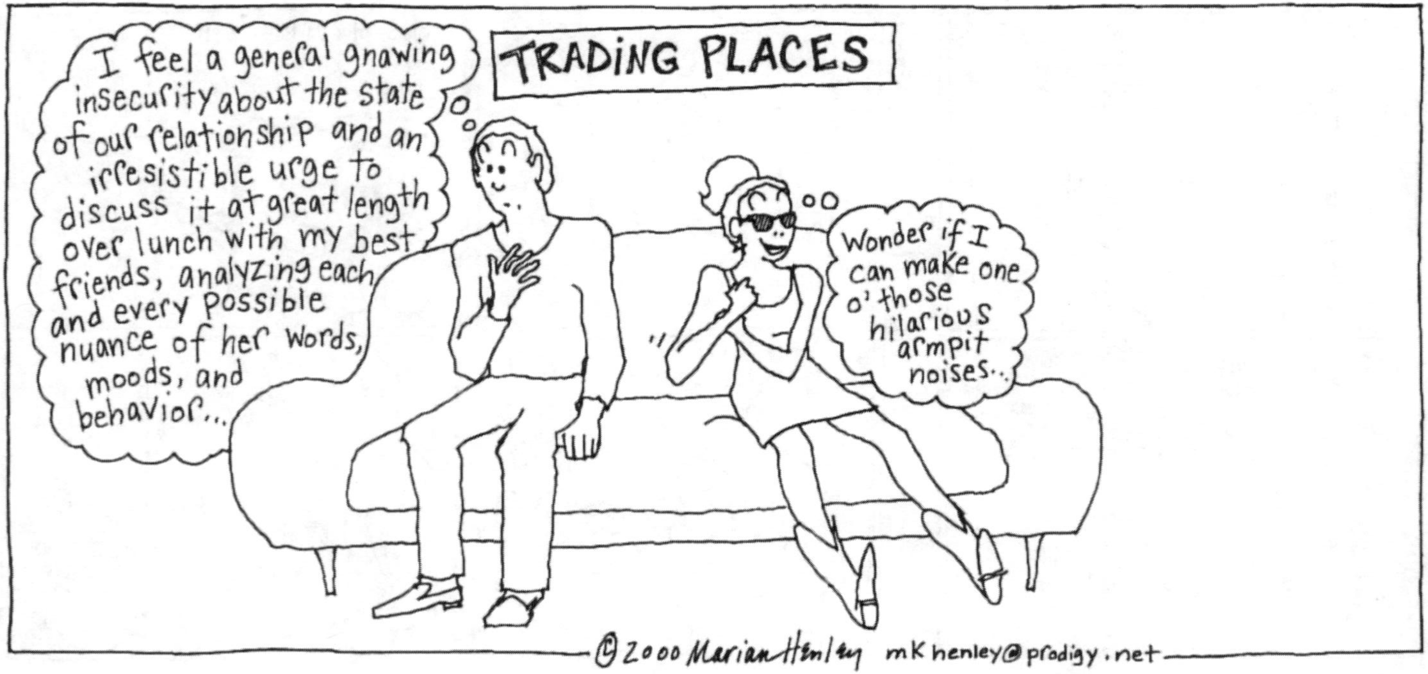
TRADING PLACES
I feel a general gnawing insecurity about the state of our relationship and an irresistible urge to discuss it at great length over lunch with my best friends, analyzing each and every possible nuance of her words, moods, and behavior...
Wonder if I can make one o' those hilarious armpit noises...
©2000 Marian Henley mkhenley@prodigy.net

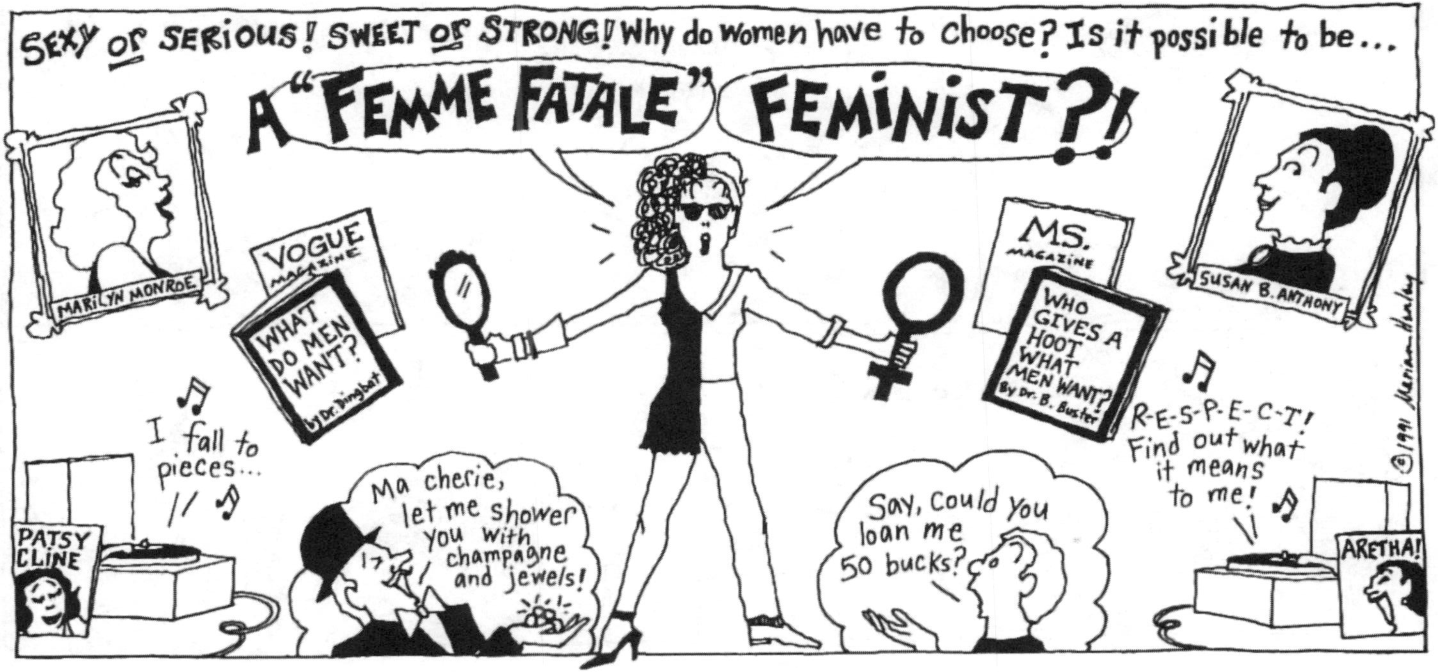
SEXY OR SERIOUS! SWEET OR STRONG! Why do women have to choose? Is it possible to be...
A "FEMME FATALE"
FEMINIST?!
MARILYN MONROE
VOGUE MAGAZINE
WHAT DO MEN WANT? By Dr. Dingbat
MS. MAGAZINE
WHO GIVES A HOOT WHAT MEN WANT? By Dr. B. Buster
SUSAN B. ANTHONY
I fall to pieces...
PATSY CLINE
Ma cherie, let me shower you with champagne and jewels!
Say, could you loan me 50 bucks?
R-E-S-P-E-C-T! Find out what it means to me!
ARETHA!
©1991 Marian Henley

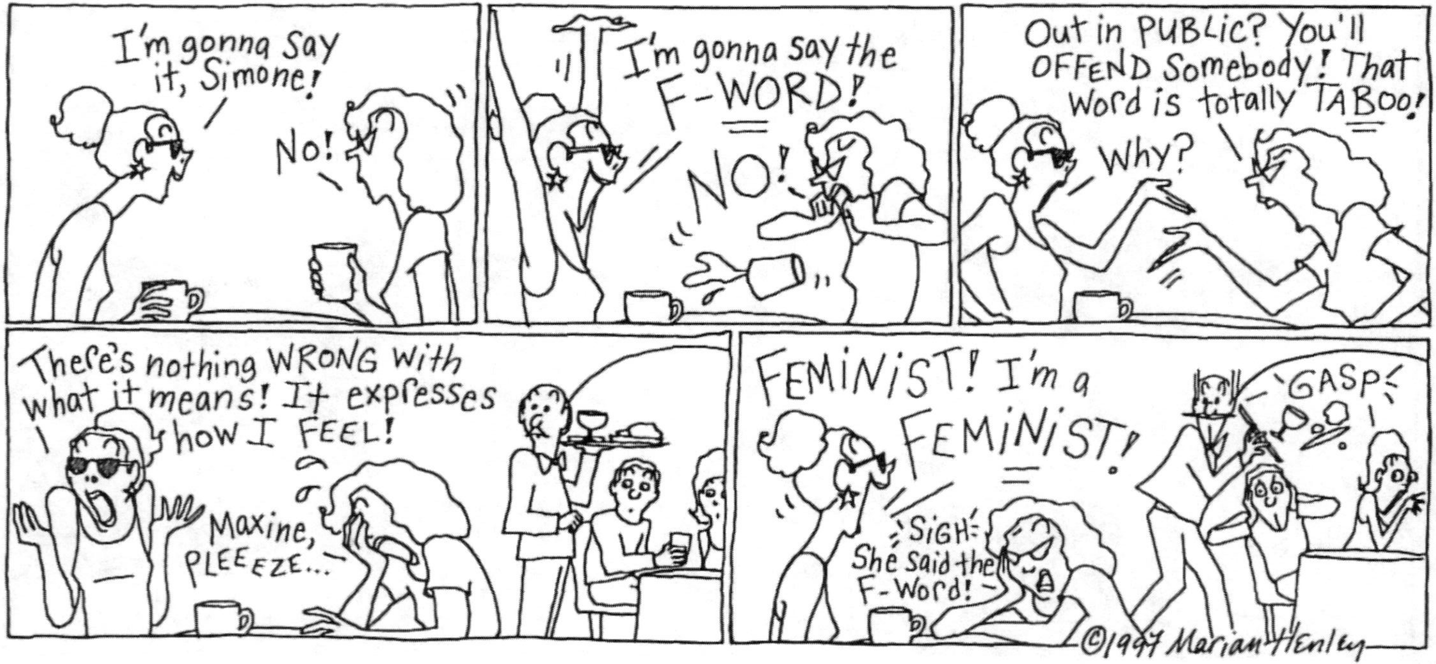
I'm gonna say it, Simone!
No!
I'm gonna say the F-WORD!
NO!
Out in PUBLIC? You'll OFFEND Somebody! That Word is totally TABOO!
Why?
There's nothing WRONG with what it means! It expresses how I FEEL!
Maxine, PLEEEEZE...
FEMINIST! I'm a FEMINIST!
GASP!
SIGH! She said the F-Word!
©1997 Marian Henley

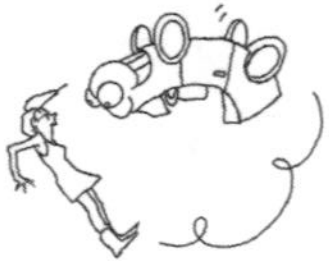

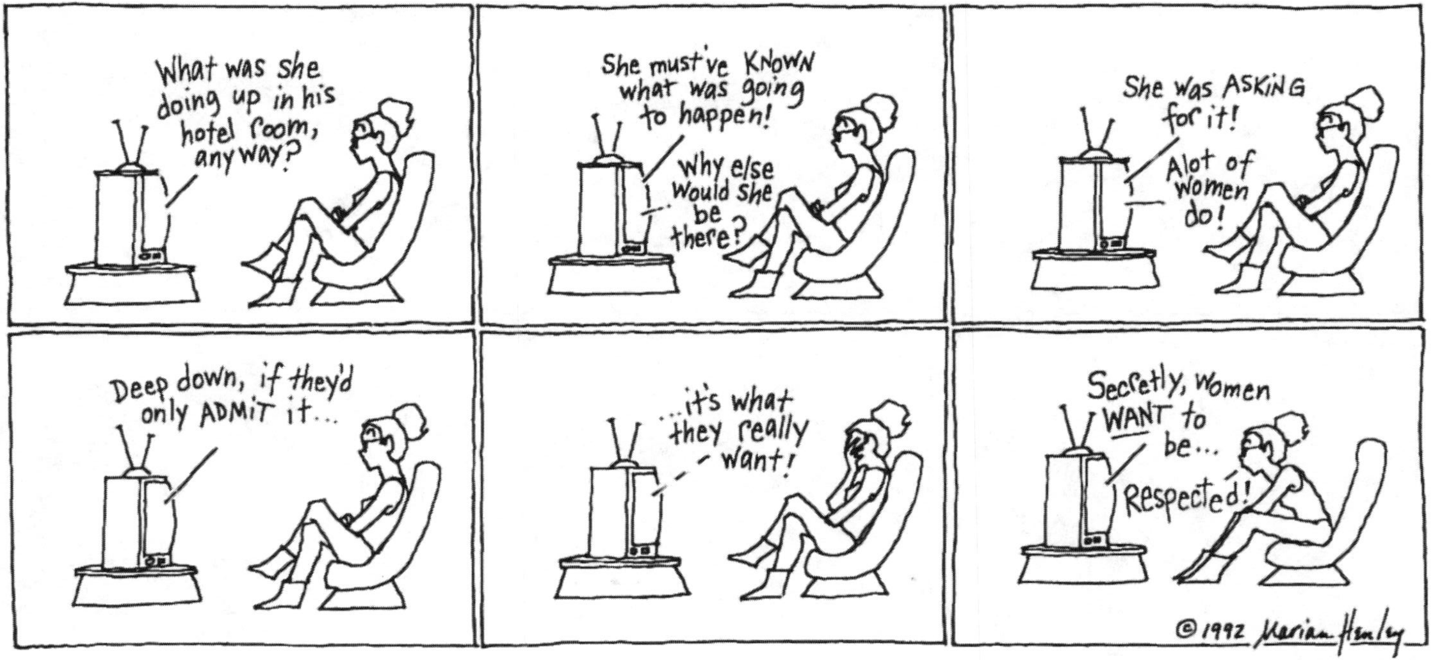
What was she doing up in his hotel room, anyway?
She must've KNOWN what was going to happen!
Why else would she be there?
She was ASKING for it!
Alot of women do!
Deep down, if they'd only ADMIT it...
...it's what they really want!
Secretly, women WANT to be...
Respected!
© 1992 Marian Henley

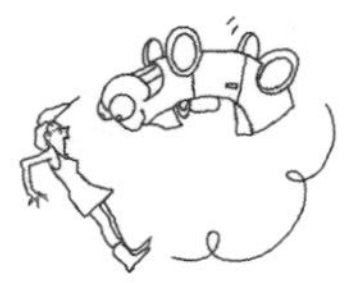

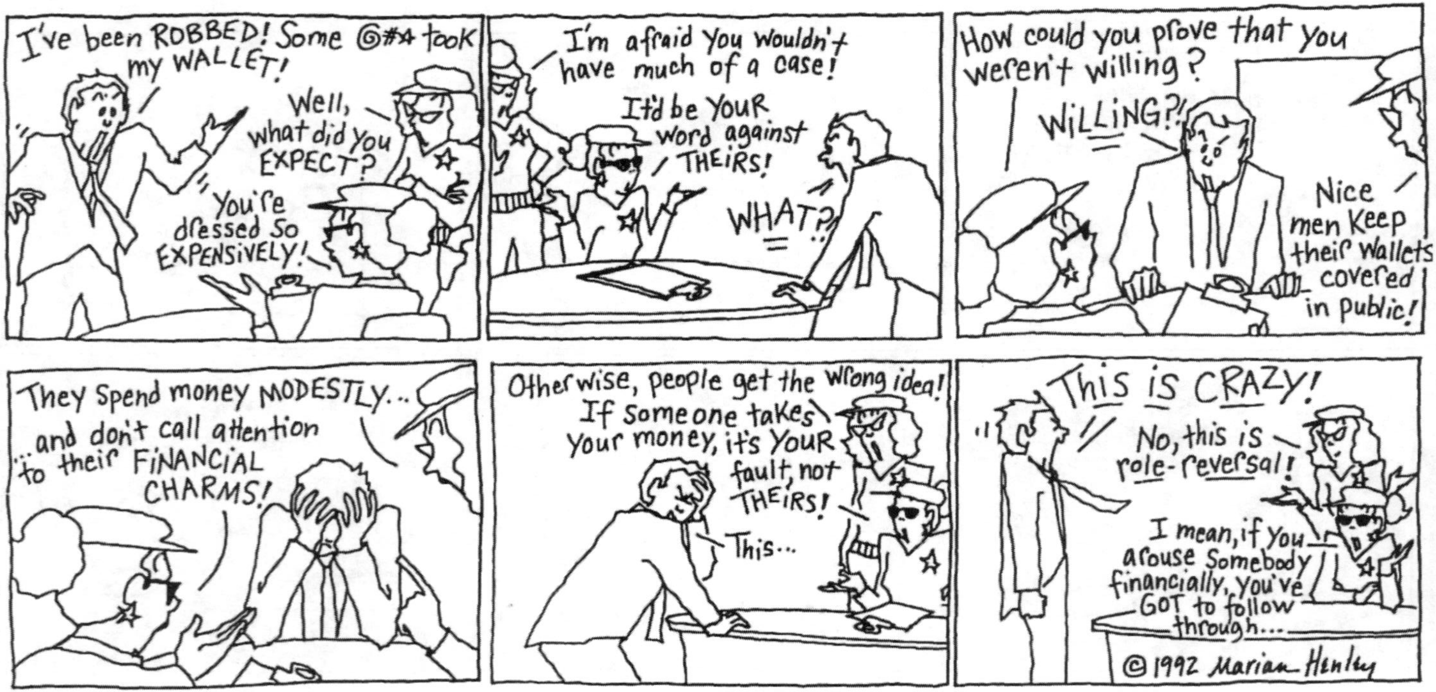
I've been ROBBED! Some @#* took my WALLET!
Well, what did you EXPECT?
You're dressed so EXPENSIVELY!
I'm afraid you wouldn't have much of a case!
It'd be YOUR word against THEIRS!
WHAT?!
How could you prove that you weren't willing?
WILLING?!
Nice men keep their wallets covered in public!
They spend money MODESTLY...
...and don't call attention to their FINANCIAL CHARMS!
Otherwise, people get the wrong idea!
If someone takes your money, it's YOUR fault, not THEIRS!
This...
THIS IS CRAZY!
No, this is role-reversal!
I mean, if you arouse somebody financially, you've GOT to follow through...
© 1992 Marian Henley

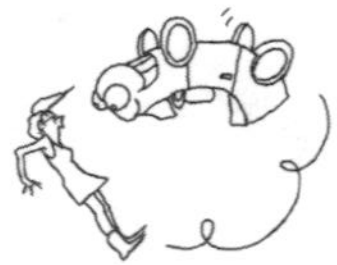

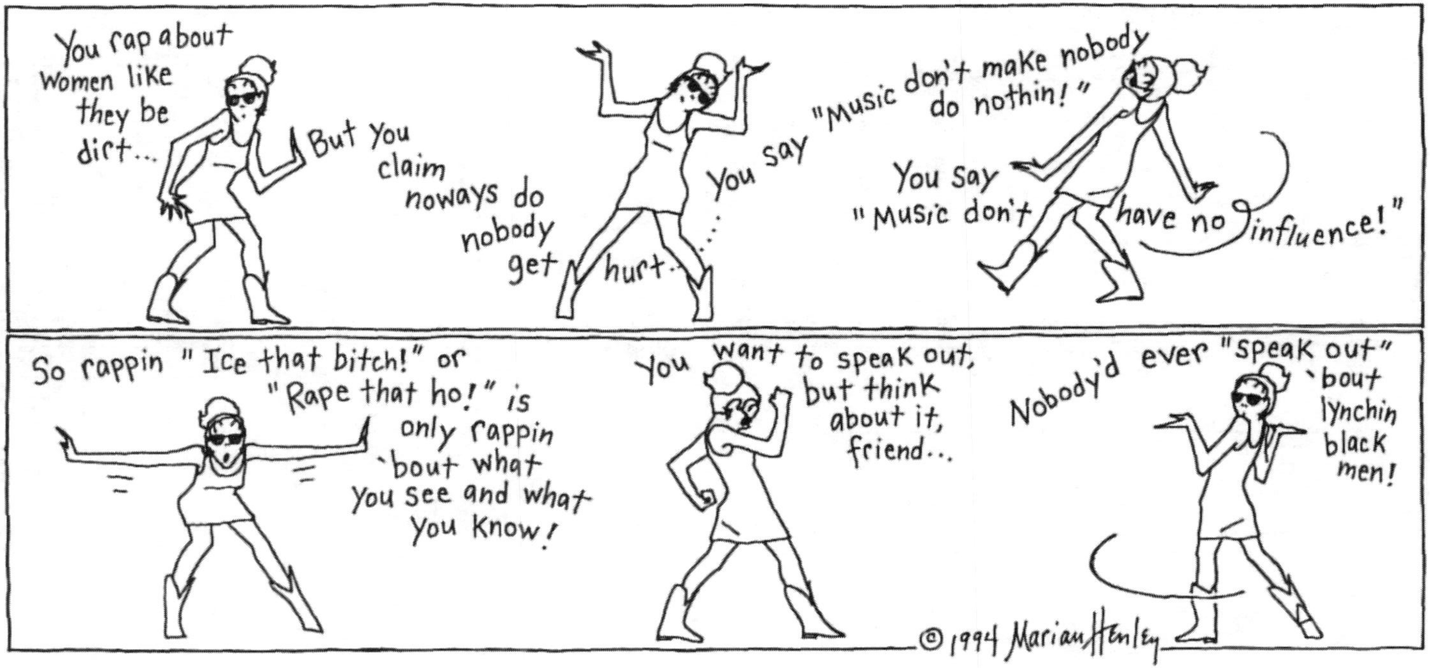
You rap about women like they be dirt...
But you claim noways do nobody get hurt...
You say "Music don't make nobody do nothin!"
You say "Music don't have no influence!"
So rappin "Ice that bitch!" or "Rape that ho!" is only rappin 'bout what you see and what you know!
You want to speak out, but think about it, friend...
Nobody'd ever "speak out" 'bout lynchin black men!
© 1994 Marian Henley

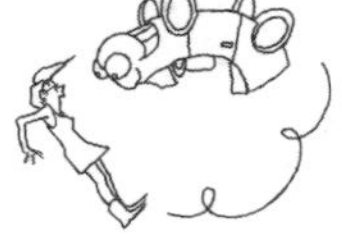

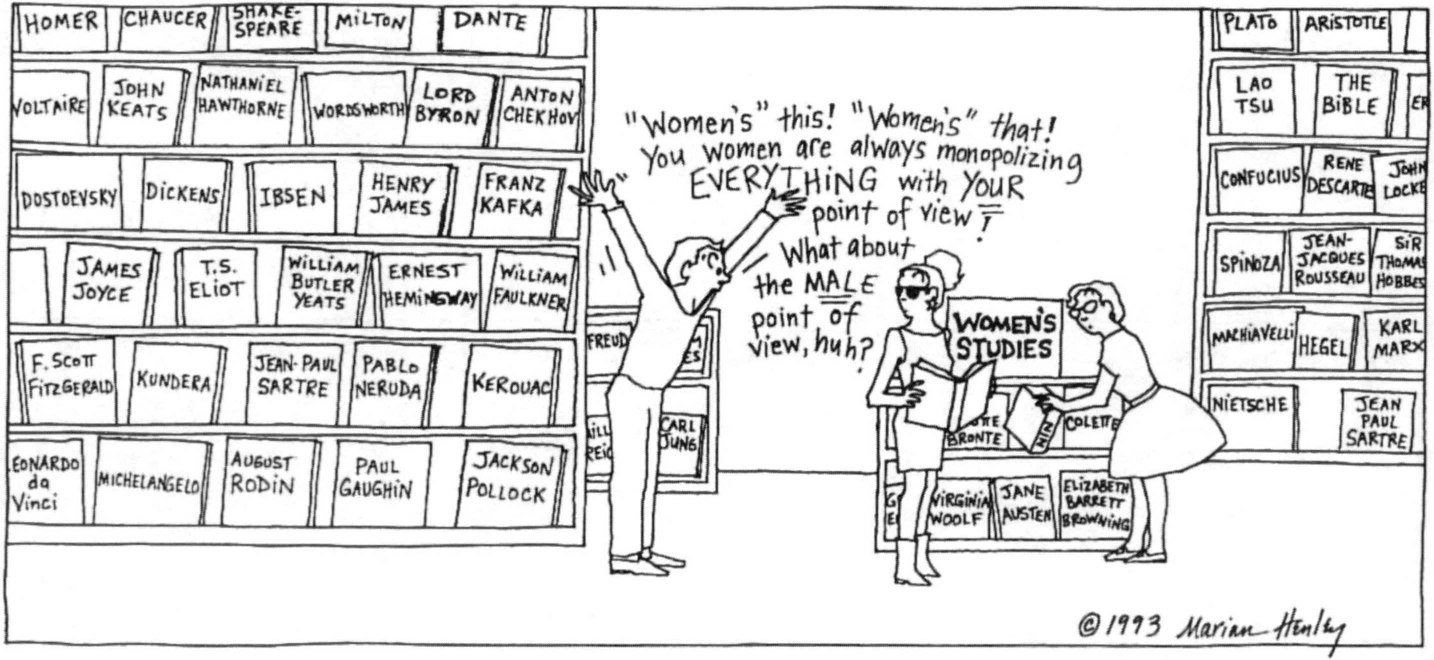
"Women's" this! "Women's" that! You women are always monopolizing EVERYTHING with YOUR point of view! What about the MALE point of view, huh?
WOMEN'S STUDIES
HOMER
CHAUCER
SHAKE-SPEARE
MILTON
DANTE
VOLTAIRE
JOHN KEATS
NATHANIEL HAWTHORNE
WORDSWORTH
LORD BYRON
ANTON CHEKHOV
DOSTOEVSKY
DICKENS
IBSEN
HENRY JAMES
FRANZ KAFKA
JAMES JOYCE
T.S. ELIOT
WILLIAM BUTLER YEATS
ERNEST HEMINGWAY
WILLIAM FAULKNER
F. SCOTT FITZGERALD
KUNDERA
JEAN-PAUL SARTRE
PABLO NERUDA
KEROUAC
EONARDO da Vinci
MICHELANGELO
AUGUST RODIN
PAUL GAUGHIN
JACKSON POLLOCK
FREUD
CARL JUNG
BRONTE
NIN
COLETTE
VIRGINIA WOOLF
JANE AUSTEN
ELIZABETH BARRETT BROWNING
PLATO
ARISTOTLE
LAO TSU
THE BIBLE
CONFUCIUS
RENE DESCARTES
JOHN LOCKE
SPINOZA
JEAN-JACQUES ROUSSEAU
SIR THOMAS HOBBES
MACHIAVELLI
HEGEL
KARL MARX
NIETSCHE
JEAN PAUL SARTRE
©1993 Marian Henley

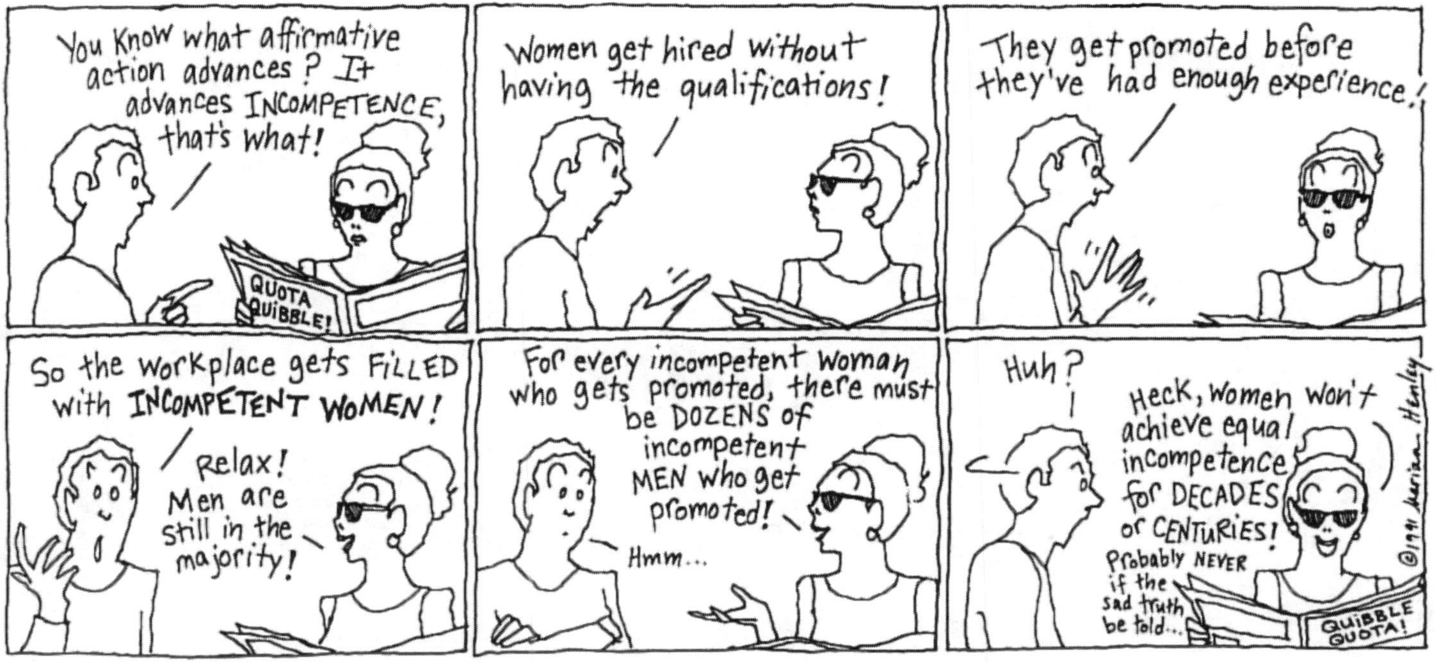
You know what affirmative action advances? It advances INCOMPETENCE, that's what!
QUOTA QUIBBLE!
Women get hired without having the qualifications!
They get promoted before they've had enough experience!
So the workplace gets FILLED with INCOMPETENT WOMEN!
Relax! Men are still in the majority!
For every incompetent woman who gets promoted, there must be DOZENS of incompetent MEN who get promoted!
Hmm...
Huh?
Heck, women won't achieve equal incompetence for DECADES or CENTURIES!
Probably NEVER if the sad truth be told...
QUIBBLE QUOTA!
©1991 Marian Henley

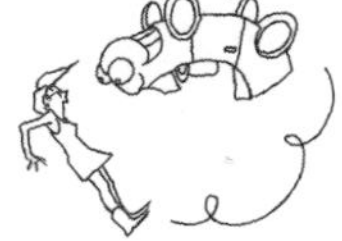

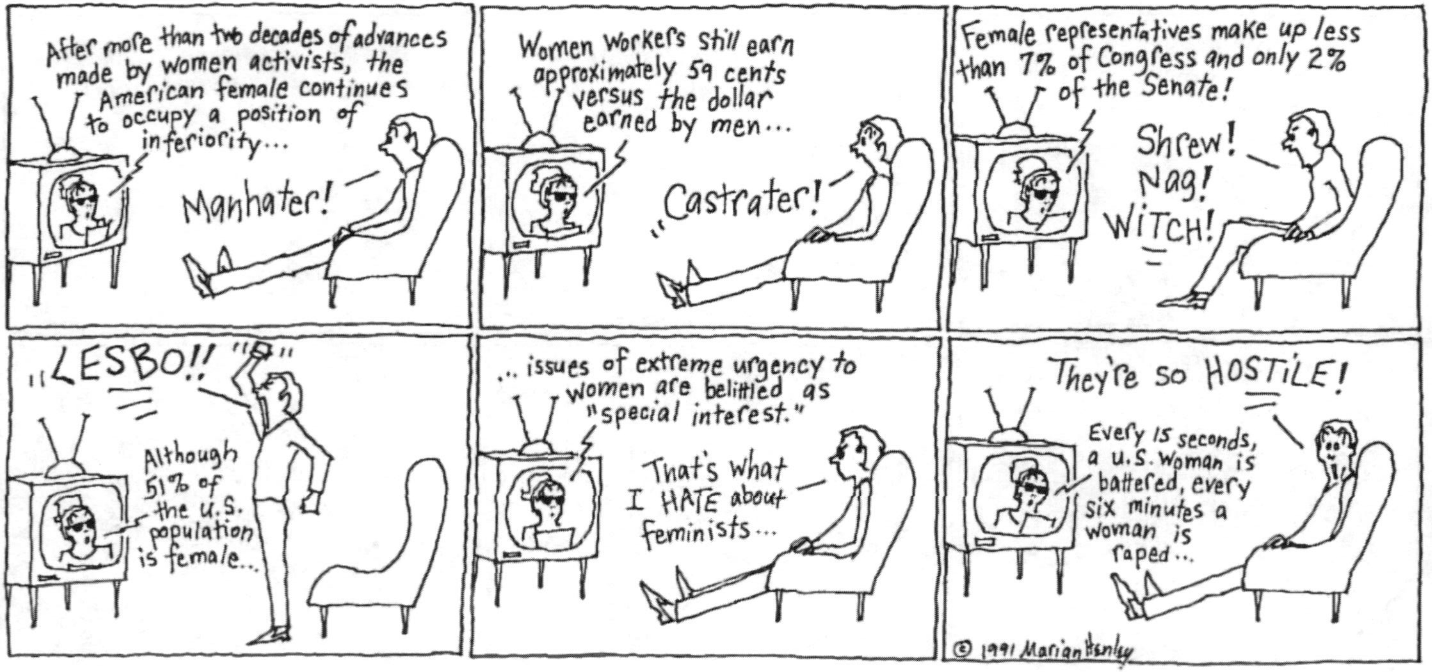
After more than two decades of advances made by women activists, the American female continues to occupy a position of inferiority...
Manhater!
Women workers still earn approximately 59 cents versus the dollar earned by men...
"Castrater!
Female representatives make up less than 7% of Congress and only 2% of the Senate!
Shrew!
Nag!
WITCH!
"LESBO!!
Although 51% of the U.S. population is female...
... issues of extreme urgency to women are belittled as "special interest."
That's what I HATE about feminists...
They're so HOSTILE!
Every 15 seconds, a U.S. woman is battered, every six minutes a woman is raped...
© 1991 Marian Henley

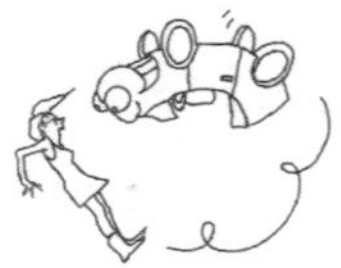

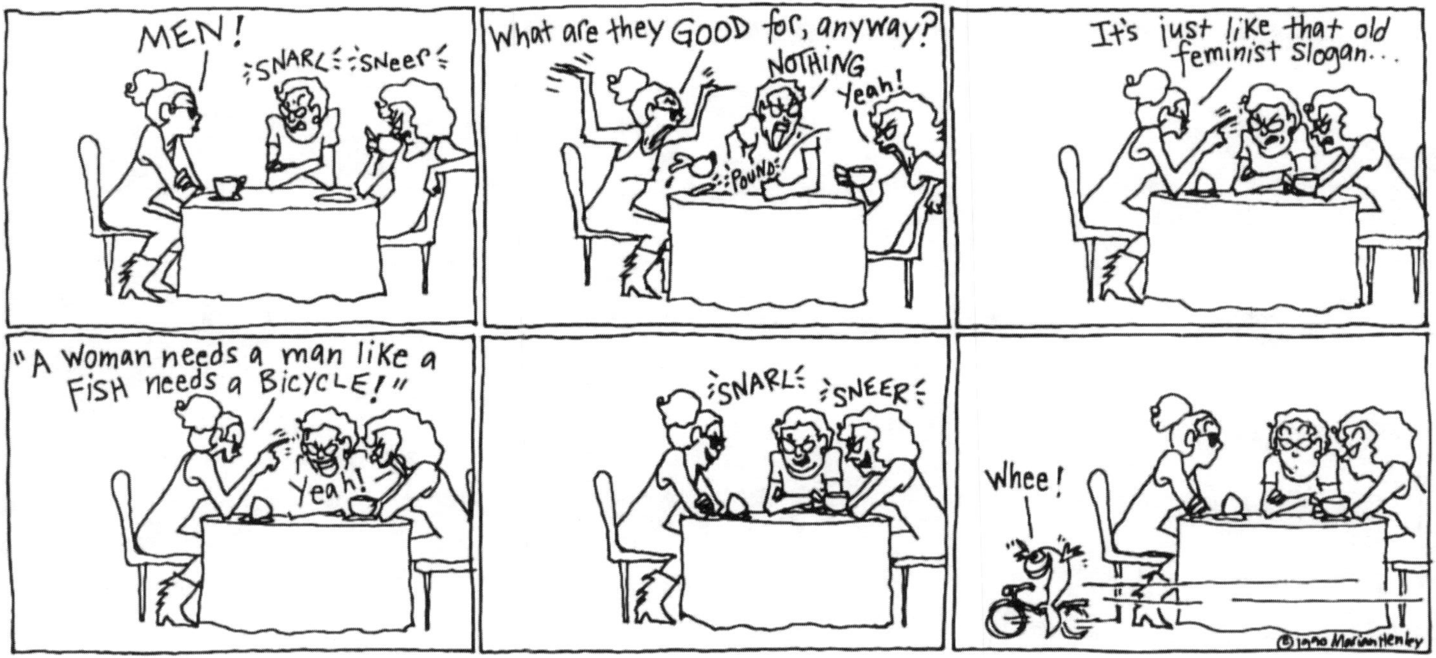
MEN!
SNARL
SNeer
What are they GOOD for, anyway?
POUND
NOTHING
Yeah!
It's just like that old feminist slogan...
"A woman needs a man like a FISH needs a BICYCLE!"
Yeah!
SNARL
SNEER
Whee!
©1990 Marian Henley

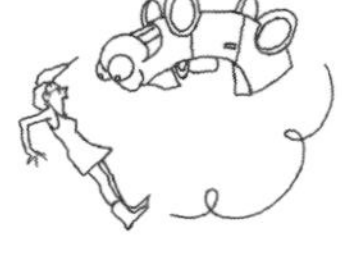

Science and Religion

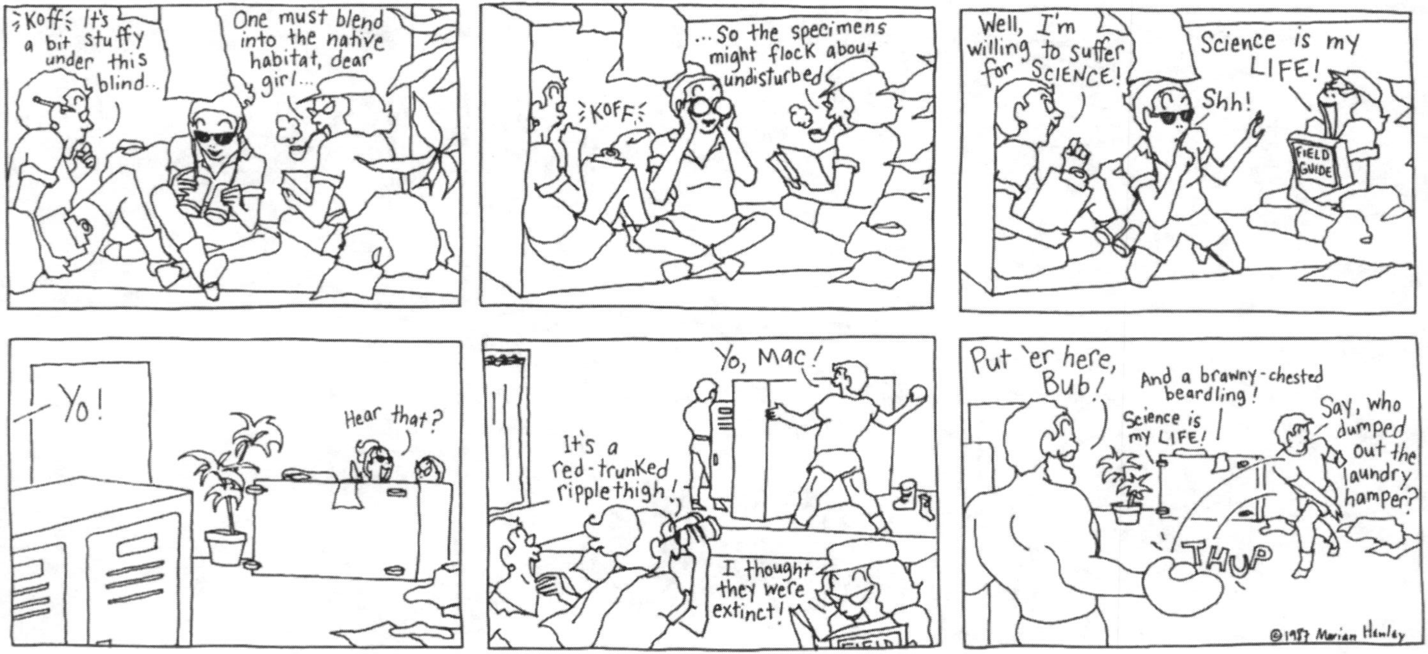
KOFF It's a bit stuffy under this blind...
One must blend into the native habitat, dear girl...
KOFF
...So the specimens might flock about undisturbed
Well, I'm willing to suffer for SCIENCE!
Science is my LIFE!
Shh!
FIELD GUIDE
Yo!
Hear that?
Yo, Mac!
It's a red-trunked ripplethigh!
I thought they were extinct!
Put 'er here, Bub!
And a brawny-chested beardling!
Science is my LIFE!
Say, who dumped out the laundry hamper?
THUP
©1987 Marian Henley

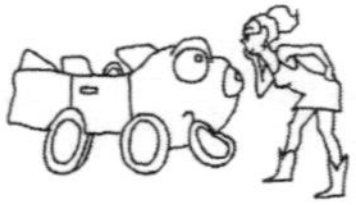

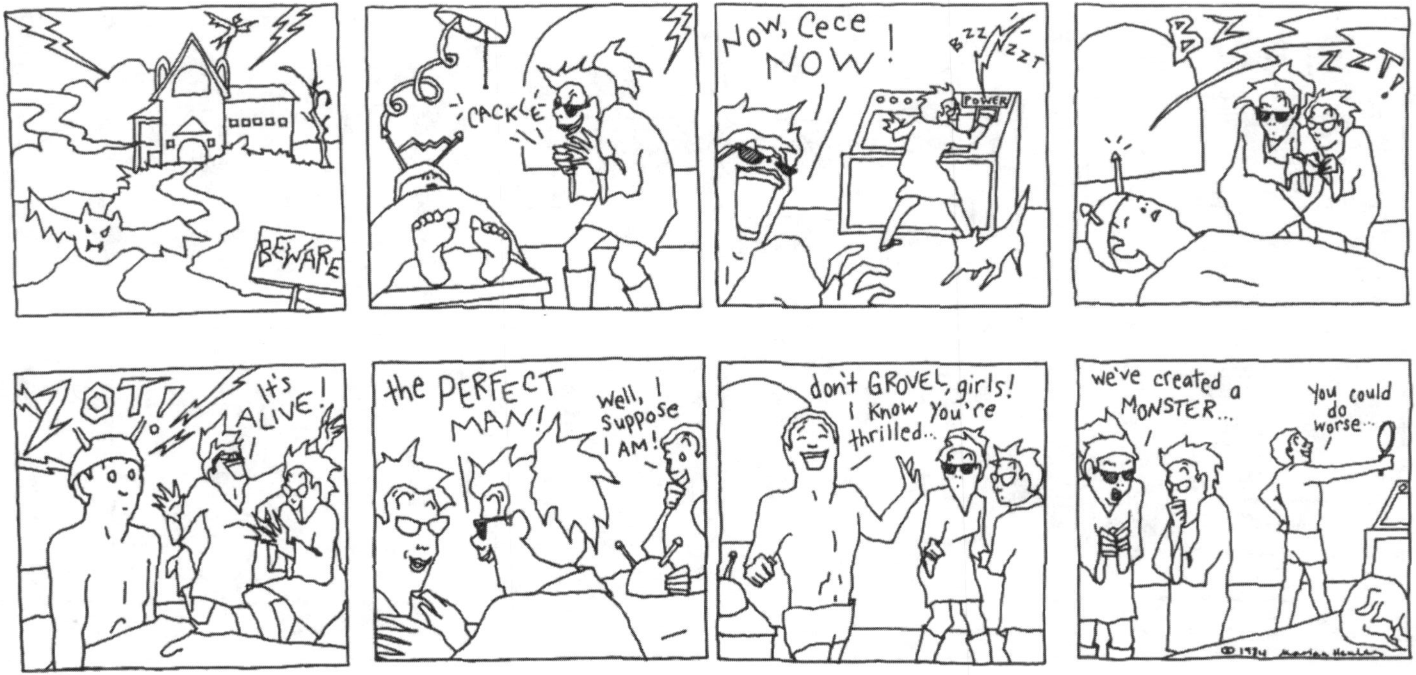
BEWARE
CACKLE
Now, Cece NOW!
BZZ ZZT
POWER
BZZ ZZT!
ZOT!
It's ALIVE!
the PERFECT MAN!
Well, I suppose I AM!
don't GROVEL, girls! I know you're thrilled...
we've created a MONSTER...
You could do worse...
© 1984

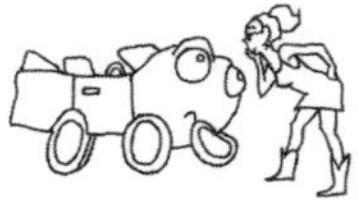

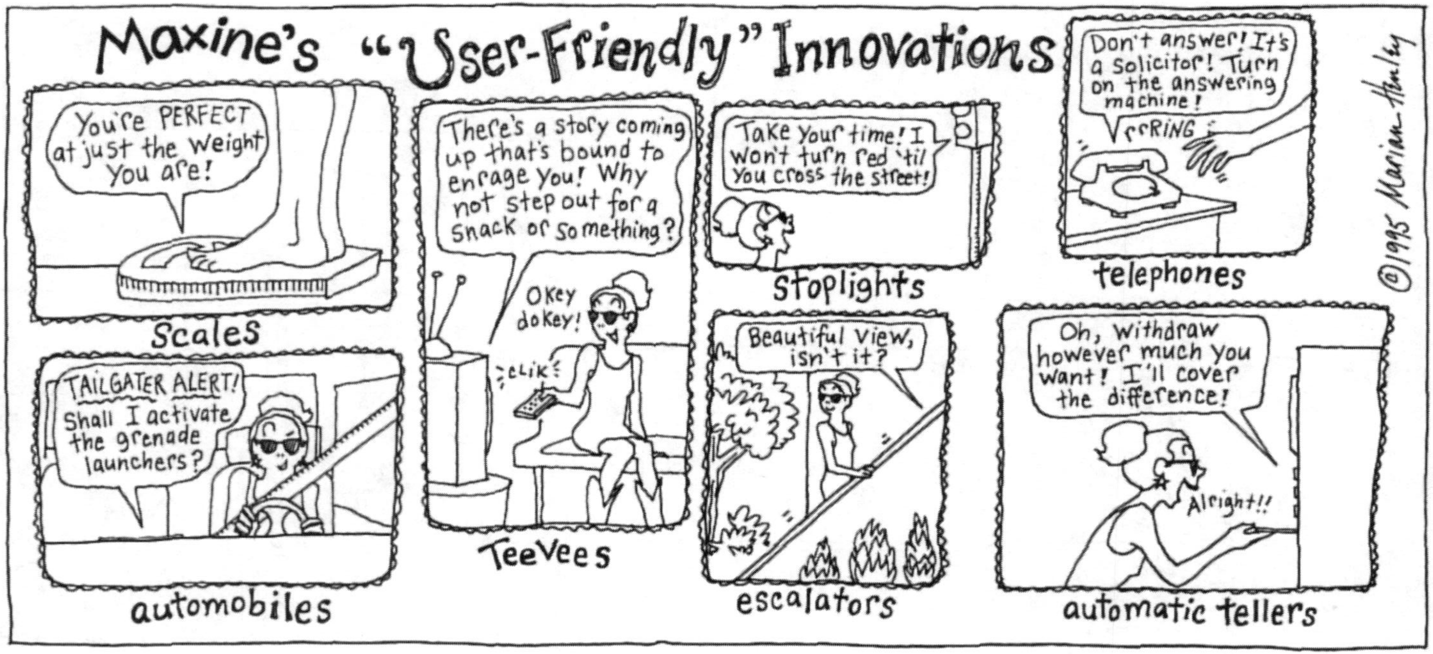
Maxine's "User-Friendly" Innovations
You're PERFECT at just the weight you are!
Scales
TAILGATER ALERT! Shall I activate the grenade launchers?
automobiles
There's a story coming up that's bound to enrage you! Why not step out for a snack or something?
OKey doKey!
CLIK
TeeVees
Take your time! I won't turn red 'til you cross the street!
Stoplights
Beautiful view, isn't it?
escalators
Don't answer! It's a Solicitor! Turn on the answering machine!
RRING
telephones
Oh, withdraw however much you want! I'll cover the difference!
Alright!!
automatic tellers
©1995 Marian Henley

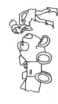

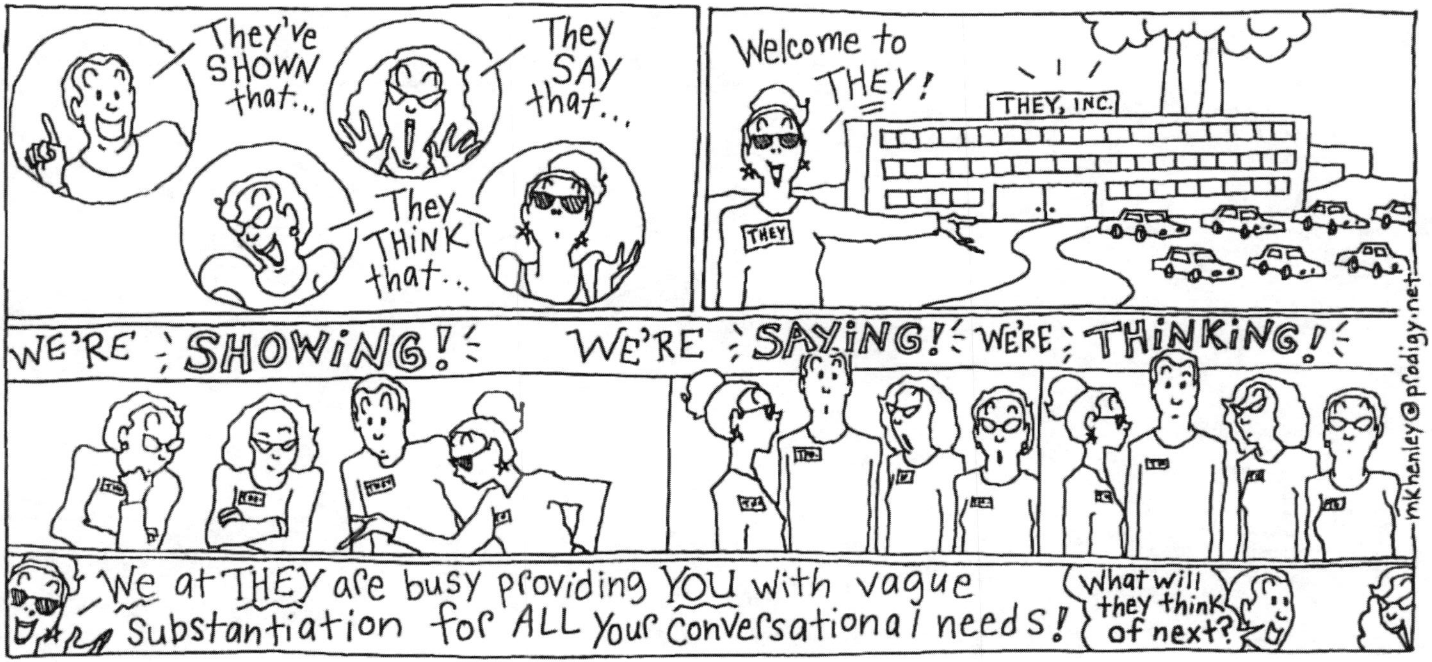
They've SHOWN that...
They SAY that...
They THINK that...
Welcome to THEY!
THEY, INC.
THEY
WE'RE SHOWING!
WE'RE SAYING!
WE'RE THINKING!
mkhenley@prodigy.net
We at THEY are busy providing YOU with vague substantiation for ALL your conversational needs!
What will they think of next?

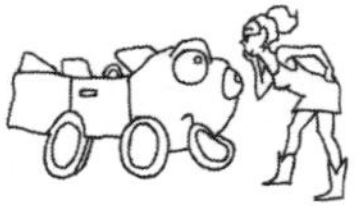

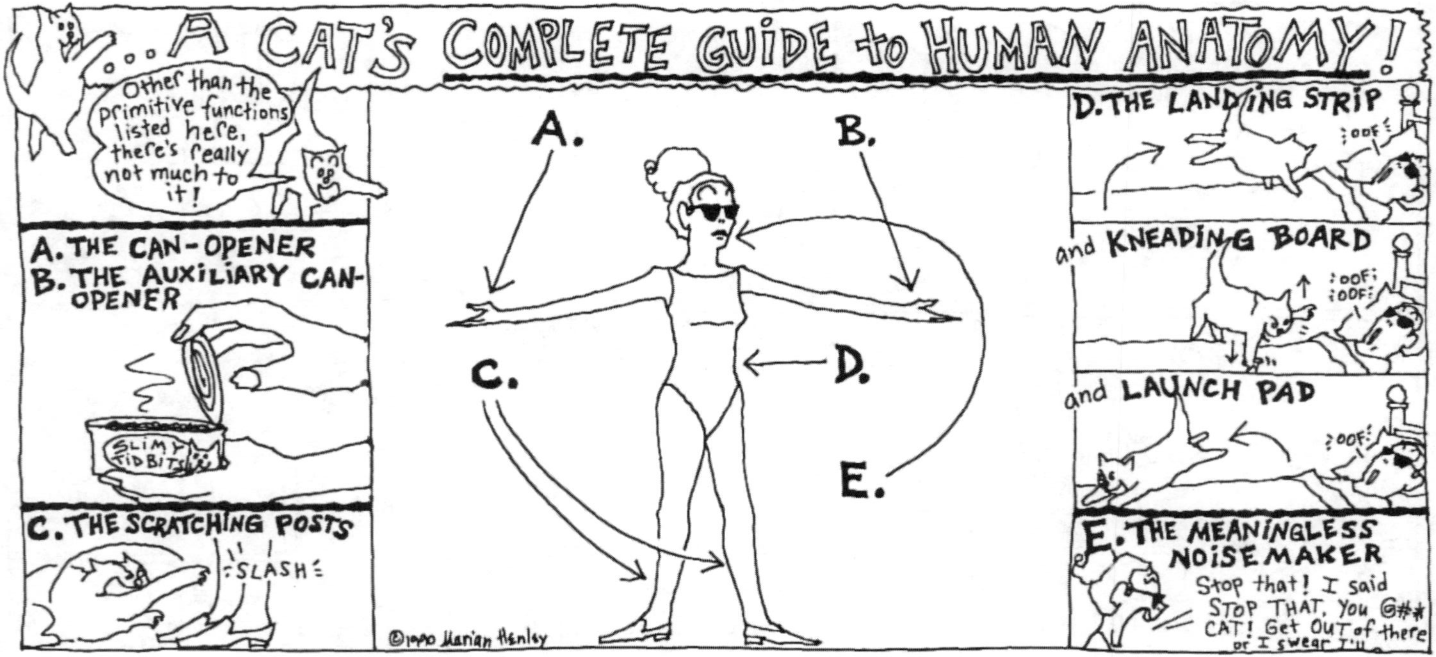
...A CAT'S COMPLETE GUIDE to HUMAN ANATOMY!
Other than the primitive functions listed here, there's really not much to it!
A. THE CAN-OPENER
B. THE AUXILIARY CAN-OPENER
SLIMY TIDBITS
C. THE SCRATCHING POSTS
SLASH
A.
B.
C.
D.
E.
©1990 Marian Henley
D. THE LANDING STRIP
OOF
and KNEADING BOARD
OOF! OOF!
and LAUNCH PAD
OOF
E. THE MEANINGLESS NOISEMAKER
Stop that! I said STOP THAT. You G#* CAT! Get OUT of there or I swear I'll

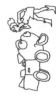

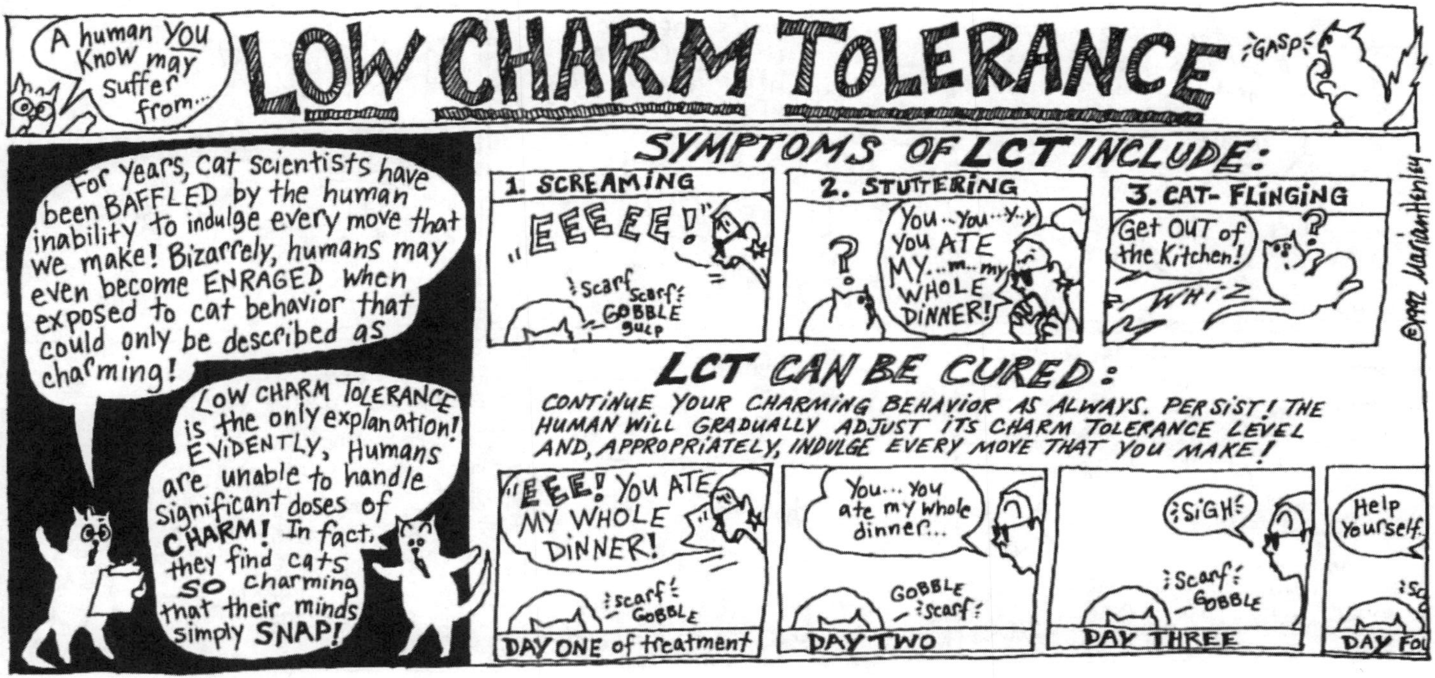
A human YOU Know may suffer from...
LOW CHARM TOLERANCE
;GASP;
For years, cat scientists have been BAFFLED by the human inability to indulge every move that we make! Bizarrely, humans may even become ENRAGED when exposed to cat behavior that could only be described as charming!
LOW CHARM TOLERANCE is the only explanation! EVIDENTLY, Humans are unable to handle significant doses of CHARM! In fact, they find cats SO charming that their minds simply SNAP!
SYMPTOMS OF LCT INCLUDE:
1. SCREAMING
"EEEEE!"
;scarf scarf; GOBBLE gulp
2. STUTTERING
?
You...You...y..y You ATE MY...m...my WHOLE DINNER!
3. CAT-FLINGING
Get OUT of the Kitchen!
?
WHIZ
©1992 MarianHenley
LCT CAN BE CURED:
CONTINUE YOUR CHARMING BEHAVIOR AS ALWAYS. PERSIST! THE HUMAN WILL GRADUALLY ADJUST ITS CHARM TOLERANCE LEVEL AND, APPROPRIATELY, INDULGE EVERY MOVE THAT YOU MAKE!
"EEE! YOU ATE MY WHOLE DINNER!"
;scarf; GOBBLE
DAY ONE of treatment
You... You ate my whole dinner...
GOBBLE ;scarf;
DAY TWO
;SIGH;
;Scarf; GOBBLE
DAY THREE
Help Yourself.
DAY FO

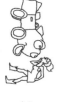

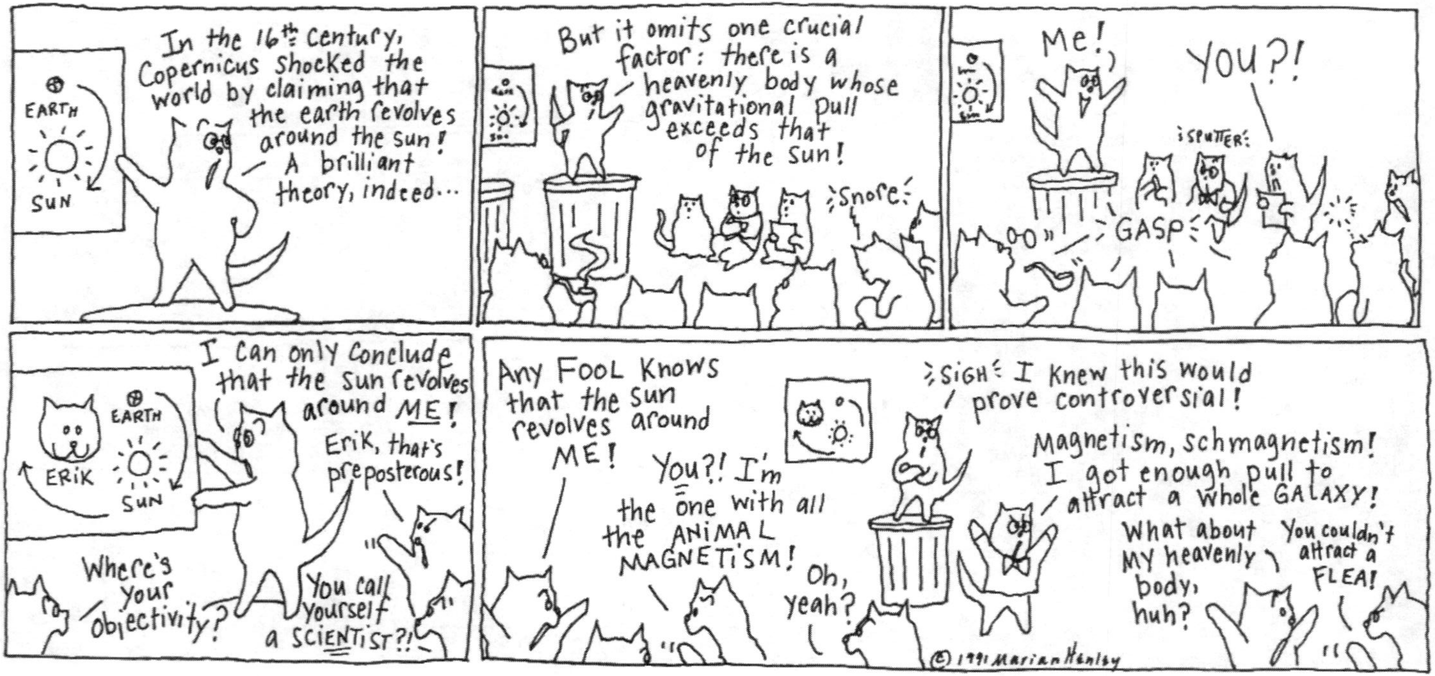
EARTH
SUN
In the 16th century, Copernicus shocked the world by claiming that the earth revolves around the sun! A brilliant theory, indeed...
But it omits one crucial factor: there is a heavenly body whose gravitational pull exceeds that of the sun!
¡Snore!
Me!
YOU?!
¡SPUTTER!
"OO"
¡GASP!
I can only conclude that the sun revolves around ME!
EARTH
ERIK
SUN
Erik, that's preposterous!
Where's your objectivity?
You call yourself a SCIENTIST?!
Any FOOL KNOWS that the sun revolves around ME!
You?! I'm the one with all the ANIMAL MAGNETISM!
Oh, yeah?
¡SIGH! I knew this would prove controversial!
Magnetism, schmagnetism! I got enough pull to attract a whole GALAXY!
What about MY heavenly body, huh?
You couldn't attract a FLEA!
© 1991 Marian Henley

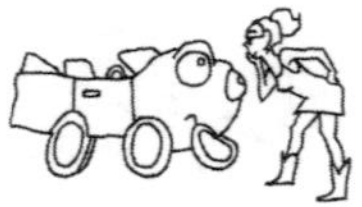

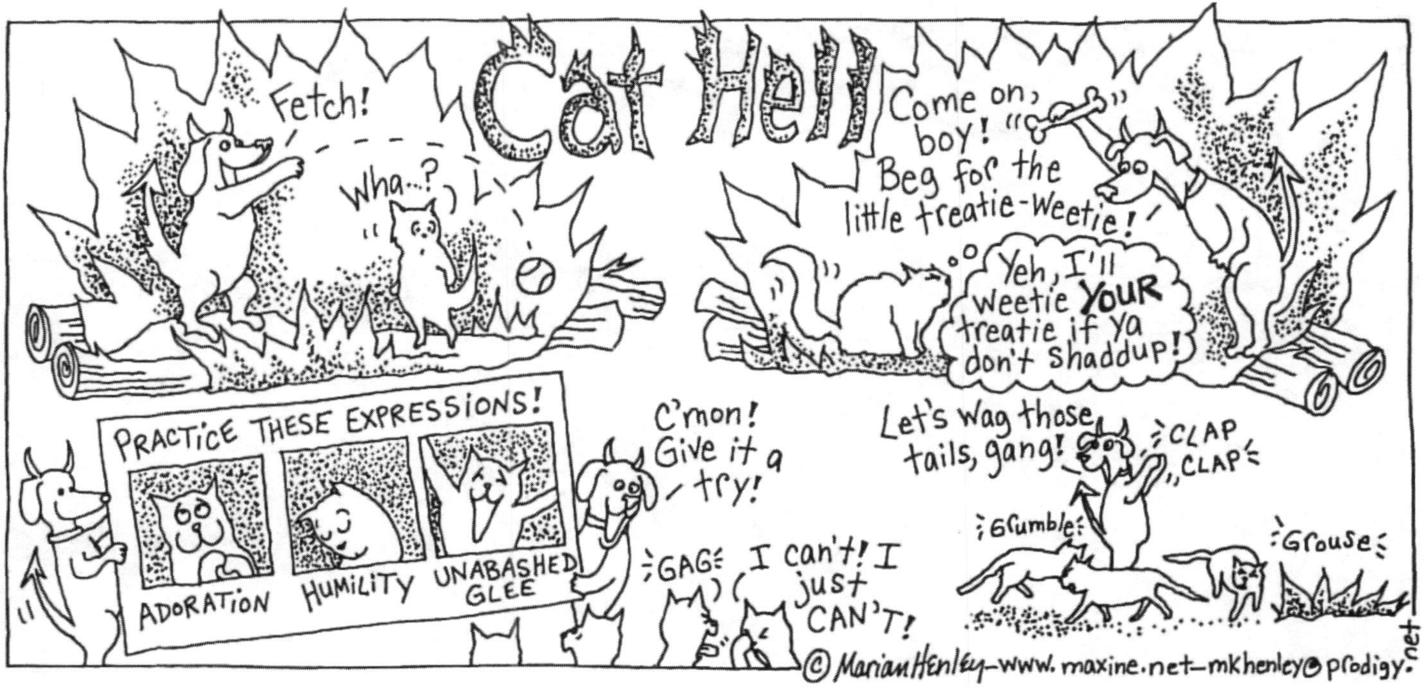
Cat Hell
Fetch!
Wha...?
Come on, boy! Beg for the little treatie-weetie!
Yeh, I'll weetie YOUR treatie if ya don't shaddup!
PRACTICE THESE EXPRESSIONS!
ADORATION
HUMILITY
UNABASHED GLEE
C'mon! Give it a try!
GAG
I can't! I just CAN'T!
Let's wag those tails, gang!
CLAP CLAP
Grumble
Grouse
© Marian Henley–www.maxine.net–mkhenley@prodigy.net

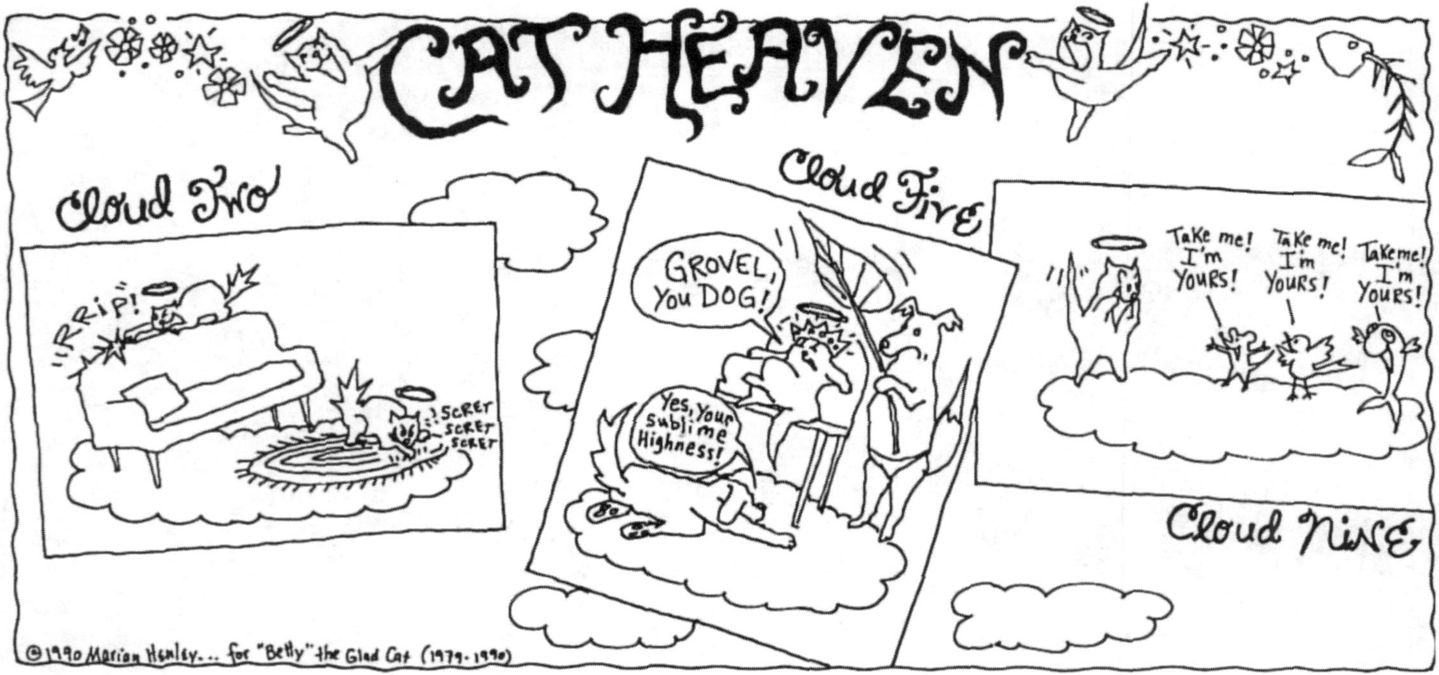
CAT HEAVEN
Cloud Two
RRRIP!
SCRET SCRET SCRET
Cloud Five
GROVEL, YOU DOG!
Yes, Your Sublime Highness!
Cloud Nine
Take me! I'm YOURS!
Take me! I'm YOURS!
Take me! I'm YOURS!
©1990 Marian Henley... for "Betty" the Glad Cat (1979-1990)

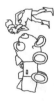

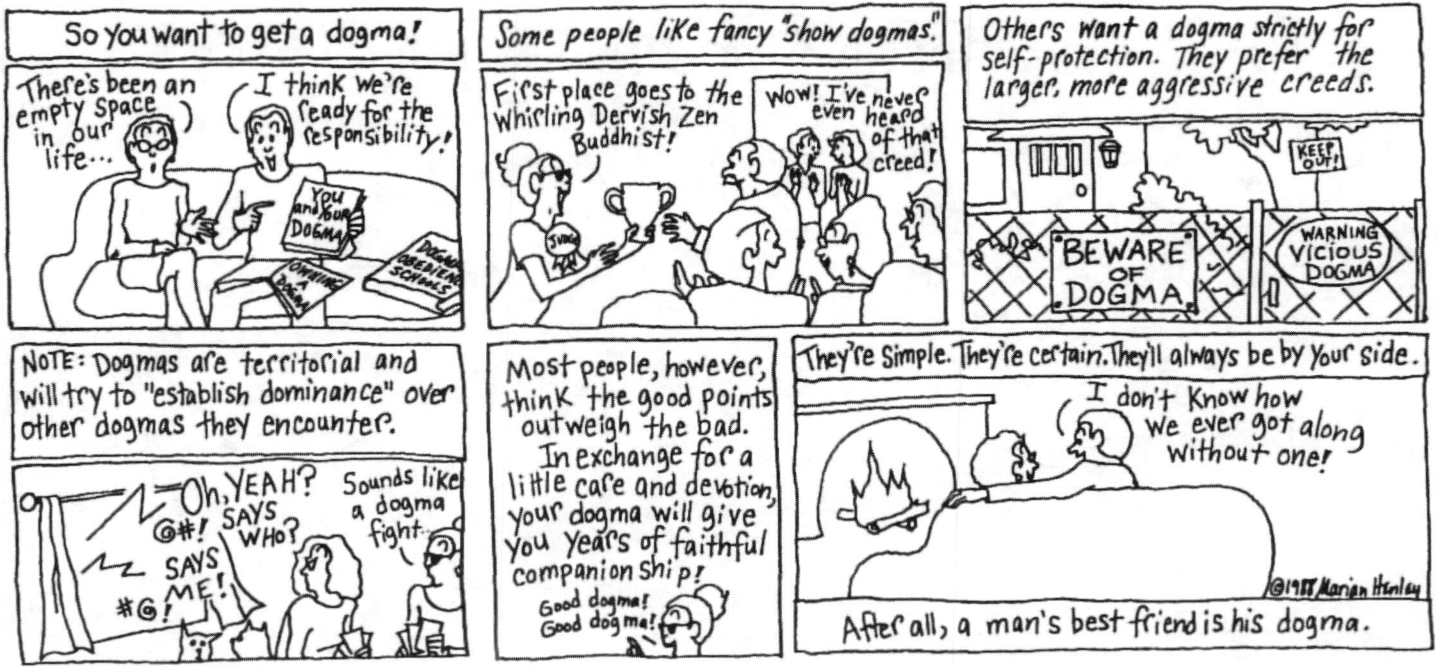
So you want to get a dogma!
There's been an empty space in our life...
I think we're ready for the responsibility!
You and Your Dogma
Owning a Dogma
Dogma Obedience Schools
Some people like fancy "show dogmas."
First place goes to the Whirling Dervish Zen Buddhist!
Judge
Wow! I've never even heard of that creed!
Others want a dogma strictly for self-protection. They prefer the larger, more aggressive creeds.
Keep Out!
BEWARE OF DOGMA
WARNING VICIOUS DOGMA
NOTE: Dogmas are territorial and will try to "establish dominance" over other dogmas they encounter.
Oh, YEAH? SAYS WHO?
@#!
SAYS ME!
#@!
Sounds like a dogma fight...
Most people, however, think the good points outweigh the bad.
In exchange for a little care and devotion, your dogma will give you years of faithful companionship!
Good dogma! Good dogma!
They're simple. They're certain. They'll always be by your side.
I don't know how we ever got along without one!
©1988 Marian Henley
After all, a man's best friend is his dogma.

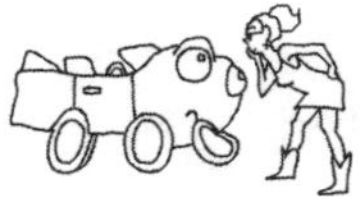

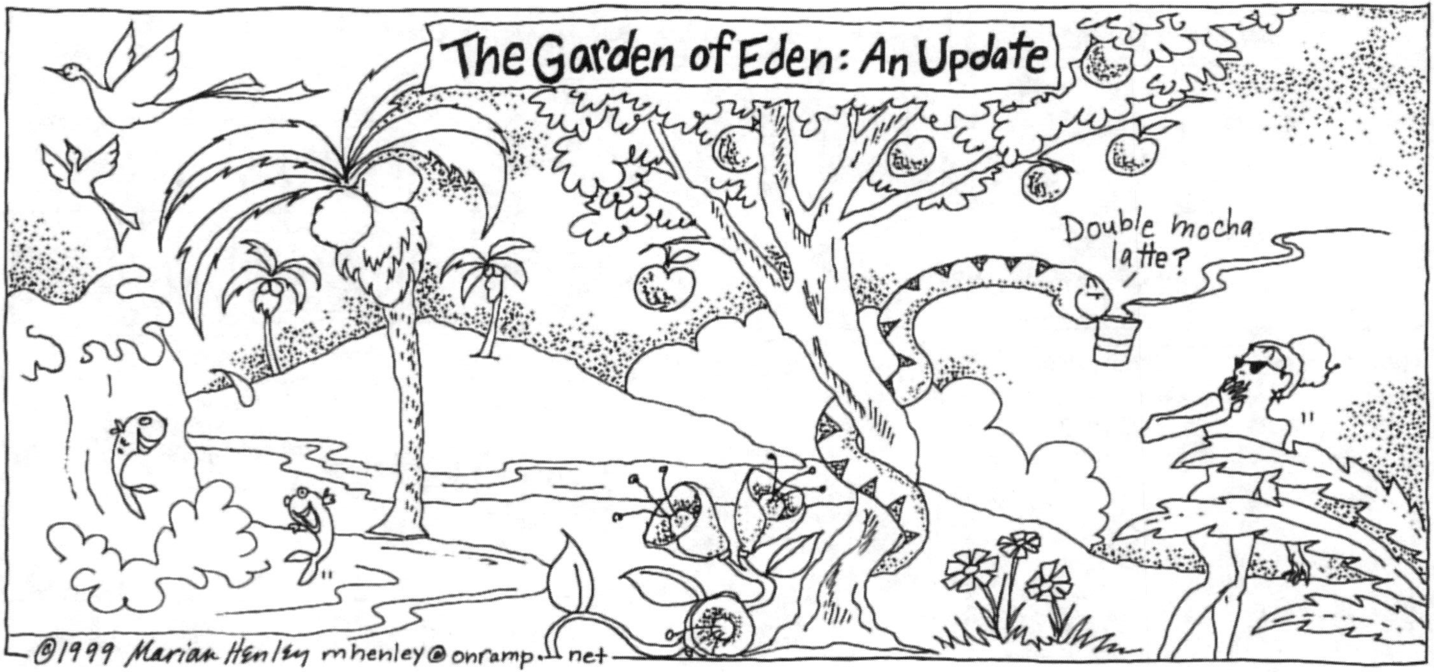
The Garden of Eden: An Update
Double mocha latte?
©1999 Marian Henley mhenley@onramp.net

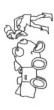

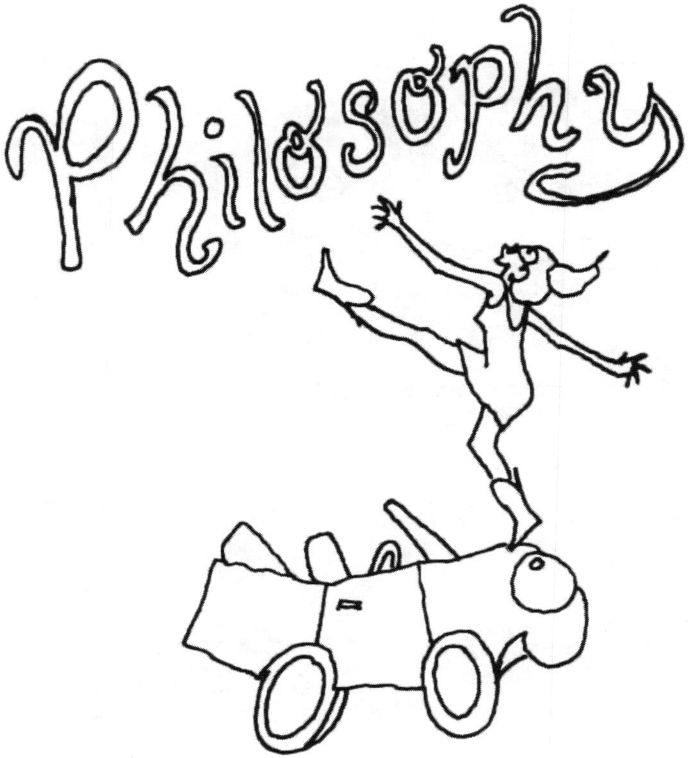
Philosophy

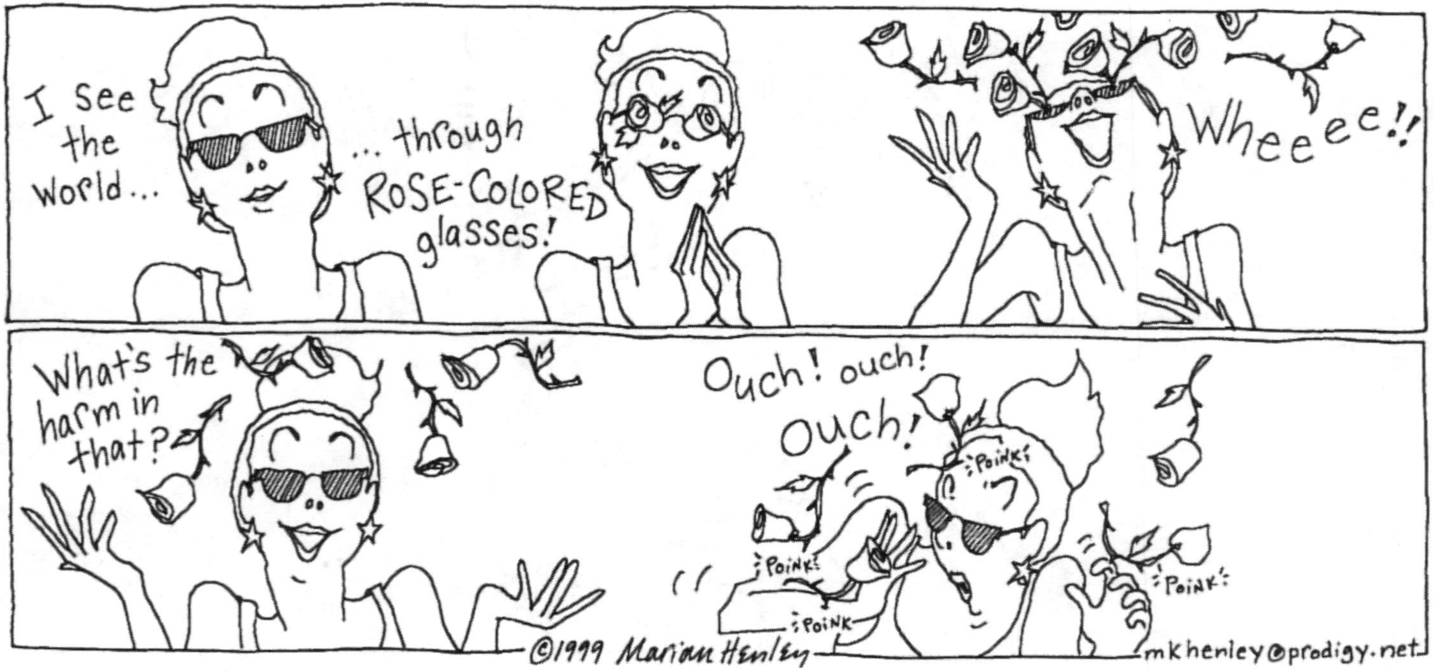
I see the world...
... through ROSE-COLORED glasses!
Wheeeee!!
What's the harm in that?
Ouch! ouch!
Ouch!
POINK!
POINK!
POINK
POINK!
©1999 Marian Henley
mkhenley@prodigy.net

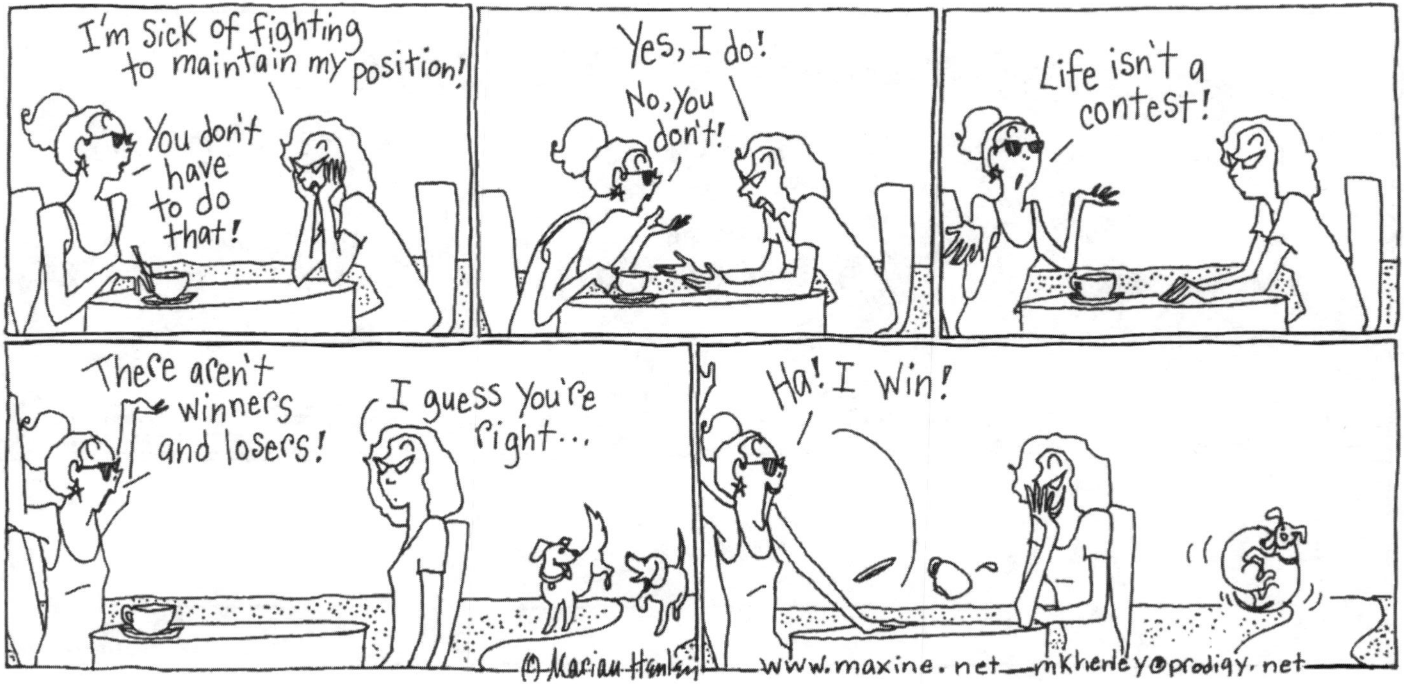
I'm sick of fighting to maintain my position!
You don't have to do that!
Yes, I do!
No, you don't!
Life isn't a contest!
There aren't winners and losers!
I guess you're right...
© Marian Henley
Ha! I win!
www.maxine.net
mkhenley@prodigy.net

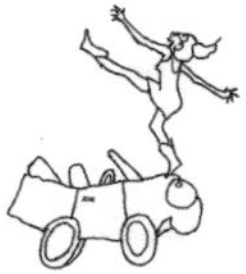

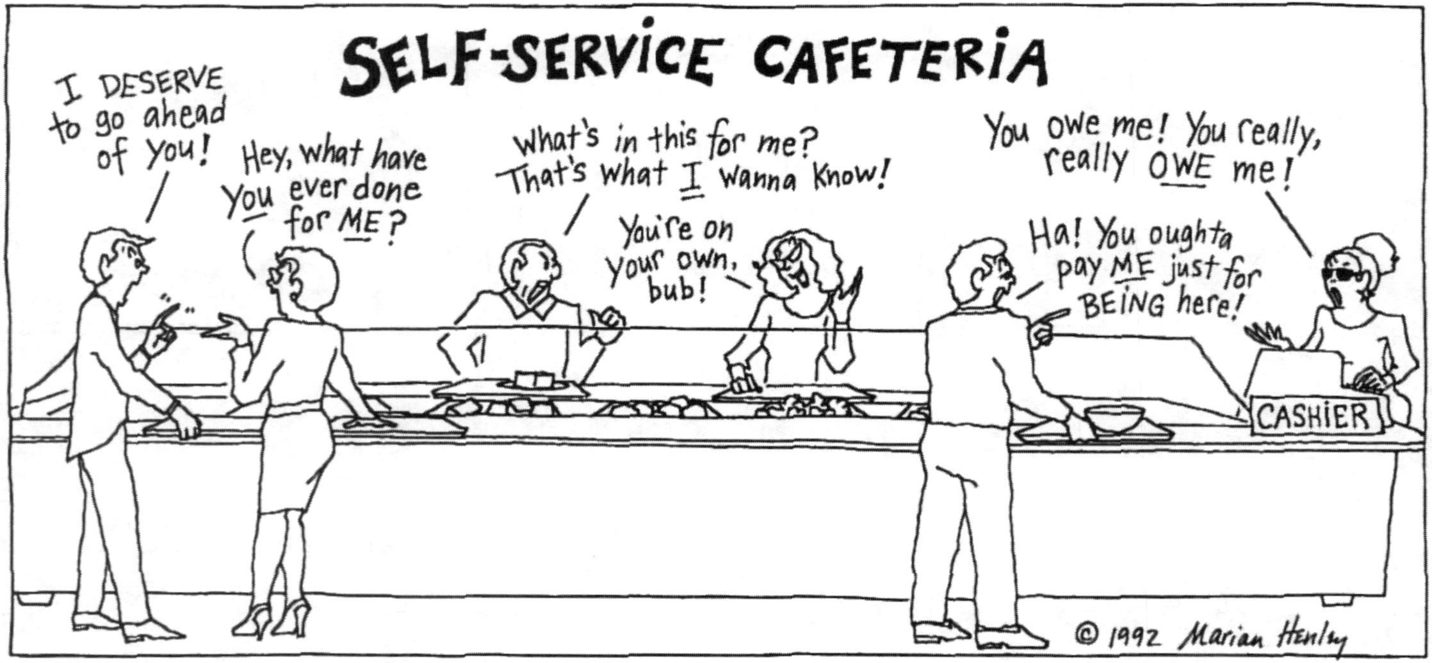
SELF-SERVICE CAFETERIA
I DESERVE to go ahead of you!
Hey, what have You ever done for ME?
What's in this for me? That's what I wanna know!
You're on your own, bub!
You owe me! You really, really OWE me!
Ha! You oughta pay ME just for BEING here!
CASHIER
© 1992 Marian Henley

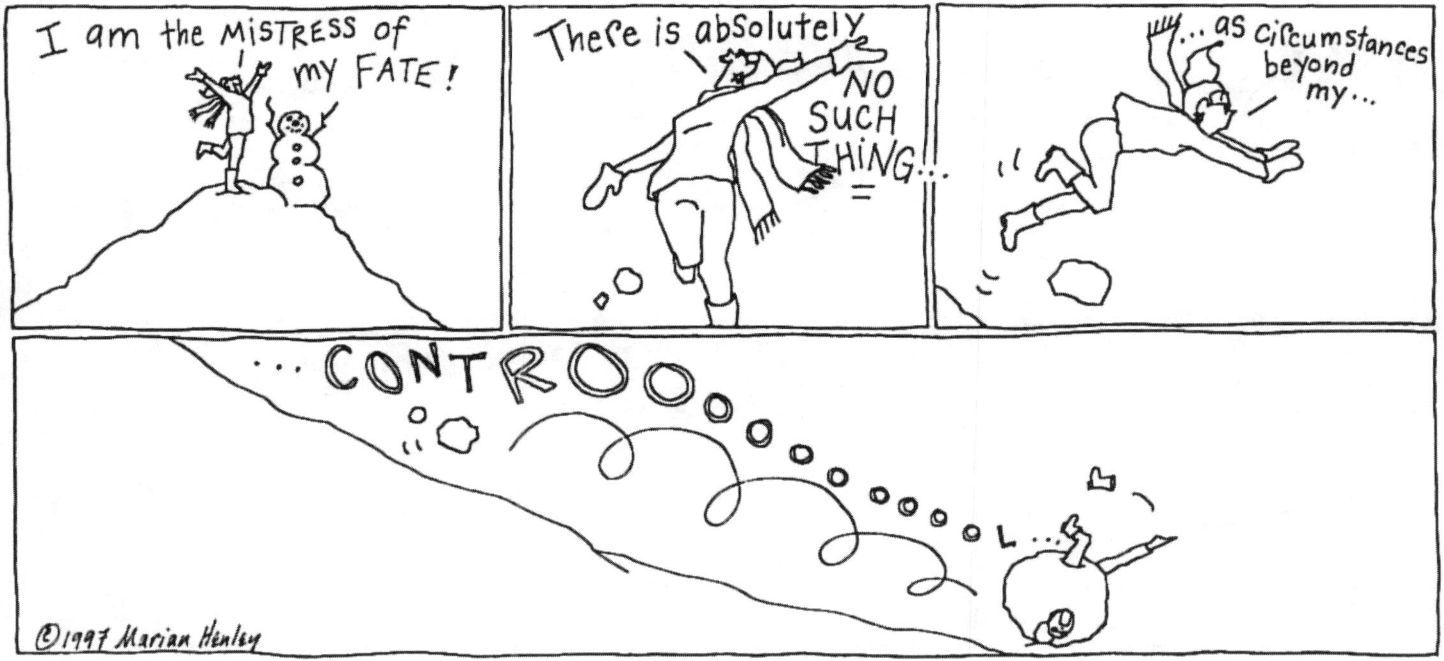
I am the MISTRESS of my FATE!
There is absolutely NO SUCH THING...
... as circumstances beyond my...
... CONTROOOOOOOOOOL...
©1997 Marian Henley

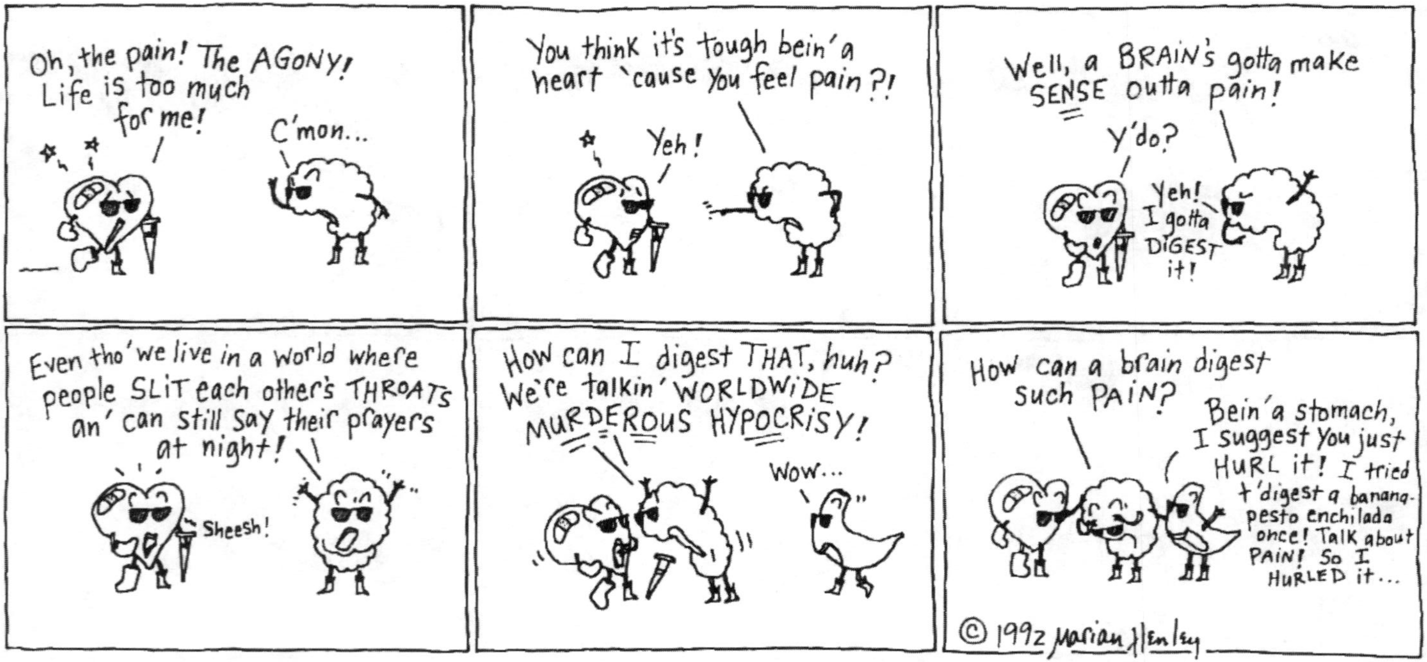
Oh, the pain! The AGONY! Life is too much for me!
C'mon...
You think it's tough bein' a heart 'cause you feel pain?!
Yeh!
Well, a BRAIN's gotta make SENSE outta pain!
Y'do?
Yeh! I gotta DIGEST it!
Even tho' we live in a world where people SLIT each other's THROATS an' can still say their prayers at night!
Sheesh!
How can I digest THAT, huh? We're talkin' WORLDWIDE MURDEROUS HYPOCRISY!
Wow...
How can a brain digest such PAIN?
Bein' a stomach, I suggest you just HURL it! I tried t'digest a banana-pesto enchilada once! Talk about PAIN! So I HURLED it...
© 1992 Marian Henley

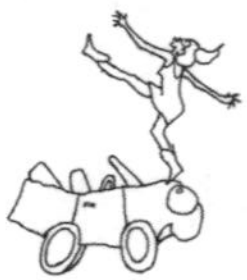

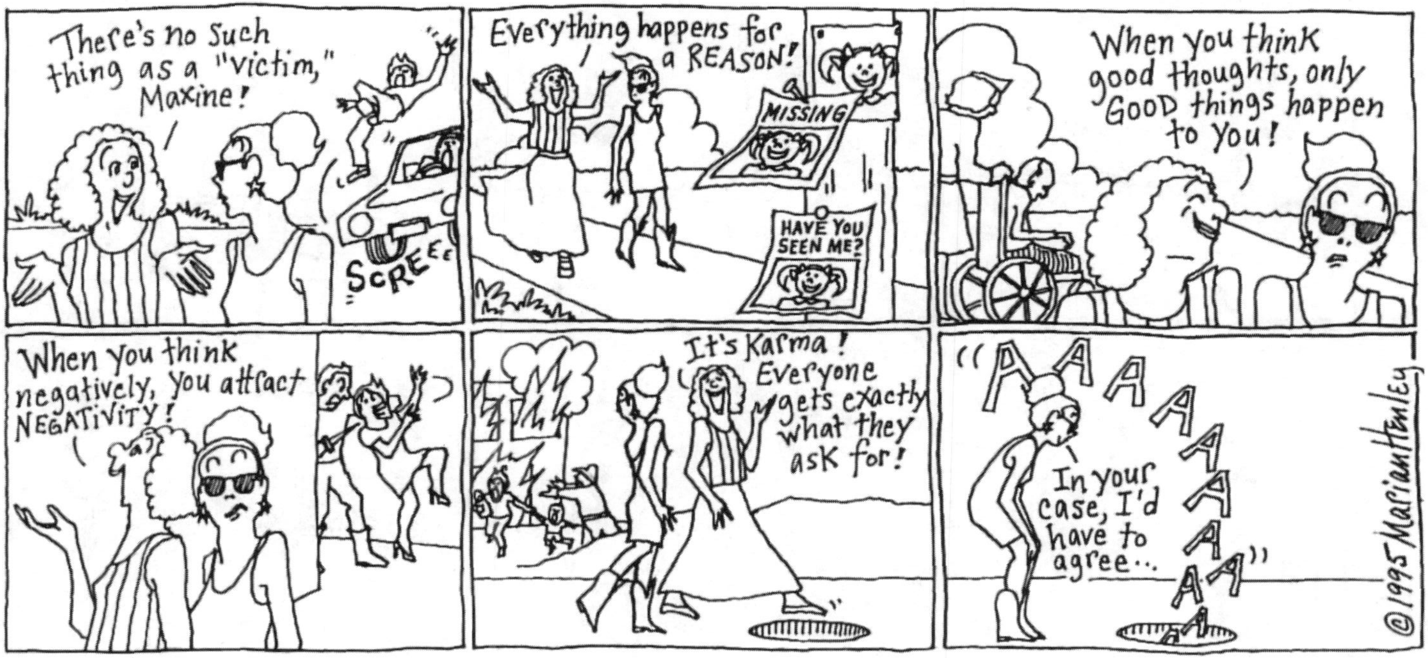
There's no such thing as a "victim," Maxine!
SCREEEE
Everything happens for a REASON!
MISSING
HAVE YOU SEEN ME?
When you think good thoughts, only GOOD things happen to you!
When you think negatively, you attract NEGATIVITY!
It's Karma! Everyone gets exactly what they ask for!
AAAAAAAAAA
In your case, I'd have to agree...
©1995 Marian Henley

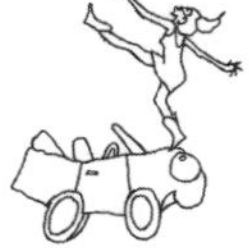

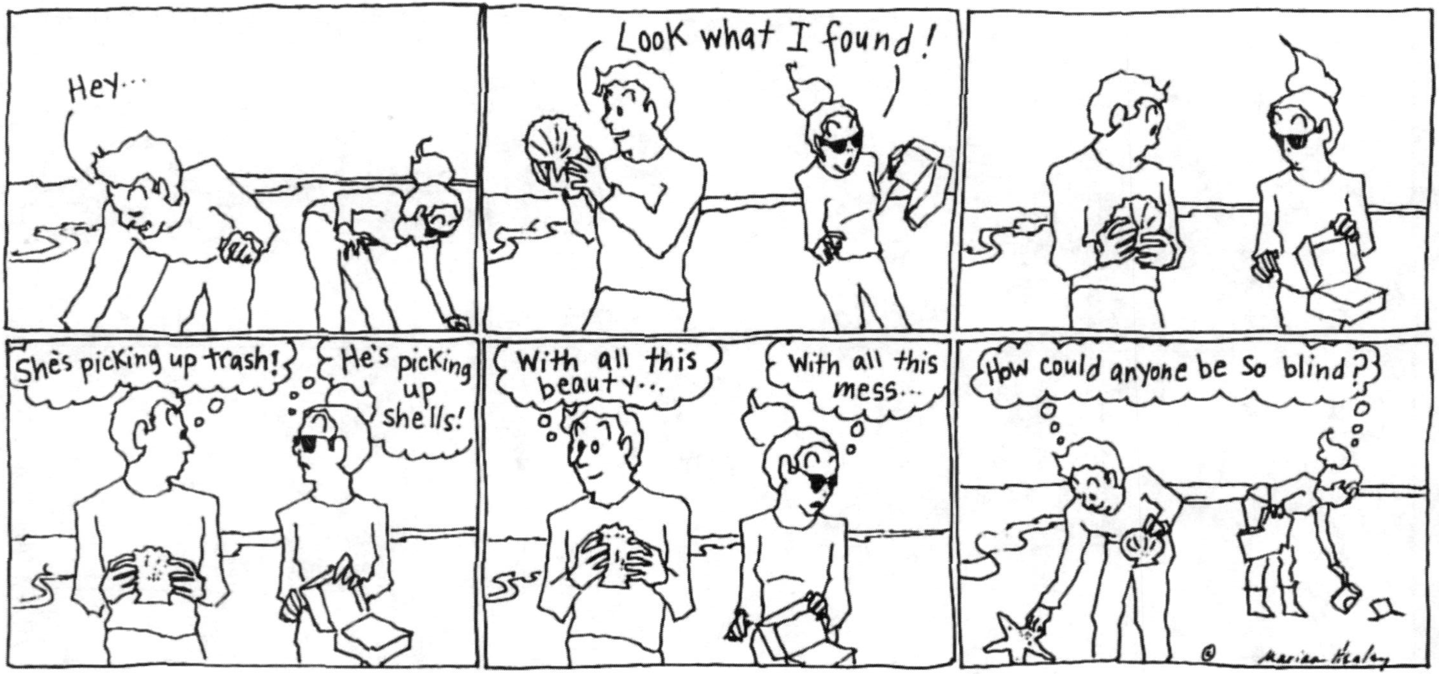
Hey...
Look what I found!
She's picking up trash!
He's picking up shells!
With all this beauty...
With all this mess...
How could anyone be so blind?
©

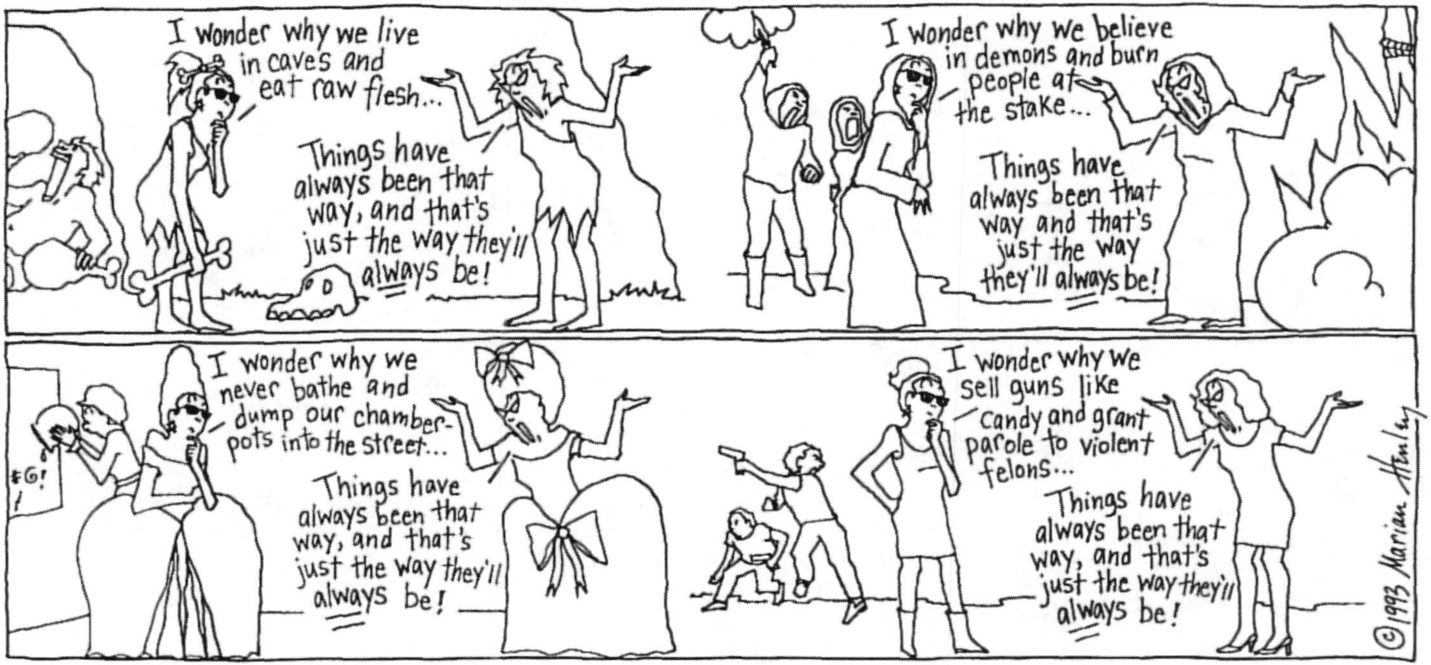
I wonder why we live in caves and eat raw flesh...
Things have always been that way, and that's just the way they'll always be!
I wonder why we believe in demons and burn people at the stake...
Things have always been that way and that's just the way they'll always be!
I wonder why we never bathe and dump our chamber-pots into the street...
Things have always been that way, and that's just the way they'll always be!
I wonder why we sell guns like candy and grant parole to violent felons...
Things have always been that way, and that's just the way they'll always be!
©1993 Marian Henley

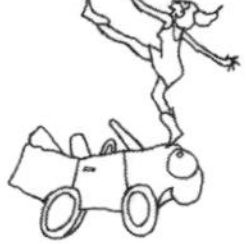

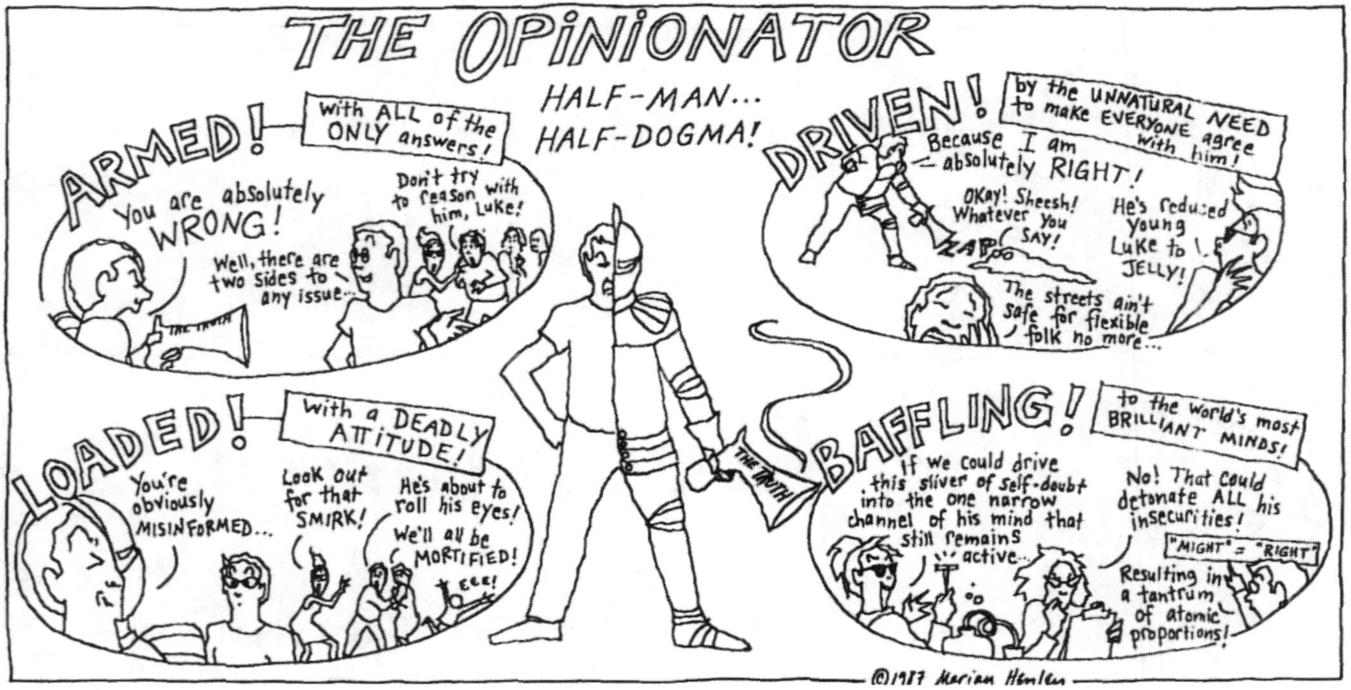
THE OPINIONATOR
HALF-MAN... HALF-DOGMA!
ARMED!
with ALL of the ONLY answers!
You are absolutely WRONG!
Well, there are two sides to any issue...
Don't try to reason with him, Luke!
THE TRUTH
DRIVEN!
by the UNNATURAL NEED to make EVERYONE agree with him!
Because I am absolutely RIGHT!
Okay! Sheesh! Whatever you SAY!
ZAP
He's reduced young Luke to JELLY!
The streets ain't safe for flexible folk no more...
LOADED!
with a DEADLY ATTITUDE!
You're obviously MISINFORMED...
Look out for that SMIRK!
He's about to roll his eyes!
We'll all be MORTIFIED!
EEE!
BAFFLING!
to the world's most BRILLIANT MINDS!
If we could drive this sliver of self-doubt into the one narrow channel of his mind that still remains active...
No! That could detonate ALL his insecurities!
"MIGHT" = "RIGHT"
Resulting in a tantrum of atomic proportions!
THE TRUTH
©1987 Marian Henley

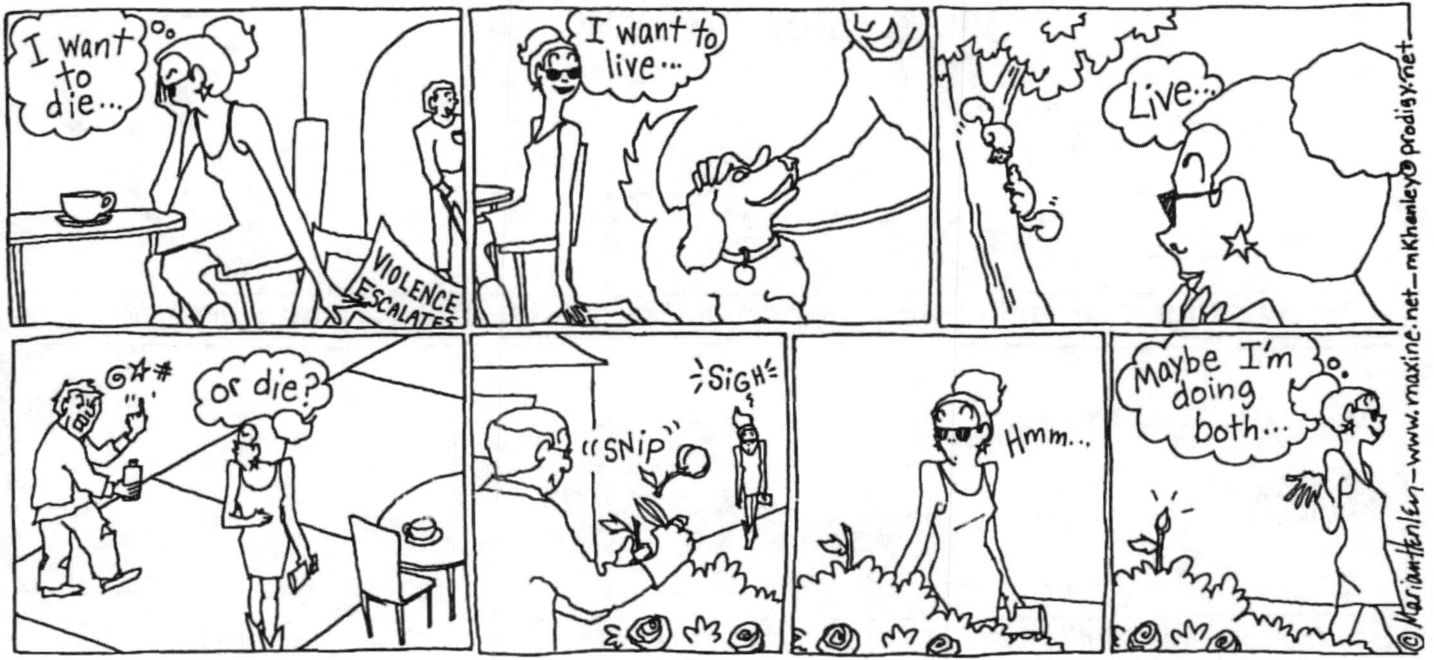
I want to die...
VIOLENCE ESCALATES
I want to live...
Live...
@☆#
or die?
"SNip"
SiGH
Hmm...
Maybe I'm doing both...
© MarianHenley—www.maxine.net—mKhenley@prodigy.net

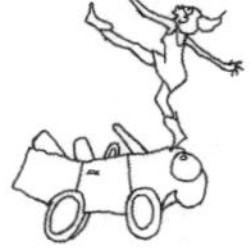

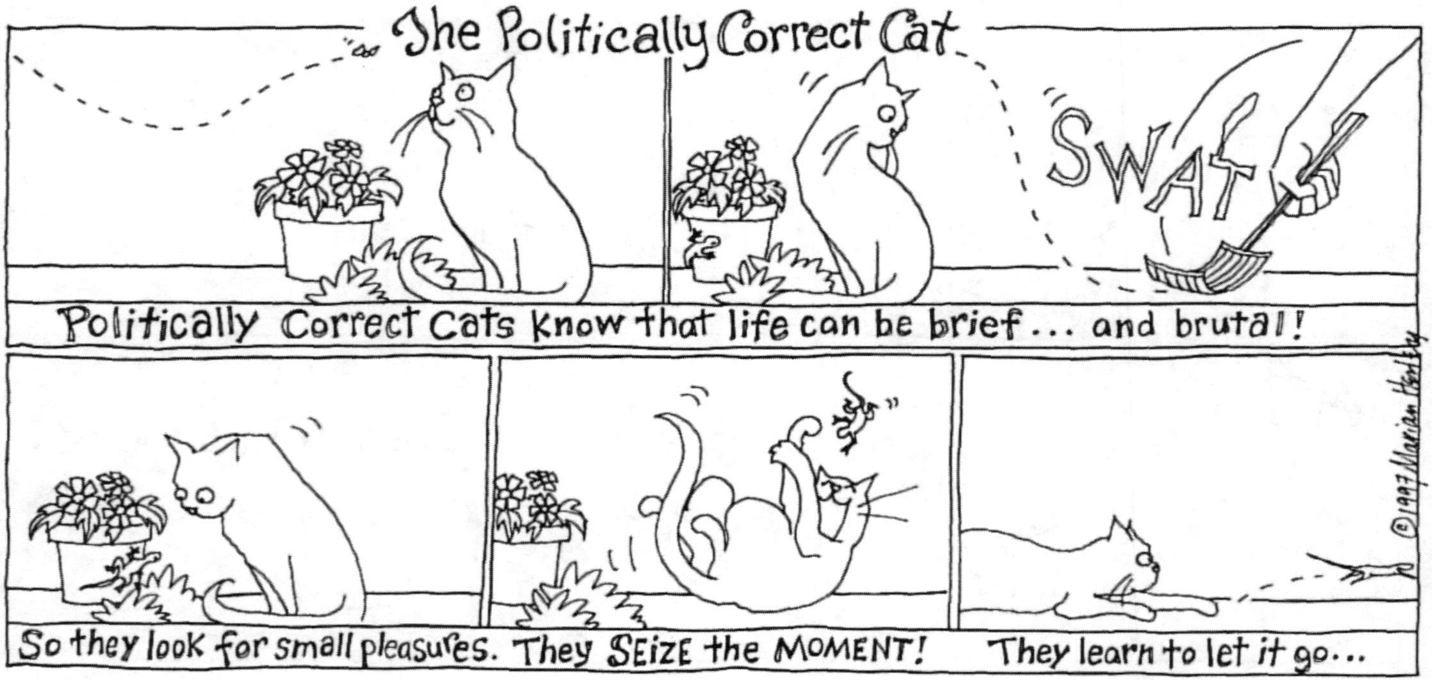
The Politically Correct Cat
SWAT
Politically Correct Cats know that life can be brief . . . and brutal!
So they look for small pleasures. They SEIZE the MOMENT! They learn to let it go...
©1997 Marian Henley

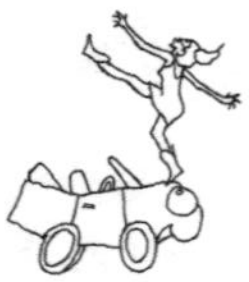

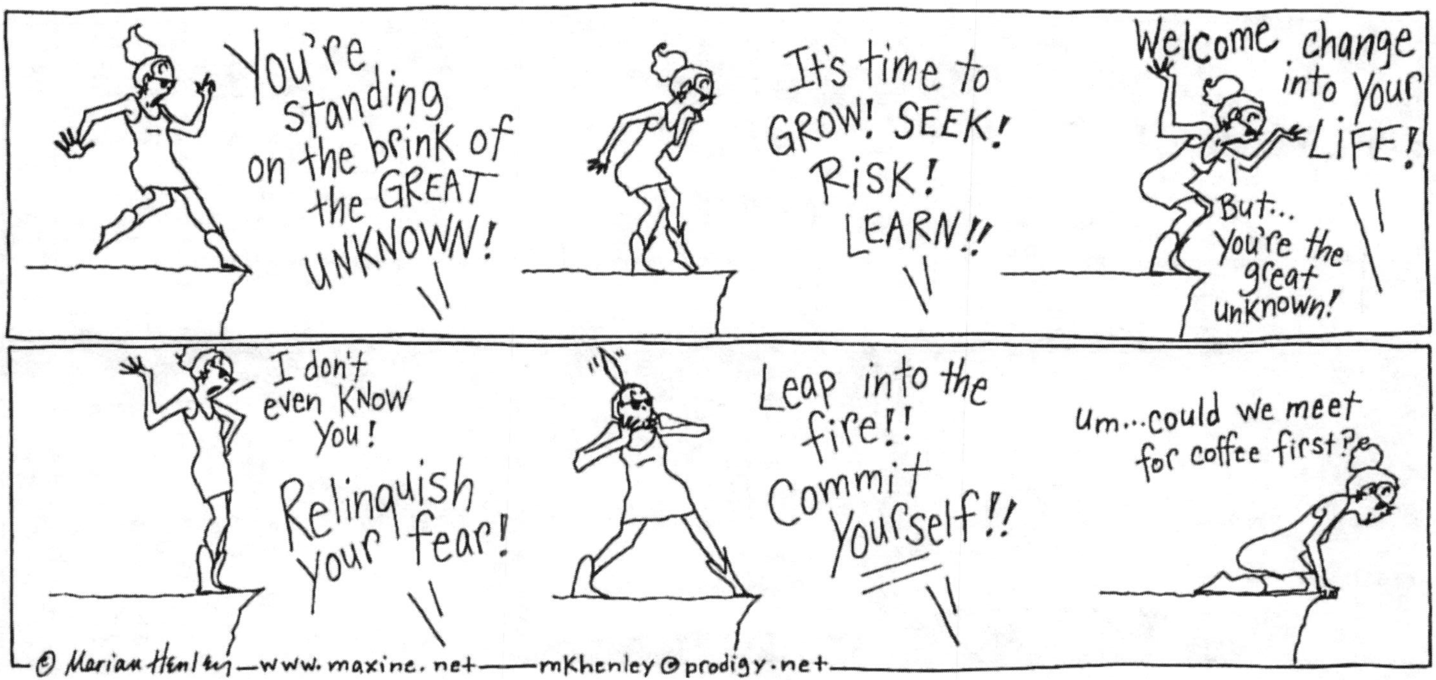
You're standing on the brink of the GREAT UNKNOWN!
It's time to GROW! SEEK! RISK! LEARN!!
Welcome change into your LIFE!
But... you're the great unknown!
I don't even KNOW you!
Relinquish your fear!
Leap into the fire!! Commit yourself!!
um...could we meet for coffee first?
© Marian Henley—www.maxine.net—mKhenley@prodigy.net

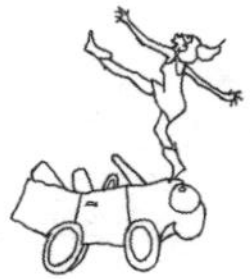

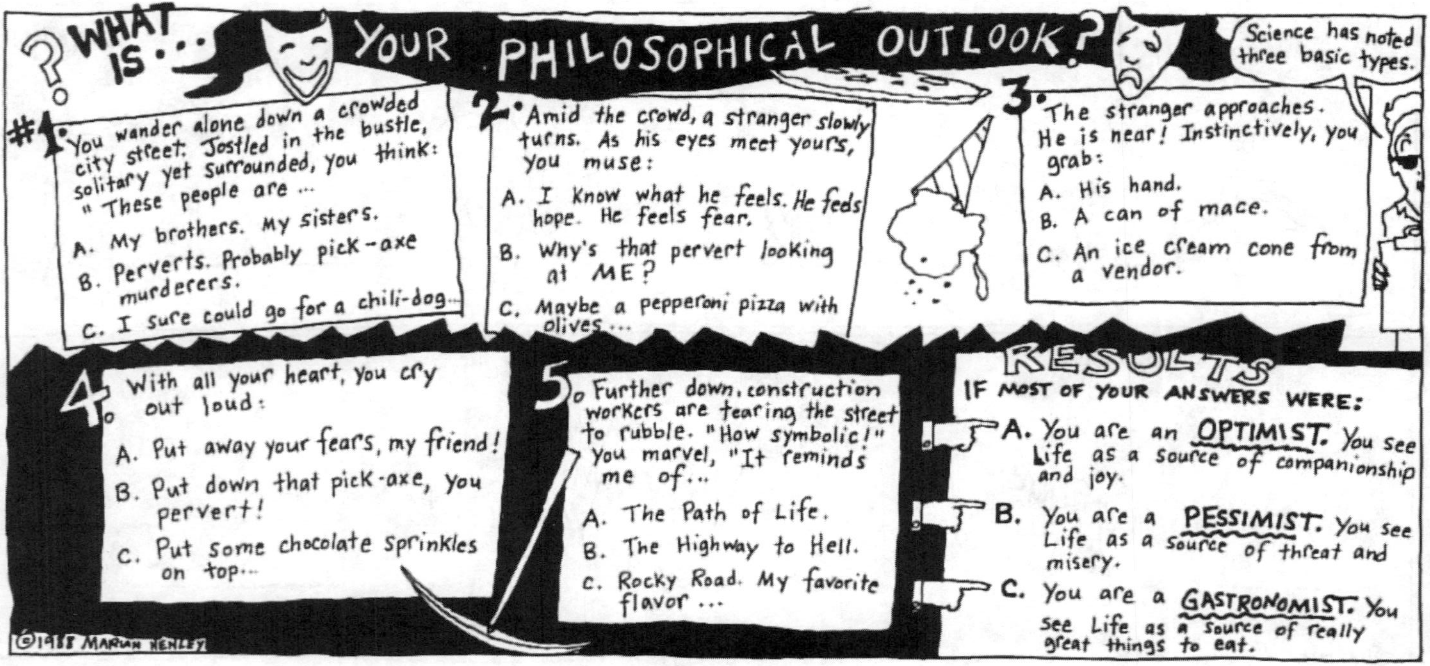
WHAT IS... YOUR PHILOSOPHICAL OUTLOOK?
Science has noted three basic types.
#1. You wander alone down a crowded city street. Jostled in the bustle, solitary yet surrounded, you think: "These people are ...
A. My brothers. My sisters.
B. Perverts. Probably pick-axe murderers.
C. I sure could go for a chili-dog...
2. Amid the crowd, a stranger slowly turns. As his eyes meet yours, you muse:
A. I know what he feels. He feels hope. He feels fear.
B. Why's that pervert looking at ME?
C. Maybe a pepperoni pizza with olives...
3. The stranger approaches. He is near! Instinctively, you grab:
A. His hand.
B. A can of mace.
C. An ice cream cone from a vendor.
4. With all your heart, you cry out loud:
A. Put away your fears, my friend!
B. Put down that pick-axe, you pervert!
C. Put some chocolate sprinkles on top...
5. Further down, construction workers are tearing the street to rubble. "How symbolic!" you marvel, "It reminds me of...
A. The Path of Life.
B. The Highway to Hell.
C. Rocky Road. My favorite flavor...
RESULTS
IF MOST OF YOUR ANSWERS WERE:
A. You are an OPTIMIST. You see Life as a source of companionship and joy.
B. You are a PESSIMIST. You see Life as a source of threat and misery.
C. You are a GASTRONOMIST. You see Life as a source of really great things to eat.
©1988 MARIAN HENLEY

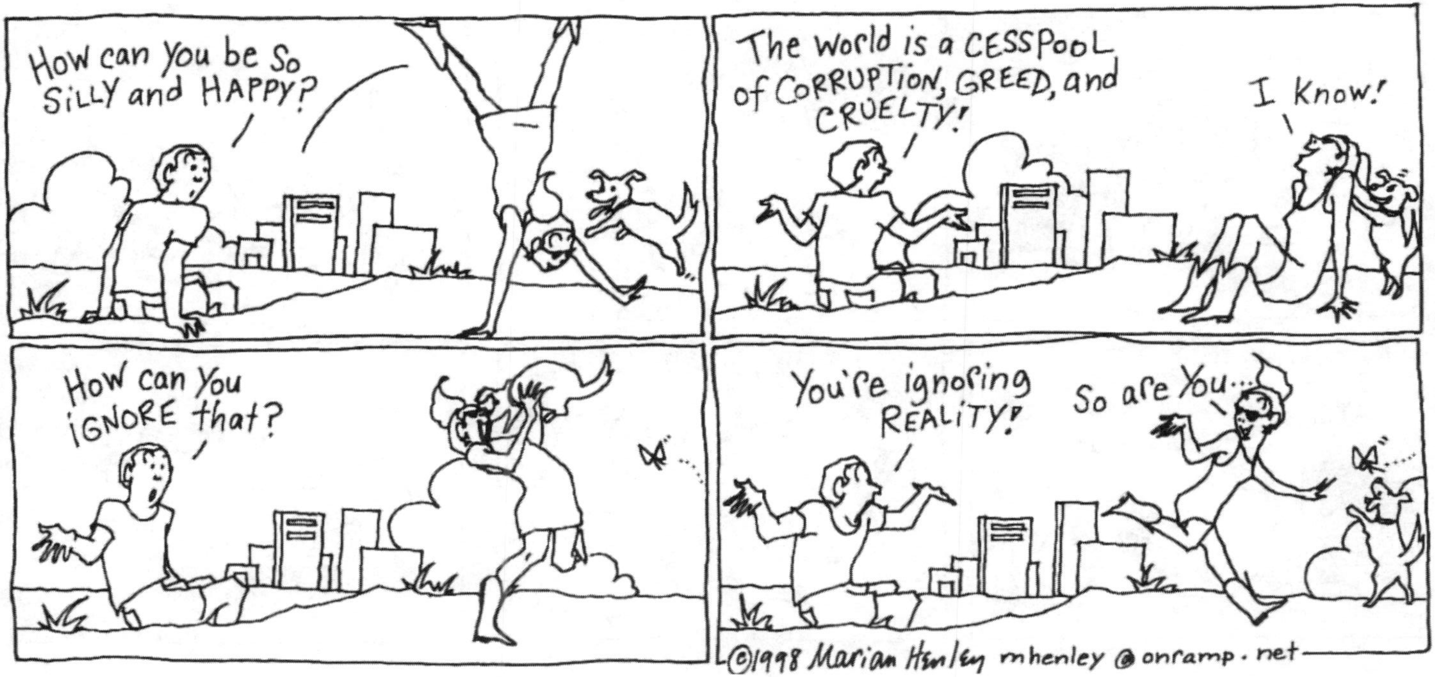
How can you be So SiLLY and HAPPY?
The world is a CESSPooL of CORRUPTiON, GREED, and CRUELTY!
I Know!
How can You iGNORE that?
You're ignoring REALiTY!
So are You...
©1998 Marian Henley mhenley @ onramp . net

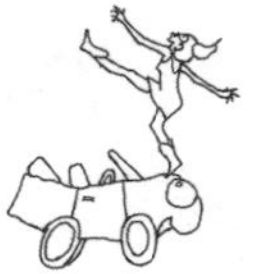

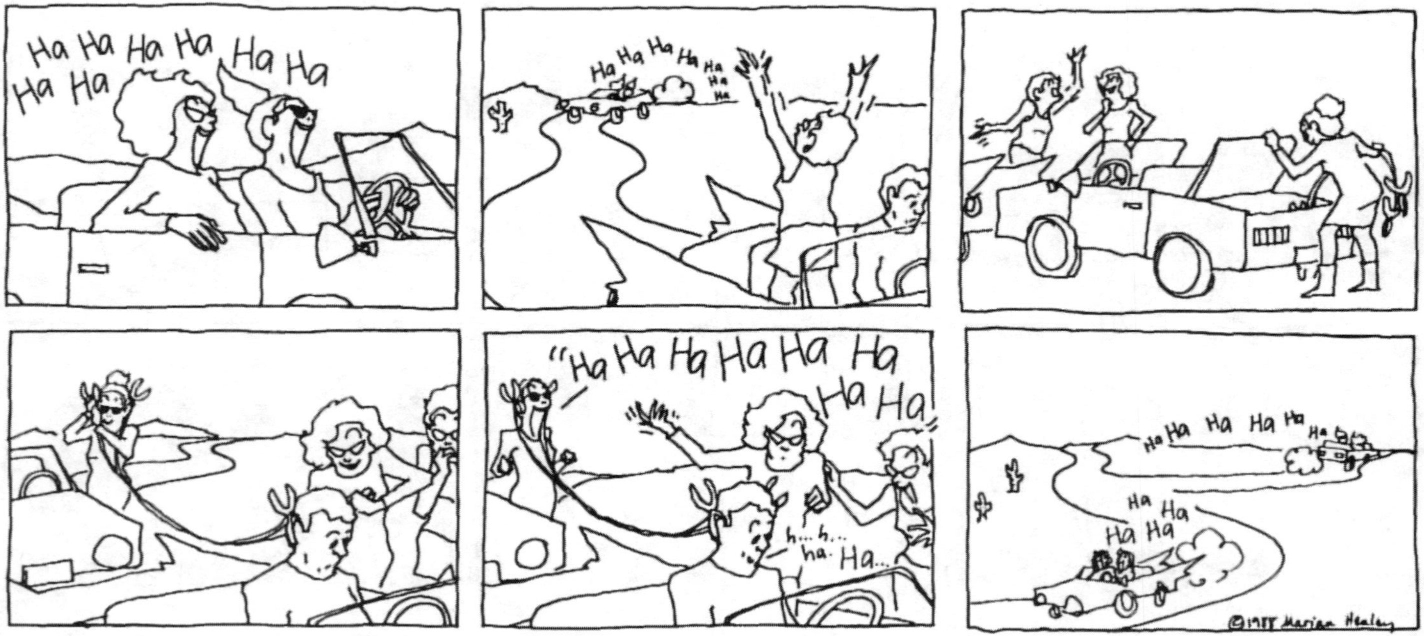
Ha Ha Ha Ha Ha Ha
Ha Ha
"Ha Ha Ha Ha Ha Ha Ha Ha!"
h... h...
ha. Ha...
Ha Ha Ha Ha
Ha Ha

Dreams

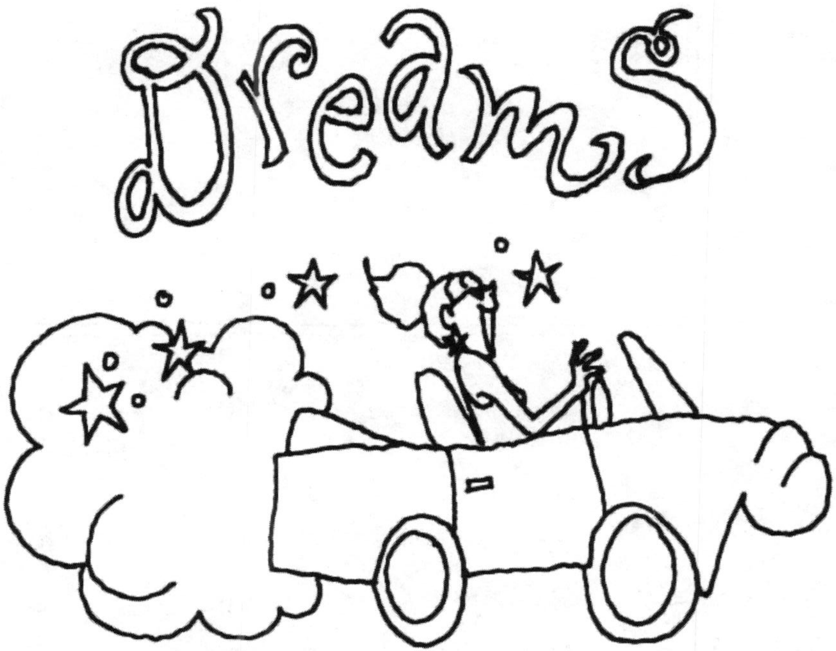

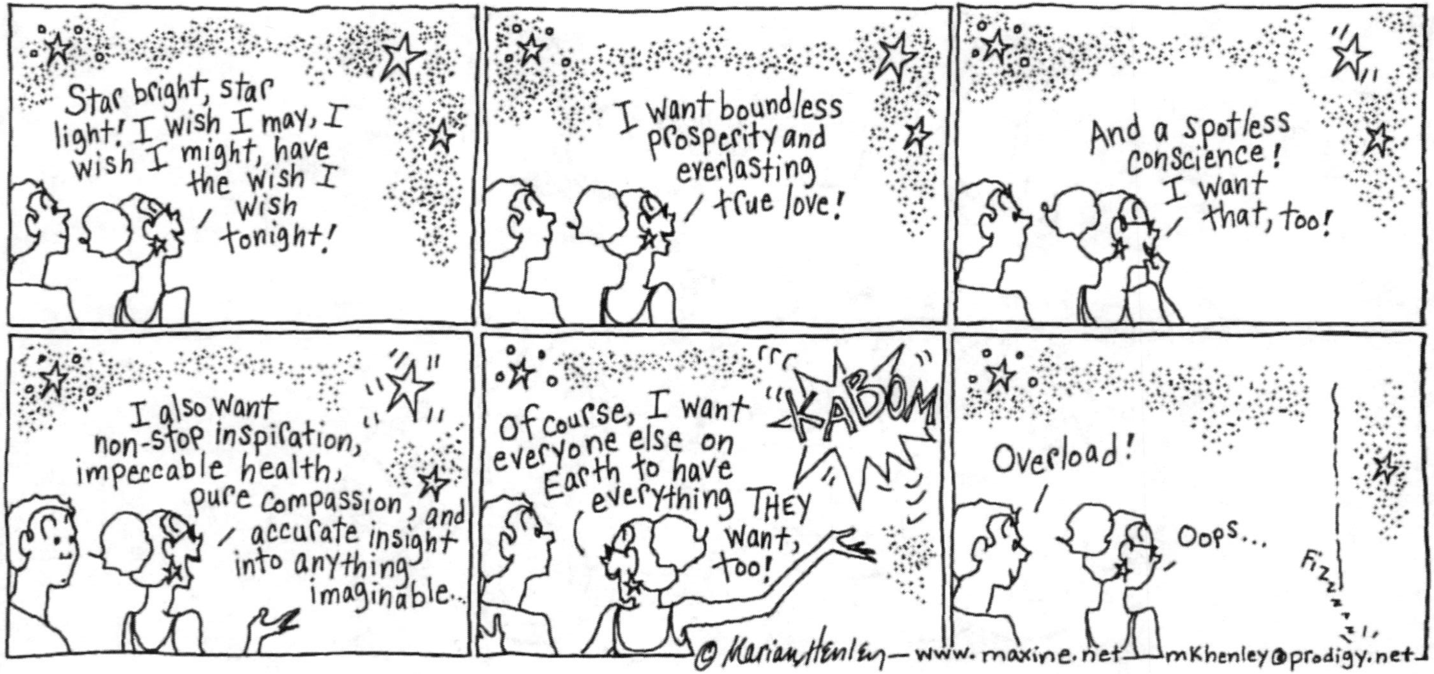
Star bright, star light! I wish I may, I wish I might, have the wish I wish tonight!
I want boundless prosperity and everlasting true love!
And a spotless conscience! I want that, too!
I also want non-stop inspiration, impeccable health, pure compassion, and accurate insight into anything imaginable...
Of course, I want everyone else on Earth to have everything THEY want, too!
KABOOM
Overload!
Oops...
Fizzz
© Marian Henley — www.maxine.net — mkhenley@prodigy.net

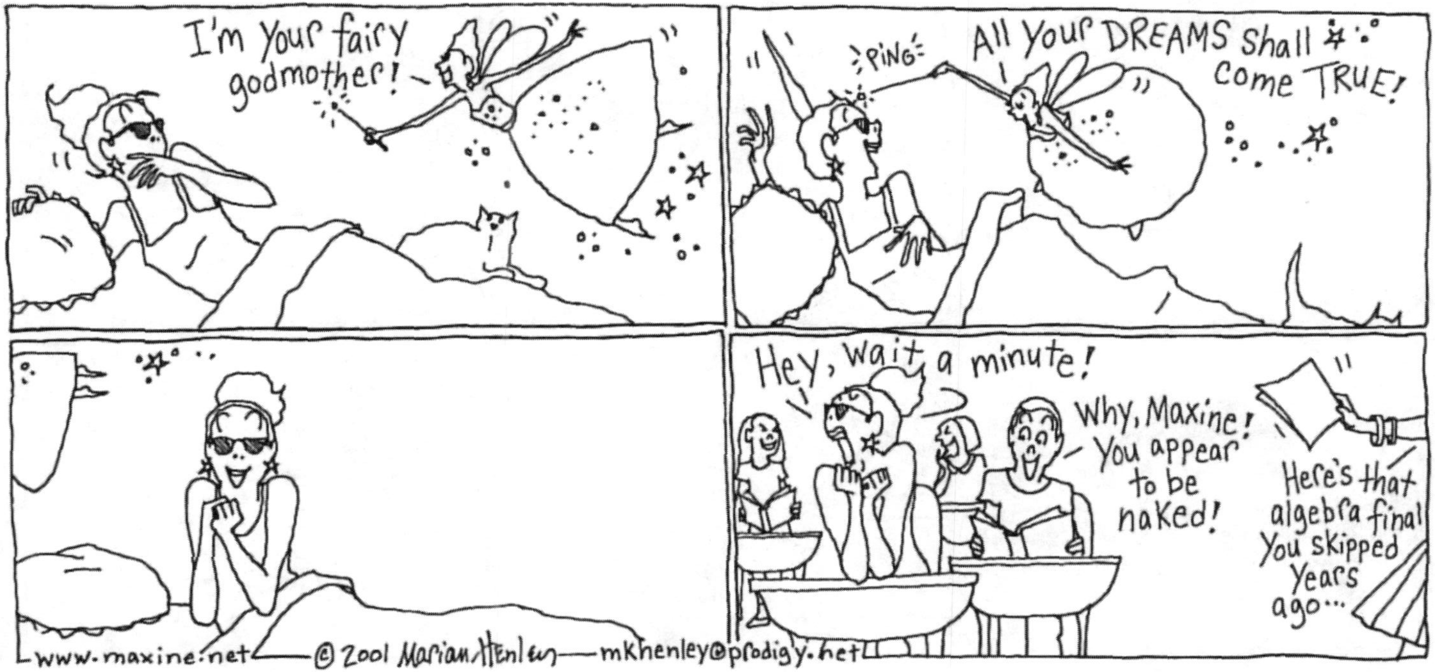
I'm your fairy godmother!
PING
All your DREAMS shall come TRUE!
Hey, wait a minute!
Why, Maxine! You appear to be naked!
Here's that algebra final you skipped years ago...
www.maxine.net © 2001 Marian Henley mkhenley@prodigy.net

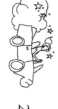

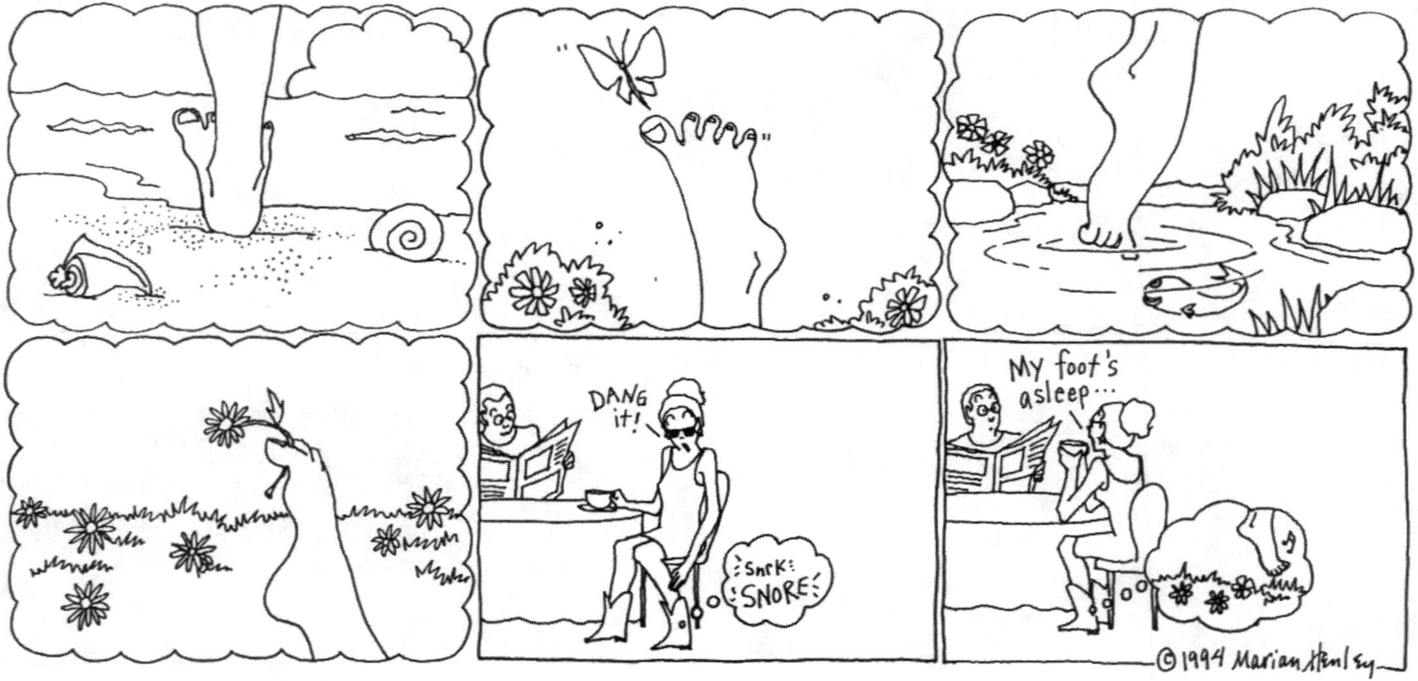
DANG it!
Snrk! SNORE!
My foot's asleep...
©1994 Marian Henley

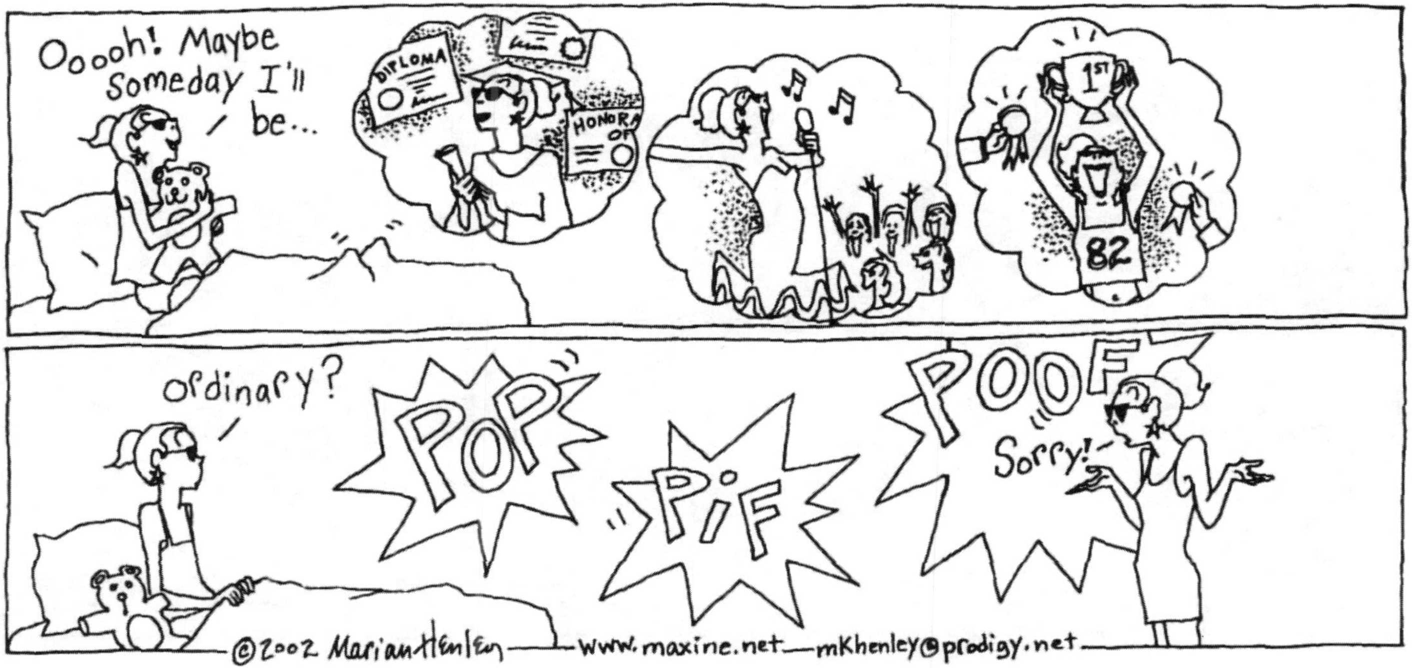
Ooooh! Maybe someday I'll be...
DIPLOMA
HONOR OF
1ST
82
ordinary?
POP
PIF
POOF
Sorry!
©2002 MarianHenley
www.maxine.net
mKhenley@prodigy.net

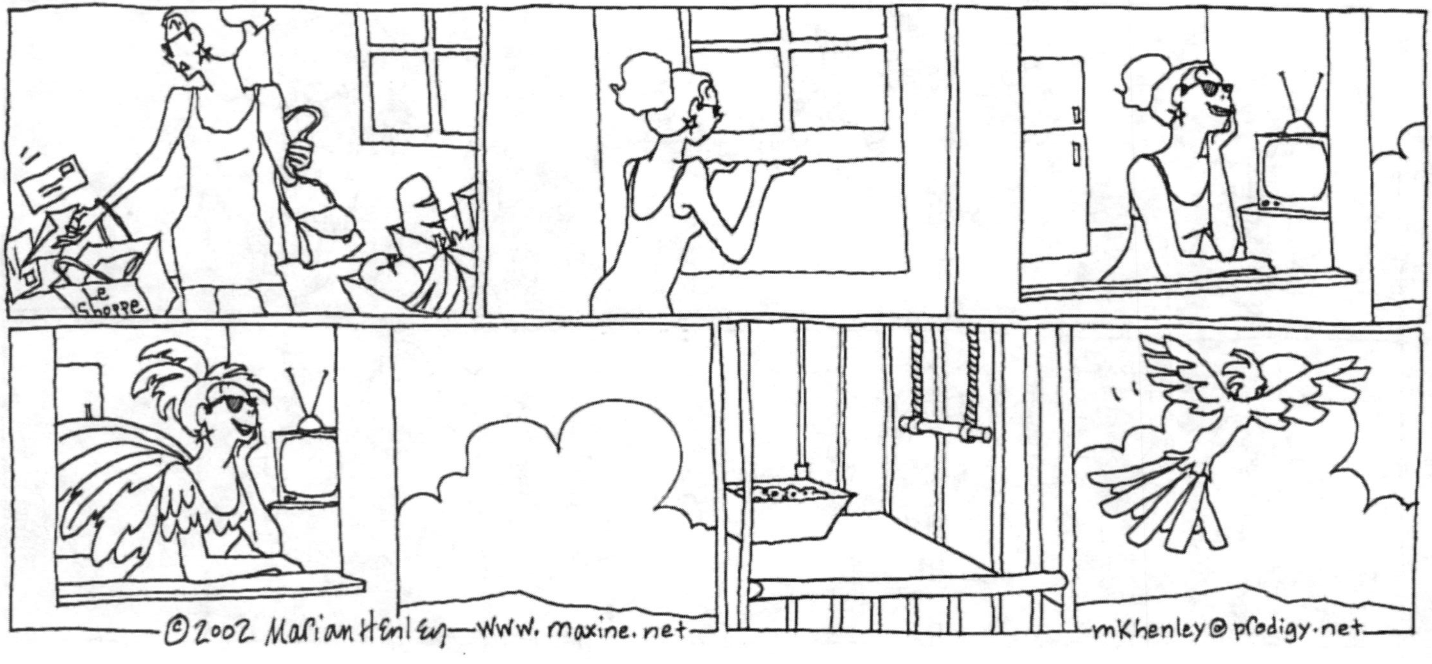
Le Shoppe
©2002 Marian Henley—www.maxine.net—mkhenley@prodigy.net

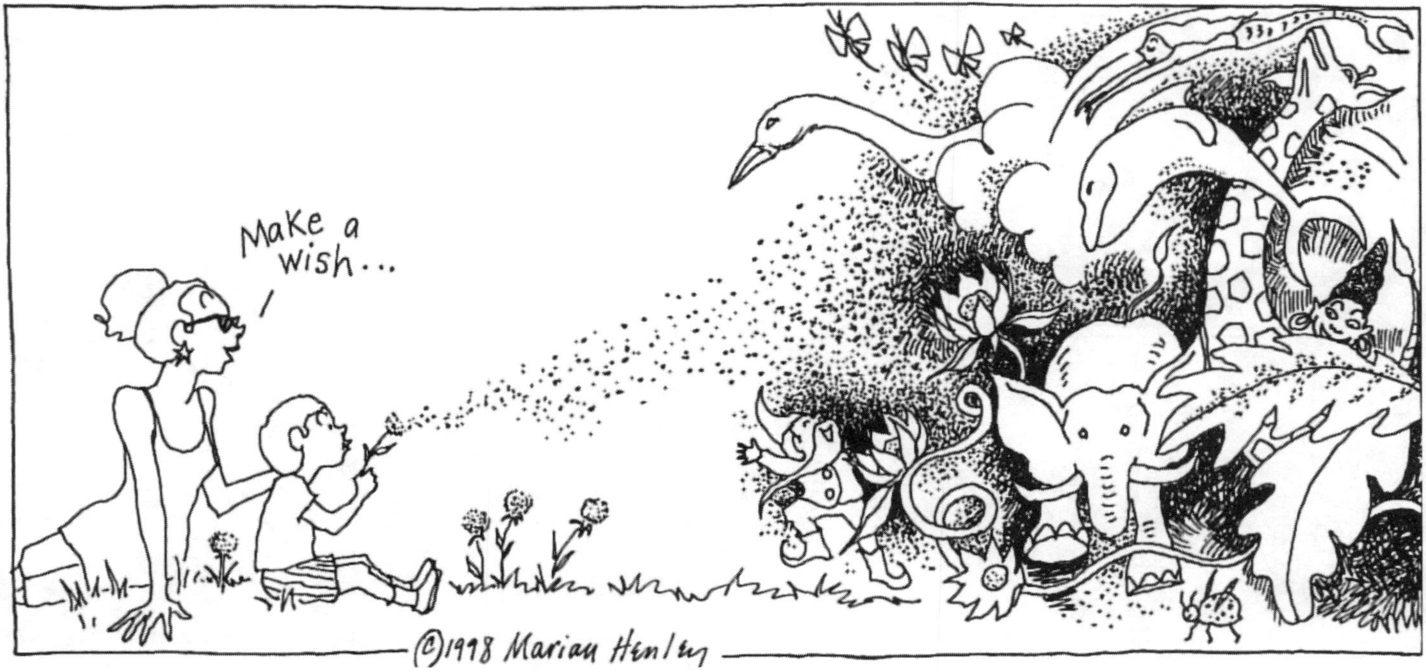
Make a wish...
©1998 Marian Henley

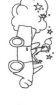